A trained art historian, **Jeremy Cooper** worked for Sotheby's before opening his own gallery in Bloomsbury in London. He has appeared on the *Antiques Roadshow* and written for the *Sunday Times*, *Observer* and *Sunday Telegraph*. In addition to his novels *Ruth*, *Us* and *The Folded Lie*, he has written several books on art and antiques. He lives in West Somerset.

··· KATH TREVELYAN ···

Jeremy Cooper

A complete catalogue record for this book can be obtained from the
British Library on request

The right of Jeremy Cooper to be identified as the author of this work
has been asserted by him in accordance with the Copyright, Designs
and Patents Act 1988

First published in 2007 by Serpent's Tail,
an imprint of Profile Books Ltd
3A Exmouth House
Pine Street
Exmouth Market
London EC1R 0JH
www.serpentstail.com

Designed and typeset by Sue Lamble
Printed and bound in Great Britain by Bookmarque Ltd,
Croydon, Surrey

10 9 8 7 6 5 4 3 2 1

··· ACKNOWLEDGEMENTS ···

The following sources are gratefully acknowledged for quotation within the text:

Four Walls, Eight Windows for the extract from *Joseph Beuys in America* by Caroline Tisdall; Penguin Books Ltd and the author's executors for the extract from Christie Malry's *Own Double Entry* by B. S. Johnson; The Random House Group Ltd for the extract from *Six Memos for the Next Millennium* by Italo Calvino, published by Jonathan Cape; Hamish Hamilton Publishers and the author's executors for the extract from *Campo Santo* by W. G. Sebald; Granta Publications for the exracts from *Waiting for Salmon* by Barry Lopez and *Pounding the Nail* by Studs Terkel, both in *Granta* 90; Sony/ATV Music for a verse from Leonard Cohen's I Can't Forget, in the album *I'm Your Man*; and Tracey Emin for several quotations including lines from *Explorations of the Soul*, privately printed in 1994.

Every effort has been made to trace copyright holders and we apologise for any unintentional omission, to be rectified in all subsequent printings.

··· CHAPTER ONE ···

WHAT MATTERS TO KATH TREVELYAN is that life does. Her own life.

The lives of others matter to her too.

Kath is no longer young – seventy-two at the present time, late in the summer of the year two thousand and four – and yet things continue to her to be ceaselessly interesting, more so in ways than when she was younger and the responsibilities of family intervened.

Kath Trevelyan intends to remain alive until the moment she dies.

There is no sign that she may be due to die, a weathered grey-haired woman in long black dresses and skirts, and a pullover in winter. Sometimes dark grey. Very occasionally white: a blouse in summer, worn free at the waist; and a smock she has been known to wear at night, with its lace trim to the collar and to the buttoned front. Kath was given the linen smock by her husband, who bought it at a charity shop in Trinity, close to their home in West Somerset. He is long dead, and their three daughters grown up, two by now with children of their own, regular yet infrequent visitors to Parsonage Farm. Most of the time Kath is alone in the old house in the foothills of The Kingsways, and is content to be so. She spends at least part of every day in her workshop, in one of the outhouses, at its heart an Albion printing press, her joy, the finest flatbed hand-press, she reckons, ever built.

Parsonage Farm has been Kath's home for more than thirty years. It is in essence a house from the sixteenth century, neither smart nor grand yet appealing, behind the hamlet's church, the home farm of some wealthy Rector of the past. It was a semi-ruin when she and Stewart bought the place, their alterations gradual, unhurried. There is more yet to do and always will be, the habit of change and renovation a way by now of life to Kath. From early on, Stewart liked to cut and mount by his own hand the glass in the restored window frames, relishing the skill he acquired to apply rills of putty and to thumb-mould them into shape. A friend of his does the windows these days, a man who used to work at the community practice he and another architect founded in the inner city of Bristol. Kath has planted a vegetable and fruit garden, surrounded on three sides by tall stone walls, facing down a southern slope and over the stream to the kitchen door of the house. She works most days there too, if only for a few minutes, strolling down the cinder paths on breaks from work in the studio.

The church is beautiful. They are around here. With squat square towers built of local sandstone, a startling purple-pink in colour. In winter the fleeces of the sheep in the fields are stained pink from the wet earth. A herd of red deer roams wild on the hills, eight hundred head of them, hunted across the heath twice a week through the season by the Kinsgway Staghounds. Feelings run strong amongst the local farmers, traditional defenders of ancient country patterns, harbourers and brushwoodsmen of descent direct from Saxon lineage, who speak still of 'thee' and 'thou' and guide the chase by marker hawthorn bushes on parish boundaries. A fallen ash seldom rests a week on common ground before being sawn on site into logs and removed by trailer to dry shelter at home. Ash burns hot, and requires no seasoning. The hunt will survive on this land as long as it possibly can, against Kath's steadfast opposition.

In the early seventeenth century a family of plasterers must have journeyed through the area, commissioned by wealthy landlords to work in a variety of properties, from manor house to tenant smallholding. There is a relief plaster panel in Kath's main bedroom, beneath the eaves, shaped to take the original angle of the roof: of Adam and Eve in the Garden of Eden, both the man and the woman eating apples, each with their other hand holding a leaf of fig to their naked bodies. There are, in fact, two apple trees in this Eden, a fat serpent entwined around one. Within a month of her husband's death Kath moved into the modest room at the eastern corner of the house, its window facing towards the rising sun, visible from the brass single bed where, ever since, she has always slept. Her daughters, and their men when they stay, use the master bedroom, with its monkey frieze and figurative plaster pair of caryatids of Hope and Wisdom to accompany the biblical panel. The family of craftsmen moved on to the steward's house at Lower Penley, on the opposite side of the hill, where they cut in limed gypsum their version of Samson slaying the Philistines with the jawbone of an ass, taken from Judges chapter fifteen. A friend of Kath's, John Garsington, lives on this same short private lane, at Grooms Cottage, with attendant barns, stable and ruined greyhound kennels. He visits her at Parsonage Farm more often than she him.

Into the world outside this rural retreat Kath seldom ventures. She used to, though. In the 1950s she was tutored to play the viola at music school in London, before leaving to teach herself, at St Bride Institute off Fleet Street, to become a traditional hard-metal printer. She still appreciates the radical in contemporary art, never dulling her mind with the reductive myths of television and the daily newspapers, instead listening several times each day to the news and music on the radio. Engagement and hope live still within her. Kath works with creative pleasure in the art-related software programmes on her Apple Mac, whilst refusing to use the Internet for anything other than email. She has always been a person of contrasts, indeed conflicts. Everybody is, she believes.

Books remain important to Kath. They are to John too, a mutual source of affection in their friendship.

At tea one day in his study at Grooms Cottage, Kath could not stop herself counting out loud on his shelves twelve books written by Italo Calvino.

'Inaccurate, actually,' he had corrected her. 'There're eleven. One is *about* Calvino, a literary biography, few of which I usually read. Or purchase.'

'Same thing, isn't it?' Kath had suggested.

'True. I invariably read only what I buy.'

'And like, on principle, every book you choose to own!'

'Of course.'

They had both smiled, sipping in silence their tea.

Kath is an artist. She is the youngest of the three children of a bishop, having lived out an idyllic childhood encircled by the fens at Ely, where her father most Sundays preached from the cathedral pulpit. Trevelyan was his name, which Kath has never changed, despite her loving marriage to Stewart Bowler, a boy from the East End, the only sibling of seven to receive a post-school education. She hates anybody addressing her as Mrs Bowler.

'I'm his widowed wife,' she tends to remonstrate. 'Not a ...'

Possession is the word tempting her. It is, however, not something she has ever felt in danger of becoming. He was a good man to her and the shape of their remembered time together is all the structure she needs for her emotions.

Kath is aware that the idyll of childhood is an illusion, that growing up anywhere is hard, no less or more so as a girl before the war in the Bishop's Palace in Ely. It makes little difference that she forever loves the memory of her father. She expresses – often – the belief that all idylls damage, that ... except, it's true, for the written dreams of Romance, the earlier the better. One of her formative experiences at St Bride Printing Library was the handling, day after day, of William Morris's edition of the Caxton *Morte D'Arthur*, taken from the original published in 1485. The typefaces and letterpress skills of Morris and his late-Victorian contemporaries have served a lifetime's inspiration to Kath in Somerset. There is no need, she maintains, for beautiful books to be as costly as Morris made them. As a student she collected second-hand volumes of The King's Classics, and frequently now takes down from her workshop shelf a book to regard. Kath's copy of *The Vision of Piers The Plowman* by William Langland, printed in 1905, cost her 1s 10d, the price, place and date of purchase noted in pencil on the flyleaf. From time to time she unfolds the filled-in form for the Honours Course of 1909 at the London School of Economics and Political Science, lodged by the book's first owner to mark a passage he valued. Kath likes to remind herself of the publisher's advertisement at the back, which quotes the *Standard* newspaper: 'The literary importance of these volumes cannot be questioned, and when it is added that each is bound in a peculiarly effective scheme of grey blue and white imitation vellum, all people who love dainty associations with the format of their books should remember that The King's Classics have every claim for their consideration and approval.' The treasure of her library is a copy of the Vale Press's *Daphnis and Chloe*, its thirty-six engravings drawn on the wood by Charles Ricketts, who wrote to a friend that 'this curiously silly, corrupt, fresh and exquisite story is an amorous romance: two foundlings brought up by shepherds fall in love, but like the Young Lady of Slough, they found they didn't know how – they are, of course, identified by their respective parents after countless fairy-tale adventures'. Ricketts lodged for his entire adult life with his lover, the painter Charles Hazelwood Shannon. They died within a year or two of each other in an apartment block in Notting Hill. Kath's gaze often rests on his black-blocked image of knights riding on horseback through a wood, captioned in capital letters: DAPHNIS HIDETH HIMSELF IN THE BOLE OF AN ANCIENT TREE FROM THE AGGRESSIVE INCURSIONS OF ARMED METHYM-NAENS. Although lower in money-value, Kath adores her less pretentious Vale volumes, with magenta-dotted yellow paper bindings printed with stylised diagonals of leaping flames, used for those texts which survived the fire on the night of Saturday, December 9th, 1899 at the Ballantyne Press in Tavistock Street. The two Charles's invested in an assortment of wedding boxes, paper lace and silk ties in which to pack up from the wreck of their printers the chunks of charred woodblocks, nuggets of Avon type and frizzled Vale paper.

In this English tradition, the limited edition books and pamphlets and posters and prints which appear, in no apparent pattern, from Kath Trevelyan's workshop at Parsonage Farm are mostly created with local friends. She works, though, from time to time with young London artists, and gives attention to a wide range of differing material from the modern movement. In her way she is, you could say, a polymath.

Kath regularly tries to persuade John Garsington to publish something with Parsonage Press, and explains to him as unthreateningly as she can the pleasure she sees them take in making a book of his essays. He doesn't write, he claims. Nothing any good, for sure, he mutters.

It's sad, for they could do something wonderful together.

But then Kath, despite her strength and independence, lacks confidence too in certain areas. She is convinced of her inadequacy. John is as defended as an island castle. They meet in moated friendship.

Other males exist within Kath Trevelyan's secluded circle of contact, notably her grandson and her brother. She doesn't much like either of them and minds, a lot, feeling this way. Particularly about Robert, her youngest daughter's third child, a boy of four whom she judges spoilt, unfunny, a barely tolerable addition to the family. Her brother Richard's character is an established mystery that ages ago she gave up seeking to understand, by now a recluse, devoted to his flock of black Welsh sheep and horde of rare gramophone records. Richard has lived nearby in the Kingsway Hills for almost as long as Kath. These days they see each other once a year, to commemorate the Bishop's birthday.

Kath keeps chickens and a farm cat, roaming free by day about the yards and gardens, and sleeping together at night in a barricaded corner of the byre – from which the cat periodically climbs through a gap below the eves to forage in the dark. Their hut is constructed from a patchwork of salvaged stable doors, old beams, redundant window frames and a lattice of rubbed ash cattle stalls. It was made by a friend of Kath's, a woman who is never satisfied with her work and strives relentlessly to master new disciplines, already an accomplished welder, carpenter and dry-stone builder, reed-thatching the latest skill to conquer. It is a kitten of hers, by now a cat, which inhabits Parsonage Farm. One day recently Kath watched in astonishment the ginger cat fall from the top of the vast sequoia beside the church. The cat's torso bounced down from branch to branch and landed out of sight by the graves beyond the wall. Kath rushed across to investigate, and was surprised not to find the body unconscious in the grass. Minutes later she spotted the cat skirt the byre and slink to recuperate in its daytime hiding place behind the woodpile, embarrassed by its inelegant error in the tree. Kath lacks sympathy for dogs. Or is her antagonism for the owners, she wonders? For the walk-rituals and oozy-coozy conversations with their fat, slobbering pets? The only dogs which she vaguely likes belong to Mike, one of her brother's sons, who walks out at dawn each day with his pair of spaniels to locate the deer in the woods, which he watches complete their night's feeding and return to shelter in secret lairs in the forest. Mike knows all the deer tracks, can guess ahead which way they intend to move and hides himself in their path to study these beautiful creatures. He is another male in Kath's life, a young man who receives her approval. Mike declines to marry the mother of his baby daughters, the four of them living happily together in a cottage on the Estate, he labouring for a local firm of country conservationists, she spending every spare moment riding out across the heath on borrowed ponies.

It cannot be denied that Parsonage Farm is large for a single person to occupy. Kath doesn't mind what people think of this, letting the gossip of the village wash away in the stream. Her home is a private place, so much so that artist-friends who stay, some for several weeks, feel unseen by the surrounding community, freed to be themselves. Don, a quiet sculptor who visits from time to time with his Japanese wife, says he senses that in being there he inhabits an entire world of his own making, especially in those chosen hours of the night when he tramps up and back alone beneath the moonlight to Anberry Stone. Kath met Don through Joshua Compston, the friend of the son of a woman with whom she had studied at the Guildhall School of Music, a boy lit by fire, a meteor. Inevitably, he died young. In his short adulthood Josh adopted Kath Trevelyan as the neglected ancient genius of his imagination, and used to turn up unannounced at Parsonage Farm, pale and pacey, where he proceeded for the rest of the day to talk at a furious lick about his latest love-loss. He was equally content to rant at random on the principles of hot-metal printing and redundant churches, or to kill, bleed, pluck and roast a cockerel, before rushing off back to London by train at a moment's notice. Kath is proud to have pressed, while he was alive, an edition for Joshua of fifteen commissioned prints, called *Other Men's Flowers*. The title was not his. He took it, with acknowledgement, from a book of poetry selected by Field Marshal Viscount Wavell GCB, CMG, MC, in its turn a quote from Montaigne: 'I have gathered a posie of other men's flowers and nothing but the thread that binds them is my own.' The soldier made this selection of favourite verse in Delhi in 1943, from where he had commanded the army at Monte Cassino, at which the principal ground-force was a battalion of Indian troops, a religious mix of Sikhs, Parsees, Jains and Ghurkas. Four thousand Indian men were killed in forlorn bravery at battle that day. Wavell used to claim this would go down as the most courageous and strongest fighting force in British military history. A piece of Don's is included in the Parsonage Press publication of *Other Men's Flowers*, together with beginning and end prints designed by Joshua himself, one of which, in bold red capitals, he persuaded Kath to transpose from a National Farmers Union poster of the 1960s: **PLEASE KEEP OUT. FOOT & MOUTH PRECAUTIONS.**

Memories of past work continue to fuel Kath's wish to print. Joshua is a continuing presence. As is Cecil Lay, a little-known Suffolk architect and mapmaker of the heaths, whose collection of poetry *An Adder in June* she published in 1978, the hardbound edition limited to one hundred copies, on Bassingwerk Parchment, the type set in 10 Baskerville series 169 with 1 point leading.

It isn't easy to describe the spirit with which Kath embarks on the working days in her studio. Habit and familiarity are important – less pedestrian qualities than might be assumed, for they breed a sense of belonging, help the beat of her blood slow, guide the rhythms of the mind into unfettered channels of experience. Kath's work, although ostensibly by others, is in fact of and from her private self. That's why it matters.

There is a physicality about the making of any art. Nothing ever is only an idea: it is based on something that has happened, and happens again in another guise as the piece finds its form. The realisation of a concept, a mental construct, is also physical, even when there's nothing to show on completion of the work. Kath loves, for example, the works of art of Rosalie Gascoigne, originally from New Zealand, the wife of a meteorologist, her starting point the place at which fine art collides and subsequently colludes with the daily routine. Now collected by major museums around the world, she did not hold her first solo public exhibition until she was fifty-seven, at the Macquarie Galleries in Canberra. Gascoigne's discovery of modern art, with its clamorous surfaces and violent juxtapositions, struck a similar note to her discovery of Australia three decades earlier. For her, art was a mode of transport and a means of becoming, as she put it, 'airborne'. For Kath too. Gascoigne's works are odes to the surfaces on which she lived. As well as speaking of an inner life of remembered spaces, the works sing a song of a day-to-day existence spent between the wide expanse of air, earth and light and a studio-yard crammed with old crates and road signs. Connected somehow to her passion for Rosalie Gascoigne, Kath also loves Bruce Nauman, dressed as a clown in outsize boots, polka-dot pantaloons and mad carrot wig, standing on one foot and shouting to camera: 'Pete and Re-Pete were sitting on a wall. Pete fell off. Who was left?' 'Re-peat,' the clown answers himself. 'Oooh!' he groans, and goes on, unendingly.

Kath reveres every morning the smell on arrival in the workshop of her old Albion press – the iron from which it is made, and the ink with which it prints. She is excited not just by the choice of type, but by the process itself of picking out the metal letters and placing them on the press, the fact that each page is slightly different, some letters being a tiny bit more worn than others, every page bearing an individual quality. The ink is never quite uniformly coloured, the choice of paper, form of binding, cover blocking and everything else always distinct, even when ostensibly the same. *Big Hart and Balls* she made in 1994 for Billy Childish and his Hangman Books of Rochester in Kent. Another contact from the art world, Billy, in his hat, is the lead singer of a rock band, a dyslexic, the misspellings of his poetry left unaltered. Kath spent days on the endpapers: a hangman's noose in pure white on jet black – working and working with her big hands till the plates felt right, each sheet pulled slightly different. She isn't a perfectionist; that would be crazy; she simply delights in getting things as complete as they can be. Billy was pleased. And she is.

Kath reckons it's impossible to have more real friends at one time than five: in order that the people she cares about feel cared for, by her – and she by them, ideally. She remembers preparing last spring for a visit from Don and wishing to treat him to the things he best likes to eat.

'I think I've thought of everything you need,' she said on his arrival. 'Decided, though, I couldn't manage to get all of what you may want!'

He laughed. 'That's fine,' he said. 'I want what I need!'

Kath enjoys this kind of exchange. For it means being understood, and saves the waste in time of explaining. Which, anyway, never works. Age, she finds, barely enters the equation, the crucial element being complicity of a sort of kindred soul, in her experience more often found in the young than the old. Nostalgia stinks. There never was nor ever will be a golden era.

Not everybody agrees with her.

Coming back into the kitchen for tea from an afternoon in the workshop, Kath is annoyed to see one of her granddaughters' crumpled crisp packets thrown onto the table – to her it's preferable that another granddaughter folds the empty packets into three-cornered hats and stands them upright, the game won if they can be pushed over with a finger and then right themselves by their own momentum.

Kath's eldest child and her two daughters are staying for the weekend at Parsonage Farm – without the husband, as everybody prefers. Their home is in South London, entrenched within Dulwich Village and its attendant assumptions. The girls go to a private day school nearby, its integral city playing fields bigger in area than the entire site of Wembley Stadium. Stewart and Kath named their three daughters Rosalind, Esther and Clementine; the first two were born in a rented bungalow on the coast at Clevedon, on the Severn Estuary; the last is quite a bit younger than her sisters, Parsonage Farm her only childhood home. Rosalind's daughters – Kath's eldest grandchildren, the girls staying this weekend – are called Betty (born in 1986) and Teresa (born in1988). Betty, although maddeningly untidy, has chosen A Level Art to study at school and in the garden makes sculptures of twigs, lichen and dried tomato shoots, which Kath cannot help praising. Teresa, the crisp packet folder, plans to be a dental surgeon. All four women are due together to arrange the flowers in the church after tea, for while Kath never attends the services, she feels obliged to take her bi-monthly turn at the task. Her arrangements are always unexpected – in spite of the fact that the congregation by now expects them to be so. Today's floral display is made entirely of plastic, much of it painted by Kath in broad strokes of colour absent in British nature.

'What's *this*?' Teresa exclaims, holding up a lemon yellow trail of leaves, striped puce.

'Plastic ivy,' her grandmother replies. 'Doctored.'

'It looks great!'

'Better now,' Kath allows, pragmatically.

Theobald Drake, a solicitor and amateur historian from Trinity, is perched at the top of a stepladder, examining in the nave with the aid of his pocket torch a three-tier brass chandelier.

'Massive! Never moved since the day it was made, at a cost of £24!' he says. 'See the date? May 1773. The names of the Rector and Parish Treasurer recorded for posterity. Splendid!'

'Spiffing!' Rosalind agrees, with a giggle, in fondness for

her teenage memories of old Theo's vocabulary.

Betty stands alone in the north aisle, looking up at a stone niche high on the wall, containing the thirteenth-century heart of Maud, a nun. She is surprised, a little shocked to accept that she has never before noticed the shrine. The body of LE QUER DAME MAUD de MERRIETE is buried elsewhere, in a cloth-makers church at the other end of the Kingsway ridge. Betty vows tomorrow to bicycle, rain or shine, from church to church in the neighbourhood to see for herself the discreet glories of her grandma's territory.

Kath is also preoccupied with private images, as she mechanically fills the conical copper vases and sets them out on the windowsills. She is thinking of her middle daughter, the odd one out by name and temperament, Esther, unmarried, a systems librarian at the Ashmolean in Oxford. Kath wonders if, as a young mother and printer, she herself had maybe been too preoccupied with the busy-ness of life, failing to give this silent untroublesome daughter the attention the girl herself never voiced a need for. Kath sees sitting in a pew the child Esther, head and eyes lowered in a book, uncomplaining of piano practice, undemanding of affection, never a hint of trouble at school. So different from Rosalind, and especially from Clem, Esther's drink-loving, party-going sisters: emotionally less self-sufficient and stable, they demanded and received more of their mother's time. Kath regrets she has maybe never made clear to her middle daughter how much she loves her. Kath also realises, in retrospect, that Esther is especially observant and sensitive, attuned to the feelings of others. Her vow for Sunday: to write a long letter to this daughter, an unsentimental statement of apology. It's never too late to change, Kath intends to affirm.

She laughs, out loud, on recall of a conversation with Esther.

'The village accuses me of "swanning" around, not taking life seriously,' Kath had complained, out on a walk one day to the farmer's shop in Great Mead.

'Swanning? Not you,' Esther said, and shook her head. 'Not wood-pigeoning either!'

They stopped in the sun to think.

'Clem does quite a lot of badgering,' Kath said. 'Maybe I robin on a bit?'

'I love wrens,' Esther then said. 'Although I'm not at all similar.'

They walked on across the brow of the field.

'I know!' Esther exclaimed. 'Wagtailing! That's you, Mum!'

At the foot of the field they crossed a stile.

'Do you remember The Rock Story?' Esther asked.

'No?'

'Don't you? I do. You told it to Frida and her kids. I remember. We were in the kitchen. You know, I really like Frida. For daring to live alone, without pretending to be outlandish. Not needing to play the role of eccentric hippie.

Everyone's so boring around her. All the same, the girls were finding their mother just a little over-sure she's different! And you said to them: "Let me tell you a story, The Rock Story. It's true, because it happened to me. One day, here at Parsonage Farm, a friend and I were together knocking down an old wall. I did the barrow work, hauling away the stones and placing them in a pile for later use, while my friend attacked the wall with a sledgehammer. The thick old thing put up a fight, but succumbed. Until, near the base, three large rocks refused to shift. Even they, though, were finally dislodged. If this woman happened to be your mother, what chance would you have against such determination? How could any of us compete? We couldn't. But we do. We all have independent strengths from which even she cannot shift us. You two too. And just think. With the power to move these vast rocks, doesn't that suggest that she must, in some part of her, be an even larger rock? To rely on. Not some stone in a sandal." That's what you said. Something like that. The last bit definitely. I can hear the words. "Stone in a sandal." You use beautiful words.'

As she assembles plastic flowers in the church, Kath reconstructs this walk, some years ago now.

Her mind moves on to a more recent event, in August, a month ago: she and Esther driving down to Cornwall for the day, to the Port Eliot Literary Festival. It was the last time they were together.

Kath loves swimming. In the parkland grounds where

the Festival is held there's an inlet off the River Tamar, with a boathouse, on the jetty of which swimmers leave their towels. Esther and Kath made it against the current all the way to the viaduct, and then back. Their bodies were eased by the effort, and they sat for a while alone on the warm stones, talking, feeling fortunate. Kath remembers a languid return through the azalea maze and the rash of tents and camper-vans set out in the home paddock for the weekend. The performances – readings and videos and art-inventions – were held in open-sided marquees within the walled gardens which extend behind the crenellated mansion. Stalls flourished beneath the oaks on the adjacent knoll, cooking and serving organic food, selling sack-wrapped blocks of Divine Earth soap, perfumed candles, mobiles, mosaics, mint teas. They arrived back from their swim in time, Kath recalled, for Fiona Banner's show, in which the artist placed herself in front of a blank canvas on an easel, facing a naked model, a gypsy woman she had met the night before in the campsite. Her portrait of the casual nude was created in words, the medium she invariably uses, painting in straight lines of black capital letters from top left to bottom right her prose perception of the figure standing in the tent pavilion. She hesitated after 'teeth', before deciding on 'bony', which Kath at first read as 'bonny': a description of herself – for sure, Banner is bonier, Kath bonnier, despite her age. The word-painter resisted escape into background descriptions of the privet hedge, floral border and brick wall, sustaining for the entire canvas a disciplined lack of compromise. After the performance mother and daughter sat on a metal bench circling the trunk of the big turkey oak, with a couple of glasses of wine, and Esther talked of the festival at Glastonbury, where she and Rosalind had regularly camped out in their teens. She didn't tell of precisely what she was thinking.

Loss. Abandonment. These, for some reason, are the words which repeat over and over inside Kath's head as she steps home with the family from the church to prepare for supper.

Rosalind mentions, for the millionth time, her mother's rejection of proposals for installing an Aga in her country kitchen.

'I've got one in Dulwich,' she reiterates.

'I'm aware of this, dear.'

'It looks ... stylish, nice. The new one. Azure enamel, with chrome lids.'

Kath doesn't argue. Her six gas hobs are what she wants. Stewart made the 'grain-cupboard' in the yard where the canisters are stored, from saved stone, terracotta pantiles and a green door with original iron latch. She loves dead Stewart. And the girls. And her grandchildren.

It's all so complicated, she finds, however simple she seeks to keep the sustaining routines of daily life.

Books are better, for they are nobody's children. Although she has never written a book, Kath does make them. They are, she feels, the opposite of children: books are ciphers and substitutes for the self; or a process of discovery, perhaps, of whom we may become. Children must be allowed to be themselves, whatever the cost of pain to mothers.

··· CHAPTER TWO ···

DAY-BY-DAY AT PARSONAGE FARM, Kath has few regular callers. The person who drops by more often than anybody else is John Garsington. He tends to call within forty-eight hours of return from his twice-monthly visits to London, where he rents the use whenever he wishes of the spare room of a house in Bermondsey. The tall town house is the home of a fluctuating gang of artists. John was introduced to them by a painter-friend and instantly liked the informality of their place, in contrast to his own manic control. The tales he tells Kath of his experiences are seldom brief.

Kath's picture of John's trial residence there, earlier in the summer, is coloured, she knows, by images of her own past. He was put up – in Kath's version – on this inaugural night in the seldom-used room of a French tenant of the household. A large wicker laundry basket was alive, the sounds starting almost as soon as he switched off the light and headed for sleep, a scraping and creaking. John switched on again the bedside lamp, dared lift the lid to look inside and root around in the dirty washing. The sound remained when he awoke in the morning: of a creature trapped in the laundry basket, unable to exit, he – and Kath, vicariously – supposed. His passion for books led John to inspect the shelves of a sort-of library in the room, including: *La Crise de la Culture* by Hannah Arendt, Georges Canguilhem's *Le Normal et le Pathologique*, and a guide to the Freud Museum at 20 Maresfield Gardens, on the cover of this a colour photo of the carpet-covered couch, with a row of ancient Egyptian artefacts ranged along the top of the radiator guard behind. A mezzotint of the painting *Oedipus and the Sphinx* by Ingres was hanging in Freud's study, John noted from a photograph in the pamphlet, together with a portrait of the psychotherapist Lou Andreas-Salomé, daughter of a Russian general and lover of both Friedrich Nietzsche and Rainer Maria Rilke, who became in the early 1920s one of the first of Freud's pupils to pursue the new discipline in a practice of her own. John never saw the books again. The tiny spare room in the basement suited him better than the Frenchman's bed-sitter. His reward? The favour of his own brass key to the front door.

Since then John has come and gone as he wishes, storing bed linen, towel, dressing-gown, wash-things and a change of clothes in a chest of drawers. He chooses to eat every London meal out – including breakfast, in a café in Borough Market - and he never sees anybody of the household (except for the occasional back view of a robed figure disappearing up the stairs with her morning glass of pressed orange juice).

Kath and John had first properly talked when he invited her out to supper at a local restaurant, a forty-minute walk from his cottage, across the fields of two farms. He's certainly different: she remembers thinking afterwards. He had punctuated the evening with speculation, in a stage whisper, as to how a table of ten further down the converted milking parlour, equally divided between men and women, could possibly be related. Three of the men were surely gay, he said, picking out a solicitous, entertaining, confident, elegantly ageing triumvirate. Maybe two of the men, judging from the shape of their prominent noses and the language of their hands, are brothers, he had suggested. By the end of the meal he had decided that the two large women, one with a limp and carrying her own cushion from bar to table, were mother and daughter.

The return walk across the fields beneath the moonlight was at moments almost magical in its beauty – at the very least, a memorable way to conclude their first dinner together.

John is telling Kath today about the Helen Chadwick exhibition at the Barbican, which he visited earlier in the week.

'Do you like her?' he asks.

'Her work, yes. I've no idea what she's like as a person,'

Kath replies.

'She's dead, of course. Visited the textile collection of the Victoria & Albert Museum on the afternoon she died. Her favourite place in the world. She was forty-two. I'm already seventeen years older.'

John looks younger than his age, much younger, almost boy-like. At other times his eyes have an ancient gleam, like polished granite, his face set in cold old lines of defence. He isn't easy company.

'Was her chocolate piece in the show?' Kath asks.

John smiles. 'Yes. Not terribly good. The basin in which it boils has a white plastic rim. Could be a gigantic lavatory seat. Splashes have the colour and consistency of diarrhoea, and are wiped off by a lurking gallery guard. I love the building opposite, an office block by Richard Rogers, for a Japanese Bank. I stood by the fountains, framed by the restored tower of St Bartholomew the Less, and watched shirt-sleeved figures pass up and down the all-glass shafts. The counterweights of the shifting lifts appear to pass through one another, as bankers halt to exit onto the atrium.'

'Ando is my favourite architect,' Kath says. 'He *is* Japanese.'

'Have you seen his work?'

'No.'

'Nor have I,' John admits.

They pause. They are in the studio, sitting in a battered

pair of leather chairs, the stable doors open to the roll of the late summer countryside. Kath registers the formality of her friend's way of speaking, wonders why he puts himself at such a distance from others, and is at the same time aware that he enjoys being with her, that he is in his way relaxed. She likes being with him, is equally eager to talk in detail about art. Maybe she isn't yet at ease either, she acknowledges.

'You're keen on Joseph Beuys, I know you are,' John says.

'I like his hat!' Kath agrees.

'He's in a mixed show at the Whitechapel.' John fishes for a pamphlet in the canvas bag he carries everywhere. 'There's a film of a performance piece he did which I'd never heard of. Washing the audience's feet!' He finds the pamphlet and reads aloud a statement by the artist: '"The world must not be as it is. The true foundation of Action Art is the element of movement ... The form in which this embodiment of Christ takes place in our time is the element of movement as such, the person who is moving."!'

Kath smiles. 'He's so funny.'

'I saw Beuys once,' John adds. 'In 1972, February. At a performance lecture. He was drawing on blackboards, and talking to us in broken German-English. Everything needs organisation, is a phrase of his I've never forgotten. On one of the diagrams he sought to define art-action to a dead hare! He did! I promise!'

Kath is still smiling, barely a line at the corners of her

warm eyes, gazing steadily at her companion. 'In 1972 Clem was nine, her sisters in their teens,' she says. 'I didn't have the time to go to London. That was the year too I did the book with Stewart. It was such an important thing. Still is. To me.'

John knows the book, has his own copy, bought before he had any idea of living in West Somerset, much less of meeting Kath Trevelyan.

'It's fine work. You're good,' he says.

'We, not me. It was mainly his. He had something worth saying, about things he believed in. And his words fitted my visual language of the time. Very political. Bold lettering printed as banners across the page. Ken Garland was my hero then, because of his Aldermaston posters for CND. I studied his manifesto, *First Things First*, where he insists that we book-designers employ our skills always for worthwhile purposes. I've never flinched from this.'

'And the falcon?' John asks. 'How did that happen?'

'My bird, the emblem of Parsonage Press? He's from here, up on the hills. A pair of peregrine falcons live in the sandstone quarry at Anberry. Their offspring, by now, I suppose. Together they chase flights of silly pigeons into the bowel of the disused quarry, and kill them at leisure.'

She stops for thought.

'There's an earlier source. From my own story,' Kath continues. 'My falcon was inspired by Whistler's butterfly in *The Gentle Art of Making Enemies*. A book I used to take down from the shelves at St Brides whenever I needed to be amused. Such a lively creature, strutting in gold across the cover's boards. Inside, Whistler added his butterfly monogram to the spiky comments on the text of his battle with Ruskin.'

'What did the critic accuse Whistler of? Pouring paint over the public, wasn't it?'

'I'm old enough these days to possess a copy of my own.' Kath rises from her chair, walks across to the shelf above her trays of type and picks out a book. 'Ruskin wrote,' she reads, '"The ill-educated conceit of the artist so nearly approached the aspect of wilful imposture. I have seen, and heard, much of cockney impudence before now; but never expected to hear a coxcomb ask two hundred guineas for flinging a pot of paint in the public's face." Good stuff! You know that Whistler won his case, was awarded a farthing's damages and had to sell his house in Chelsea to pay the victory bill to his solicitor?'

'Jesus! Things mattered then.'

'They do now. Differently.'

Together they stand at her proof-table and inspect, in detail, the three states which Kath has pulled of a woodblock she is printing for the Taunton Arts Club, a Nash-like representation of the clump of trees on the top of Granthorne Hill, where the roaming herd of ponies gathers at night. They discuss the work without affectation, both of them knowledgeable and interested and unafraid to disagree.

'Why don't I do a book of yours? You never properly answer,' Kath says.

John frowns – in truth, he doesn't know why he resists the idea.

'I ... I don't want to.' He looks away, at nothing, then back again, at Kath, for reassurance. 'I'm sorry,' he finds himself saying.

Her gaze is unwavering: 'Don't be. I wouldn't want you to do it against your will.'

Soon afterwards he goes off home.

Although this visit of John's leaves Kath feeling unexplainably disturbed – a little too alive, on the verge, almost, of elation – she quickly recovers. Her life is rich. The apparent sultriness of the late summer in Somerset is thick with incident, full of things and people to intrigue and entertain. Kath laughs, and tosses her grey head, like a girl. She is thinking of something which the tractor driver on the fields below Parsonage Farm said the other day, about the well-meaning yet dim Master of Staghounds: 'Well, he has managed to learn to brea-ea-the.'

Kath couldn't put it better herself!

The week before, passing in the car the fifteenth-century church at Soane, she read the sloped letters of the text on a billboard to say WINO IS GOD! How wonderful, she thought. And then, at a second glance, saw that the notice actually asked WHO IS GOD?

Boring!

How rich life is: she reiterates.

Parenthood, for Kath, rests at the heart of her life's richness. After the relief of feeling love for all three of her children, it's hard being unable to deny dislike of her grandson. She tries to convince herself that the antipathy is skin-deep, a reaction against the invasion by a male of her exclusively feminine family. Kath is bad at self-deception and squares up these days to the truth. Thank ... not God, because he doesn't exist ... thank nature that, from the start, she has always loved her own children.

It isn't automatic. Several women whom Kath knows are racked with guilt at not enjoying motherhood. Why should they? Because it's natural, the world insists. It isn't, Kath maintains. Love, of any sort, is a miracle.

John Garsington has never wanted to be a father: because he is terrified of hating his children – and of being hated by them. Esther is equally convinced she won't ever want to mother a child. Her reasons, though, are not the same as John's. Kath admits, to her surprise, that she hasn't dared directly to ask her daughter why.

I must.

Esther can't now, anyway, too old: Kath says to herself.

She presses down the iron plate of her Albion onto the text to accompany Taunton Arts Club's commemorative woodblock.

I should know how Esther feels because she's like me,

only worse, more sensitive: Kath tells herself.

She pauses. A look of soft surprise spreads over her features, at the even older age she knows she must be, and doesn't feel.

They were together on a coach once, going to Lyme Regis for a day by the sea, when Esther noticed a ladybird crawling across her blue bag. She was about to brush it off but held her hand mid-air, and examined the creature, the expression on her face difficult to read, eyebrows drawn into a frown. The ladybird unfurled its wings and flew up to the roof rack. Esther didn't see where it had gone, and inspected her clothes fold by fold, not wishing, Kath guessed, to squash it. Things like this were always happening to her. As a child, with her friend, Esther spent the large part of a birthday spring afternoon gathering seeds from the trumpet flowers of daffodils and scattering them in unlikely places, cherishing the idea that next year her friend's parents would find blooms appear as if from nowhere. The eight-year-old girls worked with an obsessive patience and exactitude that Esther has carried with her into adult life. She was astonished when the girl's family complained to Kath about this innocent activity and her mother then, in laughter, had explained that Esther was anyway mistaken, because daffodils propagate through the splitting of bulbs.

Kath keeps a pair of gumboots which Esther repaired, beautifully, with red bicycle patches stuck to the fractured rubber of the yellow wellingtons.

Esther was wise before her time, already grown-up in her teens in ways that others tend not to become until they are old and infirm, when, too late, they revisit childhood's perception of the world as mysterious and interesting. Kath was and is the same. They both love throwing stuff away (empty tins, finished food packets, bottles, etc.), almost all of which at Parsonage Farm is stored for recycling, making the act of discarding feel not at all destructive. Esther used to help Kath hoard old bits of iron, the two of them convinced that even if they never came in useful the bits and pieces looked great hanging in the byre, or ranked by type and shape on side-open stacks of wooden crates. There is enough by now for Kath to allow a friend to take whatever she needs, with which to make boxed collages and other things to sell. Kath dries the corpses of voles and shrews in the greenhouse for her friend to frame – the same woman who made for her the patchwork hen-hut.

Esther doesn't find the world an easy place to be. She is close, at times, to self-destruction. Kath is aware of the damage her daughter secretly does to her own body. Although Esther's purpose is to conceal the pain, it's equally important that people know – without her telling them, of course. And so, when her mother notices the brown stains on the sleeves of her cotton shirts, Esther doesn't mind, providing no mention is made of the revelation. Her socks also soak up the blood from the scars of eczema on her ankles as well as forearms, which she perpetually scratches

33

and infects. The wounds hurt. They are intended to.

Of the three daughters Esther is the most attractive. To men, that is. This doesn't please her. Given the person she is, Esther refuses to compromise, and continues to flaunt the shapely figure inherited from her mother. Her hair, though, is different, more like her father's, with tightish natural curls framing her rounded face. Stewart was also quite small, and wore browns and greens, as Esther used to, their skin-colouring similar. Kath, whose hair is thick and wavy, once dark now grey-white, is taller than both of them, with a physical presence that commands respect. Stewart had loved the ways both his wife and his middle daughter looked; they had loved being loved by him; and loved him back. He is the only man Esther has ever trusted. She cannot forget how her first boss, the professor of English for whom she worked for a time in Edinburgh, chose not to stop himself falling in love with her. 'Fall' is indeed the word. Such lack of discipline. Plain emotional indulgence. Her father recently dead, Esther gave up men on the spot, and has seen no reason since to change her mind.

When Kath last saw Esther – the month before, at the Festival in Port Eliot – her daughter had described an encounter she had recently witnessed on the top deck of a red London bus, en route to Liverpool Street after tea with a girl-friend in Bow.

An older cockney couple are sitting on the seat in front of her, staring at the screen above the window, which displays recorded news and advertisements. Sean Connery, the actor, is apparently being sued by a neighbour in California for millions of dollars for making her life a misery.

'How?' the woman asks. 'Him such a lovely man.'

The bloke doesn't reply. Transport Vision switches to the horoscopes.

'Don't have mine, do they?' she says. 'Oh yes, there it is.'

She struggles to read the text and the man – her husband, or perhaps her brother – obliges.

'Nice for the kids, anyway. Keep them happy.'

Her companion chuckles: 'Keeps you happy, and all.'

She nudges him in the ribs. 'Stop it!' she says, and together they laugh, boozy heads thrown back in unison.

As usual, Kath isn't quite sure what Esther means by telling her this story.

Kath herself is unafraid of men. She remembers, as clear as rain-water, her own stricken days of being in first-love, with the elder brother of a girl at school, on a long weekend spent at their home in the Vale of Evesham. He was perfect – the best kind of head-boy she could imagine from her seat of modesty on the junior bench. She did look older than she was – better developed, her teachers were in the habit of saying (one of them once murmured, over the semolina: 'Your mother would be proud of you, Katherine dear'). Kath was twelve, the boy eighteen, vice-captain of cricket at his school, wearing at breakfast a crested cream-white sweater over his swimming trunks. The family lived in a rabbit warren of a house, adapted piecemeal from an old mill by a weir in this neglected valley of idyll-England. She first set eyes on the boy when he rowed across the moat to collect her and Tabitha from the landing stage, to which the girls had walked from the railway station, carrying exeat cases and still wearing their Westonbirt uniforms. There was a hand-bell, like the town-crier's, which you rang to tell the household you were waiting. For Kath, who loathed the restrictions of life at boarding school, it was love at a glance, delicious escape – although by now she had quite forgotten the boy's name. The swimming was amazing, so hot one afternoon that the family had a floating picnic lunch in the millpond, with ironstone plates and tumblers of apple juice on a log table with embroidered linen cloth. Before the theatre one night nearby at Stratford, she had tried to find the mill again, to show Stewart, but it seemed to have disappeared.

The Bishop was also fond of swimming, and of boating. He and Kath, in her youth, double-sculled together down the fen lodes. Bishop Trevelyan revealed himself to his youngest daughter in ways unknown to the other children. In the giant library at Ely they used to read aloud to each other, after his sermon at Sunday Evensong, when he always left the first choice to Kath. She remembers one winter turning time after time to the *Just So Stories*, for the illustrations as much as the text, drawn and written by Kipling.

Sixty-five years on, she could recite verbatim the caption to the picture of the crocodile pulling the elephant's nose: 'All that black stuff is the banks of the great grey-green, greasy Limpopo River (but I am not allowed to paint these pictures), and the bottly-tree with the twisty roots and the eight leaves is one of the fever trees that grow there. Underneath the truly picture are shadows of African animals walking onto an African ark. There are two lions, two ostriches, two oxen, two camels, two sheep, and two other things that look like rats, but I think they are rock-rabbits. They don't mean anything. I put them in because I thought they looked pretty. They would look very fine if I were allowed to paint them.' Throughout the war, and afterwards, her father bought each edition as it was published of the King Penguin Books, beginning in 1939, when Kath was eight; she treasures the feeling of being the person privileged by him to open these slim copies fresh from the press: *Edible Fungi* by James Ramsbottom, Keeper of Botany at the British Museum, the coloured woodcut on the cover by Rose Ellenby, published in 1943, set in Monotype Baskerville; *Flowers of Marsh and Stream* by Iolo A. Williams, set in Monotype Perpetua, the stylised cover of 1946 designed by Noel Rooke.

Kath can still hear the voice of her father explaining one evening, when she was eight or nine, that while our perception of books could change with the years just as much as of people, the difference was that whereas people might drop you if they could no longer get any advantage or interest or pleasurable sensation from you, a book would never abandon you. Naturally, you sometimes dropped them, maybe for several years. But they, even if you betrayed them, would never turn their backs on you; they would go on waiting for you on their shelf, for decades. They wouldn't complain. Until one night, when you needed a book at three in the morning, although it might be a book you had abandoned years and years previously, it would not disappoint you, emerging from its place to keep you company in your moment of need. Books don't try to get their own back or make excuses or ask themselves if it's worth their while or if you deserved them or if you still suited each other, they come at once as soon as you ask. A book would never let you down, the Bishop believed.

And me, Kath asks, can't I be relied upon?

Thinking back, she has a horrid feeling that this book-idea may not have been original, that the Bishop read it somewhere else and proclaimed it as his own.

Kath knows that her father remains a key influence on her art – on everything, really. Through him and the Cornish branch of his family she is related to Humphrey Trevelyan, the Goethe scholar, and to Julian Trevelyan, the painter. In the 1950s she had stayed for four months with Julian and his wife, Mary Fedden, also a painter and print-maker, in their house on the edge of Hampstead Heath. From them she learnt of the humility in being an artist, and of the doggedness, the necessity of going on and on till something makes sense.

In retirement, the Bishop had frequently visited Kath in her early days at Parsonage Farm. He helped her plant the row of pleached apple trees either side of the top path in the garden, by now a gnarled trellis with a dependable profusion of fruit each season. He used to spend a week with Kath and Stewart and then walk with his neat guest-bag up the road for a couple of days with his son, at the school for the blind of which Richard was headmaster.

Her father is here today, seated in the cane armchair in the gazebo, catching up on unread issues of the *Church Times*. Here in spirit, Kath senses. She is leaning against the sill of the gazebo's open arch, half-turned to look out down the slope of the garden to her home. Her dark-grey skirt hides the slender length of her legs, its embroidered hem resting at her ankles, around which the faded green thongs of a pair of sandals are tied. Kath hates buying clothes and instead gathers quality hand-me-ons, wearing them till they disintegrate; she applauds the fact that John Garsington possesses a waisted black frock coat, with lapels, made in Holland, at 's-Gravenhage in 1937 by F & B Schoemaker, for a Mr van Delden, it says on the label stitched to the inside of the breast pocket. The double-roman tiles on the roofs of the main buildings of Parsonage Farm are also old, orange-red in tone, manufactured before the war at the abandoned brickworks by the bridge in Nelson. The outhouses are mostly roofed in slate, grey, from Wales. The emerald sheen of the surrounding paddocks and of the forest sweep of the hillside has faded by this time of year to the colour of Kath's canvas sandals. It is a view she never doubts, a landscape lived in and over for thousands of years, the lanes deep from use. The windows of her workshop are painted yellow: a lowish barn extending from the back of the house, once the dairy. Kath likes bright colours everywhere: except in her work, and in her dress – one explanation for her being so fond of butterflies. In a glade at Thurlbear Wood she knows the particular leaf of primrose where a Duke of Burgundy suns itself between twelve and three in the afternoon almost every day of the season, its tortoiseshell wings spread flat, black and white striped antennae ending in orange tips. They are always male, waiting for a mate, rising to ward off any rival that might arrive. Life is a tricky business for the Duke of Burgundy butterfly, this propagation thing an exhausting battle, its cycle from birth to death complete within barely a week.

Kath marvels at the elegance of nature's evolution. You know that the masculine in a particular species of bee, her father pointed out to her in the garden at Ely, in the period before the females hatch, desperate for love, mistakes a specific orchid for its destiny and flies down to impregnate the bud, is disappointed, promptly forgets the failure and attempts the same with the next orchid it sees. Thus the Bee Orchid, you understand? Subterfuge its sole method of passing pollen and reproducing another flower.

John Garsington also is keen on butterflies. Kath and he together regularly count the specimens in a sector of The Kingsways, meeting on the ridge halfway between each of their homes. John claims to have been the first to notice the return of breeding pairs of Green Hairstreak and the last to record Small Pearl-bordered Fritillaries in their patch of West Somerset, in 1996, three years before he set up permanent home in the county. Butterfly names are redolent, no description necessary. John, a tall sophisticated man, darts like a child across the heather in pursuit of a rare specimen, to affirm its sighting. Out in the hills one dusk this June, Kath led her friend to a spot where a nightjar usually sings in season. And it did, mesmerisingly, the sound more man than bird, a lament at solitude. On the enclosed plot of land outside the front door at Grooms Cottage, between the path and the byre, John is making a butterfly meadow, planning this winter to degrade the soil with pebble aggregate from the quarry, thus to suppress the rooty wheat-grass and next spring to plant plugs of wildflowers beloved by Brimstones, Marbled Whites and Purple Hairstreaks. He has a list of desirable plants, of which natural marjoram is the main ingredient, its tight blue flowers long-lived, attractive to a mass of flying insects. His book of the moment, *The Aurelian Legacy. British Butterflies and Their Collectors*, has already been allocated its place on the natural history shelves, his field glasses resting on top of the low bookcase next to the door.

He telephones Kath to share with her the joy of new discoveries.

'Listen to this, it's wonderful,' John says. 'There was a woman collector called Margaret Elizabeth Fountaine. Before her death in 1940 she bequeathed her collection of twenty-two thousand butterflies to Norwich Museum. Twenty-two thousand, pinned and labelled in dozens of mahogany Hill cabinets! Together with a black-japanned box in a canvas holdall. Locked. With instructions that it mustn't be opened till the 15th of April, 1978. They waited, till the specified date. Until the 17th, in fact, because the 15th of that year was a Saturday and the museum was closed. Guess what was in it?'

'Oh, I don't know. The last example of some extinct species? Which she, knowingly, had chloroformed to complete her collection?'

'No.'

'What then?'

'Her journal, with its daily entries for sixty years. Plus a letter. In which she stipulates this delay, till the hundredth anniversary of her first entry. To hide public knowledge of her love for a Syrian guide, Khalil Neimy. They met in Damascus in 1901, when Neimy was twenty-four and Fountaine thirty-nine. He instantly declared his adoration of her. She writes of their research. And of travelling together for years, the relationship concealed. In the end they planned to marry and settle in America, but he contracted scarlet fever and died.'

'It never works that way round,' Kath responds. 'The women are always younger.'

'Yes, odd, really,' John agrees. 'Doesn't seem fair.'

'What else does your book say?'

'How he saved her life, in India. It quotes her journal: "The roving spirit and love of the wilderness drew us closely together in a bond of union, in spite of our widely different spheres of life, race and individuality, in a way that was often quite inexplicable to most of those who knew us".'

'It must have been,' Kath says.

'Sad.'

'Why be unhappy? It's a beautiful story.'

There's nobody in John's life to compare with Kath.

They like each other's houses, sharing a taste for order. Their possessions, although different in style, are equally significant to them both. John keeps his kitchen soap in a parian mini-christening font, supplied in the 1860s to Anglican vicars for attendance at death on birth; and he piles in the airing cupboard his identical white vests in strict rotation. Whereas Kath dusts her feet morning and night in talcum powder; and retains in dated files every subscription issue of the *New Statesman*, a habit hatched nineteen years ago. John's taste in furniture is excessive for his countryman's cottage: Gothic revival bookcases and tiles designed by Augustus Welby Northmore Pugin, creator of the wild interiors at the Houses of Parliament; which John combines with some modern mischief, including a blown chicken's egg signed by Gavin Turk, and Damien Hirst's *The Three Strange Partners*, one of a series of collages made from material Hirst found in the house abandoned by his neighbour in Leeds, Mr Barnes. Kath's favourite furniture at Parsonage Farm was made for her by a local friend, William Moray, who shares with his mother's sister a farm out towards Exmoor. He designed and built her big kitchen table, of green oak two inches thick, secured to curved refectory legs, their shape inspired by the roof trusses of West Country barns. William also made the elm door leading to the hall, with brace-struts to match the legs of his table, a personal detail enjoyed by him and Kath and almost nobody else in the world. His latest involvement is with the charred black bulk of squared beech trunks, the fissures of which he adores, cut and rounded for external use in gardens and glades. Tall, with lank dark hair and an oval skull, William was for years the central defender for a minor league football club in North Devon. Together with Kath, he is one of a loose circle of artist-friends who meet in the pub at Raleigh's Cross every couple of months, to pool resources of belief.

John likes William's work too.

'What's art?' he kind-of asks. 'It all is. What's more creative than good cooking? Craft, art, invention. It's all the same.'

He and Kath talk a lot about such things, seeking

understanding.

'The other day I felt so confused,' John says. 'I mostly want to want to be wherever I am. Walking, in this case, around the galleries. The three biggest. But I didn't feel ... safe? White Cube already worried me. Its name, what it is, a minimalist rectangle of taste. Big. Subdued. The floor of polished concrete. No labels. No prices, of course! The art? It was OK.'

'What wasn't?' Kath wonders.

He shakes his head, and closes his eyes, blue, with long lashes, his face a pleasant sun-tanned brown. 'I don't know ... A feeling ... that things aren't quite right.'

'Where to next?'

'Victoria Miro, in her new premises off the City Road. A warehouse. The same concrete floors. Open to the functional iron roof. "Last chance to see these fluid, decorative paintings that refer to fluency in more than one tongue and suggest mistrust of any single version of events." Something like that, in *Time Out*. Exactly, as a matter of fact. I remember the meaningless words, and my boredom.'

Kath waits, in silence.

John smiles. 'An interlude! Pot of tea in Exmouth Market, on my walk through to King's Cross and the Gagosian stronghold. I sit outside, beneath the awning. And can't close my ears to the conversation at the table next door. Two young lawyers, with nasal voices. "Spot of luck, they failed to dock my account this month of the mortgage," one of them says. He speaks into distant air, from nowhere to nowhere, not looking at his friend, who never looks at him. "Oh yes," the same oaf says. "Camilla was doing a shoot round here the other day ... a film shoot," he feels it necessary to explain. Later they laugh at the expense of some other friend. "My God, she's mad as a hatter! Should be in Rampton ... You've heard of Rampton?" "No. Where is it?" "Dunno, actually!" They again laugh, like foghorns.'

'It's difficult,' Kath says. 'I probably sounded like that, at their age. One does, from those schools.'

'I know, but it's so ... I don't know. So predictable?'

She shrugs. 'That's fashion for you. It happens quickly. The latest place "to be seen". And there they gather. Magic!'

'The food's excellent. Do people ruin things? They need customers in order to exist, I know ... I've no idea.' John's frown hardens. 'Gagosian too. Fantastic stuff. No title or name, though, anywhere. Like we should all *know*. And people put up with it. Wander around as if they're in a cathedral. Hushed. Flushed. Proud to be in the art crowd? I hate it.'

'Isn't Gagosian showing some Agnes Martin canvases? I read a review. They must be lovely. Aren't they?'

He sighs, and gazes at Kath as she weaves at the kitchen table a garland of rosemary, her old working hands supple and accurate.

'Yes,' he agrees, 'they are.'

'And?'

'I doubt my ... self? I could be deluded, again. It's possible that I don't really like any of it. Maybe I'm deceiving myself?'

Kath stops, is still.

'I don't think so,' she says – steady, supportive. 'I think you're fine. I like you.'

He sighs for the second time, at a different pitch. 'Me you too. And I bought you something, to prove it! Wait. It's in the car.'

John goes out through the back door, returning with a framed print, quite large: a coloured etching, signed in pencil by Julian Trevelyan and marked number forty-three of a hundred. The artist has drawn his own self-portrait, a bearded figure with wide eyes and long arms, standing beneath the open arches of a high loggia, in the background the towers of Florence, the campanile of the Palazzo Vecchio in front of Brunelleschi's cathedral dome.

'I saw it after supper, in the window of a shop in Museum Street. Went back the next day to buy it.'

She is happy. He sees that she is.

'How beautiful. Isn't that the Uffizi where Julian stands? He always loved Tuscany. Thank you. I didn't know it existed.'

The gift proved nothing – other than pleasing them both – which in itself is worth a shout of praise.

Some thoughts are slow in revealing themselves, take

hours and hours of worry before finding conscious shape. Others form and complete themselves in seconds of actual time, like dreams, even when they cover decades of life's experiences. It is the latter, on this occasion, when thoughts of Julian Trevelyan surface instantly within Kath, at this moment of shared silence with John Garsington.

Thoughts of feelings of remembered friendship with her father's cousin.

It had surprised her to find how quickly she and Julian had become, despite their generational differences, such good friends, independent of the Bishop. She misses him now, regrets all the things she failed fully to listen to, assuming he'd be there many other times to ask. Stewart's death had somehow been expected, less emotional, as though she'd always known she was going to spend these many years alone. After all, wasn't it what she wanted? And maybe the death of her father had passed in simple sadness because of the attention given by him to prepare for his absence those who remained behind – the quality, perhaps, of a man of God. When Julian died Kath had been left speechless with anger. How *dare* he? When she needed him next week: to pass his eye across the proof-pull of a woodblock; to banter his own brand of droll amusement down the telephone from the cottage in Cornwall to which he and Mary had retired. To be there for Kath: her sounding-board, the exemplary artist-friend.

She glances through her window and sees a dozen house

martins swoop in and out of their homes beneath the eves at Parsonage Farm, and almost cries. The *injustice* of it! Kath remembers a spring morning of her stay in Hampstead, when Julian and Mary received in the post a parcel containing two bird boxes, quickly mounted on their house to encourage the martins to roost. They had acquired a whole colony when the time came to leave to live in Cornwall. It was their example which, quite early on, had led Kath to purchase three mud and plaster boxes of her own from the Royal Society for the Protection of Birds. On a visit from her father, she and he had fixed them below the roof – when Julian was still alive, he too had visited, to witness with her the birds' flight.

Julian was the first figure outside her family whom, as a child, Kath had learnt with love to recognise. Because of his way of seriousness with her, she had never thought of him as old: the main reason for her sense of personal insult by his death. He truly was a friend, her equal. The girl in a boiler suit and the man in baggy linen, these two had often wandered together through the fens, in search of slow worms, chatting of this and that along the paths. When cathedral work allowed, the Bishop joined them, and Kath felt he treated both Julian and she as children, with unconditional indulgence, and with steady faith in who they really were. He treated them as creators, she in retrospect interprets.

Julian was so modern, so open to newness and experiment.

To Kath, when she was young, her contemporaries seemed ten times more conventional than Julian.

'The avant-garde are ageless,' she remembers him telling her, on the veranda one night during the months she stayed with them in Hampstead. 'And dateless. Whistler, a century ago, kept a wombat in his sitting room. It used to lie across the mantelshelf, warming itself. Or was the wombat Rossetti's? One of them, it doesn't matter which.'

On another occasion, standing together in a queue for an exhibition of De Morgan Pottery at the V & A, Julian had bumped into a man he knew from the concerts he attended, a pianist, grey-haired, not young at all. The two men, each more than twice her student-age, had exchanged news of the latest events in a language that had left Kath open-mouthed in adulation. This ancient pianist performed Cage premieres, was the first European at a public concert to stuff bails of straw beneath the lid of his baby grand! Astonishing! Most of Kath's contemporaries at the Guildhall School of Music were stuck at Debussy, couldn't cope with *his* modernity!

She shakes her head, still mystified by the world's conservatism.

'What're you thinking?' John asks.

Kath doesn't reply. She is lost in another memory of Julian Trevelyan.

She feels she is seeing Julian more accurately now than at the time of her trip by train to London with him, to catch at the Institute of Contemporary Arts a play from Cornwall he had heard was special: *A Minute Too Late*, it was called, the creation of the three men from Théâtre de Complicité, who also performed it. The miners' strike was at its height, she remembers. Remembers too that Julian was frail, older than she is now, that his confidence was on the ebb – physically at the lowest low-tide (never emotionally, not him). Kath pictures as if yesterday a moment on the small stage when the Englishman is making a cup of tea and the Belgian is pretending to be both the kitchen cupboard and the stove, producing appropriate noises: of gas hissing, kettle boiling, water being poured into the teapot and tea out into the cup, and the click of the spoon stirring the sugar. With nothing there, the whole scene mimed, until in a single movement of breathtaking dexterity he plucks it seems from the air an actual cup and saucer and places it on the palm of his colleague's waiting hand.

One of the nicest things about being with John, it suddenly occurs to Kath, is the way that in his company dead people remain alive. Especially artists. In their talk of Beuys he *is*, not was. Julian too. Steam rises from Kath's cup of tea.

··· CHAPTER THREE ···

ESTHER, KATH DISCOVERS, is the author of an anarchic intervention at Tate Modern about which John had recently spoken, not knowing it was her daughter's doing. In one of the loos in the Members Room, on the sixth floor of the South Bank power station, with extravagant views down the line of the new footbridge across the Thames to St Paul's and the City, someone had altered the white-printed inscription on the black back of a door to read: TATE RELIES ON BORES. THE PAPER IN THIS FACILITY HAS BEEN DONATED BY ANONYMOUS DOE. The printing was perfectly uniform inside his loo, and John had peeked in at the other joint Male/Female/Disabled doors, where he saw that the work was incomplete, the art-alterer caught at his task and forced to escape before the deed was fully done. 'His' is only partly true, for it turns out that it was Esther who had been surprised at the patient removal and replacement of individual letters, helped by a friend from university days.

Kath recalls how moved John also said he had been on this particular visit to the Tate by the Luc Tuymans show, of canvases in subdued colours, the scratched lines in the pigment visible only in the flesh – *Wrapping Paper*, for example: bluish-pink stripes across a grey ground, the contour of the stripes incised with feverish strokes, into which the wet paint falls back. John had found other notices in the Tate equally difficult to believe. On a door exiting from the Tuymans gallery to the café is written: EXHIBITION INSURANCE. GOVERNMENT INDEMNITY SCHEME ADMINIS-TERED BY THE DEPARTMENT OF CULTURE, MEDIA AND SPORT.

'What does this mean? Why here?' he had asked her, in amusement, and with the hint also of a buried note of distress.

Out walking with her daughter, and picturing her friend John Garsington's description of this day, Kath hears in her mind the echo of the Dylan song which she and Stewart were in New York to watch him publicly perform for the first time: 'Who killed Davey Moore? Why? What's the reason for?'

Kath enjoys learning that her own daughter perpetrated the Tate joke.

They are on holiday together when Esther tells her this, booked for a week into one of the National Trust cottages at Peppercombe on the North Devon coast, at that moment tramping the cliffs in the direction of Clovelly. They stop for breath and stretch out side by side on the dry moss.

'We went twice,' she admits, in a chuckle of pleasure at thought of the escapade. 'It was hairy!'

'You're a hoot!' her mother says. 'What drives you? I do love you so.'

Esther shoves a drama-arm across her eyes. 'Mum, please! You've no idea what you're talking about!'

'I *certainly* do,' Kath insists. 'I've never said it. Not properly. That's all.'

They smile forgivingly, and stroke each other's wrists, the older woman's brown and strong, the daughter's thin, pale, brittle.

'Why is it so hard? This love thing?' Esther asks. 'I can't seem to get it right.'

'To me you do. You're the most loving of all three.'

'Oh, Mum!' she almost sobs.

'Not now, don't be upset. We're having such a lovely time.'

'It's me, not you. And *him*!'

Kath is shocked to hear her daughter refer, in the voice she uses for him alone, to a particular boy she long ago ceased to date.

'When I asked him to do something for me,' she continues. 'Something intensely important to me. Something not easy for him. He refused. That's how I knew he didn't love me. Not as I need to be. I've worked it out. Because there're times when it's essential to do, without argument, what the other asks. Unconditionally.'

Kath says nothing as they get up and walk on – though there surely is something wrong, she feels, with what Esther believes. Right, maybe, of parental love for a child. But not between adults. Not the kind of lovingness she and Stewart shared.

At a twist of the high cliff path they stop to watch a cormorant fish off the rocks below, and Kath takes the opportunity of saying: 'A lot depends on what one means by the word love.'

Esther, it is clear, is about to react angrily. She sighs. Calms herself. 'What would you say love is?' she asks.

'Love is allowing someone to be himself.'

'*Her*-self!' Esther retorts.

Kath feels the stab of mother's guilt at her daughter's audible pain and bitterness. Am I wrong, she wonders? Is mine too glib, too cerebral a definition?

'Maybe it's that love is acceptance, of self and of other. In the here and now. Celebration of the mutual freedom to be ourselves,' she suggests, no less pedantically.

They again brush arms, and both know that the conversation is over for the moment.

'Look, there's Clovelly. It's miles away!' Esther points at a harbour along the coast. 'Come on, chin up, Mum!'

Ever since discovering, from the OS map, that Clovelly is half a day's walk on from Peppercombe, Kath has been anticipating their first sight of the fishing village, in an isolated cove on the jagged coast. For to her Clovelly is a symbol of her own childhood, in the Bishop's Palace at Ely, an image of winter nights with her father in the library, the scratch of his pen and her click-clicking over and over again of stereoscopic images on the View-Master. Three images from three different discs she best remembers: Niagara Falls in snow and ice; the wave photo on the beach at Acapulco, taken from an inch above the wet sand, the bubbles of the tide almost touchable; and from Devon Scenes, England, a group of fishermen seated on stools and lobster pots in the lea of the harbour wall at Clovelly, dressed to a man in black, smoking clay pipes of tobacco. The pictures had endlessly fascinated her, shedding a light on life beyond experience, super-real, an ideal to be struggled for and never reached. Later, when graphic presentation began to matter to her, Kath had taken them out again and noted the design of the discs' sleeves, with cinema-style shaded blue lettering, the Bakelite viewer stored in its purple box, an airtight swish to the lid. She preserves this keepsake of the 1940s close at hand, in a drawer in the workshop at Parsonage Farm.

The path climbs up and down again twice more from sea-level to cliff-top, then curls along a forest track to the entrance to the village, a single steep cobbled street, access by motor vehicle prohibited. Two men struggle down from the parking space with a giant cardboard box from Panasonic: a fridge or TV screen. Residents drag wooden sleds across the stones to their front doors stacked with plastic bags of shopping. On closer inspection Kath and

Esther find Clovelly to be nothing more than a tea and souvenir trap, the quaint ex-fishermen's cottages a barren warren of holiday lets. They escape as fast as they can, the View-Master scene as much a cheat in its earlier time as today's dislocation.

'How sinkering!' Esther says.

'Totally!'

Several months ago, on June 8th, 2004, Kath had watched with all three of her daughters the transit of Venus across the sun, one of five such occurrences during the whole history of humankind, a sight last witnessed on December 6th, 1882. It dawns on Kath, as she and Esther wander silently along beyond Clovelly, that she will never see this happen again. Nor will her children. Nor her grandchildren. Everybody alive today, and many others not yet born, will all be dead by the time Venus next gets around to crossing between the sun and the earth.

Esther tells Kath of another experience, on the Underground.

'The carriage is crowded. Opposite me sit this mother and daughter. A bit overweight. They look OK, though. Until the girl leans over and whispers something I cannot hear into the woman's ear, and the mother's face creases, horribly, as she snarls: "What do you mean, he's staring at you? Of course he isn't. Who'd stare at *you*!" I didn't see the man who might or might not have been looking. I just boiled with anger. At the mother.'

Kath does not respond immediately.

'There's so much – isn't there? – which one doesn't want to hear. And is forced to listen to,' she ends up saying.

'How do we survive?' Esther wonders.

'You know May, my friend out on the levels?' Kath sort-of replies. 'She's become really quite deaf. Worse at hearing women's voices than men's. Her old sheepdog is completely deaf. And decrepit. He coughs and hawks so violently at night that she's had to ban him his couch in the kitchen. May locks the dog out now, in the barn, where he sleeps on a folded mattress. He's happy. She knows him well enough to feel certain that this is so.'

There are things that Kath likewise knows to be true, inarguably. For instance: that she and her middle daughter, Esther, are kith and kindred, drawn from their different generations towards the same spaces. To the round Reading Room at the British Museum: Kath right then happens to be thinking about – perhaps because they had together visited the alterations on a rare trip of Kath's to London. Years apart, they had both studied in the original Reading Room, Kath turning up day after day in the early 1950s to look at the library's collection of books from private presses, her favourite at the time the brief period when the Golden Cockerel was owned by Robert Gibbings, himself a wood engraver. She still loves his 1931 Cockerel edition of the *Four Gospels*, a separate volume for each evangelist, illustrated by Eric Gill's finest work on wood. Gill was good, Kath feels, and in this he is at his best, she is not alone in believing. Thirty years later Esther worked at the BM professionally, as a trainee librarian. On returning the other day they both were shocked at the Reading Room's translation into a visitor centre, endlessly recorded by tourists on digital camera. In the cases are now displayed, for glazed-in viewing instead of removal from the shelves for study, copies of books from the libraries of famous English writers: Rudyard Kipling, Compton Mackenzie, Bernard Shaw and familiar others. Esther was perplexed to look up through the internal windows at the Foster atrium beyond and to spy, from below, the crossed silk legs of fashionable women seated at minimalist restaurant tables. It was much as she and her mother before her remembered, apart from the new notices on the blue leather reading desks, pandering to the public's desire for statistics: 'This restoration of the Reading Room to its former glory required the use of 25 kilometres of 23.25 carat gold leaf and over 2 tonnes of paint'.

'Hey, Mum?'

'What is it this time?'

'I love you.'

Kath is disarmed, completely.

'Do you remember once accusing me of being arrogant? I was furious!' Esther remarks, in a tumble of laughter. 'And you regretted it, and apologised. "At least you have something to be arrogant about," you said. You did, you know.'

'It's arrogant of you to remember!'

They really do like being together.

'I've no idea why, suddenly I see the sky-blue Dinky car-transporter that Uncle Richard gave you one Christmas,' Kath continues, a little further along the path. 'To a girl! I was incredibly annoyed with him.'

'And I liked it!' Esther responds.

'I know. Life's ridiculous.'

'Who are you telling!'

'Where do we draw the line? How do we know what's beyond toleration?' the mother wonders.

'I wish I did know,' the daughter replies, without emphasis.

'You do, don't you? ... You seem to.'

The look on Esther's face, of stubborn despair, tells Kath there's something serious hidden from her. Something she isn't sure she wants to hear. She nearly asks – but doesn't. It's for Esther to choose to speak or to be silent. We all, Kath believes, have a right to our secrets.

The two women are contrastingly dressed, a mark of divergence in taste and personality, not merely a matter of generation. Alike in many ways, they are far apart in others, a source of amusement to them both. Rather than tramping the West Country hills, Esther could have stepped off the cat-walk of a fashion parade in Paris: thigh-length brightly striped woollen leggings, two mini-skirts, both of lace, the black above the white, a studded leather jacket, bovver boots and a self-knitted tassel hat – she wears the same kind of thing to work at the Ashmolean, the slimmest, chicest, palest librarian of the universe – underneath the hat, her head these days is shaven bald. Kath, as usual, is dressed in black from neck to ankle, most of her clothes second-hand. There is a damp mist in the air, and she wears a man's black Burberry mac, over-size, billowing in the breeze, her thick grey hair no longer contained in its clip, loose strands glistening with drops of moisture. Neither see themselves, only each other, and they do not realise what an odd pair they appear to the occasional couple passing by from the opposite direction, equipped with anoraks and map-carriers, and wielding collapsible ski-sticks to negotiate the coastal path.

'If lions could speak, we wouldn't understand them,' Esther says.

'That's clever,' her mother comments.

'It's Wittgenstein,' she replies.

'I'm against "if". It's nostalgic, the seeking to exist in how things are *not*. I'm afraid Clem can be a bit like that. You never, I'm glad to say. I can see Wittgenstein doesn't like "if" either. Though he's saying something else as well.'

'Many things. There's never a single explanation.'

'I know.'

'Do you?' Esther asks, on the edge of aggression. 'I think we think we know too much. The other day I saw a film, *Turtles Can Fly*. Did I tell you?'

Kath shakes her head.

'It's the first feature film to come out of Iraq since the war. It's really ... moving, important. Centred on the children in a mixed refugee camp on the Turkish border. They are armies in miniature, marauding around their shanty shacks. Such cruelty. Such belief. Such effort. Such hope. Everything. They earn pennies in the rebel mountain market selling detonators from the bombs they defuse. At terrible risk. A little boy dies. Is killed. Drowned. By his half-sister. Who then kills herself.'

Esther takes a deep breath, before going on.

'What I mean is: what right have we to judge? How could any of us possibly know what it's like to be a Kurd? An Iraqi? Any Arab? It's terrible the way we in the West imagine we always know better. When it's exactly the opposite. We know less than nothing.'

'I agree, my love,' her mother says. 'All we have the right to expose is our own lives. Art too. It's essential, I feel, to write and paint and print what we experience, directly. I don't rate research. Not really. I'm sorry.'

'Nor do I. I know I work in the Ashmolean. It's different, though. Women study there their own heritage. Not another people's culture. We don't play God.'

'Who doesn't exist!'

'I know! It's crazy!'

'Years ago, soon after I came to live in Somerset,' Kath begins to tell, 'I met an old lady, in a house with green sash windows almost to the floor. Her niece lives there now. Beautifully. Nothing ever happened. When I passed there was never anybody around. And yet the front lawn, more daisy, dandelions and moss than grass, was always trim. I wanted to know who kept this place in unchanged perfection. Surrounded by old walls. An orchard at the side, barns, the corner of a cobbled yard visible through a gap in the wooden gate. Painted green, like the windows. I asked around, and someone said that a farmer's widow lived there, the land by then sold. And one day, riding by on my bicycle, there was a woman bent over the border in the garden, wearing a floppy hat. I stopped in the road beyond. Nearly continued on my way. Then turned around and wheeled my bike to the gate. I called, quietly: "Hello, I'm sorry to disturb." She didn't hear. And I called out twice more, the last time loudly, and she quivered, looked up, frightened, her neck crooked. "Don't worry. I just wanted to say: I love your windows. Every time I pass I smile when I see them. Thank you." I turned to go. She stopped me. "Really?" she said. "They aren't original, you know. Altered in the eighteenth century." I laughed, and said: "They're lovely, though. So many have been ruined." She hobbled down to the gate and we talked for maybe fifteen minutes. She was very alive, eyes bright beneath bushy brows. At one point she stood up straight, a handsome woman. "I'm meant to do exercises. Never have time. It's marvellous, isn't it? When you're my age, someone comes out once a week to give you an aromatic massage! Don't pay a penny!" I was sad when she died. And at the same time not at all unhappy. Not for her. She was a joy till the last. To herself too, I guess.'

'What're you saying?' Esther asks.

'I'm not sure! It *was* somehow relevant. To begin with!'

Neither minded. What mattered was to be together.

'Oh, yes, I forgot to tell you, Mum. I went to Strawberry Hill the other day, on the Thames near Twickenham. There's a library in the house which we've been asked to catalogue. Amazing place! Gothick madness! You know Hugh Walpole had his own private press? They've got a copy of everything he printed.'

'Seventeen fifty-seven to seventeen eighty-nine.'

'What?'

'The press's dates.'

'Jesus, you know everything!'

Mother and daughter travel again together at Easter, in the spring now of 2005, to stay for a couple of weeks with an ex-student-friend of Kath's, Paul Annesley, the music critic. He lives in Italy these days, in a farmhouse in the foothills of the Apennines, between Lucca and Camaiore, where he passionately gardens and writes esoteric works on the history of music. Paul has never been married – although he'd like to be, to Eric, his partner of thirty years, co-author of most of the books. Since childhood, Esther has been fond of Paul and loathed Eric. Kath is more generous, less dogmatic, happy with her friends' commitment. Paul has retained his clipped good looks on into his seventies, and he and Kath make a handsome pair as supper guests at classic villas out in the Lucchesia – the cause of envy to Esther, who herself longs for their easy familiarity.

'Were you ever a decent singer?' she accuses Paul, at a trattoria one evening in the next village.

They are all slightly drunk, seated at a round table in the window. Eric fails to suppress a giggle.

'For a brief moment, I thought I was,' Paul admits. 'Soon hit the barrier. And was smart enough to become a critic ... Your mother, you know, could really play,' he adds. 'I was shattered when suddenly she wasn't there. Had taken herself off to St Brides to be a printer.'

'You didn't say. I thought you agreed. Were you pretending?' Kath challenges.

Paul's face is bathed in warm soft wrinkles. 'Not in the least. I believed in you. Still do.'

'In what? In my "talent"? Don't tell me! I hate the word!'

He breaks into open laughter. 'Dear Kath, you're a delight. You've always wanted something different. I admire you for it. I'm serious.'

'What was she like then?' Esther asks, in quieter voice.

'Very definite!' Paul replies. 'Even about her uncertainty. If you see what I mean.'

'Funny. You seem quite benign these days, Mum.'

Kath knows that her daughter, privately, is both paying a compliment and being ironical. 'I suppose things will always matter to me. Because I want them to. I owe it. To nobody, of course, other than myself. A debt for a gift? Perhaps. Because I do feel gifted. With health and education. The gift, too, of being born a woman. I never want it to stop.'

She sees in her mind as she speaks the people whose example inspired her in the 1950s, in their female-only work at the Women's Printing Society in Piccadilly. One of them, Elizabeth Friedländer, Kath several times had tea with, and was openly encouraged to give up music and join the collective.

'Did your father ever forgive you?' Paul wonders.

'The Bishop? Probably not,' Kath says. 'Though he was able to make the best of his disappointment. Welcomed me as a creator of books, and forgave the loss of his dream-daughter. The maestro musician. By the end he accepted that I just wasn't suited to the limelight.'

'But you're a star! You *are*!' Esther insists.

Paul again smiles. 'You are pretty bright, Katherine Trevelyan. You can't *not* shine. One way or another.'

'Well ...' Kath shrugs. 'Whatever you say.'

'The novelist B.S. Johnson said,' Eric intervenes to quote, from memory: '"We shall die untidily, when we did not properly expect it, in a mess, most things unresolved, unreckoned, reflecting that it is all chaos. Even if we understand that all is chaos, the understanding itself represents a denial of chaos, and must therefore be an illusion." I rather agree.'

'Grant us, God, our illusions,' Paul mutters.

'What are you on about?' Eric queries.

'Nothing. Nothing important.'

'Can believe that!'

They pay and leave.

First thing every morning Paul makes himself a demi-tasse of black coffee and wanders out to inspect his garden, beginning, normally, in the salad beds and moving on via the rose parterre to the vegetable patch. Against his inclination, three seasons ago he was forced to protect his territory from the night-time attack of wild boar, intent on digging up with their noses and tusks the young plants. A wire-mesh fence concealed on the farm-side of the laurel hedge now keeps safe his kitchen garden – where he stops on his morning walks to pick each day fresh vegetables; herbs too, designing the daily menu as his spirits revive from his usual dawn gloom, their food, which he himself always cooks, a reflection of the garden seasons. He almost always forgets the place where he lays down the small cup, and almost always finds it later in the day, sensibly displayed in a prominent position. Paul is particularly keen on composting, an art foreign to his Italian neighbours. He once tried, not unsuccessfully, the spiral method of the

Japanese, but has since reverted to the plain two-bin style of his Surrey youth, the resulting produce from the garden never failing to impress. He resists Eric's pleas, on behalf – largely – of visitors, for a swimming pool. And the old grass tennis court down below the lowest olive terrace, near the village school, he has planted out with potatoes, carrots and leeks, and black cabbage for the winter.

Kath loves being there.

'Is this a sort-of rugela?' Esther checks.

Her mother tastes a leaf. 'I reckon,' she says.

It is close to midday, and the two of them – Kath in a straw hat, Esther's bare skull brown in the sun – are out scouring the banks for wild salad leaves for lunch.

'Every time I come I forget what's what. A blank spot,' Kath acknowledges, crouching in the grass beneath an apple tree. 'I'll never be sure.'

'I'm *hopeless*!'

'Just thinking of something else.'

'Not thinking. Fussing.'

'Time, Esther. Give it time.'

'How long? I'm already ancient. Clem's got three growing kids. And she's the baby of the family!'

To Kath the dual mention of Clem and children could only mean Robert, her sole male grandchild. It is simpler to contemplate her feelings for – or against, rather – her grandson from abroad than from at home in Parsonage Farm. The violence of emotion shocks her. What's going on inside, she wonders?

Boys *are* a problem.

On a recent visit to the National Gallery, in the same room as the lances and rearing horses of Ucello's *Battle of San Romano*, Kath had for the first time seen a pair of Pessellino panels, on wood, narrow and long. One described the slaughter of the giant Goliath by young David; the second showed his triumphal entry into Jerusalem, standing on a chariot, the black-gowned figure of the old King Saul seated in the open carriage in front of him. There were horses also in the Pessellinos. And a similar dark green landscape. According to the label the pictures were acquired by the gallery in the year 2000; the viewer's attention is directed towards the kneeling figure of the female donor in the left-hand panel, and in the other to the exquisite detail of the Tuscan farms she had brought to the man she married, as part of her dowry.

Kath remembers this occasion. And also in her mind admits that, as a child, she had struggled with her brother Richard. Or something. There's a lot about this time she simply cannot recall.

'Your father, without training, really did have a beautiful voice,' she tells Esther, following on from the conversation at supper the night before. 'He was a counter-tenor. By nature. Did you know?'

'I never heard him sing.'

'He didn't much. As we wouldn't go to church.'

'Wasn't Bob Dylan his thing anyway? Not Bach!'

Kath frowns, at the memory of being taken by Stewart, as a birthday treat, to the Dylan concert at Philharmonia Hall in October 1964. It was Halloween night, and Dylan was only twenty-three, a stooped figure perched on a stool beneath a spotlight at the centre of the stage, mouth-organ strapped to his neck and large guitar lodged on his raised knee. He wore light-brown suede shoes, and the protest singer Joan Baez joined him for three of the later numbers. There were seventeen songs in all that night in New York, including the single encore. Kath loves the song – though she can't remember its name – in which he credits a particular philosopher, Schopenhauer or someone, for a quote, and then, with a chuckle, claims the next line as his own: 'That's Bob Dylan!' he says, on the bootleg tape. She recalls from this concert the singer's inner joy, his youthful surprise at having an audience, and interprets this now as clear proof of the possible unity of private with public happiness.

'Music brings people together,' she says. 'It always has for me. Think of Rachel.'

'Were you at the Guildhall at the same time?' Esther asks. 'I like her too. The viola. She draws the bow across her own guts.'

'Esther!'

'She *does*, Mum!'

'Maybe ... The other day I came across a book, *Nine Suitcases*, written by Bela Zsolt, who'd been on the same train as Rachel from Budapest to Bergen-Belsen, in 1944. One of the sixteen hundred wealthy Jews ransomed from incarceration in the ghetto for a thousand dollars each, in a deal between Kastner and the Nazis. Rachel told me how they were meant to be handed over to the Red Cross at the Swiss border. And weren't. At the concentration camp were ushered instead into the washroom. She aged thirteen, with her mother and her grandmother. Ordered to strip and place their belongings into different heaps. If it hadn't been for an air-raid siren, they'd have been gassed. By the time their guards, women as well as men, were again ready to kill them, their safe passage had been confirmed in a telegram. She survives. And does indeed play the viola, like ... like she does.'

'Does Paul know Rachel?'

'Yes.'

'It must have been hard discovering he wasn't good enough to be a professional singer. With friends all around who were great.'

'Rachel is "great", it's true. And musicians can tell. They know who's faking.'

'Don't we all? If we're honest.'

'Paul has perfect pitch. He hears and feels simultaneously. Has taught himself also to understand. It doesn't matter that he can't perform,' Kath says, returning to her daughter's previous remark.

'The composers he writes about. Ligeti and Cage.

Birtwistle, his favourite,' Esther says. 'He's always so sure of his ... taste? It's bigger than that. He claims that the quality of Birtwistle's music is no longer a matter of opinion. I remember the time ... How old was I? No more than ten! When he promised me that I'm living in the presence of a genius! Like being in Vienna with Mozart!'

Kath defends her friend. 'I sympathise,' she says.

'Arrogance?' Esther teases.

They smile at each other, pick up their baskets of salad leaves and wander up the track home for lunch.

Kath finds herself thinking of another picture she also saw on this trip to London, at the Tate Modern, a strange work by the playwright August Strindberg. Strange in itself, and even more so for its date, pre-1900: two canvases mounted as a single image, a square cut in the one to house the other, his black stark seascape framing a sunny view of the Swedish countryside, with white mountains between meadow and sky – a symbol of contradiction, the epitome of tortured human emotion. Looking at the show, Kath wrestled with a fact of life she isn't sure she likes: her suspicion that most of the artists whom we now know all knew each other. She rebels against the coterie of fame, sniffs collusion, Strindberg no exception. In the exhibition at the Tate Kath noticed a portrait lithograph of him by Munch, for which he sat six times in total silence, his loaded revolver placed within reach on an adjacent table. In Paris Strindberg was a friend of Gauguin's, and when the painter auctioned his entire studio of work in the February of 1895, to raise money for his return trip to Tahiti, the playwright was asked to compose an introduction. Strindberg refused, in an elegant letter which Gauguin so relished that he printed it in the catalogue anyway, Strindberg's expression of confusion and fear at the power of Gauguin's art an unintended hymn to radical modernism. This fact Kath definitely does like, even though the unintendedness of much of what we do does, she agrees, make life difficult to balance.

Paul, Eric, Kath and Esther drive together up through the mountain passes behind the farm into the Garfagnana, to visit the Carrara marble quarries, veiled in mists of rain from the sky and of cordite from the explosions. They stop at the Church of San Francesco in Barga and stare in awe at a fifteenth-century Della Robbia panel of the visitation in a dream by the crucified Christ. Cast in relief in great chunks of painted and glazed terracotta, the panel is enormous, the figure of Saint Francis shown kneeling in a hilly garden landscape where birds perch on the rocks nearby; he is wearing his brown cassock, a similarly clad colleague cringing in terror at his side.

The four friends also take long walks straight from the house out into the hills, where they eat picnic lunch lolling in the terraced groves and vineyards of near-deserted villages, the land still cared for, families driving up from the industrial valleys below at festive weekends to tend the lands of their forefathers. Paul leads their explorations of paths through chestnut forests, the ancient trees low-growing, arthritic, left rotting on the ground the fruit that until recently was the staple diet of both the peasants and their pigs. Working men and their motley dogs arrive these days by carloads at designated rendezvous in the hills at dawn on Saturday and Sunday mornings, dressed in camouflage gear, intent on hunting down the wild boar. Shot-guns balanced across their shoulders, they tramp their unmolested rights of public passage and let blast at every animal and bird which dares to move, an all-comers' tradition disavowed by the privileged exclusivity of hunting to hounds back home. The swifts of the Lucchesia and the stags of The Kingsways, all the same, are murdered.

'Men pick the olives as well as shoot,' Paul defends his neighbours, at supper back home, two plain carafes of red wine to hand at table. 'That's how it is.'

Esther cannot be silent: 'Doesn't make it right! It's horrid!'

'Why? The *cacciatori* enjoy themselves. The birds learn to go elsewhere. It makes no difference.'

'Aaargh! The status quo! I hate you!'

'For our first fifteen years Eric and I could have been sent to jail for living together,' Paul quietly replies. 'Some things matter more than others.'

They are sitting out beneath the newly-built loggia beyond the kitchen, made of seasoned timber and local stone, with reclamation terracotta tiles on the shallow-pitched roof, a view through to the pilgrim church behind. A giant walnut tree, hundreds of years old, overhangs their yard, where wild flowers grow between the stone slabs. They smell the rough smoke of a cigarette from the balcony window of one of the three other houses in the hamlet, none of which can they see.

'How's Richard since retiring?' Paul asks Kath.

'Much the same. Pretty weird,' she replies.

'It's some time anyway since the school closed. One forgets.'

'And for years there were barely any students. The blind are integrated, these days. Happily. My brother didn't ever really care. About the people. I never felt he did.'

'I don't know. Maybe he just doesn't fit in,' Paul suggests. 'Isn't he insanely knowledgeable about spiders?'

'Moths! Uncle Richard is a world authority on the Silver-Striped Hawk Moth,' Esther informs. 'He has, I suspect, seen more examples than anyone else alive in England. They breed in migrancy, he tells me, in particular at Bunhill Fields, the Wesleyan cemetery in East London.'

'Dad had a King Penguin on moths. With a really beautiful cover,' Kath says. 'The stylised bands reversed. One moth one way up, the other the other. On a mottled red ground.'

'Amazing!'

'What?'

'The things you remember!' her daughter answers.

'And forget. I'm surprised how much of the past is inaccessible,' Kath says. 'I don't believe it actually can be. But it seems so.'

Kath is thinking of Richard, her brother, and wondering what happened to the years of their teenage contact, which she knows must have existed and yet appear, as far as his presence is concerned, blank. Where and what was he? Who *is* he? This ex-headmaster of an ex-school for the blind, the janitor of some crumbling Victorian mansion, a Gothick monster, which it costs more to keep the rain from invading than its value justifies. Richard bought the building for a song, a fever hospital during the war, the place to which soldiers were removed to live in isolation for months on end. At the side some buildings from the later boom years of public speciality, a swimming pool and gymnasium, he rents out now to a private sports organisation. People from The Kingsways arrive regularly to swim, and to play five-a-side-football. Whilst children escape on Council-paid exeats from inner-city deprivation to stay for an hysterical week or two of freedom in the 1950s dormitories of the long-defunct junior school.

And Richard survives, a hermit, capturing moths in his traps at night.

How, Kath tries to work out, are she and he siblings? Whose child is he?

Her mother's, obviously.

And her father's?

He is, yes, he must somehow be the son of both her parents.

Kath is at once aware of how seldom she thinks about her mother – not simply because Heather Trevelyan has been dead a long time, and the Bishop, in direct temporal terms, has therefore occupied much larger a space, but because her mother had always been a lesser person.

Less to Kath, that is, not the same necessarily for Richard. Quite the opposite, maybe.

She has no idea what he felt then, nor what it is that matters most to him now. He is, she admits, one of the few people with a presence in her life for whom she does not care. Richard and Robert, the two 'R's, her brother and her grandson, neither of whom does she really like. Richard is Robert's great-uncle. What does this mean, in the context of her distaste? It's difficult for Kath to admit that she really doesn't know what she thinks about this, her vision opaque, a muddy muddle.

'Do you reckon Clem is a good mother?' Esther asks.

Kath is taken aback at her daughter's question, as if Esther had been reading her mind as accurately as a book in her library at the Ashmolean. For Kath had, in fact, been wondering whether her own mother had been any good at mothering boys; and from this had stepped on to puzzle about Clem too. Her conclusion, reached at the moment Esther spoke, being that she, she is certain, would herself have been a bad mother of boys.

'Clementine?' Kath says, stalling for time.

'Yes!'

'She's great with children. She lets them be. They're fine. Even Robert. He's a boy, that's all.'

Esther opens wide her eyes, in admiration at her Mum's willingness to talk. 'Clem's supposed to be the lost last child,' she says, in a rush of words. 'And she's an unmarried mother aged forty-two! Perfectly sure of herself. Unworried about men. Doesn't mind at all who the three different fathers are. Says she doesn't know anyway. Which I don't believe! Leaving me to be all messed up!'

'And me?' Paul intervenes to ask, pouring himself another glass of wine. 'I'm such a shining adult? Age is immaterial.'

'I know, but at least you're sorted. You and Eric. Write books and all that. What about *me*? I'm a mess!'

In the candlelight on the loggia Esther looks so beautiful, her bald head set off by radiant eyes and by earrings of polished chicken wishbones. Even she, as if seeing herself reflected in the benevolent gaze of her mother and of her mother's friends, smiles, has to fancy herself a bit. 'Oh, what the hell!' she says. 'It's Sunday!'

It isn't, but they know what she means.

Kath often dwells, these days, on the subject of age. In part because she is afraid of death, hasn't yet been able to accept her own mortality.

'Do you really believe it doesn't matter how old one is?' she asks Paul. 'Because it does. In the physical sense. I mean, some day I simply won't be here. Nor will you. Quite soon we'll be "dust indivisible".'

'"During the universal finale, at the moment of eternal harmony",' Paul quotes, in unhesitant recall from his favourite novel, *The Brothers Karamazov*, '"there will occur and become manifest something which will be sufficient not only to make it possible to forgive but even to justify all things that have happened to men – and even if all that, all of it, makes itself manifest and becomes reality, I will not accept it and do not want to accept it! Even if the parallel lines converge and I actually witness it, I shall witness it and say they have converged, but all the same I shall not accept it." Not a nothing point of view!'

'Never give up, are you saying? Is it so simple?'

'You can't, Kath. People like you go on to the end. I intend to too. We're lucky, I feel.'

'It's an invidious form of invincibility,' Eric says. 'An illusion, of course. Makes Paul feel better, though. So: what harm?'

Esther joins in. 'I wish nobody needed to do any of that. The I-can't-be-conquered gag. Who're they kidding? Themselves, more than likely. It's always the nice ones who make a mistake. Take more than they can manage and end up addicts.'

'Hazards.'

'Fences to jump.'

'Chance or choice?'

'I don't believe in destiny, if that's the issue,' Esther then says. 'Or fate. Which is much the same. It's probably something about our not being able to choose what is done to us by others, and yet becoming free enough in spirit to decide what we ourselves do in response.'

'Within the limits of our own experience.'

'Exactly.'

'And within the capacity of individual character.'

'Ditto.'

'Mmm ... interesting.'

They all four laugh, Eric at himself, aware that the other three could see that he wasn't 'interested' at all, indeed profoundly disagreed with Esther's theory.

'Mary Fedden doesn't give up,' Kath says, again serious. 'Born during the First World War and still going strong. There's always more to do if you're a painter.'

Although Kath had liked cousin Julian a great deal, indeed had loved him, since his death she had become even closer friends with his wife, visiting her at least once most months at home in Cornwall. Mary had spoken recently about being appointed in 1956 the first woman tutor at the Royal College of Art. They both agreed: it was ludicrously late. Were women so little valued? Or over-valued, maybe, and punished by men for being the ultimate essential, the single necessity in all our lives: the mother?

Artists are different, are treated by men more as equals, in Kath's experience. It is the same for Mary Fedden. The great Welsh collector John Gibbs was unusual in owning more of Mary's paintings than anybody else's, five in all. His favourite was of two young girls carrying sunflowers and offering them across a table to someone whose hand only is seen; there are wide stretches of unpainted white canvas, with pencil marks, and all the characters are black-skinned, like the Gibbs' grandchild Rebecca, at whose birth the picture was bought in commemoration. John Gibbs owned only one painting by Lucien Freud, an early work, of a dead chicken on a striped trestle table.

'He's a fraud, Freud. A socialite,' Esther pronounces.

Eric again disagrees. 'Nonsense! He handles paint like ... like he has no choice.'

'I'll agree he's sensual. Even with the corpse of a hen!'

'Isn't that the point? Creation, outside the womb, is sexless,' Paul suggests. 'Rather, is gender neutral ... Unless the ... Christ knows! Let's go to bed!'

··· CHAPTER FOUR ···

BACK HOME FROM ITALY, Esther stays on with her mother for several weeks at Parsonage Farm. She is off work, on extended sick leave after the recurrence of an illness which first made itself known when she was an undergraduate, reading History at the London School of Economics. Her doctor expects rest to be all she'll need, this time.

She and Kath call for tea one afternoon at Grooms Cottage. John Garsington welcomes them at the gate.

'It looks lovely. I haven't been for ages,' Esther says, stopping on the daisy-covered path to the front porch, the tall grasses of the butterfly meadow shaking in the breeze. 'You seem more settled.'

'I suppose I am,' he acknowledges, his voice deep-pitched, the words pronounced with habitual authority.

'It isn't easy, the country idyll. It's taken time,' Kath explains, as if defending him.

'Tea? In the garden?' he suggests.

Mother and daughter nod. 'Please,' they say, in unison.

Esther inspects the open-plan ground floor of John's cottage while he boils the kettle. The sanded floorboards are without stain or wax, practicable for a tidy bachelor, living alone. Everything is precisely in place, she notices. Just right, she feels, a perfect balance, the natural colour of untreated wood a particular pleasure.

'I love the combinations. The old with the new. When one looks closely, each object a gem of its kind. You care, don't you?'

'About my stuff?'

'Yes,' she replies.

'Of course,' he affirms.

Esther approves of John's internal order, the sense of there being nothing superfluous. Although he owns all sorts of things – books and tiles and textiles and ephemera and furniture and other bits and pieces – the house feels authentic, lived in and with. The experience of seeing again him and his home has a strong effect on her.

John leads the way through a gap in the wall, past the entrance porch of the old half of his cottage, towards the curved seat of the arbour. He carries the mugs, milk jug and teapot on a brass Damascus tray, circular, with ring-gathered carrying struts, the centrifugal force from which allows the tray to swing without spilling a drop of liquid. Hops have begun their growth up the arched poles of the arbour, the yellow leaves due in high summer to offer shade. The ground upon which their feet rest is a mosaic of swirling pattern, made of Nelson brick, fans of cut pantiles and upended bottles of Becks beer.

The talk over tea is of the rocking chair newly placed in John's sitting room, bought at auction while Kath was away in Italy. He hadn't yet told her the story of the sale in the Cotswolds of a remarkable collection descended direct from the original owner at the end of the nineteenth century, a man called Robert Weir Schultz, who had commissioned it to be made by his local craftsmen-friends, the Barnsley brothers, and their architect partner, Ernest Gimson.

Both Esther and Kath can picture the sitting room as John speaks of the ebonised elm chair with its bobbin-turned back and the wear on its chamfered rockers. For him, knowing of the creative intimacy of connection to these heroes of the Arts and Crafts movement gives this furniture a quality, a character, a beauty invaluable, far beyond monetary measure.

'It's silly, I know. But to me it matters. That Gimson not simply designed this chair, he actually sat on it!'

'A dowel is missing, I noticed. You should get it cut. William would do it for you. Happily,' Kath says.

'Excellent idea. I'll ask him,' John responds.

'What else did you get?' Esther asks.

'Oh ... this and that.' John is diffident, like a child, a shy proud boy. 'Things were awfully expensive. I was lucky with the log basket,' he admits, with undisguised delight.

'Wonderful thing! The chairs, though, they're really what the auction was about ... somehow ... to me.'

John is referring to another chair he bought, and to one he failed to purchase, despite bidding twice the sum he originally intended. The first, placed beside the walnut chest in his main spare bedroom, is a Clissett ash ladder-back, cut and shaped with great delicacy, its tall back-rods turned on the curve, the ends tapering to ringed points.

'What's the difference? Why so crucial to me? To know that an old man near Hereford, a traditional bodger called Philip Clissett, made my chair?' John's blue eyes stare into the distance, at the shape of the ancient woodland on Granthorne Hill. 'Gimson and his crew, they learnt their craft from him,' he continues. 'Sydney Barnsley had a Clissett ladder-back in his parlour at Sapperton. Exactly like mine. Which he himself may have rush-seated for his friend Schultz.'

For several seconds nobody speaks. They listen to the spring songs of the birds.

'It's important,' Kath quietly insists. 'Your valuing this simple chair keeps its maker alive.'

'Thank you. I think so too,' John says.

'And the other? The piece you missed?' Esther asks.

'I'm afraid my wish to own that was less forgivable. Because it's "by" someone. And very rare, possibly unique. It's the big W.R. Lethaby-designed oak barrel-back. Initially Gimson's, photographed by his fireplace at home in

Gloucestershire, exhibited at Barnards Inn in Holborn in eighteen ninety-one.'

'You like it, though?'

'Oh, yes, I think it's marvellous. It *is* marvellous. I just question the nature of my desire to possess it. Unfulfilled, in this instance.'

'Maybe you should be less hard on yourself,' Kath suggests.

'Or harder? You haven't known me long enough!'

A family of geese fly overhead, in arrow formation, honking.

'What a nice story,' Esther says. 'To tell and to hear.'

'It's true. More or less. Memory embroiders, I find.'

'Pleasurably.'

'Yes,' he allows. 'An Easter present to myself.'

At the mention of Easter, Esther's thoughts retreat inside her head. She ceases to be aware of where she is, lost in pursuit of clarity on an issue that has eluded her now for two weeks. Easter in Italy had taken Esther by surprise – coming early this year, everyone said, to her bewilderment. Like the moon changing its trajectory in the sky. Aren't things better fixed? How come there's so much change around the place? And what, anyway, *is* 'The Passion'? Esther had realised, in near despair, that she didn't know what her favourite music meant, that it had not until this moment registered with her that Bach's *St Matthew Passion* was a song of Easter.

Worse.

She couldn't be sure that it was indeed the Bach *Passion* which she loved best, and not, instead, his *B Minor Mass*. Was that about Easter too? On return from Italy to Parsonage Farm she had rushed to listen to the pieces, and even then had at first not been able to tell which contained the particular piece of music. Although she was almost sure it was near the end of one or the other. The bass in both, she read on the sleeves, was the same man. No help there. The *St Matthew Passion* was sung in German, she discovered, which further confused her. And then, with tears of relief, she located in the Mass the passage she was longing to hear, from the Nicene Creed: 'In spiritum sanctum ... catholicam et apostolicam ...' – these few of the many words echoing through her soul. There is much, though, which continues to mystify her. Was Bach religious? Has she missed the point of all he wrote? Is *she* a fraud?

Esther doesn't notice the flutter of butterflies across the sloped rough garden of Grooms Cottage: two Orange Tips and a Speckled Wood.

'Getting there,' John says. 'One day I'll have all the kinds that can naturally live here.'

'Where's your Buckthorn?' Kath asks.

'Haven't got any yet. So no breeding Brimstones.'

'It's nice just to sit,' she responds.

Kath cleans her spectacles with the cuff of her cardigan.

In the silence, Esther refocuses on the world outside her own troubles. 'You've reminded me of something,' she says, excitedly. 'The cleaning of Dad's spectacles! He never bothered. And you never minded. Just did it, without a word. Putting them back in his cloth case when you'd done. I always felt it was an act of love.'

'It was. It still is, I suppose, in its way, when I now do it for myself. Your father long dead and my eyesight these days weakening.'

'What do we each see?' John wonders, gesticulating from the arbour at the scene of rural seclusion. He speaks quietly, not easy to hear, not always wanting to be heard. 'Nobody knows. We sit here assuming that at least we agree on ... that.' Again he waves a hand at the view. 'And yet the one thing we *can* guarantee is that we all see totally different pictures.'

'Sculptures,' Esther corrects. 'Three dimensional, at the least.' She too gesticulates at the stepped lines of trees retreating up the hill towards the sky. 'Land sculpture.'

'I agree. This morning I cut two small sycamores from the lane, lopped a branch off a larger one that was taking light from a young copper beech, and shaped the laurel by the kennels. I'm sculpting. Not gardening. What else could you call it?'

'Does it matter what word? It's only language.'

John shrugs. 'We try. Sculpture, pictures, buildings, prints, books. Words, yes. We don't exist unless we somehow communicate.'

'But ...' Kath is about to argue, to explain to John

Garsington that language itself can never be enough, that everything doesn't have to be paraded in its full regimental colours, a band playing, the troops in ordered ranks. Feeling often isn't defined. Which doesn't mean you don't know it's there, dependable while also unknowable. 'Never mind,' she says.

Esther is again wandering around the gallery inside her head. She is picturing an incident back at the cottage, when John was slicing lemon for their tea. He had been holding the sharp knife in an awkward position and was unaware how easy it might have been for the blade to slip and slice the folds of skin between his thumb and forefinger. Watching him, Esther had remembered the fear her father instilled in her of the danger of cutting herself there, in an instant the accident locking her jaw shut. She is imagining never being able to eat again. Or talk. Imagines John maybe never again talking and thinks how sad that would be, as she enjoys his stories. Her father, Esther accepts, must in his turn have been terrified as a child by his mother's threats. Granny by her mother's. Backwards to the Garden of Eden.

'Old wives' tales,' she mutters, out loud.

Kath glances sharply at her daughter, but sees that she is far away in her thoughts. 'Clown!' she softly says.

John feels a little lost at these exchanges, and takes the last word literally. 'Do you like the circus?' he asks. And, without a pause for the reply, continues: 'As a child I used to stare transfixed by the men and women on the high trapeze.

They seemed different beings, non-humans, crossing and meeting and holding. Swinging higher than the search-lights. Right up against the stripes of the big top. Wreathed in smiles. I see them waving at intervals on their slow ascent up the rope ladder. I can't now remember them ever descending after their display. In my dreams they never return to earth. Never consent to being human. Fly forever towards each other through the sky.'

'Did we go, Mum? I remember Bristol Zoo. The stink of the hippopotamus. Did we go to the fair too?' Esther asks.

'Not with me, no,' Kath replies. 'I hate circuses.'

'I once went to a travelling circus in Cairo,' John elaborates – as if talking to himself. 'The daughter of the lion tamer was a contortionist. She bent her limbs into impossible shapes. Like a rubber doll. She was young. About ten, I guess. The lion tamer, in various costumes, was the juggler and flame-thrower, one of the clowns, and the ringmaster at the finale, dressed in a brocade jelaba, purple slippers with curled toes and an embroidered fez. I was staying with a friend from Cambridge, on my way back from buying stuff from some dealers in Tehran. He was working on flood-plain technology. Nice man. We've since lost touch.'

'My tutor at the LSE was at Cambridge. David Starkey.'

'Oh, him!'

'So? What's wrong with the Doc?'

'Nothing. Nothing at all. I used to admire him. We were

in the same college. In the same digs, as a matter of fact. During my first year, his second, I believe. Out on the Girton Road.'

'Were you?' Esther is intrigued. 'Tell me!'

'He *has* changed.'

'In what way? He was fun to be taught by. Such intellectual gusto! Hell to any student who didn't try.'

'Mild as mist, silent as a ladybird.'

'You're joking!'

'Seriously. All he did was work. How do you think he knows so much? Bided his time. Till he'd read every piece of Elizabethan text in existence as fast and as thoroughly as he could and ever since has out-argued the world.'

'Great!'

John nuzzled the corner of his lower lip. 'One January morning I was cycling down the hill into town and drew up at the Trumpington Street traffic lights behind two Girton girls, also on bikes. And the brunette said to her friend: "Cold on the cunt today, isn't it?" Nothing special. Ordinary tone of voice.'

'And?'

'I never saw Starkey on a bicycle.'

'He was born with a club foot,' Esther informs.

'Ah.'

'Is that all?'

'At present,' John says. 'Hot buttered toast? Lardy cake?'

'Thanks. Not for us,' Kath replies.

Kath, like her daughter, falls silent. Not a harsh silence, but thoughtful: about John, and the beautiful place he has created for himself, both the house and the garden. While good at such things, with a vision all of his own, her friend – in many ways her closest friend – isn't happy, she acknowledges. What's wrong with him, she asks herself? Why does he always manage to withdraw into the distance, without ever directly saying that this is his wish, his need?

She finds this part of John difficult to tolerate.

Stewart was completely different. Different from any other man Kath has ever met. Not a man at all, in the normal sense of the word. More like a woman is reckoned to be: sensitive, earth-bound, communicative. This is not Kath's view – for she has always fought against the idea that men and women are separate entities, opposition of character inevitable; on the contrary, she believes that all people are in essence the same in what at heart they care about. In memory, Stewart proves that she is right. He was, maybe above everything else, the loveliest man with whom to have children. Kath had found the business of pregnancy depressing, the years of young motherhood not much better, always wishing for more time and energy to get on with her own work, angry at accusations of 'unwomanly' emotions, while secretly racked with guilt for feeling the way she did. Not wholly alone, though: to Stewart she had always been able to talk. And by assuming his equal share in parenthood he had seen to it that she take as much time as she needed in the studio, at her old Albion, pressing the latest text. Kath assumes that her husband was the principal reason why she had come around to being a contented mother, choosing to seek for a third child on through the two miscarriages she suffered between Esther and Clementine, ceasing then to become pregnant again because Stewart died: in the armchair by the stove at Parsonage Farm, from a congenital heart attack, interrupted in the unlacing of his boots after a walk on the hill.

The mid-spring of John's garden resonates with the sound of bees, as Kath wrestles herself free from another woman-image, of those dreadful weeks of her abortion, as a student, notionally in love with a cellist in the year above at the Guildhall.

'I'm allergic to the strimmer,' John is saying. 'I'd rather the ground elder, really. Than bland strimmed grass. Its flowers *are* white.'

'And the bindweed,' Esther notes. 'It's white too.'

'Yes, plenty of that!'

'Quite studied, though, your wilderness.'

'Agreed. The casual look is contrived. I mean, I do make it hard for myself. I can't stand Roundup either. I'll dig up the docks and nettles, and brambles, rather than poison them.'

'All in the cause of art,' Kath says, laughter at the corners of her voice, her isolating dreams abandoned.

'And you? Your garden is "natural"? Your ...' John stops

himself, for once able to appreciate that he isn't under attack and that defence is therefore in itself destructive. 'Forgive me, I'm sorry. I didn't mean to ...'

'I know, don't worry,' Kath reassures. 'I'm not offended.'

'Thank you. Offence is not at all what I intend, to you.'

Esther is sitting between the two of them on the curved seat of the arbour, a witness to their understanding. She doesn't need to speak. Soon afterwards they go inside, and half an hour later she and her mother drive back home across the ridge of The Kinsgways.

The chopping board on John's steamed-beech kitchen surface has a circular burn, from an iron skillet he placed there hot from the gas ring, while taking a call from Kath on the telephone. It is the one mark of visible disorder in his whole house. He knows that this is so, and is pleased, not annoyed.

On a Friday in late April John drives Kath out across the levels for lunch at the Eel Smokery. In passing, they wander around the ruins of Muchelney Abbey, raised on a mound of clay projecting above the winter floods of the ancient sedgemoor, built by the monks at a time when Saxon peasants constructed wooden walkways of travel across the marshes. They spend forty minutes also at the cottage garden at East Lambrook, on which Margery Fish started work in the 1930s – one of Kath's earliest book projects had been a private printing of Fish's *We Made a Garden*, with wood engravings by a retired postman who had settled to private life in a reed-cutter's barn nearby – she loves, especially, the green garden at East Lambrook, composed of wild plants, without flowers. The farm room attached to the Smokery, recently converted to a daytime café, is almost full, mostly of local ladies. The talk is muted, in contrast to the tablecloths of red-check linen. John and Kath sit outside in the sheltered courtyard. Behind their bench a fig tree is rich in young fruit.

'The owner retired at fifty from school-teaching to set up this place,' John informs. 'Travelled all over Europe to learn the trade. The smoking of food has always been his passion.'

Kath lifts a forkful of hot-smoked salmon to her mouth. 'Mmm! Delicious.'

'There was a meeting here I came to. About rural development. I'm so pleased to see it's a success.'

'It's the kind of thing which drew me to the area thirty years ago. And keeps me,' Kath says. 'Local elvers. Disused farm. Field of hay beyond the fence. Bound together by natural necessity.'

John shakes his head. 'I don't know. What is man's nature? To get away with it, survive without thought? It's everywhere.'

He is thinking of a recent visit to the hairdressers in Taunton, where the same girl, a twenty-year-old, has cut his hair now for the last year, adequately enough, as short as it is possible to achieve by hand without the clippers.

'Been doing anything interesting since I last saw you?' she has been taught must be her first question, asked every time with note-flat lack of expression.

'Yes. The same as usual,' he invariably replies.

John can hear her brain churning to recall what it is that he does, unaware that he has been careful never to tell her.

Soon comes: 'Got any plans for the rest of the day?'

'Yes. Same as usual.'

'Oh.'

Slipping off the black gown at the finish she notices the plaster across a vein on the soft inside of his elbow, the result of a blood test earlier in the day at the doctor's surgery.

'Oh dear, what did you do to your arm?'

'Nothing really. The heroin is fine. I just don't fancy being poisoned by my needles, so always swab the mark,' he replies.

'That's nice,' she says. 'Got your loyalty card handy? I'll stamp it.'

John breaks the easy silence with Kath, continuing now out loud this same line of thought. 'Do people carry around a wallet-full of loyalty cards? Am I an idiot to refuse the lot?' he asks.

Kath is wearing her thick grey hair drawn into a bun, which rests at the base of her neck. Her bare arms are already brown, from spring afternoons planting vegetables and salads in her garden. She gazes steadily at John, eye to eye.

'Not at all, you're right to resist. On principle.'

'What good?' he pleads, his face smooth, tense, anxious. 'Shouldn't I be doing my bit, somehow, to help out?'

'Clear up the chaos? You can't.'

'You do.'

Kath shakes her head. 'Sadly, I can't do much to help either.'

'With the family you can.'

'That's the sadness. I can't even do it for those I bore and birthed. Time. In time they may get better. It happens or it doesn't. Think of Esther. Our lovely Esther was a disaster-child. So jealous of baby Clem that she set out, aged eight, to kill her. On two occasions she almost succeeded. Once poked a stick down the baby's throat. And another day threw her from an upstairs window. Clem, our lucky one, landed safely in the middle of a bush. The blue hydrangea by the back porch.'

'Parenthood. I could never have done it,' John whispers, as if to himself.

They are pleased to be alone together in the smokery's yard. They order coffee, hers a double espresso, his with a lunchtime dash of milk.

She asks him how his project over in the empty barns at Granthorne Manor progresses. He is proud of helping things begin to happen there, while preferring not to talk in detail, even to Kath, about his dreams for the place.

'It's like writing a book, I imagine. Until done, it doesn't exist. Only in the mind. And I'd hate this to become ... become nothing, an unfulfilled idea.'

On the return journey they call unannounced on friends of John's, an antique dealer. His wife is a potter. They are welcomed with warmth, and permitted to wander around the Victorian rectory alone at leisure. John delights in pointing out to Kath familiar treasures on the creaking landings, covered in dust – the house is stacked with hordes of magpie gatherings, things that were once ten-a-penny, now rarities awaiting resurrection: dozens of family photographic albums of the 1860s; German tin-plate mechanical toys, often in their original boxes; a roomful of Wedgwood Fairyland lustre; lots and lots more. John hasn't visited for ages, not since one of the last of the summer weekends which the dealer used to host for colleagues in the trade, a recreation of the vicarage garden party, with tennis tournament and fancy dress competition, each year a different theme. Guests used to retire to their rooms after Sunday lunch, due to reappear at tea in fancy dress and mingle in the rose garden, acting in character. The point, for most, was to be noticed. Not their host. One year he disappeared completely. Until someone realised that the woman fanning herself beneath the honeysuckle, dressed as an Ingres portrait, severe of feature, with a vast bustle, was the antique dealer in drag, his untrimmed beard of twenty years' growth shorn to smooth white flesh between lunchtime and tea. His wife, who hated their summer fête, accepted the seriousness of his pleasure. They love each other, a lot: Kath can tell this from the house itself. It's good, she finds, to do these things with John, the pleasure of his and his friends' company unanticipated, after her years of contented widowhood.

When he drops her back at Parsonage Farm, John stays on to give Kath a hand to shift the oak grain bin she has recently been given by a local farmer. They move it from temporary storage in the big woodshed into the studio, behind the door, where Kath plans to keep dry and clean her lifetime's stack of artists' proofs. John asks permission to look through them at a convenient moment, expressing a desire one day to know anything and everything she has ever done.

'Fine. Not now, though. Let's have a glass of wine,' Kath says.

'Delighted!'

They sit in the kitchen. The red Bordeaux which she opens is a present from John, part of the case he left for her on another visit, bought in Soane on his way over from Lower Penley, at the local vintner's cellar in a converted piggery. The door to the boiler-room is open, to keep watch on a black pedigree lamb which dozes there in a blanketed cardboard box, fostered by Kath when abandoned earlier in the week by a misogynist ewe of her brother's.

'He'd have let the little creature die,' she says. 'Why does he bother if he doesn't care? I don't understand.'

'He's a recluse,' John says.

'So?'

'Male.'

'So?'

'Your sibling.'

'So?'

'I've no idea how it works. All I'm saying is ... You know, I don't need to go on.'

'No,' Kath agrees. 'Let's not argue.'

The walls of Kath's kitchen are painted mustard-green, bold enough in tone to balance the floor of oiled red terracotta tiles. Facing the pair of windows the long dresser teems in colourful pottery and old decorative tins of food, with faded memorabilia made by her children and grandchildren pinned to the shelves. It is a place for use, the assortment of high-backed chairs ranged around the big busy table all bearing their different dented cushions. Coats and hats hang one on top of each other on a row of brass hooks by the door, with boots, shoes and slippers stacked on William's two-tier cherrywood rack below. The wine and the squares of local cheddar taste good.

'Sorry about the mess,' Kath says – as she almost always does.

John has learnt not to reply. He has also learnt, in the pleasure of friendship with Kath, not to apologise for his own pure white walls and immaculate order at Grooms Cottage.

He is thinking, for some reason, of the substantial holly he transplanted to beside the gate he installed a year ago at the back lane to his land. The bush appeared to have died and he was about to dig it up and try again when, yesterday, he noticed leaves pressing out to life from the bare branches to participate in the flourish of spring alongside the rest of his newly planted English hedgerow.

A copy of Stewart's sole volume for Parsonage Press has for years stood on the top shelf of Kath's dresser, beside desultory issues of the Parish Magazine.

'Tell me about the book,' John says. 'You did the printing. Who did the woodcuts?'

'Me,' Kath replies, unperturbed by his customary abruptness.

'Really? Very technical.'

'Copied from Stew's drawings. He spent months measuring on site medieval windows and doors. His number-details are printed in the captions. My illustrations are as accurate as I could make them.'

'They're more, though, than representations. You've captured ... Well, their character. The feeling of the original.'

'Thank you.'

'It's true.'

On the lower shelf a turned walnut spill vase – another of William Moray's pieces of woodwork – is chock-full of biros. John lifts down the vase and examines its contents.

'What a wild mix! Where on earth did you gather these?'

he asks.

'Esther, not me. She has a biro fetish. Can't seem to throw any pen away and leaves a trail of saved biros wherever she goes. In drawers, mugs, glasses, vases. I've got used to it.'

'Int-er-est-ing!'

'And interesting?'

'Both, actually. Esther is great as she is,' John firmly states, his fondness of Kath's daughter unequivocal.

He is absentmindedly thumbing the pages of Stewart's book on the vernacular architecture of West Somerset, stopping from time to time to examine a particular plate: here admiring the restraint of a domestic barrel vault, there pondering the narrative of a weather vane, extra-mindful of the new-found fact that Kath herself cut these firm dark blocks. John is an unusual mixture-of-a-man, historically knowledgeable and appreciative, while scarred by angry disdain for established icons of the past. His need has always been to search out the odd, the obscure, the exceptional. It's a trait of character which has caused him harm. In this case, the match of his and Kath's taste is a mutual treat.

John has moved quite a distance over the years, from being in the late 1970s a dealer in early-twentieth-century works of art, to handling a decade later some of the most inventive of contemporary artists, to precipitous retirement six months before the millennium in order to pursue an undeclared private agenda. Intent on telling nobody what drove him to the decision, he sometimes fears this may be because he doesn't personally know.

And yet there are, he can see, definite connections. At Cambridge, studying History Part I, followed by another two years reading Part II History of Art, John had visited at the beginning and end of each term Jim Ede, at Kettle's Yard, the cottage in which the collector lived, surrounded by the work of artist-friends from the early years of the modern movement, the house itself a bare wood and lime-washed cob monument to the arts and crafts ethos of the period. Jim, a sprite-like figure, the ageing English version of Cocteau's fawn, was generous and trusting in ways absent from the present time, lending to undergraduates for the duration of each semester framed drawings from his collection to hang in their rooms. John used to journey back to Cambridge a day or two early to gain first pick of the loan-cupboard at Kettle's Yard, several of his borrowings lodged forever at the forefront of his visual memory: a charcoal portrait sketch by Gaudier-Brzeska, bold and impatient; a Frank Dobson plaster figure of a nude girl; three lithographs by Muirhead-Bone of wartime shipyards on the Clyde. It is, in this sense, no surprise therefore that after half a dozen years spent cutting his art market teeth at Christie's, the London auctioneers, he opened a small premises of his own by the British Museum, selling the then-neglected first experiments in modernism. He in his turn, as Jim Ede had been, was overwhelmed by the presence of Roger Fry, a

Bloomsbury-ite of extraordinary energy, convinced of the nation's need to imbibe Continental ideals. John's reputation-setting discovery was of the Wyndham Lewis painted five-fold screen commissioned by Fry for the launch in July 1913 of his Omega showrooms in Fitzroy Square, around the corner from John's antiques shop – he came across the screen at an auction in Yorkshire, unrecognised by everyone but him, bought for a song and sold for a symphony to the Museum of Modern Art in New York. He had managed convincingly also to handle the plain oak furniture of Gimson and the Barnsleys. His guiding light, the reason for his success as a dealer, was love: the love of the art which he bought and sold.

Illustrated books of the period had always interested John; when possible, he used to pick up the wood engraving often published in a separate limited edition from the book. Prints such as *Rufus Clay the Foreigner*, drawn by Paul Nash in 1921, of two countrymen leaning on a gate, watching in the distance the naked figure of a man clamber down the bank of a derelict canal to rescue his stricken dog. The story in the text told of how both man and dog drowned, one of the observers at the gate commenting: 'A bad job that, Rufus Clay. These foreigners never do learn their way about.' Roland Penrose, also an adventurous collector of art, was another hero of John's. John kept on the relevant shelf at Grooms Cottage his copy of *The Road is Wider than Long. An image diary from the Balkans July–August 1938*, one of only ten on Millbourn hand-made paper, published with an original drawing, illuminated and signed by the author. Penrose was living at the time with the American photographer, Lee Miller, and dedicated this book of avant-garde poems to her. He wrote the words: 'Sometimes, almost never, by chance an invitation arrives to explore distant countries with a girl with whom one is in love and, should this occur, one would be an obstinate fool to refuse.' It was John's interest in hand-blocked prints which later led him to the Parsonage Press edition of Stewart Bowler's *West Country Vernacular*, and from this book finally to Kath Trevelyan herself.

Two specific happenings in the recent history of art, John reckons, were instrumental in turning him to deal in the work of his British contemporaries. He made his first step into this living world after attendance at the Robert Fraser Gallery in Covent Garden in 1975 of Gilbert and George's performance of *Red Sculpture*, a choreographed synthesis of the feelings behind a related series of violent pictures, both men wearing uniform suits and ties, the flesh of their hands and faces coated in vibrant red pigment. Accompanied by taped interjections, G and G's macabre dance lasted ninety minutes. John remembers to this day his stunned astonishment at the conclusion. By the time of the second occurrence, he had already moved from Bloomsbury to a warehouse premises in a forgotten yard off Oxford Street, where he handled, exclusively, the work of contemporary figures such as Richard Hamilton, R.B. Kitaj and Hamish Fulton, as well as Gilbert and George, of course. His experience of Rachel Whiteread's *House*, unveiled in a run-down street in East London on October 25th 1993, launched John on his last brief interlude of representing a selection of younger British artists. Whiteread resisted his advances. He contents himself these days with possession of a yellow-resin cast of the inside of her hot water bottle.

'Gates. He was keen on gates,' John says, referring to a plate in Stewart's book.

'All sorts, yes,' Kath agrees.

'Have you seen mine? It's restored now, and reposi-tioned. I found it in the undergrowth out in the woods on Granthorne Hill. Made of iron and oak. Beautiful. A hundred years ago they were everywhere on the Estate.'

'Esther mentioned it. Have you forgotten?'

'Sorry, I remember now. Sorry,' he repeats.

John notices these days how insistent he too often is on making his point – afraid, perhaps, of being ignored. The result is dogmatism, ruin of the affirmation from others which he desires. It's awful, it really is, for John, to make mistakes; he seems forever to see himself as an error, a mistaken tragedy. The repetition, over his entire adult life, of such defensiveness he has come to interpret as a form of blindness. Wyndham Lewis, the artist of the past whom he admires above most others, went blind yet continued to draw and to write. Unable to see, he published in 1954 his last novel, which he titled *Self-Condemned*, inspired by the war-time years of exile in Toronto, a fictional ordeal at the extremities of life that, thanks to the companionship of the book's wife, humanises its arrogant protagonist but finally turns him into a shell of himself after she, in despair, committed suicide. In reality, Gladys Anne – forever nicknamed by the family Froanna, after a German friend insisted on referring to her as Frau Anna – outlived her husband; and now outlives her own physical existence, in the angular portrait drawing by Lewis of her younger self which hangs on John's bedroom wall at Grooms Cottage.

Through the kitchen window they can see Kath's garden, sloping up beyond the stream to the tall brick wall, against which a peach and two pear trees grow, their pruned branches string-tied to horizontal wires. The blossom is over.

'Masses of fruit there'll be this year,' she says.

'I'm noticing, probably for the first time, what an incredible season for growth May is,' John responds. 'I think the wild yellow rattle seeds I planted in my butterfly meadow may be coming up. Don't know, though, because I've no idea what it looks like!'

Kath laughs, lovingly. 'You are odd! What sort of gardener plants something blind?'

John laughs too. 'A gardener I am not! I value what's already there. Sow little, reap less – a rose or two of the old groom's for the vase on my desk. Yellow rattle competes with the grass, I'm told. Pleases the butterflies.'

'I can give you a hand, anyway.'

'I'm glad. I need your help.'

A bird, quite large, flies low and fast down a path of the vegetable patch.

'What's that?' John asks. 'Not a thrush.'

'Fieldfare ... I think it is ... My sister was the one in our family for birds. She knew them all. A doctor in Shadwell, on the immigrant banks of the Thames. I've never met anyone who found so much natural life in the inner city. She shouldn't have died.'

'The eldest?'

Kath nods.

He continues. 'That's right, I met her son. Your nephew. Nice man.'

'Like her.'

'Like my wife, perhaps.'

Kath is aware that John was married, a long time ago. He never mentions it directly. Kath is curious to know more, but does not ask. She lowers her eyes to gaze at her own strong hands, clasped at rest on the kitchen table, hoping he will expand.

He does.

'We weren't much more than teenagers. Innocents. I shouldn't have left. And it wasn't for anybody else.' He pauses. 'There never has been anybody else.'

'Aren't you lonely?' she cannot stop herself asking.

He tries not to reply. Although part of him wants to. He

manages, somehow, to let a few words out. 'I don't allow myself to feel alone. Keep busy. Care about art, artists. I just ... well, I'm not equipped, it seems, to live with anybody. And it's fine. I'm fine. Don't worry.' He frowns, furious at this mindless phrase. 'I'm sorry, I ... God, what *am* I saying!'

She again remains silent.

'I dreamt of her the other night,' he confesses. 'Told my wife of the shame and guilt I feel at the hurt and failure. Her hurt, my failure. "Yes, it's been difficult," she says, in the dream. And I say: "It's difficult for me too. And for years and years I thought it was largely because I was bad, had got it wrong. Not now. I can see that we simply don't work together." Even as I speak, tell you about it, I experience again the pain of my dream, of her making the mistake of telling me that it doesn't matter. Of course it matters! Then as now. How could such a thing not matter?'

'It does matter. You mustn't let yourself think differently. Not for a moment,' Kath finally says.

And John feels the warmth of release, remembering an earlier conversation, when he expressed surprise at hearing of a neighbour in The Kingsways who was angry with Kath at something petty, immaterial, and of her replying: 'At my age I know I can't please everyone. I doubt if I can please anyone. Doubt if anybody can.' He loves the fact that she is unafraid of being different.

The sound floats through the casement window of the unseen call of a buzzard. Keeou. Keeou. Keeou.

'I know, you buzzard about the place! Me? I wagtail, Esther reckons,' she says.

They leave it at that, for the time being.

A week later John drives over again from Grooms Cottage to Parsonage Farm, eager to tell Kath about the four-day trip he has since made to Barcelona, to see an exhibition of drawings and models by Tadao Ando, an architect they both admire.

A tram, two buses, three trains, one tube and the car took me from there back to here, and now one more car journey to Kath's: he is thinking, with pleasure, as he slows at a corner on the narrow road.

They take tea this time within the view, on a bench set against the warm bricks of the wall, looking down towards the back door and kitchen window of the house.

After the brief quick chatter of arrival, on the bench they are to begin with both silent, content to sit and to look. And, in John's case, to pursue for a quiet moment thoughts not about Barcelona but of an incident at Paddington Station while he was waiting for the train back down to Somerset. He doesn't wish to tell Kath any of this. It's more that ... that in her presence thoughts such as these are easier to settle into whatever place John may best be able to make for them inside himself.

He is sitting outside the Costa bar beside Platform One,

with a coffee, and to the adjacent table a woman makes her way, with one child in a pushchair, another at her heels. She is carrying a paper mug; two Costa take-away bags hang on the handles of the pushchair, which is draped with coats, on the lower platform a hold-all brightly woven in plastic. The woman is not young, not rich, not slim. She is hot – wearing an overcoat, polo-neck sweater, woollen skirt and tights, in shades of brown. The little child is cross, and his mother offers him first choice of pastry. He tries not to be pleased. The mother smiles. She takes her time and the boy begins to eat. His brother smirks, gleefully, licks the powdered sugar from the top of the bun he is handed. Sitting beside Kath now, John remembers his attentiveness to each move at this family table next to his on the platform at Paddington. He hears the woman's sigh as she takes a swig of her cappuccino, before opening her handbag, delving in her coat pocket and sorting out the mass of train tickets, extracting her credit card and putting it away safely in the inside pocket of her bag. The elder boy – maybe five years old – is eyeing the chocolate-coated top of his mother's coffee. She again smiles, and shows her son how to dunk his bun in her coffee and capture the froth. The children, John notices, have rosy-red faces. They finish their food and the elder boy manoeuvres his brother's pushchair away from the table.

'Not fast, now,' the woman cautions, gathering up their belongings.

She finishes her coffee as they stand before the departure

board. Unable to locate a litter basket, she returns to place the empty paper mug on the table. And John finds himself saying: 'You do beautifully with your children.'

'Thank you,' she says, quietly, without the slightest affectation, and returns to her young boys.

Kath and John begin to talk, not of Tadao Ando and the exhibition but about the work of another Japanese man, On Karawa, whose art-in-books they both know, though not well, many of them from the early 1970s, after Kath withdrew to West Somerset and before John's obsessive involvement in the contemporary jamboree. The book of Karawa's which ages ago separately secured their attention is called *I WENT*, the single bound copy of his notes and maps of walks taken through named cities between 1968 and 1979. Maps and walks, leather binding and hot-metal text: things they together like, part of an increasing catalogue of mutual enthusiasms. Kath has seen, and describes to John, the Karawa project *One Million Years*, eleven volumes each containing the consecutive transcription of the numerals to denote each year for one million years. John responds by telling Kath of the piece with which he is familiar, created by On Karawa between April the 1st and the 15th, 1971, in New York, the artist each day sending a postcard of a different city scene to Robert Mazarguil in Paris, every one block-printed in grey with the sender's as well as the recipient's address, stating simply the time at which Karawa awoke. The postcards have identical brown 13 cent stamps with the smiling profile of President Kennedy.

'I keep the postcards I'm sent. In the big drawer of the kitchen dresser,' Kath says. 'All the unusual ones.'

'Since 1985, I've kept a copy of every postcard I've sent. None that I receive,' John says. 'I buy five, usually. Sometimes ten. And always place one aside, in mint state. I'm happy when I find a card I like.'

'You're easily pleased,' she teases.

He misunderstands. 'I'm serious,' he insists.

'Please, I *do* take you seriously. You must know that.'

John rubs a finger up and down the bridge of his nose, to calm his silly sensitivity.

'Closing doors,' he says.

'In Barcelona?' she guesses.

'You see this?' He points to an inch-long red scar above his left eyebrow. 'I bumped into a door, in a bistro. Stupid. To go in at all. I knew, from the outside, that I didn't want to. I walked in, and immediately out. And, in my haste, pulled the edge of the door shut against my own head!'

'No! Did it bleed? Did you need stitches?'

'It's fine.' He laughs. 'All my life I've been bad at closing doors. Keep things going when I should just walk away. Maybe this is the symbolic turning point.' He stops. Then adds: 'It doesn't hurt.'

··· CHAPTER FIVE ···

KATH IS BUILDING TOWARDS a major print-project of her own, in celebration of older age.

To satisfy herself, she needs to choose a topic of evident meaning, a subject in the goodness of which she has long believed. Trees, she decides, it has to be. Without difficulty, Kath persuades her friend William Moray, the cabinet maker, to write the text; for it turns out that through three decades he has been noting his thoughts about trees, their life and use and beauty. Kath will herself design and execute the woodblock illustrations.

The binding?

She is in two minds.

An aspect of her taste leans in the direction of historical precedent, towards, before all others, the incredible cover of *Examples of Ancient & Modern Furniture, Metalwork, Tapestries and Decoration* by Bruce J. Talbert, published by Batsford in 1876. Ever since first handling the book during her time of study at the St Bride Printing Library, she has held in tight visual memory Talbert's double row of stylised Japanese mon, all different, decorated in gold-leaf and set back and front against a stamped brick-red ground of florets within a rectangular grid of six golden overlapping lines.

Perfect! Of its kind.

The book-cover rival for Kath's affections is canvas-bound, with identical laid papers on the boards of both sides, the title *God's Man* blocked in capital letters above the image of an open-coated artist in silhouette against the skyscraper outline of a city, the words *A Novel in Woodcuts by Lynd Ward* printed below. The colours are black on white. Kath's copy, published in New York in 1929, once belonged to someone – man or woman? – called Byrl Walkley, the name written in fading ink on the flyleaf. The project ends in despair, the hero of this picture-tale shown in the last frame hurtling down into the abyss ... no, not the last frame but the penultimate: the final image in the book is of the devil, Mephistopheles, a skeleton in top hat and cape, holding in gauntlet hands a paintbrush.

Kath is planning to combine these two favourite designs into a piece of independent invention, something special to her. The important thing, she tells herself, is the fact that every copy of the book from beginning to end will come from her solitary personal hand.

And mind.

And feelings.

She has already chosen three images whose inclusion is guaranteed. The first will be a wood-engraving of the great oak at the head of the lane at Lower Penley, in winter, as seen from the southern window of John Garsington's library, in the left foreground the ridge of his roof, above sloping lines of double-roman tiles, cutting into the outline of a young ash beyond the gable-end. Kath hasn't yet decided whether or not to superimpose the grid of the window panes – she needs first to measure and draw out in charcoal her design for the page, aligned vertically, the thick black branches of the ancient tree unimprovable, to be depicted as they are. John's oak might even become the frontispiece of … whatever her book is going to be called.

The second image is softer, grey-toned, taken from the remains of a wood fire when, earlier in the year, she had come downstairs one morning at Parsonage Farm to find the burnt form of a log lying intact in the grate. At a single touch of the poker it disintegrated to a pile of ash. Kath hopes to communicate the fragility of this image. The opening chapter, she remembers John telling her, of Italo Calvino's *Six Memos for the Next Millennium*, the text of his Eliot Norton lectures, is titled 'Lightness': 'When I was twenty-eight, and not at all sure that I was going to carry on writing, I began doing what came most naturally to me – that is, following the memory of the things I had loved best since boyhood. Instead of making myself write the book I *ought* to write, the novel that was expected of me, I conjured up the book I myself would have liked to read, the sort by an unknown writer, from another age and another country, discovered in an attic.' It is the quality Kath aims to express in her wood engravings.

The third of her current visions is of the tall white panicle of a horse-chestnut tree, mid-pollination by a bumblebee. Though the print will be in monochrome, the bee must be seen as yellow-striped, the blossom white. Pink panicles she dislikes, for no proven reason. Her feeling, though, is that pink conker blossoms are smaller than the white, which she assumes to be the native tree, its leaves seemingly a lighter green. She loves the shape of the oldest of these trees, and as a child at Ely used to spend hours stripping the leaves with a pinch of thumb and forefinger, to render the remaining skeleton a 'fishbone'. William Moray informs her that the horse chestnut isn't in fact a native tree at all, indeed was not introduced to England until 1612, by a Dutchman called Charles de l'Ecluse, the court botanist in Vienna; and all pink flowers were once white, their colour automatically changed by pollinating bees. There does exist a rare red-flowering Indian horse chestnut, but its blossoms arrive later, in July or August, not May. It too can be a beautifully shaped tree, William feels. Kath is pleased with this information – although it doesn't alter her dislike of conker trees at the times when their blossom is pink. William tells her of his readings of the Victorian designer Lewis F. Day's book *Nature and Ornament*. He shares Day's belief that geometric design can be drawn from nature with minimal violence and no disgrace to the true principles of growth. It is out of such facts that the fantasies of artists are born, he reckons.

William keeps his own and collects other people's cherry stones to place on the path between his house and woodworking studio: for their colour and texture, and also for the sound they make when pressed together beneath the soles of his working boots.

Kath loves the stools of ancient trees she comes across in her walks through the woods on the hill, reveres the vast diameter of these fissured stumps, covered in moss and ferns.

They each have their personal recollections of trees.

'Could we do ... I don't know ... a sort-of map of the original woodlands of The Kingsways?' Kath asks William.

'When was "original"? I sense people in trees. All our woods here are man-influenced, deeply, for several thousand years. It's one of the pleasures of the place. To me,' William replies.

'Let's describe that, then. How we live together, trees and humans. Symbiosis!'

'Do you mind the marks on the trunks? The carved initials? Quaint sayings?' he in his turn asks.

'Not at all. I could cut and print a woodblock of one of them. If you like.'

William smiles, shyly, his green eyes part-hidden behind

his long hair. 'I do too,' he says. 'And the rings and grain of felled timber. And coppicing. And hedge-laying.'

'That's what I mean by maps. Records of connection,' she says.

Kath is thinking of a book she worked on in the early 1980s, *A Cellular Maze*, written by Rita Donagh and illustrated by Richard Hamilton. She admires the personal maps which Donagh created for this book about the H Block Prison in Londonderry, to record her own growing-up involvement with the political nature of home life in Northern Ireland at the time. In her private way, Kath also feels involved in politics, the presence three miles down across the fields of a nuclear power station on the coast of the Bristol Channel a subject of intermittent protest for all her thirty years in the place. She wonders how to express the need we all have of nature's respect. Fred Williams managed it, in *Sapling Forest*, a mysterious aquatint which hangs on the landing outside her bedroom door, so why shouldn't she?

She answers herself by thinking of a recent trip to London.

The main purpose of Kath's visit had been to test her memory of those significant months spent at St Bride, wanting this book to be contemporary, accurate, relevant, not at all nostalgic in its connectedness to the past ... as everything is, isn't it, whatever age you are? On the dull London morning she had first treated herself to a ramble through the upper rooms of Tate Modern, before walking down to nearby Blackfriars Bridge, on the far banks of which is the old Guildhall School of Music, behind it St Bride Institute and Printing Library. She had stood for several minutes failing to make sense of a smart metal hoarding which assumed solitary guard by the bridge: a picture of garden furniture, with wine and glasses on the table, set on a rolled green lawn beside chlorine-blue lagoon, a composite block of modern apartments beyond. The caption? Polaris World Luxury Spanish Properties. Straightforward enough in theory; in practice impossible for Kath to accept. The Victorian Gothic edifice of the school stands externally unchanged on the other side of the embankment, and although she knew that it had been sold to commerce, Kath was distressed on looking through the locked glass doors to see that the interior in which she had learnt to play the viola had been skinned and rebuilt to lower the old ceiling heights, the new floors unrelated to token retention of the façade, truncated by an utterly inexcusable street-level corridor. She hurried around the corner to discover, with relief, that the St Bride Printing Library continues to function on the second floor, largely unchanged, with the same communal table for the use of visitors. In delight, Kath purchased at the desk five identical postcards to give to John for his collection – a detail of the library's monotype cabinets, photographed, she was told, by a member of staff.

During the second week of September 1966, in the

heyday of dissent at the St Bride Institute, Herman Nitsch did a performance piece with his 21st Action of Orgies Mystery Theatre group, in which they dissected a cow, covering themselves with blood and gore. Nitsch was arrested by the Blackfriars police and marched off to the station before the performance had finished.

Sitting down now with William at Parsonage Farm to discuss their tree book, Kath reacts to her undeclared memory of these events.

'I'm not going to strive for effect. It never works. Art which sets out merely to shock never amounts to much. Often isn't even original.'

'That word again,' William murmurs.

'Oh no! I'll be banging on next about the desire to be "different"!'

'In a private press publication? Doesn't quite make sense. Isn't every Albion page "different", in one form or another? I've never made a precise pair of anything. By hand, it isn't possible. I don't even try.'

'Good. That's good.'

'Wood.'

'Pud. Like some fruit salad?' Kath offers. 'And cream?'

'Please.'

'Won't be a moment.'

Kath steps into the larder, returning with two filled pottery bowls and a jug of double cream, which she sets down on the kitchen table. They eat in silence. The elm table was the first piece of furniture William made for Kath, Stewart and their three small daughters. It has aged endearingly.

In a neighbour's backyard in Middle Mead a cider apple tree grows through the stones of an abandoned well. Kath calls by one afternoon in early June to record in a drawing the bent old tree for a plate in her book. A countrywoman, wearing a wool cardigan with big buttons, answers the knock on her door.

'Hi, Pearl. Is it OK today?' Kath enquires.

'Surely. I'll put on the kettle,' the woman responds, in the rasping voice of a smoker.

Kath settles into a weathered cane chair in the sun, sketchpad on her knee, and gazes at the tree, quickly arriving at the view she wants: a detail, almost abstract in its refinement: the leaves of a lower branch where it rests against mottled sandstone – a study in tone, the contemplation of contrast. She licks the tip of her crayon and begins to draw.

Just as she finishes the sketch her neighbour carries out their tray of tea things, with a knitted cosy on the pot, the mugs bearing the discreet stains of use.

'Beautiful day,' Pearl says, as she begins to pour. 'The mill's up for sale again,' she adds, getting straight to the topic of the moment.

'I didn't think they'd stay. Expensive?'

Pearl raises an eyebrow by way of reply. By her standards Kath herself is a latecomer. Born and bred on the main farm at Greater Mead, Pearl has spent her life with horses; happily, marriage never an ambition, she and her widowed mother now sharing the cottage in fond dispute. She has a lovely face, open and strong, her hair still cut as it was in her schooldays. Her mother plays veteran golf twice a week, on the municipal course at Uppenham.

'Sylvia doing her round?' Kath asks.

'On TV there's a channel devoted to nothing but golf. Twenty-four hours a day. Mother watches at night when she can't sleep. This is progress!'

'No! Honestly?' Kath is aghast. As someone for whom television barely exists, the family's black-and-white set dumped on the last of the girls to leave home, never to be replaced, this news shocks. 'Well, I ... how bizarre,' she says, recovering her customary equanimity.

Pearl tells Kath about the little owl she saw at dusk last week, standing on one telegraph wire and scratching its shoulders on another, slightly higher – not much higher, because these birds really are small, with stubby tail and no neck. The same night Pearl noticed three or four bats flying round and round her row of cottages, swooping and turning in the same places on each circuit, flying fast and in close formation, always at the same pace and distance from each other. In turn, Kath tells Pearl of the crow which knocks at a window of John's library. If he is already awake he hears it from his bed, banging its beak against a particular window-pane, which afterwards bears the mark – at about 5 a.m. in the summer, the crow's repeated shouts of outrage and the knocking on the glass are loud enough on occasion to disturb his sleep.

'John thinks it must be a he. Been at it for three consecutive springs. Maybe the crow was born there, in a nest on the beams, when the library was a potato store?'

'Happens. Nature's memory. Like swallows returning year after year to the same gap in a barn wall,' Pearl responds. 'I believe trees exchange information too. About where and how it's safest to grow. Mother says this is sentimental nonsense! Some land is simply better suited to germination than others, she says. Wind and things in the right direction. Right light. That's her line.'

'I could believe her,' Kath teases.

'Suit yourself, sweet.'

'I do!'

'Me too,' Pearl assures.

'Thanks for the tea. I'll give you a print when it's done.'

Back home in the garden Kath finds herself drawing, in narrow focus, the knots of wood which have formed where the fruit trees each year are pruned. These misshapen knuckles of apparent pain are the source, in effect, of the tree's fecundity.

· · ·

It is the next day that John telephones. Kath fears she must have misheard and rings straight back.

'It's me. I'm sorry, I ... I wasn't concentrating. What did you say, exactly?' she asks.

John's voice is taut, cold, excessively controlled. 'I repeat: I'm stopping our contact. We're too different. It's for the best. We'll both be able to get on with things now. Without interference. You've got your book, with William. And I'm writing this article. About the performance art of Gavin Turk. You'll get over it. Don't worry. It was a mistake. We can never be proper friends.'

'Proper! Proper! What kind of word is that?' Kath is furious. And frightened. 'We *are* friends. What *can* you mean?'

'I mean what I say. It's just too difficult. I find it too difficult,' he corrects. 'Mustn't speak for you. That'd be wrong. I'm withdrawing for my own sake.'

'What's happened? You never said. About me being difficult. Or anything. Why didn't you say? Can't we talk? There must be some misunderstanding.'

'There's nothing *to* say, Katherine. Let's forget we met. I'm busy. Goodbye.'

Several days pass before Kath is able to concentrate again on trees. She misses Julian, the only man – apart from Stewart, of course – with whom she could have shared her hurt at the loss of this last late-flowering of friendship. Although if Julian Trevelyan were still alive, the hub of her contact with John Garsington would have been differently positioned, the wheel perhaps turning at a steadier speed.

It's very complicated.

She drives down to Cornwall to be with Mary Fedden, Julian's widow, hoping to unburden some of the pain. It doesn't work. Talk eludes her. And Kath is resigned to keeping the news to herself. Nobody need know. Nobody *did* know how much she cared for him. It's only now, after John has chosen to disappear, that Kath herself acknowledges his importance to her.

Work restores her. The actual place of work, her printer's studio, converted decades ago by Stewart from the farm's dairy, begins itself to heal her hurt. She is pleased that it is summer, comforted by the feel of the warm air flowing about her bare ankles, feet resting on the stretchers of the high stool on which she has sat for some of almost every day of her working life. Alone, she allows herself to dress in a cotton skirt of dark purple, printed with entwined tulips. She wears old plimsolls on her feet.

She is experimenting with her rounded set of chisels on a block of holly, the wooden handles of her graduated rack of tools ringed with numbered bands of copper. Her tongue pokes from the corner of her mouth. In a crevice in one of the walls at Parsonage Farm she saw this morning a yellow wallflower, which she redesigns in her mind to counter the curl of the apple branch in the sketch drawn in her neighbour's garden.

She looks up, and bites her lower lip, calculating the desired height of the wild flower as she transposes it to the wall of Pearl's well, then onto the polished block of wood.

Her cabinets, Kath is distracted by noticing, grow more and more like those at St Bride. She has three storage spaces for her assorted alphabets of type. There is a heavy oak cabinet of short deep drawers, each labelled – either by her own black stencil stamps, or by brass trade plaques – with a description of its contents: 14 Point x 9390 Serr; 12 Point Serr; The Monotype Corp. Ltd. Redhill. Surrey. CONSTANT HEIGHT. Registered Monotype Trade Mark; 112468; 124027; and other professional signs and symbols. The second cabinet has narrower longer drawers, with inky finger marks around the down-curved handles, containing her collection of wooden capital letters for page headings in illuminated texts, the blocks in varied shades of colour and condition. Her last type-store is an open-shelved cabinet, the metal letter-heads wrapped in tough paper sheets of music discarded by her daughters as their grades improved, the corners of every package folded into rectangular blocks, like the linen sheets of a well-made bed. Other types are stored on the shelves in sacks, their necks tied with twine, each with a brown paper label. William made this, the third cabinet, from a chestnut tree uprooted in a storm from by the stream beside his lane. The box-like open shelves are precisely square, the structure classically proportioned, the timber left to patinate with age: craft furniture of tradition and simplicity.

Letters matter to her. The shapes of the type speak. Dates too are important. Kath is thinking of a King Penguin on misericords that she recently bought in the second-hand bookshop, dated 1954, the year after she left the Guildhall, its boards and spine designed by Berthold Wolpe. He was extraordinary, producing thousands of jackets and covers for Faber – *Door into the Dark* by Seamus Heaney is Kath's favourite, simple, in black, white and red, and distinctive, because of the trouble taken by Wolpe to hand draw the title letters for the cover. Good things need time.

The small piece of wood on which Kath works responds rewardingly. She cannot tell the results for certain, though, without testing how the cuts and touches of her chisel hold the ink. Her studio – a long open-beamed room, the eaves reaching down low over windows mounted directly below the roof-plate – is equipped by now with all she needs, the iron machines of Parsonage Press bolted in permanence to the reclamation boards, darkened with the passage of Kath's printing years. Her small test-press is a beauty, a Stansbury, its integral cabriole stand supporting an acorn-shaped collar, the plate closed by the nineteenth-century inventor's unique torsion toggle. Stewart discovered the press in a derelict customs shed in Bristol Docks, once used to print freight labels for the steamships.

The contrast of stone, moss, leaf and flower is beginning to express the self-sufficiency of texture for which she aims.

'Getting there. Getting there,' Kath mutters, out loud.

On closing the press her fingers stroke, for good luck, the maker's raised lettering along the iron stand: R. Hoe & Co. N.Y. & Boston.

Two days later Kath has done enough to show William, and visits him on his farm out towards Exmoor, where he has lived and worked in recent times. She likes it there. Which is why she goes. Kath tends only to do the things she likes.

'Why not? As I'm fortunate enough to enjoy life, why punish myself? Sadness can ... it isn't always, I know ... be a bit of an affectation,' she says. 'Don't you think?'

'Self-absorbed. Isolated. Weird.' William shakes his head. 'I've been called all these things. And more. Traits of character which don't appear to mean to me what they do to others. So I've given up worrying.'

'You're not too direct in your text, are you? I'm suspicious of statements. See these trial prints? Not many yet. Very early stages. Something in them, I hope, of ... an implication. Unsaid undertones.' Kath scratches the cuff of her long-sleeved blouse. 'Isn't this the point. That text and image shouldn't explain, let alone illustrate each other. Maybe enter into a sort-of dialogue, reverberating back and forth?'

'Yes,' he simply says.

His place is the oldest part of the working farm, the yard through which you drive to get to him an archaic medley of rural life, muddy even in summer, ducks, geese and hens everywhere. The buildings shelter at the base of a steep valley, enclosed, the road crossing a ford close to the entrance gate, large native trees hugging the line of the stream. Up on the ridge, where the road broadens out en route to Dulverton, is a cut quarry-block of stone, onto which a hundred years ago travellers dismounted from the stagecoach. There is a gang of cattle in the adjacent field. The animals wander over to the fence to check what's going on in the byre behind William's carpentry workshop. They are black, fat, firm, some with the fluffy brown vestiges of their winter coats, all young, separated from the main suckler herd grazing elsewhere on the farm – mostly steers, but heifers too, the whole bunch due in a month or two for the slaughterhouse.

'Funny creatures,' William comments. 'Look, off they career!'

With no apparent purpose, they turn and in unison kick up their hoofs and stampede out of sight behind the orchard. Kath and William sit side by side over mugs of coffee on the monks-bench in a corner of the byre, waiting for the cattle to re-emerge. Planks of timber are stacked behind them the length of the open-sided barn, sawn straight from the tree, the bark left on; divided by battens to dry, the outline of each massive trunk is preserved until the wood ceases to shrink, ready for William to use.

'A mixture of scents. Lovely,' Kath says.

'You learn, in time, to pick out the different trees. To gauge stages of maturity even within the same genus. Solely by smell.'

'Patience!'

William tells Kath about a piece of work by an artist he admires, David Nash, who lives in the hills of North Wales. When a storm brought down a two-hundred-year-old oak up on the hillside above the slate quarries of Ffestiniog, he cut the base of the trunk into a wooden boulder, natural in shape but with the mark of human formation in the blows of his axe. He rolled the boulder to the head of a stream and for the next twenty-five years returned periodically to map its progress towards the sea. Occasionally the artist intervened – as when the boulder became wedged beneath a bridge, after which it found itself for many years in a shallow basin and he did not expect it to shift position substantially again during his lifetime, looking more and more like a rock, the crisp edges rounding with erosion and its surface ageing. Then, in November 2002, a storm changed the scene rapidly. The wood boulder moved five kilometres in a matter of days, slowed again in a marsh, floating sedately on the ebb of the tide, most of it submerged, like an iceberg, and was last seen in June 2003 stuck on a sandbank near Ynys Giftan, after which it disappeared. All nearby creeks and marshes have been searched and the piece of tree is assumed to have made its way to the sea. It is not lost. The boulder is wherever it is, Nash says – according to William.

Kath wishes she too had seen *Wooden Boulder*, the video and sepia map, in the artist's recent exhibition at the Tate in St Ives.

'The cattle haven't come back,' William notes. 'Shall we go inside? I've things to show you.'

The workshop is similar in character to Kath's. Despite her familiarity with the place, she catches her breath at the size and stature of his saws and benches. William's speciality is to split poles of ash with single blows of an axe to make, in whatever form the wood falls from the blade, chairs of all kinds, from child's highchair to old man's rocker. Sections of this furniture – legs, seats, slats – lie around the space in preparation for splicing and pegging. There is masses of other stuff too. Kath and he stand beside his plan-table, big enough to display several models, intricately made of cardboard, wire, twigs, balsawood and whittled fingers of beech.

'It's my latest thing. Footbridges. I'm obsessed with them,' William admits.

Kath bends to peer from the eye-view of a pedestrian along the span of his miniature bridges. 'Do they function?' she wonders. 'What balance. Have to be an engineer, I imagine, in your trade. They're amazing.'

'I've made three real size. Only for friends. Each built to an alternative system of mechanics.'

'Where? Over streams. And ha-has? Must be fun to do.'

'They are. I love them.'

A tractor passes the window which overlooks the farmyard, and the woman in the perspex cab of the giant machine waves.

'My aunt,' William says.

'Enormous tyres.'

'She's a better driver than Uncle Herbert. He'll be with the sheep today. On the moor, rounding up the flock for shearing. I'll help.'

William came to live with his mother's sister and her husband when his wife left him, a decade ago. He regularly assists when they need an extra hand, at anything, content to be absorbed within the web of their existence, grateful for use of the old buildings. They too are pleased with the arrangement.

'Have you written more about trees?' Kath asks.

'Yes. There're some pages here.' William puts a forefinger on a brown manila envelope on the table. 'You can take it home.' Shuffling the sketches which she has brought to show him, he holds his head on one side and a wedge of dark hair falls onto his shoulder. 'These are ... they're not what I expected. Which is fine. I'm pleased in fact. We're pointing in the right direction. Shouldn't we just keep on going now?'

'You mean, without conferring?'

'I suppose I do. At present. Till we're certain of our separate voices.'

'Not till then to have our "conversation". At the making of the book itself.'

'Quite.'

Back at Parsonage Farm, Kath struggles against disappointment. While everything that William says echoes her own beliefs about the nature of their project, she feels let down, abandoned. It wouldn't be fair to blame him. She doesn't. If anybody is at fault it is herself. Which only makes the feeling worse.

She takes off for a long walk up into the ancient scrub-oak forest and out onto the top, crossing the heath open beneath the sky: her customary response to touches of despair, the timeless expanse of nature normally sufficient to revive her spirits. She tries to avoid thinking.

And can't not.

Her sadness intervenes.

With muttered self-encouragement along the drover's track, Kath diverts her thoughts towards possibilities for next undertaking something irreducibly radical.

First, though, she needs to accept the fact that the subject matter means their book of trees is bound to remain in essence conventional. It's fine, she tells herself, to cut into wood these black and white images, displaying a skill in the field accumulated through years of study and practice of the hand-press tradition.

William and I will produce a special book, I'm sure.

I do, though, want to make a difference. I honestly do. Need to create a ... Yes, there's no denying it, I want for once to be original.

Back in her studio she experiments. Around questions of paper, colours, and other materials. And with dye-stamps for tooled leather, casting several steel emblems of her own design.

One of her favourite pieces of period equipment is a bookbinder's finishing stove, kept beside the log-burner in her wide hearth: like a gueridon, on tripod legs and with a raised ring on which the wooden handles of the tools rest, the heads facing to the centre, where the removable stamping ends nestle, and remain red hot against the charcoal embers in the iron basin. She lifts up with her right hand one of the new stamps and holds it above the back of her left to test the radiated heat. And has to restrain herself from searing her skin, resists the desire to burn a scar forever.

The potential for violence – even at Kath's age: seventy-four on October 1st – dislocates the custom of work. Several things are conceivable these days, the execution of which she had previously judged herself incapable.

Kath pictures her middle daughter.

Esther has always been an outsider. What's more, for

twenty years – longer, maybe – she has damaged herself.

The making of irrational connections has become almost routine for Kath, these days.

On several occasions over recent months she has been battered dumb by the idea that Esther could be two people: her own person, of course; and also a dead baby, the child which Kath aborted. Not the actual foetus, less than three months in internal growth, but its potential of becoming a child, which seems somehow to have been reincarnated two born-daughters down the line. The man, the father of this first stirring of her womb, the cellist, was as brilliant as Esther is. He never managed, as it happens, to do anything public with his giftedness. Like Esther, he found living hard: so Kath has learnt from Rachel, her Guildhall friend, who wrote two weeks ago to tell her that the man is finally dead. Natural causes, the coroner said, on examination of the body washed up on the shore of Nova Scotia.

Kath sighs, on remembering that the young sculptor Don Brown and his wife Yoko are coming to stay this afternoon. She leaves her bookbinder's stove to cool and walks across to the house to prepare their room. The cat plays in the yard with a baby slow-worm captured on the grass verge, tossing the diapered body in the air and catching it, in pretence that it's still alive.

'I'm glad. I'm glad they'll soon be here,' Kath says, aloud to herself.

Before the car – a canvas-topped Deux Chevaux – draws

to a complete halt in the road, Kath is already opening the front gate to welcome them.

'Still squeaks!' she says, at the scrape of the gate on the stone threshold. They brush cheeks. 'How are you?' she asks.

'Great.' Don smiles, shy as ever. And looks up into the leaf-heavy branches of the trees. 'Mid-June, lovely to be down again.'

Yoko, waif-like, uncustomarily tall and thin for a Japanese, waits behind her husband, beaming with pleasure in his concealed happiness at seeing Kath. 'Hello, Kath,' she says, in lilting voice, and kisses the older lady lip to lip.

They go inside the house.

Young is the word Kath used a moment ago, in conversation with herself about Don.

How old is young? she now in silence questions.

Esther, a shaven sprite, will be fifty next year. While I, her mother, feel fifteen.

She shakes her head. And Don draws in his chin, to protect himself from the waves of emotion from his host which break over him, feelings that he doesn't understand and wants not to be responsible for. Kath presses his arm, in evident affection, and he relaxes.

Yoko and Don are the ideal guests, curious about the things they choose to see, intent upon going their own way, independent of Kath most of the time. Yoko sews linen shirts and hats, to sell in an art shop in the street-market near where they live in East London, clothes with discreetly unexpected details. Since arrival, Don has adopted a leg-thick log of ivy he found in Kath's stable-store of bits and pieces, from which to carve with his knife a figurine. The weight and diameter of the wood amaze him – as does the whiteness of the ivy's flesh. He and Yoko fabricate a day-base for themselves beside the gardening shed at the top corner of the big wall, and settle to work in the sun. The three of them tend to meet up for a cup of green tea in the middle of the afternoon, often taken in the memorial churchyard across the road from Parsonage Farm, entered beneath a weathered lych-gate with its Gothick roof of sliced stone tiles, covered in moss. Don is fond of the old cherry tree by the bench, near the poet Shelley's daughter's grave. It was the fruit of this tree that he held in mind, he tells Kath, when sculpting a pair of entwined cherries now cast in polished bronze, life-size. The first in the numbered edition of five is his gift for their visit. They are sitting beneath the tree for tea when he unveils the boxed package.

'Thank you. I'll keep them by me. On my drawing desk,' she says. 'And play with the cherries. Roll them in my hand to release ideas.'

'I hoped you mightn't be afraid to hold them,' he says.

'Oh no, I love touch,' Kath confirms.

The talk this day is of Robert Graves, the poet, whose book of essays *Some Speculations on Literature, History and Religion* Don admires, in particular for its paganism, the unabashed worship of a pre-deity whom Graves calls the

White Goddess, symbol in Don's God-less pantheon for aesthetic individualism. Kath has a story of her own to recount, about the trip out from Palma she took with her father, for a picnic on the rocks with Graves below his villa in Deya. They were on a family holiday in Mallorca, Kath then a teenage girl; the Bishop had been to graduate school in America with Graves's brother-in-law, providing their excuse to call. The poet's bronzed pugnacious features and wiry head of grey hair had mesmerised her, making speech impossible. A decade later, scouring the barrows of second-hand books on the Farringdon Road, Kath had bought for ten shillings a worm-eaten copy of *Goodbye To All That*, the war memory which Graves published in 1929. To her, the main initial delight had been the paper wrapper, damp-damaged, enough there, though, for her to recognise the patchwork style of Len Lye, a maverick amongst book designers, his work another of the pleasures of her study-time at the St Bride Printing Library. On inspecting in greater detail her prize back home, she had discovered some writing in the back, in mauve ink, the transcription of a letter sent to 'Dear Roberto' by Siegfried Sassoon, from American Red Cross Hospital No 22, 98–99 Lancaster Gate, complaining that his head was 'all crammed with village verses about daffodils and geese ... O Jesu, make it cease'. The book had belonged at some time to John Davenport, the *Observer* literary critic, whom Kath concludes transcribed the letter.

'Not that any of this matters. Just names, aren't they? Famous or unknown. Who cares?' she says.

Don frowns. 'I do, as a matter of fact. I've got to, when you think about it. If I allowed myself not to take note of the individual writer, why would I presume to make art myself?'

'For comfort.'

'Must be better ways of making myself comfortable!'

'Vanity, then.'

Don visibly withdraws, fearing attack. Yoko rescues him. 'Kath is making fun,' she says, and pulls the lobe of his ear.

'Yeah, well. Maybe.'

The girl transforms her face into a model of supportiveness – like her picture in traditional dress on the case of the pirate CD Don made in Nagasaki, presenting a copy to Kath on an earlier occasion. The disc bears a sellotaped label, dedicated by mapping pen in tiny capital letters: TO CELEBRATE THE MILLENNIUM. SOME 16TH CENTURY JAPANESE COURT MUSIC. GAGAKU. WITH LOVE. DON + YOKO. 14/10/99.

'The Bishop preferred the verse of Graves's wife, Laura Riding. The man, he felt, was a poseur. Don't ask me whether this is right or not. I seldom read poetry,' Kath says, unaware of her belligerent tone.

The conversation shifts. Kath's mood also changes – as it often does these days, tied to a gigantic seesaw that's set, it seems, in perpetual motion. She doesn't dream of telling her young friends what has happened to cause this peacelessness.

Yoko has a single request: to see English gardens. Kath's opinion, strongly stated, is that there are only four properties in the vicinity worth the kind of public visit she believes to be of value.

'Montacute's too big. Impersonal.' Kath wrinkles her nose. 'A star attraction on the NT coach tour.' Her gaze brightens. 'Lytes Cary, now that's something. Topiary tremendous. And Mary Robb at Cothay, she's a gifted plantswoman. Then there's Gaulden, mainly for its plasterwork in the drawing room, and cream tea in the dell. The best is Greencombe, over at Porlock, that's ... that's got everything. You'll see,' she adds, with the whiff of mystery.

Her guests plan their day out for Sunday, when all the properties are open. Kath accompanies them, welcoming the diversion.

Their first stop is Cothay Manor, in essence medieval, a residence of privacy where history feels part of the present, layered in feelings generous and circumscribed, ancient and fecund. Seasonal visitors enter through the meadow and begin with the relative wildness of the riverbank and bog garden, before arrival at the head of a clipped yew walk, long and tall, where Kath stops to sit on a stone bench in the shade. The creative intensity and strength of character at Cothay is palpable. She lets Yoko and Don wander on alone, hand-in-hand through gardens built in a progression of secluded rooms and corridors, difference and cohesion the living genius of the place.

'The owner-before-last was a whiplash Tory,' Kath says, peering in to the front courtyard. 'His wealth culled from colonial Africa. He and Mrs Thatcher stood shoulder to shoulder. Neither of them, not once, flinching. She relied on him. The fixer. A corrupt Cabinet Minister.'

'Fine gardener,' Don suggests.

'Lousy,' Kath corrects. 'Mrs Robb rescued the relics. She's done wonders. In twelve years only. Found the key.'

Digitalis Alba parades at selected points along the beds, in some places selected by Mary-Anne Robb, in others chosen in seeding by the plants themselves. This is as Mrs Robb wishes it to be.

The three conclude their horticultural expedition at Greencombe, not old at all, the modest house built in the late 1930s, its garden carved from the north-facing hillside overlooking the marshland and pebble beach at Bossington. Yoko is bewildered by the keeper-creator, a plump lady in straw hat, seated at a table on her terrace, reading the newspapers beneath a parasol and dispensing entry tickets, her humour difficult for the Japanese girl to follow: something about the miniature oriental maples on the lower lawn, which weep, and follow you, you suspect, when your back is turned.

'Grandmother's Footsteps. A game, you know,' Miss Loraine says, in reaction to Yoko's enchanting smile of incomprehension. 'Yes? No, never mind. It's not compulsory. Heigh ho!'

Passing her table again when they return from their walk along the woodland trails, Don tells the proprietress how beautiful he found her bearded iris, its blooms a deep summer-sky blue.

'Jane Phillips,' she tells him it is called. 'What about the Lady Mohr?'

'With double-coloured flower, oyster and chartreuse?'

'Goodness! You *do* see. Few men are what I call plant-gardeners.'

'Oh, why's that?' Don asks.

'Ladders, basically,' she replies.

'I don't understand.'

'Look. You ask a woman to fetch a ladder to do a partic-ular job, and she first asks which ladder. Then needs help to extract it from the shed. Wonders where it's safe to lean it. Confesses to a bad head for heights. In the end I usually have to get a man to do the damn thing anyway. Ladder-stuff male, planting female. Women like to get *on* with things in the garden. That's the difference. See?'

Don laughs. 'I do see. Me, on a pin.'

'Like a butterfly. Very good!' she chortles.

'Bye, then,' they call up from the entrance, on their way to their 2CV parked beneath the hornbeam beyond the gate.

As Kath is the front passenger, Yoko climbs into the bucket seat behind. They fold down the canvas top. Don's pace at the wheel is unhurried; several times he pulls in at a gateway, or on the crest of a hill, and they clamber out to admire the view.

Kath soon finds herself accustomed to their presence at Parsonage Farm, and resumes work on the tree book. The thoughtfulness of Don's comments on the project helps. She is sorry when they warn of the need soon to return to London.

On their last weekend the three of them spend another Sunday afternoon together, at the village of Albanbury, fourteen residents of which have opened their gardens to public display for the day. Built around the meeting of three picturesque hills, with vistas spreading down the farm-rich Vale of Taunton towards the sea, country people have inhabited Albanbury since Domesday, the terraced land slanted in contrary directions, amongst walls of rose sandstone. Sir Walter Raleigh's wife was born and raised in a house in this village. A field has been requisitioned for parking.

'Incredible number of cars,' Don remarks.

Kath is driving on this occasion, and is instructed by a jovial man at the gate to park beside a Bentley tourer, in bottle-green strip, hood removed to reveal a low-slung pair of immaculate leather seats. Two enthusiasts chat by the open boot, glass in hand.

'She's a peach to handle,' one of them says. 'Holds the road magnificently.'

'Even when it's wet?' the other enquires.

'Never take her out in the rain. Can't risk it. Not with a

motor of this vintage.'

Another man turns up, holding his baby granddaughter in his arms. He shows her the car, pointing out at prosaic length its features.

'What does he think he's doing? To a *girl*!' Kath splutters. 'Let's go, before I say something.'

The red-faced gatekeeper fumbles in a cardboard box for a map of the village. Kath has stomped off before he can respond. 'Ah, here it ... Oh! They've gone!'

Don, Yoko and Kath begin to enjoy themselves, nosing around tell-tale tokens of other people's lives, as interested in the architectural style of the houses, the colour of the paintwork and the choice of gravel for the paths as the plants themselves, which are all, in essence, much the same, it turns out.

'Fashion. Pull of the crowd,' Kath says. 'A few surface differences. While everyone, really, seeks an accepted identity.'

'Very Japanese,' Yoko comments, better able, after practice, to make sense of Kath's ways of expression. 'Very very English!'

'Unfortunately,' Don has to admit.

They stand in distant corners of the gardens, out of earshot of the owners, and together tease out how the beautiful shapes of much of the land could be listened to, the contours followed, not traduced.

'Is less always more?' Kath asks.

'Yes and no,' Don replies, an expert at conflicting arguments. 'Details can be exquisitely worked. Elaborate. Meticulous. Miles beyond any obvious function. Nature too. The irises the other day at the old lady's place. What reason could they possibly have for looking so exotic?'

Yoko has an answer on the tip of her tongue, but is eager to hear Kath's point of view, and remains mute, her mouth slightly open.

Kath takes her time.

'I think there might be a purpose in almost everything. Though I'm equally certain we'll never know a fraction of what it is,' she says.

'I've always believed that the one and only thing I have the slightest chance of knowing is how I feel,' Don responds. 'In my sculpture, this is what I try to define. Not what I feel that I might myself feel. Categorically not. Just the principle. That only I can ever know whatever it is that I do know. And that Yoko will only ever know what she feels. Which may be why these days almost everything I do is outwardly an image of her. If you see what I mean.'

'I do, yes,' she replies – although she doesn't in fact precisely understand.

When they load the car to leave, Don takes with him his unfinished ivy carving. The figure will become, it is already clear, a naked Yoko.

Kath misses them.

· · ·

During Esther's visit from Oxford a week later, Kath is forced to share with her daughter some of her feelings, to touch with words the hurt.

The sun is dropping out of sight behind the hill. They are sitting on the bench outside Kath's studio, watching a blackbird peck with its vivid yellow beak at a snail on the flagstones. A pair of collared doves synchronise dying swoops from the sky, coming to fluttery rest on the ridge of the main house.

'Ecstasy!'

'The pigeons?'

'Depends on your point of observation. So, Mum, what's the problem?' Esther asks. 'Come on, I need to know.'

'I'm fine.'

'You don't look it. Your hair is falling out.'

Kath claps both hands to her head. 'Is it? How awful!'

'Joke!'

Against the gable end a bushy rose climbs above the kitchen window in riotous white bloom. When Kath came to Parsonage Farm, her father, in his habit of certainty, pronounced the old rose beyond hope of recovery; she disagreed, cared for it, and receives the reward year by year of flowers to the height of the roof, up and down the ridge of which the pair of doves now patter, cooing.

'It's true, I am upset. Puzzled, anyway,' she allows. 'By John. He refuses to talk. Has decided, for no reason I know of, never to speak to me again.'

'Can't have been without warning. There're always signs,' Esther says. 'Sounds harsh. I'm sorry, I just don't think anything comes out of the blue. If you want to know.'

'It has, I promise. He's like that. Hides what's actually going on inside. We see this and forgive. It's a condition of friendship, with John.'

'That's what I mean. You knew.'

'I didn't,' Kath insists.

'You did, you said so. That he's a closed book. Padlocked. Emotionally.'

'What I meant was that I'd no idea he was thinking of not seeing me.'

'You know, though, that you can't know what he *is* thinking.'

'Don't bully. Please. I'm not a fool. I expected to be able to tell if he found me difficult. That's all. And I failed.'

'Maybe he doesn't. Maybe it's the opposite. Maybe he's in love with you!'

'Esther!'

Mother and daughter exchange quizzical glances, the shadow of the setting sun cutting at an angle across Kath's body, her head in the shade, the pleated stripes of her grey-on-grey skirt aglow in the sun's golden rays, like silver. Her capable hands lie at rest in her lap, the thumbs crossed. The two women do indeed love each other. Each of them trusts this to be an everlasting truth.

'I like him,' Esther says.

'I do too,' Kath acknowledges.

'What's wrong then?'

Kath's eyes water. Tears almost fall. 'I wish he'd permit being understood.' She brushes her cheeks with the back of a hand. Kath has never in her whole life, not even as a student, worn make-up and her skin is beautiful. 'What can I do?' she asks her favourite child.

'Nothing.'

The daughter reaches to place her own pale hand across her mother's.

They are silent. A single raven lands on the highest projecting branch of the tallest sequoia behind the church and sits there in the evening sun, looking around, uttering the occasional croak. He unfurls his wings and flaps, then digs with his hooked beak beneath each wing in turn. He lets out several more deep-throated sounds, registering his presence in the world, before flying off towards the hills – presumably in search of his mate, for they are by destiny birds-of-a-pair.

Kath considers asking about the incurable pain by which Esther is afflicted, the marks of tension indisputable. She is tired, and lets it be.

··· CHAPTER SIX ···

AFTER A SERIES OF JUNE DAYS almost too hot for work, Kath decides that if it is fine the next morning she'll take off early in the car and drive over to Piddletrenthide in Dorset, to search out Lovelace's Copse. She used to go there regularly in the 1960s and hasn't been back since, in her memory a magical place, where a Pole operated a small private printing press. He left the property ages ago, to live in France with his daughter, this Kath knows, but feels drawn now to make a kind of pilgrimage. She has retained a picture of a long low building, to enter which Count Potocki of Montalk – for that, he claimed, was his name – used to have to stoop, forced to remain permanently bent at work over his demi-folio treadle press, careless of the choice of fount, the words themselves, the poetry they formed all that mattered to him.

The countryside around is as glorious as she remembers it to have been, the wide sheep territory of the Tolpuddle

Martyrs. Kath's heart warms again at understanding the wish to defend at any cost the right to graze land such as this; she admires the determination of these men to fight the enclosing march of fence and hedgerow across their native hills. Hunting birds glide in circles through the sky, their cries child-like.

She tries several country tracks before finding Lovelace's Copse, the last hundred yards to which she walks, the lane impassable by car. Two tyre-less vehicles, their windscreens smashed, chassis enveloped to twice their height in bindweed and wild rose, have been abandoned at an angle in the ditch, facing each other. The buildings, when she comes to them, are derelict, the windows boarded. She hitches up her skirt and stretches with her long legs over the chained gate, then rounds the corner of the yard, her steps leading her involuntarily out into the orchard and down a path kept open by the passage of animals, to a stile. And there is the view she remembers from forty years before: chalk downland rolling to the horizon, spattered with groups of trees, the spinneys and copses and small planta- tions laid within the folds of landscape as if by the brush of an artist.

Potocki's assortment of farm animals are gone – more signs remain of their occupancy than of the Melissa Press, his reason for existence. Kath leaves by the way she came, in pursuit of another goal from the past, Cerne Abbas, the monastery to which Stewart used to retire regularly on retreat, a short drive away across the downs.

A childhood companion of Stewart's, his best friend at their Board School in cockney Poplar – the finest building in the district, taller than the Town Hall – had become a Benedictine monk at the close of his National Service as a paratrooper in Korea's jungle warfare. Brother Luke, as he christened himself, survived as a man of the people despite his archaic russet tunic and leather sandals. He liked to keep in personal contact with Stewart and, because Cerne Abbas is a place of internal silence, they used to exchange knowledge of their different experiences by talking at work together in the abbey's vegetable gardens, on the cultivation of which the monk had become an expert. Kath has never been there, and while she believes Brother Luke still to be alive doesn't want to meet him, merely wishes to see the place, from above, if she can, hoping to discover the path to a nearby vantage point in the hills, and maybe sit there for a time, with the sandwich and thermos of iced water she carries in her basket.

It isn't difficult. Up on top she follows a sheep trail across the horseshoe side of a hill and halts in the shade of a weather-blown hawthorn, her back resting against its trunk, the abbey buildings spread-eagled below. For several weeks Kath has been trying at Parsonage Farm to hold in focus a convincing image of her husband. It hasn't been possible, his presence dulled by the intervening years of solitude. Here, seated in the shade on a tussock of grass, looking down on the abbey to which Stewart journeyed alone for a week of every year they had known each other, his person reappears in refreshed detail. Today she misses him, without a doubt. The feeling is not familiar. Kath is critical of regret: life is too short, she believes, to indulge in missing. All the same, she at this moment wishes, very much, that he hadn't died, would have preferred him to have left her to live down there as a monk in chosen separation rather than disintegrate to dust of the earth.

She misses John too, she is able to admit in the sun and wind out here on the Dorset downs.

They didn't have the time, she and Stewart, to get upset with each other. Children, slow renovation of the house, and commitment to their separate work kept them busy both alone and together, with endless positive ideas to share. They talked themselves to sleep at night, continuing the conversation at breakfast the next morning, up early, Kath to grab an hour in her studio before the girls surfaced, Stewart off at break of day by car and train to his architect-office in Bristol. Whilst nothing could be taken for granted, the security of their relationship was never questioned. Or maybe the central question was from time to time asked, the answer always, unequivocally: Yes.

Kath replaces her things in the basket, gets up and continues on along the sheep track to explore a cleft in the hills which she can see two fields away, the sides steep, lined with handsome trees. Goyle is the word which springs to her adopted Somerset tongue – she isn't sure quite what they call these watery combes here in Hardy country, but suspects it's the same – the sound, certainly, is right.

At the base of the sharp fissure in the rock the waterfall has shaped an open pool, about ten foot wide and twice as long, before the stream rushes on through dense thickets of alder and willow, its banks a mini-forest of luxuriant yellow-green bracken. The sheep track which Kath follows twists to cross where the terrain begins to level out, and Kath turns upwards, in the opposite direction, balancing from rock to rock to the sheltered head of the pool, where she sits on a sun-warmed slab of stone. The wedge of sky above her head is pure blue, bees forage, a dragonfly skips from stone to leaf. Kath can neither see nor be seen and has the feeling no person has visited this place for years – nobody since maybe Stewart pushed his way up the banks of the stream, exploring one afternoon the landscape above Cerne Abbas. She laughs at herself, aware of the delusion.

Like a human elf, hooded looks sparkle from her eyes: at the clear clear water; at the steep secret sides of the goyle. She hears nothing but the occasional call of a bird and the rustle of upper branches in the rifts of breeze. A shrug.

Why not?

Kath takes off her clothes one by one, lays them on the rock, her basket on top and, crouching down to prevent a slip, steps into the water. She stands sharply upright and draws in breath at the cold. The stream where she enters reaches almost to her knees. Her body is white, with a bush of still-dark hair between her legs, her stomach and thighs smooth, not flabby or fat, her breasts almost non-existent. Only the creases in her face suggest age, and her grey head, and a slight forward curve to shoulders and spine, and the slackened muscles of her buttocks. She bends forward and launches herself into the pond, head held high on long neck. She turns over onto her back and kicks her legs with vigour, raising spray. The cold eases and she paddles to all corners of the pool, testing the depth of the water. Kath crawls on hands and knees back out and stretches flat out on the rock to dry, eyes closed, her arms at rest, palms upwards, ankles turned outwards. She has no need of a towel.

Kath's day away revives her energies for the book.

Good things happen.

Creatively. And in other ways too.

On a walk across the fields to the butcher in Greater Mead she drops in at the second-hand bookshop next to the garage, and buys a near-mint King Penguin to add to her collection, *Poisonous Fungi* its title. Back home in the kitchen she takes from the bookcase *Edible Fungi*, numbered K13, she notices, published in 1943, her new discovery numbered K23 on its spine, published in 1945, written by the same author and illustrated by the same artist, but the cover this time the work of Joy Jarvis – similar in style although not so effective, Kath feels. The points of difference are more numerous and significant than she had at first glance realised, the lessons of design filed in her mind for later use. She counts her King Penguins. To date she owns twenty-eight, the lowest numbered K6, the highest 74, *Woodland Birds* published in 1955 [there was no K, by then], the plates by Peter Shepherd. Her entire collection is formed of nature books – apart from *The Picture of Cricket* by John Arlott and *Medieval Carvings in Exeter Cathedral*, temptations she had been unable to resist.

At the end of another beautiful summer's afternoon, after a productive day in the studio, Kath drives the couple of miles down to the gate of the path leading to an abandoned chapel, in the graveyard of which a succession of nightingales have for years in season sung while the sun goes down. She carries with her, in the basket of woven willow-withy, a book to read, her spectacles case with its ever-present pencil, a notebook and a bar of black whole-nut chocolate. She sits on one of the benches beneath the lychgate and takes out her current book, *Campo Santo*, a collection of essays by W.G. Sebald, published post-humously. She is content quietly to wait in the shadow till the bird is ready to sing, better able these days to accept again solitude, touched with mystified concern at the reasons for John Garsington's silence, wondering all the time as she reads his favourite author what his thoughts might be – in general, and about the book, and about her.

Despite Kath's essential well-being, she cannot convincingly adjust to the absence of his phone calls, to the lack of regular sharing of the imagination. Kath takes out her notebook and pencil to record a particular passage, typical not only of Sebald's habits of observation but also of John's – and of her own predilections:

A history of the forests of France by Etienne de la Tour, published during the Second Empire, speaks of individual fir trees growing to a height of almost sixty metres during their lives of over a thousand years, and they, so de la Tour writes, are the last trees to convey some idea of the former grandeur of the European forests. He laments the destruction of the Corsican forests *'par des exploitations mal conduites'* (by misman-aged exploitation), which was already becoming a clear menace in his time ... The English landscape painter and writer Edward Lear, who travelled to Corsica in the summer of 1876, wrote of the immense forests that then rose high from the blue twilight of the Solenzara valley and clambered up the steepest slopes, all the way to the vertical cliffs and precipices with their overhangs, cornices and upper terraces where smaller groups of trees stood like plumes on a helmet. On the more level surfaces at the head of the pass, the soft ground on which you walked was densely overgrown with all kinds of different bushes and herbs. Arbutus grew here, a great many ferns, heathers and juniper bushes, grasses, asphodels and dwarf cyclamen, and from all these low-

growing plants rose the grey trunks of Laricio pines,
their green parasols seeming to float free far, far above in
the crystal-clear air.

Juniper, an excellent tree, and a beautiful word. Kath
thinks of making a wood-engraving of such a tree, standing
at the corner of a stone-walled field on the fells of Cumbria.
Cumbria too is a name she likes. In the wire tray on her desk
in the studio Kath keeps on several sheets of scrap paper
chronological note of the meanings of words that she
doesn't know and wishes, on looking them up, thereafter to
remember. Aporia was the first she noted, a decade ago, in
black ink faded now to sepia. Its listed meaning? Doubt;
perplexity. Hermeneutics she has noted on three different
occasions, each time with the same forgotten dictionary
definition: the art or science of interpretation.

The people Kath knows who live in a fine old house near
the chapel, north facing and a bit grim and damp,
recommend to guests that if they're cold it's best to open a
window! Central heating is beyond contemplation for the
owners, preservationist friends from Stewart's time. She
stops the car to gaze for several minutes at the house, with
pairs of full height window-gables either side of the portico,
built in stone, perfectly proportioned. She has never liked
the people, only the house.

On another evening, in the dry weight of late June, Kath
and Pearl together make a bonfire to burn the dug-up roots

of ground elder and other noxious plants, which it's difficult any other way to eradicate. Pearl is a veteran builder of fires.

'I could burn a wet meadow of freshly cut grass, if necessary,' she boasts.

'I believe you!'

Kath watches in admiration her neighbour's slow build up of the bonfire, feeding select forkfuls of garden debris to the cradle of red heat formed from straw, dead twigs and pieces of useless wood saved for this specific purpose: the legs of broken chairs, bashed pallets, worm-eaten floorboards.

'Keep it coming,' Pearl encourages, as Kath hauls pruned branches and things to the bonfire site behind the hen house at Parsonage Farm.

The flames leap.

'Wonderful,' Kath says.

'I'm off. It'll go like a train. Burn the lot, love. Must rush.' Pearl wipes the sweat from below her nose with a large blue hanky. 'Bye then.'

'Bye. Thanks.'

Kath pours herself a glass of wine in the kitchen and carries it to the fire. She sits down on a section of tree-trunk, her back against the wall, following with her eyes as the sparks fly up into the sky. And extinguish themselves. Float away. Wisps of matter as light as air.

···

One mid-morning in early July, a Monday, the phone on the dresser by the yard door rings.

Kath answers: 'Hello?'

'Hello.'

Silence.

She tries to swallow, twice, her mouth dry. 'It's you,' she says.

'Yes,' John replies.

They agree to meet the same day, on neutral territory, for tea in the garden of a farm cottage in the foothills of The Kingsways, where a woman serves home-made scones and cakes on slatted trestle tables set out on high summer days beneath the cider-apple trees of her orchard. When it's wet, or she happens to be away, the garden is closed, the wooden sign in the lane removed.

They pat nonentities back and forth across the table while tea is ordered and served. Left alone, conversation disintegrates.

'It's absurd,' Kath says. 'We act as if nothing happened.'

'I made a mistake. I'm sorry, I've no idea why I behaved so stupidly.'

'Explain one thing. Please.' Her words catch at the edges. 'Why did you now ring?'

'Because I want to see you,' John's voice is quiet and steady. 'I'm not excusing myself. It is, though, as you know, very difficult for me to admit to being mistaken. The possibility terrifies me. And yet, with you, this time, I'm not afraid. I was simply wrong.'

'And?' While her speech is cracked, halting, the look on Kath's face is of brightness and delight. 'I'm not letting you get away with *that*, John Garsington!'

Without direct attempt at explanation, a task which they both understand to be unachievable, the circumstances – to say nothing of the emotions – too complex for straight reason, John does nevertheless manage to communicate something of his confusion, born, he acknowledges and she accepts, in the trajectory of a lifetime's fight against ... but if he could say what it is against which he battles, then none of this might have happened.

'Won't the pain inevitably repeat itself? How can I trust that you won't hurt me another time? Maybe worse?' she asks.

'I don't mean to be obtuse. Or to drag everything back to myself. But isn't it me who must find the trust? Not in you, as I'm already certain of you yourself. What I need to do is trust our contact. Our ... duality, could we call it? I do hate the word relationship. And this is, to me, no ordinary friendship. Which may, of course, be partly why I took flight.'

'Slow down. There's no hurry. You release a thousand points, all at once,' Kath cautions.

'Isn't that it, though? With you and me? Things spill out? Without restraint?' John continues to question.

They exchange further thoughts about the strengths as

well as difficulties of their connectedness, making a tentative start at defining what it is they can depend upon each other for, and what not, on those occasions, which are bound to be repeated, when their histories intervene beyond their control and distress is caused. With visible relief, John turns to sharing with Kath his recent experiences. After six weeks of silence, his stories tumble out in a helter-skelter of sharing.

He begins with his tale of the longest day, Tuesday June 21st, when he took the midday train to London in the hope of making it to London Bridge in time to witness Ohad Fishof complete his Slow Walk for Longplayer, commenced at eight o'clock in the morning at one end of the bridge, the precise time of conclusion at the other a matter of conjecture. The purpose of this Artangel project, John explains, is to raise money for another of their artistic ventures: Jem Finer's musical composition of a thousand years in length, designed to end its continuously evolving electronic performance in the year 2,999, in Brisbane, Australia, where the piece opened in the final year of the old millennium.

'It was five in the afternoon when I arrived at London Bridge, having first dumped stuff in my room in Bermondsey. I was waylaid, you see,' he says. 'By noticing in the window of a gallery in Snowsfield an exhibition of watercolours by someone who was at school with me. Whom I never knew painted. Hadn't clapped eyes on for twenty years. And he was there, hanging the show. Bird studies. It's curious, he ... No, not really very interesting. Not to you. Nor to anybody else. Except me!'

Kath is already involved, unable not to enjoy his presence again.

'So? The mad walker?' she encourages.

'He wasn't there! It was terribly hot, so I sat down on a stone bench at the Tower side of the bridge. Behind an unusually with-it *Evening Standard* seller, with a ponytail, and white singlet, sitting beside his kiosk on a folding chair, sunning himself and reading a novel. Men in suits hurried across the river to catch commuter trains for the South London suburbs. Eager, I speculated, to fit in an evening round of golf on this longest day of the year. Shift workers shuffled out of monster monoliths to drag at cigarettes by the parapet. Mostly women. Security tags pinned to acrylic blouses. To be honest, I wasn't absolutely sure it was London Bridge at all. A torrid granite affair, with fitness club and burger bar beneath the river arches. I spotted a bronze plaque. Building of this new London Bridge commenced, it said, on the 6th November, 1967, the foundation stone laid by Cyril Frederick Lewis CBE, Deputy Chairman of the Bridge House Estate Committee. A bit interesting?'

Kath laughs, raucously. 'Slight digression!'

'That's what I thought. So I decided to walk up river to Tate Modern before it closed. And as I was crossing the bridge I saw on the other side this bloke in a cream linen tracksuit about two-thirds of the way across, progressing very very slowly in tiny steps, never for a moment stopping. It was him! His tracksuit had a hood, folded across his shoulders. The back of his neck was red from sunburn. His shoes were clean and white, soft, flat, practical. He had dark hair, looked young, fit and to the marrow serious. Behind him his girlfriend stepped in tandem, carrying in her knapsack several bottles of water.'

'Had he honestly been walking since eight in the morning?'

'Yes! I spoke to a woman on a bicycle, her feet balancing on the balustrade. I guessed she was from Artangel. Ohad began on time, she promised me, on the strike of Big Ben, heard from further down the banks of the Thames. Setting off in one direction, now working his way back in the other. The only thing which I don't think is right, and said so, is the fact that they allowed him an hour's rest at lunchtime. Oh, yes, and it wasn't his girlfriend. But a passer-by tracking his last couple of hours walk. By the time I left, two more girls had joined behind. Could have been a dozen-long snake by the end. I didn't stay. Went off to buy a ticket for the National Theatre. A production of ... No, really. I'll spare you!'

John is unstoppable. They order a fresh pot of tea. He shares with Kath another interlude.

Seated the next day on a different bench, in Hoxton Square, he watches the unloading of a van. Half of the square has been roped off, a giant rectangular box clad in galvanised iron built beneath the plane trees, the van crew carrying a score of crated canvases in through the single door. The men and women halt to plaster each other's shoulders with suntan cream. John can see inside a thin boy high on a platform of scaffold making marks in pencil on the white walls, with long steel ruler, spirit level and measuring tape. It feels to him too smart. Too official. Costly. A substantial concrete slab has been built on which to stand the edifice. John has known Hoxton Square for ages, remembering the anarchic pleasure of The Hanging Picnic ten years earlier. At which artists and their friends set out *plein air* feasts across every inch of the grass, free to hang outside for sale on the railings any work they chose. Where the trunk of one of the original London planes divides, someone nailed a pair of bird boxes, from which issued what at first seemed to be the complaints of a bevy of crows. Until, on listening more attentively, you heard a looped stream of male obscenities. Two local policemen, their professional presence redundant, entered the party spirit by tying striped red-and-white accident tape between a lamppost and the railings, labelling their self-signed artwork Roped-Off Area. Leaving the square by a different gate, John notices a plastic-coated White Cube poster excluding the public from the site, hooked to a place on the railings precisely where at The Hanging Picnic were exhibited portraits of The Brady Bunch, painted in comic colours direct onto red velvet. He regrets today's commercialism.

Money is art-approved.

'Esther's lettering has been removed from the Members' loo at the Tate,' he informs Kath. 'They've painted out the notice altogether. The doors now are plain black.'

'What a pity. Sounded pretty good to me. Isn't this the kind of expression we want? Is the Tate Modern already out of date?'

John raises his eyebrows. He may have forgotten the gentle determination of Kath's questioning. 'Possible. Probable, even,' he says. 'Don't all institutions by definition become the establishment? You're right, the most radical work is usually private.'

The flow of stories is over. For a minute or two they together wordlessly regard the antics of a gang of tits and finches in the curled apple branches above their table.

'How's the book with William going?' John asks.

'Fine. Almost done.'

'What's it like?'

'Traditional. Pictures and essays. Woodcuts and tree lore. It's the way it had to be. Can't argue with such things, can one?'

'No, that's true. Leads to falseness. I'm sure it'll be good.'

'I hope so. We've failed to find a title. Doesn't come, I don't know why.' Kath pauses. 'I'm a bit disappointed. I wanted something ... different. Naming it now I shy from.' She smiles, in warmth. 'And William is useless at deciding. Uhmmms and aaghs till the cows come home!'

'I wouldn't know what to do with them if they did!'

They both laugh.

'And your article on Gavin Turk? Did you get that done?' Kath enquires.

John's features transform; he is a boy again, pleased to be asked and in the same breath embarrassed to be caught with his feelings on display. 'Actually, I brought you a copy,' he admits, and delves into a pocket of the canvas fishing-bag on the grass at his side. 'Take it with you. I'd love to know what you think.'

Yes! Providing I like it!

Out loud Kath says, with another ripple of the lips: 'Thank you. I'll read it. With interest.'

'It's for a book of voluntary contributions, on almost anything those of us invited care to write about. My essay, I suspect, is more straightforward than most. *Gavin Turk, Artist?* the book's going to be called. If it survives the process.'

'Of?'

'The process of finding an appropriate form. It's very fluid. Unguided. Not my natural position!'

'Oh?' Kath exclaims, in ironic innocence.

'Something I've discovered. Begun to discover,' he corrects. 'Something I've got wrong all my life. About what it means to be doing well. I've always assumed that if one is lucky enough to be intelligent, well-educated, healthy. Gifted, even. Anyway a decent person. Then one's rewarded with a tolerable life.'

'Helps, definitely.'

John shakes his head. 'I just don't think it's so.' The furrow returns to the bridge of his nose. 'Genetic disposition, or bad luck, or some foolish lapse, any of these things can send you under. That's understandable. But when none of them *do* happen. You remain a "good boy", as it were. Still one can be scythed to the ground. Without warning. So the things, whatever they are, which make human beings feel OK are not what I thought they were.'

He stares at Kath, almost angrily.

'I doubt if they ever are,' she says. 'Or ever will be. We're never finished, trying to find answers.'

Whether it is Kath's tone of voice, the sense of her imperturbable place of self-safety in the world, whatever it is, John's darkness lifts. Soon the talk ceases. They drain their cups of tea and leave.

On the lane outside the cottage garden they part in opposite directions, each in their own car. They will meet again, soon, this they gratefully agree.

At home Kath changes back into her studio clothes, returns to her working table and takes out his essay to read.

It isn't long. She gets to the end and starts over again at the beginning. On her second conclusion of the piece she places the sheets of typed paper on the table, removes her spectacles, and stares into the distance. She sees John, his image sharp and clear from the pages of his writing. Kath too is clear: she likes the man she reads.

To seek to capture Gavin Turk in words on the page,
either the art or the artist, the invention or the person,
would be to miss the point. GT is elusive, he deserves to
be so, must remain undefined, a free spirit, by his own
free will able to take up and to put down anything,
everything.

It is fun, though, to study him at work, less opaquely
perhaps in the live events which he creates than in any
other of his many forms of expression. One of the most
enduring GT events of recent years was Live Stock
Market, which took place on the crucifix of Shoreditch
streets formed by Charlotte Road and Rivington Street
on FN Day 1997, Saturday August 9th, billed at esoteric
stopping places around town to be 'more sophisticated
and more demanding'. The sixty stalls set out by GT's
artist friends in the sun, accompanied by day and night
music and food and drink, attracted thousands of
visitors to celebrate ... what?

Whatever happened to happen. To celebrate being
alive, maybe.

GT's initial impetus in dedicating five of his midsummer weeks to setting up Live Stock Market was to
remember the death the year before of his young friend
Joshua Compston from the gallery Factual Nonsense,
curator of such hectic happenings as the FN First 'Party'
Conference, The Hanging Picnic and the annual Fête
Worse Than Death. This memorial event in their home

streets quickly assumed a distinct life of its own. It soon became apparent that Gavin Turk was creating something which bore his private mark, was curating his own show, his personal work of art. Conflict and contradiction were conscious presences from the start of Live Stock Market. GT's invention of the name itself incorporated enough of this necessary mix to make it a title to conjure with, containing the thought that artists had become, to a degree, animals first for sale and then for dismemberment in a market place beyond control, coupled with the idea that the work produced, whatever order dealers and collectors might seek to impose, forever remained personal stock with a free spirit. The theme had been established, with a message of sufficient definition to give the artist-stallholders an inspirational body on which to bite, while leaving them with the latitude to explore almost any matters of private concern and, it was always hoped, of pleasure. Joshua Compston's motto resounded: 'FN: no FuN without U. And fun can make you seriously FN!' The other great gavinalizing leap of imagination was the decision to print Live Stock Market's own currency for exclusive use during the day, to call the new pound-worth note One Bull, and to design and print the money emblazoned with the laurel-wreathed head of a horned bull, drawn by GT himself.

There was, though, work to be done. Gone were the days when shadowy inhabitants of the near-empty Shoreditch triangle were left to fend for themselves, no official residents around to complain about the all-night street partying which followed in the wake of Compston's original Fête Worse Than Death on Saturday July 31st, 1993, when Tracey Emin, Gary Hume, Gavin Turk and the rest of the then little-known gang danced Damien Hirst's spin-painting colours into the tarmac outside the Bricklayer's Arms. By the later 1990s Shoreditch property had begun its crazed ascent and the loft-squatting artists were expelled as fashionable wine bars and eateries grafted themselves onto the expectant spaces. Road closure permissions needed to be applied for, the fire department consulted, local flat-owners informed, live music licences secured. At the same time it felt essential to maintain the liberating sense of an event forming itself as the day progressed, fuelled by whatever the stallholders chose to bring, the principle being self-amusement, the aim to entertain each other, regardless of whether or not anybody else turned up.

As it happened, this August Saturday was spectacularly warm, and thousands upon thousands of people converged to share the GT dream. For someone ostensibly anarchic, utterly non-authoritarian, Gavin Turk managed to retain a remarkable control over the event. It was as if everyone intuitively participated in the given image. After initial incomprehension, everybody, the booze and food sellers included, agreed to deal in no other currency than GT's Bull notes, which were exchanged for pounds at polychrome booths in the street and through the black Victorian bars of Factual

Nonsense's old premises in Charlotte Road. Blocked to traffic by brightly painted farm fences, by mid-afternoon the two main routes of the Shoreditch triangle were a solid mass of several thousand people, trying their luck at the variety of stalls. The stamina and dedication of the stallholders astonished – Gillian Wearing and Michael Landy, for example, dressed in wigs and fancy dress, fully operative by ten-thirty in the morning, were still hard at work at seven in the evening, when overheard to delight in the fact that they were at last making something really satisfying of their hilarious multiple-choice four-piece Polaroid portraits. In the late afternoon a fire broke out in the overheated chip pan at the Bricklayer's and, to laughter and applause, a large red fire engine nosed a path down the road. Earlier in the day the two lone policemen designated to keep the peace had arrived to shock-horror at the uncontrollable size of the crowds, and calmed down only at smiling assurances from Gavin Turk, hand in hand with his two small children, that the atmosphere of creative joy established by the artists precluded conventional wrong-doing. What can anybody do, except swing and sway to the magic of the day?

And so the Live Stock Market delighted till the Council-designated bewitching hour of 11 p.m., when GT promptly pulled the plug on the electrics emanating from his warehouse flat, the music ceased, revellers benignly made their way to private functions of the night, and the last of the exhausted stallholders cashed their Bulls, packed up and headed for home.

Although others had helped, the essential quality and character of the event were Gavin Turk's. On the Thursday night before the Saturday happening, he claimed he had dreamt of the day ahead, had seen it from beginning to end unfold in his imagination, and from then on all his worries had disappeared. This confidence communicated itself to the fun-makers on the stalls. Mistakes were turned in a flash into successes, grumblers became enthusiasts, the earth-bound flew. Not by chance. By artistic determination. For GT is, at heart, a terrier, the ultimate wrestler with a bone. He never gives up, few themes are ever terminated, there is almost always more to say, more to see, more to be revealed. Beneath playfulness reside the consistency and discipline which give birth to works of art. Gavin Turk worries at an idea, prods and pushes, pulls it out into its constituent shapes, makes hay with it. The bull continues to smile.

··· CHAPTER SEVEN ···

AT COTHAY MANOR THERE IS a bank of pleached Oliver's lime. It becomes the last of Kath's twelve illustrations for her book with William Moray, drawn as in earliest spring, the thick trunks exactly twelve feet apart, arms reaching out to touch, growing together and forming a lattice between the windows of the medieval house and the carp pond. She admires the rigid beauty of these trees, and hopes to capture the quality in her woodcut. Kath simplifies the line of lime into an abstract pattern of design for the tooled gilt leather cover, in old gold on forest green.

Acknowledgement to John of her disappointment with the book's conventionality has had a positive effect, rekindling Kath's faith in the project. In talking to him she gave herself permission for contradictory feelings to exist. Beneath the surface of William's prose, informative, respectful, a little old-fashioned, she sees again his challenging view of the world. His imagery, given by the

174

reader time to take shape inside, is never single-stemmed – meanings multiply like the overlapping rings from fish leaping in the water of a landscaped lake. William is suspicious of the written records of woods. If we rely on documents, he suggests, we fail to learn about periods when nobody was writing, and laud the achievements of people who have too much to say for themselves. He values above academic authority the patient lessons of his own daily walks amongst the trees of West Somerset. William seeks the reality of balance. The male buds of ash, Kath reads in his text as she selects with tweezers the metal fount, are black and open up into fluffy fronds, whereas the feminine have more chestnut-like flowers. Male and female buds can flourish on the same ash tree. On the island of Britain trees survive longer than on the continent of Europe and it is our duty, William argues, to cherish them. And to care equally for the animals which share with these ancient trees the secrets of nature's meaning. He quotes the *Anglo-Saxon Chronicle* for the year 1087:

> King William set up great protection for deer and
> legislated to that intent, that whatsoever should slay
> hart or hind should be blinded; he loved the high-deer
> as if he were their father.

Right and wrong coincide, William himself wrote, she notes.

Work on completion of *The Tree* – the final title of the book – does not interfere with John and Kath's conversations about their more radical venture.

They speak of their dual wish to be new, without making a public issue of the fact.

'Issue. Not a great word,' Kath says.

'One of my problems is wanting to excel in ways not tried by others. And yet hating the idea of being labelled "experimental". I'd in a temper explain that my failed fumblings have been discarded, and that only the stuff that succeeds do I allow to be published. It's no longer therefore an experiment!'

'I agree. I do. I do,' she responds.

'Trouble is it prevents me finishing anything! Too critical,' John is able to concede.

'Silly, when you think about it,' Kath feels the confidence to add. 'Perfection isn't a sensible aim. Apart from being impossible anyway.'

'I know this. And it makes absolutely no difference!'

'Why don't we do that book?' she asks.

'We could, I suppose. If it doesn't work we wouldn't have to publish,' he says.

'Certainly not. Not even if we're really pleased with what we achieve. It's for us. Isn't that the point?'

Kath suggests using the text of John's piece on Gavin Turk. Dissatisfied with the habit of either illustrating a dominant text or writing captions to what is essentially a picture book, she wonders if there might be a way of making their two elements of expression indivisibly integral. So that his words are also her art. Not an easy concept. The form becomes vital. In the established sense, they are talking of an object which it wouldn't be accurate to call a book. Nor a visual essay.

A work of art?

There's no reason, they jointly decide, to claim any name for whatever it is they might choose in time together to create.

They progress through roundabouts and down cul-de-sacs, follow diversions, beat paths of their own towards a basic plan in which they both have faith. The aim is for pages which are themselves printed plates – etchings, in this case. It is Kath who proposes adapting one of the methods employed by Turk in his work: the series of tea-stain drawings which he from time to time sold, notably at an invited display at the Summer Exhibition in the Royal Academy. They started out life as the marks made by mugs of tea placed at arbitrary rest on cartridge paper lying around on his desk in the studio. Typically, he played with the idea, watched the blots and spills create clouds, tested the effect of a wet sugar spoon left beside the mug. It was a game, about which he grew increasingly serious. John describes his visits to Turk's studio in industrial Bow, tells Kath of the artist's delight in the colour of PG Tips. He preferred it to coffee – a more subtle tonal character. Variations in the amount of milk and the period allowed for the teabag to diffuse produced different qualities. The drawings dried beautifully, in Turk's view. Kath suggests sponging the paper for their non-book in a weak tea solution and letting it dry hung vertically to give the impression of downward movement, in the opposite direction of which to print the text. The plates to be larger than the paper, standard A4, in order to avoid indentation marks from the metal, the etched words thus to look as if hand-written. Which Esther can do for them, her spiky style of lettering individual and attractive. The sheets, Kath suggests, should be loose, unnumbered – there'd be ten in total, she has roughly calculated, including a title page and end colophon, the order indicated by nicks in the paper running clockwise from the top right-hand corner around to the top left for the last. Finally, the work could be placed in an ordinary foolscap folder, made of cardboard, modelled on the type of grey document wallet which Kath has used for years to store her papers (her brand titled, as it happens, in French as well as in English: porte document, gris for grey).

'The folder can't actually *be* a folder,' John says.

'Sure. I'll make each one. And the heavy-duty paper too. Only it won't look as though it's special. I mean, it will. Though it also won't,' Kath enthuses.

'How many? A relatively limited edition might be best. Twenty-five, say. Numbered and signed.'

'Let's both sign them. Without saying who did what. If

that's OK?'

'Excellent,' John agrees.

'I'll do something with the outside, don't worry. The title, our names. Date of publication. That kind of thing. Maybe etched border-lines, slightly lighter than the colour of the folder. We'll see, we'll see!'

It's exciting. Neither John nor Kath have experienced before precisely this kind of shared pleasure in making art. And to do it unconditionally. Without external force or reason. Seeking nobody else's approval. They are amazed.

The next day at Grooms Cottage a young swallow flies through the open granary door of John's study. It is very small, with short tail and beak, from the second brood of the season, maybe on its first departure from the nest. After flying around for a few seconds in search of the way back out, it perches on one of the beams; where it stays, little head darting from side to side, particularly animated by the twitter of other swallows outside in the lane.

What will happen to it?

It'll fly, in time, when it's ready. Won't it?

John thinks he hears the in

sistent call of the mother. The young bird seems to hear it too, and descends to the crenellated pediment of his Pugin bookcase, from there to the top of the door, then away.

He telephones Kath to share the event.

· · ·

Later in the month the two of them take a trip to London, on the train from Taunton.

As John's house is nearer town, Kath collects him in her dented estate-wagon, and parks in the municipal station yard for the night and two days they'll be away. It's a journey of a couple of hours, the countryside opening across the Levels with unspoilt views of the ruined chapels on the tops of conical mounds at Burrow Bridge and Glastonbury. They were built as ruins, citadels of Romanticism. However many times John passes in the train a mile away from the tall stone farmhouse at Aller, erected on a thumb of marginally higher land reaching out into the floodplains of the Parrett, a squat church tower and three glistening Lombardy poplars at its back, he marvels at the sight. Otherwise hidden from the roads, only in the train, or by following the footpath along the dyke beside the river does this aspect of the hamlet reveal itself, in unsurpassing grandeur of the human dialogue with nature. Generations have staked their claim here on this inhospitable territory, which at heart, with perseverance, proves a fine place to be. Further down the line, along the boundary between the counties of

Wiltshire and Berkshire, a canal bends back and forth beneath the railway track. The train slows through the station at Hungerford, and Kath feels guilt that this elegant country town is associated by her generation with news of a young man running amok down the busy High Street with a shotgun, years before massacres in schools and suicide bombers blowing to smithereens themselves and everybody else – young women as well as men who choose to escape to the after-life – taking others with them: that's what's so shocking, she finds.

Suicide? The children killed haven't reckoned on death. Kath herself isn't ready. How could they be?

To follow their early supper in the Oxo building, overlooking the Thames, John has bought tickets to the 10.15 p.m. Promenade Concert, of music by Haydn, performed by John Eliot Gardiner and the Monteverdi Choir.

Kath loves the names of the mezzo and soprano soloists: Luba Orgonàsova and Wilke te Brummelstroete.

'Can't beat a good name!' she says, sitting beside her friend on the steps of the Memorial opposite the Albert Hall, reading the programme before the concert.

'Why do people change their names?' John wonders. 'Brides or peers. "Sir" John Eliot Gardiner they now call him. He is the type, mind. Birtwistle, he's different. What made him accept a knighthood?'

'In order to get more of his music played, I hear he says,' Kath answers. 'Refuses to speak to anybody he knows who uses the title!'

'Birtwistle. A fine calling of the greatest composer alive today. I reckon, anyway,' John declares.

'Mine's not bad. Trevelyan. Solid, like me.'

'You're a waif.' John drapes an arm across Kath's sleek shoulders. 'Not at all a stray, though.'

She is leaning forward with her arms around her knees, clasping them to her chest, sleeves buttoned at the cuffs of her long loose dress, made of rumpled silk, in shades of purplish-black.

'Gar-sing-ton,' she articulates. 'A bit pompous.'

'Like me,' he murmurs.

'No. Not at all,' Kath says, and rests for a moment her head against John's chest.

He is sitting squarely erect, his hair fuzzily short, wearing a crumpled linen jacket and open-necked shirt, looking down the steps at the pair of brown brogue shoes at the end of his outstretched legs.

'Motet,' she reads. 'Words. I sometimes wish they were enough.'

'Meaning?' he asks.

'Nothing. Nothing.'

In silence, they both accept that this isn't true.

John turns to gaze at the Gothic glory of the Memorial, glowing in restored enamel and freshly gilded metal. Like a giant's jewel.

'On the sea front at Weston-super-Mare they commemorated the Consort's death rather more appropriately. With a building modest and useful, the Albert Memorial Industrial Night School,' he says. 'Have you seen it?'

'Not so I've noticed. You've been to the Stert Island Swim at Burnham-on-Sea?' she asks.

'Pass.'

'It's fun. We should go one day. To both.'

'Whenever you like, my ... um ... Kath. You know, whenever it's convenient.'

The concert ends late, at twenty minutes before midnight, and a chill night wind has arisen. Instead of scurrying down Exhibition Road to catch the tube, John hails a taxi to take them to the house where he leases intermittent use of the tiny spare bedroom. One of the Bohemian gang of artist-residents is away, and Kath has been loaned her room for the night, at the top of the narrow house. They say goodnight in the hall, and John makes for the back stairs, heading for his lair in the basement. Although the lights on the second floor landing do not work, Kath finds her way to the bathroom, washes and cleans her teeth, and goes to bed. She lies awake for an hour, thinking of many things, and absorbing the character of this borrowed room, the London home since student days of a cartoon creator, principled in choice of work, the glazed shelves stuffed with files of magazines. Most of the room is occupied by an L-shaped desk littered with materials for drawing. The woman lives for several days each week at the house she and her partner own on the south coast, at Bexhill, with their Siamese cats. Kath, who has never met the owner of the bed in which she stretches out beneath a patchwork duvet, her fingers interlocked behind her head, feels certain it is the room of a decent person. This matters. She's not sure why. Maybe it's related to her wish that every element of this visit to London with John be memorable. In a positive sense, of course. For them both.

Tonight's concert was wonderful.

So far so good!

Kath turns off the bedside lamp and falls asleep, not in the least embarrassed by these young thoughts of an old person. The house, she accepts, is in reality unlike the vision she earlier constructed to accompany John's stories of his London visits.

The next day they plan to view the galleries. Kath is happy for John to decide what and where, trusting by now that their tastes mostly coincide.

'We could see what's happening around Hoxton, if you like?' he says.

'Please,' she replies. 'Thanks.'

The great galvanised box which John saw being built beneath the plane trees in Hoxton Square is open. The exhibition, he has to admit, is stunning: down either side the three tightly hung rows each contain five large canvases, painted in clotted relief in greys and whites, soaked in what looks like metallic rust and hung with assorted iron hulks:

models of U-boats and upside-down freighters, draped in chains. They are seascapes, clearly. Beyond reality, though.

'Anselm Kiefer,' Kath says, recognising the German's work.

'*Für Chlebnikov*, it's called,' says John, glancing at the sheet handed to him by a girl at the door.

The colours inside are connected to those outside. There is writing in black ink on the blank wall at the end, as well as on the pictures themselves: Kiefer's own handwriting, white on the paintings, the words *Schicksale der Völker* on one, *Aurora* on another. He also designed the pavilion, similar in dimensions and style to his atelier in Barjac, Provence. Dead poppies coated in silver paint are stuck to several of the canvases, some of which are also draped in rusted wire and tortuous coils of recording tape.

There is more of this work in the main White Cube outside on the square. The room upstairs houses a single sculpture, the wreckage of a reinforced concrete beach building, with the drooping lead model of a battleship resting at the summit of the chaos of destruction.

Kath is pleased at John's wish to take her in the afternoon to visit Sally Stoddart, whose studio is a little further to the north, off the Kingsland Road, on the upper floor of a framemaker's workshop, one of an unaltered row of small Victorian furniture manufactories. Before going, they lunch at a fish and chip café nearby, the best in London, John says. The place is packed with taxi drivers, white to a man, the grandsons of Jewish refugees from religious persecution who a century ago made the East End their own. The cod is deliciously fresh – served with a shared plate of proper chips, small bowls of tangy coleslaw, a glass of white wine for John and cup of tea for Kath. When they leave he leads the way through a maze of side streets, past the up-and-coming villas of De Beauvoir, to the door of his friend's studio.

Kath has long admired the work of Sally Stoddart, who abandoned the academic safety of a promising university career during the early 1970s, for intricate involvement in the women's movement during its formative years, centred on an experimental group living at the time near the Round House in Chalk Farm Road. Art – if that is what the world cares to call it – came naturally to her sense of being. She has remained political in her choice of subject and individualistic in technique. As the single mother of two daughters she has never worked at anything else, whilst preserving total financial responsibility for herself and her children. By now her projects bring in more money than she wishes to use and the surplus is given away, to friends and to the actions of unknown others in need of support. Walking at John's side down the street, Kath is almost sure Sally and she will like each other – both of them interested in paper and boxes, the containers of the records of existence. She can tell, from her knowledge of the work, that Sally is the more versatile and determined a gatherer, of objects as well as of words, the result, Kath feels, of being born just after the war, a member of maybe the most idealistic generation of them all. Kath does not blame herself for being older. Rather than regret, she prefers to celebrate the inalterable conditions of individual experience.

The studio is meticulously clean and ordered. And bright, from the glazed skylight at the apex of the roof. The blank rear-end of the small factory is like a library, with double-sided stacks of open storage units poking out into the room, higher than can be reached without a ladder, neatly piled with the raw materials of her work.

They witness, on the line of plain tables in the other half of the room, the art of Sally Stoddart mid-creation. It is hard to know what to say. John doesn't need to shelter behind the cleverness of speech. He is silent. Kath too. The two of them walk slowly up and down the aisles defined by the trestle tables.

In recent years Stoddart has been exploring the use in her own pieces of the work of strangers. Not an amalgam of arbitrary objects, but the concentrated study of bodies of material produced as intended art, presented by her in a form that expresses qualities which the original creators had failed to communicate. It is, John and Kath movingly see, a delicate balance.

'Ruth Harrison was her name,' Stoddart tells them of the variously boxed and framed items at which they look, in the process of installation. 'She was convinced, until she drowned herself, that these drawings were the best things she'd ever done. Reams and reams of them. Each page completed without removing pencil from paper. Her rule. The source of art, God assured her. Almost all of them amoeba blobs. Babies. Dozens of them, close to identical. Figures from the trance of a dreaming child.'

'Did you know her?' Kath asks.

The artist shakes her head. 'No. Her teacher showed me them. After Ruth was dead and buried.'

Kath is curious, and does not hesitate to question further. 'Was she a trained painter? The drawings look perverse in their naivety. I think.'

Sally Stoddart ruffles her curly hair, begins to relax. 'Yup, you're right. Before she went clinically insane, she had pictures accepted at the RA. Pre-Raphaelite-like work in egg-tempera. Still lives which pulsate with endogenous veracity. Remarkable works.'

'You're sort of cataloguing her things. Then exhibiting your discoveries. Like a scholar.'

'Uncritically. And without exposing her: to me that's very important. Although by now I've found out a lot. About her illness, partially diagnosed in the 1960s, before she was twenty. Schizophrenia, it's termed today. She spent periods in mental hospital. Oddly, at a National Health semi-secure unit behind the Imperial War Museum in Lambeth. Which itself was built to imprison mad people. Bedlam, in the books. Bethlehem, originally.'

'Extraordinary.'

'That's my aim. Right or wrong.'

There is nothing wrong with Sally Stoddart, Kath and John agree in the Underground on their way to Paddington station to catch the train home to the West Country. Women such as her make making things worth everybody doing.

'The exceptional becomes acceptable,' Kath says.

Their carriage isn't crowded. In the warmth of return, John talks to Kath of his mother. Tells of the old lady's deteriorating eyesight and her inability to see the cracks on the teapot, and the thickening brown marks on the horrid modern tile on which the tea stands, and the finger marks on the wall beside the light switch by the mantelpiece in the sitting room, and the black flyspots on the white plastic shade in the spare bedroom. He speaks of his own hurt at this evidence of his mother's human-beingness, the inarguable signs of her decline. She has ceased to disguise her lack of interest in what John may be trying to express, interrupting him mid-sentence, saying 'Oh yes?' to cut short the uncompleted answer to her pseudo-question, returning instead to discussion of whatever it is she might be doing. 'What did you say you're writing now?' his mother asked the other day. 'A piece, about Gavin Turk. It's ...' 'Oh yes?' she interrupted, already at work again on her crossword in the *Saturday Telegraph* – looking things up in a battered school atlas on a shelf by her card table, or the well-thumbed single volume encyclopaedia, or the sellotaped leather Shakespeare which used to belong to John's father's aunt. 'You should know the answer, you're clever. Clue ten down. Read it.' His mind cannot function. He hates her never looking to see whatever is being pointed out. Never really attending to anything. Shoving down the name Che Guevara in her crossword without a thought as to what this revolutionary stood for, the complex passage of his life. No concern for what Guevara may mean to the Cuban myth, and for how the world idealises his beret-ed image.

On the train Kath is bewildered by seeing people read from cover to cover the railway company brochures, with their gloss of safety instructions and travel salesmanship. Kath had assumed they exist to satisfy legal requirements, to provide pallid conformity to some Health and Safety directive. *News from Great Western* and *Your Summer Guide to the Region*: not designed, surely, ever to be read?

Soon after the visit to London Kath completes work on the book with William. Her normal practice is to print all the pages, bind fifty copies, and store the unused sheets in metal-edged cardboard boxes, producing more finished books only on demand. Hand-press books are seldom cheap. For *The Tree* Kath charges £180. These days she has clients instantly for thirty, which covers her costs and earns as much on top as she needs, anything more a bonus. Her marketing is almost non-existent: display on the windowsill of an antiques shop in Trinity, down near the estuary – because she likes the people, enjoys their meticulous choice of half a dozen objects for sale, each with a detailed descriptive label written with an italic nib on white card; in the back room they keep a library of arts and crafts reference books, not for sale but for passers-by to study, seated in one of a pair of Lloyd Loom chairs beside the deal table.

'Nobody passes. They'll never sell,' John predicts.

'It's what I want,' Kath says, sharply.

'That's fine. I'm not suggesting otherwise.'

'What *do* you mean, then?'

'I've no idea. Some silliness.'

Kath looks hard at John, eye to eye. Before her big beautiful mouth erupts in a smile.

'Wyndham Lewis drew on any piece of paper to hand,' he says, speaking fast, in the excitement of Kath's forgiving presence. 'There's a marvellous self-portrait he did, in ink, on his British Library reading card!'

Her smile broadens, with its silent message of amusement at the rapidity of John's switches of subject.

'Yesterday I bought a new bird book, sponsored by English Nature,' he continues. 'It's got more information than you'd think any single person could ever accumulate. Wonderful words. Ferruginous Duck! Status, incidentally: near-threatened. And the Sooty Shearwater, also pretty rare – pops across from Antarctica for a few weeks each summer.

Both of them we could see, right now probably, the book says, on the mudflats at Stert Point.'

'Told you we should go.'

'Exactly!'

The shop in Trinity (there's little else: a Gothic primary school, the church of a ruined abbey, and a dovecote) sells illustrated books, when they can acquire them at an affordable price. In the past Kath has bought from them *Wiltshire Village* by Heather and Robin Tanner and H.E. Bates's *In the Heart of the Country*, with plates by C.F. Tunnicliffe, an artist she admires. This is the press tradition to which she feels the loyalty of a lifetime's practice. For the Tanners and Tunnicliffe – as for her – what mattered was the book itself, the fact of its existence, to be exchanged between collectors long long after their – and her – physical deaths.

'It's the people at the shop. Their kind. Who will keep my work alive,' she seeks to explain to John. 'I honour them now because ... I don't know. Maybe superstition. Feeling the need to reserve my spot for the future. Do I make any sense?'

'Always. To me.'

'This is where it's right that *The Tree* should be. Though it would be nice, I do see, to be working for ... well, for a wider world. Nice to be better known. Better appreciated.'

John pauses, lowers his eyes, raises his hands and holds them in front of his face, fingertips touching, prayer-like.

'With our book, I'm afraid I'd find it very difficult not to try to get it recognised,' he says. 'Reviews and things. Does this mess everything up?'

Kath is, in a way, surprised by these sentiments – surprised that he states them, not that they occur, for she ages ago realised that John felt something of this sort. She is touched by his candour.

'You're different from me. That's fine. We'll learn to do what suits us both,' she says – then adds, making a quaint girlish expression with her lips and eyebrows: 'Somehow!'

John cannot let the topic rest. 'I'm only doing the book because you've found a special form. I mean, it really can be good. And ... I'm sorry, I just want the world to know that it's me. That it's not the same as anything else. Want them to know that it's you too. That we are the creators of a significant piece of work.'

'Them? Who're these "Gods"?' Kath cannot resist remarking. She instantly reclaims the ground of support: 'No, really, I do understand. With your help, I'd also like to get our book noticed.'

He momentarily closes his eyes. When he opens them the anxiety has vanished, and he launches into another of his stories. About his recent coining of a word. While walking over to Granthorne Manor last week, John halted at the sight of a large flock of sheep newly arrived in the field by the church. They at first did something quite un-sheep-like: moved in his direction, imagining perhaps that he was the shepherd, about to feed them. They soon reverted to being sheep, pattering nose to tail at precisely the same pace away from him to the far corner of the field. Like a cumulus cloud passing in singular state across the summer sky.

'In doing this they were again being very sheep-ish, I said to myself. Then saw this was wrong. No, not exactly sheep-ish, I felt. Because that's an adjective by now given human characteristics. I tried to think what they looked like in visual reality. Dogged? But this implies a dog-like-ness, not accurate at all. Sheeppid, I decided. And remain content with my invention. Clear, concise. Note the spelling, please!'

'Next a mini-dictionary? When our Turk non-book becomes famous?'

'A manual of blank pages, we could make it,' John suggests, running along with his imagination.

'Nah, been done,' Kath says. 'And holes in the text to peer through to the dénouement. By B.S. Johnson, in *Albert Angelo*, with square cut-outs from pages 147 and 149, to read straight to 151. Published by Constable in nineteen sixty-four.'

'A commercial printing? How amazing. I've never heard of him.'

These days they revel in the to-and-fro of being together. Fortunately. For there are issues still to resolve on their project before Kath can undertake the actual making. They require, for example, a name.

'My text describes the Live Stock Market. Can't use that, though. It was Gavin's title for the day,' John says. 'What's the purpose? The character of our not-a-book?'

'Got it! In capitals. After all, it is a type of notebook, in a folder. Sounds good to me.'

'NOTABOOK, by Kath Trevelyan and John Garsington. From the Parsonage Press. Yes, a ring to it.'

'Maybe Esther should write the title too. For me to print on the folder's flap.'

'The containing colour?' he asks.

'I like grey. Except it's over-used,' Kath replies.

'A particular grey. Like old Welsh slate. Crumbling, covered in lichen. Textured. We could find the paper to do that, perhaps.'

'We'll see, we'll see,' she says.

When Esther next comes down from Oxford for the weekend they discuss their ideas with her. She approves. And experiments with the size and shape of words on the page, searching for fluidity in the script, the visual feeling of a text in the process of composition. She suggests the introduction of crossings-out – not in violence: the measured deletion of a false phrase by a single line, following on with the chosen term; the occasional incision of a word or two above the line, signified by the angular sign she likes, uses a lot in writing her own letters; and the lines themselves quite far apart, not always straight.

Like John, Esther also tells Kath the tales of her life, as camouflage, at times, for concealed pain. She disrupts their concentration in the studio to share with her mother two things observed on a visit the weekend before to Kenwood, on Hampstead Heath. Esther describes in animated detail a seven-year-old boy arriving at the outside café fresh from a game of cricket, down on the lawn where it flattens towards the lake. Rewarded with a Coke, he talked non-stop to his mates, barely a moment to suck on the straw in the iconic bottle. 'Oh, there's Lucy, she's going to the bog,' he said, already fluent in prep-schoolese.

'This Lucy must be his sister,' Esther says. 'Which neither explains nor excuses anything.'

'I didn't know such language remained in use,' Kath comments. 'Not good, I agree.'

The second incident occurred inside the house at Kenwood, where the Iveagh Bequest of Old Masters is on permanent exhibition. A man from Bethnal Green was showing the pictures to his northern boyfriend. Both had the air, in Esther's version, of ill-adjusted malehood. No criticism is implied, and she doesn't elaborate the point, keen to reach the crux. Which turns out to be the moment when the first man said, with intense delight: 'Now this is the most beautiful picture in London,' referring to the sunlit girl with a lute, by Vermeer – a guitar, according to the caption.

As usual, Kath isn't certain quite what Esther implies.

'Didn't you once do a Gavin Turk print for Joshua?' the daughter asks – interrupting her mother's unfinished examinings of the Vermeer story.

'What? ... Yes, he was one of the artists in *Other Men's Flowers*. I never met Turk. Don is the only one I know. He did his best print ever, I think. A letter-press list of activities. Hundreds of them. With no obvious order. Or meaning. I remember it begins with Passengers; Luftwaffe Band; Rock Climbers. And ends on Councillors; Pen Pals; Servants; Air Traffic Controllers; Draughtsmen. It took me ages to type-set. Although he did help, in his way.'

'Turk seems fun.'

'Joshua called him the Surrey dissident!'

'And John? Are you and he getting on with it again?'

'No ... well, yes. Don't be so nosy!'

'Such a tiny world, isn't it? So many connections.'

Esther's words articulate Kath's underlying view quicker than she perceives it for herself. The world does indeed, at times, feel frighteningly small, everyone's fate entwined with everyone else's. Which is increasingly true of the globe as a whole, regardless of individual circles of connectedness. Perhaps it always has been. Wasn't it St Augustine of Hippo who wrote, in his *Confessions*: Even if mistaken in my thinking, I exist. And Karl Popper who forged a positive response: We can return to the beasts. But if we wish to remain human, there is only one way, the way into the open society.

Kath is constitutionally unable to trust either of these powerful men. Esther feels the same.

John joins them for lunch on the Sunday, at the kitchen

table in Parsonage Farm. Kath is a natural cook, the things she chooses to buy and eat reflecting the taste of the moment. In her kind of country life the seasons matter. The preparing and presenting of food to friends is an act, she believes, of love. They talk while she chops and stirs at the remaining details of their meal. John complains about Gavin Turk appearing everywhere on his recent trip to London ... no, John doesn't in a negative sense 'complain', for he likes the way these things happen. He was sitting, he says, in the café at Tate Britain, having a salad, when he looked up and noticed on the wall a framed photograph of Gavin and his eldest son, the boy dreamy, the father caught on camera at a moment of haunting introspection. Later, in another institution, there he was again, alongside Chardin and Goya and Bellini in The Stuff of Life, a special exhibition: his black-painted bronze bin bag mounted on a low plinth of parquet, identical to the rest of the floor. Esther drops in and out of the conversation, dipping periodically back and forth from her book. Since a child, she has always read at table. And likes to recite aloud passages as she reaches them, whatever the relevance of her subject to the concerns of others. Today it is a passage from the latest *Granta*, an essay by Barry Lopez on the chinook salmon which spawn each year in the river outside his cabin in a remote valley of Oregon:

During several years of exposure to different societies of

traditional people – remnant Ainu on Hokkaido, Inupiaq Eskimo in Alaska, Pitjantjatjara Aborigines in the Northern Territory – I've encountered individual men and women who possessed what seemed to be a staggering expertise in natural history: a knowledge of the ecology of fire and the signs of coming weather; an ability to predict when a particular creature might be found in a particular place; an understanding of the links between plants, insects, humidity and temperature; an ability to decipher the very recent past, revealed, for example, in faint scribes on the surfaces of snow and sand. What I learned from this welter of examples were two things. First, to endure as a people you have to pay attention. Second, no individual exclusively possesses this expertise. It's the community's collective creation. The long-term stability of the community depends on the regular and uncalculated sharing of empirical information by close observers. The individuals most impressive to an outsider in their local knowledge are often merely the most adept communicators of their society's experience. The response to such people to changing or dire conditions is not to call on experts, as that term is commonly used in the cultural West, but to gather the best minds, those that not only observe but listen, that see something else at stake in life besides a professional reputation.

Esther says nothing on finishing her passionate recital. Chin held high in defiance, she looks directly into the faces of the other two.

John reaches across the table for the paperback, which she hands to him. He thumbs the contents. He is frowning.

'I never noticed,' he mutters. 'Ah, that's why.' He smiles. 'I went straight to Doris Lessing. On chairs in provincial auctions!' He returns the book to Esther. 'Thanks. Terrific. I'll read mine at home.'

Esther has flipped into combative mood. 'You were married, I hear,' she says in pursuit of John. 'What was she like?'

'Young. We both were.'

'And?'

'Plenty. Private,' he insists.

'*Then*, maybe. Now it needn't be,' Esther argues. 'What has she become?'

'Please, Esther, don't press,' John requests – gently, his fondness for Kath's middle daughter transparent. 'All I will tell you is that she is a writer. And that we've travelled, apart now for twenty-five years, along similar roads and in the same direction. Which allows us finally to be friends. I've no idea how I got it into my head to leave such a fine woman. I did, though. Presumably because I needed to. Had to, actually. Satisfied?'

Esther smiles. She is pleased with this information. 'Thank you,' she says.

They talk over lunch of many other things. Of garden vegetables. Of skin rashes. Of James Joyce. Of the Noh theatre in Osaka and the zippy series of coloured woodcuts produced there for fanatics to collect. They speak of the moon. Of new wave cinema. Of museums. Esther remembers noticing in the loos at the Tate that the World Dryer Corporation's hometown is Berkeley, in Illinois not California. John informs them that the urinals at the Gemeentemuseum in The Hague are oval, Mondrian-like, mounted beside them two lidded aluminium containers labelled Incontinentiebox. It is almost his favourite building in Europe, he says, constructed of coloured brick with verdigris-ed copper roofs, flat, the interiors set with smooth grey tiles and waxed slate. A modernist masterpiece.

'Do you still see Starkey?' Esther asks.

'Not since Cambridge, no,' John replies. 'We went opposite ways. He to Elizabethan history, me, eventually, to contemporary art. The undergraduate seeds were sown, I think, by Nicolaus Pevsner and his book *Pioneers of the Modern Movement*. He was a guest lecturer, on English Architecture. I'm afraid I may have acquired his tendency towards aesthetic absolutism! Pevsner spoke with a clipped Würzburgian accent and illustrated his talks with photographs projected onto the screen by a whirring epidio-scope.'

'Charming!'

'Arbitrary, isn't it, the stuff which sticks in the mind,' Kath says. 'When and why it surfaces.'

It is a lovely midsummer's day and John drives the three

of them after lunch for a walk by the sea, an hour away on the surfing sands of North Devon. Like kids, in the car as it travels across the wilds of Exmoor they vow to compete for first sight of the ocean – when it comes, blue against a steep green curve of grazed hillside, the view is so magical that no one speaks, subsumed by beauty.

The waves, they see when they arrive at the long water's edge, are peopled by dozens of figures in black wetsuits, paddling their boards out into the surf. These one-time heroes of the beach are tortoises compared with a new breed of surfer hurtling behind the eyebrow curves of multi-coloured kites. They tack at will, jump the waves, or let themselves shoot in on the breaking surf, immediately turn about-face and are borne by the wind out again to sea, never parted from their shortened boards, leaping at times for aeons, it seems, into the air. The bay curls into the hazy distance. Kath, Esther and John follow the tracks in the sand of a dog – until Esther identifies the marks as the paw-style soles of some fashionable training shoe. They walk on beyond families of castle-building children, of retired pairs of folding chairs, and of sun-bathing couples stretched semi-naked on towels in the dunes. The woman of the shoes appears never to have returned – unless, as Esther it is who again points out, the tide is coming in, her back-track already obliterated. Kath wants to dive into the pounding waves, free here of the surfers who flock together within easy reach of their exhausted cars. She hasn't a costume, and is not relaxed enough with John to remove her clothes for a skinny-dip.

Before the journey home they take a late tea in the only café on the strand. John struggles to decide which bun to buy, and hunches his shoulders, acutely uncomfortable. Kath watches him, wondering what's going through his mind, trying to guess the feelings her friend is endeavouring to deal with. She is aware beneath his ordered exterior of raw flesh. Kath understands, with regret, that there is little she can do to help.

When John drops them back at Parsonage Farm, instead of escaping to his own place he hangs around, assists with the washing up from lunch. Esther disappears to her room with another of her books, and Kath sees that John wishes to talk. This time she is prepared for his openness.

'I noticed you notice my distress in the café,' he says.

'Was it all the people? The smell of a done-day by the sea? Ice lollies and cigarettes? I couldn't tell.'

'All of that and more. From my own family's days on the beach. When I was a boy. Polzeath. Southwold. Harlech. The location of summers past.' He stops. Pulls with his fingers at his lips, the furrow on the bridge of his nose deepening to the blackness of a stagnant ditch. His eyes too have darkened. 'Occasionally, in a burst of leisure, Mummy would agree to stopping at the kiosk. I was desperate, always, for an Orange Maid. Very occasionally she let me have one. Mostly we had vanilla ice-cream, between wafers. Her own favourite. Or maybe the cheapest. I don't know. We were grateful for whatever she gave us. A treat.'

Kath realises that in order to continue he needs her first to respond.

'It doesn't seem to me that you had any reason for gratitude,' she says.

John looks puzzled.

Kath expands the boundaries. 'I'm thinking of parents. They choose to have us. Are we meant to thank them? You needn't answer. You're not a father. I can, though, say what I feel for myself about being both child and mother. Which is, that there are no rules.'

'She used to be cross,' he reveals, 'if I or my sister failed to eat our wafers in the required manner. Or if my father got it wrong. In self-defence, I soon learnt to do it perfectly.' His features register the memory of success, not of pleasure. 'We – my mother and me – sometimes smiled at each other. Conspiring to agree we're better than the rest.'

'And swimming?' she asks.

He shakes his head, and at the same time nods, in contradiction. 'We're strange creatures. I used to shiver with the cold. And yet never wanted to get out of the water. Surfing then on tummy boards. Everyone. Men and boys. My teeth chattered all evening, till I fell asleep. In our caravan. On the bunk above the front window.'

To fill the ensuing silence, Kath shares a detail of her own childhood: 'We almost never went on holiday as a family.

Dad's busy time at the cathedral. So Mum took us off to stay with relations. On a farm in the summer. Her brother's. In north Norfolk. I loved it.'

John cheers up. 'I bet you did!' he says.

They both laugh. Kath washes a saucepan. John hangs the tea-towel on its hook. They leave it at that for now.

Next time, she intends to go for her swim regardless of towel and costume, as she normally would if alone.

They do not do everything together, needing, it is clear to both of them, to retain the independence of separate friendships. Friends, especially the long-established ones, are to them their emotional cement, an essential to well-being.

Kath takes to making her own occasional trips to London, staying for a night or two mostly with Rosalind in Dulwich, in part with the hope of coming better to understand her grandson on his home ground. She catches one day a train from King's Cross to Ely, the first time she has returned to the place for over thirty years. It is early March. She is alone. Staring out of the carriage window at the flat lands beyond Cambridge, Kath marvels at the peat-blackness of the ploughed earth, the richness of which she had quite forgotten, the smell of its fecundity suddenly within her, despite the hermetic seal of the train's windows. In fields by the railway track are heavy-footed horses, with mackintosh coats laid across their bowed backs, and in the distance the shine of the galvanised tin roofs and angled ventilation shafts of chicken farms.

Ely Cathedral is incredibly venerable. So solid.

Kath walks slowly down the nave, storey after storey of rounded arches rising above her to the painted vault, the side aisles flanked by rows of tombs of the bishops of yore. Her father isn't there. He refused a memorial, making his favourite daughter promise to scatter his ashes from the cliffs of Devon into the sea. Kath feels like a child again, delighted by the heat still of the great old iron stove outside the Chantry Chapel of Bishop West, at the very bottom of the cathedral, where she used to escape the body of the service to sit and read, looking up now and again at the complexity of carved stone tracery of this luxury-retreat of the man who in the early sixteenth century lived, they claim, 'in the greatest splendour of any Prelate of his time'. Kath sits again in her old place. She is building up the strength to go out through the side door to the house of her childhood. It was her father who had abandoned the grandeur of the Old Palace for a house which, in Kath's memory, is quite old and grand enough for anyone. She wants to see too the boathouse down on the river, near the Maltings, which were working then, where they kept their double-scull.

'Ahaah,' she sighs, out loud.

Outside, Kath's faith in childhood revives. She sees, up in the roof, the window of her bedroom, facing the length of the cathedral. She sees that the room which the Bishop made into his library was indeed big, part of a medieval hall. She sees that their garden was indeed surrounded by the tallest of walls and went right up to the external wall of the nave. There *is* a park. And there ... yes, behind their house, near one of the school's buildings, is Prior Crauden's Chapel, where in the heat of summer she used to ... yes, again to read, free from the day-trippers, a place of privacy. As a girl she was always reading, she remembers.

Kath is glad to have visited. And sad. There was a sense then of the cathedral rising from the fertile earth, the centre of an extensive rural community, for centuries quietly prosperous and self-contained. These days the place is full of old people disgorged from coaches to hobble around the knick-knack shops and sit at café tables, in silence. Nothing left to say. Getting through another day.

She cannot admit, even to herself, on her return to The Kingsways the extent of her pleasure in John's gentle enquiries into her visit to Ely, ever ready to listen to her feelings, should she choose to share them.

'I made a discovery,' Kath says.

'I imagine. Several!'

'No, for you, not me.'

John is surprised, looks a little anxious. 'Oh?'

'You know your big encaustic tiles? Armorial. On the chimney breast. Above your wood-burner.'

'Of course. I'm fond of them,' he says. 'They're fake, in a

way. False crests. Some Victorian family creating a history for itself.'

Kath chuckles. 'I don't think so,' she responds.

John smiles, aware of her warmth, her indelible beauty. 'Tell me?'

'On the altar steps at Ely. Beyond the choir stalls. Are five diamond tiles, one of which is identical to one of yours!'

'Really!' He is astonished. 'I don't believe it! I mean ... I believe *you*. Always, It's just ... Do you know, I've had that tile for thirty years. More. And I never knew!'

··· CHAPTER EIGHT ···

ONE MORNING IN THE STUDIO Kath places an old Bob Dylan record of Stewart's on the turntable of her gramophone. She has never been tempted by compact discs, preferring the removal of LPs first from their cover and then from the inner sleeve, enjoying the measured ritual of lifting by hand the needle-arm to the start. Kath takes care of her records, over a hundred in total – including Stewart's, all of which she has kept. The familiarity which has grown over the years with the cover designs is part, by now, of her own aesthetic. She mostly listens to classical music, often early works, Machaud and Pérotin her present passions. These daily sounds have affected her making of books, more so perhaps than the exterior visual styles of the covers. She can still just about read the fading note which Stewart pinned to the record she is listening to – from the May 1963 radio interview of Dylan by Studs Terkel: 'Nowadays it's just, I don't know how it got that way but it doesn't seem so simple. There are more than two sides, it's not black and white any more.' Kath wonders how this boy from Minnesota has managed to bear the public weight of history.

On her break for coffee Kath decides on the place for a period iron latch, a present weeks ago from her hoarder-friend. She sees it, in a forward flash, on the door to the lavatory in the back passage of the main house, most frequently used direct from the garden, this old thumb-latch larger than the modern reproduction to which Stewart was reduced, for want of an original. Without further delibera-tion, Kath grabs bradawl and screwdriver and installs the replacement. She is pleased with the result, time and again lifting the latch to balance the weight and feel the rubbed smoothness of touch of thumb, and to hear the solidity of the sound as it falls shut. The door-plates of the latch are the shape of the ace of spades, the handwork a hundred years ago of the local blacksmith.

Kath returns invigorated to the studio.

To her surprise, it is again difficult to concentrate.

She recalls, with a smile, the sign John has recently erected on the lane-wall of his house: the name Grooms Cottage in rounded script fashioned by him from a coil of wire, nailed to the sandstone of which the house is built. If you didn't know it was there, you'd never see it, wire and mortar similar in tone. It makes no difference, improves nothing for guests, nor for van-drivers delivering packages. John himself admits that after the initial excitement he has forgotten it is there. He adapted the idea from a house in Nailsborough, their sign black-painted against lime-white plaster – an old man whom John saw cutting the verge said that it was his father's idea, and that the next day a boy in the village had knocked on the door to warn that someone had scribbled on his wall.

John has become a considerable distraction; and Kath, it seems, doesn't object.

The other day he turned up with some tree information, too late for inclusion in the William book but nevertheless interesting. His theme: the way even the most beady-eyed of us look without seeing. He explained how he had been living at Lower Penley for two years before he noticed the tall locust tree in one of his copses, with naturally rutted trunk and craggy branches, its lightness of leaf and white tumbling blossom, up high in the sky, previously concealed by some evergreen laurels he had cleared. The point he was eager to make to Kath was the morning's further discovery, from the forester of the Granthorne Estate, that this type is known as black locust, originally recorded in a select area of the Southern Appalachian Mountains, but so admired both for the durability of its wood (as fence posts it seldom rotted) and for the capacity of its fallen leaves to cleanse the soil that itinerant suppliers of saplings in the nineteenth century sold it widely over the whole of North America, and thereafter to Europe.

The increase in John's unannounced appearances leads Kath to suspect him of selfishness. She is capable, when angry at herself for allowing him to disturb her peace of mind, of extending this to accusation of his leading a life of irreversible self-indulgence. A bachelor, with money in the bank and a mother he seldom sees, he accepts responsibility for no one; and grants permission to not a single soul to approach close enough to soothe his own chosen solitude.

She never directly mentions any of this to John.

Why, she wonders?

It dawns on Kath, at her desk in the studio, a Dylan song playing in the background, that he *is* self-indulgent, and that there's nothing wrong with being so; that it's how we all could best behave, when you think about it: enjoy ourselves, only do things which have a chance of bringing satisfaction.

I want to too, she says to herself.

I do!

Kath is unable to contemplate the possibility that she may have come to love John for helping her, however late in the day, to be comfortable with feeling this way.

She gets up to have yet another look at the latch.

Mmm! Not bad!

· · ·

John is in a subdued mood when he next calls, by invitation, for lunch, just the two of them. After his previous withdrawal he accepts that ending their contact is no resolution to unease, which he today again feels with Kath. He is awkward in his movements. His voice catches in his throat and his eyes avoid hers. He hates himself for the evasion. From what? Nothing wrong with her, as far as he is consciously aware.

Sight of a photograph on the kitchen sideboard, an image he has often noticed before, has an unexpectedly calming effect. It is a snapshot, in imperfect early colour, of Esther aged four, looking cross, seated in a wing chair, her short legs stuck out in front of her, with Stewart leaning over the back of the chair, incandescent with delight at fatherhood of this child. The little girl wears a home-knit pullover, denim skirt and Christmas tights. Her hair is cut in a bob. The photograph embodies everything John values in the life of this family, with whom he is thus reassured in feeling happily involved.

He is alone in the room for several minutes while Kath steps out to pick salad in the garden. His thoughts turn to a telephone conversation earlier in the week, with Peter Simpson, a man of seventy now, a photograph of whom is stuck by transparent corner-mounts into John's only album. In this picture of thirty years ago Peter, his blow-dried blond hair shoulder length, is wearing a purple T-shirt. He holds visor-like a hand to his eyes, blinded by the sun as he approaches the table around which a group of them sit at lunch, on the pavement outside a trattoria on a back canal in Venice. John's wife is there. Until the other day Peter and he had not once spoken since the divorce. They talk of Anne, his wife, with whom Peter maintains contact. John admits he doesn't understand why he left her. 'Well, fuck you, is all I can say!' Peter says. There is no rancour, on either side. John doesn't feel a need to defend himself. 'All that mayhem I caused, and I don't know why I did it,' he says. They promise to meet up sometime. He doubts that they ever will.

Over lunch Kath and John agree to accompany each other in a fortnight's time to a picnic to which William has separately invited them, at his aunt and uncle's farm in celebration of their fiftieth wedding anniversary. There will be lots of people. John and Kath feel doubly daring: for admitting one to the other their mutual fear of crowds; and for giving the locality wink-and-nudge excuse to mark them a couple. This weekend they arrange a 'test' excursion to the cinema club in Street, to see *Million Dollar Baby*, the Clint Eastwood movie about boxing. They enjoy the joke of pretence, acting out before the show over a drink in the bar the shyness of bare acquaintance. The film cuts short their game.

'Powerful. Eastwood's right, that's *not* a boxing film,' John comments during the interval.

Kath is shocked by the physical violence of many of the scenes, particularly the suggestion that a woman's path to feeling decently about herself is best met through hitting back. She is about to say something to this effect when a man in an immaculate pink shirt stops to say hello. Kath hardly recognises him and doesn't attempt a conversation. John manages to contain his amusement till they are again alone.

'Incredible! I overheard that fellow talking earlier to someone in the foyer. The decanted accent! Do you know what he said? "Cheer up, Deirdre, just another hurdle in the steeplechase of life." He did!'

Kath rolls her eyes. 'Chest hairs at his open neck.'

The second half is due to begin. The end of the film risks sentimentality, and is all the more impressive for teetering on the brink before declining to supply an easy answer. It refuses to offer any definitive answer at all.

On the way back in the car, three-quarters of an hour's drive home across the levels, Kath finds herself talking to John, in confidence, about something Esther told her when she visited last weekend.

'I'm getting braver. At asking difficult questions. What is it, I wonder, I always fear hearing? It isn't good what she told me. I'm really glad I know, though.'

The truth had emerged by chance, almost casually, as she and Esther knelt side by side weeding the asparagus bed. The position reminded her, Esther said, of cultivating cannabis in the squat in Primrose Hill where she lived for a couple of years during and after study for her degree at the London

School of Economics.

'I didn't know it was a squat,' Kath had said.

'You did, I told you,' Esther claimed.

'You didn't, I promise.'

Esther shrugged. 'Oh, well, maybe not.'

'What else don't I know?' Kath tells John of then asking her daughter, instantly, without stopping to think.

'About drugs. Addiction. Hospitals. Years and years of the fight to free myself,' she had replied, without emphasis, as a matter of plain fact.

'It explains so much that I couldn't understand,' Kath says in the car as they drive down the long straight dykes home from the cinema, the half-moon low in the sky ahead of them. 'Addicted to heroin. Our sweet Esther. Concealment as much a habit as the drugs, I suppose. And I was easy meat. Silent about my own insecurities. Pretending, for the girls' sake, to be a reliable mother. Of course I didn't want to listen. Not to that kind of stuff.'

'You mustn't punish yourself,' John cautions. 'Cannot help now.'

'I feel so sad for her. It has affected everything. Not marrying. Never trusting anybody. It was the boy, you see, who got her hooked. The one she loved. What was she trying to prove?'

'That she wasn't afraid?' he suggests.

'I loved him too. Sensitive. And weak. A liability, it transpired.'

They are alone on the road, surrounded by silence.

Kath continues to speak. 'Not his fault. Maybe she has other reasons anyway for not wanting children. Like you. There's nothing wrong about not being a parent. I wouldn't have been, were it not for Stewart.'

John remains supportively silent at the wheel.

'You'd have been a good father,' she says. 'You give time to things. Are interested in what young people mean. Reassure them, somehow, that you accept whatever it is they truly think. Can take their worst without losing your own place in the puzzle. It's a gift. Esther likes you more and more.'

'I like her. You know I do,' he says – also as a matter of inarguable fact.

At the front gate at Parsonage Farm, before parting for the night, John folds his arms around Kath and hugs her longer and more tenderly than it has occurred to him to do before. She leans against him, her hands behind his back, and in the dark of the lane they rest together for a minute or two down the full length of their slender frames.

'Good night,' they say, almost in unison, and hold hands as they step apart, she turning towards her house, he to his Mercedes, relinquishing touch at extended fingertips.

··· CHAPTER NINE ···

WORK ON NOTABOOK TAKES TIME. It provides them with a reason for being together that they need not question. The experience strengthens their relationship.

'There's no hurry,' Kath says. 'Got to get it right!'

John has learnt not to overreact to this mild teasing. He is able to smile, and not to speak when he's nothing to say. It is now the spring of 2006. The book is almost done. They are seated at Kath's kitchen table, just the two of them, in the Windsor armchairs at either end, both with gold-rimmed quarter spectacles on the end of their noses, across the tops of which they gaze at each other.

'So?' one of them says.

'So what?' the other says.

'The quantity.'

'A hundred, I'd like.'

'Then a hundred it'll be.'

'Nice round number.'

'Exactly!'

The limited edition of their not-a-book has grown in numerical size and dropped in price. Seventy pounds is the cover charge they fix today, discounted to forty a copy to any shop buying to sell – paid up-front, a condition which John buttresses Kath's desire to impose, in conflict with the standard sale-or-return arrangement expected by retailers.

'Don't have to stock it if they don't want, do they?' he protests. 'We need *some* commitment!'

'Can't charge the shop in Trinity in advance,' Kath points out. 'Wouldn't be fair.'

'Of course not. They'll be the exception.' John's smile broadens at her frown of concern at the other end of the table. 'You said yourself there are no rules. So we aren't breaking one!'

Kath doesn't attempt to conceal her pleasure at his consistent grasp these days of the point of it all, without her needing to explain, the courage of his conviction exceeding her own. A problem shared is a problem doubled, Esther always says. Wrongly, Kath decides – in her case, as it is now, with John's steady presence in her life and work.

He has changed his mind about promotion of the book, content for the main method of sale to be by direct order, by letter or telephone to Parsonage Press. Kath doesn't possess, or want, a website and sales through the Internet are therefore impracticable. John accepts the slower system, managing to stop initial worries of limited attention to his

... baby, it feels to him; except that this would make Kath its mother, not a sensible way of thinking ... their co-creation, he defines the project, unable for the moment to find a less clumsy phrase.

'What about reviews, etcetera?' Kath enquires.

'That's a problem,' John acknowledges. 'We can't send out, willy-nilly, seventy quid books. On the off-chance of a mention. And yet I really do believe it deserves to be noticed.'

'What about some sort of extract? Or facsimile? We could Xerox the etched sheets, write a press release describing the folder itself and the general nature of the edition, and mail these to the newspapers and radio programmes. Whom were you thinking of contacting?'

'Art critics, I suppose. The book people. Some painter-friends. TV director or two. Whoever might be interested.'

'What's wrong, then, with my idea of photocopies?'

John again smiles, and removes his spectacles, waving them somewhat extravagantly in the air. 'Nothing, my love,' he says.

'That's it, then,' she says.

Over the next three weeks Kath completes the final touches to the full print-run of NOTABOOK. On placing all the pages in their folders, they decide to tie around each a piece of undyed garden twine, sealed with a small square of lead, stamped GT.

Their first port-of-call, before posting a single facsimile

text to reviewers, is the antique dealer in Trinity.

John has never been before. They park alongside a substantial granite kerbstone in the main market street. The shop itself is eighteenth century, a double-fronted house, its modest pair of bow windows painted fig-green. On the sill, where copies of their work will be displayed, is a decorated Wedgwood dish, signed on the back by Louise Powell, the label says: a blue-brush country scene of trees, pasture and a cottage. Notice is directed to Fig. 38 in *Good Citizen's Furniture. The Arts and Crafts Collections at Cheltenham*, a copy of which John possesses – the description on the card does not claim equivalence, merely proposes related qualities to the illustration referred to, the famous Daneway bowl by Louise's father Alfred.

'My God, they're rare,' he says. 'I might have to buy it!'

'Ownership, again?' Kath notes. 'That's fine. It's why these nice people exist, to pass on to others their discoveries. And to buy more. Sell more. Selectively, in their case.'

'And mine!'

'True!'

They briefly clutch hands, pull the bell and enter.

Over demi-tasses of espresso coffee served in the study section of the shop, enthusiastic discussion of a proof copy of NOTABOOK fuels their belief in the project.

It must, it must work, John tells himself – then takes a deep breath, tries to alter the pressure-pattern for success, seeks release from his habit of control.

With Kath, on the other hand, nothing is obligatory.

Launch party? Public signings? Author photographs? Colour supplement fandangos? None of this has to be, if one of them doesn't want it – for whatever reason – or for no logical purpose at all. Alternatively, they are allowed to agree to all of it. There really are no rules in this private process of coming close.

All the same, it is tiring for Kath, when the biggest to the tiniest of things are to John negotiable, insistent on voicing his convoluted views at each decision.

'Let's toss a coin,' Kath is reduced, on a later occasion, to proposing. 'I honestly don't care. And you, you've a dozen plus *and* minus preferences!'

'That's how it is. I'm not going to pretend it's easy. When it isn't.' They are alone in the studio at Parsonage Farm, John gesticulating in that excessive way he behaves in distress. 'Look, I find life complex. What's more, I believe it *is* complex. If you can't accept this then ... No, I'm sorry, I know you know. I just ... It's difficult. I'm difficult! We'll be OK.'

Kath passes the palm of her hand from his forehead down the bridge of his nose, over his lips (which he air-kisses), to his chest. She presses his breastbone, and says: 'We already *are* OK.'

The issue under discussion is a planned celebration, the desire to share their book with friends and family in some special marking of the day. Whom to invite is the point of contention. In particular: John's mother.

Kath risks a final solution.

'Maybe this is something to trust me to decide? Personally, I'd rather you didn't burden yourself with the woman. It's too late. She'll never listen. And if she could, I doubt you'd any longer want to tell her anything important.'

John places his hands flat in front of him on the iron bed of Kath's Albion press and leans forward, rocking back and forth on the soles of his shoes. He is in pain. He always will be. Feelings about his old mother mustn't again be allowed to harm him: that's what matters now. There's no dispute. Kath is right. The most important fact of life to him, John knows, is her. He wouldn't dream of defiling love for Kath by telling his mother how he feels. Ever.

'Let's not send her an invitation,' he says. 'She can stay with me some other time.'

The launch party is on the second Sunday in March, thirty-five people for lunch at John's place, served at tables inside and out, cooked – as a favour to Kath – by Lorna Wardell, the closure of whose café in Taunton two years ago is a loss to the community not yet replaced: a tragedy, some say, to be deprived of her lemon meringue pie. These days Lorna designs gardens, with lavender paths and bay tree topiary. Guests at Grooms Cottage sit wherever they wish and eat whatever they want. The wine, like the food, is especially good. His neighbours on the Granthorne Estate are all invited, queen of the day the grandmother who worked after the war as a housemaid in the demolished mansion, custodian since then of the *Samson and the Philistines* relief in her tied cottage at the head of the lane. Kath adores her on sight, a woman of limitless dignity and restraint. The Trevelyan/Bowler family arrive in force, including the children's children and a couple of cousins. Only Esther declines to come, on grounds with which both John and Kath sympathise: a conviction that almost everybody would praise her work on NOTABOOK in terms she'd hate. It's one of the few things I've done I'm really proud of, Esther writes in a long letter to them, and I'd like it to remain this way. What I want to do, is walk to the top of May Hill that day, with a half-bottle of champagne, and drink it sip by sip in the spring sunshine all on my own. Thinking of you two. And of me. Pleased to be alive.

In the lull of mid-afternoon Kath finds herself and brother Richard in the shade of the arbour, sharing the curved seat, with nobody else in the immediate vicinity. She stares at him as she might at a stranger. Which he is, she feels. Her brother, Kath is prepared today to admit, is distinctly different from the man she assumed him to be. For a start, he is elegantly bald, his smooth skull fringed by a cropped horseshoe of auburn hair. Of the greatest significance: he isn't blind. On the contrary, the eyes, which she had pictured lacking in the capacity to express a flicker of interest in the world, are fiery bright.

Laughter tumbles forth. 'This is absolutely idiotic, I know,' Kath says. 'But I'd got it into my head that you became – I've no idea when! – a blind man. Fat. Pale. With a white stick. Of course it was a *school* for the blind you set up. And you closed it because … Why? Not because you yourself couldn't see!'

Richard too is amused. He may have drunk a couple more glasses of wine than intended. 'No matter,' he says. 'I always thought you thought I was a bit of a slug. You probably said so. When we were children.'

Kath's childhood contact with her elder brother remains a topic she is determined to ignore. Her smile freezes. A blanket drops, muffling sense and memory. She rallies. 'On what is it you're so expert? Spiders?' she asks.

'Yuh, that's one of my interests,' he replies. 'It's the Silver-Striped Hawk Moth, though, which is … well, my primary concern, you could say.'

Kath is stuck for a response. Richard recognises her plight, and comes to the rescue: 'Didn't you sort of curate Dad's King Penguins? I'm sure you did. Anyway, it was one of them which set me going, all those years ago. *Some British Moths* by the Keeper of Entomology at the BM. I'll never forget reading that only two hundred specimens of Silver-Striped had ever been seen in the British Isles. The majority in the Wesleyan burial ground at Bunhill Fields. Its nick-name, the book said, is the Stranger.'

'Really?' Kath is intrigued. 'I've got a copy of my own. I

collect them. The ones on nature. It's almost my favourite cover.'

'How nice,' Richard says. 'We do, after all, have a shared history.'

'The spines. Have you noticed? The title runs bottom to top,' she says, again refusing to be drawn into memory-land. 'Most books did then. They changed direction in the 1960s. And have never looked back.'

The brother's eyes sparkle. 'Design-wise,' he remarks.

These two old siblings hold each other's gaze and, without words, agree to be amused, to bury anger. There's no point. It's too late to sort it out, she tells herself. Might as well be friends.

'The hops are good this year,' Kath says, referring to the profusion of growth on John's trellis, the yellowy-green leaves of which conceal and cool them. 'It's the same everywhere in The Kingsways. Trees and shrubs and things, they all flourish.' This conversational comment makes her think of the formal gardens at Richard's abandoned school. 'How do you cope with the gardens, without any staff?' she finds herself asking.

'I don't! Clear as much as I need for my moth traps. Tend the plants on which they feed and breed. And leave the rest to itself.'

Kath is surprised by the emotion of relief. 'Sounds sensible,' she says. 'I'm glad you manage.'

'More than "manage". I do exactly what I want!'

'Hopes are good too,' she says, pats Richard on the knee and goes off to see if she can give John a hand.

Kath finds him in the greenhouse, discussing with his landlord's sister the merits of spaghetti squash. He is not a cook of talent. He isn't, in reality, a cook at all.

'A provider of wholesome-enough stuff to eat, is as much as I might claim,' he says. 'Unless someone else creates the food!'

Kath is pleased: she can see that John is happy with the day.

'Why bother, then, with a greenhouse?' his guest, a gardening enthusiast, enquires.

'Because ... I like it. It's so ... appropriate. Don't you think?' He spins around, pointing through the glass roof at the glade behind. 'I found it in abandoned sections, in a woodsman's yard. Bought the bricks from the reclamation boys. And set it here.'

'It's an idea, made manifest,' Kath says. 'The smell of tomatoes. The warmth of the air. Autumn afternoons in a chair with a book. Mug of tea on the potting table!'

John strokes the sleeve of her dress. 'We do things differently. But have similar feelings,' he says. 'And NOTABOOK is the proof.'

The reviews, when they begin to appear in the art magazines, praise their work. The project is written up in a Sunday supplement, beside a posed photograph of the two of them at lunch with Gavin Turk, in a transport café near his East End studio. The Formica table-top is yellow, the plates green. Turk wears his orange denim jacket, with a machine-woven silk label at the back of the neck, visible in the photo, inscribed with his name. His professional signature, reproduced on the designer label and used a lot in his art, is different from the way he signs his cheques. 'Gavin Turk' (in inverted commas, written in the air as he explains) is an artist – although the distinction from Gavin Turk, the man himself, is getting by now a little blurred, leading to confusion – which may be helpful to the cause, of course, he says, with his usual optimism. On the way to Cornwall a week later with his partner and kids in their camper van he calls by, and offers John a work of art.

'My latest. Shall I do you one?'

John hesitates. 'Where?' he asks.

They are having a late breakfast in Grooms Cottage. Caesar, the youngest son, aged five, so named for being born by caesarean section, is singing to himself on the floor. Gavin points to the wall against which the staircase rises, with light streaming in from the only tallish window in the house, the plain plaster painted, like everywhere else in the building, white.

'Hammer, six-inch nail and sheet of decent paper. All I need,' Gavin says.

'Fair enough.' John has decided to accept whatever it is his friend plans. 'Won't be a moment.' He speedily returns with the requested materials. 'Over to you.'

Gavin Turk steps halfway up the stairs, assesses the skewed shadow of the window-frame on the wall, looks up at the softer sunlight spreading down from the double glass doors of John's study, picks his spot and bangs the nail through the paper into the wall. The rectangular piece of paper hangs at an angle, onto which the sun projects an image of the nail, shifting in colour and position in response to the movement of clouds across the sky and to the position of the sun. Gavin walks up then down the stairs, inspecting the effect.

'Not bad,' he says, signs and dates his work in pen at the bottom right-hand corner of the A4 sheet, and hands back the hammer. 'Kinetic art. Always changing.'

At night, when they've gone, John sees that the moon also casts a shadow, in a grey wedge, the head of the nail blurred and big. Like a silver-point print. Or the delicate hatched lines of a hard-lead drawing. He wants to telephone Kath to share his delight. With difficulty, he waits till morning to tell her.

There's another thing to tell: of his observation earlier in the day of swallows in the field beyond his study, to which the Aberdeen Angus have recently been moved, and his noticing the birds' absence from the adjacent fields; such a beautiful combination, swallows and bullocks and grass – there is a reason, he realises: seeing the cattle ceaselessly flap and swish their ears and tails, it is clear that they and their dung attract flies, and that the flies attract the swallows, swooping back and forth close to earth, maybe a hundred birds in frantic pursuit of food, passing each other at incredible speed, no hint of danger of collision.

A friend-of-a-friend invites them to give a fringe presentation at the Cheltenham Literary Festival, which they decline.

'Done. It's time to move on,' John says.

'Oh, where to?' Kath queries – as ever, less sure of herself than him.

He is preoccupied by other thoughts and impatient with her uncertainties. He tut-tuts. Disliking the sound he hears himself making, he stops this disagreeable progression of behaviour. John attempts to look at things from her point of view, and is able to see that he hasn't, in fact, shared in any depth with Kath his involvement in the project over at the old barns at Granthorne, about which right then he is thinking.

'I'm sorry. I imagine all these things and forget I haven't told you them. To me, you're part of everything.'

'What nonsense!' she retorts. 'If you don't share?'

Over the eight months since getting back together again, much has changed. Everything is different, it could be said – most importantly of all: the nature of their commitment – a state of affairs which it isn't possible to describe, the usual words too easily misinterpreted, inadequate for this personal and particular purpose.

To say that Kath then smiles is accurate in itself; but the myriad qualities of her expression can only be felt, by John.

'Tell me now, please,' she adds.

'It's the principle, basically, about which I care. A refusal to play the game. Disdain for maximisation of profit, for charging as much as you dare and then a little more.'

'John Garsington, you are a little ... er, indirect, shall we say? So, OK, I do know what you're talking about. That for the last two years you and Nick Strutton have been renovating the redundant farm over at the Manor. I even know that the columns of the big barn are Romanesque, pillaged from the church.' She is enjoying herself. 'Actually, you've told me more of that sort of thing than anything else. I can only guess, from random snippets and your funny anxious face these days, that it's due soon to open?'

'Correct!'

'And?'

'Lots. Might be simpler, probably, definitely quicker, if you ask a question.'

'What is expected of you?'

'Ah, now that's a difficult one. Expected of me by myself or by others?'

'The latter, please.'

'Yes, let's not get diverted.' He pauses. 'I'm glad you asked. You know I'm not quite sure. Nothing full-time, I really have made that clear. I suppose in ways I've done my bit already, helping get it off the ground. I mean, I may organise an exhibition or two. Mount a couple of concerts. A friend In London says he'll persuade Les Arts Florissants to give us an evening of music. The barn is an astonishing space. I doubt if there's anything anywhere in the West Country quite like it. Next question?'

'Do you love me?'

'That's inarguable. Yes.'

The conversation continues. They have lunch together, after which Kath returns to her studio at Parsonage Farm, while John walks over the fields to Granthorne to check on the name-signs about to be erected around the complex of converted barns.

The next day, in a charity shop in Taunton, John buys for Kath a copy of Edward Fitzgerald's translation of *The Rubáiyát of Omar Khayyám*, from the Carillon Series, bound between block-printed paperboards and with illustrations by Robert Anning Bell. He chooses it for its graphic design not for the title. And for the artist, a framed colour-relief by whom he owns, *The Lily Girl*, the label on the back of which records that it was a wedding gift from Anning Bell and his wife to a Mr and Mrs Taylor, in 1893. John loves labels. He doesn't tell Kath about any of this, not wishing to demand attention for his own obsessions; the book is a mark of John's concern for her, not a statement about himself. She is pleased with her present – carillon, a ring of bells, a word she likes, yet has no desire to emulate – an imprint she hasn't seen before and will, one day, make use of in her work, of this Kath is certain.

The relationship of Kath to her work continues to evolve, leading her into caves of the imagination she had never expected to explore. Music has reclaimed its hold on her – modern music, tossing into the air the rules of harmony, quavers and staves falling back onto the keys in the multiple languages of the world today. Not that she attempts to play again the viola. Her instrument is bound by now to be the old Albion printing press in her studio, a machine capable in her hands of almost anything. Kath's confidence glows. She opens up the palms of these hands of hers, looks down at them, and feels safe. By chance, as if to illustrate the point, she notices that a day-flying moth has trapped itself inside the shade of her desk lamp. Kath encloses the moth in her hand, opens a window and releases it, watching its bright orange flight across the yard in the sun. A small bird darts from its hidden perch inside the hydrangea, catches the moth and in an instant eats it.

She frowns.

It must be a simple matter for birds to capture as many bobbing moths and butterflies as they like. They don't, though – not that Kath remembers having seen before. Why not? And why did this particular sparrow grab at this particular moth? Did it mistake it for something else, something potentially scrumptious discarded from her window?

Kath seems to have more time these days to observe

events, more time in the mind, for all sorts of things. On her bicycle in town she has to pull hard on the brakes to avoid a woman in a dither with her electronic invalid's buggy. 'Sorry, don't know where I'm going,' the old lady says, with a silvery smile. 'None of us do,' Kath calls out as she recovers her balance. Minutes later she passes ranks of identical maroon buggies parked on the pavement outside Price Is Right; and then observes that many of these Borough chariots are ridden by quite young women, without obvious disabilities; all the machines in Taunton are maroon, she sees, the labels on the back inscribed, in sloping letters, Shoprider. It is the men, mostly, who have cigarettes dangling from their mouths as they trundle in their Shopriders along the street.

There's another wallflower in her wall!

How did it establish itself? Appears to be no earth at all.

The nourishment must exist, unseen between the stones.

Elsewhere there is no food to feed on. Only violence. How can a boy born into terror, growing to adulthood in the knowledge of inalterable cruelty, of the powerlessness to resist degradation and disease, have respect for the life of man? Or woman? Or child? He can't. Humanity is a word without meaning to him without experience. Mao Tse Tung didn't know what it meant. When relatively young, in the hinterland of China, a friend records sitting beside Mao at a village circus, when a girl on the trapeze falls to the earth and impales herself on a tent peg. As the crowd gasps in horror, Mao alone laughs, spontaneously, the emotion of human sorrow beyond his comprehension. Hurt, mutilation, death are to him normal. And to many others: in Indonesia, Siberia, Northern Ireland, Nepal, Sri Lanka ... in Africa ... in Asia ... in the Middle East. Mao for sure allowed, maybe intentionally caused the deaths of twenty million of his own people, individual human sacrifices to the idea of the whole, their existence no more to him than hieroglyphs on a map.

Other people kill on an intimate scale, murder half a dozen others by also blowing up themselves.

Kath is thinking of John, as she always does these days. She thinks of his anger, turned in upon himself, as befits a man of his advantages. Violence all the same, isn't it, his culture of civilized despair?

Love: to many merely another word, difficult to learn the meaning of in later life, without earlier experience.

Not impossible, though.

It happens, on occasion.

And John is at the same moment thinking of Kath, as he always does these days. He is on the train to London, on his own. Not far from the city the track passes through the town where John spent his boyhood, and from the viaduct he can look out of the window onto paths along which he used to walk the family's dog at night, on a lead, until it relieved itself in the gutter and he turned immediately for home. In his parents' house affection was channelled through the dog. No one was affectionate to anyone except through the dog. He too made a fuss of the dog, and is grateful for it having been a sensible and loveable dog. John has passed this spot several times on the train with Kath, in silence, telling her nothing, aware that the feelings which these scenes touch in him are of no communicable significance, the private memories of his youth, capable of resonance only with another's youth. He doesn't want this, not with Kath. They are adults. He needs her for who she is now. And for whatever he has become.

In the rain he spends the afternoon at the National Gallery in Trafalgar Square, for the first time at any length in fifteen years. Endlessly, room after room, he is astonished by the beauty man is capable of fabricating from the placement of paint on canvas. Such complexity. Such simplicity. John is happy.

It doesn't last.

The next night, at a film, he is confused by the degradation of the life depicted, by an artist, Asia Argento, choosing to expose the relationship of a mother to her son in terms of the starkest distress. Not exaggerated, not dishonest. All things which people do. Which people make films of them doing. Which people watch them being filmed doing. Which he watches, sitting in safe collusion in the main cinema at the Institute of Contemporary Arts, in the Mall, fairly late at night, a few hundred yards from his country's sleeping Queen, the grandmother of Buckingham Palace.

Right now, back home, both Kath and John are thinking of Esther, as they often do when they are together these days. In her they witness versions of themselves at different periods of their lives, Esther's lack of emotional disguise a mirror to their own feelings, brought into sharper focus than often they can recognise inside themselves.

'The things she comes across in the streets of Oxford. And tells us about, here at Parsonage Farm. What hope in Lesotho?' Kath says.

John's nostrils flare. 'It's what people say. The hatred in their voices. Screams of abuse from ordinary mothers at ordinary boys. That's what gets to me.'

Kath places the fingertips of her hands against her closed eyelids, briefly, then looks at him across the table. She smiles, and says: 'None of us three have given up. Now that is something!'

He also smiles. 'What did Esther say the other day? About Wittgenstein? That he reckoned in philosophy one shouldn't banish or tidy up some crude but troubling thought. Rather, should give it its day, its week, its month in court.'

'I see how you'd agree with that!'

John laughs out loud. 'I forgot to tell you! You know, now that I'm in London again a lot, how I've gone back to the man who cut my hair years ago in Bloomsbury? Yes, well, when I walked in nothing had changed. Twenty years on! Same old ladies toasting the same old perms beneath the same old helmet hairdryers. "Hello, it *has* been a while," Ivan says. And when I stupid-sort-of-coyly ask: "Do you give appointments to ancient clients?" he replies, quick as light: "Cut the hair of anybody who walks in that door." I do like Ivan. No sentimentality there!'

Over time, John is filling in for Kath gaps of information about certain aspects of his past. They tend not to speculate on the causes of his eager telling of some stories and rocky silence around others, both having learnt that there's nothing to gain by direct enquiry, as the net result with him is firmer forbearance. From the outset of their friendship they have spent many hours talking about the art they both, often differently, love. The work itself is what always matters, but by now Kath also knows the basic narrative of John's dealing career. Details of his contacts with individual young artists, however, emerge piecemeal – more a measure, in this case, of discretion than secrecy.

'I've just realised that most of the artists I represented were women,' he says. 'It wasn't intentional. They were the best. And half of them were never tempted anyway. Rachel Whiteread's work I've always adored, and I've never even met her. Same with Gillian Wearing. A lesson to everyone when she won the Turner Prize, and refused point-blank all interviews. She might have welcomed attention before the award. Afterwards, no need! Do you know Rebecca Warren's sculpture? Incredibly intense. She I failed to spot. Ah, well. Too many names. It's good I packed it in.'

'Not completely,' Kath suggests.

'Exhibitions in the Great Barn at Granthorne? We'll see. Maybe,' John concedes.

'If Joshua were alive, he would,' she says, almost to herself.

John also tells Kath bits and pieces about his mother. About her passion for the dancing of Scottish reels, which she used to practise every fortnight through the winter in a borrowed school gym, with a group of fellow enthusiasts – in those suburbs visible from the train. She also loved to sing and was a member of the local choral society – *The Dream of Gerontius* is the work he best remembers her performing, in the assembly hall of some other school. The concerts were free, her membership too. Money mattered enormously to his mother's wartime generation. The habit of thrift is impossible for the old lady to abandon, and on most Sunday afternoons she hobbles from her flat down the road to Waitrose minutes before it closes at 4 p.m., to purchase the reduced-price food: half a cucumber, two croissants, a loaf of bread, a bunch of wilting flowers and nameless other arbitrary items to a total of £3.48 – she fusses and puzzles over the change.

'A single night in her flat is as much as I can occasionally take,' John says. 'I don't expect things to improve.'

'They don't,' Kath agrees.

It's lunchtime. Seated at the oak table outside the open byre at Grooms Cottage, they squeeze lemon onto their smoked eel, toss the garden-green salad and begin to eat. John cuts a couple of slices of the cottage loaf.

'As I came out of the dairy the other day in Greater Mead, three horse-drawn traps passed by,' Kath says. 'The occupants in pairs, wearing identical logo-ed sweatshirts and baseball caps. Their faces warm and rural, enjoying themselves. Why the ugly gear?'

'Why do you and I get so upset?' he questions.

'I'm not.'

'I am!'

John hates the bearing of brands. Where his mother now lives, the street after street of tedious wealth depresses him: the retirement homes with double-barrelled garages, brash Tudorbethan semidom, in every spare space a building, with heaps of gravel in new drives, awaiting distribution – yellow, clean, weedless, inches thick and hell to walk through. Ranks of competing yucca plants on the patios.

'Kids do live there. You see them at the mown grass corners, huddled in scruffy groups with their bicycles. How do they survive the anaesthetic?'

Kath had been thinking something of the kind a few days ago. About the powers of human survival. 'People do,' she says. 'We just do.'

'Like the Sunny Jim doll!'

She laughs, in surprise – pleasurable – at the workings of John's funny mind. 'Ah, um, yes ... Explain?'

'On the Force packet? The cereal? You must remember. If

you collected enough coupons you could write in to Nestlés for a rag doll.'

'Huh!'

'I was never allowed to. Treats restricted to tea-cakes with millions and billions scattered across the pink icing. Same period. Seriously. You haven't forgotten?'

'Hundreds and thousands.'

'What?'

'That's what those coloured bobbles are called.'

John wags a forefinger – at himself. 'Exaggeration. You're as bad as your mother!'

Kath's voice ripples with laughter. 'Worse! Because you have the advantage of knowing me!' she says.

The talk turns to books, in particular to their placing on the shelf. Kath confesses how much it matters to her that the books she likes are positioned next to other books she likes, the less favoured authors segregated to higher shelves. Date, or alphabetical order, is immaterial. Although colour does come into it. And the writer's gender – three of her fiction shelves are of books written only by women. She fiddles with juxtapositions, registering distinct satisfaction at moving the literary essays of V.S. Naipaul to beside her two James Wood collections of reviews, and at the placing, in a spare bedroom, of Hilaire Belloc next to G.K. Chesterton.

'Esther is always mucking up the order,' Kath says. 'I think she does it on purpose!'

Numbers are another issue. In their new series, Great Ideas, Penguin has numbered the spines in the order of original creation, from No. 1 *The Shortness of Life* by Seneca to No. 20 *Why I Write* by George Orwell. She hasn't got them all, only the volumes which interest her – Michel de Montaigne's *On Friendship*, originally of 1580, for instance: 'As for marriage, apart from it being a bargain where only the entrance is free (its duration being fettered and constrained, depending on things outside our will), it is a bargain struck for other purposes; within it you soon have to unsnarl hundreds of extraneous tangled ends, which are enough to break the thread of living passion and to trouble its course, whereas in friendship there is no traffic or commerce but with itself.' Pocket Penguins are also numbered, from 1 to 70, to celebrate seventy years since the imprint's foundation. The few volumes Kath has of these also bear the numbers on their narrow spines and are ranked accordingly on her shelf – except that No. 64, Kafka's *The Great Wall of China*, is placed at the end of the run, to stand next to the same author's *Metamorphosis*, from another modern series the design of which she admires, cover and typeset by Fraser Muggeridge for Hesperus – printed, apparently, in the United Arab Emirates.

'Pinched from King Penguins,' she says. 'The numbering idea, I mean.'

John taps both hands on the side of his skull. 'And I thought I was a maniac!'

'Common sense.'

'Sense, yes. Common? I think not!'

'It's how I do it, anyway,' Kath defends.

'Don't stop being you. Promise.' John turns to stare, sightlessly, at the branches of the old apple tree poking above the roof of the garden shed. He gets to his feet. 'Finished lunch? I'll clear the plates.'

Before Kath returns to her studio over the hill, they together inspect the edge of the paddock, where John is thinking of planting in the autumn a line of pleached English lime, to form a sculptural break from the back garden of one of the cottages at the end of the lane, where the flowering shrubs are a bit too bright, to his taste. The idea was Kath's, and John is pleased to leave the ordering of the trees to her. He can picture the change, and feels fortunate in his closeness to this lovely woman.

There remains a slight awkwardness to their partings, on both sides, neither of them wishing to make assumptions, and thereby to assert precisely where and when they'll next see each other. Things are left a little in the air.

That evening John happens to hear the sound of a chainsaw in the nearby wood, part of the Granthorne Estate, and strolls over to investigate. It is one of the locals, a man whom he knows and respects, recently switched from rearing sheep on hired land on The Kingsways to logging, a pleasanter as well as a more profitable activity, Timothy maintains. When John began restoration of the end of his cottage, roofless and abandoned, once a dwelling but utilised for the previous two centuries as a cattle stall and barn, Timothy was incredulous, and after a theatrical pause commented in his Somerset drawl: 'Youse must want som'at to do-o-o.' John invites him to call by for a beer when he's filled his trailer with logs. They sit at the outside table, the timber of which Timothy recognises, the bulk of it recovered from ruined buildings on the Estate and adapted by traditional methods to its new purpose. They talk of this and that. John remembers his country friend, a solitary middle-aged man, telling him on an earlier occasion about a tough childhood, forced by his father to live with him in a caravan parked at sites around the county, wherever itinerant labour as a thatcher could be found. His sisters stayed with their mother – to whom Timothy returned on the day of his sixteenth birthday, legally freed to decide for himself where to live. John asks after her, and hears that she died two months earlier, of cancer, which she had suffered uncomplainingly for ten years, removed to hospital after the final attack, where she died within five days. Tears form in Timothy's eyes and run down his stubble cheeks. He rubs his face with the back of his fist, leaving trails of sawdust in the wet.

'She be a strong woman. Didn't complain. Nothing no one could do. Never knows a half of it, does thee? I miss her. And ain't ashamed to weep at her leaving us.'

··· CHAPTER TEN ···

IT ISN'T LONG TILL THE opening celebrations at Granthorne Barns, to be held over the two days of April 28th and 29th, a Friday and Saturday. The public task which John has taken on is the museum area, dedicated to the life of the Estate, with maps and photographs and objects and artefacts reaching back towards its medieval origins.

John is proud of what has been achieved. Nicholas Strutton, the owner of the buildings and land, a working farmer, has sustained the momentum of this daunting project with courage and principle. Inheriting the property in his early thirties, with mounting debts and the threat of dereliction, Nicholas refused to capitalise on the Estate's assets and has never sold a single field or building, preferring financial hardship to jeopardising the character of this special place. In consequence, there really is nothing anywhere in the West Country quite like Granthorne – it is why John is here, convinced that his home and surroundings feel the way they do through remaining unavailable for purchase, saved from the intervention of alien tastes. Beauty of this quality cannot be bought; Granthorne, as it is, is priceless. The custodian of history, Nicholas intends to pass on the Estate in prime condition for unchanged survival for another century, in the charge of his son, at present a pre-pubescent boy. John is happy to contribute to the protection of this rarity.

'Not left to his daughters, of course. Even though they're older,' Kath points out.

'Maybe. Who knows?' John responds.

'You can be *so* annoying! You disapprove, I know you do. Why won't you just agree with me? They'll do whatever they want anyway. Doesn't make it right!'

Kath is helping set out the display cases in the museum. John rests his back for a moment against the newly plastered internal wall of the old granary. With the support of her presence in his life, he finds it easier at least to acknowledge contradictions between how he feels and what he expresses. He is not much nearer, however, to understanding whatever it is which causes him to remain tight, inflexible, in need, mostly, of having the last word to say.

'No, I know. I just ... I don't know. If Nicholas wasn't who he is, a bit difficult, secretive, these barns wouldn't exist to preserve. And I feel I have to defend him. Even with you! Idiotic. I'm sorry.'

They carry on with their work in silence, confident in

each other's ability to select and position without discussion these Granthorne things around the room. Kath has printed the descriptive labels, in Baskerville, within a double border, the lines of different thickness; they pin these to the wall and place them in the cabinets beside the objects on display. There are hundreds of different ways of doing the job. This particular choice is theirs. It is distinct. And appropriate, in Kath's and John's view.

The fabric of this old home-farm, gathered around four enclosed courtyards and flanking the Jacobean manor, with its own gatehouse, triumphal arch and walled garden, is seen now in the restoration to be exceptional. John maintains that this fact was never in doubt, that decisions along the path were answered by the architecture itself. Everything was already there, waiting to be discovered.

Today's revived flow of water is perhaps the most revealing mark of renewal.

At first inspection even the iron waterwheel was hidden, walled up in the dark below the disused granary, the wooden teeth of the grinder-cogs undamaged, only the buckets of the Victorian wheel rotten. Some rooting around in the undergrowth above the property disclosed the extent of the pond from which the water originally flowed to power the mill, channelled down a still-existing stone leat and on into a matching drain beneath the farm track. Although the dam had been deliberately breached in several places and the stream descending from Granthorne Hill diverted, its restoration was straightforward. The water once emerged below, John discovered, into a mediaeval carp pond beyond the manor, abandoned generations earlier to the invasion of alder, ash and willow and by now almost impenetrable. The retaining stone wall remained, over ten feet high. And a brick bridge-arch sluice, through which the water from the wheel used to be discharged a hundred yards distant into this lower pond via another square-section stone drain, punctured by later excavations in only a few places and simple to repair. The water again now falls uninterrupted from top to bottom of the sloping site, the Vale of Taunton stretched wide and lush beyond, bordered by the soft contours of the Brayburgh Hills separating land from sky.

In the museum John stops work for a moment to lean down over the glass and steel splash barrier to the rotating water wheel. 'The sound, it's sustaining, I feel,' he says to Kath.

'There're a pair of dippers nesting in the millpond,' she replies.

'Are there? Nature's approval.'

'And I've been for a swim in the carp pond!' Kath adds.

He is delighted, and kisses her on the lips. 'We're doing okay,' he whispers.

The Friday celebrations begin in the morning at ten, with coffee and patisserie for local villagers at their private view of the project.

Where the new staircase leading up from the main

entrance turns left across the back of the waterwheel to John's museum and exhibition gallery, to the right is the public door to the Great Barn, an amazing space fifty foot high and eighty feet in length, its double doors in the centre opening into thin air above the arched columns of the lower room. From these tall barn doors bales of hay and straw used to be tossed down to the cattle sheds, with sufficient bays in the milking-parlour to service a hundred cows at a time, the Granthorne dairy herd numbering in the nineteenth century over a thousand. The keystone above this door is dated 1852, the year the Great Barn was moved stone by stone from the southern side of the Manor and re-erected on this site, where it didn't interfere with the family's view of the valley. They were rich, then, the cost of the builders' wages immaterial. Romanesque columns removed in the fourteenth century on expansion of the Estate's church were installed at this time at the base of the barn, framing now the glass-panelled doors to the Food Store, full on this opening day of farm produce and home-cooked delights culled from as close as the neighbouring fields to as far away as the olive groves and chestnut woods of Tuscany. They sell fine wine, and organic chocolate, and bottled kidney beans, and lots of other things. The L-shaped farm building on the opposite side of the barn to the exhibition hall is a café on mornings and afternoons and in the evening a restaurant. There is a bakery in the blacksmith's forge, a stonemason in part of the cow stalls, a tractor hire company in another section, and a tree specialist in the hen house. A society-saddler has set up shop where the cider press used to be. According to the oldest surviving farm labourer, a resident these days of the almshouses nearby in Wilton Musgrove, before going out into the fields on a summer's morning each of the team of twenty harvesters, scythes shouldered, drank a quart of cider from the racked barrels: so he says, in fond recall of times long gone, when the church was full every Sunday with the men and women who worked on the Estate, walking over in converging groups from their tied cottages on the family's fifteen farms, strung across the southern ridge. John documents in the museum how the Second World War destroyed provision of the home farm's already parlous state of being.

This new adventure is a kind of renaissance, a rebirth of sorts.

As the sun sinks below the horizon a crowd gathers in the courtyard in front of the Great Barn, the doors at the centre of the building fold inwards and a spotlight figure steps to the threshold to sing. She has a microphone pinned to the breast of her taffeta ball-gown, and her voice resounds through speakers in the courtyards below. Sarah Leonard is her name, a professional soprano, the niece of a friend of Kath's from her brief period of study at music school in London. A pianist accompanies the singer. The tone is pure, her notes held without wavering, music from the neglected period of English song at the beginning of the twentieth century, by Warlock, Howells, Ireland, Bridge and Gurney. The title she has chosen for the recital is 'Renewal', her third song a composition by Frank Bridge, the words translated from a collection of poetry published by Rabindranath Tagore in 1913:

> Day after day he comes and goes away.
> Go, and give him a flower from my hair, my friend.
>
> If he asks who was it that sent it,
> I entreat you do not tell him my name
> for he only comes and goes away.
>
> He sits on the dust under the tree.
> Spread there a seat with flowers and leaves,
>   my friend.
> His eyes are sad, and they bring sadness to my heart.
> He does not speak what he has in mind; he only comes
>   and goes away.

The poem was taken by Tagore from a traditional Bengali text, about the unconsummated love of a high-caste girl for her father's gardener. It is not necessary to know this story, the music in itself filled with meaning, different to different people. To John it is a lament, the sense of loss in the slow ascendant notes of 'he only comes and goes away' touching deep within, the final 'away' by the singer repeated, like an echo.

Esther is down for the opening. She and Kath walk

together across the fields to Granthorne from John's place, the approach from which is along a bridle path through the middle of a field of ripening corn, terminating at the door to the fairytale rose-stone turret of the church, St Thomas of Canterbury, where generations of the Strutton family are buried, one couple in a mausoleum, their figures carved in alabaster, wearing elaborate ruffs and narrow square-toed boots. Esther has stopped asking her mother about John, for the two of them are obviously happy, and she, as it happens, is not in the least bit jealous. Well ... a tiny bit, maybe.

'I'll never manage it,' she says.

'What?'

'You know!'

'I don't.'

'You should.'

'I do hate that word, Esther. Please don't say "should". Say you're disappointed in me. Or you want to be chief librarian. Or the world is shit. Just don't tell me what I should or shouldn't feel.'

'Sorry.'

They link arms. There is already a large crowd in the ex-farmyard when they arrive (this second time, having already spent most of the day helping in the office). The sound of a song greets them, and as they round the corner of the walled garden they see Sarah, a slight and slender figure despite her performance dress, caught in the eye of the concert spotlight, in full, indeed beautiful voice.

The grandmother from the farmhouse at Lower Penley is there, with her memories of the previous era's end: of the childless old man who used to own the place, a recluse by then and judged by many mad; to her, though, a decent fellow, hiding away for most of the day in a secret corner of the overgrown garden, where he grew his own vegetables.

'Uncle Tom, we all called him,' she says. 'Dressed in rags, by any standard. When they pulled the mansion down, the manor here then let, he came to live in the cottage next to mine. With the man who, in the days when they kept the finest stables in these parts, used to be his personal groom. The two of them bachelors. Lord knows what they ate. Raw carrots and tinned rice pudding, wouldn't be surprised.'

'Must have been hard for you,' Kath says.

'Lost my job within the year of starting it. I was young, mind. First of the boys on the way. My husband he was a forester. Always work hereabouts with trees.'

'What happened to him?' Esther asks, quick with questions.

'Drink. Sent him to an early grave, right where he deserves to be, in this churchyard. I'm not sorry, and don't care who knows,' the bold old woman declares.

A photograph of her hangs in the museum, standing in the kitchen yard at the big house, in her starched pinafore and cap, sharing laughter and a smoke with the cook. In essence she has not changed – still works at her own uniform pace, living in the same home, taking the same breaks for her mug of tea and cigarette (Silk Cut instead of Players Plain), as trim and philosophical as ever.

'You and I, we're the same age,' Kath says.

'Battle horses,' the woman replies, and laughs. 'Lovely what they've done with the old place, isn't it?'

Esther's serious expression melts, her round face bathed in smiles, as it once used to be, briefly, for a year or two in her late teens. 'You! You're lovely!'

'Listen?' Kath intervenes. 'The interval is over. Sarah's singing again.'

They drift with a section of the crowd from beside the bakery out again into the main courtyard, where Kath and Esther walk down a gravel path to the end of the newly created knot garden, ending in a holly hedge by the low wall of the drive to the manor, with a stone bench on which they sit, facing the singer sixty yards away on the balcony of the Great Barn.

> I will go with my father a-reaping
> To the brown field by the sea,
> And the geese and the crows and the children
> Will come flocking after me.
> I will sing to the tan-faced reapers
> With the wren in the heat of the sun,
> And my father will sing the scythe-song
> That joys for the harvest done.

When the recital finishes they make their way up the

main stairs and into the hall of the barn, where food is laid out on trestle tables. There is room for everyone, almost three hundred people standing to talk and drink, spreading out into the exhibition space beyond the waterwheel. Sarah returns after changing in the office into a loose black trouser suit. Kath has been looking out for her and goes immediately to her side, with a glass of wine. They drink each other's health, and serve themselves plates of polenta, grilled cod and salad. Later they try a slice of the chef's apple tart. It tastes good. The sense of completion, Sarah of her recital, Kath of different unsaid things, unifies the night.

Is there rest? Can it ever be good enough?

Kath, happy though she is, doesn't fully believe John will be able to hold to his word.

The next morning at Granthorne Barns they celebrate the opening of the covered market. A variety of fresh produce from local farms is displayed on the dozens of stalls ranked beneath the crown trusses of the milking parlour, supported along both sides by the old oak posts, smoothed at the waist where the cattle used to rub, without walls or divisions, exactly as it was built. The feeling is of times past, a market of the type unseen in use since before the war. An image cherished by John is central to this concept: the gathering under one roof twice every week, on Wednesday mornings as well as all day on Saturdays, of the barrows seen on West

Country lanes laden with flowers, fruit and vegetables surplus to the household's needs, unpackaged, non-standard, delicious to eat – with jars of honey from different hives, gathered from different flowers, deliciously different in taste, and sealed bottles of roast squash soup. Whilst welcoming the presence also of locals from the Farmers Market, the principal aim is to offer a place for the distribution, at minimal cost to all concerned, of the stuff of life which commercial reality decrees must otherwise go to waste. John has devised a system by which clutches of a dozen stalls are run by a single person, the amateur growers required simply to turn up at the beginning of the day, lay out the season's specialities, name their price and trust the public to fill the brown paper bags provided and pay the lady at the desk. He spent many days driving around the villages of the district, stopping at any farm, cottage or country house with a substantial garden and explaining the nature of his idea to whoever would listen. Today he is rewarded, his alternative solution by buyers and sellers alike embraced.

At the market John speaks to a character he's heard about from several sources but until now has never met. The fungi-man is how everyone refers to him, by no other name known, his appearance on the heath and in the woods irregularly observed, the attempts on occasion made over the years to follow him ending in abandonment in some wild thicket, far from the beaten track – even further, John's informants wistfully conclude, from the conceivable site of a single edible mushroom. The man is of uncertain age, with fleshy face, large teeth, one missing at the top centre, and an uncut bush of auburn hair. He places himself impassably in John's path between a line of stalls.

'Want any mushrooms?' he asks.

The voice is deep, in an accent difficult to decode, the man's eyes sparkling with inner amusement.

John answers the challenge with an implacable look of his own, instantly aware to whom he's speaking. 'I do,' he replies.

'Early in the season yet. Could get you a basket or two of pleurotus for Wednesday. And I've my eye on some polyporus which'll be as succulent sulphur-yellow as man could wish in a couple of weeks, I reckon.'

In hidden delight John pummels his thighs with the fists as usual tucked inside his trouser pockets. This, precisely, is the point of his idea. Since moving to Grooms Cottage he has tried to make himself into a mushroomer, aware that The Kingstons are renowned for collection from beneath their ancient beech droves of the best chanterelle in the country. A woman who spent her childhood on the Estate's farm at Okethorn told him only yesterday of walking home from many a Sunday School and picking in the fields enough penny buns for a tea to die for: thinly sliced and sharp-fried by her mother in a cube of butter in an iron skillet on the log-range, served with chopped parsley fresh from the garden and eggs from their hens, placed on the plate beside three rashers of bacon from the back of a Granthorne pig and a wedge of white bread baked, as always in those days, that very morning. John is thinking, as he listens to the fungi-man, not only of this but also of an incident the previous autumn. On the third consecutive sunny afternoon last November, after a week's rain, he had taken a stroll up the hill with a wicker basket and knife on his last forage of the season. In the warmish wet, with winter rays of sunshine angled low, he will never forget coming across the extraordinary sight of dozens of tall mushrooms on the slope of a field bordered by a row of ancient beech: a child's picture-book image of the nether world, the shaggy-topped mushrooms with wide umbrella rims like toadstools, the brown older ones six inches in diameter, their younger cousins poking whiter flesh above the turf, drop-shaped, not yet opened by the sun. *Macrolepiota procera* is their scientific description, parasol in the vernacular, the only choice fungus John is confident occasionally of finding in abundance. His private dream in creation of the covered market is to display the mushrooms that he plans this autumn to gather, to be admired by others, and bought for a few shillings, to eat, if they dare – a delicacy, the flesh thin, white, soft, the taste sweet, smell slight, uncommon, edible, excellent: the essential book assures us.

John and the fungi-man move aside from the throng, to sit together on the wall and talk – not for long, as an arrangement simple and secret is quickly secured.

It is a marvellous thing to happen, this meeting. The man is a Pied Piper, whom the rest will follow, and fill the stalls with free wild food. Later in the year the pickers of blackberries and blueberries and sloes and hazelnuts and the hips of the dog-rose will arrive, while others will bring marsh samphire from the estuary, bladderwrack from the sea; next spring will come the hedgerow foragers of leaves of wild garlic for salads and soups, young stinging nettle for teas, elderflower for cordials, long white roots of dandelion for coffee, burdock for beer. There need now be no end to any of it.

The following week an accident in his garden at Grooms Cottage frightens John.

In retelling the events to Kath he tries to dismiss their significance. Nothing serious happened – nobody was hurt. A careless act. In the midday heat, the muscles of his back aching, instead of laying aside a piece of brick unearthed from the vegetable patch which he was digging to remove to the rubble pile later, he threw it with his left hand towards the undergrowth behind the byre. Conscious of risk to the greenhouse, he hurled the brick high and hard. He misfired and it struck an overhanging branch of the poplar, fell vertically down and smashed a pane of glass.

The sound shocked him. In the extreme. As if the jagged glass falling from the roof onto the concrete floor and a second time there shattering into finer shards, had entered him, lacerating flesh.

In haste to clear up the mess he went about the task unthinkingly and dropped the dustpan of debris on the path to the garden, creating trouble and danger in another place. He heard his boot crunch on an unseen piece of glass in a corner of the greenhouse. Saw the sharp glint of fragments in the soil beneath the tomato plants. Managed to cut his finger, draw blood.

Kath is supportive, does not criticise.

This helps.

He fears, all the same, that he may never be able to forgive himself. Damage to the beautiful old greenhouse which he rescued from neglect, restored and rebuilt on the edge of his woodland glade, threatens ... Disintegration? ... Annihilation? ... Threatens the self-destruction of every single thing about which he cares.

I've done it before: John tells himself. I could again.

Mustn't. Mustn't.

With Kath's encouragement, John puts his mind to plans in the autumn for an exhibition at Granthorne Barns of contemporary art.

'Don't want a survey. Do we? The lax smack of academia. Pay attention now, boys. Or you'll miss the crux. The crucifix. Stations of the cross in snooker balls. Butterflies at flutter-death in house paint.'

'Why not a virtual gallery? You could exhibit the *concept* of an exhibition!'

'Excellent plan. All the paraphernalia of a show. Slick invitation cards. Stories in the press, and the slipping of a meaningless image or two to the *Daily Mail*. Sponsorship by Bombay Sapphire gin. Twenty identical confessionals stood in astrological symmetry around the Great Barn, each hung in black velvet, on the seat inside a headset to cover eyes, ears and nose. Projection through this of the close-up sight and sound of the chatter at a private view. The whiff in your nose of the breath of the Minotaur.'

'Seriously.'

'I am.'

'I know.'

'What, then?'

Kath declines to reply to John's rhetorical question. She waits for him to calm down and tell her his actual hopes.

Together they explore an idea that is, in effect, a survey of John's private and professional experience in dealing with contemporary art. From the beginning, when in the solitude of school holidays he used to take the tube train from his family's home in the suburbs into town and look at everything anybody chose anywhere to present as the work of creation. To the end, when he closed his premises, liquidated the company and moved away with whatever remained of his stock to live in Somerset.

He begins to make a list of the things he'd like to exhibit – efficient in practical matters, John's choice of objects is made from collections already known to him, whose private owners or public curators could be persuaded, he reckons, to lend their possessions. This initial list feels to John like the chapter headings of a book, inscriptions on a piece of paper of his patterns of interest.

(A) *Leap into the Void* (1960). A copy of the photo-montage by Harry Shunk of Yves Klein in his black suit, arms outstretched and chest spread in a swallow-dive from a wall above the pavement on the back streets of Paris.

(B) *Devil's Darning Needle* (1999). In its perspex box, Samuel Pepper's damselfly pinned by thistle quills to a leaf, as if caught in flight, attached at the synthorax to its double pair of hyaline wings.

(C) *Water Tower* (1998). A hand-collaged photoprint and plan of the see-through tank which Rachel Whiteread erected on the rooftops in New York.

(D) *Study of a Nude* (1952–3). The oil painting by Francis Bacon, small, grey, the back of a naked man, his arms raised above his head.

(E) *Straight Miles and Meandering Miles* (1985). The text representation printed in capital letters by Richard Long of a 294-mile walk from Land's End to Bristol, walking nine straight miles along the way. The straight miles: Carnaquidden Downs, Cornwall; Brockabarrow

Common, Bodmin Moor; Hurston Ridge, Dartmoor;
Dunkery Hill, Exmoor; Wills Neck, Quantock Hills; The
Foss Way, Somerset; Queen's Sedge Moor, Somerset;
Berrow Flats, Somerset; Dolebury Warren, Mendip Hills.

(F) *Crossing Stones* (1987). Another walk-work by Richard
Long, of 626 miles in 20 days, a stone from Aldeburgh
Beach on the East Coast carried to Aberystwyth Beach
on the West Coast, and then back again.

(G) *John Peel* (2005). A memorial portrait of the disc jockey,
in his jumper, with a cup of coffee and quizzical smile,
admired by the Glaswegian artist Michael Fullerton for
his lifelong commitment to the avant-garde.

(H) *Break Down* (10–24.02.2001). The ring-bound record of
Michael Landy's demolition and recycling (executed in
the empty ex-C&A store in Oxford Street) of his every
single possession, listed and numbered. From: A1,
Abigail Lane *Blue Print* framed print of Judith Rees' bum
circa 1993. Through: MV1, Saab 900 Turbo 16S. To:
S1078, 11 shots of work based on bowler hats and
tongues on 35mm slide film 1986.

(I) *Quayside Picnic* (1999). Blocks of geometrically cut
black-burnt oak by Jim Partridge.

(J) *Dulling* (2003). Eight of Tobias Rehberger's 637 different
pages of the text 'all work and no play makes Jack a dull
boy', typed out and published by Counter Editions in
Courier 12 pitch on an antique impact printer.

(K) *The House that Jacques Built* (1992). Peter Doig's painting of a hunting hut in Canada.

(L) *Fluxus 1* (proposed 1961–2, realised winter 1964–5). A wooden box with burnt title, containing manilla envelopes and translucent sheets bolted together, documenting printed scores, a variety of ready-made and constructed objects, printed photographs, etc, of work by György Ligeti, Ben Vautier, Emmett Williams, La Monte Young and others, put together by George Macunias.

(M)*The Donald Parsnips Academy* (14th November to 4th December 1997). Twelve chalk drawings on schoolroom slates, documenting the dictionary definitions of some of the thousand new French words invented by Adam Dant and his students.

(N) *Ruth Harrison's Babies* (2006). Sally Stoddart's compilation of drawings by Harrison, mounted in lidless rows of baize-lined miniature coffins.

(0) *Relic (Cave)* (1991–93). The blue hereditary plaque for GT's degree show at the Royal College, displayed propped on its side in a white vitrine. It reads: Borough of Kensington. GAVIN TURK Sculptor worked here 1989–1991.

(P) *Magazine Sculpture* (1969). Double-fold portrait spread of *Gilbert The Shit and George The Cunt*, first exhibited – in a glass case – at 3 p.m. on the Saturday afternoon of the 10th of May that year, to a private audience invited by

G & G (also an early postcard 'sculpture' by them?).

(Q) *Self-Portrait and Autobiography* (both 1983). Two pieces of the same size by Susan Hillier, the first in liquid gold leaf on a photograph, mounted on linen, the second in liquid silver leaf.

(R) *Cell (You Better Grow Up)* (1993). A seven-by-seven-foot wire cube containing many made-things by Louise Bourgeois, of which she writes: First there is fear, the fear of existence. Then comes a stiffening up, a refusal to confront the fear. Then comes the denial. The terror of facing ourselves keeps us from understanding and subjects us to the repetition of acting out. It is a tragic fate.

Reading back through the list, he finds that one of the questions which these ideas for an exhibition seem to be asking is the most basic of them all: what is art?

Different things to different people. Whatever anybody likes. An impulse towards individual creative expression combined with the desire to communicate. Beauty. Skill. Passion. Invention. Imagination.

Partial truth. Not good enough.

It's easier, maybe, to say what art isn't.

Art is not the physical work. Think of music. That Beethoven was an artist nobody doubts. Doesn't by now doubt. For the greatest period of his life, though, he couldn't actually play an instrument – he could barely hear. Mozart played his piano compositions with a brilliance unmatched;

yet even he couldn't manage to be an entire symphony orchestra. In music, what is the physical record of creation if it isn't the score, all the notes of every instrument transcribed by hand and reproduced for centuries? And does not the art itself exist only in the making of the sound of these written notes, every time the music is played? The meaning of music, its shape, the relationship of sound to sound, its emotional touch, the soul of music is withheld from us all, from the composer too, is denied Beethoven himself until it is performed.

Giotto didn't paint his frescoes in the Arena Chapel, not all of them, not one of them, hardly a single figure solely himself.

Berthold Lubetkin didn't personally build the Penguin Pool in the zoo at Regent's Park.

Benvenuto Cellini didn't cast and glaze his porcelain group of *Ganymede and the Eagle* in the Musée Jacquemart-André.

Picasso didn't etch his own *Frugal Meal*, from the drawing of two circus performers at table, a man and a woman, in gaunt despair.

In contrast, each and every brushstroke in a Rembrandt van Rijn is his, and every dash and flick of paint is also his in a Joseph Mallord William Turner – is by Turner, of course, not Rembrandt – although T comes after R, and was influenced by the older man, inspired by him, to a degree.

No, lists aren't the answer.

John tries again.

The idea in art and the idea of art are what matter.

Matter to John. So does an individual's perseverance with this and other ideas for a long time, until death. Conflict and contradiction are inevitable, in the making of art and in the perceiving of it. John hates exclusiveness in any would-be artist, whilst having to admit to feelings within himself, as an observer of art, of what is by many called elitism.

Not right either. Too ... prissy!

Is the art of fiction easier to define than the art of art?

The craft behind art. Crafty: John can hear Gavin Turk tease.

Let's be frank. In John's involvement with contemporary art it is the artists themselves who interest him as much as the stuff they do. Possibly more. He likes them (even when he doesn't know them, even when they died centuries ago) for the art-person their work suggests to him they might be (even when he knows that in actual life they're flawed horrid people).

I mean, Rembrandt must have been a good bloke, he just must have been: John says to himself. Like Gavin is. Gilbert and George also, in their infuriating way.

That's my opinion. What's yours?

I can hear your scepticism as to what the point might be of marking a map with the route of a circular walk across Dartmoor, and noting by arrows on a sheet of paper the direction of the wind at each night's pitching of the tent, then exhibiting the two together mounted, glazed and framed.

Art is the point, I say. Like it or not.

And what *is* art?

Ah ... well ... yes ... not easy to answer.

The snail mound which the tenants at Granthorne have raised in the vegetable garden in what was once the school paddock is art of its kind, with a kind of purpose: to look down onto the tops of the apple trees in the orchard and check when the fruit is ripe. There are, though, it's true, less laborious methods of assessing the harvest's prospect. And it is really beautiful to sit at the summit of the mound, its spiral path lined with lavender, and look up from reading your book to gaze out across the Vale of Taunton.

John talks to himself, Kath to herself, tendencies the two of them have developed through the years of living alone. There is great tenderness in both their self-talkings. The mutual quality of many of these feelings, being separately experienced remains as yet separately known.

One of the things of which Kath's aware is that she hasn't, not for years now, missed the absence of the sound of sharing the house with Stewart. She remembers again now the one fact about his death which she hadn't anticipated: the not hearing of the inconsequential, not consciously noted sounds of his presence in the house: the cushioned thud of the fridge door closing, the flush of a toilet, a clearing of the throat. It's a very long time since she last missed these sounds. Maybe it's somehow because John lives at the other side of the hill, where the light as well as the external noise of country life arrive from the opposite direction, that Kath hasn't, before this moment, been aurally aware of John's absence, her denial of loneliness until then perfect and complete.

John's private amazement is of a different kind of sensuality, and concerns comfort in the soft touch of Kath's skin. This he felt the instant they first brushed cheeks, in a slightly awkward goodbye gesture. It's easier now, his physical awareness of her grown fuller, though no less beautiful and astonishing than at that earliest moment. He talks to himself about the loss for too many years of any physical closeness akin to this.

Both of them have become lovingly attuned to each other's vulnerable grace.

··· CHAPTER ELEVEN ···

AT THE END OF APRIL, with the Granthorne project successfully underway and exhibition plans best allowed the private passage of time to find their shape, John and Kath travel together for ten days, initially to Jerusalem, the Golden City. Neither of them has been before, although at different moments in their separate pasts they both had meant to. It's no use waiting till the place is safe and stable, they decide. They acknowledge that there have been better years to visit Israel – and worse, in the tortuous history of a land known under many names. Palestine they decide on the plane between themselves to call it.

They are staying in an old courtyard hotel beyond the English church, in no-man's-territory, on the divide between the Jewish West and Arab East of the city, ten minutes' walk from the Damascus Gate. It is a charming place, once the home of a European archaeologist, built by him around a fountain, with the bedrooms opening singly off the covered precinct, the double storey at one end containing the reception and the dining room on the ground floor, and on the upper floor couches and cushions and kelim rugs on which to sit and talk, with views through full-length shutters towards Temple Mount. Almost all the internal walls are tiled, in Iznik style, turquoise and ultramarine intertwinings of the leaves of clematis in patterns of endless rhythmic repetition. The architecture is why they are here: to experience for themselves the accretion of forms and spaces in this walled city of ancient holiness to three faiths. They are here also to spend time alone together, in a culture-of-being unfamiliar to them both.

They intend to walk everywhere, eager to see with their own eyes as much as they can. Apart from the bus ride at night from the airport at Tel Aviv on the three-quarters of an hour journey up the slowly climbing road to Jerusalem, their first true sight of Palestine is from the unbroken city walls the next morning, beginning at the fortress bulk of the Damascus Gate and from there walking along the top of the ramparts through the Arab Quarter, around the gardens of the Al Aksa Mosque, not until then turning towards the City of David. John, in particular, is entranced by the view from there across the Kidron Valley to the colonial hospital on the summit of Mount Zion and, with a swift sweep of the eye to the right, sight in the foreground of the Tomb of Absalom. He has never seen anything comparable: the strangest dome, in stone, like an inverted ear-trumpet; supported on a double-stack of articulated pediments; applied Ionic columns visible on three sides; and all this in a building not much bigger than a four-poster bed. When, in the afternoon, they wander through the streets and cloisters in the old city, within the ramparts below, Kath takes special delight in the gate to the Cotton Market in the west wall. She loves the intimate pair of barred windows in a room on the roof, with its striped walls, sandstone and rose, and the inverted cascade of blind arches, with the row of triangular piles of terracotta cylinders across the top – a dovecote, she presumes. Their joint favourite of this first day in Jerusalem is the whole district of Mea Sharim, which they explore on their way back to the hotel, designed in blocks by a resident of the German community under Ottoman rule, Conrad Schick, who died in the same month as Queen Victoria, aged seventy-nine. The area's architectural uniformity pleases them, doors and windows similarly arched in plain stone, with small synagogues in the upper floors of several domestic houses, a presence signified by projecting bays to hold the Ark of the Law. Ownership of Mea Sharim has since been acquired by the severest of religious sects, the men in the shops and squares wearing fur hats and long black coats in the heat of early summer, the women with ugly wigs and pale pale skins. On return to their tiled haven John and Kath are exhausted, but content with each other. Supper of marinated lamb tastes delicious, with couscous, and a sharp salad of herbs, tomatoes and chopped baby courgette.

The next day, on the recommendation of a Syrian fellow-guest, they find a taxi-driver to guide them along the hazardous road that follows the river Kidron down towards the Dead Sea. Mar Saba, their architectural target of the morning, is situated towards the base of this valley, on the hills of Engedi, looking out across a corner of water to the biblical Mountains of Moab on the Jordanian side of the sunken salt sea. Greek monks still live in the cells which climb up the sides of a cliff, nestling close to the gilded dome of the basilica. Pilgrims can stay on retreat in the two small towers at the gate of the monastery, with a fall of olive terraces to the door of the church. Sitting together in the shade of the porch John reads to Kath from his Baedeker a transcription of the notes made by the painter David Roberts, on his visit to the Convent of St Saba, as it was then called, on April 4th 1839:

> The Dead Sea lies in a deep Caldron, surrounded by cliffs
> of limestone rock, utterly naked, the whole giving the
> strongest look of sterility. The surrounding region too is
> a naked desert; it has an Egyptian climate, and from its
> exposure for seven or eight months of the year to the
> full power of the sun, it is obviously condemned to
> hopeless aridity. The height of the surrounding cliffs so
> generally screens the Lake from the wind that it but
> seldom loses its smoothness of surface. Yet, though the
> utter solitude of its shores, especially in connexion with
> the history of the buried Cities, impresses the spectator

with the idea that he is looking upon a mighty Sepulchre, the immediate aspect of the waters is bright and even sparkling; they lie like a vast mirror, reflecting with almost undiminished lustre every colour and radiance of the bright sky above. Flocks of birds too, with their flight, and even with their songs, enliven the scene; yet under every aspect, it impresses the mind with a sense of the mysterious and monumental.

In the monastery's olive grove they eat the picnic supplied by the hotel, and replenish their flasks with cool fresh water from the well.

'You don't mind, really? Driving on to the Dead Sea?' Kath asks. 'We're so close, I'd feel silly not seeing what it's like swimming there.'

'That's fine, my love. Of course,' John replies.

'It's probably awful. Loads of tourists.'

'Plastered in mud!'

'Floating in the water, with white sun hat and black glasses, reading the *Herald Tribune*!'

When they reach the resort on the side of the lake the scene is tranquil, surprisingly unspoilt, with a dozen families lounging in the shade beneath reed-thatched canopies and almost nobody bathing. The troubles in Gaza, and the bomb in a police station in Galilee three weeks ago, are keeping travellers away from the West Bank. Kath and John, when they are together, find it easier to be philosophical about the danger of death. She tries to swim, backstroke, but the drops of water falling from her raised arms sting her eyes. You have to move incredibly slowly, there's no choice. Kath succumbs, and for half an hour literally sits in the sea, shoulders and arms clear of the water, reading her book.

'I'm glad I did it. Thank you. Quite an experience,' she says to John as they return to the car for the drive back, via sweet tea and a quick tour of the mosaics of the Hisham Palace and fallen walls of Jericho, to Jerusalem.

On both journeys, out and back, they have to pass through check-points in the steel and concrete wall built by the Jews to keep out the Arabs. It is an unpleasant experience.

On their third day they visit the Holocaust Memorial, Yad Veshem, two Hebrew words of sombre resonance, in a language reinvented for titular use in this adopted land. The majority of those very very few survivors of the death camps emigrated to Palestine and have managed, in most cases, to erect a liveable new narrative for themselves, their children and their children's children. The threat, though, of disintegration of the State of Israel feels today terrifyingly real. In the early evening, hoping to lift a cloud of foreboding, they walk through the old residential district of Yemin Moshe to have supper on the terrace of the Cinemateque and to go afterwards to the movies.

The site is spectacular and the whole place abuzz with bright young life, in bookshop, bar and café. The steel and stone terrace overhangs the Vale of Hinnom, with an uninterrupted view up towards the Jaffa Gate and the citadel.

John is glancing again at his Baedeker. 'Have a swig of wine,' he says to Kath, his face wreathed in smiles. 'You'll need it! Guess what this is called?' He waves at the bare rocks and scrub olives disappearing below them around the curve of the hillside, with the occasional gravestone and derelict quarry, bare of human dwelling in this most crowded of cities. 'The Valley of Blood!'

'God!' she says, laughing.

'Whose?' the girl with whom they happen to share the table interjects.

Kath looks at her, and again laughs, pleased with what she sees, the girl's cheeks freckled, her hair spike-striped in henna; and pleased also with what she hears of the couple's Kiwi drawl, when the four of them talk more about their impressions of Jerusalem. The boy is a film buff and warns that tonight's movie is unlikely to prove much of an antidote to the fearsomeness of these troubled times.

'Got one of my favourite cinema lines,' he says. '*Ich bin ein Schauspieler*,' he whines, in imitation New Zealand Deutsch. 'I'm just an actor,' he self-translates. 'As if *that's* an excuse for collaboration with the Nazis! As if he's nothing else, will die if he cannot act. And the play he's doing, in Berlin in 1942? You'll never believe it! Yeh, he's playing Mephisto, with shaven head and white make-up. It's great, I tell you.'

He isn't a boy, of course; nor is she a girl. They are probably thirty. Young by comparison with Kath and John.

In bed that night, in their scented room, John fits his naked body to Kath's, coupled front to back in the night-train, his arms crossed over her breasts, their paired thighs drawn up towards their chests, holding each other's hands. He talks quietly into her ear.

'It's silly, I know. I can't help it. To begin with, talking to the New Zealanders, I felt open and confident, quite natural. As if the difference in age didn't matter. She was an attractive woman. Unusual. Him too. Then I suddenly saw myself as they must see me. A funny old man, good for a holiday laugh. Don't you remember the unquestioning assumption, when we were young, that older people were a different species? While you and I, we now discover, are more like children. Very human indeed. It's they, their generation, who are the adults. Not us. We're just starting out.'

Kath disentangles a hand and strokes his wrist. 'We're getting there. Don't worry.'

John closes his eyes. He hates it when she uses this phrase. 'I do "worry",' he says. 'Less than before, being with you. I may never stop, though. Worrying.'

'What about, this time?' she asks.

'You really want to know?'

Kath turns around in the bed, their faces inches from each other on the long double pillow. She rests one knee on his hip and stretches her lower leg out down the bed. 'Yes, I do,' she says.

'It's not edifying,' he says, defensively.

'Things often aren't.'

'I was reminded why I gave up dealing. Rather suddenly. One of the reasons, anyway. Coming down into the gallery from my office one afternoon I saw a young woman looking at the current show. An art student, I could tell. She glanced up as I passed and smiled at me. And I said "Hello" or something. "Need anything?" maybe. Anyway, we talked. I felt charming and knowledgeable. Slightly flirtatious. As soon as I was out in the street, off to the bank as originally intended, I was devastated by the idea that I had become exactly what I used to despise in the art market. One of those dirty old men. That's what she must have thought, I thought. It's what I would have thought. What I did think. Do think. So I packed it in. At the end of the season. Removed myself from ridicule.'

Kath exhales, sharply. She is trying to contain her fury at him for this little speech. The self-indulgence. His complete evasion of the central point.

'In that case, I must be a particularly foul old woman,' she says.

John is silenced. He is wrong. No argument. He doesn't move. Nor does she. They stare unblinkingly at close quarters into each other's eyes.

Eventually, he speaks. 'I left London because I was afraid I was no good. As a dealer. A person. It had nothing to do with any art student, male or female. I've always failed to feel good enough. I always will fail. Will tend always to set myself ridiculously exaggerated goals.'

Kath in an instant forgives him. 'Designed by you to fall short?' she wonders.

'So I've every excuse to quit? Start anew? Perhaps,' he accepts.

'Please don't.'

'Leave you? Never.'

'I love being here, with you. I'm afraid it's taken the last drop of my courage to let it happen. I can't be alone again,' Kath says.

No reply is necessary.

Ten minutes later they are still lying wide awake in each other's arms. Different feelings toss for attention. By now, after eight months of escalating intimacy, they welcome their differences, with pleasure encourage each other to explore whatever feelings separately occur. Kath and John do feel the same, though, in one important respect: the sense that neither needs the other to change, to become anybody but themselves. This means they are free to concentrate on being together, without wasting more than an occasional anxious moment agonising about whether or not it's right to have committed so much. The moon shines into their room through the half-open shutter, spotlighting their clothes on a chair, Kath's trailing on the floor, John's neatly folded across an arm, in the order in which he will put them on in the morning, underpants uppermost. The Middle Eastern night is as bright, almost, as British day. And Kath finds herself thinking that you can tell more about a man's basic colour preferences from his pants than from anything else. In the middle-aged male, underpants cease to be chosen for external effect; they need to be loose, comfortable and – in John's case – either dark blue or dark grey; these undoubtedly are his favourite colours; and those, as it happens, which suit him best. Kath attempts to remember what colour Stewart's underpants were. She can't.

I chose them anyway: she says to herself.

This, as she knows, is unfair, for as often as not it was the other way round: Stewart who bought her knickers, rather than she his pants. Both of them were reluctant shoppers, dividing equally between them responsibility for the household and family chores, one of which was buying underclothes at Marks & Spencer.

'No rules. Things can be true sometimes and not true at other,' Kath says, out loud.

'Better slightly salted,' John says.

'What?'

'Butter,' he replies. 'Better a little salt than no salt at all. In my opinion.'

Kath has no idea how John arrived at this subject. She doesn't need to know. He has. That's good enough for her. And he deserves a response.

'Rock salt,' she suggests.

'In butter? You reckon?'

'Pulverised.'

'Well ... yes ... That's possible.' He yawns. 'I'm tired.' He kisses Kath, on the mouth and on her tummy button. 'Good night, my adored. Till the morning.'

They both sleep peacefully, drawing breath with barely a sound.

At the weekend they pack their bags and take the short flight – via Cyprus – to Amman, capital of the Hashemite Kingdom of Jordan. Trans-Jordan, like so many of the so-called countries around here, isn't a proper place at all. It too was Palestine, until the British gave both the western and eastern banks of the river, a parcel of the desert, half of Jerusalem and the whole of Bethlehem and Jericho to Abdullah bin Hussein, the ex-Sharif of Mecca, in reward for tactical maraudery during the First World War, in the process raising him to the official status of His Royal Highness King Abdullah of Jordan, great-grandfather of the present ruler. Warfare changed the shape of this territory again: having been ejected from Mecca in 1910 by a rival tribal chief, the Hashemites were exiled in 1967 by the Israel Defence Force from care of yet another holiest-of-the-holy sites of Islam, Jerusalem the Golden. They haven't done badly, John and Kath decide. Amman is adequate, the hill-village of Salt delightful and the catacombs of Petra sensational. The stone of Petra is genuinely pink, not some photographic trick of the light, as John had until then assumed; while the fort at Azraq is black, built of basalt, the temporary home of Colonel T.E. Lawrence, myth-made in his *Seven Pillars of Wisdom* into 'a place of unfathomable silence, steeped in knowledge of wandering poets, champions, lost kingdoms, all the crime and chivalry and dead magnificence of Hira and Ghassan, each stone and blade of it radiant with half-memory of the luminous silky Eden which had passed so long ago'. It's true that walls do matter in this desert, which during the day is blisteringly hot and at night chill, cheerless. Different kinds of walls matter: walls lined with camel-skin rugs in tents; walls of triple-thick stone in the caravanserai stationed along the ancient trade routes; walls spanned by flat roofs and painted white or sky-blue in mud villages. The eighth-century walls below the low domes of Qasr Amra are decorated on the inside with human figures, reclining in a garden – one of a string of desert retreats built at the time by the Omayyad rulers of this arid land. Kath is intrigued. Did artists imagine into life walled rose gardens in the sand? Or did peoples of the past know the secrets of persuading the desert to flower? Like Derek Jarman, the magician of Prospect Cottage, on the shingle beach at Dungeness, to the left of his door as you face the sea: lovage (with shoots of pale green leaves), iris, cistus and chicory (which with the cornflower has the bluest of blooms), a verbena, rosemary, cistus again, wallflower, artemisia, santolina, day lily, two Mrs Sinkins pinks, the whole fringed by sedum.

VERSES

(Addressed by Waladata, daughter of Mohammed
Almostakfi Billah, the Kahlif of Spain,
to some young men who had pretended a passion for
herself and her companions)

When you told us our glances, soft, timid and mild,
Could occasion such wounds in the heart,
Can ye wonder that yours, so ungoverned and wild,
Some wounds to our cheeks should impart?

The wounds on our cheeks are transient, I own,
With a blush they appear and decay;
But those on the heart, fickle youths, ye have shown
To be more transient than they.

They are ready for home. Holidays, they accept, are not
really for them. They need a reason to travel: to work, or to
visit a dear friend, pleasant though it has been together to
experience this part of the Middle East. Their return from
abroad proves to them how rich their lives already are, how
much they still have to see and learn about the world of
West Somerset.

There is one moment, only, of dizzying despair: when
they separate at the end of the journey for homes on
opposite sides of the hill. It is a feeling they are aware that
both are suffering, and the more quickly therefore subsides.
There are no rules, they say to each other. And mean it.

· · ·

Contradiction and conflict are concepts with which Kath has become familiar in her relationship with John; they do not frighten her. The third of this 'c'-word trilogy, confusion, is new to Kath. In the past she has been content with either knowing something or accepting ignorance; there was seldom any confusion; mistakes, yes, and forgetfulness, and changes of mind, but not confusion, not of which she was conscious. For several weeks after returning from Palestine Kath has felt confused. Not about John in himself, nor about her feelings for him. Not about their connectedness. Not about his or her house. Not about the attitude of her children to John, nor about his reactions to them. In fact, it doesn't seem to have anything to do with him. And yet she knows herself well enough to be certain that it must.

How?

A bumblebee is banging its head again and again against the window of her studio, anxious to get on with the job of gathering pollen. It is a large long-haired bee with tawny collar and striped yellow and black bum. Bumblebees, Kath happens entomologically to know, developed from a specific kind of hunting wasp and in the process turned vegetarian. It is making quite a noise bashing the glass. She opens the window and with a sheet of foolscap pushes the creature out into the late-spring air. Honeybees Kath treats with greater circumspection, as they're more inclined to sting. She finds it perverse that parents explaining the 'facts of life' to their children used to talk about 'the birds and the bees' – given that birds, unlike humans, hatch out of eggs, and most honeybees do not engage in sexual activity at all. For teenagers acquainted with nature, this euphemism must have resulted in no end of confusion. Bees provide a discouraging model for adolescent love, one in which all the boys want to sleep with the same girl, and the only ones who manage to do so are castrated at their moment of ecstasy and promptly expire, whilst the rest live out their drone-of-a-life forever celibate.

Caterpillar attack. Last August caterpillars of the Large White butterfly devastated in a single night the nasturtiums in her walled garden at Parsonage Farm, the flowers of which she likes to add to salads. Over the next two nights the mottled black and lime caterpillars moved on to the perpetual rocket in the bed next door, where, fortunately, they progressed to the next and penultimate stage of butterfly existence before finishing this off too. Kath hopes the attack won't repeat itself this year. The heads of Large White caterpillars are decorated with a fetching yellow diamond; they smell strongly of mustard, to discourage the birds from eating them. Listen to the things munch! Can't be fun being a nasturtium at caterpillar time; fennel is a safer bet, with its own protective smell.

I know, I'm meant to be working out what's confusing me. I am. Indirectly. The plan is to catch, if I can, the trouble by surprise. Spot my confusion sunning itself in a secret glade and creep up to have a good look.

It isn't easy being ... seventy-four now, seventy-five on October the 1st. And in love with a man about to be sixty, with whom you spend at least a couple of nights every week naked in bed, either at his place or yours; long mornings too, talking about the most unexpected things, laughing a lot. The difference this time: you've just spent ten consecutive days and nights continuously in his company.

Kath misses John. And her eyesight isn't what it was. And she has a worrying pain down her left side, which gets worse not better.

It occurs to her that, when she was a girl, the Bishop was the one who broached the subject of sex. Kath's mother didn't tell her about periods or pregnancy or giving birth to a child, it all came from her father. Quite naturally, in front of the fire at Ely in the library after supper, just the two of them as usual. She remembers she was reading a novel by Tolstoy, *The Death of Ivan Ilyich*, which she had taken down the previous evening from her father's bookshelves:

> And he could not understand it, and tried to drive this
> false, erroneous, morbid thought away and supplant it
> with other proper, wholesome thoughts. But the idea,
> and not the idea only but as it were the reality itself,
> kept coming back again and confronting him. And he
> summoned in place of this thought other thoughts, one
> after another, in the hope of finding succour and
> support. He tried to get back into former trains of

thought which in the old days had screened him from
the notion of death.

Kath doesn't claim to remember what the Bishop was
reading, nor indeed whether or not he, like her, was also
immersed in a book at the time. He might have been making
notes on the wad of paper he kept butterfly-clipped to a
plywood board, rectangular with rounded corners, balanced
on his knee. She is sure, though, that he would have been
gentle with her.

'Katherine, sorry to interrupt,' he had said – something
of the sort. 'I was wondering. It's necessary that somebody
ask. How much do you know about … um … the birds and
the bees? What a ridiculous phrase that is! About having
children, is what I mean.'

Kath doubts that she knows any more now than she did
then. Less, in a sense, since coming to believe how much
there is that we'll never understand about being a parent.

'Oh!' she exclaims.

She has caught a glimpse of her confusion hiding in the
undergrowth: the problem is being a child, she sees, not
about bearing a little girl in your belly. All parents were once
children. Every single person began life in the womb of a
woman. Kath's confusion, unaware that it is being watched,
shifts position. It isn't only hers, this particular confusion,
she observes, it belongs also to John.

You're not responsible for everything, you know!

Herself, she means, not just John. And her father. And Esther. And Stewart. All the people she cares about, alive and dead.

Which may be an important point: that there's nothing wrong with caring equally about yourself. Indeed it could be said that our own feelings are the only thing any of us can hope to know.

And understand?

You're joking!

To say nothing of politics. Of the fact that, not long ago, Saudi Arabia was plain Arabia, known in Latin, the language of the maps, as Arabia Felix, criss-crossed tirelessly by the women explorers of the nineteenth century, who wouldn't have been at all happy to learn that the colourful Bedouin tribe of Wahabis near the desert village of Riyadh, under the leadership of young Ibn Saud, were allowed to drive the ancient Hashemite lineage from Mecca and Medina north into Palestine. Oil, of course, was valueless then. Whereas now ... well, now it's different.

Kath shakes her head.

She reaches for Don's pair of bronze cherries on her desk and rolls them in the palm of her hand, smooth and cool to the touch.

A chicken clucks in the yard beyond the window of her studio. The rain continues to drift in from the estuary, not hard but steady, the landscape wet. She thinks of the bumblebee, wonders if it might not have been better off inside this morning. She tidies away into a cubby-hole of its own in William's storage-unit the stamps and tools she had made specially for NOTABOOK. This work is finished; it's time for the next. Kath needs a clean sheet before being able to begin another project and judges this to be the right kind of day to dust down her studio, check materials, make a list for replenishment from the suppliers in Bristol and rub clean with linseed oil her old Albion. She likes doing this. Takes note to remind herself, when the weather is dry, to chamois-leather the studio windows and buff-sparkle the glass with her duster – which, currently, is a discarded white cotton undervest of John's. Like her father, Kath writes down her ideas on lined foolscap – although not on a clipboard but on a tear-off pad, keeping the notes in a series of identical folders, titled according to subject: Books to Buy, Esther's Stories, House, Me, Nature, Unpaid Bills, etc. The folders are filed alphabetically on the open shelf on the wall to the right of her desk. After tea, the studio prepared, she reaches to remove from its place her folder of Future Projects and begins to read.

By now, after years and years of note-taking, she has many different ideas to consider. She finds interest in them all. Although most of the time she ends up making something she had never thought of before.

··· CHAPTER TWELVE ···

JOHN CHOOSES TO BE BUSY. Although he accumulated more than enough money dealing in art not to need to work for a living, he continues to want always to have something interesting to do.

'Mmm, inter-est-ing,' Kath says, with deliberate emphases.

'Not everyone's taste, I agree,' John says – about the idea of his they're discussing.

'Better than *The Archers*, I'll give you that.'

'My mother follows religiously,' he responds. 'So long as she can listen daily to *The Archers*, blind, drip-fed, limbless, she'll soldier on.'

Kath ignores John's excess. 'At home we competed to be the one to turn off the radio, before a note of the theme tune,' she says. 'Then time the switch-on, again to miss the music. You had to get it right. No curtailment of the weather forecast before, nor loss of the programme after. Forgotten what it was. That Ron and Eth thing, maybe.'

'Bet the Bishop pounced to effect.'

'He did. Me too.'

Neither John nor Kath own a television set, or buy newspapers, liberating extra time for other things. John tends to talk exaggeratedly about what he might do; this has become a bit of a game, his fevered chat a tangential expression of delight at Kath's presence in his life. The actual projects on which he embarks are focused, ambitious and invariably successful. John requested approval for the latest from his landlord soon after their return from Amman, in a report he christened the Granthorne Park Bathing Pool Project. The draft plan contains some gratuitous phrase-making which will need later to be removed. Kath can't understand why he left in certain bits in the first place – one of the sentences about funding, for example: 'Any public money which might be available to assist the Granthorne Park Bathing Pool can be accepted only if nil onerous conditions need be attached: this is private land, the work is of personal note and motive, raising no issues at all of rule-bound official concern'. Pretty silly. It is his Outline which she likes:

> Granthorne Park is a creation of the 1820s when,
> following the building of a vast mansion (in 1968 totally
> demolished), the original medieval park was
> 'landscaped' to incorporate the great old existing oaks
> into a roll of pasture, with a long drive winding past a

large artificial lake. Over the other side of the stream the family's Jacobean manor, the thirteenth-century church and their fine farm buildings (the great barn incorporates Romanesque columns) remain intact, the main lake fed by three pools, the water guided down its path through brick sluices. One of these pools has a tall retaining Anberry quarry dam, with a stone-cut runnel at the top channelling the water down a twenty-foot sandstone cascade. All this work is more-or-less intact, and this is where the bathing pool is to be resurrected (the owner's sister remembers swimming regularly there in the early 1960s). In the mid-nineteenth century Monterey pine, sequoia, copper beech, Scots pine and cedars were planted near the pool, and these also remain. The access is by an ancient track, a grassed continuation of the lane at Penley which passes the late-sixteenth-century farmhouse, and four other period tenanted properties. A beautiful secret combe opens up in the small valley at the head of this pool, with the woods beyond climbing up towards the crest of Granthorne Hill. A recent grant from English Nature has insured return of all this parkland to grazed pasture for a minimum of the next thirty years, including the select planting of native trees to replace the originals when they eventually die.

John can summon to almost-life a vision of the completed pool. Beginning at the top, at the mouth of the combe, where watercress grows in the level bed of pasture:

here, on the right as you look down the valley, by the gate across the grass track, is the first of the ornamental trees, a biblical grey-leafed cedar. This is where the land starts its sharp descent towards the bathing pool, and a few yards down from the tree he will construct a small dam, to establish a feeder pond in which to collect silt washed with the stream from the hillside, to be regularly emptied, saving from sedimentation the main pool below. The goyle – Kath's word – is greatly overgrown, making it difficult as yet to see quite where to open out the reclaimed pool, in a horseshoe shape ending at the existing stone dam. The sides are steep and must be cleared of scrub. John has a feeling old brickwork will be revealed, guiding the course of the stream through the dams and sluices and lost lily ponds, under the now-broken footbridges, to terminate in the grand lake, with its picturesque boathouse and railinged oval walk, strategically placed at the edge of the lower park to formalize the view from where the mansion once stood. The plan for John's section is modest in scope by comparison with the original scheme. Excavation of the pool, restoration of the dam and cascade, clearing and replanting of the banks above and below: this will be easily achieved, he feels. He intends, furthermore, to design a new bridge to cross the stream at the head of the bathing pool, out of timber from the Estate, connected to a pontoon reaching towards the centre. The boards of the pontoon will be laid with a sisal runner; it will be hidden from sight by the trees at the edge, a place to stretch out at rest in the sun and from which to dive deep into the cool water.

Kath is the swimmer. The pool project is in part for her – when it's finished, John promises to reconsider his habit of refusal to bathe in the open air.

The point, though, his own main point, is the art.

The artists have already been chosen, and shown the site. Four, only, friends of his and with one another. The work is not done; it has not directly been spoken about, for the decisions are theirs alone to make when they're ready. There is plenty of time, many logistical matters for John first to organise. Just the principle has been agreed. That they will create one piece each, to take four self-selected places without alteration of what is already there and at the same time changing perceptions of the pool. Modern interventions, so that in a hundred years' time people who may come by surprise upon the scene will find, in parallel song, landscaped art of the early 1800s and 2000s.

Gary Hume, Gavin Turk, Georgie Hopton and Don Brown.

A list of names. Their art?

We'll see, we'll see.

The 25th of July 2006 is John's sixtieth birthday. There can be no party, no incitement to fancy dress, no kissostrippogram, no celebratory speech of welcome by the birthday

boy. It wouldn't be fair to ask, would bestow on him punish-
ment not pleasure. If it wasn't for Kath he'd be passing the
date without notice, private or public, like any other
Tuesday. Even so, nothing much is happening. Or a lot is,
depending on one's point of view: Kath, Esther, John and his
mother are having dinner together at Parsonage Farm. A
long slow dinner, with separate sequential tastes, each dish
served with a single fresh glass of appropriate wine. Kath is
the cook, John the vintner, the other two their chosen
guests.

Chosen by them both – chosen by both of them.

Esther's inclusion was uncontested; the decision to invite
Mrs Garsington, on the other hand, followed several
difficult conversations. In the end, though, it is how Kath
and John equally, in their different ways, want it to be.

On the afternoon before the dinner Kath briefly met Joan
Garsington for the first time, over at Grooms Cottage.
Tonight, greeting the old lady in her own home, she is able
to see her less suspiciously as a person, not merely as the
mother of ... of John – his name is enough, Kath no longer
needs to label him.

Joan Garsington is a widow. Her mother was a widow.
She comes from a family of long-lived women. Joan
Garsington likes going out, is at her best with people she
doesn't know, strong-voiced, neatly dressed, plumpish and
slightly stooped. She wears drop-pearl earrings, her hair is
modestly dyed and the powder on her face isn't caked, the

lipstick cherry red. Her son and she mutually miss everything good within each other. The tension between the two cannot be hidden; once seen, though, it can be ignored, Kath finds; it must be, or she'd be too angry with John to speak, his behaviour child-like, ungenerous, petulant.

Esther is in a better position than Kath to assess the state of things between John and Mrs Garsington. The old lady certainly doesn't listen, to anybody. Esther is amused – it's typical, quite loveable in someone you like. John, though, doesn't like his mother at all, the reason obvious: he sees and fears how similar he is to her. Mrs Garsington doesn't need to listen, she's old, she's heard it all before. She's lively, talks a lot, about Basra, where she was stationed during the war, a nursing sister in the army; she is interested in her son's recent trip to the Holy Land simply as a trigger to reminiscences of her own. This upsets John. There is no resolution. In the lounge at Parsonage Farm, a room infrequently used, the only person who appears relaxed over coffee after dinner is Mrs Garsington, choosing the upright chair, leaving the others to loll uneasily at a lower level on the battered chesterfield and sagging pair of armchairs, playground trampolines to generations of children.

Esther isn't really there, has fallen into reverie.

John, Esther is thinking, is closer in age to her than to her mother: ten years downward against fourteen years up.

It's all arranged, she tells herself. Mum'll die and John and I will comfort each other. Ros and Clem and their grown-up kids can share this place, I'll have retired from work, be wise and benign and pass my declining years in John's annexe at Grooms Cottage. Plenty of books, fine wine and elevated chat. What more could one ask?

I won't feel alone.

The key'll be for us to enjoy our arguments and not interpret them as some kind of threat or criticism. John's defensiveness isn't going to disappear overnight; nor is my conviction that men will always let me down. And although I *know* all this, I'm just going to have to accept the old habits kicking in from time to time, touching pain within us both. We're similar and we're different and that's good!

These are Esther's ... let's call them thoughts.

John isn't thinking directly of the current conversation either. He is stuck in childhood, walking the dog in the local park, eyes closed as he trudges along the dead-straight tarmac, muttering to himself. Right now, in Kath's sitting room, the trouble is that he can't remember what he was saying to himself all those years ago.

It must have been important.

He smiles. At the Leonard Cohen song suddenly running through his head:

I stumbled out of bed. I got ready for the struggle.
I smoked a cigarette and I tightened up my gut.
I said this can't be me, must be my double.
And I can't forget, I can't forget, I can't forget but I don't
    remember what.

He tries out, still in his mind, Cohen's almost-speaking voice and reckons he could probably do it too. His version. He smiles again, pleased to recognise that he doesn't want to sing and therefore will never be able to. Not out loud. Only in his imagination.

Kath is seldom thinking of only one thing at a time, and while listening to Mrs Garsington's tales about the tent hospital on the outskirts of Basra she is also wondering about John. And about herself. She is wondering if maybe she spends too much time preoccupied by thoughts of him. Of them. It's a bit exhausting: she admits. Then she too smiles, confident of how much she enjoys the company of this funny unexpected man.

And Mrs Garsington?

Nobody knows what she's really thinking about. It'll certainly be something. Everybody is always thinking about something, even when they claim they're not. The old lady notices that both Kath and John are smiling; her pleasure at this refreshes the vigour of her story, and she spreads her narrative out to include VE Day and the impromptu celebrations in the desert. She makes it sound as if the patients threw away their crutches, in an instant regrew bomb-blown legs and danced the tango with her in the moonlight.

John's mother doesn't stay long. Two nights is enough. She is as relieved as he that they manage it without a serious quarrel.

'Now, dear, you've got to tell me what you want for your

birthday,' she says, sitting on the bench outside the front door at Grooms Cottage, her suitcase by her side, handle pulled out, ready half an hour early to leave for the station. 'New saucepans. Whatever you like.'

John is silent, biting his lip in the effort not to take offence. What about *her* saucepans! Reduced to clear, I bet.

Joan is eyeing the tall brown grass in the 'butterfly meadow' at the other side of the path, full of ... weeds, in 'normal' terms. It doesn't occur to her that it might be better not to say: 'I'd willingly contribute to a proper lawn. How much would it cost? Your father would've done it himself. Okay, okay, it's not your style. Say something. I'm not going until you tell me what I can give you for your birthday.'

'A tree,' John replies, too weary to resume battle. He gestures at the paddock beyond the gate. 'That's going to be an orchard,' he says. 'It'll be planted this winter. You can pay for the quince, or a plum, if you insist.'

'I'd prefer an apple tree. Get a Golden Delicious, something nice. I'll do you a cheque, get it over with.' She fiddles in the handbag on her knee, removes chequebook, spectacles case and biro. 'Eighteen pounds? Should cover it. Easily,' she says, as she finishes writing and hands John his present. 'Come on, must be going. Can't stand being late. So unnecessary.'

Kath has chosen her new project. The year 2006 is the tenth

anniversary of Joshua Compston's death and she has decided to print, in letter-press, a commemorative edition of his FN ephemera. The task today in her studio is to search through the accumulation of material she has kept on Joshua and make an initial selection of things she might do.

She has barely begun when two rediscoveries define the project. First: Joshua's visiting card, printed on one side with his name and address and on the other with an Egyptian-style frieze of artists at work, below the title of his enterprise, Factual Nonsense, in oak-leaf green on cream cartridge paper. Second: a statement in the letter he wrote to her in July 1988, a month after his eighteenth birthday: 'I am worried that I shall perish to this world. Before this happens I must try and leave something worthy of the great bloody mother – Art.' The visiting card she will re-cut on a small block and print double-sided exactly as the original. The excerpt from the letter she'll need to design for transformation into a piece of appropriate ephemera. Thinking about this, she comes to another decision: that whatever she does will be relatively small, to avoid confusion with the folio of art-prints she produced for Joshua's *Other Men's Flowers*. This follows, naturally, into the idea of presenting the commemoration as a canvas-covered hard folder, opening like an old spectacle case at the short side, the lid as long as the rectangular box out of which the separate items are then shaken. She doesn't know how many. Maybe twenty-five, one for each year of his life? She wants it to open with a sw-oo-oo-sh, like the purple box for her Sawyer's View-Master, made in Portland, Oregon, USA.

The corner cabinet in Kath's bedroom contains bits and pieces connected to friends, Joshua included – the double bedroom, with the Adam and Eve plaster relief, into which she has moved back from the dormer room. She walks across the yard from her studio to the house and goes upstairs to check what's there. Lots of things! In particular a booklet made by the son of her ex-Guildhall friend, with whom she went to Factual Nonsense's very first Fête Worse Than Death. Alister, the son, was one of the artists involved with Joshua and made – she can't quite remember when, or why – a cotton-threaded booklet the shape and size of an electric plug, each of its thirty pages printed with different instructions for the wiring. The number of variations is surprising. Kath plans to print a invented plug-label of her own for the FN folder.

She finds that she's kept an unfinished packet of Joshua's cigarettes, Sweet Afton, decorated in tints of grey against corn-coloured ground, with an oval portrait of the poet Robert Burns hovering above a Highland scene and a quotation from his verse:

Flow gently, Sweet Afton, among the green braes,
Flow gently, I'll sing thee a song in thy praise.

The smell of Virginia tobacco brings Joshua closer again: an anachronism, born out of his time, smoking unfiltered cigarettes and rushing about in charity-shop waistcoats; and in the same breath such a ferocious proclaimer of the new. Adam Dant is a similar mixture of a man. At most FN events he used to set up stall to execute and distribute ever-updated hand-written issues of his Daily Journal. In the corner cabinet Kath also comes across one of these, composed in the crowded street outside the last private view at Factual Nonsense, of the show *Slugs and Snails and Puppy Dogs Tails*:

DONALD PARSNIPS DAILY JOURNAL
(OF THE NOW FOR THE THEN & WITH THOROUGH
REFERRALS TO THE OTHER)

PRESENTS

NEVER SAY NEVER

A SHORT GUIDE TO THE POSSIBILITY
OF ETERNAL LIFE ON EARTH
FOR HUMAN BEINGS

(THERE'S NO TIME TO LOSE LIKE THE PRESENT)

Kath reads a bit and then puts the pocket-paper down, disappointed at the text's ironic tone. She likes the drawings, of a cartoon boy with striped bowler-type hat and pebble glasses, the author's alter ego. A woodcut of the cover she can see herself doing, and enjoying.

As with Kath's involvement in John's bathing pool, so he plays his part in her project. For one thing, Factual Nonsense

was nearer the heart of his world than hers. The only event
Kath attended was the first, her Parsnips journal a later gift
from Alister; whereas John went regularly to FN inventions
(interventions, Josh called them) and was friendly with
several of the artists working at Factual Nonsense. John and
she could, in theory, have met there then. Kath is glad they
didn't, happy with her peripheral connection to the East
London hullabaloo, her contact based on Parsonage Farm
and the visits initially by Joshua, later by his friends Don
and Yoko.

Kath's re-examination of these possessions leads to the
thought that, despite her outward friendliness, she might
prefer objects to people, and that John may in practice be
more sociable than she is. She takes down, in its undyed
linen case with the appliqué initials TE in crimson on the
flap, her copy of Tracey Emin's book *Exploration of the Soul,*
which Joshua had persuaded her to pre-buy for fifty quid,
characteristically messianic in his collection of the money
Emin needed at the time before being able to produce the
work. Kath loves the object itself. And she is excited by ideas
for making a related memento of her own. Perhaps a small
folded card, on the back of which she might reproduce the
prize which Emin and Shaw gave to winners on their Rodent
Roulette stall at the second Fête, with the drawing of a
mouse in a sweat-shirt, signed by the two artists. On the
front of her piece Kath thinks of printing a phrase of
Joshua's, recalled in Tracey Emin's words: 'We're going to do

this thing – Yeah – And we're gonna do it right.'

What on the centrefold?

Kath removes the book from the case, all two hundred of the edition hand-stitched by a working party of Tracey's friends, Alister amongst them, tipped in to each one on the end page a unique monoprint. She notes on the pad of lined foolscap a possible quotation from the book:

> I sat up in bed – the night silence
> burning my mind – the covers pulled
> up close around my face – my body
> saturated in my own piss – too scared to breathe –
> my eyes darting around in the semi darkness
> The house was creaking – like it was alive,
> as though it was breathing –
> And everything became dark – like a black
> sea – it would sweep over me

There's no shortage of FN material, rich in Joshua-language, 'no FuN without U' one of his signature phrases. He loved concocting exhibition titles, the choice and size of lettering important to him: Utopic Space Manifest; seamless cream; HARDCORE (part II). His handbill promoting the sale of a Gavin Turk T-shirt begins

FACTUAL NONSENSE
purveyors of the
ND(SFM)
Notorious Dream (Struggle for Modernism)

and ends

Above all remember: FN *makes sense*
so wear your T-shirt with pride
in the founding faith of the idealist exchange
mechanism

Kath puts aside selected invitation cards and programmes and manifestos and other things to think about some more.

Another guiding principle of the project pushes to the fore: that it's nowhere near good enough to make a folder of ephemera of concern only to FN initiates, to the haphazard few – Kath both wants and needs a wider audience, an emotional resonance with the unknown outside. She's happy to take her time. Happy too to have already had a decent time in life to get to where she is right now. And also sad: that Joshua is dead. Killed by accident-on-purpose. If that makes sense. By risking it, let's say, as he had often done before.

Did he intend, this time, not to get away with it?

Everything he ever did was meant to mean something. Something monumental.

Maybe he simply made a mistake.

A paragraph Kath reads in one of Joshua's letters reminds her of the conversation in Jerusalem with the young New Zealand couple. They, like she and John, think a lot about the process of creation, the way things are made. It's important, these days. Has been for centuries, to those engaged in making art. Music included, of course. And film. The New Zealanders told them of the Robb Lectures that they went to at the University of Auckland, given in their graduation year by an Englishwoman, Marina Warner. Kath's remembered impression of what they said Warner said is: that contemporary technologies of weaponry and film-making have altered the nature of the literal, by confusing act with representation, the event as performed with the image as perceived. Kath recalls – precisely, she believes – the sentence 'Leakage between simulated and actual reality is not trapped inside the cinema or Gameboy'. Kath has the feeling that Tracey Emin's attention-seeking strength comes from her dealing with a basic form of experi-ence far removed from the magical illusions of *The Lord of the Rings* movie, say, and from the equally unreal 'reality' TV of *Big Brother*. Kath hasn't seen either. So what? Doesn't mean her opinions are wrong! And Tracey's book was written years before she became famous. It's not the Gospel, not seminal truth-telling, not mass consumption. It is imagination. Necessity.

So? What's this all about?

Why is Joshua dead?

She wishes Esther was at home, to help her work out what these jumbled images signify.

It's a beginning, just the start of things, no need to worry yet about making sense, she lectures herself.

Kath's face softens into one of her long smiles, lips in an

open curve, as she recalls to mind an Esther quote, from Wittgenstein, her favourite man: The joy of my thoughts is the joy of my own strange life.

. Kath's eyes, like her mouth, are flowingly alive.

On Thursday evenings – twice a month, usually – John and Kath meet at seven for the Adult Swim at the pool that used to be part of her brother's school, revived by the retired PE master as a local sports complex. The title courts modernity; the style and nature of the pool and its small gymnasium is old and intimate. They sometimes have supper together afterwards, their hair still wet, at the bistro-café in Greater Mead. If not, Kath cooks at home in Parsonage Farm and John stays the night, often two. He keeps an extra toothbrush and set of shaving things in Kath's bathroom and has been allotted a drawer of his own in the painted pine chest in her big bedroom. She too leaves extra underwear, some gardening clothes, spare gumboots and other odds-and-ends at John's place. The time is likely to come when they'll want to live together and it won't be easy, they know, for either of them, to accept the change. Not yet, though. She's not ready yet. Kath realises how the relative informality in her placing of things around the house is in fact intensely particular – less obviously so than with John at Grooms Cottage, where most of the objects are art-works of some kind or another: things with names, 'by' someone; names people in the know have heard of; things precisely in position. Kath's stuff matters just as much to her, maybe more, emotionally. She is beginning to believe that John, despite his possessiveness, is right to claim that the works of art themselves he could do without, if he had to. Their financial value, to him, represents freedom from worry about money. He has no shares, no pension, no insurance. The art, if necessary, will be sold, in order to avoid having ever again to deal to live. These days, Kath admits to being more attached than he is to the personal meanings of things. She is reluctant, all the same, to make the connection to a central difference between her and John: her being the mother of three children, and the grandmother of five; compared to his familial solitude.

There is purpose to the regular swimming sessions: they plan this August together to register their names for the Stert Island Swim, from the beach at Burnham-on-Sea across the estuary to the island, 2,400 metres there and back – at spring tide, it needs to be, when the water is at its highest and the slowest swimmers more easily avoid being stranded on the slip of uninhabited land. An hour and a half is the maximum time permitted, after which stragglers are rescued from the water in a rubber speedboat. In 2003 the first person home was a woman, Sarah Hartshorn from Bath, re-crossing the line drawn in the muddy sand twenty-seven minutes and twenty seconds after the starting bang of an old pistol. Wetsuits are encouraged, as water temperature rarely rises above eighteen degrees. Kath will be the oldest competitor, by one year – several other seventy-year-olds have already booked, amongst the expected final total of almost a hundred, the age and hometown of each listed in the programme of the day. Last year Jane Tull travelled down for the weekend from Dymock, in Gloucestershire, and Oliver Le Cheminant drove over from Dawlish, Devon, aged thirty-six and forty-three at the time, respectively.

Swimmers are requested to arrive by half-past nine for the ten-fifteen start.

John and Kath leave it till the last moment, the sellers of souvenirs already busy setting up stall on the esplanade, a crowd of onlookers milling around. At midday begins a children's competition to build the best sandcastle, a notice informs. A line of donkeys awaits a couple more customers before the first of its half-dozen perambulations of the tidal beach; little boys already in the saddle kick at the donkeys' sides; the animals, oblivious, budge not an inch. It is the height of the summer season at Burnham-on-Sea, the caravan sites full, candyfloss and chips and everywhere a sense of potential celebration. It is sunny – a Sunday. Another notice promotes the Sedgemoor District Council's weekend Word Search and a Promenade Quiz. Taunton Canoe Club has volunteered to escort the swimmers back and forth to the island. It felt different last year for John and Kath, free to sit at a distance on a wooden groin and observe, curious to see what was going on. Today it is they at whom people have come to stare.

They have changed at home into their swimming gear and in the tarmaced municipal car park now take off their clothes and remove from the boot long towelling bathrobes and flip-flops.

'Got the entry form?' John asks.

Kath senses his wish to be somewhere else. Anywhere else. She feels the same. 'We don't have to,' she says – knowing that this isn't really true, that it would be more difficult to give up at this late stage than to go through with it.

John manages a smile. Within his own distress he is able also to see what a silly, brave thing this is for Kath to do. Less silly for her than for him, as she has always been a swimmer. Braver, though. Much braver, as she isn't young. He loves her. 'If it's too much, we'll stop,' he says. 'Call a canoeist to the rescue!'

On the beach the organiser of the race sits at a wooden table, beneath a parasol. She is warmly welcoming and hands them each an official rubber skullcap, noting the colour beside their names, for recognition in the water. The fastest swimmers wear orange, the youngest red. Theirs are gold. They turn towards the other swimmers in the roped-off section of the sands, doing stretching exercises, chatting in groups and zipping up their wetsuits. There are yellow caps, blue, dark green and pink. One only, so far, is white. Kath and John find an empty spot and remove from a bag which they carry with them a bottle of animal oil to rub onto the bare flesh. They each have a pair of goggles. Several others, they see with relief, like last year, wear ordinary costumes. A young man wanders over to introduce himself: the leader of the swim, a farmer from a couple of miles along the coast, born and bred and working on land Kath has often walked across on her way to the nearest beach from Parsonage Farm. This year the Mayor of Burnham-on-Sea will fire the starting pistol, he tells them, eyebrows raised in amused respect. His wetsuit is grey-blue not black, with white and sky-blue stripes. It fits perfectly his athletic body.

'Surfed as long as I can remember,' he explains. 'Proper nutter for the waves! You'll do fine, don't worry. Calm as a bath. With the taps on! Great you're here.' He looks at his waterproof watch. 'Fifteen minutes to go.' And gives the thumbs-up sign to a friend he spots on the esplanade. 'See you,' he says to them, and trots off to greet the next newcomers.

John spreads a tarpaulin on the sand and sits down, arms behind him, elbows locked for support, legs stretched straight out ahead. Kath kneels beside him.

'We'll stick together. Won't we?' he checks.

She pats him repeatedly on the shoulder, as if beating out the time of a viola piece playing in her head. 'Oh no, don't leave me,' she replies – superfluously.

Five minutes before the allotted time the good-hearted young man summons the swimmers to the starting line, drawn by him with his heel in the sand. They stand in a long line facing the silted salt water of the estuary. The rubbered man, his brown face bright in the sun, stands facing them.

'Well, thanks for coming. Great to see you all,' he says, smiling at the motley sight. 'Look, I don't need to tell you this. All the same, I will. The Stert Island Swim is a challenge, it isn't a race. It's old. It's ours. Something they used to do years ago. Years and years ago. My grandad remembers. Never did it, mind. Only watched as a boy, before the war. So me and some mates, at the millennium we decided to set it up again. And we've done it every year since. It's ... well, you'll see, it's a nice feeling. You're mostly local. Like me. That's our farm.' He turns and points to the land along the coast of the estuary, some fields green, others golden to the cliff's edge. 'We help each other along. Right? Hope the pistol works! Any questions? No? Sure? All yours, Mr Mayor.'

Nobody mentions the towers of the nuclear power station, dominating the coastal fields on which it stands.

When the gun fires, with a little dance and whoop of joy, the younger men and women run into the waves. Kath and John walk to the sea, on into the shallow water. The mud of the estuary pushes between their toes, and when the water reaches to the depth of their thighs, off they swim for the island.

Fals

Arlene Hunt is originally from Wicklow, but now lives in Barcelona with her husband, daughter and a mêlée of useless, overweight animals. *False Intentions* is her second novel.

Also by Arlene Hunt
Vicious Circle

ARLENE HUNT

False Intentions

HODDER
HEADLINE
IRELAND

For Anne

First published in 2003 by Hodder Headline Ireland

The right of Joanne Plott to be identified as the Author of the
Work has been asserted by her in accordance with the
Copyright, Designs and Patents Act 1988.

A Hodder Headline Ireland paperback original

A CIP catalogue record for this title is available from the
British Library

ISBN 0 340 83264 9

Typeset by Hodder Headline Ireland

Printed and bound by
Clays Ltd, St Ives plc

Hodder Headline Ireland
8 Castlecourt Centre, Castleknock,
Dublin 15, Ireland
A division of Hodder Headline
338 Euston Road
London NW1 3BH

ARLENE HUNT

False Intentions

**HODDER
HEADLINE
IRELAND**

For Anne...

First published in Ireland in 2003 by Hodder Headline Ireland

A Hodder Headline Ireland paperback original

A CIP catalogue record for this title is available from the
British Library

ISBN 0 340 83364 9

Printed and bound in
Clays Ltd, St Ives plc

Hodder Headline Ireland
Castleknock, Dublin 15, Ireland
A division of Hodder Headline PLC
338 Euston Road
London NW1 3BH

1

The return was much harder than he had anticipated. Visibility was non-existent, and the howling wind had whipped the spray into a frothy maelstrom. A thin fork of lightning streaked across the sky, illuminating the furthest point of the cliff face before it vanished, plunging him into darkness again.

James 'Kelpie' Kilburn had fought the water for over forty minutes. He glanced up and realised the rapidly rising swell and the ferocious tide had forced his jet-ski off course. He was being pulled back towards the foaming water at the estuary mouth. He dashed at the spray across his mask and realigned the ski. If he was sucked in there, the light vessel would be no match for the rocks and rip-pools.

His original plan had been to crest the sandbank a few hundred yards further up the coastline and let the ski drift back to the set-down point, lessening the chance that anyone might hear the engine. Now – because of the storm – that option had been rendered impossible. Although he doubted anyone would be out on such a filthy night, Kelpie knew he had to risk being seen if he was to make it to shore.

He adjusted the goggles, shifted his weight and throttled towards the small inlet to the left of a rocky overhang. The spray sliced across the bow and lashed his face. He swallowed great gulps of freezing salt water. It burned his throat and made his stomach heave. Twice the engine stuttered and threatened to leave him to the mercy of the tossing waves. It took all of Kelpie's remarkable strength and sheer willpower to force it on.

Finally he rose over the last sandbank and entered the slightly calmer water of the secluded bay. He searched for the beam of the infrared lamp he had earlier placed high up in the grassy dunes. If he could not locate it, he might accidentally come in too far down the beach and tear the blades of the ski on the rocks hidden below the waterline. It took a few anxious moments to locate the faint red glow, but eventually he spotted it. He whooped and renewed his efforts.

A few metres from shore, Kelpie shut the engine off completely. He jumped into the inky, chest-high water and pushed the jet-ski towards the bank. The current, even this close to the shore, was treacherous. The freezing water swirled and battered against him, tearing at his wetsuit, waiting for him to make that one slip. By the time the ski blades scraped against the shingle, Kelpie's entire body trembled with fatigue.

He hauled the ski onto the shore, knelt,

removed his mask and retched, voiding his stomach of the bitter sea water. He wiped his mouth and immediately felt better – still shaky, but better. He staggered to his feet, rolled his shoulders and flapped his aching arms, willing some heat to return, willing the blood to flow to the surface. He glanced at the waterproof rubber cube hooked to the back of the ski with heavy-duty spring-ended rope, and for the first time in three hours he allowed his face to relax. Kelpie grinned. It had been worth the hassle. No one would ever suspect a route like that. Hell, it was almost suicidal. Patrick was one smart fucker, no doubt about it. Even in the middle of a storm, the GPS unit had easily traced the inflatable cube containing the bags, just as Patrick had told him it would. This had been the third time they'd used this route, although this was without doubt the biggest delivery yet.

Kelpie straightened up and pulled the black life jacket over his shoulders, deflated it and slipped it into the nylon backpack. This was not the time to be congratulating himself. The job was only half done.

The bitter night air was black as ink, and the rain, whipped up by a vicious northerly wind, slewed across the small beach, lifting sand like a sheet. Kelpie was impervious to it. He snapped on his night-vision goggles and glanced up the beach, waiting for his eyes to become accustomed to the green shadows.

He ran through the plan in his head. Although he had studied this area in detail and knew the shortest route, Patrick had warned him he was to leave nothing to chance – and Patrick was the man when it came to planning. Kelpie travelled a different path each time. He was to go over the first dune, left along the sandbank for a quarter of a mile, then turn right and make his way through the scrub grass near the mouth of Carrily Woods for another half-mile. A clean car would be waiting there, locked, the keys taped to the underside of the left wheel arch. He would have to make the journey twice. The bags weighed seventy kilos each, there was no way he could manage both at the same time. Once he had secured both bags in the boot, he could come back and deal with the jet-ski. Patrick had told him to coast it back down to the beginning of the estuary, drag it up onto the small beach and secure it behind the rocks, where it could be picked up by one of the trucks from Naughton's quarry later that night.

Kelpie wiped the sand and salt water off his face. He took a deep breath. One wrong turn and he could find himself stuck in one of the many mazy gullies that ran between the shore and the secondary road. The road meant danger. Someone might spot him, and that was something he definitely didn't want – not when he was carrying this much shit.

He glanced back at the marker and nodded. He had drifted slightly, but it was nothing he couldn't handle. Patrick always said to allow for slight alterations.

Kelpie untied the cube, opened two sealed zips and parted the heavy-duty rubber lining. Inside were two locked waterproof cases. Kelpie pulled these out, deflated the cube, rolled it up and stashed it under the ski. He hefted the first case onto his broad shoulders. Staggering slightly under the weight, he set off towards the first dune.

He moved quickly, despite the chill and his aching arms. He was eager to be done with this end of the job, eager to get into dry clothes and get back to his hotel and make his calls, eager to kick back and enjoy some well-deserved R&R.

Ashley Naughton's toes and calves ached in the ridiculously high heels. As she clicked down the deserted cobbled street, each step reminded her that it was her own stupid fault her legs ached. Her shoes were brand-new Prada slingbacks, shoes made for standing, not for walking the mile and a half home. And of course it had to rain. And of course there wasn't a cab to be had, not on a Saturday night, not in Dublin.

She sniffed loudly and dashed at the tears of self-pity spilling down her cheeks. She should have stayed home. The whole night had been a total washout. She should have slapped Claudia back, that's what she should have done – shown her she couldn't get away with that. Was it *her* fault Claudia's boyfriend had come on to her? God, and that stupid Megan had been totally wasted. Was it any wonder she didn't know what was going on? Well, screw them – screw them both; she didn't need them anyway. It wasn't like they were really close any more, anyway. Claudia was spending more and more time with that jerk, and Megan – well, Megan was Megan.

Ashley neared the front door to her apartment building and fumbled in her pockets for her keys. In her haste she pulled them out too fast, spilling coins, keys and bits of tissue onto the wet street. Her favourite lipstick rolled off the footpath and into the overwash running down the side of the street. She heard a little splash as it continued its journey down to the sewers below.

'Ah, shit!'

Ashley tucked her damp blond hair behind her ear, bent down and fished her keys out of a puddle. She sniffed loudly. This was the worst night ever. God, Claudia had been so angry. Ashley closed her eyes tight for a second, remembering the expression on her friend's face. Self-righteous anger flared instantly. How could Claudia have called her those names? Hypocrite! Everyone knew she was the biggest bike in first year. And it wasn't like she'd meant it to happen, it just had. She couldn't believe Claudia hadn't believed her. What sort of friend was she?

Ashley shook the water off the keys and stepped off the cobbles onto the pavement. The lights in the communal hall seemed blurred, and her hand left rainbow tracers before her eyes when she tried to lift the key to the lock. Jesus, she was really trollied. Ashley squinted hard, took two steps forward and rested her forehead against the security glass, struggling to concentrate on unlocking her front door. She was oblivious to the large shape looming over her shoulder.

'C'mon…' she said out loud. 'Stupid bloody—'

A hand came over her shoulder and snatched the keys out of her grasp.

'Hey!' Ashley jerked her arm back and tottered wildly on her heels. She turned around. 'Excuse me—'

The man stepped out of the shadows and leaned in close, his shoulder edging her off the step. He wore a dark woollen cap pulled low, almost over his eyes, and the collar of his coat was turned up.

Ashley backed up and hit the door behind her. Irritated, she pushed at the man, her pale hand slapping against his chest. 'I don't need any help, okay?' She lunged for her keys. 'Give me them!'

The man moved out of range slightly. He looked up the street, and the light of the streetlamp fell across the lower half of his face. Ashley stared at him in confusion and shook her head. 'Hey! What are—'

The man flicked out his wrist and grabbed a fistful of her hair. He twisted it viciously, pulled her head towards him, then snapped it back, knocking it on the doorframe. Ashley Naughton grunted, her eyes rolled up and she sank on her buckling legs.

Before she hit the ground fully, the man threw his arm around her body and pulled her upright. If anyone came along, it would look like she was drunk. Carefully he pocketed her keys and moved off down the street. It had been that easy.

He turned the corner into Temple Bar and pressed the remote alarm he carried in his right hand. A black Transit van parked on the kerb flashed its lights in response. The man opened the back doors, shoved Ashley in and climbed in after her. Once inside, he bound her hands and feet and taped her mouth. She moaned softly but didn't regain consciousness. Satisfied, he threw a blanket over her and left the van.

The man closed the doors, locked them carefully and hurried back to the apartment building. He let himself into Ashley's apartment, using her keys, and left a note on a coffee table. Then he went into her room, grabbed a few of her things and bundled them into a hold-all he found at the bottom of her wardrobe. In less than ten minutes he was ready. He left, locking the apartment door behind him.

He started the van's engine and pulled slowly out onto the empty street. No rush, no fuss. At this hour of the morning, he knew he didn't need to worry about attracting attention.

14

The office of QuicK Investigations was little more
than a cold, damp, gloomy room at the top of a
building on Wexford Street – a building that should
probably have been pulled down years before, but
which, by dint of having an original Georgian
façade, had avoided the wrecker's ball. Still, owing
to its poor maintenance, the rent was cheap, and it
offered an address as close to the city centre as the
motley crew of tenants could afford.

The ground floor housed a dingy grocery
shop, useful only for milk and papers and cigarettes. It was run by an increasingly senile old woman
who stored cardboard boxes in the communal hall,
despite the fact the local fire brigade had warned
her on numerous occasions that she was creating a
fire hazard.

On the first floor was Freak FM, a pirate radio
station owned by Mike Brannigan, a local hustler,
gadfly and self-proclaimed entrepreneur. Freak
played hardcore house, speed garage and chillout
trance, 24/7. In between the music, the teenage
DJs played heavily coded and often rambling

requests to friends and enemies alike. The local cops knew it existed and largely ignored it, though they would have liked to catch Mike Brannigan in action. They never did. Mike wasn't the sharpest knife in the drawer, but he wasn't that stupid, either. He was twenty-two, street-smart and work-shy and never on the premises. And the cops knew they would get nothing from the sullen teenage boys who rushed around in hooded tops and oversized jeans, lugging record boxes and CDs up and down the stairs at all hours of the day and night. None of the boys looked a day over four-teen, yet any time he met them on the stairs, John Quigley – co-owner of QuicK – marvelled that they had the latest phones hanging from their huge belts, the newest, whitest trainers, the biggest bling-bling dangling from scrawny necks and wrists.

The second floor was home to Rodney Mitch-ell, a skinny, sandy-haired, middle-aged solicitor with a fondness for Bushmills when he had the cash and cans of anything when he didn't. Rodney's second vice was an undying and unrequited love for Sarah Kenny, John's partner in the inves-tigation business. Rodney was often missing from his office for days at a time, out on one of his mammoth benders, destroying what was left of his liver and his bank balance. He frequented busy pubs, where the pitch of human chatter took his mind off his own miserable, solitary existence.

And at the top of this dilapidated building was QuicK Investigations, John Quigley and Sarah

Kenny's two-year-old, slipshod, failing detective agency. The office was situated directly under the eaves, where every sound from Wexford Street below was magnified and the ancient sash windows rattled each time a gust of wind or a heavy lorry rolled by. In winter it was freezing. Whatever heat the heavily painted radiators could produce was sucked out through the neglected rafters and missing roof tiles. In summer, the heat was suffocating. Layers of yellowing gloss pinned the windows closed and the vents were stuffed with old cobwebs and tissue. Here, amid the cheap second-hand furniture, pound-shop prints and dusty fake houseplants, many a happy marriage crashed and burned.

Sarah Kenny sat behind her scuffed plywood desk, chewing on an already well-chewed Biro. She wore a crisp white shirt, black boot-cut trousers, comfortable black boots, headphones and a frown. She stared at the keyboard of her computer as if the keys were in Greek. No matter how often she typed out a report like this one, she felt bad, almost seedy. It was as if seeing the deeds in print made them worse. No wonder women always flung the reports away as if they were poison.

Sarah pressed Play on the small tape recorder, cracked her knuckles and attacked the keyboard with renewed vigour, her fingers clacking across the stiff keys. She had spent much of the previous night stuck in a small hotel bar in Carlow, chatting to and being chatted up by one Mr Pat Flynn, butcher *extraordinaire*. For the best part of two hours she had smiled and let him tell her all the things he'd do to her if she gave him half a chance. The drunker Pat Flynn had become, the more lewd and persistent he had been. Mary Flynn – his wife – wanted every word verbatim, both in print and on tape. It was a tall order for such a short time. Sarah had been typing for over an hour, and barely half of the conversation had been transcribed. Sarah tapped the keys harder. God, the butcher had been such a ribald windbag...

Across the room, John Quigley glanced up from the newspaper he'd spent half the morning buried in. 'Hey, you break that, you buy it.'

Sarah pressed Stop and slid her headphones down to her neck. 'What?'

John repeated what he had said.

'John, you couldn't give this piece of shit away.' She looked at her computer and shook her head. 'One of the kids from Freak was up here the other day, bumming cigarettes, and he actually laughed when he saw what I was working on.'

'Did it take long to get Mr Flynn's attention?' John jiggled his eyebrows at her. One half of his six-foot-two frame lay kicked up on his desk, the other slumped low in his chair. His light-brown hair could have used a trim and he was in dire need of a shave. As usual, he wore a denim shirt so faded it was almost white, Levi jeans and scuffed motorbike boots. He had a cigarette tucked behind his ear.

'Nope. The wife was bang on. Soon as he spotted the blond hair, he was slobbering after me like a randy old dog.' Sarah's own long, near-black hair was held high in a ponytail. The night before she had pinned it down flat and covered it with a Farrah Fawcett wig, complete with winged side-fringe. She thought she had looked ridiculous. Pat Flynn's jaw, however, had almost hit the floor when she'd walked up to him and asked him for the time.

'Can't say I blame him. You looked hot in that dress, and the hair...mm-hm. Maybe you should think about a colour change. You know what they say: blondes have more fun.'

'Is that so?'

'So they tell me.'

'Speaking of which, are you meeting Cindy tonight?'

John shrugged one shoulder. 'She's busy.'

'Doing what? Surely even she can paint her nails in under an hour.'

John grinned. 'Meow, Sarah! Jaysus, pull the claws in. What's your problem with her, anyway?'

'I don't have a problem.'

'Sure you do. Come on, out with it.'

Sarah shook her head and returned to her typing. 'I told you, I don't have a problem with her. I just don't think she's your type.'

How could she explain her dislike to John? Cynthia Conlon, his latest girlfriend, was twenty-two going on thirteen. She was five foot two, curvy, pretty, bubbly and a total airhead. Her interests were fashion, fashion magazines, watching *America's Next Top Model* and shopping. Sarah didn't understand Cynthia, and Cynthia sure as hell didn't understand Sarah. The temperature dropped a few degrees whenever they were in the same room. But then, Sarah never liked any of John's girlfriends.

John scratched the two-day growth on his chin. 'Cynthia's a cutie, and fun – you remember having fun, don't you? It's something people like to do when they aren't working. You should try it sometime.'

Sarah snorted. 'I might *try it sometime* if I weren't the only one *trying* to keep a roof over our heads.'

'Hey, babe, there's more to life than fretting over money.'

'Easy for you to say, you don't have a mortgage to pay.' Sarah pushed her headphones back onto her head. Her dark eyes glittered. 'Look, I'm trying to get this report ready. One of us has to try to earn some cash.'

'Okay,' John said. He lit his cigarette, shook out his paper and resumed reading.

'John, you know it's illegal to smoke that in here, right? This is a workplace.'

'Sarah, the day I kneel before the Nanny State in my own frigging office is the day I give up breathing.'

'I wish I could give up breathing. That's a disgusting habit. Why don't you at least try to stop?'

'Are you nuts? Remember the last time?' John shook his head. 'It was torture.'

'Well, I'm not paying any damn fine if you get caught.'

'Nobody asked you to.'

Sarah tapped the keyboard harder than necessary for the next few seconds, furious that he could annoy her so much. These days it seemed as though he didn't give a shit about the business. All he ever thought about was chasing skirt. He thought he was such a catch... Jesus, Cynthia wasn't even that good-looking, not when you took away the inch-thick makeup and the Toni & Guy shag cut. She was nothing more than a carbon copy of all John's other conquests. And as for his attitude to work... God, Sarah thought, I could murder him with my bare hands.

John eyed Sarah over the top of the *Sun*. He took in her tight face and tense jaw muscles and knew he shouldn't have ribbed her. But he couldn't help it. Lately all she ever did was jump down his throat. Okay, so maybe things were a little slow; shit happened that way sometimes. Business would pick up.

If only Sarah would open up a little, talk to him. He'd known her nearly his whole life, and yet she still remained a mystery to him. She needed to let her hair down, loosen up, have a little fun. Christ, she was only thirty-one.

John studied her. Sarah Kenny was five foot ten in her socks, slim without being skinny, dark-eyed, dark-haired and private. She was a good-looking woman, with her pale skin, sooty eyelashes and deep, brown, intelligent eyes. She had a throaty, dirty-sounding laugh. He knew loads of blokes fancied her – at least two of his mates had asked about her – but when he told her, she laughed it off and told him to stop trying to fix her up. She claimed she was happy alone. And that, thought John, was half her problem right there. It wasn't healthy to be alone all the time.

He puffed on his cigarette. Sarah was right about one thing: Cynthia wasn't his type. Truth be known, he probably would have given her the elbow three weeks before if he hadn't enjoyed pissing Sarah off so much. Not that he still harboured any romantic notions about Sarah, not after the last time, but he enjoyed the fact that she was acting a little jealous. What man wouldn't?

The phone on his desk rang. He picked it up, listened, said, 'Okay,' and hung up.

'That was Mrs Flynn. She'll be in around three this afternoon.'

Sarah nodded. 'Fine.'

'She sounds kind of pissed off. You want me to tell her?'

'I can do it.'

'Suit yourself. Don't blame me if she slaps you.'

Sarah didn't look up.

'Suit yourself.'

Breaking bad news to wronged wives could be

22

a tricky business. They either fell apart and wept or grew angry and offensive. Sarah had been slapped by distraught women twice in the last eight months and was beginning to tire of it. John preferred to handle the husbands. Men didn't slap. He got the stony face, the jaw-clenching and fist-tightening – good wholesome repressed anger, just the way John liked it. Of course, he knew that anger surfaced somewhere, and the wife probably got it when confronted with her goings-on, but that wasn't his problem. If you don't want to get burned, don't go poking different fires.

John exhaled a cloud of smoke and stared up at the largest of the cracks in the ceiling. Of course, it wasn't just the cheated they had to deal with. If he took into account all the phone calls they got from the cheaters – threatening to break every part of their anatomies, threatening to burn the office down, threatening, always threatening – he'd have a persecution complex.

Sarah turned off the tape recorder and glanced at him from over the top of her ancient 486 computer. Her dark brows tightened into a knot. 'Are you going to do any work today?'

John stubbed out his cigarette in an over-flowing ashtray. 'I'm thinking about work. Does that count?'

'Will you please make a start with the invoice for Grady Insurance? It should have been sent three weeks ago, for Christ's sake. We need that money.'

John sighed, dropped his feet off the desk and pulled open his drawer. 'Where's the time sheet?'

Sarah tutted loudly and threw him a dirty look.

'Sarah, where is it? Did you move it?'

'Maybe if you tidied up that tip you call a desk, you'd find something once in a while.'

John moved a few papers and three empty cigarette boxes in a fruitless attempt to find the time sheet. 'Can't find it.'

'Oh, Christ!' Sarah stopped typing and rubbed her hands over her face. A wave of exhaustion washed over her. She wanted to scream at him until her throat hurt. Was he deliberately trying to wind her up? Couldn't he see how dire their circumstances were, how desperately close to breaking point she had come? Was he really that stupid? 'John, we need that invoice sent in *today*! You promised me you'd do it. There's hardly enough money in the account to run the phone line, and we barely made the rent this month.' She took a deep breath and forced herself to keep her composure. 'So please, I'm begging you—'

'Aha! Here – chill out, I found it.' John pulled a crumpled, tomato sauce-stained piece of paper from under a pile of similarly stained documents. 'Drama over, untwist your knickers.' He chuckled and smoothed the sheet out on his desk.

He didn't notice Sarah's shoulders stiffen, or the look of cold fury that crossed her face. If he had, he might have found some reason to spend the rest of the day out of the office. Sarah, through a supreme effort of will, swallowed her rage and resumed typing. But she knew that, one of these days, she was going to let him have it. Either that or she would walk out the door and never come back.

At five to three, in an effort to appear helpful, John offered again to break the news to Mary Flynn. Sarah shook her head and glanced through her hastily finished notes.

'I can do it, John. It's not like I haven't done it before.' It was a source of pride to Sarah that she never backed away from a difficult situation.

'Think she'll be a crier?'

Sarah sighed. 'I hope not. All that bawling…' She shook her head. 'It's not like they ever *leave* the shits.'

'Yeah, well, they can't all be tough cookies like you, babe.'

Sarah tapped the face of her watch. 'Don't you have somewhere to be?'

John hauled himself out of his chair, grabbed his mobile and beat a hasty retreat down the stairs to Rodney Mitchell's office.

Rodney had once been a good solicitor, too good to be rotting away in a shit-hole on Wexford Street. But he was a chronic alcoholic, could never seem to get himself straight for longer than a month or so. He was separated, with no kids, forty-four but he looked like he was in his late fifties. He was an inch taller than John and about half his weight. He had wispy reddish-blond hair and a seriously shabby wardrobe in various shades of brown. Beneath that wispy barnet there lurked a keen mind, if he'd only stayed off the booze long enough to use it. But he was a decent bloke, when sober, and he threw regular work QuicK's way: insurance scams, fake injury claims, worker's comp cases – boring Mickey Mouse stuff that paid the rent and kept the wolf a few paces back from the door.

John tapped once and let himself in. He grinned when Rodney's face lit up. The solicitor wasn't happy to see John per se, but he figured that if John was there Sarah might not be too far behind. John shook his head and closed the door.

Poor Rodney was arse over feet in love with Sarah, who hardly gave him the time of day. She might have been more inclined to talk to him if he hadn't turned into a blushing, gushing, bumbling fool every time she was within a fifty-foot radius of him, and if he had managed to stay off the drink. Once Rodney had ill-advisedly tried to express his undying love to Sarah by groping her while reeking of Scrumpy Jack and vomit. Sarah had kicked him down the stairs; he'd landed on his face. A shocked John had carried Rodney into his office and left him on the floor to sleep it off. Fortunately, Rodney had been so drunk he remembered nothing of his encounter the next day, and John saw no reason to cause him any more embarrassment by telling him the true reason for his many bruises. Better for him to think he had fallen asleep in the street and been set upon by a gang of youths. Sarah, to her credit, never mentioned it either.

'What you doing, big man?'

'Hello, John. Nothing much. You?' Rodney dropped his hands under the desk so John couldn't see them shaking. He'd been off the booze four weeks and he was close to his personal breaking point.

John pulled up a cheap wooden chair and dropped into it. 'Making myself scarce while my lord and master breaks another heart.'

Rodney glanced up towards the ceiling. 'I hope she doesn't get slapped again.'

'She'll be okay. She's getting good at ducking.' John tipped his head at the paperwork on Rodney's desk. 'Tell me you've got something for us to work on. The bank account runneth low.'

Rodney glanced at the papers and shook his head. 'I'm afraid not. Probate tax and property deeds. But if something comes in, I'll come straight up.'

John smiled. He knew Rodney would; any excuse to moon over Sarah.

The walls in the Wexford Street building were paper thin, so when Mrs Flynn buzzed the intercom, John heard it in Rodney's office. He listened to her footsteps on the stairs outside, heading towards the certain heartbreak on the next floor. He and Rodney exchanged grim, manly winks and waited. If she was a crier, they'd soon hear it.

The two men sat and held their breath. So far, so good: nothing but the creak of footsteps overhead. John heard Sarah's low voice, then nothing. Sarah was probably playing the tape. This was usually the tears part. John sat forward in his chair and noticed Rodney's bony shoulders visibly tighten.

John's mobile phone burst into life, making both him and Rodney jump. John lunged for it.

'Oh my God, you are *so* not going to believe this.'

John slapped his hand to his forehead. 'Cyn. Didn't I ask you not to call me on this number?'

'You know I'm supposed to be going out tonight, right? Well, nuh-uh! It's cancelled. There's no *way* I'm going out with that Tanya Hegarty after what she said to me today. Oh my God, you should have heard her! Get this: she said that the only reason Daddy bought *my* apartment was for tax reasons, and that the one *her* daddy bought wasn't, and then I said to her—'

'Cynthia, I can't talk right now.'

'Can you believe she said that, to *me* of all people?' Cynthia snorted loudly. 'I mean, puh-lease, she's a fine one to talk. Everyone knows her father barely escaped without a prison sentence for having all those offshore accounts. Does she think I don't *know* about that? *Hello*, does she think people don't *talk*?'

John closed his eyes and let calming thoughts drift over him. After ten minutes of mind-numbing drivel, Cynthia finally hung up. John checked his phone and cursed softly when he saw how low the battery was. If he was going to keep seeing her, he'd have to start carrying a spare. The girl could talk the hind legs off a donkey.

'Was that the little lady?' Rodney was looking at him with a certain degree of sympathy.

'Yeah. That was her.' John's mobile bleeped. He stared at it in dismay. Cynthia had sent him a text message: 'I love you' and a line of Xs.

'I'm glad things are working out for you.'

John glanced up, and for a moment he could have sworn he saw Rodney smirk. Before he could say something, he heard footsteps overhead. They listened to the slow descent down the creaky stairs. Mrs Flynn was leaving the building, armed with the lethal tape. God help Mr Flynn.

A few minutes later, Sarah popped her head around the door. She nodded politely to Rodney. 'Rodney.'

Rodney blushed ketchup-red. 'Hi, Sarah.'

Sarah pretended not to notice. 'Come on, John, the coast's clear.'

'How'd she take it?'

'Like a man.'

Sarah disappeared back up the stairs. John shrugged at Rodney, who was staring wistfully at the door, and followed her up. Back in the office, Sarah waved a cheque under his nose. 'Look at this: she gave us a hundred quid extra.'

'Yeah?' John grabbed the cheque and

scrutinised it before handing it back. 'No wonder, it's drawn on the husband's account.'

Sarah swept her fringe out of her eyes, sat behind her desk and grinned. 'So? Who cares where it comes from? But guess what else?'

'What?'

'She's going to recommend us to a friend of a friend of hers. The woman's daughter has run away. Could be worth a decent wage if we play our cards right.'

'Yeah?' John sat down behind his own desk and folded his arms across his chest. 'Who's the girl?'

'Ashley Naughton, eighteen years old. She came up to Dublin from Wicklow back in September, to study at Trinity. She went missing over a week ago.'

'Eighteen's a bit long in the tooth for a runaway.'

Sarah shrugged. 'I know, but that's what Mrs Flynn said.'

'Cops on it?'

'Apparently the Gardaí aren't interested because it's flight by choice. Anyway, Mrs Flynn says the mother, Margaret Naughton, is going out of her mind with worry. The family's not short of money, either.' Sarah stopped smiling and looked around the office. 'We probably won't get the job, though.'

'No reason why we wouldn't.' But John knew what she was thinking. Even if this Margaret

Naughton were to hire an agency to look for her daughter, it wouldn't be a shitty one like theirs.

Sarah looked at the cheque again and drummed her fingers on the desk. 'We're not exactly equipped to handle a missing person, either, are we?'

John picked up a pen and doodled on his sketchpad. 'Shit, Sarah, how *equipped* do we need to be? Look, this kid is eighteen, right? She probably buggered off with a new boyfriend for a few days. Or she's had a row with the folks and is refusing to call home. I mean, if the cops think it's not worth bothering with, it can't be that big a deal, can it?'

Sarah nodded slowly. 'Maybe not.'

'You know how kids are at that age. Bet you a fiver she's had a bust-up with the folks, so she goes off in a snit to teach them a lesson.' John doodled some more. 'Shouldn't be too hard to find her. If this woman calls, we'll take the case. You're seriously thinking of saying no to money? Weren't you just telling me earlier how skint we are?'

'Yes, but—'

'Well, there you go, then.' John smiled over at her and quickly changed the subject. 'I didn't hear any crying. How come Mrs Flynn was so easy about the husband's roaming hands?'

Sarah picked up the cheque and sniffed it like a cigar, her dark eyes sparkling. 'Oh, she's some cookie. According to her, Pat Flynn's been sleeping with her younger sister for months now.

31

That's why he was staying in the hotel that night – the sister was supposed to meet him there. Only Mrs Flynn made it her business to turn up at the sister's door, roaring and crying, with an overnight bag tucked under her arm – which put the kibosh on her plans.'

John scratched his head, puzzled. 'So where do you fit in? Why did she want him on tape trying it on with you?'

Sarah grinned. 'Because Mrs Flynn is going to pretend she doesn't know anything about *their* affair and play our tape for her sister, claiming Mr Flynn's been a naughty boy with someone else.'

'Ah, now I get it.' John shook his head and started to laugh. 'The crafty old… Her own sister will lynch the bastard, thinking he's playing away with someone else.'

'And he'll go crawling home with his tail between his legs.' Sarah tightened her ponytail and laughed. 'Serves him right. The cheeky git told me last night he'd never done anything like that before in his life.'

3

The next morning John woke up flat on his back, with Cynthia's hair in his mouth and her slightly chubby leg resting across his bladder. He groaned, checked his watch and tried to peel her off without waking her. It was like peeling off Sellotape. Cynthia liked to keep the heating on full blast, and his skin was sticky with sweat. John made it to the bathroom and urinated forever, cursing softly to himself.

In his opinion, there were two main problems with staying over at her place. First, none of his stuff was there – toothbrush, shaving kit, maybe some fresh clothes – and, second, it mucked up his routine. And if he wanted to add a third – which he didn't – the hangovers were really wearing him down. Why was it he always wound up so drunk on nights out with Cynthia? Did he need that much drink to make her bearable?

He yawned. Why couldn't he have sex, enjoy a post-coital fag, get dressed and go home? Why did women always make such a big deal about staying the night? Who cares where you are once you're asleep?

He went back into the bedroom and scrambled around in the dark looking for his clothes, stepping painfully on his belt buckle and cursing again. Jesus, he was almost thirty-three, and yet here he was, sneaking around at six in the morning, trying to get dressed in the dark, all because Cynthia liked to use his body as an extra pillow. Disgusted with his own failure to put his foot down, John located his shoes and tiptoed towards the door.

'Johnny? Are you *leaving*?'

Caught. John sighed heavily and turned back. 'Yeah. Sorry, I didn't want to wake you.'

Cynthia turned the bedside lamp on and sat up. Traces of mascara were smudged around her eyes and her hair stood on end. She dragged the duvet across one shoulder. 'It's the middle of the night!'

'I've got to get home and take the dog out for a run before I go to work.'

'Can't I at least have a kiss before you go? You know I hate it when you sneak off like that.' Her voice was sulky. 'Makes me feel like a…a hooker.'

John sighed, walked back across the room and kissed the top of her head. 'See you later.'

Cynthia flopped backwards and yawned sleepily. 'I'll see you at lunchtime.'

'What?'

'We're having lunch, remember?' she said, sliding back down under the bedclothes.

John didn't remember saying any such thing. 'I don't think I can meet up today, Cyn. Cynthia?'

She was asleep, or pretending to be asleep. John couldn't be bothered trying to fight such blatant acting. He let himself out of the apartment and braced himself for the cold morning air.

Dublin in the morning smells unlike any other city. The pungent sea breeze blankets the city in wet, damp air, interwoven with the molasses tang from the Guinness factory. At the first whiff the nose revolts, struggling to separate the sweet from the sour and fetid, but after a few breaths the heavy, contrary air is oddly reassuring, pure Dublin. John stood outside the door of the apartment block and took a deep breath, savouring the smell and enjoying the peace and quiet of the softening shadows, silencing the mocking chatter in his tired, hungover brain.

He had parked his car near Leo Burdock's, a famous chipper by Dublin Castle. He set off, zipping up his jacket against the damp, wispy air and feeling guilty about the way he had treated his dog. This was the second time in a week he'd left Sumo alone all night. Cynthia would have to go.

John turned the corner, his fingers crossed in his pockets in case his car wasn't where he'd left it. This was a habit he'd acquired when his first car, a clapped-out Metro, had been stolen from behind the Stella Cinema in Rathmines one night. He firmly believed that if he crossed his fingers, his car would magically be waiting for him, that Dublin's horde of little bastard joyriders would have bypassed her in favour of another.

And there she was, parked just where he'd left her – his silver-grey, pristine, two-door, low-slung, petrol-guzzling '85 Opel Manta Berlinetta. John rubbed the bonnet lovingly. She was his pride and joy. He had bought her for a song at an auction four years previously, only she hadn't looked anything like she looked now. John had changed the old brakes to disks, lowered the suspension, had the side strips removed and resprayed and upgraded the engine to 16v. The whole interior had been painted and painstakingly restored, and he had recently inserted a top-of-the-line stereo system.

He rubbed the car again. This was another reason Cynthia had to go: he couldn't risk leaving his baby in town overnight. One of these days his crossed fingers might fail him. The thought of some little bollocks tearing through the streets in his car, changing up through the gears with no thought for her…he had no words for such a horror. Trembling slightly, John deactivated the alarm and climbed in, eager to get home.

Home was Ranelagh, a nice area barely south of the city, with a good mix of student flats, old money and new money to keep the place interesting. It had plenty of pubs, good laundrettes and enough eateries for people like John, who didn't do cooking. John's street ran perpendicular to the main drag. It was a quiet cul-de-sac, all neat lawns and lace curtains and neighbours who arranged their bins properly and tut-tutted about students and disc parking. He was lucky, if you could call it that, to live there. When his father had died back in 1990, two years after his mother, John and his older sister Carrie had inherited enough money to buy their own homes outright. John had chosen well. The mid-terrace, two-bedroom cottage he'd bought back then was worth absurd amounts of money now. Still, he'd rather have had the old man back any day.

John locked the car and walked up to the dark-green front door, his humour lifting with each step. It was going to be a glorious day. The night was breaking up, and even this early John could see there wasn't a cloud in the sky. The last of the stars disappeared and a soft red glow spilled across the Dublin Mountains.

John shook his head and smiled. He wasn't being fair to Cynthia. She was a sweet girl, and maybe if he gave her a chance she'd grow on him. All this nonsense about needing to sleep in his own place was probably some knee-jerk fear of commitment or some shit. Carrie slagged him off constantly about his bachelor leanings, demanding he settle down and produce some cousins to play with her own rapidly expanding brood. Maybe she was right. Maybe if he tried harder and wasn't so set in his ways, things would be okay; maybe if…

He opened the front door, and the smell hit him immediately. That leafy, coppery smell could only mean one terrible thing.

'Shit!'

John flicked on the hall light. He noticed immediately that the door to his bedroom was ajar – and he knew he hadn't left it that way. A sinking feeling crept along his spine.

'Sumo?'

A low, rumbling growl came from his bedroom.

'Sumo, come here, boy.'

The smell grew stronger with each step. John pushed the bedroom door open fully.

'Oh, you fucking dirty…'

Sumo had been busy. The cream and blue curtains that Carrie had hung not three weeks before were in tatters. Strips from John's best wool jacket poked out from under the dog's massive body. He probably would have chosen the bed to lie on, if he hadn't already used it as a toilet and his own personal playground. John shook his head, amazed at the damage. His duvet was ripped to shreds, and feathers from both pillows lay everywhere. It looked like an explosion in a battery farm.

John gripped the door handle in fury, afraid to let go in case he made the mistake of charging the dog. In hand-to-paw combat, the dog would easily win. John's vet believed Sumo to be half Irish wolfhound and half German shepherd. John believed him to be half horse, half Sherman tank.

'I'm going to kill you.'

Sumo bared his teeth and growled. John sighed. He knew the growling meant business. It said, 'I accept I've done wrong, but you shouldn't have abandoned me, and if you touch me I'll tear your throat out.'

John relaxed his grip on the door and forced himself to back out, turn and walk down the hall to the kitchen. He'd have a cigarette and a cup of coffee. He would count to a thousand. He'd go for a run and deal with the mess when he came back. He would not get angry.

Sumo clearly sensed victory. Seconds later, he joined John in the kitchen, waving his enormous fan-tail as if nothing had happened. John reached down and patted the massive, wiry head. 'Mutt,' he said. 'I'm going to have you neutered.'

Sumo gave him another half-wag. He was black and tan, rough-coated, with comical, wiry eyebrows. John shook his head. He couldn't really stay angry with him. Sumo was as unfriendly as he had been the day John had found him, three years before, ripping through the bins behind McDonald's on the Naas Road. John had taken pity on the mangy-looking pup with plate-sized feet and thrown him into the car. Sumo had growled all the way home and slept at the end of the bed that night.

No, there was only one person at fault here. Cynthia would have to go.

After a quick coffee, John rinsed out his cup and returned to his bedroom. He was relieved to see Sumo hadn't yet mastered the art of opening drawers. He pulled out an old tracksuit and changed in the bathroom, then he used a plastic bag to pick up Sumo's deposit from the bed, stripped the sheets and bunged them into the washing machine. The duvet was beyond help.

By the time he was ready to leave, the sun had managed to climb into the sky. John checked he had everything – keys, body-warmer and evil, ungrateful mutt – then got in the car and drove to Phoenix Park. Sumo stood on the back seat with his head out the window over John's shoulder, his tongue lolling.

Phoenix Park, the biggest enclosed park in all of Europe, was John's favourite place to run. At that hour of the morning it was fairly deserted, and a gentle mist covered the grass. John parked the Manta off the main road, past the old cricket house. He looped his keys around his neck on a string, snapped a harness on Sumo and connected an extendable fifteen-metre lead to a special belt around his waist and to the ring on Sumo's harness. He warmed up and set off for the gallops, with Sumo loping along beside him. It was a five-mile run and he did it at least four times a week, rain, hail or shine. The harness was an absolute must: fallow deer roamed freely about the park, and Sumo thought of them as fair game. And the stupid things were so tame you were nearly on top of them before they bolted. John had spent too many mornings traipsing after the dog to take the chance.

John had discovered running by accident. When he'd realised the usual dog walks didn't tire

Sumo out, he'd had to think of something else, and short of tying the dog to the back of his car, running was his only option. Now he loved it. John liked a pint and he smoked too many cigarettes to be fit, but he didn't jog, he ran. He ran until his legs ached and he felt like coughing up the crap coating his lungs. He hit the gallops at a steady pace and ran along by the football pitches, feeling his anger fade. Sumo loped three feet ahead of him, leaving the rope slack, his ears cocked, scanning the dew-laden grass for any unwary deer.

John ran and sweated, about Cynthia and his destroyed room, forgetting about Sarah's tense face and his failing business. He pushed up the pace on the final lap of the gallops until his chest screamed and his legs felt like lead. And after he finished the run and collapsed, wheezing against the bonnet of the car, ignoring the contempt on his dog's face, he felt good. He had no idea why, but he did.

John went home, fed Sumo and put him outside with a rawhide bone to chew on. He hoovered up the bulk of the feathers, showered, changed and went to work, content with the world. He parked the car two streets from the office and strolled, whistling, into work.

Sarah was there ahead of him, drinking coffee and leafing through a fresh stack of bills. She looked anything but content. John took off his jacket and hung it behind the door. He nodded to her.

'Hey.'

'Don't "hey" me. I thought you paid the insurance on the Fiesta?'

'We did.'

'Bollocks!' Sarah flung a sheet of paper at him. 'This is from the insurance company. Last month's cheque bounced sky high. We've been driving around with no cover.'

'So I'll transfer some money across. Chill out. I'll take care of it.'

'Don't tell me to chill out! What if we'd been in an accident?'

'We weren't.'

'We need that car, John.'

'We can use mine for a few weeks.'

'Hah!' Sarah said, flinging the paper down. 'Your car is too bloody obvious, and it's too expensive to run, anyway.'

'Sarah, it's not going to kill us to use it for a week or two.'

'That's not the point! Jesus, John, don't you realise—'

'Sarah, I said I'll take care of it. Don't give me a hard time over it. Jesus, I've had a right bleeding morning already. Got home and Sumo had done a hatchet job on my bedroom.' John dropped into his chair. 'I'll take care of this today, okay?'

Sarah raked her hair with her fingers. 'What do you expect? Poor Sumo, if you keep leaving him on his own there's bound to be trouble. He's not a toy, John.'

'I knew you'd take his side.'

42

She raised her eyes to the ceiling and went back to her paperwork. She wore black jeans and a black tight-cut T-shirt, and her hair was still damp from her morning shower. John let his eyes roam all over her when he was sure she wasn't looking.

'I'm not taking sides,' she said, turning a page. 'You shouldn't keep a dog if you're going to abandon him every time some bit of fluff comes along. You've no sense of responsibility at all.'

This was too close to the bone for John. 'I didn't *abandon* him. I stayed over with Barbie last night.'

'You mean Cindy.'

'Cindy, Barbie, what's the difference?'

'Barbie has more class.'

John opened his mouth, then closed it again. He wished he could think of something clever to come back with, but, as usual, he couldn't. He would later, probably on the way home, but by then it would be too late.

'What have we got on today?'

Sarah pointed to his desk with her chin. 'Margaret Naughton's coming in to see us.'

'Who?'

'The mother of the missing girl, remember? We talked about it yesterday. Jesus, you remember yesterday, right?'

John pulled open his drawer and looked for time sheets with a resigned air. 'Shut it with the sarcasm and give me the details.'

'Mrs Flynn called her last night, singing our praises. She'll be here around eleven.'

'You were talking to her?'

'First thing. Phone was ringing when I got in.'

'How'd she sound?'

'Upset.'

John glanced around the shabby office, taking in the vinyl wallpaper – circa 1973 – the swirling red and green carpet and the mismatched furniture. He figured Mrs Naughton would take one look at their rag-tag operation and hit the road. He caught Sarah doing exactly the same thing. 'Think we ought to tidy up a bit?'

Sarah put her coffee cup down, on a desk covered with thousands of circles. 'I don't think a quick dust and hoover is going to make any difference to this place.'

'So you don't think we need to tidy?'

Sarah shook her head. 'I'll get the Hoover, you clear up that awful desk.'

Margaret Naughton buzzed the intercom at twenty past twelve, just as John was beginning to wonder if the outside of the building had put her off. Sarah buzzed her in and turned to him, her face deadly serious and pinched with warning.

'Now listen – don't act the eejit, John. This case could be worth a few quid if we get it. Please, I'm begging you, be on your best behaviour.'

'Jesus, Sarah, I'm not a complete gom.' John rolled his eyes. 'Relax. I'll be a good dog, I promise.'

'John, I swear to—'

There was a soft knock on the office door. Sarah pushed back her chair and began to rise.

'Come on in,' John roared. 'It's open.'

Sarah flinched, threw him a filthy look and slammed back into her chair.

The door opened. 'Hello?'

Margaret Naughton was nothing like they'd imagined her. For a start, she was much younger than they'd expected, in her late thirties. She was about five foot three, trim and well dressed in a cream trouser suit and a chocolate-brown silk shirt. She wore soft leather Bally shoes and carried a dark-brown Louis Vuitton bag the size of a small car. Her hair was subtly highlighted and cut in a short, choppy style that flattered her tiny features.

'Come in, Mrs Naughton, please,' Sarah said politely.

'I'm so sorry I'm late,' she said apologetically. She closed the office door behind her and looked around, her eyes travelling slowly about the room. 'I couldn't find a place to park.'

'Not at all, not at all, Mrs Naughton.' John stood up and offered his hand. 'I'm John Quigley. Please, do take a seat.'

Sarah's expression hardened at his false tone.

'That's my partner, Sarah Kenny.' John beamed at her.

'Mrs Naughton.'

If Margaret noticed the tension between them, she didn't let on. She nodded politely and shook their hands. John's eyes widened at the size of the rock on her wedding finger, and he had to hide his delight: the Naughtons were obviously more than just middle-of-the-road wealthy.

Mrs Naughton accepted the chair John offered her and glanced around the room again, as if trying to take in every detail. 'Thank you for seeing me.'

'That's our pleasure. How can we help you, Mrs Naughton?' John said, keeping up his very best behaviour.

Mrs Naughton cleared her throat, and Sarah noted the purplish shadows that ran deep under her carefully made-up eyes. 'I'm not sure...you know. About this.'

'We understand this is difficult, Mrs Naughton,' Sarah said. 'If we can be of any help to you, we will.'

'Mary Flynn says very good things about you both.' She tightened her grip on her handbag, holding it across her chest like a shield. 'I don't know what else to do.'

'Let's start at the beginning,' Sarah said. 'Did you bring the things I asked for this morning?'

Margaret's head bobbed again. She shook the bag at Sarah. 'I brought everything I could lay my hands on. The Gardaí have dismissed Ashley's disappearance as' – she wrinkled her nose in disgust – 'some kind of prank.'

Sarah smiled and opened her notebook. 'Well, if you'd—'

'Imagine!' Mrs Naughton snapped, her face

tightening in anger. 'What sort of people do they think we are? My daughter would not put me through this sort of worry for a *prank*. One of them even had the gall to suggest Ashley had probably *hooked up* – that's the term he used – with some boyfriend and gone off...' She let the sentence trail away.

'And is that a possibility?' John asked. 'I mean, girls—'

'Mr Quigley, I assure you, Ashley would never do something like that.'

'Call me John.'

Mrs Naughton raised her chin and glared at him. 'My daughter is missing. She hasn't been in contact with anyone – not me, not her father, none of her friends. Believe me, Mr Quigley, when I tell you something has happened to her.'

Sarah narrowed her eyes warningly at John. 'I think what John means,' she said softly, 'is that people, especially young people, often don't think of the consequences of their actions. They often do things – reckless things – without malice, but also without responsibility.'

'Why do the cops think it's nothing?' John persisted. 'What makes them so sure?'

Margaret lowered her head and stared at a stain on the carpet for a long time. Finally she sighed. 'My husband discovered that both of Ashley's bank accounts are empty. She had over five thousand euros in each of them in August – we'd put it there for college, you know, for her to

47

use to buy groceries and things. It was supposed to last the year… And it's gone, all of it. Edward reported it to the Gardaí.' She curled her upper lip slightly. 'Then there was the note.'

'Note?'

'That's where they got their idea that Ashley is on some kind of…' She splayed her hands out in front of her, lost for words. 'I don't know, shopping spree. Her flatmates were in Galway for the weekend, and when they got back they found this note Ashley is supposed to have left. It's nonsense, complete—'

'What did the note say?' John asked.

Margaret glared at him for a second. 'It said, "I'm sorry, but I need some time alone. Ashley." It doesn't even look like Ashley's handwriting.'

'You don't think the note was written by your daughter?' Sarah said.

'No, I do not.'

John glanced over at Sarah and raised an eyebrow. This woman was kidding herself. If Ashley Naughton had cleaned out her accounts and left a note, it stood to reason she was off somewhere, living it up. 'She definitely took out all her money?'

'Yes, but that doesn't explain anything.' Mrs Naughton's voice vibrated with tightly controlled anger. 'I know my daughter, Mr Quigley…John. I know that at eighteen she's classed as an adult, but she's not an adult. She would never have taken off without calling me. Ashley's an only child, and she would never have done this...never.'

'Look, I'm not saying she—'

'Mrs Naughton,' Sarah said, cutting John off, 'we're going to need some background information on Ashley – friends, addresses, the last person to speak to her, that sort of thing.' She leaned across her desk and grabbed a fresh, unchewed Biro from a jam jar. 'If you tell us to go ahead, then we'll look into it. I promise you, if she's run away, we'll find her.'

Margaret leaned back in her chair and glanced around the room again. Her eyes roamed over every crack and grubby surface. Sarah followed her gaze and felt a dull blush creep up her neck. God, the place looked so shabby. She'd probably tell them to forget about it.

'My husband doesn't think much of detective agencies. He says this is a complete waste of time and money.' Margaret's pale eyes returned to Sarah. 'Edward thinks the Gardaí are right, that Ashley will come back with her tail between her legs when her money runs out...'

'They get along?' John asked.

'Oh, those two...you know fathers and daughters. Always arguing.' She tried a smile. 'But he's wrong, absolutely and utterly wrong. I know Ashley better than anyone. She wouldn't do this. She'd never hurt me this way. She wasn't that type of girl. Something has happened to her, I know it.' Her eyes glistened and she put her hand over her chest. 'I feel it.'

Sarah nodded. 'I promise, we will do our utmost to find out what happened.'

Margaret smiled then, and it was a genuine smile that spoke volumes. Sarah felt the gratitude flow from her in waves. She guessed that since the discovery of the empty accounts, Margaret had been fighting a losing battle to convince anyone to treat her daughter's case seriously.

'She's been in Dublin how long now?' Sarah asked.

'Two and a half months.'

'She live alone?'

'No, she's sharing an apartment in Temple Bar with two friends, but she hadn't even had a chance to move all her things there yet.' Mrs Naughton's voice wavered. She looked at Sarah with tears in her eyes. 'You know how it is – she kept saying she'd get round to it. The truth is, she'd been coming home less and less. There was always something going on.'

'I see.' Sarah wrote something on her pad. 'Did she go out much in Dublin? Have a favourite bar? Nightclub?'

'I don't think so.' Margaret pulled a face at the word 'bar'. 'I never heard her mention any place in particular.'

'She never mentioned a boyfriend or anyone special she might be seeing?'

'No.' Margaret shook her head emphatically. 'Ashley and her flatmates are joined at the hip. That's why I didn't really fret that she didn't come down. I know how close they all are.'

'And they don't know anything about her disappearance, nothing at all?'

Margaret shook her head again. 'Ashley was planning to go to Galway with them that weekend, then she told them she'd changed her mind and was going to come home instead. The last they saw of her was on the Friday night. She was still at the apartment when they left to catch the train from Heuston Station.' There was a catch in Margaret's voice. 'They said she was fine. Her usual happy self.'

'We'll talk to them. And we should come down to your home, Mrs Naughton, and look through her room. And if you could make a list of Ashley's friends and their telephone numbers tonight, we can make a start with them.'

Sarah's brisk tone seemed to soothe Margaret, and she relaxed her shoulders for the first time since she had stepped into their office. Clearly the fact that they were willing to do something galvanised her into action.

'I have the names here,' she said, dipping into her shoulder bag. 'I brought them with me.' She extracted an envelope and practically hurled it across the desk at Sarah. 'I have the names of her teachers in Trinity, her friends, her doctor. My address is there on the front, and there's a photo of Ashley taken during the summer. Everything I could find is in there.' She took a deep breath. 'I don't know what to do next. I've spoken to everyone who knows her.' She searched for a tissue in her bag, found one and blew her nose long and hard. 'I'm sorry,' she said. 'You've no idea… I've been going out of my mind.'

'I'm sure. You must be so worried.' Sarah took up the envelope. 'But try to keep calm. It could be something simple. Maybe she had a row with someone, or she's finding the course and the move a bit overwhelming. Maybe she just needed a break.'

'I hope so.' Mrs Naughton smiled weakly. 'Please, call down tomorrow. You can go through her room then.'

John decided to step off the sideline at this point. 'It would be better if we went today. The quicker we begin to search, the quicker we find your girl. We'll need a word with the other family members, too, if that's all right.'

'There's only my husband and my mother-in-law. And they don't know anything either.'

'You'd be surprised what people know and don't realise.'

Margaret chewed hesitantly on her bottom lip. 'Oh, well, of course… I mean, my husband is very busy right now, and… Well, the thing is…' She looked between Sarah and John, her face anguished. 'He's very upset about all this.'

Sarah raised one eyebrow.

'As far as he's concerned, this is all nonsense. Please – I haven't told him I'm hiring anyone. Give me a chance to speak with him first, then come down tomorrow. I'll be there.' She got up, clutching her bag so hard her knuckles went white.

'My address is there on the front of the envelope.'

'Mrs Naughton, we will need to speak with your husband,' Sarah said evenly.

Margaret looked longingly towards the door. Finally her shoulders drooped and she turned her face to the floor. 'I'll let him know to expect you. If you can leave it until after twelve, I would greatly appreciate it. He should be home by then.'

John came around his desk and showed her to the door. 'Don't worry, we'll just ask a few routine questions. We won't take up much of his time.'

'Thank you. Thank you both so much.' Margaret turned on her heel and left.

After she'd gone, John closed the door and turned his attention to Sarah. 'What do you make of that?'

'Weird, huh?' Sarah said, her gaze straying to the door.

'The kid's probably a little troublemaker. Maybe the father knows her better than the mother.' John slapped his hand against his forehead. 'Shit, I forgot to talk payments.'

Sarah massaged the back of her neck. 'Don't worry, I spoke with her about it over the phone.'

'You did?'

'Yeah.'

'What about discussing it with me first?'

'What was there to discuss?' She opened the envelope and spread the papers on her desk. 'We need the work.'

John folded his arms and waited patiently,

trying hard not to get annoyed. More and more often, lately, Sarah was doing things without consulting him. 'Well?'

'Well what?' Sarah picked up the picture of Ashley Naughton and studied it closely. The girl was seriously pretty. In the photo, she wore her long blond hair pulled back into a ponytail. She had pale, clear skin and even white teeth. She was perched on a low wall, wearing an old rugby shirt, pulled tight over her knees. She smiled shyly towards the camera. Sarah had to agree with the mother: she didn't look like the type of girl to cause trouble.

'How much? How much are we charging her?'

'She's paying us three hundred a day, plus expenses.'

'Each?' John said hopefully.

'No.'

'Ah, are you fucking pulling my leg, Sarah? That's only a hundred and fifty each. I could earn that on one spouse gig in less than an hour. And don't tell me she's not loaded. You saw that ring, right? You should have asked for more.' John pressed his fingers into his forehead. 'Jesus Christ! We're not a bleeding charity.'

Sarah leaned back in her chair and eyed him. 'That's true, John. But before you start whinging, check your diary – if you can find it. Tell me something: how many gigs do you have this week?'

'I don't need to check,' John said, 'and that's not the point.'

'No?' Sarah tapped her Biro hard on the desk, a sure sign her temper was beginning to get the better of her. 'Gee, I thought it was. I thought making some money was very much the point.'

'Yeah, but three fucking hundred quid—'

'It's three hundred quid a *day*! And we have less than two hundred in our business account!'

'I *know* that, but—'

Behind him, the door opened. Sarah's face darkened as Cynthia sailed in.

'Jesus! Don't you ever knock?'

John wasn't exactly pleased to see her either. 'Cynthia, how did you get in?'

'Well, hello to you too! Did I interrupt something?' Cynthia sashayed across the room, sat down on the edge of John's desk and crossed her legs.

'Yes.' John glanced at Sarah, but she was already leafing through the papers again, her mouth drawn into a tight, angry line.

'Who was that woman I met coming down the stairs? She looks familiar. You must be coming up in the world, baby. She's hardly your usual customer.'

John sat down at his desk. 'What makes you say that?'

Cynthia rolled her eyes dramatically. 'Her shoes and that bag, of course – Louis Vuitton, *hello*. This season, too, the lucky old cow. There's a waiting list in Brownies for that bag, at *least* three months. You should have seen her face when I asked her, as if she couldn't believe I'd know what they were. Don't know why she's bothering – mutton dressed as lamb. Are we still on for lunch? I'm *starving*! Oh my God, wait till I tell you about the day I've had.'

'Let me get this straight.' Sarah's head snapped up. 'You were hassling our client over her clothes and bag? You're some piece of work. Could you not see she was upset?'

Cynthia wrinkled her nose. 'I only asked her about her bag, Sarah. No biggie.'

John felt the beginning of a headache flutter behind his eyes. 'Cynthia, you can't ask clients *anything*. They value their privacy.'

Cynthia glared at a space somewhere to the left of Sarah's shoulder. 'She didn't look upset to me. But, then again, I'm not the great Columbus you are, Sarah.'

'Columbus?'

'Oh, puh-lease, you know – the guy in the raincoat, on *telly*.'

John stole a quick glance at Sarah, who was staring at Cynthia in disbelief. 'I think that's Columbo, Cyn.'

'Whatever.' Cynthia stood and tapped her watch. 'Look, can we eat now or what? There's a new place in Westmoreland Street. Daddy was there, he says it's got *amazing* seafood and a great wine selection…'

John glanced at Sarah, but she waved him away. 'Go on, I'll make a start with some of these phone numbers.'

'Are you sure? I can stay if you need me.'

Sarah glared at him. 'John, I'm sure Cynthia has *something* to get back to.'

John nodded and grabbed his coat. The look said it all: *Go, and take that dumb bitch with you.* Columbus. Jesus Christ. Cynthia would have to go.

4

The heavily lined curtains were drawn tight across the windows of Vinnie York's penthouse apartment, shielding the interior from the cool, grey winter light. Six floors below, Baggot Street bustled with office workers and the bars began to fill up with early-release blue collars. Couriers tore breakneck through the build-up of evening traffic. Car horns blew and people yelled, roared abuse, laughed and conversed as they hurried from offices, eager to reach the shops and the bars and then, finally, home.

Vinnie rolled over on Egyptian cotton sheets, threw an arm across his face and slumbered until the day grew dim and darkness fell again. In winter Vinnie might go whole months without ever seeing sunlight. He was the anti-Cinderella, only truly coming alive after midnight. Vinnie's heart hammered hardest when the doors of Tempest, his hip nightclub, opened to the throngs of scantily clad people queuing patiently to get in. Then he was truly awake.

At 5.00 p.m. on the dot, the silver Bang & Olufsen phone by his bed trilled. Vinnie pushed the aloe vera sleep mask up onto his forehead, opened one eye, leaned over and picked it up.

'Yeah.'

'Yorkie, you up, man?' It was Davey Clarke, his head doorman.

Vinnie yawned. 'I am awake. Do you have news for me?'

'Not on the gear.'

'Fuck. Nothing at all?'

'No. But we've to meet with the other problem at nine.'

'We'll discuss that over breakfast.'

Vinnie hung up, rolled onto his back and stared at the ceiling. For a moment he had forgotten the terrible predicament he was in. Now it came flooding back, irritating the lining of his stomach and darkening his humour. *Merde*, he thought.

Normally he took pleasure in his day, enjoying every waking moment, but this last week... And now the old man had run out of patience and was coming here, to his turf – acting like he, Vincent York, needed help in sorting this mess out. Vinnie ground his teeth together in annoyance.

After half an hour in the power shower, he was fully awake. He dried himself off with a fluffy towel and switched on his sunbed. Vinnie spent half an hour on it every day to ensure his skin remained golden. Best money he'd ever spent, that sunbed. He could be out half the night and still manage to avoid the pasty-faced, sick look his patrons and staff wore.

After the sunbed, Vinnie opened his closet and pondered what to wear. Vinnie didn't do colour. He wore black, grey and white, sometimes all black and very rarely, perhaps in the summer, all white. He was proud of the fact that he didn't own a single pair of jeans. At thirty-eight, he had to take his appearance seriously. He had noticed the signs of age creeping in, and he was damned if he was going to assist them by sloppy dressing.

He chose a crisp white shirt and a black, single-breasted Hugo Boss suit and carefully laid them out on the bed. He returned to his en-suite bathroom and moisturised his entire body with cocoa butter, paying particular attention to the skin around his neck. As his skin soaked up the cream, he brushed and flossed his teeth, gelled his black hair, trimmed his goatee beard – filling in any grey with a mascara wand – and finally splashed himself liberally with Aramis aftershave. Vinnie smiled at his reflection in the mirror. He still had it, still liked the cut of his own jib. He winked, shot at his reflection with two cocked index fingers and switched off the light.

By 6.45 he was heading at a brisk clip to one of his five favourite restaurants for a late and calorie-controlled breakfast. Here he would meet with Davey Clark to discuss the night ahead. A creature of habit, Vinnie York performed this ritual five days out of every week, taking only Monday and Tuesday off.

Vinnie had opened Tempest a couple of years

before, in response to a growing demand for proper clubs in Dublin. Once, his only serious competition had been Spirit, the Pod, Red Box and Lillie's Bordello. But Lillie's was small and ridiculously elitist, and the Pod had gone to the great nightclub in the sky, and he'd heard Red Box was struggling to make its numbers. Spirit was a challenge, but it was on Abbey Street. Of course, there were other places, but they didn't trouble him unduly.

Tempest was a roaring success because Vinnie York didn't give a shit *what* came in his door, as long as it wasn't a total scumbag and had money to spend. His club had a hip, mixed crowd, carefully cultivated by Vinnie himself with the help of hand-picked doormen – he had gained a reputation about town as a tremendous host. He kept his feet on the ground and was hands-on in every aspect of his business. If one weekend was slow, he wanted to know why. He flew in top DJs from every underground club in England. He organised speciality nights, free mike nights, hip-hop and drum-and-bass guest nights. He succeeded where others failed. He was a star.

He was also fast becoming the number-one coke and ecstasy supplier in Dublin. Truth be told, he didn't really need Tempest at all. But Vinnie was a new breed of drug dealer. He'd witnessed a lot of men lose out to the CAB over the years because they'd had no way of showing where they garnered their income. And he was fucked if he was going to lose any of the things he'd worked so hard for, especially over something as stupid as income tax. Tempest offered security and a laundrette for his funky money – and, frankly, he loved the place.

Vinnie York's opinion of himself was high. He believed himself to be an innovator. He accepted the unwavering fact that the most spectacular night out for his punters involved drugs, easily located and in plentiful supply. Instead of trying to cull dealing in his club, he harvested it greedily. His men knew what to look for in a crowd. Anyone caught dealing was dealt with swiftly, had his stash confiscated, was ejected with more force than necessary. Vinnie had drugs in his club, but they were supplied and controlled by his own men, not by some greasy junkie fuck who'd probably poison half his punters before the night was out.

Vinnie was nothing if not meticulous. He didn't like problems and he didn't like hassle. He worked hard and he played hard. While drugs were his main source of income, the club was a constant source of pleasure to him. And now that pleasure was under threat. If Patrick had listened to him, they would never be in this position. He would never have made such a mistake.

Vinnie finished his breakfast and checked his watch. He ordered a pot of Turkish coffee, lit one of the few cigarettes he smoked a day and relaxed in his chair. At 7.30 on the dot, a huge, muscle-bound figure materialised behind his shoulder.

'Boss.'

'How's it going, Davey?'

Davey Clarke pulled out a chair and eased his considerable bulk into it. At five foot nine he wasn't exactly tall, but what he lacked in height he more than made up for in sheer mass. He weighed in at an impressive sixteen stone, almost all of which was chest and arms. He could bench-press two hundred and sixty pounds without breaking a sweat and had been known to take easy money from unsuspecting hard men willing to try arm-wrestling. He didn't talk a lot, relying on body language to make his message clear. Tonight he wore his usual uniform of black jeans, a tight black T-shirt and Doc Martin boots. His sandy hair was buzz-cut to within an inch of its life, his nose was flat from one too many breaks and his skin was pockmarked from a youthful bout of severe acne. He didn't drink and, as far as Vinnie knew, had no interests other than work and weight training.

'Well?' Vinnie blew out a stream of smoke. Normally he liked to chat with Davey before the business talk took over. Davey was a mate from way back when. He was big, strong, loyal and on the payroll, the way Vinnie liked his friends.

'Same old same old,' Davey said, turning his bulldog face towards the window. He watched the passers-by for a second or two with an expression that would make most people bless themselves and cross the road. 'Spoke to all the movers, nobody's caught a sniff of any action.'

'Has the ski been found?'

'Nope. It's like the fucker vanished into thin

air. Checked out his hotel passport under the mattress, same clothes hangin' in the wardrobe, and I know he ain't been back there. Got one of the bellboys keepin' tabs. Minute he shows his mug, I'll get a call.'

Vinnie felt frustration bubble inside him. Not only was his business threatened, but the losers and shakers would surely have spread the word that something was amiss *chez York*. He'd be a laughing stock soon. 'He could have used a fake passport.'

'Takes a bit of time to organise moving the gear out again.'

Vinnie raised an eyebrow. 'Well, if he hasn't moved it on, then it's in the fucking country, and if it's in the country, someone has it. I mean, Jesus, it didn't fucking disappear into thin air. The GPS unit proved it made it to shore.'

'Yeah, I know that.'

'Naughton's stonewalling me. Got quite fucking lippy, too, when I tried to sound him out.'

'Yeah?' Davey shrugged one massive shoulder. 'That prick Dougie's actin' real hinky, too.'

'The Landlord? Fuck, that's all we need. You think he's got wind?'

'If anyone has, it's likely to be him.'

'You know, I never liked him.' Vinnie tapped his fingers together.

'Don't he and Naughton go back?'

'All those bastards go back. Well, perhaps we should have a chat with him.'

'I'll set it up.'

Vinnie nodded. He didn't like the fact that Dougie Burrows was in on his act. Dougie Burrows was a renowned fence and had no loyalties. Worse than that, Dougie had contacts and could sell sand to a fucking Arab. If Kelpie had enlisted his help in moving the gear on, Vinnie would have to act fast. 'Did you get a chance to talk to that queen Nolan?'

Davey smiled suddenly, showing perfect teeth. 'I sure did.' He glanced down at his hands, and Vinnie noticed the skin on his left knuckles was swollen and slightly bruised. 'He's offered to phone us the second he gets wind of anything.'

'How kind of him.'

'Yeah.'

'So it's a waiting game.' Vinnie scowled. '*He*'s not going to like that, now is he?' He inhaled deeply and changed the subject. 'Tell me, Davey, how is the family?'

'That fucker Willy's makin' noise about the car again. Asked me ma if she'd help out with the repayments.'

Willy was Davey's older brother, a hopeless case who had worked all his life and resented every penny Davey had because he never had any of his own. He was the bane of Davey's life.

Vinnie feigned interest. 'Really? What did your mother say?'

'She asked if I'd help the cunt out, throw a few bob his way.'

'And will you?'

Muscles bunched in Davey's jaw. 'I suppose I'll have to. It'll get him out of me ma's kitchen, at least, the whingin' fuck. The guy's forty years old. You'd think he'd have some respect for himself and not be hasslin' me ma for cash, wouldn't ya?'

Vinnie nodded, looked sympathetic and kept his trap shut. It was one thing for Davey to bad-mouth his brother, quite another for anyone else to do so. Vinnie had once watched Davey almost kick some guy to death for making a minor disparaging remark about the Clarke family. That had been three years before, and the guy still talked funny. Blood was blood, at the end of the day. 'I'm sure you'll sort it out, *mon ami*. How is your mother? Is she keeping well?'

'She's grand. She'd be a lot better if she didn't have to waste so much of her fuckin' energy worryin' about that prick.'

'Well, tell her I was asking for her.'

Davey flexed thick muscles in his neck until the veins stood out under the skin like pipes. 'Yeah.'

'What about the shifts for the weekend – are they sorted?'

'Yeah. Me and Jas'll do the front door Saturday and Sunday. Jimmy and Mark inside, upstairs is covered by the Donkey brothers.'

'I probably won't be around much over the next few days.'

'Figured as much.'

'So much going on.' Vinnie poured another

coffee and offered one to Davey, who refused.
'This guy we're meeting tonight – you've had him
thoroughly checked out, right?'

A look of scorn passed over Davey's face. 'We
wouldn't be meetin' him if I hadn't. Give me a
fuckin' break, Vinnie. What do you think I am?'

Vinnie leaned across the table and jabbed his
index finger at Davey's face. 'Don't you get fucking lippy, *David*. I'm asking a simple question.'

Davey scowled. He hated it when people
called him David. It reminded him of the old man,
who had used his full name when he was about to
beat the living shit out of him. 'Sorry, man, but
come on…' Davey spread his shovel-shaped
hands. 'I'm not goin' to set up no meeting with
some cunt I haven't screened, am I?'

Vinnie straightened out his cuffs and flicked
an imaginary piece of lint from his jacket sleeve.
'What do I know? That's why I ask questions,
n'est-ce pas?'

Davey smiled his shark-smile and rested a
thick forearm across the table. 'Yeah, well, he's
small fry. But after tonight this guy's gonna know
the score, boss.'

Mollified, Vinnie sipped his coffee and gazed
out onto the street. He wouldn't stand for anyone
trying to muscle in on his turf, especially in his
own club. Next thing he knew some punter would
have overdosed on rat poison and be lying curled
up on the floor in *his* toilets, foaming at the mouth,
heels rattling off *his* tiles. The Drug Squad would

close Tempest down, or make renewing his drink licence even more difficult than it was already. Vinnie had enough hassle on his plate right now, he didn't need any more aggravation.

'Boss?'

'Hmm?'

'About tonight?'

Vinnie set his cup down. 'You know what to do.'

Davey nodded and stood up to leave. 'I'll meet you at ten to nine, right?'

Vinnie frowned. 'I don't want this to get messy, Davey. Just make sure the fucker knows we're not going to tolerate dealing in the club. No rough stuff. You can't imagine the trouble I had getting the stain out of my shirt the last time. *Sacré bleu*, what a nightmare!'

'No problemo.' Davey smiled slowly. There wouldn't be any problem, if the guy acted smart. If he didn't…well, that was different.

'And we can't waste time hanging around afterwards. I need to get to the airport. It's bad enough that *he*'s coming here. I can't be late picking him up. You know how waiting upsets him.'

'I've got the flight time.' Davey tapped the side of his head with a thick index finger.

'He *hates* waiting.'

'Yeah.

'I can't believe he'd even set foot on Eire's fair soil. He always swore he wouldn't. There are plenty who still hold a grudge.' Vinnie smiled softly. 'Plenty of people who'd love to get wind of his arrival.'

Davey didn't answer. There were more than a few people who hated Patrick York. The fact that he was taking the risk of flying into Ireland showed how panicked he was.

Vinnie looked slyly at his friend. 'You know, Davey, Dougie Burrows would be very interested in information like that.'

Davey shrugged. 'Probably.'

'It might keep the filthy shit on side.' Vinnie drummed his fingers on the tablecloth and frowned. 'The biggest haul we've ever tried, disappearing... I don't believe in coincidence, do you?'

Davey shook his head.

'Patrick's a fool. I never trusted Kelpie, and Naughton's a tricky bastard.' Vinnie settled back in his chair as if exhausted. 'You know, I'm tired of dealing with the old school, Davey – tired of it. At times like this I feel I need to make a few changes. Hmm?'

Davey said nothing. He was tired too, tired of listening to Vinnie prattle on. Tired of the tantrums, the coke binges, trying to keep him on track, trying to keep him from fucking up. And now he was at it again, threatening this and that. Vinnie was like a rattlesnake: he liked to make a lot of noise before he struck.

'It seems I do all the running around, and they reap the rewards.' He sighed theatrically and gave Davey a weary smile. 'Go on now. I need time to think. *Adieu, mon ami, adieu.*'

Davey grunted goodbye and stalked out of the restaurant. And the French was another thing. Vinnie knew about as much French as Davey did, but ever since he'd banged a French bird over the summer he kept using stupid French phrases in his speech. Thought it made him sound *cultured*. Crazy fucker. That shit got on Davey's nerves. Still, he had to admit, it was better than the year before, when Vinnie had insisted on speaking like he'd been born and raised in 'the hood'. Davey grimaced, remembering Vinnie ordering him to 'sit your ass down, homie'. Nah, compared to that the French wasn't bad at all.

5

Francie Bolger waited behind the disused railway bridge in the dilapidated flank of the East Wall. From there he could keep an eye on the yard but still remain hidden. He had a runny nose, and he wiped it constantly on his sleeve. He was nervous. This was his big moment, his chance to hit the big time. Any minute now, if the bouncer hadn't been pulling his chain, Vinnie York would arrive and he could make his pitch.

He rubbed his hands together, spat on the ground and hopped from one foot to the other to keep warm. At twenty-three, he knew he was never going to be any taller than five foot six, and at times like this he wished to God he were packing a bit of muscle. Nerves were affecting his stomach, and he belched loudly into the still night air. He tasted the Big Mac he had scarfed down earlier, as his older brother Niall had gone over what he should say.

Francie knew they were small-time. They sold ten-spots of hash (sometimes with peat briquette crumbled in) on street corners, and occasionally, when they could get it, they flogged small amounts of ecstasy – nothing major, just twenty or thirty at late-night parties when people felt the first lull in their buzz. But things were changing. Lady Luck had tossed a bone their way. They were moving up.

Less than a month before, at a rave in Tyrone, Niall had been introduced by a mutual friend to two dealers from Belfast. High as a kite on a ball of speed and two doves, Niall had boasted about the deals he could make in Dublin. The Northern boys were interested and assured Niall they would have no problem getting coke and vast quantities of pills, if he wanted it. Niall had played it cool, although he'd nearly shat himself. He said he'd think about it. He took a pager number and promised to get in touch over the next few days with an answer. Then he excused himself and ran off to find the nearest john.

Two days later, he'd called the Northern boys and said game on. Then he just had to find the money.

Not a car, house, shop or lone walker within a six-mile radius of the Bolgers' neighbourhood had been safe. At one point they'd had so many car stereos they'd had to enlist a cousin to store some of them. Together Niall and Francie had pawned, scrounged and robbed the ten thousand quid required for their first payment on a bulk order. Now they had sixty grams of coke and four thousand ecstasy pills waiting to be shifted. Niall, who was better at maths, reckoned they'd make at least twenty thousand in profit, easy – once they moved it on, of course. With the proceeds, they could buy bigger next time and make twice that. With shining eyes, Niall told Francie they would be driving BMWs and living the good life in no time. They'd have pussy on order, flash gear, whatever they wanted. Niall began to eye up a serious fourteen-carat gold chain hanging in the window of a jewellery shop in Henry Street.

They'd used their two younger sisters to move the gear into the nightclubs across town, knowing that the girls could get in anywhere and wouldn't be searched. Niall had soon got wind of the lack of dealers in Tempest. Realising the fresh market potential, he had tried his hand there the weekend before and had shifted almost fifty pills and five grammes in ten minutes, before he had been rumbled and evicted forcefully from the club. That hadn't bothered Niall – he'd expected it – but then the doormen had pulled him round the back of the club, roughed him up and relieved him of his stash. Nearly two hundred pills and fifteen grammes of coke disappeared, poof, inside a pocket.

But the doormen hadn't called the cops, and, considering the amount he'd been carrying, that struck Niall as suspect. So he'd checked around. It hadn't taken long to find out that the Tempest hard men pulled the same stunt with any dealer they caught. So Niall had set up the meeting and sent Francie to call the club's bluff. They couldn't afford to be three grand down so soon into their new business venture. The doormen had to return either the stash or the money for it. If they didn't, Niall was going to make more trouble than they could handle.

Niall wasn't stupid, and he wasn't about to talk to them himself: they already knew his face, and he needed the club to believe there was a crew involved. Crews were dangerous, crews were feared – look at the West Side Crew, or the Finglas Posse. Nobody fucked with them. That was where Francie came in. The club would never know he was Niall's brother. It was genius.

Francie cleared his throat and spat again. He was growing ever more twitchy, and he dipped his hand into his pocket and gripped the Stanley carpet-cutter he always carried. If there was any trouble, he'd slash open the face of the first fucker that crossed him and run like the clappers. Francie had heard stories about the Tempest doormen. They were known as a hard bunch, but that didn't worry him unduly. He'd seen hard men before. They all looked the same when they were rolling round on the ground trying to hold their cheeks on.

At nine o'clock Francie heard the crunch of tyres over the rubble. He ducked down, dodging the arc of the headlights, and positioned himself behind a wall, where he could see who was coming to the meeting.

Three men climbed out of a black Cherokee jeep and glanced around. Two were obviously doormen, big and dressed in black from head to toe. The other man was older, slim and dressed in fancy clobber. Francie watched as he wrinkled his nose at his surroundings. That had to be the owner, York. Francie thought he looked like a queer. This would be even easier than he'd expected.

'So where is he?' York said. 'Come on, Davey, I haven't got all night. I thought you said he'd be here.'

Francie watched the two doormen exchange looks and grinned. They probably hated working for the guy. That was good too: they wouldn't be too eager to save his skin.

The bigger bouncer, the one Niall had told him to watch out for, shrugged and glanced at his watch. 'He'll be here,' he said with calm certainty.

Francie waited and watched them for another few minutes. Finally he took a deep breath and stepped out from behind the wall. The three men turned in his direction, and for a split second Francie got the distinct impression he should have stayed behind the wall. The moment passed.

'Oh, look,' the queer said, 'the rat's come out of its sewer.'

Francie nodded and tried to look braver than he felt. 'You Vinnie York?'

'Why, no, I'm Tom Cruise, slumming it for the day. Movie research. You know how it is – has to look authentic.'

Francie frowned. 'What?'

Vinnie stared at Francie's confused face and gave up any attempt at humour. It was clear the little shit was as thick as two short planks. 'Get over here, will you?'

Francie spat on the ground, puffed himself out and strolled across the waste ground towards them. 'What's the story, bud?'

'"What's the story?"' Vinnie mimicked perfectly. 'Move! I haven't got all fucking week.'

Despite himself, Francie picked up the pace a little. He noticed the doormen fanning out slightly, and he slipped his hand into his pocket and gripped the blade. If there was even a hint of trouble, he'd go for the big one first, gut him like a fish.

'You Vinnie York or what?'

The older man bowed deeply. 'I am. Now hurry up and tell me why you wanted to see me. And, *mon fils*, it had better be worth my trip down to this dump.'

Francie halted a few feet in front of the trio. 'All right, bud: I want what's mine.'

'I see.' Vinnie nodded and stroked his goatee. 'And that would be?'

Francie nodded at the doormen. 'Your mates here went and messed with the wrong fella last week. Took shit that didn't belong to them. We want it back.'

'Do you hear that, Davey?' Vinnie tapped his head doorman on the shoulder. '*Sacré bleu*, we messed with the wrong crowd. What would you say to that?'

'I'd say he's got some fuckin' nerve.' The big

76

man rolled a mean eye over Francie and cracked his knuckles.

Francie ran his tongue over his lips. He was aware that his legs trembled slightly, and he hoped it wasn't too noticeable. Niall had warned him to keep it tight, not to show fear. 'Think of Scarface,' Niall had said.

'I'm only tellin' yous the score. You messed with the wrong fuckin' crew last week.' He forced his voice to sound harder. Something about York's grin bothered him. 'Yous don't want to go messin' with this lot. They're hardcore.'

'What crew?'

Davey Clark began to laugh.

'The Darndale Devils,' Francie said, and immediately wished he had thought of a better name. Now the other bouncer was laughing too.

'You said "fella" a second ago, now it's "crew". Try to get your story straight, at least.' Vinnie smiled and folded his arms. He was beginning to enjoy himself.

Flustered, Francie tried again. 'Look, if you don't give the stuff back, then it's out of my hands. I have to go back to my boss and tell him yous want to go about this the hard way.'

'What hard way?' Vinnie said. He leaned one elbow on the bonnet of the jeep and raised an eyebrow.

Francie glared at him. Was this guy fucking simple? Time to play his trump card. He made an attempt at a sly smile, but somehow he couldn't pull it off. 'My boss knows yous don't report what you get to the cops. He knows you're keepin' the gear yourselves. So here's the sca: if you don't give his stash back pronto, you're gonna find all kinds of trouble knockin' on your bleedin' door.' He curled his upper lip in a perfect, much-practised sneer. 'Me boss has friends in the right places, you know what I mean, bud? He ain't gonna put up with no more shite. Either the gear's given back or he's gonna bust the fuckin' score wide open.'

There was absolute silence for all of about five seconds. Then Vinnie, Davey and the second doorman – Jason Healy, known as Jas – burst out laughing. They doubled over and howled.

Francie was so startled that he backed up a few steps, but his fright soon turned to humiliated fury. He bunched his hands into fists. 'Laugh all yous want, bastards! Yous'll be fuckin' sorry!'

Vinnie waved at the bouncers to quiet down. He pulled out a pristine handkerchief and dabbed at his eyes. This guy was too much. If his 'boss' had had that many friends, he wouldn't have sent this gobshite to do his talking for him.

'Oh my. And that's the situation, is it, *mon fils*?' Vinnie composed himself and refolded the handkerchief. 'That's what your *boss* says?'

'Yeah,' Francie snapped. 'That's what he says. It's no bleedin' laughin' matter, neither!'

Vinnie snorted a little. 'Oh, you're so right. Well, then, we'd better give him what he wants. Can't go making enemies in our line of work –

isn't that right, Davey?' Vinnie patted Davey on the back. 'The Darndale Devils…we don't need that kind of *merde*, do we?'

'We sure don't.' Davey smiled with such undiluted menace that Francie felt the hair on the back of his neck prickle.

Vinnie pushed himself off the jeep and walked towards Francie. 'This boss of yours – he wouldn't try and deal in my club again if I gave him his stash back, would he?'

Francie eyed Vinnie suspiciously. 'Nah, he wouldn't. He knows the score.'

Vinnie smiled and extended his hand. 'If that's the case, we must forget all this unpleasantness. Come, *mon ami*, shake on it. Your boss will get his gear back if he keeps his dealers out of my club, okay? I worked hard on that club, can't risk Tempest getting a reputation. You do understand that, don't you, dear?'

'Eh…sure.' Francie had already spent his share of the haul in his head. This had been so easy. He hadn't expected York to be such a pussy – but then, if the guy was a queer… Francie withdrew his hand from his pocket and offered it to Vinnie. He was surprised when Vinnie clamped his wrist in a vice-like grip and swung him around, into the waiting arms of Davey Clark.

'Hey! What the fuck—'

Davey punched him twice in the kidneys. Francie doubled over, and Jas stepped forward and kicked him square in the mouth. Francie

79

pinwheeled backwards and hit the deck hard. Davey grabbed him by the hair and dragged his head up. Francie groaned, coughed, tried to breathe and spit at the same time. The kick had split his lip open, and blood ran down his chin. One of his front teeth slipped underneath his tongue.

Vinnie loomed over him. With a deft movement, he slipped his hand into Francie's pocket and extracted the Stanley knife.

'Well, lookie here: this little kitty has claws.' Vinnie passed the knife back to Jas. 'You could have somebody's eye out with that, couldn't you, *Francie*?'

Through his pain, Francie's heart sank further. Vinnie York had called him by name; he knew who he was.

'Oh yes, indeedy-doody-deedy – very dangerous, playing with weapons you can't handle.' Vinnie squatted down on his hunkers to face him. A wave of overpowering aftershave rolled over Francie and his stomach flipped. He retched softly.

'You see,' Vinnie said, smiling pleasantly, 'I *know* your game, Francie. That fucking halfwit brother of yours – what the hell is his name?' He clicked his fingers twice. He knew the name perfectly.

'Niall,' Davey said.

'Ah, *merci* – Niall. He sent you along to tangle with us. That wasn't very nice, now was it?' Vinnie stretched out a hand and ruffled Francie's damp hair. 'Personally, I wouldn't send my brother out to fuck with someone on my behalf. You two mustn't get along.'

'Motherfucker...don't know what you're talking about,' Francie said blurrily. His tongue flapped over his thickening lip. The tooth dribbled out and landed on his chest. Francie stared at it in dismay.

'Sure you do.' Vinnie smiled and leaned in closer. 'Your brother, Niall, was selling in my club. Davey here caught him and confiscated his gear, and now the little prick wants it back. So, instead of cutting your losses, you come down here and threaten *me* with going to the cops – which, in fairness, Francie, we both know is bullshit.' Vinnie tilted his head. 'How am I doing so far?'

'Fuck...you.' Francie struggled to get to his feet. Davey pushed him back down easily.

'Oh Francie, Francie.' Vinnie laughed. 'Don't be like that. I understand where you're coming from. It's hard to make a living these days, *n'est-ce pas*? Worse if you lose your gear. Oh, trust *moi*, the irony isn't lost.' Vinnie smiled and tilted his head. 'You boys must be pretty desperate. You're taking a lot of risk for a few bags of charlie and some pills, wouldn't you say?'

Francie listened to Vinnie's calm, reasonable voice and felt a new form of fear. He had expected anger, and he had expected threats, but this shit... He wished he'd brought some back-up. He wished he had a crew. He wished Niall had come with him. Niall would know what to do. Niall wouldn't be afraid of this guy.

Vinnie stood up and brushed at the knees of his trousers. 'Francie, lad, let me tell you something about business, something that will stand to you in the years to come. Davey, let him up, will you?'

Davey released his grip on Francie's hair, grabbed him by the scruff of the neck and hauled him up onto his feet.

'*Merci*, Davey.'

Davey grunted.

'You see, Francie' – Vinnie stretched his arms wide – 'business is like nature. It's all about the survival of the fittest. Now, I know you're probably thinking that's an old cliché, but you've got to admit, sometimes the old clichés are valid.' Vinnie smiled. Expensively capped teeth shone in the half-light from a distant street lamp. Francie watched him and wished more fervently than ever that he had stayed behind the wall.

'Now, take me – what would I be, Davey?'

'A lion.' Davey had heard this routine a hundred times before. He hated it, thought all this waffle was stupid, but Vinnie loved the sound of his own voice.

'Right.' Vinnie's smile broadened. 'So I'm the lion, king of the jungle. And you, Francie, you are a cat, a raggedy little alley cat. You can kill birds and chase mice, but if you stray onto a lion's patch, what do you think the lion will do? Hmm?'

Francie blinked slowly. His head was fuzzy and his back ached where Davey had punched him. He was desperately trying to draw breath down into his lungs. He knew he would puke if he didn't, and he didn't want to puke in front of this man.

Vinnie frowned and clicked his fingers impatiently in front of Francie's bloodied face. 'I'm not talking Latin, am I, Francie? I know your limited brain is probably struggling right now, but you understand English, don't you?'

Francie narrowed his eyes. He wasn't sure what Vinnie York wanted him to say. A single thought sounded in his skank-addled brain, and his swollen lips formed that one thought: 'You're a fuckin' headcase.'

Behind him, Davey Clarke sighed. Now he'd done it. Why couldn't people nod and get it over with? Why did they always act the hard man? A fucking dog could tell that Vinnie York wasn't playing with a full deck.

Vinnie's jaw tightened, and he took a step closer to Francie. 'I don't know. You try to teach people something, and all you get is abuse. It's simple, you fucking philistine. I'm the lion and you're the cat, right?'

'All right, man – fuckin' chill.' Francie spat more blood and tried to keep from crying. 'You're the fuckin' lion.'

'Good. Now you, little pussy, should have kept to hunting in your own back yard and not come meowing and creepy-crawling into *my* jungle.' To

Francie's dazed horror, Vinnie York curled his hands into claws and pretended to stalk around. 'Little pussies shouldn't take on bigger prey, Francie. You know that, right?'

'Yeah, whatever. Listen, man—'

'No, *you* fucking listen.' Vinnie lunged forwards with lightning speed and grabbed Francie by the throat. 'I'm not finished, you little cocksucker, and I *so* hate to be interrupted. That club is my jungle. You think I have time for this shit? You think I don't have bigger problems? Don't fucking mess with the lion, Francie. I have big fucking teeth, and I see all. Those sisters of yours, the little blonde bitches with the big tits – I can have them picked up. I can gobble you up. Rarrrr!'

Francie swivelled, breaking free from Davey's grip on his neck. He knew he had to get as far away from Vinnie as he could. If he ever got out of this, he would kick Niall in the nuts for sending him here. This guy was stone crazy. His brother had sent him to deal with a basket case.

'All right! Keep your fuckin' hair on!' Francie backed up as fast as he could. 'Stay the fuck away from me. You're crazy, man. Off the wall.'

Vinnie accepted this assessment of his character with surprising good grace. 'I am a little erratic, I admit, Francie, but I have problems – oh, *mon ami*, problems like you wouldn't believe. I don't have the *time* to waste on these matters. I need you to understand me when I say my club is off limits.'

'Whatever. Stick your club up your arse.' Francie was almost crying. He could feel the tears burning at the back of his eyes. He wanted to go, badly.

Vinnie threw up his hands in mock horror. 'Francie, darling! Why so sullen? Don't tell me you're scared, are you? Davey, do you think Francie understands my position?'

Davey shrugged. 'Dunno.' Jas advanced on Francie, unnoticed.

'I didn't think so either,' Vinnie said sadly. 'It's such a shame when it comes to this.'

Francie edged further away. If he could make it to the wall, he'd hop over it and run all the way home. Fuck the gear, and fuck Niall too. If he wanted it that badly, let *him* come down here and ask—

'Francie, I'm not finished with you yet.' Vinnie clicked his fingers.

Jas stepped forward and twisted Francie's left arm behind his back. When Francie struggled, he bent back his little finger to breaking point. Francie stopped struggling.

Vinnie looked almost apologetic. 'Francie, baby, the lion doesn't squeak, the lion roars. The lion can't let the pussycat piss all over his territory and walk off – oh, no. The lion must be seen to be *active*, otherwise every fucking tomcat within a ten-mile radius will be all over his patch. Do you understand what I'm trying to say, Francie?'

Francie nodded vigorously, because Jas had

applied even more pressure to his finger, and because Davey was smiling. He was sweating, despite the cold. He tasted bile in his throat and swallowed. 'I'll sort it. I'll say it to my brother. I swear on me ma's life. He won't go near your place again. None of us will. I *swear*!'

Vinnie looked over his shoulder and winked at Davey. 'Do you hear that, Davey? He *swears*.'

'I heard.'

'Francie…' Vinnie leaned in closer. For the rest of his miserable life, Francie would tremble violently whenever he caught a whiff of Aramis. 'Francie, I don't think you're a bad lad – I don't want you thinking that. It pains me that you should have a bad opinion of me, really, it does. It's so unfortunate it has to come to this.' Vinnie nodded his head.

Jas snapped Francie's finger. Francie screamed, high and long, a scream that stopped abruptly when Vinnie hit him in the throat with the side of his hand.

Ten minutes later, Davey hauled the barely conscious Francie across the waste ground and manoeuvred him into an upright position against a crumbling wall. If someone happened to pass, they'd think it was just another junkie skagging out. He did a quick search of the kid and found his mobile phone. Davey examined it. It was a good phone, probably hot and worth a bit of money. Davey flipped open the back and pulled out the SIM card. He pocketed the phone and flung the card far into the sludgy waters of the canal, where it sank with barely a ripple.

Vinnie squatted down and cupped Francie's battered face in his hand. Francie's eyelids flickered. He groaned once and, as far gone as he was, tried to roll away.

'I'm glad we had this little chat, Francie. Now, make sure you explain to that prick of a brother: no dealing in my club, not now, not ever. And Francie, if you try to create trouble, your sisters will be the next family members I talk to. Somehow I doubt they are as tough as you.'

Francie slipped down the wall onto his side. His breathing was loud and uneven, whistling through his broken teeth. He batted feebly at Vinnie. 'Please...'

Vinnie sighed and shook his head. 'Davey, hand me that blade of his.'

Davey took the Stanley knife from his pocket and passed it over. Vinnie bounced it up and down in the palm of his hand. 'This reminds me of a scene from *Crocodile Dundee*, Francie. You remember that film? You know that part when he's being mugged and they threaten him with a knife, and he pulls out his own? He says, "Call that a knife? *This* is a knife."' Vinnie put the Stanley knife on the ground, reached into his pocket and pulled out a long, pearl-handled straight razor. 'That's not a knife. *This* is a knife, Francie.'

He slashed Francie across the face twice, opening him up from just under his left eye to his chin. Francie shrieked and raised his broken fingers to protect his face, too late. Dark blood ran down over his jaw and dripped onto the frozen ground beneath him. Francie saw it and began to make a strange keening sound.

'Stop that noise, would you, Davey?'

Davey punched Francie hard in the side of the head. Francie slumped. He tried to lift his hand to his face again, but passed out before he reached it. The blood began to pool under him.

Vinnie stood up, tossed the Stanley blade into the canal and wiped his razor on Francie's back. He gave him one last pitying look, turned and walked back to the jeep.

Davey followed him. 'Why did you cut his face like that? He was gone, man.'

Vinnie sighed, pulled out his handkerchief and wiped blood from his hands. 'Do you watch the National Geographic Channel, Davey?'

Davey shook his head.

Vinnie stuffed his hanky into his breast pocket. 'I'll bet Francie doesn't either. You should – it's very educational.'

Davey nodded. He hadn't a clue what Vinnie was on about.

'I'm merely marking my territory, Davey – marking it for all to see.'

'Oh.'

'Come on, Davey boy.' Vinnie draped an arm over Davey's shoulders. 'The airport awaits, and things are...well, things are never as bad as they seem.' He paused and glanced down. 'By the way, I meant to ask earlier: do you think these shoes go with this suit? They're hand-made, you know.'

'Yeah, nice.' Davey looked down at the shoes. They were black leather. He couldn't tell if they were any different from the shoes Vinnie normally wore. 'Classy.'

'Thank you, Davey.' Vinnie smiled and got into the back of the jeep.

Davey climbed in and started the engine. Jason was in the passenger seat, cleaning blood from his steel-toed boots with a baby-wipe. Vinnie pulled out his mobile and called the club to check how many complimentary passes had been allocated for that night. Davey glanced at him in the rear-view mirror, listening to the calm, controlled way Vinnie spoke, as if he hadn't a care in the world. No doubt about it: Vinnie York was the wrong man to cross.

6

Forty minutes later, Vinnie waited in the harsh light of the arrivals hall, leaning against an advertisement for a Howth fish shop and cleaning a streak of dried blood from under his nails with a toothpick. He was humming 'I'm Every Woman' under his breath. On the surface he was the very model of composure, but underneath his nerves twanged like stretched catgut.

It had been a long time since he and the old man had had a face-to-face meeting. Patrick thought it was better that way: no one could connect them if they never shared the same room, breathed the same air. In truth, the arrangement suited Vinnie too. He disliked Patrick, and he got the distinct feeling that the sentiment was mutual.

A group of passengers came flocking through the arrival doors. Vinnie scanned their bags, noted they had flown in from Amsterdam and straightened up. He fidgeted with his sleeves and stood on tiptoe, his eyes roaming over the sea of weary faces. All around him, people hugged and gave excited whoops of delight – families reunited, loved ones claiming back their own. An overweight woman in a lime-green sweater jostled him as she swept past with more suitcases than she could manage. Vinnie elbowed her hard in the nearer of her massive tits. She yelped and jerked away, giving him a confused, disbelieving look. 'Hey!'

Vinnie ignored her. It was typical of Patrick to refuse to be collected by one of his men. He liked playing top dog, liked having Vinnie at his beck and call. Time obviously hadn't mellowed the old bastard out completely.

'Hey!' the woman repeated in a heavy Dutch accent. 'You did that on purpose.' Vinnie stared at her, without expression, until she grew fearful and backed away.

Seconds later, he caught sight of his father walking swiftly in his direction.

Vinnie was slightly irked to see that Patrick looked remarkably well. Although he was pushing sixty, Patrick York trained in a gym three times a week and was careful to the point of obsession about what he ate. His shoulders did not slouch, and as far as Vinnie could see his body looked as hard and uncompromising as ever. Patrick wore dark trousers, a knee-length leather jacket and a flat cap pulled down low over his eyes. He was an inch and a half shorter than Vinnie, but he wore two-inch-heeled cowboy boots, which gave him the edge. He carried a plain black leather sports bag in his left hand, a newspaper in the right; he was travelling light. Vinnie liked his new nose – it was so good, it had to have cost a bundle – and something else about him was different, too, but Vinnie couldn't put his finger on it. All the money in the world couldn't change Patrick's eyes, though. The eyes remained the same, cold blue chips constantly scanning the surroundings, alert to all forms of danger.

Vinnie fixed a smile on his face, moved forward and extended his hand. 'Good flight?'

Patrick didn't answer or break stride. He grabbed Vinnie above the elbow and spun him around, forcing Vinnie to wheel on his heels to keep his balance. 'Any word?'

Formalities over, Vinnie allowed Patrick to hustle him along. 'Ah, no. But like I told you on the phone, I have everyone looking—'

'Kelpie?'

'No. Davey checked his room. Everything is exactly the way it—'

'Get Naughton on the blower, tell him I want to see him in an hour.' A fat cigar seemed to materialise from thin air. Patrick jammed it into the corner of his mouth with his bag hand. 'Car outside?'

Vinnie pried Patrick's fingers off his arm. This was another annoyance: Patrick would not use or enter a car park, not even in a busy place like Dublin Airport. He had been stabbed in the ribs in an underground car park in Holland, back in '97. The blade had missed his aorta by the smallest margin and kept him in hospital for four months. It pained Vinnie to think how close he had come to being an orphan. If only the assailant had taken more time to steady his hand. And Vinnie had paid the useless fool his money up front – money that he had no hope of reclaiming, since the failed hitman was now buried deep under the foundations of an apartment block near Kilmainham.

'Parked right outside, as per orders.'

Patrick eyed a 'No Smoking' sign with disgust and chomped down hard on the cigar. 'This fucking country! Right, let's get out of here.'

'I have a suite booked at the Burlington. I hope you'll—'

'*Suite*? Fuck that shit. I'll kip at your place for a few days. I'm not going to be here long enough for hotels.' Patrick glanced at him. 'I don't see you ringing Naughton. What's wrong, don't have a phone?'

Vinnie glanced at his watch, his brain scrambling. He hadn't expected Patrick to want to stay with him. 'You want to ring Naughton right away?'

Patrick switched the cigar to the other side of his mouth with his tongue. 'What am I, talking fucking Swahili? Yeah, get him now. Tell him to meet us at your gaff, and tell him I want to see him alone. Make sure he doesn't bring the other cunt. I don't want that bent bollocks to know I'm here. If I see him, I'll cut the fucking eyes out of his head.'

Vinnie pulled his lips into a thin line. 'I need to stop off at the club to see—'

'Fuck the club.' Patrick glared at his son

angrily. 'Five years it took me to open a line with the Turks. Five long fucking years of piss-small deals and arse-licking.' He shook his head and bit his cigar so hard it began to crumble around his teeth. 'You think they're gonna wait another week for their money? Think they're *all right* with this fucking situation?'

'Well, I've had some pretty pissed-off buyers calling me, too—'

'They won't pull your spine out through your arse, though, will they?'

'No.' Vinnie pulled his mobile from his pocket. 'I'll call Naughton.'

The electric doors parted with a gentle swoosh. Patrick stalked outside and rolled a cold eye over the people and taxis, his ears adapting to the familiar accents. He'd sworn many years before that he would never set foot in Ireland again, and look where he was: back in the fucking hole from which he'd fled.

Where the hell was Kelpie?

He glanced over at his son and noted Vinnie's expression of barely contained hostility. They were not close. Vinnie displayed none of the fierce loyalty Patrick had witnessed over the years between Turkish fathers and their boys. Those boys would take a bullet for their old men. Vinnie would be more likely to put one in him. Not that it was completely the lad's fault. Patrick hadn't been involved with much of Vinnie's upbringing, having had to go on the lam while the lad was still only a nipper. But he'd sent money back and paid for the kid to be watched over, long after his wife, God rest her, had passed on. It hadn't been his fault the foster family had treated the lad badly. Shit, he'd done his best. Still, Patrick knew Vinnie regarded him as a father in name only. And that made him as dangerous as a cornered rat.

Patrick chewed on his unlit cigar. The Turks were more than edgy. If he didn't recover the gear, he would have to make restitution, and that left them back at square one – worse: ten years of business would go down the fucking Swanee. The club would have to go, and their apartments and their cars and whatever other luxuries they had acquired over the last decade. The Turks wouldn't accept less than the wholesale price. And he could pay them everything and still wind up floating face-down in the Singel Canal.

Patrick glanced at his son, taking in the Tag Heuer watch and the suit that had probably cost more than three grand. Vinnie would not like the alternative to his current standard of living. 'Where's the car?'

Vinnie inclined his head towards the jeep. Patrick followed his gaze and squinted. A hulking shadow moved behind the steering-wheel.

'There's someone in it.'

'It's Davey. He's driving.'

'I told you to keep my visit on the QT! What is this shit? If I wanted a fucking welcoming committee, I'd have fucking asked!'

Vinnie opened his mouth, but before he had a chance to protest, Patrick strode away, muttering obscenities under his breath.

Incensed, Vinnie trotted to catch up. 'Davey's not a mouth! You know that! *Mon dieu,* he's like a brother to me.'

'Well, he ain't your brother. I don't know nothing about the cunt, except that he's stuck to your side like a fucking growth.'

Davey got out of the jeep and acknowledged Patrick with a nod, nothing more. Patrick grunted and passed him the bag. Davey took it without any obvious attitude and put it into the boot, then climbed back into the driver's seat. Patrick got into the back, leaving Vinnie the front seat. Davey glanced at him once in the rear-view mirror and glanced away.

Patrick stared at the back of Davey's shaven head and listened to his son talk to Naughton's wife. Less than ten minutes in the country, and already his unease was crippling. Patrick wasn't pleased that Davey was constantly around, wasn't pleased that he said nothing but heard everything. He wasn't pleased that Davey Clarke knew he was in Dublin so soon. He wasn't pleased that Vinnie had ignored his explicit instructions. He wasn't pleased that Vinnie was obviously as high as a kite. He chomped hard on his cigar and glared out the window at the city of his birth, a city he had prayed he'd never clap eyes on again.

★

By the time Edward Naughton entered Vinnie's penthouse two hours later, Patrick's humour had not improved. He had been on the phone since he got to Vinnie's place, tracking down old contacts and putting out feelers in the 'community'. With a shipment as large as his, someone had to have heard something. Someone had to be in the market. It was a simple plan: find the buyer, find the supplier, break the supplier's neck. Regain the shipment. Sell it. Pay the Turks. Simple.

And yet, as Patrick paced across the pale marble floor of Vinnie's sitting room, a dull ache had settled deep in his spine, as if the weight of his responsibilities were grinding his bones to dust. He fought against the rising tide of panic. If only the Turks hadn't taken Anouk, his lover, hostage; if only he had had the good sense to hide her when he had first learned of the cocaine going missing. But he had been in a state of shock. He hadn't been thinking. Kelpie wouldn't have betrayed him. He didn't believe it for a second.

Naughton, on the other hand…Naughton was a different matter. Patrick glanced at him, noting that he was sweating heavily. He was a big man physically, both broad and tall, but where Patrick was fit and lean, Naughton was a prime candidate for an early heart attack. His huge belly – the result of too many steak dinners washed down with double cognacs in expensive restaurants – strained against the buttons of his shirt. He had an expensive mistress and a high standard of living, and even though he made good money with his construction company, he attracted attention from the Inland Revenue and other sources. Patrick had been planning to get rid of him – he was too much of a liability. Maybe Naughton had got wind of that fact; maybe that was why Patrick's biggest consignment had simply vanished into thin air and his right-hand man was nowhere to be found.

Patrick watched Edward hover at the living-room door, smoothing his tie nervously. He wore an extra chin like a scarf under his florid face. Even his once-magnetic green eyes had sunk deep into twin balloons of shining flesh. He disgusted Patrick.

They had been friends once. They had grown up on the same streets, chased the same girls, played knick-knack and smoked their first fags together – soggy-tipped Carrolls filched from Patrick's old man's packet when he came back from the pub for a kip. They had a shared history, a shared business. But money always changed people's loyalties. If Ed was involved in this, then he had signed his own death warrant.

'You look a bit hot there, Ed. Why don't you sit down, take a load off?'

Normally Naughton was the life and soul of the party. He liked a laugh and liked to play the lord of the manor. He cultivated the image of a poor boy made good, a hard-working philanthropist willing to be a shining example to the weaker man. He honestly believed that every man he met envied him and every woman found her knickers wet from the waves of his charm. But at that moment Edward Naughton was feeling less than comfortable. The roof of his mouth was sawdust-dry and his shirt was stuck to the small of his back. He stopped a few feet inside Vinnie's sitting room and fidgeted with the large gold ring he wore on his pinky. When his wife had got hold of him and passed on the message that there was a problem and the 'foreman' wanted to see him, his stomach had flipped.

'I said sit down.' Patrick lifted his glass in a mock toast.

'Patrick, I...I can't believe you're here.'

'Me neither.'

'It's good to see you.'

'No, it ain't. It's very fucking bad to see me. You seeing me means there's a fucking problem.'

Vinnie slouched in a black recliner, holding a flute of champagne to his lips, and watched Naughton. The man repulsed him, from the top of his greasy head to the soles of his ugly brown shoes. He reminded him of a lizard. Vinnie would have liked nothing more than to open his patio doors and hurl the fat fuck six floors to his death. He probably would have done it if he hadn't believed that Naughton knew where the cocaine was. There was no point in killing the bastard until they had the delivery back. There'd always be time for that later.

'Well...' Edward tried to look calm, but his

voice failed him: it was pitched several octaves higher than normal. 'I don't know what else I can tell you.'

'My boy here called you hours ago.'

'I came as soon as I got your message. I was in Waterford on a—'

'You kept me waiting here like a prick.' Patrick crossed to the curved, stainless steel bar. 'I don't like waiting, Ed. It makes me nervous.' He filled his own glass and another tumbler with hefty splashes of Jim Beam and chucked two ice cubes into each glass. He left his own drink on the counter and carried the other over to Naughton.

Edward's skin looked grey and sickly. He spread his hands wide. 'Patrick, I—'

'Here, have a drink. How's the missus – she holding up all right? Heard the kid is missing.'

Edward reached for the glass. As he took it, Patrick slapped him across the side of the face.

Edward dropped the glass and reeled back in shock. Patrick advanced on him, slapping him about the head and neck. The blows weren't hard, but Edward covered his head with his hands and shrieked like a woman. Enraged by the noise, Patrick swung one fist upwards and caught Edward flush on the cheekbone. Edward tumbled backwards as though he'd been struck by a mallet.

'Think you can leave me waiting around, Eddie? Do you?' Patrick's face was red with rage. 'Think I've nothing better to do than sit here sweating fucking gallstones?'

Edward rolled over onto one elbow and looked at him imploringly. 'Patrick—'

Patrick slapped him on the ear. 'What the fuck happened, Eddie? Huh? What the fuck happened to the gear?'

'I don't know! You've got to believe me! I didn't – I don't—'

'Where's Kelpie?

'*I don't* know!'

'You telling me you didn't see him?' Patrick drove the sentence home with a kick towards Edward's ribs. He missed, but Edward still screeched as though he'd been shot. 'You telling me he drowned?'

'No, I swear. The car was still at the pick-up point, but I know he came in – I know he did!'

Vinnie eyed the spilled bourbon spreading across the floor towards one of his hand-printed angora rugs. He put his drink down and got out of his chair. Much as he despised Naughton, he could see no use in battering the fat bastard unconscious – not on his floors, anyway. He glided across the room and inserted himself between the two panting men. 'This is pointless.'

Patrick glanced at Edward's teary face, swore softly and whirled away. He strode back to the bar and upended his drink in one long swallow.

Naughton wiped at his face with shaking hands. He rolled over onto his ample arse and struggled to his feet. Vinnie didn't offer to help.

'Why did you do that?'

Vinnie stared at him, disgusted to hear tears and self-pity in the man's voice.

'You think I had anything to do with what happened?' Edward stepped forward, wringing his hands. 'I don't know any more than you do. I waited for the call, same as you. It didn't come. I drove down to the beach to pick up the ski myself. It wasn't there. But I saw the tracks. It definitely came ashore.'

'Funny, your kid being missing too.'

Edward jerked upright. 'What do you mean?'

'I said it's funny how your kid's gone walk-about right now.' Patrick refilled his glass and glared at Edward. 'Out of harm's way.'

'I don't know where she is! I'm worried sick about her. And I don't know what happened to the cocaine, but I think it was an inside job, all right. Definitely.' Edward shook his head warily, but his eyes strayed involuntarily to Vinnie. 'It has to be someone who knew about the operation.'

'What are you looking at me for?' Vinnie took a step towards him and jabbed him in the shoulder. 'Eh? What are you looking at me for?'

Edward cringed. 'I'm not saying it was you, I'm just saying someone has to know something.'

'It wasn't my idea to use the coast for operations,' Vinnie snarled. 'Or to send fucking Kelpie out like a fucking surfer.'

Patrick snorted. 'No, that was my idea. It's too much gear to risk Customs nabbing it at the ports. We've brought it in by the coast before, you

102

ungrateful bollocks. You heard about the warehouse in Blanch getting raided, didn't you? I didn't see you whinging when the last three deliveries got though all right.'

'Why would I whinge if it gets through?' Vinnie snapped back. '*Mon dieu!* The other deliveries were shit compared to this one, and what do we have now? Nothing, zip, *rien de rien.*'

'Vincent, shut it. All that French crap is upsetting my fucking stomach.' Patrick dropped into the nearest armchair. The last week had sucked the life out of him, and he was reaching the end of his tether. He took another sip of his drink and glanced at his friend. For a moment he felt a twinge of sympathy. Eddie looked terrible. Maybe the kid really was missing. Maybe it was all unconnected.

But then a more powerful image entered his mind: Aziz Dinmuher, that one-eyed Turkish freak, holding a serrated hunting knife against Anouk's pale, beautiful throat, her liquid brown eyes blinking in pain and shock. It reminded Patrick that he didn't have time to waste on sympathy.

He waggled his empty glass at Vinnie. If he didn't find the merchandise soon, he might as well drink himself into a stupor. Maybe that way he wouldn't feel the pain so badly when Aziz finished with Anouk and came looking for him. Maybe it wouldn't hurt so much when he was gutted like a piece of fish.

'Ed, we're going to go over everything again.' Patrick belched softly and patted his chest. 'Vinnie, get him a drink. Eddie, sit down. Go from the beginning and leave nothing out.'

Edward eased his bulk onto a velvet chaise longue. Vinnie filled two fresh glasses and thrust one at him. 'Here.'

Edward accepted the fresh bourbon with shaking hands and gulped some down. 'It's not much, Patrick. I've tried everyone I know, and I've got nothing.'

'Tell me anyway.'

Edward wiped his chin and told Patrick everything he knew.

7

John collected Sarah from outside her apartment building on Patrick Street at eleven the next morning to drive the forty-six miles to Ashley Naughton's family home. It was a clear, bright winter day, and as the city fell away and the dual carriageway opened up before him, John put his foot down, enjoying the speed and power of the Manta as she cruised easily down the motorway.

'Do you want to get us arrested? Slow down and stop driving like an idiot.' Sarah fidgeted with her seat belt. 'You can't afford any more penalty points on your licence.'

John sighed and slowed down. Another simple pleasure shot down. This morning Sarah was as cranky as a cat with a clothes peg on its tail.

'Do you know where we're going exactly?' John asked.

Sarah unfolded the road map on her lap and studied it. 'We drive down to a pub called Jack White's, take the first left and follow that road for another two miles, then take another left and the house should be a couple of hundred yards in on the right.' She refolded the map and stuffed it into

105

the glove compartment. 'The house is called Claremont. Look out for big black gates with lions on either side.'

'Lions?'

'Yeah, lions.'

John switched lanes to overtake a guy talking on his mobile. 'Jack White's…isn't that the pub where your woman had the husband shot in a fake robbery?'

'Yeah.'

'Maybe we'll stop off for a pint of Bloodweiser on the way back.'

Sarah shook her head and looked out the window.

John scowled. She used to laugh at his crap jokes. Come to think of it, she used to *make* the odd joke. He glanced at her pale, drawn face, her shadowed eyes fastened on the hills and greenery of Wicklow.

He'd known her almost all his life. Their families had lived four streets apart in Clontarf – not the posh part, but a good part. A year older than Sarah, John had nonetheless found time in primary school to pull her hair and blast the ball at her really hard whenever she was in goal during big break. By the time they'd progressed to secondary – he to the Brothers, she to the Holy Faith Convent – they were friends, in a way, or at least they knew a lot of the same crowd. They had shared the same bus into town, making eye contact, smiling and nodding – only he sat down the back with the cool guys, smoking fags and shouting out the grimy windows, acting the hard lad, while she sat up front with her girlfriends, whispering and giggling about whatever it was teenage girls whispered and giggled about.

When Sarah passed her Leaving Cert and got into college to study art and design, she maintained her ties with local friends. She didn't suddenly become a knob, like a lot of other college nerds John knew. He'd always admired that about her, her sense of loyalty. He'd retaken the Leaving, scraped through the second time round and got his first full-time job in Fitzsimmons', a local bar. Sarah drank there on Friday nights with a band of screeching, catcalling mates. It was around then that he began to look at her as more than just a girl he knew. She wasn't like the other girls. She was quieter, more thoughtful, and she had a way of tilting her head when you spoke to her, as though she was really listening, as if you were the only person on the planet. And, of course, she had blossomed into a real looker.

One Friday evening at closing time, he plucked up the courage to ask her out, prepared to be sarky if she said no. He was mentally practising his put-down when she looked at him with her deep brown eyes and surprised him by saying yes.

They had dated for almost a year and a half – and they had, despite huge differences in opinions and manner, been pretty happy. Right up until the night Sarah came down to the pub to surprise him and caught him rolling around the car park with a blonde barmaid. John had thought of theirs as a damn good relationship.

Sarah had dumped him faster than you could say 'cheating bollocks'. And despite his many pathetic attempts to woo her back, she remained aloof and disinterested. If she happened to run into him she was frosty as a glacier, but always polite. John wondered if she had ever really felt anything for him, convinced himself she hadn't and began to act like he was the wounded one.

Three months after they'd split up, Sarah dropped out of college and left to work for a textile firm in Manchester. In less than a year, she had disappeared off the map altogether. John made some minor inquiries, but nobody really knew where she was or why she didn't come home any more. As time went by with no sign of her, there were the usual rumours, especially in the local: she'd joined a cult, had a drug problem, was a lesbian. John didn't buy any of it, but unfortunately the rumours were all he had to go on. The people who could have enlightened him, like Sarah's older sisters, wouldn't give him the time of day. Helen – the oldest, and the bitchiest – threatened to do him physical harm if he ever asked her about Sarah again. John figured they had probably heard about the barmaid incident.

Sarah had been in England five years when her father died. Old man Kenny died as he'd lived, blind drunk and probably too far gone to feel a thing. He'd taken a lift home from the Submarine Bar on the back of a Honda 50 motorbike driven by an equally drunken friend. The bike never made it round the first corner. Bystanders reported that Mr Kenny's head had split like an overripe tomato on the poorly surfaced road. 'Mangy' Benjy Moxley, the driver of the ill-fated Honda, sustained no injury, serious or otherwise: he was found flat on his back under a rhododendron bush in the front garden of a nearby house, snoring gently, a crushed cigarette still dangling from his lips. The responding Garda reported that when they finally got him awake, Moxley refused to believe them when they told him that he'd been in a crash.

As is often the way with men like him, Anthony Kenny – who, in life, had been regarded as a shitebag – in death swiftly became a pillar of the community. The funeral was huge; St Michael's Church was packed. John Quigley was seated three rows back in the side aisle when he caught sight of his ex-girlfriend. He would never have known it was Sarah if she hadn't been flanked on either side by her sisters, Jackie and Helen.

Sarah had looked a shadow of her former self. Her long dark hair lay limp and ragged down her back, and she was deathly pale. As John watched, she slipped forward in her seat, resting her forehead on the heels of her hands. Jackie grabbed Sarah gently by the shoulders, whispering in her ear, trying to straighten her up. John looked at her hollow cheeks and gaunt frame and wondered if the stories about drugs were really so far-fetched after all.

Sarah looked dazed, as if she had been sedated. She huddled in her oversized black coat for the whole ceremony, her head bowed as though the effort of lifting it was simply too much. Occasionally Jackie and Helen exchanged worried glances behind her back. Jackie leaned in again and put her arm over Sarah's shoulders, murmuring softly in her ear, but Sarah didn't respond. The only sign that she was aware of them was when she edged slowly along the seat, away from Jackie's anxious concern.

John lost sight of Sarah after the service, but when he reached the graveyard he searched for her. He found her standing near the now-empty hearse, listening, dead-eyed, as a drinking buddy of her father's bent her ear about what a great man Anthony Kenny had been. John was pushing his way through the mourners to reach her when Helen Kenny grabbed his arm with vice-like fingers and shoved him behind a moss-covered headstone. Over her shoulder, John saw Jackie rescue Sarah from the barfly mourner and steer her through the crowd, like a schoolteacher hauling an errant kid in from the yard.

'Don't you even *think* about it,' Helen whispered in a voice that could strip bark from a tree. 'You stay the fuck away from her, John Quigley.'

John tried to turn his head away, but Helen

moved directly in front of him. Her dark eyes, so like Sarah's, blazed with red-hot hatred.

'What's wrong with her?'

'Our father's dead, you stupid shite. What do you think's wrong with her?'

'Jaysus, Helen, I only want to talk to her. Pay my respects.'

'Your *respect*? What respect have you ever shown her?'

People glanced their way. Helen fixed a strained smile on her face and lowered her voice. 'Look, the last person she wants to talk to is you, get it? You've done enough damage to her, you fucker.'

John stared at Helen. 'Did she say that? Or are you talking for her now?'

Helen tightened her grip on John's arm. 'You're a waster, Quigley – always were, always will be. Stay away from my kid sister. Got it?' She released him and stepped back, her face white with anger, her dark hair whipping wildly about her head. Behind her, the graveyard was filled with mourners eager to bury her father and get to the nearest pub. 'Don't make things any worse. I'm warning you.'

Then Helen turned on her heel and marched away to stand by her mother, who was watching John with a puzzled expression, as if she couldn't quite place him. Jackie and Sarah were nowhere to be seen. And that was the last he'd seen of Sarah Kenny for another fifteen months.

Then, one quiet night while John was drying

glasses and watching reruns of *Friends* on the bar's wall-mounted portable, the side door opened and Sarah walked in and sat down at the counter.

John blinked in surprise. 'What can I get you?'

She didn't look friendly, but neither did she look hostile. She didn't remove her coat or even unbutton it. 'Baileys on ice.' The years in England had changed her voice. Her accent was still Irish, but it had lost some of its soft Dublin burr.

John poured the drink, studying her while he fussed with ice cubes. She looked different – still too thin and pale, but more together. Her hair had been cut to just below her shoulders and shone glossy under the dim bar lights. Her cheeks had lost the sunken shadows that had shocked him at the funeral.

Aware that she was watching him, he set the drink down in front of her and searched for his usual line of blather. For once he came up empty-handed.

'How much do I owe you?' She made no move to extract any money.

'Nothing; my shout.' John leaned against the counter, aware that he was grinning at her like a slack-jawed idiot and incapable of doing anything about it.

'Thanks.' Sarah took a sip and looked around the smoky room, taking in the ripped cloth on the pool table, the wood-look wallpaper and scuffed tables and reused beer mats. John followed her eyes, suddenly ashamed of his surroundings. That made him angry enough to talk.

'You home for a holiday or what?' He injected a level of disinterest into his voice.

She shook her head. 'No, I'm back for good.'

'Yeah? That right?'

'Yes.'

For some inexplicable reason, this delighted John. He beamed again. 'So what are you doing? You got a job lined up and shit?'

'Nothing yet.' Sarah took another sip of her drink and shrugged. 'Maybe I'll reapply for college. I've got a bit of money saved, so I'm not in that much of a rush. Something will turn up.'

'Yeah, sure it will.' John wiped at a non-existent mark on the bar. He couldn't decide if she wanted to talk to him or not. But why would she be here if she didn't? 'Listen, I never got a chance to tell you – I'm sorry about your dad. I remember when my old man passed on. It took ages—'

'I heard about that. I'm sorry I couldn't come home for it. He was a wonderful man.' She lifted her head then and looked him straight in the eye, and for a moment John felt his heart lurch: she looked so vulnerable, and at the same time so angry. The words dried up in his mouth.

'Well, you know what I mean,' he finished lamely. 'I'm sorry too, okay?'

'Okay.'

'Sorry for everything.' He wasn't sure what he was apologising for, but something passed between them.

'Thank you.' Sarah's mouth twitched slightly. 'So, you still in the bar trade, then?' She waved a hand around the dingy pub, changing the subject quickly. 'You must like it.'

John admitted something that he had only recently begun to realise himself. 'It's all right, but I can't see myself sticking at it much longer.'

'No? What are you going to do?'

John picked up a mouldy dishcloth and began to twirl it in his fingers. 'Don't know.'

Sarah raised one eyebrow. 'I remember that look: you've got something up your sleeve. Why can't you tell me?'

'Nah, you'll laugh.'

'Try me.'

'It's stupid.'

Sarah took another sip of her drink. 'Must be, if you won't even admit what it is.' She shrugged and looked bored.

John glanced around the bar. It was still early evening, and most of the usual reprobates had yet to turn up, but the few who were dotted about were watching their exchange with interest. John could tell they were listening, too: old Malachy at the end of the bar hadn't taken a sip of his pint of Harp since Sarah had sat down, and Malachy wasn't known for slow drinking.

John leaned in closer to Sarah, his face tight with wariness. 'All right. If you must know, I'm thinking of opening a' – he glared at Malachy's profile again and lowered his voice further – 'a detective agency.'

Sarah barked a laugh. She instantly regretted it

when she caught the look of embarrassed hurt in John's eyes. But this was the last thing she'd expected to hear.

'Are you serious?'

John began to move away. 'Yeah, see, I knew you'd laugh.'

'I'm not laughing because it's stupid. Only because it's…unexpected.' Sarah looked at him with renewed interest. 'Why do you, of all people, want to do something like that?'

'Why not me?' John picked up an ashtray from the bar and emptied it into the bin. 'It'd be great. You get to be your own boss, work your own hours… I'm thinking of specialising in insurance scams. Shit, Sarah, I could do it, too. I'd be great at it – driving around, watching fat cats play golf even though they're claiming bad backs…'

'Have you even thought this through?' Sarah said, wonderingly.

'Hey,' John said. 'There's a guy who comes in here now and again. He works for Axa Insurance, he's a claims assessor. I've done a few nixers for him, when I'm off – handy money for a couple of hours' work. Anyway, we were talking one night, and he reckons there's a real market for that line of work in Ireland – private, like.'

Sarah snorted softly. 'If it's that great, why doesn't he do it?'

John's scowl deepened. These were questions he didn't want to consider. He didn't know why he felt he had to justify his dream to her, anyway. 'I don't know. He's connected with a company, he's got kids… But anyway, that's what he says. I want to do something different than stand here, listening to the same shit, day in, day out. I'm sick of it.' Malachy huffed gently at the end of the bar and John glared at him.

Sarah drained the last of her Baileys and stood up. 'Now *that* I can understand.' She dug her slender hands into her pockets. 'Well, good luck. I hope it all works out for you.'

John would never know why he said what he said next, not in a million years. Maybe it was something about her disbelieving expression, or maybe it was something he felt he owed her. Maybe it was because she looked pretty when she smiled.

'If I open an office, you want to come work with me? You know, if something hasn't turned up.'

'Me?' Sarah laughed again, a good, clean, natural sound. This time it didn't offend him. 'Doing what?'

'PI work.'

'Spying on people?'

'It's not spying,' John said. 'It's…it would be helping people.'

She stopped laughing and looked at John thoughtfully. 'Helping people, huh?' She shook her head gently. 'Tell you what. You organise something like that, and if I still haven't got anything on, give me a call.'

He could tell she didn't believe he'd ever do it, and that annoyed him. 'I'm going to do this.'

Old Malachy took a deep gulp of his drink and beamed at Sarah.

'Sure.' Sarah winked at Malachy and left the bar, still shaking her head.

John ran his fingers through his hair and made himself a promise. He would do whatever it took so that people could never look at him as a chancer again. He would make something of himself, even if that meant working at it day and night. He would open his damn office, and he would call her. See how smug she was then.

Less than five months later, he rented the top floor of one of the worst buildings in Wexford Street. That same week he called Sarah Kenny on his newly installed phone line and offered her a job. To his delight, she actually had the good grace to sound impressed. Then she said okay, she would come along and take a look at his set-up.

She had come down the next day and stared in bemusement at the shabby office and his one-line Golden Pages ad. She asked John what he had to offer her, and John admitted he had nothing.

'If I put some money into this venture...' she had said as she walked slowly around the office, running her fingers through the inch of dust that rested on a dado rail, 'what about making me a partner?'

John had grinned, eyed her breasts through her jumper and said okay. If she wanted half of nothing, she was welcome to it. Sarah nodded and said she was willing to invest three grand of her savings into the business, take it or leave it. John, who had used every penny to pay the first three months' rent in advance and had no money left to get business cards printed up, stopped acting like a jerk and agreed to her terms.

'There's even a solicitor downstairs, I think,' he had said. 'We can get him to draw up a partnership deal.'

'I don't want my name on anything,' Sarah had replied. 'I'll be a silent partner. I'll draw a salary, but I want my name on nothing.'

'Why?'

'Because that's the way I want it. Got it?'

'Got it,' John said.

QuicK Investigations was born.

'We'll check with the Gardaí later today, see what their take on this is,' John said, trying to break the silence. 'Make sure we aren't treading on anyone's toes.'

'Yeah.' Sarah rested her head against the passenger window. 'The last thing we want is to annoy the Gardaí. Only an idiot would do that.'

'They can't hold that against me for the rest of my life.'

'I wouldn't bet on it.'

'And neither can you.'

'I wouldn't bet on that, either,' Sarah said, but she smiled to soften her words.

In March of that year, John had spent two weeks stalking the wife of one Detective Inspector Sean Dillon. Unfortunately, John had had no idea that he was working for a Garda, and Sean Dillon had seen no reason to enlighten him. John had followed Mrs Dillon as she went shopping, picked up the kids, went to the gym and did nothing of any great importance – that is, until the last day of the second week, when he had tailed her to Bewley's Hotel on the Naas Road and got a beautifully detailed shot of her canoodling with another man in the car park. Then they had disappeared into the hotel for well over an hour and come out wearing the self-satisfied smirks of people who have got away with something illicit. John had been particularly amused by the obscene gesture the man made to Mrs Dillon as she climbed back into the family Ford Focus. John wasn't sure what it meant, but it had made her blush like a teenager.

The trouble was, the man who had made Mrs Dillon blush so hard turned out to be a colleague of Detective Dillon. John had identified the man from his car reg and reported back to Sean Dillon with the immortal words, 'She's seeing a bleeding Garda – shit, that's grounds for divorce in itself!' Then he had handed over the excellent pictures of Mrs Dillon, giggling, with her suitor's hand most of the way down her blouse.

Detective Eamon O'Shea was a well-liked man who, after Detective Dillon was finished with him, had to have his jaw rewired and his arm – the one he'd put down Mrs Dillon's top – set. He also had to have some fairly sharp glossy prints removed from another orifice. It took three men to pull Sean Dillon off him and another two to drag the enraged cuckold fifteen feet down the hall to a holding cell to cool off. When the uproar finally died down, Sean Dillon got a nice cushy transfer to the arsehole of nowhere, and John Quigley's name was mud with the Gardaí. Dublin was very small sometimes.

'We'd better make sure we're not interfering with an ongoing case, that's all.'

'I'll give them a call.' Sarah pulled her notebook out of her bag and flipped it open. 'Detective Sergeant Michael Dwyer took the complaint. He's a Pearse Street boy.'

'A local boy for local problems,' John said, doing a poor imitation of Royston Vesey. 'Hey, maybe we can call in on the way back, see how long it takes them to toss us out onto the street.'

'You go in and I'll time it.'

'I'd say, depending who's on the desk, about one minute.'

'A fiver says less than that,' Sarah said, grinning.

'Maybe it would be better if you went in.'

8

Claremont House was pretty impressive, in its own way. John whistled softly as they drove along a winding drive lined with weeping willows and the full size and scale of the property came into view. Only an enormous amount of money could have built such a masterpiece of poor taste.

The house was a sprawling, three-storey, mock-Tudor affair with mullioned windows and high Gothic arches. The top half of the house wore a necklace of black wooden timbers set in gleaming white plaster. A chunky watchtower sat, squat and out of place, on the western side of the pitched roof. Heavy silk curtains the colour of day-old oysters were gathered in busy sweeps, covering every window. It should have been imposing, but from the wrought-iron guttering down to the massive limestone steps, the whole place was a clashing mish-mash of styles and eras. It reeked of money, new money.

The Manta rumbled across the pale gravel, did a slow lap around a four-tier fountain and pulled up in front of an iron-framed conservatory that ran along the west side of the house. John and

Sarah could see that the large gardens were land-scaped to within an inch of their lives. No blade of grass was longer than half an inch, no indigenous plants had been allowed to nestle among the neat box hedges and Japanese maples. A large pond, fringed by achingly neat clusters of pampas grass, lay still and watchful to the left of the shorn lawn. A lone lily pad bobbed forlornly, facing the washed-denim sky.

'Phew,' John said softly. 'What does Naughton do again?'

'He's a property developer, owns Zara Con-struction – you know, that crowd that threw up all those apartments near Eden Quay.'

'I know the ones you're talking about. The Safety crowd threatened to close them down after a couple of hoddies fell off the scaffolding.'

'That's him.' Sarah unbuckled her belt and reached for the door handle.

They climbed the flagstone steps and stopped in front of a ten-foot-high wooden door – which, to John's delight, actually had a brass knocker shaped like a lion's head. To either side of the door, stained-glass windows gleamed in the pale winter light.

'Do you want to knock or shall I?' John said, glancing at the lion. It was almost as big as his hand.

'Man, that's tacky.' Sarah laughed. 'When was the last time you saw anything like that?'

'Sarah, I've never seen anything like this.' John

reached up and seized the huge ring caught in the lion's teeth.

Before he got the chance to rap it, the door opened and a scarily thin old woman appeared before them. She was a couple of inches shy of five foot and almost entirely grey – grey hair, grey cardigan, grey skirt and grey skin. Everything was grey except for her teeth, which were a curious dusky yellow.

'Hiya,' John said, plastering on his best 'sure, I could be your son' smile. 'We're here to see—'

'I know why you're here.' The grey lady squinted over his shoulder at Sarah. Her expression suggested they'd both crawled straight up from a sewer. 'She's expectin' yous.' She stepped aside by about one inch and wrinkled her nose as they slid past her. John got a distinct whiff of mothballs.

The hall was a long, wood-panelled affair, bigger than Sarah's kitchen, bathroom and bedroom put together. The walls were hung with heavily framed landscapes and hunting scenes. The air reeked of furniture polish, pot-pourri and plug-in air fresheners. The parquet floor gleamed from buffing. In other circumstances, John would have taken off his shoes and slid the whole length of it. Instead he and Sarah followed meekly behind the grey woman, trying not to gawp.

'I suppose you'll be wantin' tea?' she said over her shoulder.

'Coffee would be nice.'

'I should've known tea wouldn't do yous.'

'Gives me the runs,' John said cheerfully.

'What?' The old lady stopped and peered at him.

'I said I'd love some buns.' John smiled his best smile again. 'Didn't get much of a breakfast this morning.'

'Pity about you.' The old lady shook her head and shuffled away.

Sarah nudged John hard in the spine. 'Stop.'

John shrugged. 'I thought all old ones loved to feed young men.'

'That's *Father Ted*. This is real life.'

At the end of the hall, the old lady ushered them into a small, over-bright living room. It was a claustrophobic room, crammed with doilies and dainty tables covered in figurines and dried flowers. In the tall, skinny antique fireplace, a log fire burned away brightly. The mauve carpet was covered in embroidered rugs, and they matched embroidered cushions arranged on the chairs and the floral, high-backed sofas.

The old lady jerked her jaw at them. 'You wait here; I'll get her.' She shot John another withering look and disappeared out the door.

'I like the welcoming committee.' John perched on the edge of the rock-hard sofa and pulled out his cigarettes. He looked around for an ashtray and sighed when he couldn't find one. 'She probably thinks we should have used the servant's entrance.'

Sarah strolled around the room, studying the many photographs dotted about. Her eyes came to rest on a framed picture on top of a heavy mahogany sideboard.

In this picture Ashley Naughton looked about sixteen, gawky and impossibly long-limbed, and she wore a school uniform. Her blond hair was in pigtails and she had train-track braces on her teeth. Sarah mentally compared it with the picture Margaret had shown them the day before and marvelled at how easily goofy girls, with the right clothes and a little make-up, could transform themselves into beautiful women almost overnight.

The door opened and Margaret Naughton walked in. She wore a navy trouser suit with a silvery blouse – the dark colour added about ten years to her age. She had a pearl choker at her throat and no make-up on. John rose to greet her, but she waved him back down with an impatient gesture. She glanced uneasily around the room, and Sarah realised she had been crying not long before they'd arrived.

'I wasn't expecting you quite so early,' she said.

'No real traffic, so we made good time.'

'I see.' She looked at the carpet, refusing to make eye contact.

'Mrs Naughton,' Sarah said, 'have you heard anything?'

'No.' Margaret retreated a step closer to the door. 'I expect my husband home shortly. Do you still need to talk to him?'

Sarah glanced at John and back at Margaret. 'Yes, we believe it would be better if we did. Was there anything else you'd like to tell us?'

'No, I can't think of anything off hand…' She fiddled with the choker and glanced around the room again. 'You know, I keep replaying conversations, over and over. Did I miss something? But there's nothing. Ashley wasn't upset. She wasn't acting strangely. This is all so…so totally unreal.'

'No arguments or fights?'

'No.' Margaret glanced hastily over her shoulder. 'Not with me.'

Sarah noted the emphasis. 'Who was that lady who let us in?'

'That's Ashley's grandmother, Emily.'

'Your mother?'

'My husband's mother.'

'Does your mother-in-law live with you?' John said. His sympathy for Margaret went up ten fold.

'Yes.' Margaret sighed and closed the door. 'Look, Emily's not all bad, but she doesn't think I should have got you – or the Gardaí, for that matter – involved in family matters.' She absently brushed at her fringe; two bright spots of colour burned in her pale cheeks. 'I've upset everyone.'

'I see,' Sarah said, although she didn't. If her granddaughter were missing, even for one night, she would have as many people as possible trying to track her down, over-dramatic or not. What kind of people wouldn't?

'I'll go and see what's keeping the coffee.'

Margaret glanced at her watch and inched backwards towards the door. 'If you will excuse me.'

'Sure, go ahead,' John said, spreading his arm across the back of the sofa. 'I could murder a cuppa.'

Margaret offered him a tense nod and bolted.

'What's wrong with this picture?' Sarah said. 'What's going on here?'

John scratched at the stubble on his chin. 'Yesterday she was begging us to help, and today she's pissed off that we're here.'

Sarah heard a noise outside in the hall. She shook her head and held up her hand. The grandmother appeared at the door. John noticed there were no coffee cups in her hands.

'Come on up and see the girl's room. My son'll be home soon, and I don't want to upset him havin' you lot here. If you ask me, there's been enough fuss over Ashley.' She folded her arms across her chest and glared at them with open hostility.

'Maybe we should wait for Mrs Naughton,' Sarah said coolly.

'She's in the kitchen.'

'Maybe she would like to show us Ashley's room.'

'What difference does it make who shows you?'

John stood up. He knew Sarah was threatening to dig her heels in, and that usually resulted in a row somewhere. 'Okay, lead on.'

'And we'll need a word with Mr Naughton, when he gets back,' Sarah said, glancing at her watch. 'When do you think he might get here?'

'I'll show yous the room, but you're not to be botherin' my son. He wants nothin' to do with this carry-on. Neither of us does.'

'That's a strange one, isn't it, Mrs Naughton?' Sarah said, with exaggerated politeness. 'I'd have thought you'd want to know what's happened to your grandchild. Aren't you worried about her?'

'Of course I am.' The old lady's rheumy eyes snapped in her direction. 'But she's a young one, and young ones are always doin' stupid things. She'll come back when it suits her. That one always was a right little madam – not that I blame her. Takes after the mother, that one, can't be told nothin'.'

'Okay,' John said. 'So if we can just see her room...'

'This isn't the first time Ash has run off. All this fuss... You wait and see, she'll be back when it suits her.'

'She ran away before?' Sarah said.

'Oh, aye. She didn't tell you that, did she?' She glanced back at the door, a smug look on her face. 'She was missin' for a few days then, too. I don't remember where she was, mind, but she came home with her tail down in the end. We didn't need no *detectives* to find her then, either.' Emily stalked out of the room.

John shook his head slightly. 'Told you: runaway.'

'Shut up, John.' Sarah brushed past him. 'You don't know that.'

They followed Emily up the highly polished stairs and along a thickly carpeted landing crammed full of end tables and stiff-legged, heavily gilded chairs. There were more country-life paintings dotted here and there – mournful Constable rip-offs, a collection of ornately framed hunting scenes, the type where packs of baying hounds fought for space with swan-necked, Arabic-faced hunters. John wondered if Edward Naughton had bought the furnishings in bulk to add a sense of rustic charm to his pile.

Emily pointed at a heavily panelled door and carried on around a corner without a backward glance. Sarah exhaled in relief. 'I thought she'd be hovering over us the whole time we were here.' She rolled her eyes and opened the door. She'd only been there twenty minutes, and already she was sick of Claremont House. If Ashley Naughton *had* run away, she for one wouldn't blame the girl.

Ashley's room was at the back of the house on the second floor, overlooking a large red-brick garage and a small patio. It was large and airy, with a few pieces of dark, heavy furniture. The walls were painted a chalky white and someone, probably Ashley herself, had made a half-hearted attempt at liming the floorboards to match. A massive colonial-style double bed sat in the middle of the room, covered in a soft white duvet. The walls were blank except for a large oval mirror. A shimmering silver disco ball hung from the ceiling over a white two-seater sofa covered in caramel-coloured suede cushions.

'Jesus, teenagers these days,' John said, taking a step into the impossibly neat room. 'Where are all the posters, the clothes on the floor?' He looked around and shook his head. 'Talk about anal.'

Sarah closed the door. 'It's a girl's room, Johnny. We're not all pigs like you, you know.' She crossed the floor and opened the door of a huge wardrobe. Rows of clothes hung, in order of length, on wooden hangers. Only a few hangers were empty, and Sarah wondered why Ashley hadn't taken many of her clothes when she moved to the city. She opened the other door and found jumpers and T-shirts, all neatly folded. Eight shoe-boxes were neatly stacked, with the labels facing out, on the floor of the wardrobe.

'You think this room was given the once-over for our arrival?' John said, moving towards the bedside locker.

'Maybe, or maybe Ashley's just a neat kid.' Sarah opened a chest of drawers and flipped through the pile of neatly folded jumpers. She did the same with the next drawer, then the next. 'Mrs Naughton probably tidied up when she was looking for information.'

John opened Ashley's locker, lifted out note-books, papers and magazines and plonked them on the bed. 'What are we looking for, exactly?'

'A note saying where she's gone would be nice. Failing that, a diary, receipts – anything that might give us a hint about how this girl spent her time.'

John pulled out a set of photographs of Ashley and a group of friends making goofy faces at the camera. Ashley had her arm thrown around the shoulders of two girls – another gorgeous blonde with a sultry, posed expression, and a plain redhead with masses of frizzy hair and a sweet smile. John shook his head and threw the picture on the bed. 'I don't like looking through a girl's stuff. It's wrong, somehow.'

'Keep looking.'

They searched the room quickly and methodically, but after a good forty minutes all they had learned about Ashley Naughton was that she was neat, liked *Elle* magazine, read Stephen King and Anne Rice books, looked after her clothes and kept her CDs in the right covers.

'I don't know…' Sarah looked up from the pile of notebooks she had been leafing through and brushed a strand of dark hair out of her eyes. 'You find anything?'

John dropped onto the bed. 'Nope.'

Sarah sat on the bed next to him and gazed around the room. 'This is a waste of time. We're not going to find anything here.'

John put down a shoebox full of hairclips and scrunchies. 'She didn't take much with her when she moved out, did she?'

Sarah frowned and shook her head. 'It's weird, that. If you're moving away from home, wouldn't you bring most of your things?' She picked up a copy of *Elle* and flicked through it idly. 'I'd like to get a feel for the girl – but shit, John, there's nothing here to say what she was like. There aren't even flyers or ticket stubs or anything lying around. And I'd like to know why Margaret didn't tell us she'd run away before.'

'Because she wanted us to take this seriously, and maybe she thought we wouldn't if we knew.' John shrugged. 'Who knows?'

'Something's not right.'

John stood up. 'One thing I do know: we'll never find out sitting here. Let's go check out her flat.'

Sarah pocketed the photo of Ashley and her friends. 'Okay.'

On their way down the stairs, they heard raised voices coming from a room on the ground floor. Sarah slowed to a crawl and waved at John to do the same. It was difficult to hear the words, but it was definitely a man's voice and he sounded angry.

John tapped her on the shoulder. 'I'll bet that's—'

'Shh.' Sarah eased her way closer to the door, hoping the stairs wouldn't creak.

Before she could get into listening range, Emily yanked open the door and stepped out. 'What are you doin' creepin' about?'

Jesus, Sarah thought, *she must have ears like a bat.* 'We're finished with the room. Is Mr Naughton home? We'd like to have a word with him.'

'Would you now?'

'Yes, we would.'

'What did I already tell you? You're to leave my son alone. It's bad enough that Ashley's missing without him havin' to talk to a pair of shysters.' She folded her arms across her chest. 'Why don't you ask them tramps where she's gone, the ones she was shacked up with?'

Sarah had put up with enough belligerence for one day. She took the last three steps in one jump. John's mouth twitched as Emily took a hasty step backwards.

'I don't want to waste any of your precious time,' Sarah said, towering over the older woman, 'so if you could ask Mr Naughton for a moment of *his* time, we won't have to sully your day any longer.'

'Don't speak to me that—'

'Ma, leave it. Go on, inside.' The voice was gravelly, with a curious mixture of accents – polished inner city, Sarah thought. Edward Naughton appeared behind his mother's shoulder, gently grasped her waist and steered her back into the room in one fluid movement. 'Go on now, I'll be back in a sec.' He closed the door on her protests, leaned against it and crossed his arms in an exact copy of his mother's actions.

Sarah and John hadn't been sure what to expect, but after the elegant Margaret Naughton, the man before them was not it. Edward Naughton was fat and greasy looking, and his charcoal-grey John Lewis suit only emphasised his rotund physique. A nasty yellow and purple bruise covered the left side of his jaw. A gold pinky ring, as big as a bottle top, glinted in the dusky light of the hall. On any other day, he was probably a real charmer, but at that moment he was glaring at them as if they'd tracked dog shit across his favourite antique rug.

John came down the steps and held out his hand. 'Mr Naughton, my name is John Quigley, and this is my partner, Sarah Kenny. We were hoping we'd get a chance—'

The corner of Naughton's fleshy mouth sank. 'I know who you are, Quigley, and I know why you're here.' He glared at Sarah. 'What the fuck gives you the right to go talking to my ma like that?'

Sarah flushed. 'Mr Naughton, I was—'

'I don't give a shit. That poor woman's nearly out of her mind with worry. Are you that much of a cunt that you can't see when someone's too upset to be bothered?'

Sarah's flush spread down to her neck. 'Cunt' was her least favourite word in the world. 'Mr Naughton, I'm sorry if I appeared rude, but John and I felt it was important we spoke to you.'

'Hey, listen to what I'm telling you.' Edward Naughton stepped closer, using his bulk to intimidate. All the polish had vanished; the thug had come out from beneath the veneer. He jabbed his finger almost into Sarah's chest. 'We've nothing to talk about. If Margo wants to hire two detectives to scrounge around in our private lives when it's obvious Ash has fucked off for a break, I can't do jack-shit about it, but let me assure you, girlie, you won't be talking with me. My daughter's eighteen; she's a grown woman. If she wants to fuck off for a few weeks without telling anyone, that's her lookout.' He jerked his head towards the front door. 'Now if you'll excuse me, I'm sure you can find your own way out. I think that's your piece of shit cluttering up my drive.'

'Sorry you feel that way,' John said tightly. 'That's a nasty-looking bruise you've got there, Mr Naughton. Looks painful.'

'Accident at work; occupational hazard.' Naughton stared at John. His green eyes were flat, almost empty. 'Now get your stuff and get out.'

'We should speak to Mrs Naughton before we go.'

'Margo's gone out. She left while you were snooping around Ash's room. Hope you left everything the way you found it.'

Sarah stuck out her hand and said, with heavy sarcasm, 'It was a pleasure to meet you, Mr Naughton. I hope we can find your daughter.'

Naughton walked back into the room and closed the door in their faces.

'Arsehole,' John said loudly, almost daring him to come back out.

Sarah stood looking at the door for a few seconds. Finally, she shook her head. 'Come on, let's get out of here.'

★

Edward Naughton waited for the front door to close, then he watched through the window of his office as the Manta roared off down the drive, spewing gravel all over his neat lawn. His heart thumped uncomfortably in his chest and he fought hard to control it. He needed to regain his composure and think. Now was not the time to panic. He went to his hostess trolley and poured himself a stiff brandy.

'Where'd Margo go?'

'How should I know?' Emily rubbed a hand over her face. 'That one's always runnin' here and there.'

Edward turned to look at her. His mother sat slumped in one of the leather chairs in front of the hand-carved teak desk he'd imported from Italy the year before. The sight of the desk comforted him. The sight of his mother did not. She was wringing her hands as if they were wet, a habit he detested.

'I'm tellin' you, son, watch your back with them. What did I always tell you? You can't judge a book by its cover.'

Edward's shoulders tightened. His mother had a saying for every moment in life. 'Shut up, for God's sake, and let me think!'

He pressed his fingers to the bridge of his nose and forced himself to breathe slowly. This was the worst possible timing. Margo was kicking up the stink of the century, and now he had two more problems to take care of... Racked with self-pity, he turned from the window. Where the fuck was Ashley?

'I need to make a few calls.'

Emily flinched at her son's tone. She gripped the desk in her arthritic hands and pulled herself up slowly. 'There's no need for that mouth on you.'

'Ma, I'm sorry, but I've got calls to make and I need to be alone for a while.'

Emily tilted her head high and strode for the door. When she was gone, Edward loosened his tie, picked up the phone and punched in a number.

'Pascal, it's me. We have a problem.'

'Tell me something I don't know.' As always, Pascal Mooney sounded as though he was just coming out of a coma. It was the thick Galway accent. Pascal's voice was always laconic, especially when he was furious.

'She's called in private detectives to look for Ashley.'

'Margo?'

'Of course, Margo. Who the fuck do you think?'

'You said she wouldn't. You said she'd be all right, like.'

'I tried to stop her,' Edward said. He knew he was whining, but he was feeling more hard done by every second. Why did everyone blame him for everything?

'Not hard enough, obviously.'

'She's very upset.' Edward sat down heavily. Even to his own ears, he sounded pathetic.

'I'm pretty fucking upset myself,' Pascal Mooney reminded him. 'I can't believe you're backing out on me.'

'I can't do anything, not with Ashley missing.'

'You don't know York has her.'

'It's too risky.'

'Everything's risky now. Anyway, it's too late to back out. What are you going to say – "Oops, I found it, sorry about the mix-up"?'

'Oh, for Christ's sake—'

'How're you going to explain Kelpie being missing? Going to pull him out of a box too?'

'That wasn't my fault.'

'Give me their names – the detectives. I'll have them checked out.'

'QuicK Investigations. They've a place on Wexford Street, I'll find an address for them. Christ knows where Margo dug them up.'

'No need for an address.' Edward heard the click of Pascal's lighter and the deep pull on a cigarette. 'QuicK, huh? Never heard of them.'

'That's good, isn't it? They don't look like much. A guy and a girl – he looks as thick as pigshit, but I don't know about the girl.'

'Nothing about this is good, Eddie. This is getting more fucked up by the minute. And the last thing we need is someone else on top of us at the moment. You were supposed to be in control of your end.'

Edward ran his hand through his thinning hair. 'I know, I know.'

'Dougie's not going to wait forever.'

'I know that.'

Mooney sighed heavily. 'Tell me again about Patrick. How'd he look?'

'Angry.'

Pascal said nothing for a few seconds. Edward's heart beat painfully in his chest. He wished he had never confided any information to this man. Mooney was as unpredictable as the weather.

'He gonna talk to anyone in particular?'

'He didn't mention any names.'

Pascal dragged on his cigarette again. 'He ask about me?'

'He warned me not to tell you he was here.'

'Did he now? The prick.' Pascal laughed suddenly. 'It must be fifteen years or more since he was here last. He must be sweating it.'

Edward fingered his bruised cheek nervously. 'He's not a happy man, I'll tell you that.'

'What's he thinking?'

'I don't know what the fuck he thinks. That bastard Vinnie is playing him like a song. He keeps suggesting I'm behind it.'

Pascal gave a low chuckle. 'Vinnie never liked you, that's for sure.'

'He's not too fucking fond of you, either!' Edward gripped the phone so hard his hand trembled. 'What do you think Patrick's going to do – I mean, if he can't trace it?'

'He'll never trace it; no "if" about it. Dougie Burrows would never deal with the Yorks.'

'Then what?'

Pascal took another long drag of his cigarette and exhaled before he answered. 'We sit on it for a while, wait till the shit dies down.'

'What about Vinnie?'

'If push comes to shove, we can always get rid of that shitepipe too.'

'What a complete arsehole,' John repeated as he tore up the road towards Dublin.

Sarah nodded. She was barely listening to him. She was thinking about Edward Naughton. His reaction to them was hardly normal, even if he didn't relish their presence. He had struck her as a man struggling to keep a lid on things.

'No wonder Ashley's done a runner,' John said, jamming a cigarette into his mouth. 'She legged it to get away from that lot. I don't blame her.'

'I wonder what he's so afraid of,' Sarah said, more to herself than to John.

'Afraid? That fucker's not afraid. He thinks we're scum.'

'He was nervous about something. What do you think happened to his face?'

'Hopefully someone kicked the crap out of him.'

Sarah glanced at John, noticing for the first time how furious he was. She found that almost as odd as Edward Naughton's anger. Normally, other people's opinions or behaviour didn't make the slightest impact on him. 'What the hell's wrong with you?'

John accelerated through a yellow light and kept his eyes on the road. His lips were pulled into a thin, pale line.

'Come on, out with it. What is it?'

'I think he's an arsehole and he knows nothing about cars.'

Sarah turned her head and looked out the window to hide her smile. Only John could take an insult to his car so personally. Edward Naughton had burned his name into John's bad books. Nobody called his baby a pile of shit.

9

By the time they reached Dublin, John had calmed
down a little. He dropped Sarah off in Pearse
Street to talk to the Gardaí and drove back to
Wexford Street alone. He bought a lukewarm
chicken-and-mushroom pie from the Spar shop
across the road and returned to the office, where
he went to work on the names Margaret had given
them.

He tried calling Ashley's apartment and got
the answering machine; he didn't leave a message.
He wasted an hour contacting old friends with
whom Ashley had long since parted company. By
the time Sarah came back to the office at half-four,
he was frustrated and bored.

'What kept you so long?' he snapped.

Sarah hung up her coat, shook her hair out
over the collar of her shirt and raised her
eyebrows. 'Excuse me?'

'Sorry,' John sighed and waved a hand at the
paperwork on his desk. 'I've been chasing down
the Ashley Naughton fan club.'

'Anything?'

'Nada. Everyone I've spoken to says she's a

nice kid. So far I've learned she's really good at maths and hockey – oh, and she can do three somersaults in a row.' John ran his fingers through his hair. 'I don't even know why Mrs Naughton gave us half these numbers. Ashley hardly kept in touch with any of her old school friends. The only ones she still hangs out with are the girls at the apartment, and I can't find them. What about the cops, what was their story?'

'Much the same.' Sarah turned on the kettle and blew on her hands to warm them up. 'Ashley was reported missing by her mother on Monday. They sent someone down to talk to Margaret on Tuesday evening, but by then Edward Naughton had found out about the note and the money coming out of her account. So he apologised for wasting their time and the whole thing was called off.'

John laced his hands behind his head. 'So that's that.'

Sarah made herself a cup of coffee and sat down behind her desk. 'Sergeant Dwyer – he's the one I was talking to – thought there *might* be more to it, but since Ashley's legally an adult, their hands are tied. And apparently Edward Naughton was extremely vocal on the subject of backing off.'

'Yeah? I wonder why.'

'He kept saying Ashley had run off before and she was always threatening to do it again. Sergeant Dwyer says he doesn't think that's unlikely. He did say he thought Naughton was acting hinky, but he put it down to the fact that – you're going to love this – Naughton's done a bit of time.'

John grinned. 'Has he now? For what?'

'He wouldn't say, but it'll be easy to find out. Dwyer reckons Ashley is probably a bit of a wild child too.'

John shrugged. 'I'm not surprised about our boy Edward, but Margaret makes Ashley out to be an angel. So has every person I've spoken to today – except for Granny.'

'Yeah, well, people change, John. Maybe when she left home she came out of her shell.'

'So they're not looking into this any further?'

'Nope.' Sarah flicked on her computer. 'It's you and me, Johnny boy, out on our own.'

'Well, I've got less than you. Like I said, I spoke to most of the friends on the list Mrs Naughton gave us, and I got zip. Same shit each time: Ashley Naughton's quiet, she's nice and she keeps herself pretty much to herself.' John scratched his chin. 'This Dwyer sounds like a helpful bloke. Don't suppose you mentioned you worked with me?'

Sarah snorted and tapped at her keys. 'I wanted him to *help* me, John. We can't always have everyone against us. Life's hard enough as it is.'

John didn't like the way she said it. 'Look, Sarah, I know things are a bit...well, shit at the moment, but it'll pick up, you'll see. We'll get another case in—'

She spun in her chair and opened the filing

cabinet behind her. 'I really hope so. I mean, if we hadn't landed this case, we'd have been totally skint.'

'I know. But hey, we've always pulled through before, haven't we?'

'I'm tired of skimming through by the skin of our teeth.' Sarah turned back to him. 'I don't want to fight with you, John, but I do need you to pull with me just now. We need to make this business work.'

'I know.' John nodded. 'And you were right the other day: I know I've got to pull my weight more. And I will, okay?'

'Can I get that on tape?' Sarah broke into a grin. 'You never know when I'll need proof that you said that.'

'You don't need a tape, I promise.' John raised his fingers and crossed them. 'Scout's honour.'

'You were never a Scout.'

'Man, you're tough.'

Sarah smiled and shook her head. 'Okay, then.'

'We good?'

'Always.'

Sarah cleared her throat and glanced at the notes on her desk. 'Tell you what: I'm going to look into Naughton, see what he was inside for.'

John nodded. 'I'll crack on with talking to the flatmates.'

He dialled the number for Ashley's apartment again, got the machine and left a message telling the remaining flatmates he would be calling on them later that same day. He hung up, picked up his pen and chewed on the end of it.

'If Ashley Naughton wanted to get away that badly, why now? She had left home, for God's sake. She could have stayed up in Dublin and just gone home for the odd weekend. Round my way, every bleeding shop is full of students working on the weekends.'

Sarah looked up. 'That's true. Why would she bother running away?'

John doodled some more. 'It doesn't make sense. What's she supposed to be running from?' He stood up. 'I'm going to track down those flatmates. Want to come?'

Sarah shook her head. 'You go ahead. I'm going to make a few calls, find out a bit more about Edward.'

'Catch you later.' John grabbed his jacket and left.

Sarah looked through the photos of Ashley. She particularly liked the one of Ashley and her friends that she had taken from the bedroom. They were just a bunch of girls, out having a good time... Where was Ashley? And what was up with Edward Naughton? Regardless of what John thought, she knew he was fearful about something. It came off him in waves. Was he simply worried about his daughter? But if so, why did he not want them on the case? Maybe it was sheer snobbery – or maybe not.

Sarah picked up the picture again. 'I hope

you're all right, girl,' she said softly. 'I really do.'

It was easy to find the apartment Ashley shared with her friends. It was in the heart of Temple Bar, only a few minutes from the gates of Trinity College. A tiny studio apartment in this neighbourhood could cost as much as a three-bedroom house anywhere else.

He rang the intercom and got nothing. It had been a long shot, but John was tired of ringing people. Anyway, this gave him a chance to have a look around the area where Ashley lived, and see if anyone knew her or remembered seeing her on the weekend she went missing. There was an Italian restaurant three doors up from the apartment, a shoe shop next door to that and a trendy hair salon blaring rap music under the apartment itself.

John canvassed the three businesses to see if they knew anything about Ashley. The pink-haired manager of the salon asked her staff and drew a blank. The girl in the shoe shop was friendly, but she didn't normally work in that store. One of the waiters in the restaurant knew the girls John described, but not individually; he'd just seen them walking down the street when he took his cigarette break outside. John figured from the guy's goofy grin that there had been a certain amount of catcalling involved.

John went back down the road and tried the apartment again. There was no answer. John stepped off the kerb and glanced up. As he did, he caught sight of a head ducking back behind the curtains in a bay window on the second floor. Margaret had said Ashley's apartment was on the second floor. John raised an eyebrow and played a hunch. He rang the bell again. This time he left his finger on it for a good ten seconds, then gave it two more long bursts.

And – bingo – the intercom was answered by a nervous female voice. 'Hello?'

'Hey, it's John Quigley, I called earlier.'

'Oh, hi… Em, listen, there's no one else—'

'I'm not going anywhere, so you may as well open up. I'm here about Ashley Naughton.'

There was another, longer pause, then she said, 'Come up. We're number—'

'I know which flat it is.'

She buzzed him in.

John climbed the stairs to the second floor and knocked harder than necessary on the door of number 6. He waited what he considered a long time before the lock rattled and the door opened about two inches, on a thin chain. A pair of wary grey eyes, fringed by pale eyelashes, peeped out through the gap at him.

'Do you have ID?'

John laughed. 'You serious?'

'My mam says I'm to let nobody in unless I know them. And I don't know you.'

John shrugged and fished inside his battered leather jacket for his wallet. 'Your mother was right.' He held out his driving licence.

A pale, freckled hand slipped out and took it.

She studied the photo, then him, then the photo again. Finally satisfied John was who he said he was, she closed the door and took the chain off. 'Sorry about that. Can't be too careful...'

'That's okay.' He didn't have the heart to tell her he could have booted the door in as easily as he could butter toast.

'I'm Megan Lowry.' She stuck out her hand and he shook it. He recognised her as one of the girls in the photo they'd taken from Ashley's room. Megan was about eighteen, five foot eight, skinny and flat-chested. She had frizzy, shoulder-length red hair and the palest skin John had ever seen. She wore grubby navy tracksuit bottoms that sagged at the knees and a grey cardigan a couple of sizes too big for the fattest man John knew. Her long, pale feet were bare. The nail varnish on her toes was neon green and badly chipped.

John let go of her hand and smiled reassuringly. 'You're a hard crowd to get hold of.'

'Oh, are we?' She chewed on her bottom lip and stared somewhere at his chest. John could see she was as nervous as hell. What the hell was it that made people jumpy around him? He'd have to work on his smile.

'Claudia's not here yet. I mean, she's on her way – it's just that...' She blinked. 'I finished early.'

John nodded and tried to look like he believed her. He guessed Megan had skipped some classes. Judging from the hair and the clothes, she'd fallen out of bed when he buzzed the intercom.

'Would you like some coffee, Mr Quigley? I think we have coffee.'

'Sure, coffee sounds grand – and you can call me John. "Mr Quigley" makes me feel old.'

Megan didn't laugh, only nodded and led him down the hall into the sitting room. It was large, painted pale yellow, with two floor-to-ceiling bay windows and an expensive-looking maple floor covered in sisal mats. The furniture was good quality and not exactly student style: John recognised some of the pieces as French antiques – his sister Carrie would have wept if she'd seen how they were being treated. It should have been a nice room, but it was wasn't. It was crammed with old takeaway boxes, ashtrays full of butts and half-empty cups, and there were clothes everywhere – drying on radiators, hanging over chairs, tossed on the floor. It was the filthiest room John had seen in a while.

Megan caught him looking and blushed. 'Sorry about the mess.' She scooped some clothes off one of the sofas and, lacking anywhere else to put them, tossed them onto a chair. John picked a deep red sofa to sit on and watched as Megan surreptitiously picked up an ashtray full of roach-ends and carried it into the kitchen. He wondered how the almost pathologically tidy Ashley had coped with the mess here.

Megan came back out of the kitchen and stood fidgeting at the door, looking sheepish. 'We don't have any milk left. Do you take milk?'

'Black's fine.'

'Cool.' She disappeared again and came back a few minutes later with two cups of black coffee. She handed him one, pushed some magazines off another chair and folded her long body into it. 'So did…have Ashley's parents asked you to look for her?'

'Yes, they did. You know her folks?'

She shrugged one bony shoulder. 'I've met them a few times, at school concerts and open days. Claudia knows them better than I do. Ashley used to stay over at her house for weekends and stuff. That's why Ashley moved in here, because of Claudia.'

'Just the three of you here?'

Megan blinked, rummaged in the deep pockets of the cardigan and pulled out a battered packet of Marlboro Lights and a box of matches. 'That's right.'

'Claudia…?'

'Claudia Delaney. Her parents own this apartment. Me and Ash are supposed to be helping with the rent.'

John glanced around the untidy room again and wondered if Claudia's folks realised how their tenants treated the apartment. He put his coffee down on the floor and pulled out his notebook. 'How do you girls know each other? Were you all in school together?'

Megan lit a cigarette and nodded. Her fingernails were bitten right down to the quick.

'Good friends, then?'

She shrugged one shoulder again. 'Uh-huh.'

'Do you share rooms here?'

'No, there's three bedrooms – well, two proper-sized bedrooms and one boxroom. Claudia has one room, I've got the other and Ashley has the boxroom. I would have taken it, but Ash said she didn't mind. Claudia will probably get someone else in if Ash isn't coming back...'

John leaned forward in his seat. 'What makes you think she won't be back?'

Megan shrugged again. She picked at a loose thread on the hem of her cardigan, avoiding eye contact. 'I'm not saying she won't, it's just... Well, if she's not here, you know, there's no point in letting it stand empty and all that. Ash wouldn't *mind*.'

'Why wouldn't she mind?'

'She just wouldn't.'

'Was everything all right here? I mean, you girls all got on okay?'

'Sure. Why?'

'Well, did Ashley ever mention anything to you about wanting to leave?'

'No, she didn't say anything.'

'So don't you think it's strange that she took off like that?'

Megan flushed again. 'Sure.'

'Where do you think she is, Megan?'

'I dunno.'

'Don't you think it's strange that she would up

and leave without telling her best friends where she was going?'

'I dunno.' Megan did the one-shouldered shrug again and studied the box of matches in her hand. 'Ash was very…you know, odd, when she wanted to be.'

'Odd? How?' John wrote, '"Odd." Possible fight?' in his notebook.

'Just…she could be really moody sometimes.'

'In what way?'

'Oh…you know.' She began to chew on her lip. 'Just moody.'

For the next twenty minutes or so, John struggled to make small talk with Megan. It wasn't easy; she was on edge the whole time. He discovered that she was studying science, that both her parents were pharmacists and that she couldn't really smoke – she didn't tell him the last part, but after watching her nearly choke on her Marlboro Light he figured it out for himself. The one subject Megan seemed happiest to talk about was Claudia – Claudia says, Claudia thinks. John got the feeling Claudia was the queen bee of this hive.

Eventually, as John was exhausting his reserves of conversation, he heard the front door slam. 'That's Claudia now.' Megan jumped to her feet with palpable relief and scurried out to the hall to warn Claudia they had company. She closed the door behind her, but it didn't catch and John could hear the exchange.

'Shit, Meg, you look awful. Are you still hung

over?' The voice was deep, smooth and self-assured.

'Shh! Listen, there's a private detective in the sitting room. He's here about Ash.'

'Shit. Why did you let him in?'

'I had to. He saw me at the window.'

'God, Meg, you're such a total idiot… I've never seen a real detective before. What's he like? Is he old?'

'Dunno. About forty.'

The smile faded from John's face.

John almost whistled out loud at the ravishing blonde who walked in behind Megan. She was cute in the photo, but up close and personal Claudia Delaney was a knockout. She was about five foot five, slim, but with curves in all the right places. She wore a long red coat, knee-high boots and a short denim skirt. Her mid-length, honey-blonde hair glowed under the apartment lights and her perfect nose had a smattering of sun-freckles, which for November was pretty impressive. *Damn,* John thought, *what's happened to students over the years?*

'Claudia, this is Mr Quigley.'

John extended his hand, trying hard not to drool. Claudia Delaney examined him closely before offering hers. 'Meg tells me you're a detective,' she said. Her voice was polished and husky; she sounded ten years older than she should have. 'Did Ash's parents really hire you?'

That was the second time in less than an hour

he'd been asked that. He wondered why there was so much surprise. It struck him that maybe he wasn't the only person to find the Naughtons a bit strange.

'Yes, they did.'

Claudia pulled a face and took off her coat, which she threw over the back of the sofa. She moved with the easy confidence of someone who knew her own effect on the world and was used to being admired. 'I'm surprised old Daddy Naughton called in outside help,' she said. 'Hardly his style.'

John sat back down on the sofa. 'What makes you say that?'

'Megan, is there any coffee?' Claudia asked, ignoring his question.

Megan jerked towards the kitchen as if on a string. 'I'll get you one. Mr Quigley, another one?'

'I'm good, thanks.'

Megan picked up the empty mugs and scurried off. Claudia dropped onto the sofa, crossed her legs and kept her cool gaze on John. He felt her eyes travel all over his body, and he got the distinct impression she didn't care if he noticed or not.

'Megan tells me you and Ashley Naughton are close friends,' he said.

'Yes. Ash was in my class at boarding school, and my parents have a summer home in Brittas Bay, near her parents' house. We used to sail a bit when we were younger. That's how we met first.'

'So your parents are friends.'

'Hardly.'

John blinked at the abrupt tone. 'They're not?'

'No.'

'What do your parents do?'

'Daddy works for the Bundelbank in Switzerland.' The corner of her mouth twitched slightly. 'He commutes home every other weekend.'

'And your mother?'

'My mother is dead.'

'I'm sorry to hear that.'

'That's all right. She died when I was very small. My stepmother, however, stays home, orders the staff about and takes a lot of pilates classes.' She flashed a sarcastic smile and took one of Megan's cigarettes.

'Any brothers or sisters?'

'None, thank God.'

'Do you have any idea where Ashley might have gone?'

Claudia blew a perfect smoke ring before answering. 'London, Paris, Milan…' She smiled again. 'Seriously, I haven't the foggiest.'

John leaned back on the sofa and studied her. She was lovely to look at and had a body that would make grown men weep, but she was like a really fancy vase: everything on the surface, nothing inside. Her eyes, while beautiful, were cold and flat, and he sensed her pauses were perfectly timed to allow her to consider each question carefully.

'She never mentioned anything to you about taking a break away? Never gave any clue she might be planning to leave Dublin?'

'Nope.'

'Did she ever mention she was unhappy?'

'No. Did she say anything to you, Meg?'

Megan carried a fresh cup of coffee back into the room. 'What?'

'Ash. She never said anything to you about being unhappy here?'

'No.' Megan frowned at John. 'I told you, she was fine the last time we spoke to her.'

'Remind me, when was that exactly?'

Megan handed Claudia the cup and climbed back into her chair. 'Last Friday.' She glanced towards Claudia. 'It was Friday, right, Claudia?'

Claudia flicked her blond hair over her shoulder. 'You know, Mr Quigley, we've told Margo all of this plenty of times.'

'Who?'

'Margo.' Claudia looked at him as if he was an idiot. 'Ash's mother.'

'Oh, I didn't know she was called that. Tell me again anyway.'

'Didn't Meg tell you this?' Claudia shot Megan a glance. 'Friday was the last time either of us spoke to her. Megan and I went to Galway that weekend to see friends of ours, didn't we, Meg? We caught the five o'clock train. When we left, she was sitting right where you are, watching some crap on telly. She was fine. She certainly never said anything about leaving. She said she was going to go home for the weekend.'

'Was she going out that night, or planning to meet up with some other friends?'

'What other friends?' Claudia snorted. 'Honestly, Ashley hung around with us. I don't think she'd have blown us off for—'

'What about boyfriends? Was she seeing someone? Could she have gone somewhere with a boyfriend?'

Claudia narrowed her eyes slightly. John could see she didn't like being interrupted. 'She wasn't seeing anyone in particular. Like I said, we've *told* Margo this already.' She wrinkled her nose in irritation. 'You know, Ash was my friend and everything, but the way Margo's going on about her is ridiculous. She was quite unpredictable, you know – hardly the sainted innocent Margo makes her out to be.'

'I see.' John nodded and wrote 'unpredictable' in his notebook under 'odd'. Despite what she said, he got the impression Claudia didn't have a lot of time for Ashley.

'What age are you?' Megan said suddenly.

John glanced at her in surprise. He'd half forgotten she was there. 'Fast approaching thirty-three. Why?'

'What's it like, being a detective? Is it exciting? Do you, like, get to go on lots of dangerous jobs and things?'

Claudia snorted from the sofa. 'Oh shut up for God's sake, Megan. It's not like in the films, is it,

Mr Quigley? I bet it's dead boring really.'

John glanced at Megan's disappointed face and wiggled his eyebrows in his best Magnum impression. 'Actually, it has its moments.'

Meg smiled shyly.

Claudia scowled at her and rolled her eyes back to John. 'Look, Mr Quigley, is that all? I mean, we've told Margo all of this, and I really don't see why we have to keep repeating the same thing over and over. Ash left a note, you know.'

John nodded. 'I know. Her mother says it's not her handwriting.'

'She would say that, wouldn't she?' Claudia sniffed. 'Her precious baby would never do anything as common as run off – oh no, it has to be some big fucking drama.'

John wrote 'Claudia angry' in his notebook. 'How was she doing in college? Everything okay?'

'Ash was doing well; she's always been good that way.' Megan smiled. 'Not like me – I think my lecturer is speaking double Dutch or something half the time.'

'Maybe if you went *in* occasionally you'd understand him better,' Claudia said.

Megan blushed bright red and shot a guilty look at John. Claudia flicked ash into her cup and smirked. She was letting him know who was alpha female in this little group. John decided he didn't like Claudia. She was a looker, but he didn't like her. He sat forward in his seat and let a little ice creep into his voice.

'Why didn't Ashley go to Galway with you, seeing as how you're such good friends and everything?'

If Claudia caught the tone, it didn't show. She shook her head. 'I don't know. We asked her to come.'

'Strange that she didn't go.'

'Not really. She doesn't know our friends down there that well. Does she, Meg?'

'No.' Megan buried herself deeper in her cardigan, so that only the top half of her face showed. John had to concentrate to hear her.

'I'll need the names of your friends.'

Claudia stared at him. 'Why?'

So I can check on your bullshit story, John thought. 'No reason. Better to have them, though.'

'Bloody boring, Galway.' Claudia ground out her cigarette against the cup and dropped the butt in. 'Jesus, what a shit-hole.'

'I like Galway.' Megan poked her head a little further out. 'It's got some good bars.'

Claudia sighed as if any opinion Meg might have was too annoying for words. 'Anyway, if you ask me, Ash was a little pissed off because we didn't try to persuade her to come to Galway with us. But, like I always say to Meg, we're not joined at the hip.'

John smiled. 'Megan, whereabouts in Wicklow do you live?'

Megan frowned. 'Ashford. Didn't I tell you that?'

She had, but the more Claudia prattled on, the more the whole Galway story smelled like a crock of shit, and John wanted to see what Megan looked like when she was telling the truth.

'Oh, that's right. How did you find Galway?'

Megan blinked at the sudden change of subject. 'I…it was great, really good fun.'

Satisfied she was lying, John decided to steer things back to the Naughton family. 'Ashford? I passed through there yesterday, on the way to the Naughtons' house.'

Claudia threw her legs over the arm of the sofa. Her skirt rode up and John could almost see the tops of her thighs. 'Don't tell me you were asked down to the *manor*?'

'Of course I was.'

'Awful, isn't it? All that money, and look what he built. Daddy says it's one of the ugliest houses he's ever seen. And the way Daddy Naughton goes on about it…' She looked out from under her eyelashes at John. 'Of course, you can't buy taste.'

'Really?'

'I'm not *saying* anything.' Claudia laughed suddenly. 'Was he happy to see you there?'

'Why do you ask?'

Claudia rolled her eyes. 'Because Daddy Naughton hates anyone calling to the house. If you don't believe me, ask Meg. He's a total freakazoid, a control freak. What's he like, Meg?'

'He *is* kind of scary,' Megan said with a little shudder. 'Ash's mam is really nice, but Mr

161

Naughton…he scares me. He always seems really angry; he's always shouting. Did you meet the witch?'

John had a fair idea who she was referring to, but he had to ask. 'Who's the witch?'

'Ash's grandmother. She'd give anyone the willies – always creeping around, spying and listening outside doors. Ash said she even caught her snooping through her room.' Megan bit at her lip and blushed. 'God, can you imagine?'

John nodded. He knew how dangerous teenage girls could be about their privacy. Carrie had once bloodied his nose when she caught him rooting through her room in search of paper.

'Horrible old bitch,' Claudia said. 'The things she used to say to Ash…'

'Like what?'

'You know, horrible things. Mind you, she called me plenty of things too. She doesn't like "my sort", whatever that's supposed to mean. I mean, have you heard her speak? She's a total knacker. Every time I was there she found some way of insulting me.'

'She was always fighting with Ash,' said Megan. John glanced at her. She caught his gaze and looked away.

'And now they're all wondering why Ash ran off? Duh! If I was her, I would have high-tailed it long before now.' Claudia caught John looking at her legs and smiled. John looked back at his notebook.

'I heard she ran off before. Do you know what happened?'

Megan sat forward in her chair. 'Oh my God, that was *so* bad. Ash got caught smoking down behind the basketball courts, and that old bitch Sister Eithne suspended her. Rang Mr Naughton in work and told him to come and collect her that afternoon.'

'Miserable lesbian.' Claudia sniffed.

'Ash was hysterical,' Megan said, her pale eyes huge at the memory. 'Well, who wouldn't be, with Daddy Naughton on the warpath? So, instead of hanging around, Ash legged it.'

John made another note. 'Where did she go? How long was she missing for, exactly?'

Megan pulled a face. 'Only for a few days, but my God, the fuss! Mr Naughton was livid. He threatened to sue the school and everything – he totally went ape-shit! We don't know where Ash actually went, she never said, but when she came home Mr Naughton went mental. She had bruises for weeks.'

John leaned forwards. 'Wait – are you telling me he hit her?'

Megan glanced guiltily at Claudia and closed her mouth. Claudia jumped in straight away. 'No one knows what happened, exactly.'

'But she had bruises,' Megan said quickly.

'Shut up, Meg! You could be sued for that kind of talk; it's slander.' Claudia turned her attention back to John. 'Look, I don't think this has anything to do with now. Ash's probably gone off on the tear somewhere. She took money, didn't she? I heard she cleaned out her accounts.'

'Who told you that?'

'Margo. And if she took money, it's probably because she's planning to spend some time away. Right? So all this fuss is for nothing.'

John rubbed his hand over his eyes. Everything she said was true, so why did he get the feeling there was more to it? 'Which of you found the note?'

'I did,' Claudia said. 'That was so typical of Ash – the drama. She gets it into her head she's going to do something, and that's it. Isn't that right, Meg?'

Megan nodded and shrank further into her cardigan.

'When we came back from Galway on Sunday evening, we did think it was weird she hadn't come back from Wicklow, but like I said, we thought she was pissed off because we went off without her. Then on Monday evening Margo called asking to speak with her, and that was that.'

'Did she take any of her things from her room?'

'Some clothes,' Megan said softly. 'I'm not really sure if—'

'We don't know,' Claudia interrupted. She sat upright and glared at John. 'Jesus, I'm so sick of this. We have Margo calling morning, noon and night, Daddy Naughton barging in here and yelling the place down… Anyone would think Ash was a child of six or something.'

'When did he call here?'

'Like, about an hour after Margo called on the Monday,' Claudia said. 'He came storming in here, demanding to see her room, screaming at us—'

'He was so angry,' Megan said, her pale eyes blinking at the memory. 'I burst out crying. I feel silly about it now, but seriously, it was like – like he'd totally lost it.'

'He'd no right bursting in here like that,' Claudia snapped. 'Anyone would think we'd hidden her under our beds, the way he was going on. Accusing us of the most ludicrous things.'

'He went ballistic,' Megan said mournfully.

'Which was a bit rich, if you ask me,' Claudia said. 'He'd never set foot in that door before to see how she was. He wouldn't even help Ash bring her stuff up from Wicklow. Margo did it. He was dead against her moving in here.'

'I see,' John said. 'And what happened when he realised neither of you had seen Ash since the Friday?'

'Oh,' Megan said, 'he tore out of here like a madman.'

'Way to ham it up, Meg.' Claudia shot John an exasperated look. 'And now Margo's been ringing us day and night to see if we've heard anything, and we haven't. I *know* Ash. She'll turn up when she runs out of cash.'

'Speaking of cash,' John said, 'Margaret Naughton tells me there was close to ten thousand euros in Ashley's accounts – a sum that's now nearly gone.'

'So?' Claudia said, warily.

'Well, ten grand – that's a lot of money to go through in less than three months. Isn't it?'

'I don't think so. Look, Ash likes to shop.'

'But still—'

'Look, John, ten G might seem like a lot to you, but it isn't. Not to us.'

'Was Ashley taking drugs?'

Megan's head disappeared completely, and Claudia glared at him. It was a moment or two before she replied.

'Look, I know you have to ask questions, but this is getting ridiculous. Ash has taken off, and I'm not going to sit here and answer any more questions.'

John closed his notebook. He knew he had just touched a nerve. 'Look, I don't care if she was or not. I just want to find her and let her mother know she's safe. So if either of you hears from her or remembers something useful, I want you to call me straight away. I'll leave you my number.'

'God, this is all *so* OTT,' Claudia said. 'She'll probably turn up next week with a shitload of clothes from London or something. Honestly, all this fuss over nothing. She's just looking for attention.'

John stood and pulled his card out of his

wallet. Ashley's supposed best friend seemed more upset by the fuss than by the fact that her friend hadn't been seen or heard from in over a week. 'Listen to me,' he said, unable to keep a note of anger from creeping into his voice. 'If she calls here, I want you to contact me. Got it?'

'All right! There's no need to get sniffy.' Claudia snatched the card out of John's hand and tossed it onto the table without even looking at it.

'Can you show me Ashley's room?'

'There's nothing there that can help you. We've all looked. Margo's been in there twice.'

John shrugged. 'Which way is it?'

Megan pointed at a door leading off the sitting room. John slipped his notebook into his jacket and crossed the room.

'You're wasting your time,' Claudia called.

'Maybe so.' John closed Ashley's door behind him and leaned against it.

It was a purely functional room, with cream walls, a beige carpet and floor-length cream curtains. And it was tiny: the bed, wardrobe and matching locker were as much furniture as you could squeeze in and still leave room for one person to stand. The bed was neatly made up and clothes were hanging in the wardrobe – not the preppy clothes Ashley had had at her parents' house. John pulled out a pleated skirt so short it would have barely covered Ashley's backside. At the bottom of the wardrobe he found three pairs of Skechers runners, a pair of strappy sandals with

Perspex soles and a pair of thigh-high leather boots. The sneakers he understood, but the others were hardly casual wear. Christ, how could women even walk in heels that high?

John searched the rest of the room in less than fifteen minutes. Ashley Naughton clearly felt more comfortable leaving personal things around here: there were two well-kissed posters of the R&B singer Usher taped to the door, and the bedside locker held a handful of CDs and some postcards. John flicked through the postcards. Two were from Megan, the other was from Claudia, sent from somewhere in the Alps. Under the bundle he found a photo of Ashley, Megan and Claudia, dressed to kill, standing outside the Front Lounge bar.

John stared at the picture. The girls were obviously plastered. Ashley looked stunning in low-rider jeans and a red tank top cut off about two inches below her breasts. Claudia looked seriously hot, too, all in black, and even Megan was looking pretty sharp in a red-and-black kilt and knee-high boots. He put the picture back, wondering if Margaret Naughton knew her daughter wasn't the polo-shirt-wearing baby she thought she'd reared.

There were some more photos stuck to the mirror on the wardrobe: two of Ashley and Megan drinking pints in a pub somewhere, and one of Claudia and Megan posing by the Molly Malone statue. In a wicker basket on the dresser was a collection of metal bracelets, hair clips, ticket stubs and small change. A glass jar held some pretty grey and pink seashells. John shook his head. Ashley had only been here a few months, and already this little boxroom contained more of her personality than her room at her home.

He sat on the end of the bed. Cute as the photos were, they didn't tell him anything except that she liked to have fun with her mates. He felt frustrated and a little out of his depth. How the hell were he and Sarah ever going to find Ashley if they hadn't a clue where to start looking? He closed his eyes and listened to the murmur of the other girls. What were Claudia and Megan hiding? Was Ashley in trouble of some kind? Were they covering for her? There had to be something he was missing.

John switched on the bedside lamp and began to search the room again. He lifted the mattress: nothing. He opened the curtains and ran his hand along the top of the window, but all he came away with was a fingerful of dust. He flicked though the bundle of magazines by her bed and emptied her wastepaper basket. He pulled out the folders stacked three deep under her bed and flicked though her coursework. She was a good student from what he could see, but hardly remarkable.

John slid the last folder back into place and sat on the bed again. As he leaned across to switch off the lamp, his eyes fell on the carpet by the locker. He tilted his head slightly. It definitely bulged a few inches to the right of her locker.

John grinned, suddenly grateful he had shared a house with a teenage sister. He knelt down and ran his hands along the carpet. There was something under there. He slipped his fingers under the skirting board and gave the carpet a gentle tug; it rolled back easily. He reached underneath and pulled out a small bunch of flat, silver keys. There were eight of them, neatly fastened together with a red ribbon.

John dropped the carpet back into place and sat on the bed to examine his find. He turned the keys over in his hand and smiled at the name stamped along the leg of each key. He'd heard about these. These keys weren't for any lock. They were complimentary passes, and all for one club: Tempest.

10

Dougie Burrows sat back in the armchair and grinned at Vinnie, showing off a mouth only a barracuda would be proud of. Vinnie smiled wanly back. The armchair he sat in was faux leather and leaking stuffing. It made him want to sneeze.

Dougie was a ruddy-faced man of about fifty. He wore brown corduroy trousers, a padded plaid shirt and a brown sleeveless jacket with net pockets. Dougie's top jaw was so overcrowded with teeth that they overlapped and protruded from his mouth, and his bottom jaw wasn't much better. It was often said Dougie could eat an apple through a letterbox. His thick, coarse hair defied gravity and stuck out from his head in a mushroom-shaped bush. Dougie 'the Landlord' Burrows was part tinker, part trader, all crook.

'So you want me to put the word out that no one's to bite on any big delivery? You want me to keep an ear to the ground, that right?'

'Exactly.' Vinnie pressed his linen hanky against his nose and inhaled in shallow drags. Dougie's front room reeked of wet dog, urine, Jeyes Fluid and the petrol Dougie used to wipe down the coats of his fighting dogs. In the corner, a huge, ancient television played *VIP* with the sound turned down. Dougie had earlier explained that he liked to watch Pamela Anderson, but not to 'listen to her shiteing on'. Vinnie had laughed benignly, giving a remarkable impression of savouring the little freak's foibles. Now, however, his humour had evaporated in a plume of *eau de chien*.

'Perhaps we can go out for a drink?'

'My home not good enough for you?'

Vinnie brushed dog hair from the leg of his Armani trousers. 'Of course it is, but you know me – I hate to intrude.'

'You're not botherin' me, I told you.' Dougie eyed him slyly. 'So tell us this and tell us no more – this must be a right big load if you're down here.'

'It's big enough, yes,' Vinnie said, somewhat warily. Dougie was a little too keen.

'How much we talkin' about?'

'Enough.'

Dougie scratched under his balls. 'If you don't tell me what I'm lookin' for, how would I know when I see it?'

'One hundred and forty kilos, pure and uncut.'

Dougie began to laugh. 'No wonder you're here with that puss on you.'

'I don't see what's so funny.'

Every time Vinnie spoke, four pit bull terriers, individually caged by the door, shifted their weight and craned their massive necks to stare at him intently. They were ugly dogs, battle-scarred, squat and big-headed, with small mean eyes and ears cut tight against their skulls. Disturbingly, they reminded him of Davey. A fat rottweiler lying by Dougie's feet farted in her sleep, increasing the stench. Vinnie swallowed his indignation and pressed on. 'Look, Doug, everyone knows you're the man to see in these situations. Why, you're practically a legend.'

'What makes you think Naughton's gonna approach me?'

'I never mentioned Naughton.' Vinnie eyed him suspiciously. 'How do you—'

Dougie grinned. 'Everyone knows you and that fat fuck are in cahoots. If you've been stiffed, stands to reason it might have been him.'

'All right, then: if he approaches you, I want to know.'

'Look, York, a shipment that size is worth a lot of money. Now, if it falls into bigger hands than mine…well, there's fuck all I can do about it.' Dougie's grin widened. 'And if Naughton were to approach me—'

'Dougie, there is not a doubt in my mind that, if he has it, then he will come to you. He'd be a fool to try anyone else. Like I say, you're the best at what you do.'

'Go on, you cunt you!' Dougie Burrows threw back his head and howled with laughter, slapping his thigh as if this was the most fun he'd had in months. 'The fuckin' tongue on you! Any smoother and you'd be dribblin' down my leg.' He stuck his little finger in his ear and waggled it about, then wiped off whatever he'd located on the leg of his pants.

Vinnie tried to smile, but couldn't quite pull it off. He couldn't take another minute trapped in this room. He desperately wanted a line, and he couldn't seem to stop his leg from jiggling up and down. He was sick of waiting for this toothy retard to stop talking bollocks. His patience was shot.

'Dougie, I know you will help me.'

Dougie stopped laughing. 'Oh?'

Vinnie stared at him, his eyes raking over the ragged clothes, the filthy nails and rough hair, and marvelled that such a disgusting pile of scum could be a multi-millionaire. Dougie's wealth stemmed from the fact that he owned almost every hideout, bolthole and lock-up in Ireland. He rented the most elusive of addresses, north and south of the border, to the underworld, he provided lead-lined underground bunkers for stashing arms and he supplied safe houses, complete with generators, untraceable phone lines and dry food supplies, for men who might need to lay low. He owned lock-ups specially kitted out for stolen trucks and containers, purpose-built warehouses with hydroponic lights for cannabis-growing, small factories containing top-of-the-line equipment for the mass production of ecstasy and speed. He had elaborate pits, dug out under remote sheds on even remoter farms, in which he staged twice-monthly dogfights, his main and highly lucrative hobby. He rented stylish apartment to pimps and freelance prostitutes from Galway to Cork to Dublin. He owned dozens of large refrigerated buildings, ideal for butchering thousands of illegal cattle and pigs. If you required the space, Dougie supplied it. He wasn't called 'the Landlord' for nothing.

Vinnie knew Dougie's village-idiot act was just that – an act. Dougie was a shrewd fucker, and not a man to make a mistake. Vinnie caught the gleam of intelligent patience in his host's eye and smiled. He would play the game.

'Tell me now, why should I help you?' Dougie eyed Vinnie.

'Why wouldn't you help me? We've done good business before, haven't we?' Vinnie leaned closer, in a conspiratorial manner.

'Business *is* business, Vin. You know that. So why the fuck would I turn someone down just to deal with the likes of yourself?'

'Because a man like myself is a useful man to know, Dougie,' Vinnie said in a low, ominous voice. 'A man like myself is a man going places. And there's only so much a man like myself is willing to put up with.'

The dog by Dougie's feet shifted in her sleep and raised her head. She turned one wall-eye in Vinnie's direction and sniffed the air as though she could scent the threat seeping from his skin.

'Shh, whisht now…' Dougie made a soft cooing noise and rubbed behind her left ear.

'Don't mind him. He's only messin'.' Dougie tightened his hand on the back of the dog's neck. She growled and bared an impressive set of teeth. Suddenly she didn't look so old and infirm. 'Aren't you? You wouldn't be tryin' to threaten the likes of me, now would you?'

Vinnie blanched slightly. He'd never liked dogs, especially big ones. He wished Davey had been allowed to come inside with him, instead of being left to scratch his arse in the comfort of the jeep.

'*Mon dieu,* Dougie – what a thought! No, no, I'm not saying that at all.' Vinnie leaned back in his chair, putting as much distance between his face and the dog as possible. 'Look, you're a business-man, Dougie. I know you would never turn down an opportunity, should one come your way. But there are opportunities and then there are mistakes, hmm? Personally, I think dealing with the likes of Naughton is always going to be a mistake. You know he can't even piss without Pascal Mooney to hold his cock.' Vinnie raised his eyebrows. 'Do you want the pig knowing your business?'

'Why are you dealin' with him, then?'

'I don't,' Vinnie said. 'If it were up to me, I would have nothing to do with Naughton either.'

'Now that's a fact. I never did trust a man who'll run with the fuckin' pigs.' He leaned over the side of his armchair and spat. 'Course, I don't much like smooth cunts like yourself, either – six of one, half-dozen of the other. Tell me this: why should I bother my arse gettin' involved with you?'

'Because I can give you something you want, Dougie. Something that would definitely be of interest to you.'

Dougie stared at the television screen, his face betraying nothing. Vinnie had been dancing around something since he got there, and Dougie knew it.

'Go on.'

'Supposing,' Vinnie said lightly, 'I were to offer you an incentive to deal strictly with me.'

'What kind of incentive?'

'The wiping clean of an old slate.'

Dougie turned his head, his eyes narrowed and suspicious. 'Which slate would you be talking about?'

'Albert.'

Dougie blessed himself and spat over the side of the chair again. When he raised his head his face was stony, his eyes hard and flat.

'Well?' Vinnie asked, although he already knew the answer. 'You know how suspicious he is. I can make sure you get your chance.'

'You'd do that?'

'In a heartbeat.'

Dougie rubbed coarse red hands over his jaw. 'You bring me that cunt, and I'll waive my usual fee for a change-over.'

'Consider it done, *mon ami*.' Vinnie clapped his hands and instantly regretted it: the dogs in the cage began to bark, and the rottweiler jumped to her feet and snarled. Vinnie slammed back in his chair.

'Lie down out of that!' Dougie yelled at the top of his lungs, and the dogs were instantly silent. The rottweiler sat down, but kept her good eye firmly on Vinnie.

'Jaysus, York, are you tryin' to get yourself killed or what?' The Landlord roared laughing at Vinnie's stricken face. 'Don't be clappin' in here. You're liable to get yourself eaten. Them cages wouldn't hold them for long if they really wanted to get out.'

'I see,' Vinnie said softly. He cleared his throat and inched forward in his seat. 'Well, then, are we in agreement?'

'Aye. One thing: you bring him yourself. I don't want to clean the slate and then have you fucking running round sayin' you knew nothing about it. Right?'

'*Myself?*' Vinnie's squeal set the dogs off again.

'Aye, that's right – yourself. Nothin' personal, like,' Dougie said. When he got them quiet again. 'You're some hard-nosed cunt, York;. Never thought you had it in you. It's a dog-eat-fuckin'-dog world, no doubt about it.' Then he glanced at his penned dogs and roared laughing again.

Vinnie stared at him and ground his back teeth together. The crazy bastard had worn him out – but Vinnie knew he'd never get his hands on the goods without this loon. No matter who was selling what, Dougie would catch a name from the wind. Without him, Naughton would sell the cocaine on and Vinnie would have nothing. 'Okay, *mon ami*. We have a deal.'

'Good.' Dougie spat on his hand and offered it across the head of the rottweiler.

Vinnie stared at the pool of spittle gleaming in his palm, aghast.

'Shake on it, you fucker, like a gentleman.'

Vinnie swallowed his disgust and repeated the gesture. They shook. Dougie grinned and hoisted his body out of the chair.

'Come on down to the kennels, I'll show you the new litter – I'll give you the pick if you want. Best fuckin' stock I seen yet: only a week out of the mother, and one of the little bastards is already trying to tear the faces off the other cunts.'

Vinnie glanced down at his Gucci loafers. They were new, he had only worn them twice. 'Really, I'd love to, Dougie, but the thing is…well, I'm not really a dog person.'

Dougie looked at him in disbelief. 'You don't like dogs, is that what you're sayin'?'

'Oh, no, I *love* them. They don't seem to like me, though,' Vinnie back-pedalled. 'I certainly wouldn't be able to keep one. I live in an apartment and keep such odd hours…it wouldn't be fair to the poor animal.'

Dougie grunted. 'Come on and see them any-way. You'll never see a finer-looking litter. Took me more than eight years to get bloodlines like this.'

Rather than insult a man who might hand him his future on a platter, Vinnie mourned his shoes and followed Dougie through the rest of the disgusting cottage, past rows of gleaming cages and out across a muddy, shit-filled, freezing yard, to look at an animal he despised.

By the time he got back to the jeep, he was apoplectic with rage.

'Well?' Davey glanced at his boss's face. 'He tell you what you wanted to hear?'

'The moment he hears anything, he'll call.' Vinnie pushed the heater up to full and stripped off his shoes. They reeked of dog shit and were soaking from the puddles he hadn't been able to avoid. '*Mon dieu,* he dragged me down to see his fucking *pups*! Look at these – they're ruined.' Vinnie rolled the window down and hurled them into a nearby hedge.

Davey started the jeep and rolled down the rutted, bumpy lane. 'If he showed you the dogs, he must be on side. I hear they're his fuckin' pride and joy.'

Vinnie rubbed his hands together and blew on them. 'How can he live like that? How can he stay in such a shit-hole?'

'He's a weirdo.'

'Yes,' Vinnie said, searching his pockets for his wrap of coke, 'but a useful little toad. I wonder how he knows so much about the deals people make? I mean, he knew about Naughton. How do you suppose that is?'

'He travels all over. You know you can't shit in this country without someone commentin' on the colour.'

'I'd love to know how he gets away with everything he does.'

'I hear he's connected up North.'

'Connected?' Vinnie opened his wrap and took a deep sniff. 'The only thing *connected* to that fucker is disease.'

Davey said nothing.

Vinnie folded his wrap back up and cleared his throat softly. 'I was right about one thing.'

'Yeah?'

Vinnie grinned like a shark. 'He'd do anything to get his hands on Patrick.'

Davey said nothing.

'The only thing is, he says I have to deliver him personally.'

'Suppose that's normal.' Davey shrugged. 'Just covering his arse.'

'Yes. Now I have to work out how to get Patrick to him without attracting attention or suspicion.' Vinnie sighed and stared out the window at the gathering darkness. 'Oh, Davey, sometimes it's hard being the lion.'

Davey reached the end of the lane, turned on to the main road and put his foot down. If Vinnie was going to start on about the lion again, he was going to get to Dublin as fast as humanly possible.

11

'Anything new?' John asked Sarah when he got back to the office.

Sarah shook her head, looking bored. She was on hold, and had been for almost ten minutes. 'No. You?'

'I'll tell you when you're done.' John dropped into his chair and pulled out his notebook.

Sarah pulled a face. Every line of inquiry she had tried was a washout. Ashley hadn't taken her passport so it was unlikely she had left the country, and there was no record of her on any of the flights or ferries to England. She hadn't used her credit card since the fourth of November, two days before she had vanished. A slow burn of anxiety began to gnaw deep in Sarah's gut. The girl had vanished into thin air.

Eventually someone came back on the line. 'Yeah, hi... No? Really – nothing at all? ... Okay, yeah – that's fine. How much?' She wrote something down in her notebook. 'Thanks a million for your help.'

She hung up. 'That was Ashley Naughton's bank, in case you were wondering. She didn't take out that money in one go. She's been spending like a good thing since she came up to Dublin – five hundred here, two there… Every Friday she pulls out the guts of five hundred quid. No wonder the accounts are empty.'

'Shit. What's she spending it on?'

'I couldn't tell you. There's been no activity on her card since last Wednesday, and no tickets bought with it. The only thing Ashley paid for with her card in the last few weeks was a pair of Prada slingbacks from Brown Thomas.'

'Yeah?'

Sarah shook her head. 'Prada, John? She's eighteen, and she just waltzes in and buys a pair of shoes that cost more than I earn in a week.'

'She wouldn't be the only one of her crowd who could do that. You should see the other two at the apartment.'

Sarah raised an eyebrow. John lit a cigarette and told her about Megan and Claudia and finding the keys.

When he'd finished, Sarah looked decidedly unimpressed. 'They don't exactly sound like friends to me. Weren't they worried about her?'

'I think maybe Megan was. Hard to tell what the other one thought.'

'You think they know more than they're letting on?'

John laced his hands together behind his head, leaving his cigarette to dangle from his lips in a way he thought looked cool. 'I think they're bullshitting me about Galway. You should have seen Megan Lowry's face when I showed them the keys. She's a pale kid, but she managed to go about four shades lighter. Next thing I knew, Claudia was falling over herself trying to convince me they'd never heard of the place.'

'Maybe they hadn't.'

'Give me a break, Sarah. That Claudia probably knows every club in the city – and even I've heard of *this* place. The other thing I got was that they hinted that Naughton once roughed Ashley up.'

Sarah's head snapped up. 'What?'

'Yeah, the last time she ran off. The girls say he went mental and Ashley was covered in bruises for weeks.' John shrugged. 'That could explain why Ashley's had enough and doesn't feel like spending time at the old ranch.'

Sarah said nothing for a moment. She was thinking of the bruising to Edward Naughton's face. Was it possible he had done something to his own daughter – and maybe she had fought back? Maybe that was why he had been so uneasy about finding two detectives on his stairs… 'Do we know the keys were hers for sure? They could have belonged to whoever had the room before her.'

'Claudia Delaney's parents own that apartment. Nobody rented the room before Ashley. The keys are hers, Sarah, I'm sure of it.'

Sarah ran her fingers through her hair and considered it. 'What if they are hers? So what? What does that mean?'

184

'It means she probably went there,' John said sarcastically.

'You know, a lot of clubs leave things around in pubs and stuff, to drum up business. She could have picked them up from a table anywhere.'

'Not this club.' John pulled the keys out of his jacket pocket and tossed them over to her. They landed on her desk with a jingle. 'I rang Cynthia to see if she knew about them. She says you only get the keys if you're a member or a guest of a member.'

Sarah picked them up and shuffled through them. They were silver and beautifully designed, with the word 'Tempest' stamped on the leg in a Celtic font.

'And another thing – why did she hide them?' John said.

'Okay, so we need to talk to the club, find out if she's a member and if she was there the night she vanished.'

John looked at his watch. It was after seven. He hadn't eaten anything since the chicken pie and he was exhausted. All those late nights with Cynthia were beginning to take their toll.

Sarah shuffled the keys and looked thoughtful. 'Those places usually have CCTV cameras on the doors. If she did go there, they might have her on tape. What do you think?'

'Sure, they might.'

'It's a start, at least.' Sarah glanced at John and caught him yawning. 'Look, John, why don't you head home?'

'What about you?'

'I'm waiting for a call from Helen,' Sarah shrugged. 'While I'm waiting, I'll give Tempest a ring.'

John shook his head. 'I'm fine. I don't need to go home.'

'You should go home and get some rest,' Sarah said firmly. 'There's no point in the two of us sitting here twiddling our thumbs. I'll give you a bell the minute I hear anything.'

John slipped his jacket on and rummaged for his car keys. 'Helen, huh? I hope the devil knows his time at the top is limited.'

As soon as the words were out of his mouth, he knew he shouldn't have said them. Sarah gave him a dark, unreadable look, shook her head once and turned her back on him.

John felt like a gobshite all the way home. He knew he shouldn't have said anything about Helen, but he couldn't help himself. He was tired and fed up. He'd have to stop all these late nights with Cynthia – especially now that she was starting the 'time to meet the parents' crap. John could think of nothing, short of plucking his pubic hair with tweezers, that would be more painful than meeting her folks.

His humour improved slightly when he got home and discovered that Sumo hadn't managed to open the new bolt on the bedroom door. The big dog was under the kitchen table, sulking. John opened the back door and let him out into the garden, where Sumo extracted his revenge by urinating on the only healthy plant John had.

John made boiled chicken and rice for Sumo and beans on toast for himself and pulled a can of Heineken from the fridge. He carried the whole lot into the sitting room and sat down to watch television, but found he couldn't concentrate. He kept thinking about Sarah, how irritable she was lately. He wondered if she was starting to regret coming into business with him. Maybe she was thinking of moving on. Shit, what would he do if she left? She was his better half when it came to business. And she'd been getting an awful lot of phone calls from Helen lately. Maybe Helen had finally persuaded her to leave QuicK and try something else. God, how he despised Helen. She was everything Sarah was not – bitter, stuck up and a total bitch – and she hated John with a passion bordering on obsession.

John ate half of his pathetic dinner and let Sumo lick the plate clean. Just as he was getting into the shower, the phone rang.

'Shit.' John hopped out of the shower, stumbled out to the hall and grabbed the phone.

'Hey, it's me.' It was Sarah.

John tried not to drip onto the phone. 'Listen, can I call you—'

'You were half right about the keys.' Sarah shuffled papers in the background. 'They're only given to members, so either Ashley was a member, or she knows one. I spoke to a woman called

Sophie Allen – she's head of PR – and asked if she can get me a copy of the members list. They do have CCTV, but they're not exactly eager to help. She says she'll check with the boss, but she asked if we could hold off for tonight. Friday night's pretty busy, apparently, and she doesn't have time to run through the tapes for us.'

John wiped water out of his eyes. 'When can we see them?'

'She says she'll talk to the owner and hopefully we can see the tapes tomorrow or Sunday.'

'That's too late. Did you tell them this is a missing person?'

'Of *course* I did.'

'Sorry. So what now?'

'Honestly?' Sarah sounded disillusioned. 'I don't know. I've called every name on Margaret Naughton's list, and nobody can give me anything. Frankly, I don't bloody well have any other ideas.'

'Okay.' John wanted to say more, but he couldn't think of a single thing.

'What do you think?'

'I think we can talk about this tomorrow, maybe when I'm not naked and freezing my bollocks off.'

'Oh, sorry. Okay, sure – tomorrow.' Sarah hung up.

John climbed back under the hot water. As he shampooed his hair, he thought about Megan Lowry and how pale she'd gone when he'd shown her the keys. Why? And why had Ashley hidden the keys under the carpet? Who was she hiding them from? Her father? Her friends?

John rinsed the suds from his hair and worked on a plan. He'd get dressed and take the dog for a walk, then he could head into town, grab something decent to eat, maybe head to Mulligan's for a few pints and catch up with some of the lads. Ever since he'd started seeing Cynthia, he'd neglected his mates. He'd definitely have to spend some quality time on a barstool to make up for it.

Just as John switched off the water, the phone rang again. His shoulders sagged and his mental image of Guinness started to shimmer and dissolve. He wrapped a towel around his waist, stepped back into the hall and lifted the receiver. 'Forget something? Or do you want to come over here and wash me?'

'What are you talking about?' Cynthia's voice split through him like a knife.

'I thought you were Sarah.'

'Why would *she* come over and wash you?'

'She called before, when I was in the shower,' John sighed. 'I was being sarcastic.'

'Oh.' Cynthia lost interest immediately. 'Baby,' she said in a sweet purr that made John suspicious, 'what are you doing tonight?'

John looked at his face in the hall mirror. He had shadows under his eyes and he looked pale. He had barely recovered from the night before. Maybe the ten-year age gap was starting to show.

Cynthia never seemed to be tired. 'I…I think I'm working.'

'On what?'

'We got a case in today. Very last-minute.'

'It must have been.'

John knew she didn't believe a word of it. He decided against trying to sound more convincing. Maybe if she realised he was lying, she'd get annoyed and leave him alone. 'If there was any way I could get out of it, I would, but, you know … Why do you ask?'

'I promised my friends you'd meet them. We're only going for a few drinks and maybe on to a club or something. I said you'd go. Now you're going to make me look like a total idiot.'

'I don't think I can get out of this one. It's probably an all-nighter.'

'Can't *she* do it?' Cynthia's voice rose an octave. 'It's not like *she's* exactly going to be busy on a Friday night.'

John let that one go. 'Hey, come on, Cyn. We can go another night – next weekend, maybe.'

'I told them you'd go! They're expecting you.' She was whining now. 'God, John, sometimes you act like you don't want to be with me at all.'

'Cyn, don't be like that.'

'It's true!'

John sighed. 'Look, we have fun, don't we? We go out, we have a good time – but we don't need to see each other every night.'

'I *told* my friends you'd be there,' she whined.

'John, come on, *please*. It'll be fun. We're doing Lillie's first, before it gets crowded, then probably Spirit. I don't see why you can't at least make an effort. It's not like you ever do anything I want—'

Suddenly John had an idea. 'I'll come out if we can spin by Tempest. Could we get in there, do you think?'

'Well, *duh*, of course. We're going out with Sondra, and she knows *the* best places in town for dancing. And that's one of them, according to her. The owner's a bit of a dish – I've met him, you know, out in Lillie's one night. He's cute and everything, but a total coke fiend. Wasn't at all friendly. I don't think it's really my scene – it's quite underground, from what I've heard, and it's supposed to be *full* of knackers – but Sondra goes a lot and I think she has a good time. But then, she'd have a good time at a funeral. But we *could* try it if you want. I mean, it's not like I won't try somewhere different. It's good to try—'

John took a deep breath. 'So that's yes, then?'

'Why do you want to go there?' Cynthia sounded suspicious and confused at the same time.

'No reason. I just heard it was a good place.'

'Really? What about your gig?'

'I'll give Sarah a buzz and tell her something came up.'

'Oh, Johnny, that's brill! Listen, I'll come over early and we'll decide what you'll be wearing. Then I can—'

'What did you just say?' John thought he'd misheard her.

'Clothes, Johnny! No offence, baby, but you can't go to Tempest looking like you normally do. You wouldn't get in.'

'What the hell is wrong with my clothes?'

Cynthia paused. 'There's nothing *wrong* with them, exactly. It's just that they're a little...well, you know.'

'No, I don't know!' Now he was truly offended.

'Well...'Cynthia paused again, longer this time. 'They're a little dated – *nothing* we can't fix, baby. I mean, we can... Look, never mind. Wear black and I'll pick you up in a taxi about ten. Okay? Got to run – bye, baby.'

Cynthia hung up first, something she'd never done before. John stared at the phone in astonishment. What the hell did she mean about his clothes? Goddammit, his clothes were practical and comfortable. Nobody had ever passed judgement on them before. To hell with that and to hell with her: he'd wear exactly what he liked. To hell with the whole thing, actually – he'd call her back and cancel. Mulligan's was more his style anyway, and as far as he knew nobody had ever passed a dress code for it.

And yet, at ten o'clock, he was dressed in black Levi's and a black suede shirt and he'd attempted to polish his motorbike boots.

12

Down in Tempest, things were heating up.

'Where the fuck is Alejandro?' Vinnie screamed at the top of his lungs. 'Tell the little spic I want to see him – not in a minute, not in a second, *now*! *Now*!'

The floor-girl bolted down the steps to find the missing barman.

'For fuck's sake! We open in two hours and the bars haven't been stocked properly. Is this what I'm paying him for? *Sacré bleu*, I'm away for a few hours and the whole place collapses around my ears!'

Vinnie flung himself onto a sofa in the members' bar and tilted his head from left to right. His brain was running full-pelt from the long line of coke he had hoovered up seconds before. He could barely contain his desire to get up and start pacing. 'No, take it down. I don't like it there.'

Davey stared at him and then at the huge, gilded mirror that had taken him and one of the Donkey brothers almost an hour to put up. 'You sure?'

'Of course I'm sure. It's completely wrong up

there. *Mon dieu*, David, I don't know how I let you talk me into it in the first place.' Vinnie waved a disgusted arm at the mirror. 'I want it moved to the landing, *toot sweet*. People always look at themselves when they're climbing stairs.'

Davey counted to five in his head. It hadn't been his idea to stick the mirror over the seating area – not that it mattered, when Vinnie was in this humour. Patrick was upstairs on the phone, having spent the day snapping orders. The old man was playing his cards close to his chest, refusing to tell Vinnie who he was talking to, and Davey knew Vinnie's paranoia was shifting up through the gears. The news that the PR department had received a call from detectives looking into the disappearance of Edward Naughton's brat of a daughter had almost pushed him over the edge.

'We're supposed to be doing a vodka promotion tonight.' Vinnie held up a half-empty bottle to the light. 'This tastes like *merde*.' He threw the lime-green and pink bottle halfway across the room, where it bounced off a table and rolled harmlessly under another sofa. 'You couldn't *give* the stuff away. How are we supposed to make any money on it? And get hold of Sophie. Tell her to get her arse up here. Fucking idiot. Imagine admitting that we keep the CCTV tapes.' He shook his head and sniffed loudly. 'Fucking Naughton… Fuck him and fuck her.'

Davey headed off to get the ladder and the PR girl, his face carefully neutral. Vinnie had been practically foaming at the mouth for over an hour now, and Davey was sick to death of the sound of his voice.

He found Sophie at the main bar, a gin and tonic in front of her. As usual, she was scribbling into the big Filofax she carried around like an extra appendage. 'He's lookin' for you,' Davey said to her.

Sophie turned on her stool and raked back her black hair. 'Is he still mad?'

'About the same.'

'Fuck!'

Davey walked past her to the storeroom at the back of the club. He punched a good-sized hole in the boiler room door and grunted with satisfaction. Then he licked the blood from his knuckles, picked up the heavy metal ladder and tucked it under his thick arm. He took his time walking back to the members' bar. Sometimes even he needed a few minutes away from the reek of madness.

Cynthia's friends were a nightmare, and John knew he was in for a hellish night the second he clapped eyes on them. But he didn't bolt. He fingered the photo of Ashley in his pocket and put on a brave face.

First there was Rebecca. She was a drama student, even though she was at least three years older than him. She was tall, bony and loud, with masses of curly blond hair and a laugh that could shatter glass at twenty paces. Gavin, a skinny, trendy number who worked in advertising, was even worse. He wore his hair in some kind of mullet, gave John an embossed business card and kissed him on both cheeks. Next was Sondra – John suspected the 'o' had originally been an 'a'. John wasn't sure what the hell she did because he could barely understand a word she said. The woman didn't talk, she screeched, in a faux-American accent she'd picked up while spending a few weeks in New York. Then there was Adam. Of all of the wastes of space John met that night, Adam was the closest to normal: he was a computer programmer, he didn't hand John his card and he didn't kiss his cheeks.

They met in the Bailey and moved on to Tempest. As they walked up Grafton Street, John wondered if this was worth the earache he was suffering. He didn't think he could bear another of Rebecca's ripping laughs, and if Gavin brushed against him once more, he would deck him. He looked at Cynthia's beaming face, thought of Sarah and fixed a grin on his face.

Tempest had once been an old, almost derelict leather factory on the corner of Pleasant Street. It had been due for the wrecker's ball when Vinnie York had stepped in and bought the place for a song. Vinnie had gutted the place, reinforced the walls and ceilings, backhanded the leader of the local residents' association and applied for a drink licence. He had installed fifty grand's worth of speakers, a springboard floor, a state-of-the-art bar designed by a hot London design duo and a whole array of dazzling lights, and now it was one of the hottest night spots in the fair city, regularly turning away hundreds of people on the weekends.

John heard the dull thud of a heavy bass pounding from its walls, growing fainter as they turned the corner to the steel front door. They waited behind three irate lads arguing furiously with two huge and neck-free doormen.

'Why can't we come in?' one of the lads shouted, getting dangerously close to jabbing the bigger of the men. 'You let our friends in earlier on.'

'Sorry, lads. Regulars only.'

'This is bullshit, man! They weren't regulars, and they got in. We're supposed to meet up with them.'

The doormen looked bored. 'Regulars only.'

Sondra strode up to the door, all big smile and jutting chest. 'Hey, Davey. What's happening?'

The uglier of the doorman glanced at her briefly and then over her shoulder, his eyes scanning the little group, resting longest on John. He had summed them up in a heartbeat.

'Right, lads, you'll have to move away from the door,' he said, using his meaty arm to swipe the three protesting men out of the way. He waved John's group in. He nodded to Adam, but his eyes showed no sign of recognition. He had preferred the look of them, nothing more.

John slipped past the two lads and muttered, 'Sorry.'

There were immediate howls of protest. 'You're letting them in and not us? But we were here first!'

'I'm not tellin' you again, right? It's regulars only, lads. You can stand there until tomorrow if you want, but—'

John paid the anaemic-looking cashier forty quid for himself and Cynthia, and another four quid to check their jackets. Stunned by the cost, he rounded the corner, pushed through thick velvet curtains and stopped dead.

It was as if he had stepped into another world. A wall of sound hit him, enveloped him and came up through his feet. The sheer heat made him wobble for a second. He could feel the throb of the bass through his chest. The place was heaving. PVC, see-through T-shirts, chunky silver jewellery and more hair gel than you could shake a stick at – and that was the men. The women were pushed and stuffed into slinky dresses, done up to the nines, hair and make-up styled to perfection. The dance floor was a sea of writhing, sweating bodies, all facing a raised DJ box designed to look like a pulpit. Giant cardboard clouds hung all around it, making the DJ look like he was playing in the middle of the sky. Sean Paul boomed from the massive speakers. Sets of strobe lights flashed at random intervals, like lightning, changing the sky scene to a storm. Dry ice machines spewed more clouds high above the crowd. It was a far cry from Mulligan's.

'Coming to the bar?' Adam shouted.

John nodded and pushed off into the throng, dodging spilled drinks and lethal spiked heels. At the bar he paid far too much for two drinks, passed one to Cynthia and leaned back to take in the crowd.

They were a mixed bunch, eighteen or so up to forty, with a few older people dotted here and there. Absolutely everybody was dancing. Even the people talking on the edge of the dance floor swayed in time with the beat. Cynthia was already on the dance floor, having a ball. John stood awkwardly on the fringe. This wasn't his kind of music, and he wasn't about to humiliate himself by hopping around like a lunatic. The heat was making his shirt stick to the small of his back, and, even though he was standing stock-still, he appeared to be in everyone's way. He took a long gulp of his beer. He'd never felt so out of place in his life.

He took another slug of beer and turned to the bar. Two guys worked frantically behind it. They were like chalk and cheese: one was tall, blond and Nordic-looking, the other was small, dark and built like a jockey. John waited until the blond one made eye contact.

'What can I get you?'

'Can you have a look at this?' John yelled, and passed Ashley's photo across the bar.

The barman pulled a face. 'Do you want a drink?'

'No, I have one. Just have a look at the photo and tell me if you know her.'

The barman gave it a cursory glance and shook his head. 'Nah.' He moved off and took another order.

'What about your friend?' John bawled after him.

'Look, man, we're snowed under.'

'I only want to ask him if he knows her, if she was ever here.'

The barman rolled his eyes. 'Hey, Carlos, come here.'

The second barman threw handfuls of crushed ice into three glasses and poured Bacardi over them. 'What? I am busy.'

'This guy wants you to check out a photo.'

'What?'

'Wants to know if you've ever seen a girl here.'

Carlos ground up some mint leaves and flung them into the glasses. 'I am busy.'

'He's busy,' the first barman said. He poured a pint and took two more orders.

'It'll only take him two bloody seconds!' John said.

'Carlos! Two seconds – get this guy off my back.'

Carlos threw up his arms theatrically, stomped down the bar and looked at the photo. 'No, I don't know her.'

'You sure you've never seen her?'

'I say no,' Carlos snapped, and spun on his heel.

John took Ashley's photo back. 'Yeah, thanks a lot.'

He pushed off the bar, edged over to Cynthia and grabbed her arm. 'Where's the members' bar?'

'What?' She cupped her hand behind her ear and leaned towards him.

'Where's the members' bar?'

'What?'

'Is there anywhere quieter in this place?'

'*What?*'

'*Quieter*! Is there anywhere we can *talk*?' he bawled.

Cynthia nodded and pointed over the bopping heads towards a neon door in a wall. 'Chill-out room!'

John offered her a lame thumbs-up sign and pushed his way towards the door. He turned back to ask her if it had a bar, but she was gone again.

'Shit…' He contemplated diving back through the crowd, but he couldn't face it. Cynthia could come and find him if she wanted him.

The chill-out room wasn't as packed as the main floor, but it was pretty full. It was a long room with vaulted ceilings, soft velvet sofas and dainty wrought-iron tables, each with a thick church candle burning in its centre. Soft lighting and a slow Sade number filled the room with soothing vibes. To John's delight, it had a separate bar – smaller than the main bar, but well stocked, and that was good enough for him. After the noise and heat of the main room, this was an oasis of calm.

John went through the photo routine with the two slightly less harassed barmen and came up empty. He tried a few of the friendlier-looking people around the bar and got the same reaction. Nobody, it seemed, knew Ashley or had ever seen her there.

He remained in the relative comfort of the chill-out room for the rest of the night. He stood at the bar, nursing his drinks and watching the people around him steadily becoming louder and more animated. He guessed this high level of animation had less to do with the drink than with the small white pills everyone was openly popping. And it wasn't just pills. When he went to the men's bathroom and discovered the queue for the cubicles, John realised the club was awash with cocaine. Every so often a bouncer pushed through the crowd, scanned the room and mouthed something into a small headset, but John noticed they turned a blind eye to the obvious use of drugs. He wondered what exactly the men *were* looking for.

An hour had passed before he caught a glimpse of Cynthia's head bobbing up and down by the door. He raised his beer to her, and she waved and came rushing over.

'*There* you are! I've been all over this place

looking for you.' She pouted and fluttered her eyelashes at him. Her pale-green dress was sweat stained, her make-up had slid down her face and she seemed to be having trouble focusing. She licked her lips and took a deep drink from the bottle of water she carried, her pale throat bobbing crazily with every gulp. John thought she looked slightly repulsive.

'You knew I was in here.'

'Not all night!' She put her hand on her hip and cocked it. 'I've been looking for you *everywhere*.'

John grinned. He knew she hadn't been looking for him. Cynthia had been dancing her arse off outside. She had probably come to find him only because she'd remembered he had the ticket for her coat.

Cynthia waved her arm around. 'Well? What do you think of the place? Isn't it *so cool*? That's DJ Croza spinning outside. God, he's, like, amazing. Rebecca says he only plays one night a week, even though there are *tons* of clubs looking for him, because he thinks playing too much saps his creativity and he wants every performance to be a totally mind-blowing experience. Isn't that so cool?'

'Yeah. Lucky him.'

'Gavin's friends Blue and Arancha are inside. They're throwing a party afterwards, and guess what?' Cynthia clapped her hands together with delight. 'We've been invited!'

'Blue?'

Cynthia either didn't hear him or chose to ignore him. 'They're, like, famous for their parties. I've never been to one before, but Sondra says they're *amazing*, with proper decks and lighting and—'

John grimaced. Cynthia was spitting all over him. 'You go. I'm going to head on home.' The thought of being stuck in a house full of people named after colours filled him with dread. He dumped his empty glass on the bar. The whole evening had been a waste. If Ashley had come here, he doubted that any of the pill-heads would remember her.

'Johnny, don't be a wuss! They're all *dying* to meet you.' Cynthia pressed her sweaty body into him, pushing him back against the bar. She leaned in and nibbled, none too gently, on his earlobe. 'Come on, baby, it'll be so cool.' Her teeth bit down hard.

'Ow!' John prised her off. 'Jesus, Cyn, that hurt—' He stopped. Cynthia's pupils were coal-black and huge. She wasn't drunk; she was totally off her face.

'Cynthia, what the fuck have you taken?' He took a closer look at her. 'Your eyes are like piss-holes in the snow.'

She yanked her arm free and gave him a playful slap across the chest. 'Oh, don't be such a bore. What the hell's wrong with you? Look, it's only a Mitzi, okay?'

'A what?'

'A Mitzi. You know, Mitsubishi? E?' Cynthia laughed at John's angry face. 'Don't freak out, Johnny. I got you one too.' She laughed and lunged at John, pulling his head close and sticking her tongue deep into his mouth.

John tasted Juicy Fruit and Red Bull. Repulsed, he pushed her off. 'Cynthia, I'm going. Here' – he dug her ticket out of his pocket and pressed it into her hand – 'don't lose this. I'll call you tomorrow when I get a chance.'

Cynthia's face crumpled. 'John, don't be like that…'

'I'd rather be like this than like every other knob in here.' John sidestepped her and strode towards the door. The main room was like a furnace. Strobe lights flickered and hundreds of tightly packed bodies were wedged between John and the exit. His eardrums winced when, beside him, some guy in spandex stuck a whistle in his mouth and blew long and hard. John was considering ramming the whistle down his throat when he spotted something that grabbed his attention.

At the far end of the dance floor, a girl poured into a red leather catsuit moved through the crowd, carrying her drink over her head. She was breathtaking. Her long blond hair was twisted up in bunches and tied with silver ribbons, and the catsuit was zipped open almost to her navel. John watched as Claudia Delaney bounced along to the heavy bass, oblivious of everyone around her.

'Never heard of the place, my arse,' John said.

He stepped back into the throng and pushed his way towards her, but it was tough going and by the time he reached the spot where he'd seen her, she was gone. John stood on his toes and searched for her. He caught sight of her silver tassels moving along the edge of the dance floor and disappearing up a tiny stairway beside the DJ's pulpit.

Shoving people roughly out of the way, he eventually made it to the foot of the stairs. There was a velvet rope stretched across the entrance, and behind it a formidable, ponytailed bloke wagged a thick finger at him. He had a smooth, Italian-looking face, only slightly marred by a mole the size of Denmark on his left cheek. He was chewing gum.

John pointed over the bouncer's shoulder. 'My friend's gone up there, the girl in the red leather.'

The bouncer moved the gum to his cheek. 'Yeah? You a member?'

'No, but—'

'Sorry, mate. Members only.'

'But my friend—'

The big man folded his arms. 'Not interested, pal. Move it along.' He began to chew again, a bored expression slipping down over his eyes.

John nodded and stepped back. There was no point in arguing. The bouncer followed him with his eyes until he melted back into the crowd. From deep in the dance floor, John traced the line of the stairway and saw a large, smoky window set high above the crowd, running the length of the dance floor.

'Johnny! There you are.' A sweat-drenched Adam slapped him hard on the back 'Cynthia's looking for you. Did she find you?'

'Yeah, she did.' John pointed to the window. 'Adam, what's up there?'

'VIP, baby. That's where the beautiful people go to get away from the rest of us.' Adam slapped him again and spilt some of his vodka down the back of John's shirt.

'How do you get up there?'

Adam shrugged. 'You've got to be a member, I think.' He frowned and stared hard at some girl beside him. 'Hang on a sec, Johnny.' Then he was gone, weaving his way through the crowd.

John bought another beer and hung around for the rest of the night on the main floor, hoping to catch another glimpse of Claudia, but she never reappeared. When the music stopped and the harsh overheads came on, he allowed himself to be shepherded out into the cold night with the last of the bedraggled clubbers.

'Johnny! Still here? You change your mind? Are you coming to the party?' Rebecca twirled around the car park, swinging a bottle of Bud by the neck. She stumbled, and John grabbed her by the shoulders and steadied her. Her eyes were huge and unfocused. It was clear she was on the same stuff as Cynthia.

'Sure. You guys go on ahead and I'll catch you up.' He noticed Cynthia and Adam sitting on a wall, their arms entwined. They were obviously talking about him. Every so often one of them shot him a not-so-furtive glance.

'Don't worry – lovers' tiff, eh?' Rebecca laughed and wrapped her arms around him. 'Happens to the best of us. Okay, Johnny, you follow on. You know where it is, right?'

'Yeah.'

Over her shoulder John watched Gavin and Sondra sharing a deep snog and wondered if taking E blurred all the boundaries. Shit, he thought, if it straightened Gavin up, it must be something. After more hugging and declarations of love, and one blubbering apology from Cynthia, the group finally moved off. John waited around in the cold until the last clubber had wandered off to pastures new, but there was no sign of Claudia Delaney.

John decided to call it a night at four o'clock, when the bouncers came out, gave him the evil eye, climbed into their cars and left. He walked home with his hands in his pockets, thinking. Claudia had been dancing her arse off in a club she'd sworn blind she didn't know existed. And she had got into the members' bar, no less, past the big ape on the stairs.

John bought a bag of chips in Portobello and ate them walking home along the canal. He wondered why Ashley's flatmates would lie to him.

And, if they'd lied about Tempest, what other porkies had they told him?

Claudia Delaney… John shook the chip bag and licked salt off his fingers. She looked pretty hot in leather.

13

Vinnie woke up with a start. He'd been dreaming that someone was shouting at him. He pushed the sleep mask up on his forehead, opened his eyes and quickly realised it was no dream: someone *was* shouting at him. His father's face loomed in the half-light of his bedroom.

'Come on, shift your arse.'

'What—' Vinnie jerked away and rolled to the other side of the bed. He switched on his bedside lamp and fumbled groggily for his watch. His eyes were gritty with sleep and his hair stuck out wildly from his head. 'What time is it?'

Patrick strode across the room and yanked the curtains back. Outside, dawn was breaking across the sky. 'It's seven-fifteen. Come on, we're moving.'

Vinnie shielded his eyes with his forearm and squinted at Patrick. 'Are you fucking *crazy*? I've barely been asleep two hours. If you think—'

'One of the lads just called me on the mobile.' Patrick marched back to the bed and jabbed his finger into the middle of Vinnie's forehead, his eyes blazing. 'Now get up. We're going to

Smithfield – going to meet him in an early house there.'

'Why don't you call a taxi?'

Patrick stopped moving. 'What did you say?'

'Nothing.' Vinnie threw his covers back and got out of bed. His head was fuzzy and his sinuses were completely blocked. 'Who's the source?'

'Never mind who. Let's go.'

Half an hour later, Vinnie huddled in his overcoat opposite a locked-down bar at the back of Smithfield market, waiting for Patrick to return to the jeep. His father had been in the bar for almost five minutes now. Who the fuck was he talking to – and why didn't he want Vinnie to know? Did he suspect something, or was he just being the careful bastard Vinnie knew him to be?

Vinnie checked his watch again and swore. This was bullshit, waiting around like a fucking lackey. He pulled out his phone and dialled Davey.

'Yeah?'

'Davey, it's me.'

'Boss?' Davey sounded surprised. 'Everything okay?'

'No, it's fucking *not* okay.' Vinnie sniffled and told Davey where he was.

'What you doin' there?'

'*He*'s inside. He got a call an hour or so ago: someone's come up with a name.'

'What name?'

'I don't know, do I? He has me waiting on him like a…like a fucking *chauffeur*.'

211

'So go in.'

'I can't. He insisted I wait here, the bastard.' Vinnie glanced balefully at the door. 'Look, do you know anyone around here?'

Davey said nothing for a few seconds, thinking. Then he cleared his throat. 'I got a cousin lives near there. I'll call him up, see if he'll go down and have a look. He's a regular bar-hopper, so there's no problem with him goin' in. It won't look dodgy. That's if you want.'

'Oh, I do. I do want.' Vinnie stamped his feet to get his blood flowing. 'Tell him to get a description and a name, if he can. How long will it take him to get here?'

'If he's home, fifteen minutes or so.'

'Make it so, *mon ami.*'

Vinnie snapped his phone shut, ran across the road and climbed back into the jeep.

'You are sly, but so am I,' he sang as he stared at the pub's front door. If Patrick thought he could keep him in the dark, well, he had another thing coming.

Patrick accepted a second Jameson's on ice. He sucked on his cigar and looked around the lounge of O'Sullivan's, taking in the hard, worn faces of the dockers, traders and early birds dotted about. A few people were talking quietly amongst themselves at one of the small round tables, but mostly the bar was silent, save for the soft *fleadh* music playing in the background. But it was a companionable male silence. There were no women around to stir up the blood and create a need for bravado. The air was thick with smoke. Even the sharp-eyed barman chewed on the nub of a tightly rolled fag as he flicked idly through an early newspaper. It would have taken a health inspector with a neck like a jockey's bollocks to come into this place and try to enforce the smoking ban.

Patrick sat back deep in the shadows of the snug and felt a moment's composure, the first he had felt since he'd set foot back on this cursed isle. He understood this place, where men took simple pleasure from solid male company and the easy nature of drink.

'How can I help you, Mr York?'

Patrick's companion, Philo Redmond, was a small, fidgety man with a bad complexion and tar-stained fingers. His front teeth were rotten due to his many years as a smack-head. Philo was no longer a junkie. He had beaten the drug by pure chance. Three years before, he had crossed against the traffic on North Circular Road, on his dazed way to find a fix, and had been struck by a car travelling fast up the bus lane. The impact had broken both his legs and left him in a coma for nine months. When he eventually awoke in St Vincent's, he was three stone lighter, had a limp and was free from the poison that had blighted both his life and the lives of all those who knew him.

That had been his one and only lucky break. Philo Redmond was a known fence and was currently looking at a long trip to the 'Joy due to a turncoat cousin who had squealed like a pig at the slaughterhouse door. Philo was an angry man, filled with self-pity for himself and remorseless to others.

Patrick eyed him. 'You know me and your old fella went back a long way. He was a good man, Philo, a good man.'

Philo raised his Jack Daniels and smiled bleakly. 'Aye, he was that. He was fierce grateful to you for all your help, like – never forgot how you looked after me ma when he went down.'

Patrick shrugged one shoulder. 'In those days a crew looked out for one another.'

'Those days are well and truly fuckin' over,' Philo said. His lip curled into a bitter sneer. 'Nowadays even blood would roll on you when their backs are against it. There's no loyalty left, Mr York, and that's the bleedin' truth.'

'That's the truth,' Patrick agreed, and shook his head.

A back door opened and a gaunt man with sleep-sodden eyes slunk into the bar. He wore blue overalls and hobnailed boots that hadn't been laced up. He sat at the bar and rubbed his unshaven face. The barman nodded to him and set up a whiskey without being asked. A regular, then. Patrick eyed him with disinterest: another miserable soul in need of the hard stuff.

'To Philly Redmond,' Philo said suddenly, and raised his glass.

Patrick clinked his against Philo's and took a deep sup. Philo's father, Philly, had died of cancer two months after being released from the 'Joy on compassionate leave. That had been ten years before, when Philo was barely in his teens, and still Philo's eyes watered at the memory. Patrick wondered how Vinnie would react to his demise. His hand automatically rose to the eight-inch scar under his left arm, where the surgeons had fought frantically to repair his collapsed lung. Would there be tears? Would Vinnie drink a toast to his father's name? Or would the little bastard be the first to dance on his grave? Patrick shuddered softly. Death was all he seemed to think of these last few days.

He closed his eyes and tried not to think of Anouk. Where was she now? He should have sent her into hiding when he learned of Kelpie's disappearance, but he hadn't thought Aziz would act so swiftly. After all, they had history between them. He had been a fool. Men of his business had no trust. Anouk... He pictured the sheen of the afternoon sun on her café-au-lait skin, her easy smile, the slightly crooked front tooth that she tried to hide. The sickening ache of terror settled deep in his bowels. His eyes snapped open.

'Philo, I need you to contact everyone you know, about a delivery of mine that's gone astray – a big delivery, cocaine. It's high grade and liable to be sold in—'

'Mr York, that's why I called you.' Philo put his glass down on the table, his face pale and serious.

215

'Dougie Burrows has already put out the word for it. And the word is that no one's to touch it. It has to go directly to him.'

'Burrows?' Patrick felt his stomach tie up into a knot. 'How the fuck does he know about it?'

Philo shrugged. 'Dunno, but he does. And that slippery cunt'll stop at nothin' to get his hands on it. And, now that the word's gone out, whoever has the gear is gonna find it pretty fuckin' tricky to locate another buyer – including yourself, if you know what I mean.'

Patrick wiped at the sweat that had suddenly broken out on his forehead. He thought of Anouk's brown eyes, how they looked like they were made of chocolate.

'Does Burrows know I'm here?'

'I reckon if he knows about the gear he knows about yourself. Seems to me someone's leaking info on you, left, right and centre.'

'Jesus fucking Christ.'

'Look, I've still got a link there,' Philo said softly. 'I'll look into it, see what I can dig up.' He leaned in closer still. 'I'm not tryin' to tell you your business nor nothin', but if you've got a leak, the only thing you can do is plug it.'

Patrick gulped some of his drink down. Dougie Burrows. This was the worst possible news. He leaned forward and tried to catch his breath. He could hear his blood rushing in his ears.

'Mr York, are you all right?'

'Philo,' he said thickly, 'let's talk plumbing.'

14

'You sure it was her?' Sarah raised a sceptical eyebrow. She put down her toast and took a small sip of scalding tea.

They were sitting in her tiny, bright-yellow kitchen. John nodded. He couldn't answer without spitting crumbs halfway across the table, and Sarah had already warned him that the next time he did that he'd be out on his ear.

It was still early on a cold but sunny Saturday morning. John hadn't been able to wait until they went into work. He had called over to Sarah's apartment to tell her about his discovery. Once he'd finished laughing at her Rupert the Bear pyjamas and giant tiger-striped slippers, she had grudgingly offered him breakfast.

'You're sure? How many beers did you have?'

John took a hefty gulp of his milky tea. 'Not enough, let me tell you – too damn expensive. It was definitely her, Sarah, dolled up to the nines and poured into a leather suit that left nothing to the imagination.'

Sarah raised the other eyebrow. 'No wonder you noticed her.'

John grinned and took a bite of rock-hard toast. 'Hard not to, all right.'

'So why do you think she lied?'

'Dunno.' John shrugged. 'But I'll bet you twenty quid Ashley Naughton was at the club the night she went missing, and I'll bet you Miss Claudia knows a lot more than she's letting on.'

'What do you want to do?'

'We get a look at the CCTV tape, see if any of the girls turn up on it. If Ashley was there, we need to know who she was with and why the flatmates are lying.'

Sarah nodded and tried to cover a yawn with the back of her hand. John looked at her a little more closely.

'You look wrecked.'

'I am, a little.'

'Yeah? How come – late night?'

'Well, actually…' Sarah blushed slightly and leaned forward in a conspiratorial gesture that made John grin. 'I took some of your advice. I had a date last night.'

John felt the toast giving him heartburn. He swallowed the last bit and asked casually, 'Yeah? Who with?'

Sarah picked up her cup and hid behind it. To John's amazement, she was blushing to the tips of her ears. 'Come on, out with it! Who's the guy?'

'His name is David Fenshaw. He works with Helen at the head office of Eircom.'

'*Helen* set it up?' John put down his cup a little

harder than necessary. 'You told me you'd never go out with one of her cronies. Please, you have got to be shitting me.'

Sarah blinked, surprised at his harsh tone. 'You're the one who told me to get out more.'

'Yeah, but not with one of *them*.'

'He's a nice guy – very charming, in an old-fashioned way. Holds chairs out and gets the door and stuff.'

'Oh, *my*,' John said, falsetto. He tore off a chunk of toast and popped it into his mouth. 'What a *gentleman*.'

Sarah took a sip of tea. The blush had gone from her face and she wasn't smiling any more.

'I'm just saying.'

'Of course you were.' She eyed him icily over the top of her cup.

John snorted and changed the subject. 'So what's next with the case?'

Sarah drained the last of her tea and stood up. 'Stick with the club, I suppose. It's all we've got to go on.' She picked up her plate and went to the sink. 'John, much as I love your company, I have to go and have a shower, so if you don't mind…'

'Ah, sure.' John dropped his plate into the sink. 'Thanks for breakfast.'

'Next time, maybe warn me before you call over this early.'

John held his palms out and faked his best innocent face. 'You wanted me to show a bit more initiative.'

'I did, didn't I?' Sarah pushed her dark hair over her shoulder and tilted her head to look at him. John couldn't make out the expression she wore. She walked him down the hall, opened the door and waved when he waved, but John couldn't shake off the feeling he'd hurt her feelings.

The last thing he wanted was for her to think he was jealous or something. She was his friend. If she was dating, getting out into the world again, why would he be jealous of that?

Pascal Mooney threw a few coins into a payphone and dialled Edward Naughton's number. Even though it was still early, Naughton picked up on the second ring.

'What?'

'We have a problem.'

'Jesus, Pascal, what is it?'

'Cops down in Wicklow have located the jet-ski.'

'Fuck. That was quick, wasn't it?'

'Bits of it washed up on shore not too far from Arklow harbour. I got the call from one of the lads I'm friendly with, went down myself this morning and had a look.'

'Patrick's going to know Kelpie was knocked off.'

'Who's to say he didn't do a bunk?'

'But his gear – it's all at the hotel. It's obvious he never went back there.'

Pascal Mooney leaned his elbows on top of the

phone and ran his fingers through his thick grey hair. He was forty-five years old, broad across the shoulders and fairly fit from playing seniors' hurling twice a month, although he was developing a bit of a paunch. His heavily hooded brown eyes and enormous Roman nose made him appear lazy and dull-witted, which he definitely was not. 'Look, this changes things. With the ski located, don't you think it's time we made a move, sold the gear on?'

Naughton didn't want to talk about the deal. Even thinking about the deal was making him sick. 'Are you sure it's Kelpie's ski?'

'Positive. The forensic unit pulled the serial number off the engine chassis, traced it back to the robbery in Wexford. It's definitely the one Kelpie used.'

'Oh. Well…maybe Patrick won't find out about it.'

Pascal lit a cigarette and listened to the fear in Edward's voice. 'Don't be fucking thick. He'll probably get the same information I have by the end of the day. Any word on your kid yet?'

'No, nothing.'

'Weird, her just vanishing like that – same day as the delivery and all.'

'That's what Patrick said,' Edward muttered. 'Of course it looks fucking bad. It's that Vinnie. He has her – I know it. He's fucking psycho! He never wanted me on board. He'd do anything to fuck me up.'

Pascal shook his head and sucked on his cigarette. 'How would he know you were picking that night to pull it?'

'I don't know.'

That was something else that was troubling Edward. He liked to believe he had been scrupulously careful in the run-up. He'd covered all the bases, or so he thought. But he'd never once considered something happening to Ashley. Why would he have? She didn't even live at home any more.

'You really think he has something to do with her vanishing like that?'

'I don't know,' Edward replied miserably.

Pascal closed his eyes and smoked for a minute. 'I think you should talk to Burrows, make sure he knows we're not fucking him around.'

'No,' Edward snapped. 'It's too risky, Pascal. We need to wait, bide our time. At the moment, Patrick's not buying the Kelpie angle. We can't risk it. We need some way to convince Patrick that it was Kelpie.'

'What about the sister?'

'Josie?'

'Yeah. Stands to reason that Patrick's gonna want to talk to her.'

Edward said nothing for a long moment. 'There's no love lost between them.'

'Right. So supposing I go sound her out a little – maybe offer her a few quid to sort of…suggest that Kelpie's done a runner.'

'I don't know…Patrick's pretty fucking sure Kelpie would never have betrayed him.'

'Nothing erodes a man's trust quicker than losing that much money.'

'You know,' Edward said, 'last I heard, Josie was pretty much on the skids.'

'Good. She'll be willing to take a handout.'

'Okay, do it – but don't, for fuck's sake, mention my name to her.'

Pascal didn't answer. He just wanted to sell the gear on and get his share of the money. They had planned this to perfection – and now Ed was starting to stall. Dougie Burrows was not a man to fuck with, any more than Patrick York was, and he was already starting to wonder if Edward was up to the job. Pascal was heartily sick of Edward Naughton and all the shit that came with looking after him. But he also knew that Dougie would never keep him on the books alone, no matter how many favours he'd done him over the years. Dougie still regarded Pascal as the enemy, a dirty cop, a ratbag. The only way he could stay in the game was hitched to Edward, and that meant keeping the fat son of a bitch alive. At least while he was useful.

'I checked out those detectives, the ones Margo hired.'

Edward's voice was breathless. 'And?'

'Small-time, but still, you got to make her get fucking rid of them. Can't have them snooping around. We've enough to be worrying about.'

'I'll get rid of them.'

'Good. Do it.' Pascal hung up.

Edward replaced the receiver and sat back. He pressed his hand against his chest and felt his heart hammering behind his ribs. He felt ill. He wasn't sleeping, and his blood pressure was through the roof. The sooner he got rid of the gear and got the hell out of Ireland, the better.

He stared listlessly out the window at his garden. If only he knew where his daughter was – if only he were certain she was safe… But if Vinnie had her, why hadn't he called to offer a trade? Why hadn't he called Edward's bluff? What was he up to?

Outside, a cold sleet fell. It drifted across the gravel and coated the steps, making them slippery and treacherous.

15

Sophie Allen was tiny. She looked as though she weighed about the same as a wet Labrador. She wore a black leather jacket over a black polo and black trousers, and her raven-black hair was pulled back from her bony face in a thin metal band. She had a curious habit of shaking her head every few seconds, almost a twitch, which Sarah found very hard not to mimic.

They had found her hunched over a makeshift desk in a cramped office-cum-storeroom in Tempest, chewing her lip and scribbling furiously in a bulging Filofax. John and Sarah, squeezed in behind her waiting for her to play the damn security tape, were breathing through their mouths: the smell of Gió perfume was overwhelming in the tiny room.

'You're lucky we still have this, you know.' Sophie tapped the tape with hard red nails. 'We would have used it last night if you hadn't called. I hope you realise how helpful Tempest is being. The weekend is our busiest time, you know.'

'Like I say, we're very grateful,' Sarah said, for the second time in as many minutes. She lowered herself onto an upturned beer crate.

'Okay, let's see here.' Sophie inserted the cassette into a player bolted under the desk and flicked on the television screen. 'Any particular time you're looking for?'

'Not sure.' John stood behind them with his arms folded. There was barely enough room for two, let alone three. He was sandwiched between a crate of empties and eight boxes of single-ply toilet paper.

'Oh.' Sophie's shoulders sagged. 'If you knew, we could narrow it down a bit.'

'Sorry,' John replied, without sounding in the least sorry. Sophie pulled her lips into a thin line and pressed Play.

Instead of one decent picture, they got four grainy images on one screen: the ticket box at the door, the bar, the cloakroom and one overhead of the dance floor. It occurred to John and Sarah that Tempest was more interested in watching its staff than in watching the punters.

'This is from the start of the night, when we open up first,' Sophie said. 'See, there's Davey, the head doorman.' She tapped the screen.

John recognised the guy who'd been on the door the previous night. On screen, Davey unlocked the huge main doors and walked out into the night air.

'Normally there's nothing for a while, not until – shit.' Sophie's phone shrilled. She pressed Pause while she checked the number. 'Look, I'm really sorry, but I have to take this.'

'Go ahead,' Sarah said. 'I'll fast-forward along, save a bit of time.'

'Oh, I can't. I'm afraid someone from the club would have to be with you.'

Sarah shrugged. 'Okay, but it's going to take all day if we have to stop every time you get a call.'

Sophie hesitated. Her twitch intensified.

'Especially since we don't know what time we're looking for exactly,' Sarah said sombrely. 'It could take ages.'

Sophie's bottom lip disappeared completely. Finally she pressed her phone to her ear. 'Sophie Allen... Who? What do you mean, he can't make it?' Her free hand grabbed the bulging Filofax. 'I don't want to hear it! That gig was booked over three months ago... What? It's fucking Saturday evening! Where am I supposed to find a replacement at this short notice? ... I don't give a shit how sick he is, he can't pull out now! Wait, wait...' She clasped her phone to her chest and turned to Sarah. 'Look, run through it, okay? I'll be back in a few minutes.'

Before Sarah could reply, Sophie raced out the door. They heard her arguing with whoever was on the phone all the way down the stairs.

John slumped into the chair Sophie had vacated. 'Jesus, I thought that freak would never go. What do you think she takes? Speed? Coke?'

'Nothing, probably. Some people are like that.'

'I don't know *anyone* like that.'

Sarah pressed Play. 'Helen's like that.'

John had forgotten about Sarah's sister. No wonder he had disliked Sophie Allen on sight.

Sarah scanned through the earlier parts of the night quickly. On screen, the club filled up rapidly. The quality of the tape wasn't as bad as they'd first thought, but it was still eye-watering work. John and Sarah concentrated in silence, but after half an hour, John was ready to admit defeat. They had fast-forwarded, rewound and paused through most of the tape and found no sign of Ashley Naughton.

'She wasn't there,' John said quietly, stretching his cramped neck.

'Mmm,' Sarah said. She pressed Rewind, then froze the screen. 'You know something? There are people in this club who didn't go through the front door.'

'What?'

'Look.' She pointed to the square showing the bar. 'See that guy with the white hair – there, to the left of the frame?'

John followed her finger and saw a silver-haired youth with a nose ring the size of a towel-holder. 'Him?'

Sarah nodded. 'And there's another one further on... Hold on for a sec.' She fast-forwarded the tape a little and froze it on the bar again. This time she picked out a girl with a shaved head and a spiderweb tattoo etched across the backs of her bare shoulders.

'Nice paint job.' John stared at the screen. 'You're saying what, exactly?'

'I'm saying some of these people didn't come in the front door.'

'You sure? I can barely make out half the people that did come in.'

'Well, I can, and those two definitely didn't.' Sarah tapped the screen in front of her. 'Think of the guy with the white hair for a second. He was the easiest to notice.' She rewound the tape back to Davey opening the door, then rolled it slowly along until the end of the night. It took another five minutes of stopping and starting, but by the end of it John knew she was right.

'There must be another entrance.'

'No shit, Sherlock,' Sarah said.

John clapped his hands together. 'That's how I missed Claudia on the way out. Members' bar, members' door.'

'Probably.' Sarah rewound again and concentrated on the crowd. She spotted two other people who she was pretty certain hadn't come in the regular way.

John drummed his fingers on the desk. 'We need to see the members list.'

'I asked Sophie, and she shot me down on that one. They have to respect the privacy, blah-di-blah.'

'Screw the privacy. I don't give a shit about the other members. I only want to know if Ashley Naughton was a member.'

'We don't know that she was here at all,' Sarah reminded him.

'What's the owner's name again?'

Sarah glanced at her notebook. 'York, Vincent York.'

'Right, so we ask him if he knows her.'

'And if he doesn't?'

'I don't know.'

'Then we turn the screw on the flatmates.'

They left the tiny office and went in search of Sophie. She was downstairs at the bar, still on the phone.

'Hi.' John tapped her on the shoulder. 'We've finished.'

Sophie waved him away. Sarah pulled out a stool and sat at the bar to wait. John decided to have a look around the club.

It looked different in the daylight, smaller and dirtier. The sprung floor was filthy, stained and covered with thousands of fag burns. The lighting system hung from dull metal bars and was covered in grime. The plastic clouds looked cheap and tacky. John grinned. For all its coolness and hip music, Tempest was just another dump. John shook his head: to think people paid twenty quid a pop to come here... He stopped grinning when he remembered he had been one of those people not twelve hours before.

The only other people working were the cleaner, a sprightly sixty-year-old named Breda Quinn, and a young man called Daz who was stocking up the bar. John had a quick chat with Breda, but she couldn't help much: she worked two hours every morning and knew none of the club's patrons. John thanked her and turned his attention to Daz.

Daz was about twenty-three and lightly built. He wore his dark hair cropped short, with spiky red tips scattered throughout. His jeans trailed under the soles of his huge runners, and his T-shirt stopped two inches above his waistband. John stood in the door of the storeroom, waiting for the barman to acknowledge his presence. It was only when Daz leaned forward to grab a crate that John noticed his earphones. He tapped the barman on the shoulder. The barman turned round, frowned and flipped a tiny switch on his earphones. He had ultra-pale skin and glazed, bloodshot eyes. 'What?'

'You work behind the bar on weekends?'

'Yeah. So?' Daz picked up a crate of Budweiser and carried it from the storeroom to the bar. John followed him. Daz gave him an irritated glance.

'I didn't see you last night.'

'I was working the members' bar.'

'Do you normally work there?'

'I work in whichever one's busiest.'

'You ever seen this girl?' John slid Ashley's photo across the bar.

Daz picked it up, gave it a brief glance and threw it back to him. 'Dunno. Bit young for here.'

'She might be a member.'

'Like I said, I don't normally work the members' bar.' Daz turned away and started to unload the Bud into a cooler, carefully wiping each bottle with a filthy cloth.

'I thought you worked in whichever bar's busiest?'

'Look, man, what do you want?'

'This girl – her name's Ashley Naughton – she might have been here a couple of weeks ago, maybe with a group of her friends.'

Daz shrugged. John shook his head and glanced up the bar. Sophie was off the phone and talking to Sarah.

'There was another girl here last night – blonde, same age. Claudia Delaney. That name ring any bells?'

'Nah.'

John tried again. 'She was in red leather, an all-in-one thing. She could be a member.'

Daz scratched at his bandanna, and John caught a glimpse of the massive purple hickey behind it. He was surprised that this kid had summoned the energy to get that far with another person.

'Look, mate, I can't help you, yeah?' Daz leaned an elbow on the bar. 'I come in, do my job and go home, yeah? This place is so packed some nights, I don't even see faces, never mind what they're wearing, yeah?'

John picked Ashley's photo up and slipped it back into his pocket. '*Yeah.* Thanks.'

Daz went back to the bottles. John turned away, but then he thought of something. 'Hey,

Daz, can you give me the names of the other guys who work the members' bar, and the guys who were off? They might remember more.'

Daz sighed heavily and dropped the cloth into the crate. 'Fuck, man, I don't know all their names.'

'Give me the ones you do.'

'Got a pen on you?'

John gave him his pen and notepad and waited while Daz laboriously wrote down six names. 'You're wasting your time,' Daz said as he finished off the last name.

'Which of these guys works the bar upstairs?'

Daz gave John a weary look. 'Alejandro Cortez. He's foreign.' He pointed to the last name on the page. 'Mixes mad cocktails and shit.'

'Only one guy in that bar?'

'Only needs one, unless it's mad busy. It's a small bar. There was another guy used to do it, Alan, but he's gone now.'

'Gone where?'

'Huh?'

'Gone where, and when did he go?'

Daz fiddled with his bandanna and squinted at the ceiling. 'Let's see… He left about two weeks ago, thereabouts. Think he might be in the Westbury or somewhere.'

John leaned on the bar. 'Why'd he leave?'

Daz scowled. 'How should I know? We wasn't mates, yeah?'

'Know this guy's address?'

'Nah.'

'You sure he's gone to the Westbury?'

'Nah, I just heard someone say something about it. Listen, I got to get moving on this shit, yeah?'

John had had enough of the stimulating conversation. He muttered, 'Yeah,' and rejoined Sarah.

'Where's Sophie?'

'Gone on another call. Come on, let's get out of here. This place is manky.'

'Did you push her about the members list?'

Sarah strode towards the door. 'Yeah, but she's digging in her heels. The privacy of the members is sacrosanct. But I checked, and there is another way into the club, behind the fire escape at the back of the building. It's used by staff.'

'And guests?'

'Don't you know it?'

'What about Vincent York? When do we get to talk to him?'

Sarah buttoned up her jacket and opened the door onto the street. After the gloom of the club, the harsh sunlight blinded her momentarily. 'She was cagey about that, too. She says she'll try to get him to give us a call, but the guy's very busy and he wouldn't know anything about Ashley anyway.'

'Wow, so eager to help, this lot.'

'So what now?'

John unlocked the car, got in and started the engine. 'The barman in there told me another guy left a couple of weeks ago. The timing's right. Maybe he's connected with Ashley.'

Sarah held out her hand. 'John, at the risk of bursting your bubble, we don't even know if Ashley Naughton ever set foot inside Tempest.'

John lit a cigarette and inhaled deeply. 'Okay, then: first things first.'

'What?'

'It's still early. I say we squeeze the girls again – confront Claudia with what I saw last night.'

Sarah snapped her seat belt on. 'From what you say, Claudia's a pretty cool customer. She'll have a story lined up.'

'She might, but I'm betting Megan Lowry won't be quite so slick.'

Sarah looked at him in surprise. 'You think she goes there? You told me she wasn't the type.'

'I think that wherever Claudia goes, old Meg's not far behind.'

Vinnie waved Sophie out of his office and closed the door behind her. He picked up the phone and dialled the mobile Patrick was using. His father answered immediately.

'Guess who I've had here?'

'Who?' The reception was thin and crackly, and Vinnie wondered where Patrick was.

'Detectives, asking about Ashley Naughton.'

'Gardaí?'

'No, private – guy and a girl.'

'*Fuck!*'

Vinnie held the phone away from his ear. 'I told you Naughton was trying to cause trouble for me. I told you he was too—'

'I'll call you back.' Patrick hung up.

Vinnie waited. Exactly two minutes later, the phone rang.

'It's that stupid bitch Margo. She hired them.'

'His wife?' Vinnie rubbed his hand over his tired eyes. This was really too much. Couldn't the fat fuck even keep track of his fucking wife?

'Don't worry, I've spoken to him. You get the address for Kelpie's sister yet?'

'I have it here in front of me.'

'Go see her.'

Vinnie ground his teeth and tapped manicured nails on the desk. 'Letting her call detectives in like that…it proves Naughton's lost control of the situation, wouldn't you say? *Sacré bleu*, wouldn't—'

'I told you to cut out that French crap, Vincent. I ain't one of your ladies.'

Vinnie scowled.

'If Naughton's behind it, then Kelpie's dead.'

'More likely they're working together. I don't see Naughton getting the drop on Kelpie.' Vinnie closed his eyes.

'That's *bullshit*!' Patrick exploded. 'Kelpie would *never* fuck with me. I've known him half my fucking life.'

'You can never tell, though, can you?' Vinnie said sagely. 'That's why I always said it should have been kept strictly in the family.'

Davey slipped into the office. Vinnie raised a finger to him. Davey nodded and sat down.

'Don't tell me how to run my business, Vincent. Go talk to Josie.' Patrick hung up.

Vinnie replaced the receiver and lay back in his chair, his fingers steepled in front of his face.

'Well?' Davey raised an eyebrow.

'Naughton's wife called the detectives.'

'The dumb cunt.'

'Patrick says he doesn't believe Kelpie would do him over.'

Davey snorted. 'He's losin' it, man. Going soft.'

'I agree.' Vinnie closed his eyes.

'I'm telling you, Yorkie, you should be runnin' this show. You're the one put the work in, made the contacts, done all the runnin'… Don't seem right that someone like Naughton should be eating from the same plate. You don't need him, man. He's a fuckin' liability. This proves it.'

'I couldn't agree more.' Vinnie nodded and opened his eyes lazily. 'You get a name from this morning yet?'

'Yeah. The guy your old man was talking to is a fence for Dougie.'

If Vinnie hadn't been tanned within an inch of his life, the colour would have drained out of his face. 'What?'

'Yeah, guy called Philo Redmond, lives over in the 'Brack.'

'Shit.' Vinnie rubbed his face. 'Is Patrick

planning on dealing with Dougie through this guy? God damn it, we need Dougie.' Vinnie suddenly snapped bolt upright. 'Jesus, what if that little fuck knows about my visit to Dougie? What if he told Patrick? Why would Patrick be talking to someone like him?'

'We need to find out what they chatted about.'

'Get the jeep.' Vinnie lit a cigarette with a shaking hand and waved him towards the door. 'We've got to visit Kelpie's sister, too.'

Davey nodded and hauled himself out of the chair. 'What about Dougie?'

'I don't know, I don't know. First things first: we need to find out what Patrick and this fucking fence spoke about.' Vinnie dragged hard on his fag.

'Don't sweat it until we know what was said.' Davey went to the door. 'I'm pretty sure Patrick don't know what you're thinking, boss. He's just scratchin' around in the dark. This guy Philo, he's pretty far down the ranks of Dougie's men.'

Vinnie watched his bouncer's massive back disappear through the door. He smoked for a while and forced himself to calm down. Patrick couldn't know about his visit to Dougie. If he had, he would have said something on the phone.

He closed his eyes. Davey had only stated the obvious: Patrick was clearly losing it, and he, Vinnie, should be calling the shots. It was his turf. He had set up the apartments and bought the compressing machine. It had cost him the guts of nineteen grand to organise the whole operation. And was there any recognition of this? Where was the consideration of his investment and time?

Vinnie inhaled another lungful of smoke and rolled his shoulders to ease the ache that seemed to have settled there over the last few days. Even being in the same room as his father infuriated him. They were like the lions on the Serengeti: there was only room for one king.

Vinnie closed his eyes again and began to hum 'Things Can Only Get Better' under his breath.

16

Philo Redmond watched his eleven-month-old daughter trying to haul herself up onto her pudgy feet. She gripped the edge of the table and slowly, deliberately stood up, weaving slightly. When she was completely upright she turned her head to him and broke into a wide grin, showing off four gleaming front teeth.

'Look at you, Destiny.' Philo beamed at his daughter. 'Look at the big girl, standin' all on her own. Come here to Dada.'

Her grin widened and she squealed with delight. She was a beautiful baby. She had bright blue eyes and a head full of dark curls, exactly like Philo's sisters. She didn't look a thing like her fucking tramp of a mother, Philo thought gratefully. How he had ever climbed on Tracy in the first place was a mystery to him; he must have been locked out of his mind. She disgusted him, with her tracksuits, her rolls of fat and her greasy, unkempt hair. She wasn't fit to have a kid like little Destiny.

'Come on, chicken, walk to Dada.' He held out his hands to her, kicking the takeaway Chinese bags out of his daughter's way. That was another thing: the house was manky. The fat bitch never cleaned the place. She and her bloody mother were junk-food junkies, the two of them – chips, curries, pizza… He hadn't had a home-cooked meal in four weeks or more. She even had the kid on a diet of chocolate buttons, chips and buttered bread. His ma told him kids Destiny's age should be eating vegetables. But when he complained, Tracy ran bawling across the road to *her* ma's place, and then he had to put up with the two of them in his fucking house, whinging and carrying on. Philo would have liked nothing more than to kick Tracy's ma out the door on her arse, but he knew that if he did, Tracy would leave and take the kid with her – and, seeing as he was about to go away for two years, he couldn't afford to lose any time with Destiny.

Philo shook his head and raged at the injustice of his life. Caught on a fucking nixer, of all things, for his cousin Coolie Black out in Malahide. He should have known there would be more than three cameras operating in a warehouse that size, should have known Coolie would never have cased the place properly, should have known Coolie always squealed like a stuck pig when he was caught, should have known to get rid of *all* the DVD players. Judge Barry had flung the book at him. And now Dougie fucking Burrows was refusing to help him out. After all the shit he'd done for him, Dougie was turning his back on him in his hour of need, all because he hadn't been on Dougie's payroll that night.

Well, fuck Burrows: from now on Philo was going to operate solo. The only person he would watch out for was his girl, his baby girl. Everyone else could go fuck themselves. He hoped Patrick York remembered his help when Philo made it outside again. He probably would: Patrick was old-school, not like the clowns going around now – fucking Muppets, every one of them. Patrick York had class.

'Come here to me – come on, baby.' He leaned forward on the couch and wiggled his fingers again.'

Destiny's grin faded a little as she contemplated the gap between the coffee table and her father. It was more than a few steps. Philo watched her blue eyes size up the distance and felt his heart swell with love for her, his angel, the only thing he had ever done right in his whole miserable life.

'That's right, baby – that's right… Oh, you're such a brave girl. Dada will catch you.'

The doorbell went. It played the theme music from the movie *Titanic* – 'My Heart Will Go On', Tracy's favourite song in the world. Philo winced; he hated that stupid doorbell. The bitch must have forgotten her keys again. He tried to ignore it, but Destiny was looking towards the front window, her little face curious.

The doorbell went again, for longer this time.

'All right!' Philo hauled himself to his feet and stretched. He scooped Destiny up in his arms, smelling Johnson's baby shampoo on her curls. She said, 'Dada,' and patted the stubble on his cheek.

'Yeah, baby: Dada. Don't you never forget that,' Philo whispered, nuzzling her little neck. 'Dada, that's me.' He stepped into the tiny hall and opened the front door. 'Why don't you use your key—'

'Greetings and salutations,' Vinnie York said, smiling, high as a kite. 'Interesting musical choice.'

Philo froze. Without realising it, he clutched Destiny closer to his body, making her whimper slightly. 'What the fuck do you want?'

'A word.'

Davey Clarke moved into view and pushed the door open further, and he and Vinnie stepped inside. Suddenly the little hall felt very crowded. Philo backed up a step. Destiny stared at the two men in amazement and wound her tiny fingers tightly in her daddy's hair.

Vinnie surveyed the hall and grinned. The wallpaper was striped pink and yellow below the dado rail, with yellow and pale-blue flowers above. Tracy's mother had picked it. Philo hated it, but Tracy had screamed at him and he had relented. He didn't give a fuck what she did with the house, as long as she left him alone.

'My, Philo, I didn't realise you were such a decorator. *C'est magnifique.*'

'I asked you what you want,' Philo repeated.

Vinnie stopped smiling. His over-bright eyes swivelled towards Philo. 'My father met you this morning. What did he have to say for himself?'

'I didn't meet no one this mornin'. Sure, I'm only up a few minutes.' Philo went down the hall to the back of the house. He stepped into the small, untidy kitchen and stared at the back door in dismay. It was locked. He'd never make it out in time, not carrying his girl. He felt sick to his stomach. Why had he answered the door? Why hadn't he checked first, the way he normally did?

Vinnie and Davey crowded into the kitchen behind him. Vinnie leaned against the worktops. 'Really? You're sure you didn't meet him?'

'Your old lad? Shit, man, I ain't seen him for years. He back?'

'He is indeed.' Vinnie glanced at Davey. If the little freak was lying, then he had something to hide – something Patrick must have said. 'You sure it wasn't you?'

Philo put Destiny into her high chair and smoothed her hair with his hand. He opened the fridge and found a small carton of Orangina. He needed to act normal; he didn't want York to see he was nervous. 'Nah, man. Someone must have got me mixed up. I got the kid to look after, can't be out all hours like I used to.' He rinsed out a purple Barney beaker and filled it with the Orangina. 'So, like' – he screwed the cap on and turned to give it to Destiny – 'someone must've—'

He froze. Davey had picked his baby girl up out of her high chair and was holding her, with no expression on his face. Destiny was smiling uncertainly and playing with the zip on the collar of his bomber jacket. She looked across at her father, and the smile fell from her face. She held out her pudgy arms to Philo. She looked like a tiny doll in the bouncer's massive arms.

'Dada?' she said.

'Ahh,' Vinnie said. 'Hear that, Davey? She wants her Dada.'

'Give her to me,' Philo said, his voice high and terrified. He put the beaker on the worktop and took a step towards Davey.

'I wouldn't even try it, pal,' Davey said. He raised one hand and rested it under Destiny's chin. Philo stopped.

'She's a pretty little thing.' Vinnie smiled. He turned on a gas ring, lit it with his lighter, fiddled with the knob and watched as the blue flame climbed higher. 'You know, *mon ami*, the thing about pretty babies is that I hear they grow up to be quite ugly. Tragic, eh? Imagine how hard that must be – spending your whole childhood being adored, only to turn into something repellent.'

'Listen, Vinnie—'

'So I'm thinking, what if I made her ugly now? It might give her time to learn to live with it. To accept the inevitable.' He held out his hands to Davey, and the bouncer passed the baby over. 'What do you say, Philo? Do you think she'll be grateful in years to come?'

Vinnie flipped Destiny over his arm and lowered the baby's face towards the flame. Destiny wriggled. Her lower lip shot out and she began to cry.

Philo thought his heart would stop in his chest. 'All right, I'll tell you! Let her go!'

He leaped forwards to snatch her from Vinnie, but Davey backhanded him hard across the face. Philo's nose exploded in agony. He gasped once, saw stars and fell back against the cupboards. When he raised his hand to his face, it came away bloody; Davey had broken his nose. He looked up at Vinnie, tears streaming down his face. 'Please, for the love of God, don't hurt her. I'll tell you what you want to know!'

'What am I, Davey?' Vinnie said triumphantly. Heavens, this was much easier than he'd imagined it would be. He moved the rug rat away from the flame slightly.

Davey scowled. 'Boss, we don't have—'

'What am I?' Vinnie snapped, glaring at the bouncer.

'A lion.'

'Right! I'm the lion, Philo. You should have told me what I wanted to know the first time I asked. Now I have to teach you a lesson. The lion cannot be seen to be *weak*!' Destiny's crying turned into a high-pitched, hysterical wail. Vinnie pulled a face and raised his voice. The little bitch was ruining his speech. Couldn't she see he wasn't actually going to burn her? God, he hated babies. 'The lion doesn't meow, Philo, the lion *roars*! And the lion wants to know what you and that bastard father of mine *talked about* this morning!'

When Vinnie yelled, Destiny screamed in fright. The sound made Vinnie flinch slightly – and it made Philo think Vinnie had burned her. Bleeding and confused, he didn't see that Vinnie had moved Destiny away from the flame. All he knew was that his baby was screaming.

Vinnie York had misjudged Philo Redmond. He was a coward and a rat, but there was one thing for which he would fight to the death, and that was his daughter. He leaped up with an inhuman roar, grabbed the nearest thing to him – which happened to be an old-fashioned stainless-steel toaster – and swung it hard, catching Davey flush on the side of the head. Davey crumpled with a startled grunt. Then, with Destiny's terrified screams ringing in his ears, Philo launched himself across the floor to save his daughter and to rip Vinnie York's throat out.

'Shit!' Startled by this sudden turn of events, Vinnie did the only thing he could. He flung the child at Philo.

Philo caught Destiny in mid-air, before she could crash into the presses and break her tiny neck. He put her – screaming blue murder – on the floor, then he pulled a carving knife out of a block beside the fridge and leaped across Davey's prone body to reach the man who had hurt his baby.

Vinnie backed up fast. 'Davey! Get up!'

Philo slashed out frantically. The blade didn't reach far enough to do any real harm, but he did manage to slice open Vinnie's fine wool gabardine and the suit jacket beneath it. Vinnie stared down at his ripped coat. 'You bastard! That's *Armani*!'

Philo lunged for him again, but this time Vinnie neatly sidestepped the swing. He grabbed Philo's wrist in an expert lock and smashed it against the side of the kitchen door. Philo dropped the knife. Vinnie released him and hit him hard under the chin with the heel of his hand. Philo's head snapped back and he staggered slightly, but he didn't go down. He lunged forward, hands outstretched to gouge out Vinnie's eyes. But Vinnie's height advantage came into play: before Philo reached him, Vinnie stretched out a long arm and hit him on the bridge of his broken nose.

Philo howled in agony. His hands flew to his face. His head was buzzing; he felt sick. Destiny screamed and screamed. He had to get her out of here—

When Philo removed his hands from his face, Vinnie was holding a pearl-handled straight razor. His face was a mask of rage. Before Philo even knew what was happening, Vinnie had slit his throat open with a vicious flash of his wrist.

Philo staggered backwards. He turned his head. Destiny sat on the greasy lino, huddled in the corner. Her beautiful blue eyes were squeezed shut, her face red from screaming. He couldn't tell if she was hurt; for some reason his eyes wouldn't focus. He smiled at her and tried to tell her that she was all right, that she was Dada's beautiful girl, but his voice wouldn't respond. He hoped she remembered him; he hoped...

Philo pitched forward onto his knees and collapsed. He reached out to his girl and touched her chubby leg with bloodstained fingers. Then he lay still.

Vinnie wiped the razor on the sleeve of his ruined coat and slipped it into his pocket. Ignoring the screaming child, he stepped over Philo and shook Davey by the shoulder. The bouncer snuffled, coughed and sat up.

'What the fuck?'

'Let's go,' Vinnie said.

Davey looked at him. Vinnie's eyes were glazed and calm, his voice a dull monotone. Something was wrong.

Dave rolled his jaw and rubbed his throbbing ear. He looked around and saw Philo lying in a rapidly expanding pool of blood, his sightless eyes pinned on his screaming daughter.

'Davey,' Vinnie repeated in the same flat voice. He stepped around the human mess and walked out the door.

Davey stood up unsteadily, straightened his jacket and followed his boss out of the tiny, sun-filled kitchen, leaving Destiny to scream for her dada, over and over again.

17

John pressed his finger on the buzzer of Claudia and Megan's apartment and held it there while he counted slowly to ten.

'They're not there, John, or if they are they aren't answering. Come on, leave it, will you?' Sarah pulled up her collar and stamped her feet in the cold. 'Maybe they went home for the weekend.'

'Well, Claudia didn't.' But John stepped away from the door. There were times when even he had to admit defeat. 'All right, we'll try them again later.' He ran his fingers through his hair, at a loss. 'Are you hungry yet? We can head over to the Parliament and grab something.'

'I've no money with me.'

'My shout.'

'Well, why didn't you say so?' Sarah grinned, her dark hair whipping in the wind like a sail.

John kicked the door of the building, put his hands in his pockets and walked with her up the street. 'You think the club is dodgy?'

'Probably not, but I can't think of anywhere else to start. If Ashley was planning to do a disappearing act, she did her homework. No phone calls, no credit card activity, no tickets bought…'

'She wouldn't be the first woman to disappear into thin air in this country.'

'Don't say that.'

'Okay.'

Sarah stopped in her tracks and turned to John. Her face was pinched and serious. 'I mean it. I don't want to think like that.'

'Okay.'

They began to walk again. John stuck a cigarette into his mouth and lit it. 'Hey, if we do get hold of the flatmates, how will we get them to talk? Will we try good cop/bad cop?'

'That doesn't work, you idiot.' Sarah grinned.

'It works in *Law & Order*.'

'That's a television show.'

'Exactly. So it must be true.'

'John, some day you and reality are going to collide head-on, and I can't wait to see it.'

They had reached the bar. It was lunchtime, and the place was busy. Sarah began to unwind her scarf. 'They make a decent soup here, don't they?'

'Yeah, but I don't know about getting a table, it's bleeding packed. Look, why don't we try—' Suddenly John began to grin.

Sarah frowned. 'Why don't we try what?'

'Why don't we see if that girl will share a table with us.' John pointed to a pale girl with masses of curly red hair, who was doing her best to hide her face behind an open menu.

Sarah followed John's finger. 'Flatmate?'

'You betcha.'

They walked over to Megan Lowry. A half-drunk pint of Carlsberg and an empty chip basket sat on the table by her Indian print bag. The closer they got, the lower her head sank behind her menu.

'Megan.' John pulled out a chair and sat down across the table from her.

Megan glanced up and did a poor job of pretending to be surprised. 'Hey, hi… What are you doing here?' Her wild hair stood out from her head in a thousand ringlets. She wore a turquoise hippie shirt and deep indigo jeans that flared far over her Nike runners.

'We were up at your place, thought we might drop in and see if you girls were around. Isn't this lucky? This is my partner, Sarah Kenny.'

Megan looked at the unsmiling Sarah and smiled nervously. 'Hi.' Sarah nodded to her.

'You waiting on anyone?'

'Claudia was supposed to meet me here, but she said she'd be late.' Megan put down the menu and began to play with the ends of her hair. 'So why were you looking for us again? Have you found Ash?'

'You mind if I sit down?' John said. She shook her head. 'No, we haven't found her, but we think we know where she was the night she disappeared.'

'Oh…really?' Megan somehow managed to look even more uncomfortable. John beamed at her. He was in no hurry. He wanted her to sweat a little.

'Don't you want to know where she was?'

'I…yeah, where was she?'

'Come on, Meg.' John winked at her. 'Who do you think you're codding?'

'I don't know what you're talking about.' Megan's eyes searched the room over his shoulder. John knew she was on the lookout for Claudia.

'Tempest nightclub. Like it said on these keys I found in her room. The place you girls didn't know anything about.'

'Oh, right. Really? That's – that's interesting.'

'We know you two were lying about that.'

Megan looked sick. 'I don't know anything about—'

'Cut the crap,' Sarah snapped, playing bad cop. 'Why did you lie about knowing the club?'

'Look…' Megan glanced nervously at Sarah and back to John. 'I…I mean, we were in Galway. So if Ashley *was* at this club, like you say, we didn't—'

'Do we look like bloody idiots to you?' Sarah rapped her knuckles off the table. She was still standing, forcing Megan to look up at her. 'You might want to think long and hard about the hole you're digging for yourself. Anyone would think you don't give a shit about that poor girl.'

'I don't know what you mean.' Megan tugged

at the hem of her shirt, winding it over and under her fingers. 'We're frantic about Ash going off like that. If we knew anything, we'd have told you.'

'Why are you frantic? I mean, from what John's told me, you think she's gone on some kind of a shopping spree,' Sarah said. 'What are you so worried about?'

'Well, I…it's just that we haven't heard anything. You know?'

'So now you're worried.'

'Yes – I mean, no… We—'

'Maybe you think something happened to her? Maybe something to do with Tempest?'

'What?' Megan tried to cover her alarm. 'Why do you say that? What makes you think she went there?'

'I checked out Tempest last night,' John said. 'And I saw Claudia there with my own eyes. So don't sit there and bullshit us about how you lot don't go there on a regular basis.'

'What?'

John could see that Megan's surprise was genuine. 'That's…now I know you're lying! Claudia went home yesterday. I know she did. So she couldn't have been there last night. She wasn't.'

'She travel down to Wicklow with you?'

'Yes.' Megan's eyebrows knotted together. 'We caught the bus together. So she couldn't have been where you say she was.'

'You two joined at the hip?' Sarah asked

sarcastically. 'How do you know where she was? Maybe she came back up, you ever think of that?'

'I know where she was because I *called* her,' Megan said. '*Okay?*'

'Last night? What time?'

'Around nine, nine-thirty.'

'On a land line?' John asked.

Megan scowled at him. 'On her mobile. We *always* use our mobiles.'

'So,' Sarah said, 'she could have been anywhere.'

Megan glared at Sarah. Two bright spots of colour appeared on her cheeks, and her right leg began to bounce under the table. 'If my friend says she's at home when I ring her, why wouldn't I believe her?'

'What are you getting so upset about?'

'I'm not upset about anything.'

'You sure about that? You seem upset.'

'Whatever.' Megan gave Sarah the 'talk to the hand' gesture beloved of teenagers the world over, but Sarah could see doubt had set in. She pushed on, smelling blood.

'Maybe she didn't want you to know she was going to Tempest. Maybe you were cramping her style. I mean, from what John tells me, she's quite a looker. She probably gets a lot of attention, doesn't want a hanger-on.'

Megan's lip wobbled slightly. 'Claudia's not like that…and anyway, she wasn't *there*!'

'I *saw* Claudia Delaney in Tempest last night,'

John said. 'Wearing some red leather suit. Had her hair all done up like a poodle.'

'Leave me alone.'

'She was dancing on the podium with—'

'I don't believe you!' Megan yelled suddenly.

Two women at the next table stopped talking and turned to stare. Megan lowered her head and gripped her leg to stop it bouncing up and down.

John glanced over at Sarah. 'Sarah, you want to try telling this girl I don't hallucinate any more – not since I gave up licking toads?'

Sarah tapped her fingers on the table. 'What I'd like to know is why Claudia was able to go upstairs to the VIP bar. Is she a member?'

'I don't know what you're talking about.'

'Why are you lying about it?'

'I'm not—'

'You think you're helping Ashley? Think you're doing her any favours?'

'I – I don't—'

John knew Megan was beginning to crack. 'Come on, Meg,' he said softly.

Megan shook her head, refusing to meet his gaze. Her pale hands twisted over and over again in her lap.

'You can talk to us.' John leaned in closer and softened his tone. 'What's going on?' He rested his hand on her sleeve, but Megan pulled her arm away.

'Look,' Sarah said, 'you'd *better* start talking to us. Because if something has happened to that girl and you know what it is, you are in serious shit.'

Megan flinched at her tone. When she spoke again, her voice was soft and defeated. 'I…we were there, okay? Ashley…she left. She told Claudia she was going home. I swear to God, if I'd thought anything was going to happen I'd have gone with her.'

'And this was on Friday the sixth.' Sarah nodded triumphantly at John.

John patted Megan's hand. 'Good. That's great. Look, Meg, we don't care about you going to the club. But we need to know if Ash met somebody there that night. Maybe she was seeing someone who worked there, eh? Maybe she left with someone? Anything you can tell us would be great. Please, Meg. We need to find her. Her poor mother is frantic.'

'Yeah,' Sarah said, 'and this time, no more fiction.'

Megan lifted her head, and her pale eyes were brimming with tears. 'But I keep telling you I don't know anything! You think Claudia and me know where Ash is, but we *don't*. Why would we keep it a secret? How can you even think that?'

'What are we supposed to think?' John said. 'You both lied to us from the start.'

'I'm sorry! Vinnie said we shouldn't mention the club.'

'Vinnie?' Sarah said. 'Vinnie York?'

'How do you know him?' John leaned forward.

'I met him through Claudia.'

'She a friend of his?

Megan shrugged.

'Is that a yes or a no?' Sarah said.

'Yes.'

'Why did he ask you not to mention her being at his club?'

'He said that, since Ash had left his premises, her going off like that was nothing to do with Tempest, and he told us not to mention that she'd been there.'

'When did he say that?'

'A day or so after she disappeared.'

'How did he know she was missing?'

'Claudia probably told him. I don't know. He just asked us not to say anything.'

'What?' John frowned. 'And you said yes?'

Meg hesitated, then nodded miserably.

Sarah could see that Megan was already beginning to regret opening her mouth about Vinnie York, so she hopped on her fast, before the girl clammed up. 'How do you know this guy? I mean, how do three eighteen-year-olds who've barely been in the city a wet month know a man like York?'

Meg's head dropped lower. Her pale hands plucked at her shirt. 'I don't really,' she said eventually. 'I...I...'

'You what?' John stared at the top of her head.

'Meg?' Claudia Delaney appeared at Sarah's shoulder. 'What's going on?'

'Oh, Claudia...' Megan's voice was barely

audible. 'They keep asking me about the club!'

John stared at Claudia. She was wearing a short suede jacket and sprayed-on black trousers. She looked tired, but still very, very hot. 'Hey, Claudia, we were just asking about that club you've never heard of.'

'Yeah,' Sarah said. 'The one where you were dancing last night.'

Claudia cocked her head high. 'I don't know what you're talking about. I don't even know who the fuck you are.'

'I'm Sarah Kenny.'

'Yeah, well, Sarah Kenny, why don't you back off and leave my friend alone?'

'Because we're trying to find another friend of yours, and you two keep bullshitting us.'

Claudia stepped closer to Sarah. She was shorter, but at that moment she looked ready to punch Sarah straight in the face.

Sarah smiled. 'You want to get out of my face, girl.'

Claudia returned the smile. 'Come on, Meg. We're going.'

'Why did you lie about the club, Claudia?' John asked.

'Meg, come on!'

'Don't ask this one anything, John. Don't waste your breath.' Sarah sighed. 'Megan, the night Ashley disappeared – why did she leave early?'

Claudia actually flinched. 'Meg, what have you told them?'

259

'They wouldn't leave me alone.' A note of self-pity crept into Megan's voice. She turned to Sarah. 'I mean, I don't know why you keep asking me all these questions.'

'Don't give me that. What happened this particular night? Why did she leave?'

Megan pulled her legs up onto the seat and hugged her knees. 'I don't know.'

'Didn't you ask her why she was leaving?'

'No! I didn't see her actually go. But I think…well, maybe she could have been upset about something.'

'Yeah?' Sarah frowned. 'About what?'

'Right, that's it – we're going.' Claudia grabbed Meg by the hand and hauled her out of the seat.

Megan allowed herself to be pulled up. She stared bleakly at Sarah; tears spilled down her cheeks. 'I don't know anything. Look, I was really drunk, okay? I don't remember what happened. That's it, *okay*?'

'Hey, let go of her.' Sarah grabbed Claudia by the arm.

Claudia whipped around, teeth bared like a dog's, and slapped Sarah's hand. 'Don't fucking touch me!' Megan dropped her head again and began to snivel.

John got up, fast, and moved between the two women. Sarah turned back to Megan. She was furious. Anything could have happened to Ashley Naughton, and her so-called friends had been lying from the word go. She wanted to know why.

She clicked her fingers under Megan's nose. 'Is there anything else you're not telling us?'

Megan shook her head.

Claudia said, 'We're out of here,' and with that, she pulled the still-crying Meg out the door and away.

'Right.' John stood up. He was sure there was plenty Meg wasn't telling them, but he knew it would be no use trying to push her any further – not with Claudia there. 'Let's go. We need to talk to Mr Nightlife.'

Sarah's lip was curled in disgust. 'Wow. That girl is a total bitch.'

John grabbed her arm and steered her towards the door. 'I know.'

Outside, a biting wind had picked up and the sky was thick with black clouds. They walked back to John's car in silence. Sarah's head was down and her shoulders bunched. She was seething.

'You were a bit hard on Megan,' John said.

'She deserved it.'

John sighed. 'She's not a bad kid. Just easily influenced by Claudia.'

'Claudia Delaney…' Sarah said as they reached the car. 'I'd love to give her a good slap.'

John unlocked his door and got in. 'I *knew* they were lying about something.'

Sarah slid into the passenger seat, slammed the door and blew on her hands to warm them. 'That girl's been missing for seven days, John. Anything could have happened to her. This Claudia girl deserves a kick in the arse.'

'I'll call Stevie and see if I can get a bit of information on Vinnie York. Maybe there's a reason he didn't want the cops sniffing around his club.'

'Why did he let us see that tape if he didn't want anyone to know Ashley was at his bloody club?'

John shrugged and started the engine. 'Why wouldn't he? None of the girls were on the tape. That's *why* he showed it to us. It puts him in the clear.'

'The sneaky shit.'

'Bad move on his part. If he'd said she was there and she left, I wouldn't have given him or his club another thought.'

'Me neither,' Sarah said. 'Guess he wasn't as smart as he thought.'

18

In the gathering darkness, Vinnie and Davey waited on a deserted street just off North Circular Road. The rising wind flung leaves and pieces of paper across the windscreen of the jeep, momentarily obscuring their view of the dilapidated five-storey house where Josie Molloy rented a bed-sit. They had been there for over an hour.

Vinnie was freezing, but they couldn't put on the radiator. That would mean running the engine, and they didn't want to attract any attention to themselves. He shivered, fidgeted and fussed with the cuffs of his fresh shirt. The strange calm that had filled him earlier had long since vanished, and doubt had set in. He worried about the wisdom of leaving Philo Redmond's body behind. What if someone had seen them enter the house? The street had been deserted, but that didn't mean they hadn't been observed. What if someone remembered the jeep? They had parked two streets away, but people remembered the oddest things…

Anyway, it hadn't been his fault. If the stupid fucker hadn't tried to stab him, none of it would have happened. But he should have asked questions first. As it stood, he was still none the wiser about what Philo and Patrick had said to each other. And when Patrick got wind of Philo's death, he was bound to be suspicious.

Vinnie sighed and glanced at Davey's brooding profile. The big man hadn't said more than two words in the last two hours, and Vinnie was beginning to think he'd suffered some kind of damage from the blow to the head. How could he be content to simply sit there and watch the building like a gargoyle? Was he not worried, was he not anxious? Was he immune to the cold?

Vinnie blew on his hands. Davey's silence aggrieved him. 'This is ridiculous, you know, *mon ami*. A complete waste of time.'

'Could be.'

'You know, *David*, I don't know why you're so pissed off. I was the one who had to handle the situation. *Mon dieu*, you were out cold.'

'Yeah.'

'He tried to stab me.'

'Yeah.'

'So it was self-defence. *N'est-ce pas?*'

'Yeah.'

Davey spoke without moving his head. It hurt whenever he moved it. He had a lump the size of a grapefruit behind his ear and spreading up into his hair. He'd let himself get knocked out cold by a guy who was built like a jockey, and because of that, Vinnie had been left, unsupervised, to his own fucked-up devices. Davey was disgusted with himself – and a little worried about Vinnie's growing tendency to use his blade. It was another sign that he was losing it. Davey wasn't sure if that was a bad thing or a good thing.

Vinnie sank down further in the seat and mourned his Armani coat. He'd had to burn it, along with his suit and his saturated shirt. The suit he could replace – it had only been Hugo Boss – but he had loved that coat. He had bought it three years before, and it had fit him like a second skin. Armani didn't do that style any more, either; he wouldn't be able to replace it. It was a terrible waste.

Further up the street, an obese woman carrying two shopping bags turned the corner and walked towards the house. Davey shifted in his seat. 'She's here.'

Vinnie squinted through the window. 'That heifer? That *can't* be her.' He snatched a photo from the dashboard, stared at it and thrust it into Davey's hands.

Davey glanced down at the photo, mentally ageing it twenty years, and back at the woman. 'That's her all right.'

The woman stopped in front of the house and began to climb the steps to the front door. She moved slowly, using the rusted handrail to haul herself up one step at a time.

'*Mon dieu*,' Vinnie said in an awed voice. 'She's a behemoth.'

For once he wasn't exaggerating. Time had

not treated Josie Molloy well. She had once been a renowned beauty, but now her frame buckled under almost twenty stone of blubber. Her dark hair was streaked with grey and pulled back from her puffy face in a tiny, greasy bun. She wore a shapeless grey dress with a long, grubby beige raincoat over it. Her swollen ankles spilled over her scuffed, flat loafers.

'How *vile*.' Vinnie sighed. 'Honestly, people really let themselves go, don't they? I couldn't *live* if I looked like that.'

Davey pulled on a hat and grunted. He'd seen worse. 'What are we doin' again?'

'Patrick wants us to talk to her, that's all.' Vinnie pulled a face. 'See if the fat sack has heard from Kelpie.'

'Think she'll tell us if she has?'

'I don't know, do I? I'm only following orders, remember. If the great Patrick wants us to talk to her, then talk to her we shall.'

They waited while she unlocked the door and went inside the building. Josie Molloy's bed-sit was at street level, to the left of the ancient, peeling Georgian doorway. Confirming this, her pudgy face came briefly into view as she pulled floral curtains across the cracked sash window.

'Ready?'

Vinnie pulled a woollen hat over his black hair. 'I suppose we'd better get this over with.'

They got out of the jeep. Twenty feet from them, on the steps of a derelict house, three teenage boys huddled in oversized parkas sat passing a joint between them and brazenly giving the jeep the once-over. Davey went over to them, singled out the one in the middle with the earring through his lip, leaned in and murmured something Vinnie didn't catch. The boys suddenly remembered places they needed to be. They melted away into a nearby alley without even a backward glance – not exactly running, but moving faster than their normal tough-guy gait allowed.

Vinnie pulled on a pair of black calfskin gloves and watched them move off. Davey pulled on a woollen pair and patted the heavy sap he carried in his jacket pocket. He had collected it from his house on the way here. He wasn't taking any more chances today. Josie Molloy was a woman, but she was a big woman, and when you dealt with scum anything was possible.

They crossed the road together. While Vinnie kept sketch, Davey checked the nameplates beside the front door, but they were old, faded and of little use. They would have to work it another way.

'Remember,' Vinnie said softly, 'keep your wits about you this time.'

Davey felt a flush of embarrassment. 'Yeah.'

He slipped the old Yale lock with a used telephone card and pushed open the door. The front hall was a mess of bikes, litter and rotting carpet. A padlocked payphone was bolted to the wall and the peeling wallpaper was covered in hundreds of scrawled numbers. Cigarette butts lay almost an inch thick under the phone. The place stank of damp, mould, mouse shit and a thousand other odours that had ingrained themselves into the walls over the passing years.

Vinnie closed the door gently behind him and pulled a face at the smell. He flicked open his mobile, read the number off the payphone and dialled it while Davey unscrewed the single bulb dangling from a frayed cord.

The phone echoed loudly in the hall, and less then ten seconds later a door opened and a small Chinese man popped his head out. On seeing Davey and Vinnie standing in the shadows, he pulled it back in and closed his door.

Davey hooked his thumbs into the belt loops of his jeans. 'Smart fella.'

Vinnie snickered. The phone rang and rang. Eventually, the door to their left opened a crack. The persistent shrill of the phone continued. They heard a muttered 'Fuck', then Josie Molloy heaved her huge frame through the doorway, grumbling under her breath.

Davey spun away from the wall and stepped out into the open. Josie gasped and jerked up her arms, but Davey shoved her hard in the chest with both hands. She stumbled back a few feet. Before she had a chance to steady herself, Davey clapped his hand across her mouth and walked her backwards into her flat. Vinnie followed and closed the door behind him.

'Fabulous place. Very bijou.' Vinnie leaned

against the door and surveyed the room, distaste etched across his face. It was truly a dump: a one-room bed-sit with high, dirty ceilings and a threadbare carpet. There was a sagging camp bed pushed up against the far wall and a kitchenette complete with a hot plate and mini-fridge. A huge, old-fashioned wardrobe dominated the room, its speckled mirror reflecting the decay around him. The whole room smelled of stale sweat and sour milk and something else Vinnie couldn't put his finger on. A red Formica table held the only thing in the room that wasn't on its last legs: a brand-new, thirty-two-inch TV.

'Nice.' Vinnie walked over and traced a gloved finger across the screen. 'Do they give these out on the welfare?'

Davey had forced Josie back onto the bed. He knelt on her massive stomach with one knee and gripped her chin, forcing her face in his direction. Her eyes locked on his. 'If I take my hand off, no screamin', right?'

Josie nodded once. Davey removed his hand and stood up, slowly.

Josie remained on her back, breathing hard. 'I don't have any money.' Her voice was deep and raspy, the voice of a forty-a-day smoker.

'Clearly,' Vinnie said. 'But then, we're not after money.'

'Jaysus, what do you want, then?' Josie whipped her skirt down to cover her legs.

Vinnie reeled backwards, thoroughly disgusted.

'*Sacré bleu,* we definitely don't want that, either! Look, has Kelpie been here? Have you heard from him?'

'My brother?'

'Yes.'

'No. Why would I have?'

Vinnie sighed and rubbed at his forehead. He was getting another of his headaches. 'Do you know who I am?'

Josie squinted at him. 'You're Patrick York's boy. You've a look of him.' She rolled her head to look at Davey. 'Who're you?'

Davey shrugged. 'Doesn't matter who I am.'

Josie grinned. 'Strong silent type, huh? I'm tellin' yous, I don't know where Kelpie is. I haven't seen him. Why don't you check with that whore he keeps over in Ringsend?'

'We did. She told us to check with you.' Vinnie cocked an eyebrow.

'Why you lookin' for him? I thought him and your old man were as thick as thieves.'

'Tell me, where did you get the money for this?' Vinnie pointed at the television.

'You think Kelpie gave it to me?'

'Maybe he was feeling generous.'

Josie laughed, a guttural, phlegmy sound. She heaved herself upright with a huge grunt, leaned down and pulled a tan pop-sock up to her dimpled knee. The nylon ripped under the strain, and a ladder raced up her calf. She shook her head sadly. 'Can't keep these things from tearin' – and I hand-wash them, like you're supposed to.'

270

Vinnie grimaced. He doubted Josie Molloy washed much, and she was flashing far too much wattled flesh for his liking. 'I asked you a—'

'Look, whatever he's gone and done now, it's not my problem. He's my brother and all, but I ain't seen him since last December, right? Even then, it was only for a minute or two, when he threw me a few quid. He don't contact me or nothin'.'

'So where did you get the money for the television?'

'Not from Kelpie, that's for sure. He doesn't look up or down at me. He never has.'

'Oh, really?' Vinnie said. 'That's a crying shame. Families should keep in touch. Why, I was only saying that to Davey earlier. Wasn't I, Davey?'

He reached out a gloved hand and shoved the television off the table. It crashed to the floor. The screen exploded, spraying shards of glass everywhere.

Josie leaned back on her hands and rolled her eyes again. 'Here, listen, wreck what you want. There's nothin' in this shit-hole worth worryin' about anyhow.'

Vinnie scowled at her, disturbed by her obvious lack of concern. She wasn't frightened of him, and that irritated him further. He paced back and forth across the broken glass. 'I never worry, Josie. Not my style.'

Josie snorted. 'So what are you doin' here, then? Course you're bleedin' worried.' She searched Vinnie's face with cool, sharp eyes. 'What's he done?'

'Your brother was supposed to make a delivery, last week. He failed to show up.'

'Yeah? Well, I told you, I haven't seen him.' She grinned, exposing dirty, uneven teeth.

'I'm going to give you a number. If he should get in contact, I want you to call me immediately.'

'What's in it for me?'

Vinnie laughed. 'I let you live for another few pathetic years, you fat piece of shit.'

Josie laughed and pulled at her tights. 'Not good enough, York. If you want me to rat out my own flesh and blood, you'd better be offerin' something as a...as an incentive.'

'Incentive?' Vinnie glanced at Davey in disbelief. '*Incentive?*'

'Why shouldn't I have somethin' for my troubles?'

Vinnie crossed the room in quick steps and slapped Josie across the face. 'I'm not asking you, I'm telling you.'

Josie brought her hand up to her face. Her eyes had turned small and mean. 'Go fuck yourself.'

Davey sighed softy and slipped his hand into his jacket to finger the sap. She was a game old bird, no doubt about it. Why the fuck hadn't Vinnie just slipped her a few quid? She'd have told him anything he wanted to know. Why did he always have to do things the wrong way?

'What's it worth to you? Seeing as now I have

to go out and get myself a brand-new telly?'

Vinnie slapped her again, harder. Josie jerked her head and hauled herself onto her feet, her thick hands bunching by her sides. 'You dirty fucker. I suppose it makes you feel like a big man, hittin' an old one like me.'

Vinnie's pupils dilated, and the corners of his mouth stretched into a tight smile that Davey recognised as bad news.

'Josie Molloy…' Vinnie whistled softly. 'My father says you were a hot piece of stuff when you were young. Look at you now. I was saying to Davey earlier, it's terrible when people let themselves go.' His hand shot out and he slapped her again. 'You fat piece of *shit*. You think you can put the squeeze on me?'

Josie's lips curled back over her teeth. 'I'm going to knock your fuckin'—'

Davey hit her on the shoulder with the sap – not too hard, but hard enough to get her attention. Josie cried out, and as she turned to him he shoved her in the chest and knocked her back down onto the bed.

'Not the way to play this,' he said simply, and let the sap bounce on the palm of his left hand. His eyes warned her not to mess about. He didn't want another bloodbath on his hands. 'Be smart.'

'All right – all *right*!' Josie rubbed at her shoulder and glared up at him. There were tears in her eyes and a red mark on her cheek where Vinnie had struck her.

Vinnie balled his hands into fists. 'All right, *what?*'

'All right, if I hear anything, you'll be the first to know.'

'Good. That's better.'

'Give us a number.'

It was as if someone had thrown a switch. Vinnie took a step back and beamed at Josie. His eyes sparkled with warmth and humanity. He felt his shoulders loosen and the slight throb over his left eye recede. He pulled out a hand-tooled silver card-holder and extracted one of the pressed linen cards he'd had specially imported. He flipped the card into Josie's face. She made no attempt to catch it, and it fluttered down onto the bed.

'Don't let me down, Josie,' Vinnie said. 'I don't like it when people go back on their word.' He jerked his head at Davey, but as they moved towards the door, Vinnie turned. 'Of course, it goes without saying that we never had this conversation. Remember that, will you, *mon amie*? Because if I have to remind you, I will carve the words into your fat flesh.'

He opened the door and sauntered out. Davey gave the old woman another glance. Her eyes were on Vinnie's back, and they held a burning hatred.

'Why're you workin' for shite like that?' she said softly, over suppressed tears.

Davey looked at the old woman they had just humiliated, at her smashed television and the squalor in which she lived. He slipped the sap back into his pocket and closed the door behind him. Some days he asked himself the same question.

After they left, Josie wiped away the trace of blood where she had bitten down on her lip. She hauled herself off the bed and made her way wearily to the hall. She pulled a piece of paper from her bra strap and dialled the mobile number Pascal Mooney had given her.

She knew her brother was probably dead. Despite what she had told Vinnie, he had often sent her a few quid here and there. With him out of the picture, she would need an extra helping hand. If the cop wanted her to play ball, he had better be offering more than a telly for her help.

19

As soon as John got home, he placed a quick call to the only police friend he had left in the world: Detective Sergeant Steve Magher.

Steve was thirty-eight years old and almost a sixteen-year veteran. He was stationed in Tallaght, a hot spot if ever there was one – although Steve claimed it wasn't half as bad as Blackrock, where he'd worked before. He reckoned that in Tallaght, at least you knew exactly what you were dealing with, whereas in Blackrock money and expensive solicitors muddied the waters. He was happily married to a great lass called Ailbhe and had – at last count – five little girls, all under the age of seven. Steve desperately wanted someone he could train to be the next champion Cork hurler, and John figured he was going to keep trying until Ailbhe either produced a son or cut Steve's dick off while he slept.

John and Steve knew each other from the early days of John's detective career, when Steve had been sued. Nicky Shaw, a first-class delinquent and small-time crook, had been after him for assault, grievous bodily harm and anything else he could get his bottom-feeding solicitor to add to the charges. At Steve's request, John had trailed Shaw for three weeks solid, taking only the minimum time off for sleep and food. He watched as the young man hobbled around Tallaght on a pair of crutches, dragging his legs as though the very touch of air caused him tremendous agony. He watched as Shaw's mother helped him in and out of the car outside the post office where he collected his dole. He watched as Shaw hobbled out the door to pick up the post and dragged his body back into the house, his teeth clenched with pain and effort. He always wore a neck brace, and he never, ever slipped up.

Shaw claimed that Steve had robbed him of his chance to become a plasterer and turn his life around. He had ended his many years as a juvenile delinquent and chosen a different path in life, he said: the very week Steve had knocked him off his bike, he had become an apprentice. He claimed his back had been so severely injured that he could barely climb a flight of stairs, let alone ladders and scaffolding. He was eighteen years old and crippled for life, he said. Shaw's solicitor sent Steve's solicitor letters that reeked of pathos and smug self-satisfaction – and a letter from a local building contractor, who happened to be Shaw's uncle, claiming he had taken the lad on only days before Steve Magher had 'mown him down and ended his dreams of working with his hands'.

Steve's version was somewhat different. Steve

admitted clipping the bike and running over the back wheel as he looked for a parking space in the Tallaght shopping centre on a packed Friday evening – although he questioned why Shaw had been stopped on a dangerous curve with no reflective bands on his jacket or bike, and why the two guys handing him money had bolted as soon as Steve stepped from the car. Steve had got out and asked the kid if he was all right. The kid had got up, spat at him, called him a 'dozy country wanker' (Steve was originally from Cork) and said he was going to sue him for the bike and his injuries. Steve apologised for hitting the bike and offered to show the kid what real hurt was like. Unfortunately, Steve made his outburst just as a woman and her two teenage daughters wheeled past with a packed shopping trolley. He took a step towards Shaw, who fell on the ground shrieking as though hot coals had been stuffed up his arse. Steve heard the woman gasp, 'Oh my God, did he hit him?'

That was Steve's first mistake. With a crowd gathering and Shaw looking for an Oscar, Steve remembered his Garda training and leaned over the kid to check for injury. Another onlooker yelled, 'Leave the poor boy alone or I'll call the police!' Steve roared back that he *was* the police, and that they should all shut up and let him 'assess the little prick's non-existent injuries'. This Steve did, squeezing Shaw's body all over and hauling the moaning lad to his feet while roaring, 'Does that hurt?' Mistake number two.

The official complaint said Shaw was suing Steve for slander, intimidation, dangerous driving and, of course, police brutality. Although Steve had been off duty at the time of the accident, the brass didn't like the stink rising. Steve was hauled into a meeting and practically ordered to settle the case out of court. When he refused, he was threatened with a formal reprimand. Steve thought of his wife and kids, looked at the Superintendent's bloated face and hundred-euro haircut, and decided he needed outside help. He contacted John Quigley. QuicK was cheap, and it was one of the few agencies that didn't have any moonlighting cops working off the books.

Thanks to John's dedicated camera work, his ability to climb slippery walls and Shaw's hormones, the case was dropped. Three weeks into the case, John had followed Shaw to a nice semi-detached house where, through the poorly drawn curtains, he was able to photograph the reformed delinquent's acrobatics with his fourteen-year-old girlfriend on her parents' sofa. It was these pictures, taken while the girl's folks were at bingo that sealed the deal. The twelve colour prints came out perfectly and proved once and for all that Shaw was uninjured, was extremely agile and could be done for sex with a minor. Steve Magher gave the prints to his solicitor, went home, kissed his pregnant wife and didn't waste another minute fretting about Nicky Shaw. At Sarah's insistence, John had waived the last week's fee, only asking that they could call on Steve now and again if they needed too. QuicK had made its first useful contact.

So, while Sumo soaked the remaining healthy plants in his back garden, John called Steve's mobile. It was answered on the second ring. 'Hello?'

'Steve, it's John Quigley.'

'Well, fuck, so it is. How's it hanging, Magnum?'

'All right. How's the driving?'

'Fuck off and tell me what you want, because I've no doubt you want something.'

And so, with the pleasantries over, John gave him Vinnie York's name. Steve took it down, complaining mildly that he wasn't John's personal assistant, and promised to call back within the hour.

John wasn't overly worried about York. It was natural enough that he hadn't wanted his club mentioned: it was bad publicity. But warning the girls to say nothing struck him as a little off.

An hour later, while he was eating cold Heinz beans out of the can and watching the nine o'clock news, John got the return call.

'I thought you'd forgotten about me.'

'Chance would be a fine thing,' Steve drawled down the line. 'Listen, boyo, you're heading for trouble with a capital T. Time to pick up and get out of Dodge, like.'

'Yeah? Wouldn't be the first time. What's the juice?'

'Remember, you got none of this from me.'

'Yeah, I know.' John put the can down and reached for a pen.

'I wouldn't go fucking with them Yorks, Magnum, if you know what I mean, like.'

'There's more than one?'

'There are always a few cockroaches.'

'What's the story with them?'

'Dirty fucking shower. Patrick York – that's Vinnie's father – ever heard of him?'

'No. Should I have?'

'He's probably a bit before your time. He was involved in all manner of shite – armed robbery, GBH, gun running, protection rackets, at least one murder linked to his name, money laundering... You getting my drift? Great fella for being around whenever there was trouble. Left Ireland a good few years ago now.'

'And the son?'

'The apple doesn't fall far from the tree. Vinnie's a head-case. Got locked down years ago for beating his foster father half to death. He just came home from school one day and completely flipped out. He was fourteen, so he didn't stay inside. But Jaysus, Magnum, the damage. He beat that man until his face was pulp – left him in intensive care for weeks.'

'Jesus,' John said, and thought of Ashley Naughton's pretty face. 'And now?'

'He's clean – as far as anyone can tell, like. Although there's many a rumour that he's involved in all sorts, like the old man.'

'What sort of rumours?'

'That he's using the club as a front, that he's got a pipeline to bring drugs into the country. I heard he's cleaning out the local dealers, too, heading for a monopoly. But sure, look, you know yourself, Magnum, rumours don't mean shit – not if you can't back them up. And he's cute that way. Nobody's willing to pull the plug on him. And it's an interesting fact that he has a lot of heavies working for him.'

'Heavies?'

'Yeah, fellas who all know the layout of the 'Joy,' Steve said. 'I wouldn't want any of them fuckers knocking on my door. His main man is a guy called Davey Clarke – a tough nut with a sheet as black as a whore's. So if you're treading on their toes, watch your back.'

'Ah, Stevie, I didn't know you cared so much about me.'

Steve Magher laughed. 'You never know when I might need a man of limited talent. That it?'

'Thanks, Steve. Drive safe.'

'Go on, you prick you. Tell Sarah I said hello.'

'Will do.' John hung up and leaned down to pat Sumo's wiry head. 'Hear that, Sumo? Limited talent.'

He dialled Sarah's number, but it was engaged, so he went to his room and changed into a tracksuit to take Sumo out. As he slipped the dog's collar on, the doorbell rang.

Sumo began to bark furiously. John grabbed his collar, dragged him down the hall to the kitchen and shoved him inside. Then he opened the front door. He was very surprised to see Davey Clarke standing on the step, looking massively wide and chewing gum.

'It must be ESP. I was just talking about you.'

'Hope it was a good conversation.' Davey looked him up and down. 'You look familiar.'

'People say that to me a lot.'

'You been down the club?'

'What club?'

'Oh, a smart cunt.'

'Thanks.'

'Hear you're going around stickin' your nose into Tempest's business.'

'Did Claudia call you?'

'It don't matter who called me. Fact is, I'm here.'

'I'm investigating the disappearance of a girl, and the club keeps coming up.'

Davey transferred the gum from one side of his mouth to the other and cracked his knuckles. 'Yeah, well, you've done your questioning, so back off.'

'Or what? You'll come to my door and chew gum at me?'

Davey flexed the muscles on his neck and sneered. John sneered right back. They did that for another couple of seconds, until John got bored with it.

'Get out of here.' He stepped back and began to close the door.

Davey shot out a meaty paw and knocked the door back into John's shoulder, sending him stumbling backwards into the hall and falling flat on his arse. Davey stepped in and closed the front door behind him.

'Maybe you're fuckin' thick, I dunno. Let me explain somethin' to you. I'm not askin' you to back the fuck off. I'm tellin' you.'

'Whoa! Cool it, okay?' John scrabbled away. 'I get the message. Now get out of here before I let my dog out.'

Davey didn't seem to hear that. He took another step towards John. 'You go around messin' with the wrong people, it upsets everyone. Now, my boss has been very decent to you, lettin' you see that tape and all, but there's a limit to his patience.' Davey hauled John up by the front of his shirt and hurled him against the wall. John felt the air whoosh out of his body.

Davey grabbed him again and pulled him close. His breath reeked of Bubbalicious gum. If he was worried about Sumo's vicious barking and scrabbling at the kitchen door, it didn't show. 'Now, I don't like havin' to talk to you, bud. I've other shit to be doin'. So if I have to come round here again, you and me are gonna have a serious conversation – got me?'

'Loud and clear,' John wheezed. 'So I guess this means we won't be copping a look at the members list any time soon?'

Davey said, 'Tsk.' The next thing John knew, he was sailing through the air like a model airplane. He landed against the kitchen door with an almighty crash.

'You really are a dumb fuck.' Davey rolled his neck, apparently preparing for his next attack.

John decided it was time to call in the big guns. He wrenched the kitchen door open. As Sumo came bursting through it and over him, he grabbed the dog's harness line and held on, but Sumo still managed to drag him a couple of feet. He was snarling, ears flat against his head. Foam and splinters of door were streaked along his muzzle and neck. It was all John could do to hold him.

'Get out of here or I'll let go,' he gasped.

Davey finally looked impressed. He said, 'Fuck,' and backed up to the front door with genuine haste. He jabbed a finger in John's direction. 'Stay out of shit that doesn't concern—'

John loosened the lead by a couple of inches. Sumo sprang forward, his hind legs scrabbling for purchase for the leap that could rip Davey's throat out. Davey bolted out the door and slammed it shut behind him.

John let go and Sumo bounded to the door, barking furiously. John sat up gingerly against the wall and waited to catch his breath. His back and shoulders ached from where he had struck the door, and he was so shocked by what had happened that he could scarcely believe it had been real.

He was still sucking air back into his body when the phone rang. He crawled along the floor towards it, pulled it down onto his lap and answered it. 'Hello?'

'John?' It was Sarah, and she sounded angry and upset.

'Uh-huh.'

'Guess who's just been here.'

'Can't have been Davey Clarke, so I'm guessing another bouncer from Tempest.'

'Edward Naughton.'

'Edward Naughton?' John leaned against the wall and crossed his legs. 'Thought he didn't approve of the likes of us.'

'He asked me – no, *ordered* me – to drop this case.'

'He what?'

'And get this: he's prepared to pay us for our time, *and* for two weeks extra, if we do.'

John waved a furious hand at Sumo, who, out of sheer frustration, was beginning to gnaw at the front door. 'Why would he want to do that?'

'He didn't say.'

John rubbed his back with his free hand. That was a hefty chunk of money for nothing – money that could go into their account and cover some of their expenses, money that wouldn't involve being thrown into walls. 'So what do you want to do?'

'Something's screwy about this, John. I don't

like people who try to tell me what to do. So I'll tell you what we're doing: we're going to find that girl for her mother. If *she* wants us to stop looking, that's a different story.'

'Did you tell him that?'

'I did. He wasn't very happy about it. I believe he called me a "stupid cunt". You know, John, that's the second time that man has called me a cunt.'

John grinned. It sounded like Sarah was making a face.

'You think I should have just taken the money?'

'No, I think you're right.' He knew Sarah wouldn't take the easy route. 'Okay, let me give you an update. Guess who called here throwing his weight around?'

Behind him, Sumo gave up trying to eat through the front door and threw himself on the ground, sighing heavily. He closed his eyes and pretended to go to sleep, but John could see by the cock of his ears that he was listening.

Vinnie opened the door of his apartment, eager to take a long, hot shower and grab some shut-eye. He barely made it inside before Patrick was on his back.

'Well? What did Josie have to say?'

Vinnie shook off his coat and hung it in the hall closet. 'She hasn't seen him.'

Patrick ran his hands through his hair. 'Shit.'

Vinnie walked past him into the sitting room and went straight to the bar. He poured a large glass of Jack Daniels and tossed it back. 'She says she'll call if he gets in touch.'

Patrick leaned against the door and stared at the floor unblinkingly. Vinnie poured another hefty shot of Jack and sipped it. While he drank, he allowed himself time to study Patrick carefully. His father seemed to have aged dramatically in the past few days. He was pale, and shadows were etched deep under his eyes. He wore a hunted expression Vinnie had never seen on his face before. He looked stooped, shrunken, diminished. Vinnie was delighted.

'You heard from the Turks?'

Patrick raised his head slowly. 'Yeah, I heard from them.'

'And?'

'And they're running out of patience.' Patrick ran a hand over the stubble on his chin and exhaled loudly. 'If we don't find the gear in the next day or so, they're gonna start looking for compensation.'

'Compensation?' Vinnie didn't like the sound of that. 'What kind of compensation?'

'The deeds on the club, for one thing.'

'My club?' Vinnie felt like Patrick had just punched him in the stomach.

Patrick's head jerked up. 'Yeah, the fucking club. And it's not your club, it's *our* club, and don't you forget it. I gave you the fucking money to start up, remember? This fuck-pad's going to go, too. My place in Holland – all of it. You thought they'd just say, "Not to worry, lads, shit happens"? Shit, Vincent, sometimes I think you're not playing with a full deck.'

Vinnie put down his glass. He hadn't moved a muscle, but somehow his legs had locked and cramped. 'How long are they giving you?'

'The end of the week. After that, we can kiss everything we ever worked for goodbye.' Patrick closed his eyes and fought to control the rising panic. Aziz had let him speak briefly to Anouk. She had tried to sound brave, but he knew she was terrified. She had assured him she was being treated well. She had said that she loved him and that she knew he wouldn't let her down. Her trust had made him weep. When Aziz had come back on the line, Patrick had known that Anouk had very little time left.

He glanced at his son surreptitiously. Vinnie's face was pale and taut, his eyes black and unfocused. *God*, Patrick thought, *he looks out of it*. Was it possible that Vinnie really didn't realise how much danger they were in?

20

The next morning, John and Sarah met in Bernie's
Café for breakfast. Sarah had a lukewarm
cappuccino and a fresh croissant with marmalade.
John had a full Irish breakfast with fried bread and
a pot of tea so strong you could almost stand a
spoon in it.

'I'm telling you, it stinks. Why would he pay us
not to look for his own kid?' Sarah swirled the
dregs of her coffee, wondering how John never put
on any weight when he ate like a pig. 'And I don't
like the sound of this club, either.'

John used the last slice of bread to mop up the
baked bean sauce, popped the whole lot in his
mouth and swallowed. 'Did you try the PR girl
again?'

Sarah shook her head and frowned. 'She's not
taking my calls. Five times I called that office and
her mobile. I've left numbers and everything. Zip.
Another one who seems to have dropped off the
face of the planet.'

'Davey Clarke sort of hinted the club might
not help us any more, right before he threw me
down the hall.'

'You should have called the Gardaí. That's assault.'

'And have them traipsing around my house looking bored? Don't think so.'

'I'm telling you, John, the more I hear about this guy York, the more I'm scared for Ashley Naughton's safety.'

'Me too,' John admitted. 'I got hold of Alejandro last night, after I talked to you.'

'Who's he again?'

'Another barman from Tempest.'

'And?'

'And nothing. He nearly broke his arse trying to tell me what a great place Tempest is and how fantastic Vinnie York is. Every time I tried to ask him about Ashley or Claudia, he changed the subject.'

'Everyone's shutting us out big-time.' Sarah snorted and downed the last of her coffee. 'Well, if Steve's right about the Yorks, I'll do a bit of digging around, see what I can find out.' She reached behind her and unhooked her coat from the chair. 'What are you going to do today?'

'I'm going to give Mr Nightlife a call.'

'Good.' Sarah stood up. 'I'll tell you something, John: Naughton really freaked me out last night. He was sweating and pacing, banging his hands on my desk and yelling…' She swung her coat on and zipped it up to her chin. 'He looked really scared.'

'Maybe he'd had a chat with Davey too.'

'Maybe so. Look, I'll see you later.'

John watched her walk out the door and dodge traffic as she ran across the street. He paid the bill and wandered down the street to the office.

He spent another futile hour trying the club. Finally, at nearly ten to twelve, someone answered the phone in Tempest. John recognised Daz by his sparkling demeanour.

'Yeah?'

'Hi, this is John Quigley, the det—'

'Yeah.'

'Listen, I'm looking for your boss. He there?'

'Mr York doesn't come in on Sundays.'

John drummed his fingers on the desk. It was like pulling teeth. 'Do you have a home number for him, or a mobile number?'

'Can't give that out.'

'I need to talk to him today.'

'You leave a number and I'll make sure he gets the message.'

'Get him to call me on my mobile.' John gave him the number. 'And Daz – my partner's been trying to reach Sophie Allen. She around?'

'Nah.'

'Know when she gets in?'

'Nah.'

'If you see her, ask her to give Sarah Kenny a call. She has the number.'

'That it?'

'Yes. Thanks for—' He didn't get to finish. Daz, the tosser, had already hung up.

★

'Well?' Vinnie asked Daz across the bar. He'd only been in the club ten minutes and already he was feeling better. He nursed a hefty glass of vodka and Red Bull, trying to cure the raging hangover coursing through his body. He'd drunk the best part of a bottle of fifty-year-old malt whiskey the night before, to rid himself of Patrick's words. He'd woken up on the couch at nine o'clock, cold and still wearing yesterday's suit. The first thing he'd done was stagger to the bathroom and throw up. His face was puffy, his head was fuzzy from fatigue and his mouth was dry and furry. The only saving grace was that Patrick had left the apartment early, and he had managed to go wherever the hell he'd gone without Vinnie's help.

Daz nodded. 'Yeah, it's the same crowd.'

'*Merde.*' Vinnie drained the last of his drink, crossed the dance floor and painfully climbed the two floors to his private office. He would have to do something about those detectives. Clearly Davey hadn't made a damned bit of difference.

'I want a word with you.'

Vinnie shrieked. He fell back against the door of his office, clutching at his heart. 'How did—'

Patrick whipped around in the chair. 'You want to explain to me what the fuck you're playing at?'

'How did you get in here?' Vinnie felt his voice spiralling higher. Patrick remained seated in *his* chair, with his feet up on *his* desk, chewing on a

293

cigar and reading a newspaper. The back of Vinnie's scalp prickled with irritation. 'Jesus Christ! What are you doing here?'

Patrick waved the newspaper. 'Just went out and got the paper. I thought I'd come down and check out the operation you've got going here.'

Vinnie felt the colour drain from his face as he saw what Patrick was reading. It was a copy of the *Sunday World*, and blazoned across the front of it was the headline 'Man's Throat Slashed as Baby Watches'. He tried to swallow, but his throat had turned to wood. He wondered if Patrick had spotted the dead man's name.

'Well?' he said, keeping his breathing soft and his face neutral. 'I think it's a bad idea, you being here. *Mon dieu*, what if someone sees you?'

'I can't stay cooped up in that apartment all day, every day. And I've already told you: don't talk that French crap to me.' Patrick shook his head in disgust. He put the paper down and came around the desk. Vinnie backed up a step.

Patrick came towards him fast and stopped a fraction in front of him. Vinnie felt a thin trickle of sweat run down his back.

'Vincent, I'm going to take a piss. You want to move out of my way?'

'Oh – of course.' Vinnie side-stepped quickly and waited until he heard Patrick's footsteps moving down the stairs. Then he took a deep breath and attempted to swallow again. He went to the desk and speed-read the newspaper story, taking careful note of the descriptions of the two men seen leaving the scene: both wearing black, one stocky, the other tall and possibly foreign. Vinnie wondered at that briefly. Foreign? How odd. He exhaled. The descriptions were vague – they could be of anyone, really – and there was no mention of the jeep. Gradually he felt a smidgen of control return to him.

'Philo Redmond? I know that name…he's one of Dougie Burrows's men, isn't he?' he said aloud, practising. 'What the fuck makes you think I'd know anything about this? How dare you!'

He considered getting rid of the paper, just in case Patrick hadn't read the article, but he knew that was stupid: it would have been the first thing he'd read. But why hadn't he said anything about it, anything at all – even a comment to suggest he'd known the dead man?

When Patrick came back in, Vinnie got such a fright he jumped and dropped the paper.

'Okay there, Vincent? You look like you've seen a ghost.'

Vinnie shrugged and picked up the paper, folding it so that the headline was no longer visible. 'That's…no, I'm fine. Why wouldn't I be?'

Patrick leaned in too close to him. His breath was like sandpaper on Vinnie's face. It smelled of cigar smoke and Rennie's antacid tablets. 'Don't know. Why would you be so nervous?'

A noise like the far-away buzz of a thousand crickets began in Vinnie's left ear, and he began to see spots before his eyes. His hand dropped to his coat pocket, searching for his blade, but just as his fingers found its comforting shape, Patrick stepped back. Vinnie reeled away from him and slumped down onto the sofa.

Patrick turned and reclaimed his position behind his desk. 'Fuck off out of here for a while, Vincent, will you?'

Vinnie stared at him. 'What do you mean?'

'I've got a few calls to make.'

'This is *my* office.'

Patrick slammed his fist onto the desk. 'Don't make me ask you again.'

'I wanted a word with you,' Vinnie said suddenly.

'Not now. I've other shit on.'

'I'm not sure offering the Turks my club is such a good idea.'

'Do you not? Surprise, surprise.'

'I will not lose this club because Naughton has screwed us over.' Vinnie wiped his hands on the legs of his trousers. His left eye twitched uncontrollably. He was unable to regain his composure, and that was scaring him. 'I won't sit here while our business falls apart.'

'You'll do what I fucking say, Vincent. If you don't, you will be one sorry fucker.'

Vinnie narrowed his eyes. 'You're threatening me? Your own son?'

'You better believe it. Now beat it. I need a bit of privacy.'

Vinnie didn't trust himself to speak. He stood

up, executed a sort of half-bob and left the office as fast as he could. His features remained frozen, but inside he fizzed and popped with rage. He had been threatened on his own turf. Nobody threatened him – nobody.

Whatever doubts he'd had about betraying Patrick vanished. Dougie Burrows would have his justice, and by God, Vinnie was going to enjoy watching him claim it. Deliver Patrick to Dougie? He would deliver him wrapped up and tied with a bow.

Patrick ran his fingers through his hair and sucked hard on his cigar. The boy was a fucking nut, pure and simple. He unfolded the newspaper and stared at the shocking story again. He didn't feel guilty that Philo was dead – after all, Philo had only contacted him because he had an axe to grind – but he was furious that Vinnie had been so free and easy on his way out. What if someone had recognised him, or given a better description? The cops could have been crawling all over them this morning. Shit, Vinnie was a fucking liability. In more ways than one.

He picked up the phone and dialled a number. This was a call he had been putting off for various reasons, but now he had no other choice. There was too much at stake for errors.

After only a single ring, the call was answered by a clipped male voice. 'Trenton Security. How may I help?'

'This is Patrick York for Alonso... Yeah, I'll wait.'

The line went through another set of extensions. Moments later he heard a deep, honeyed voice that he knew well, even after all these years. Patrick closed his eyes. He was dealing with the devil himself, and he knew it.

'Alonso, man... Yeah, I'm good. How you doing? ... Yeah, yeah, long time no see. Look, let's cut to the chase. I need a guy – two, actually. I need someone who can tail. Has to be someone good, discreet... Yeah, I'll wait.'

He took another few puffs on his cigar while he waited. 'Yeah? ... Good. I want one to tail my son, Vincent, and the other to watch a guy called Davey Clarke – he's a bouncer, works for Vincent. You know him? ... Oh, yeah, I should've figured. I want to know everyone he talks to, everyone he sees, and I want it to start straight away. Where do you want the payment made?' He picked up a pen and wrote down a number. 'Yeah, got it. Oh, and another thing – I need a piece... Nah, nothing fancy, just something that's clean and works... Not yet, probably in the next couple of days... Great. You want me to add that into the payment? ... Nah? Cash? Ha, just kidding... Sure, no problem. Yeah, we'll do that, next time I'm over. Good talking to you, man.'

Patrick hung up and smoked his cigar. He had been in the game a long time, and the most valuable lesson he had ever learned was that you trusted no one. Not even your own son. Especially not his son.

Dougie Burrows watched Pascal Mooney's huge, shambling figure heading his way. He pulled a cob pipe out of his breast pocket, filled it and struck a match. He sucked noisily, waiting for it to draw. By the time he had it lit, the big cop was at the van door.

Pascal opened the door and slid in, wrinkling his nose at the stench.

'Aye, whiffs a bit, doesn't she?'

'I'm surprised to hear from you. Thought you didn't deal with my kind.'

Dougie grinned. 'It's a stupid cunt that stays too rigid, Pascal. Sure, you must know that.'

Pascal kept his gaze straight ahead. His hooded eyes were alert, scanning the Tesco car park for signs that he was being watched. 'What do you want?'

'You're a smart enough fella for a pig, Pascal,' Dougie said mildly. 'I'm surprised to see you making such a fuckin' eejit of yourself with Naughton.'

Pascal's face was stony. 'Oh?'

Dougie scratched under his balls with his pipe stem and popped it back into his mouth. 'See, let me tell you somethin'. I have two dogs back at the kennels – big fuckers, the pair of them, shoulders on them like you wouldn't believe. They could pull a Mini up a hill on a wet day.'

'That's nice.'

'Aye. But here's the thing: only one of them boyos can fight worth a fuck. The other fella can't go the distance, see? He's not built for the long haul.'

Pascal turned his head slightly. 'What are you saying here?'

Dougie shrugged. 'Sure, I'm not saying a word. I'm only tellin' you about my dogs.' He sucked on his pipe contentedly. 'I like to know the animals I deal with. I'd hate to be in a situation where I'd be backin' the wrong dog, do you know what I'm sayin'?'

'You think I'm backing the wrong dog?'

Dougie grinned. 'Jaysus, will this weather ever let up, do you think? I may look into building a fuckin' ark next.'

Pascal took the hint and got out of the van. He gulped fresh air deep into his lungs and vanished back into the crowds of shoppers.

Edward Naughton was history.

21

On Monday John was in Rodney Mitchell's office, eating a bacon and melted cheese roll, when Sarah came back from wherever the hell she had been half the morning. John was bored. He had stayed in the office, not because he wanted to, but because he hadn't anything better to do. He had called everyone he needed to call, and short of consulting a psychic, he was at a loss. The Ashley Naughton case was slithering into no man's land before his very eyes.

'I knew I'd find you here,' Sarah said, sticking her head around Rodney's door. 'Why aren't you upstairs manning the phones?'

John picked up his mobile from Rodney's desk and waved it at her. 'See this, Sarah? It's got this wonderful new technology known as call divert.'

'Come upstairs, I've got news for you.' She acknowledged Rodney with a wink. 'Honestly, Rod, I don't know how you get any work done with him lurking about.'

'Oh, I don't mind, really.' Rodney blushed so badly it looked like he'd been scalded.

'Way to play it,' John said, and wiped his mouth.

'What?' Rodney said, looking even more uncomfortable.

John grinned and let him off the hook. Sometimes slagging Rodney was like shooting fish in a barrel.

Upstairs, Sarah pulled out her battered notebook and a bundle of papers. She flipped through the pages until she found what she was looking for. 'Wait till you hear this. I did some checking on Naughton.'

John dropped into his chair and grinned at her excited face. 'I take it you've got good shit?'

'Yep. Steve said Vinnie York's father was a criminal legend, right?'

'Yeah.'

'Well, what if I told you Naughton is a bit of a crook himself?'

'I wouldn't be too shocked.'

'Would you be shocked if I told you our reluctant employer was a close friend of Patrick York, back in the day, and probably knows his son?'

'Now that would surprise me.' John sat up. 'He knows Vinnie York?'

Sarah nodded. 'Oh, I'd say they're more than passing acquaintances.' She dropped a bunch of pages onto John's desk. 'I've got most of it here. Have a read of this and tell me what you think.'

'Where did you get all of this?'

'Newspaper archives.'

John picked up the bundle and leafed through

it. There was a recent photo of Vincent York, his hand wrapped around a glass of champagne, smiling like a pro for the camera. Under the photo was the line, 'Mr Vincent York enjoying the hospitality.' John studied the photo, taking in the perfect smile and the expensive-looking suit. He shook his head.

The other pages were a collection of photo-copied newspaper stories and grainy copies of photos. John recognised Edward Naughton in one of the photos: he had been thin back then, but he had the same belligerent expression on his face, as though the fact that he was handcuffed to a Garda was nothing more than a minor nuisance. John relaxed in his chair and read.

Back in 1965, Edward Naughton had been nothing more than a petty criminal, with a juvenile record as long as John's arm – nothing major: shoplifting, nicking cars. But in '71 a group of men had robbed a lorry-load of goods from a loading bay on the East Wall. A security guard had stumbled across the little gang as they were loading everything that they could into an old van. In the ensuing hullabaloo, the security man got a knock on the head. He didn't wake up. He died three weeks later in the Mater.

'And?' John waved the article at Sarah.

'Three men were seen fleeing the scene. And guess who got caught selling the gear two weeks later?'

'Naughton?'

'Exactly. But since the cops couldn't prove he was actually in on the raid, they got him for handling stolen goods instead. This time the judge took a longer look at Naughton, and he landed in the loving arms of the 'Joy for a four-year stretch. Naughton never admitted his involvement in the robbery and he never named anyone who might have been with him. He was released in 1974 after serving two, and kept a clean nose for a while after that.'

John lit a cigarette. 'Okay, so we know Naughton was trouble. Now why doesn't he want us looking for his missing daughter?'

'Shut up and listen. After he got out of the 'Joy, he moved down the country, worked on the building sites and pretty much stayed away from the Dublin scene. There's no record of him anywhere in the country after 1975, so it's assumed he moved over the water to England, looking for work.'

'Yeah, him and half the country,' John said. He blew twin streams of smoke through his nostrils. His own father had gone to England during the 70s, and until the day he died, Tony Quigley had never got over the way he'd been treated on the building sites of London and Birmingham. *Mick, Paddy…* Dogs; they'd been treated like dogs.

'Yeah,' Sarah said, 'but Naughton came back in less than two years, flush with cash. That's when he set up Atlantic Development, his first construction company.'

'So far, so legal.'

'Read the second-last page in front of you,' Sarah said, scowling. Sometimes she thought John deliberately acted obtuse, just to annoy her. 'Guess who's on the original board of directors with him.'

John flicked to the page, read a few lines and sat up straighter. 'Patrick York?'

'That's right. Interested now?'

'Very.'

'There's a little bit of background information on him there, too. But not too much.'

John whistled through his teeth and studied the photo of Patrick York, circa 1977. Patrick wore the big hair and questionable clothes of the times, but even to the untrained eye, he and Vinnie bore more than a passing resemblance.

'Naughton re-registered the company in '88 as sole director,' Sarah said. 'Ten years later, he folded outright. He formed Zara Construction the following year – again, as sole director.'

John nodded. 'Okay. So that's the connection between them – building?'

'Don't be thick, John. Patrick York wouldn't know gravel from ice cream. The man is a professional criminal, only he's more low-key than most – did his utmost to keep his face out of the courts and the papers. From what Steve says and from what I've found today, you name it and he was linked to it.'

John nodded. 'Steve said he was bad news. He said there was at least one murder connected to him.'

Sarah checked her notebook. 'Yeah. Back in the early seventies, one of Patrick York's known associates was a man called Albert Burrows, known as Bertie. This Bertie was a genuine hard man, a head-cracker, and he and York allegedly had a hold over a lot of the pubs in central Dublin – but, of course, nobody can *prove* anything. Anyway, this Bertie had a temper and was known for shooting his mouth off – even York couldn't control him fully, and apparently York's quite a head-case himself. Sometime in early '72, Bertie vanished – poof, just like that. He was never heard from again. The story was that he got into a fight with some IRA men over protection money, but nobody really swallowed that. The Gardaí reckon York had something to do with it, but they couldn't prove a thing. Less than a month after Bertie Burrows's disappearance, York left Ireland. He hasn't been back since.'

John put out his cigarette and rested his chin on his hand. 'Interesting company Edward Naughton keeps.'

Sarah's smile stretched from ear to ear. 'Yeah, isn't it?'

'Okay, so Naughton and Vinnie York probably know each other. So why is Naughton's daughter missing? Has Naughton done something to piss York off? And what about Margaret Naughton – you think she knows about all this?'

'She's got to, hasn't she? She's married to the man.'

'That doesn't mean anything.' John drummed

his fingers on the desk. 'Does anybody know where Patrick York is now?'

'I checked with the Garda assigned to the case back then – he's nearly retired now – and according to him, the last the Gardaí heard Patrick York was living at a hotel called Hoksbergen, near the Singel Canal in Amsterdam.' As Sarah glanced down at her notebook a curtain of dark hair swung across her face. 'That was a couple of years ago. Nobody knows where he is now.'

'We need to talk to Vinnie York, find out why he was so keen to keep his club from being mentioned.' John lit another cigarette and sucked on it furiously. After a few minutes he picked up the phone and dialled Tempest.

'Yeah?'

John winced. Once again, he had the dazzling Daz on the line.

'It's John Quigley, Daz. Your boss call in?'

'Yeah.'

'You gave him my message yesterday?'

'Yeah.'

'And he knows it's important.'

'Yeah.'

'Did he say he'd call?'

'Didn't say nothing, just took the number.'

'Right.' John felt an almost irresistible urge to drive over there and slap Daz's skinny, chewed-up neck with the back of his hand.

'Let him know I called, *again*.' This time he hung up first.

He leaned back in his chair and studied the cracks in the ceiling. 'I'm going to ring Margaret Naughton.'

'And tell her what?' Sarah said, without looking up.

'Tell her Ashley was at Tempest, for a start. See if she knows this York guy.' He dialled the number. The phone only rang twice before it was picked up. Margaret Naughton must have been sitting beside it.

'Hello?'

'Mrs Naughton? Hi, it's John Quigley.'

'Have you found Ashley?'

It bothered John to hear such hope in her voice. He couldn't begin to imagine what she must be going through. 'I'm sorry, no. But we're making progress. We now know where Ashley was the night she went missing.'

Margaret's voice was unnaturally hushed. 'Where was she?'

'She was at a nightclub on Pleasant Street, a place called Tempest. You ever hear of it?'

'Tempest? No…I don't think so. I don't think I ever heard Ashley mention it.'

'Here's the thing: she was there with Megan Lowry and Claudia Delaney. They'd been there a few times before.'

For almost twenty seconds he got no reply, then: 'They were *all* there? But…the girls told me they were away. They told me they didn't see Ashley that night. They said—' Margaret's voice

308

cracked with disbelief. 'They said they were in *Galway*.'

'They lied. They never went to Galway that weekend.'

'They *lied*? But why?'

'They were told not to mention the club.'

'I don't understand. Who told them that – who?'

John rubbed his hand over his head. 'Mrs Naughton, the owner of the club is a man called Vincent York. You ever heard of him?'

She didn't reply, but John heard a sharp intake of breath and figured that name meant something to her, all right. He decided to go for broke. 'He's the son of Patrick York.'

'Oh my God! Patrick York – I…I haven't heard that name in years. Why…why would this man – Vincent, is it? – why would he tell the girls not to mention that Ashley was at his club? I don't understand any of this! What are you saying?'

John closed his eyes. 'Sarah and I think Vincent York may have had something to do with Ashley's disappearance. I've been trying to get hold of him, but so far no luck. Mrs Naughton, I know your husband had dealings with Patrick York in the past. Is there anything we should know? Anything that you're not telling us?'

'Like what? Edward knew Patrick, of course. They practically grew up together. But as far as I know, they haven't spoken for years.'

John wrote 'grew up together' and 'history' on his pad.

'But…you're telling me Ashley was definitely at his nightclub?'

'Yes. I'm positive.'

She took a deep breath. 'I didn't know Patrick even had a son. I don't understand this. Why would the girls lie to me?'

'I don't know,' John said evenly. 'Can you check with your husband, see if she mentioned anything to him about the club? Can you do that, Mrs Naughton, and get back to us?'

'I…of course.'

'I intend to find out why York didn't want his club mentioned. It could be nothing, but it's the only lead we have to go on.'

Margaret sounded as though she was crying.

'I'm really sorry I don't have anything more to give you at the moment,' John said softly.

'I…keep expecting her to…to walk through the door any minute.'

John nodded, even though she couldn't see him. 'I know, I know.'

'Thank you for calling.'

John hung up and shook his head. 'Jesus. That poor woman.'

Sarah closed down her computer and dragged the phone directory off the shelves behind her. A few seconds later, she found a pen and wrote something down in her notebook.

'What are you doing?'

'You want to talk to Vinnie York, right?' Sarah stood up and put on her coat. 'You know the best way to get someone to talk to you?'

'What?'

'Stand right in front of him.'

John snapped his fingers, delighted to be given a reason to get out of the office. 'I'll get my coat.'

22

John parked the Manta a few doors up from the rear entrance of Tempest and settled in to wait. Sarah had taken Vinnie's address from the phone directory and was at that moment camped in a coffee shop opposite his apartment building. She rung the bell but there was nobody home.

It was bitterly cold, and a raw wind forced darkening clouds across the November sky. John shivered and clapped his hands together. This was a long shot – Vinnie York could be anywhere – but with no other way to contact him, all they could do was wait.

After an hour had passed, the staff door at the side of the club opened. Two men came out and walked quickly across the road to a black Jeep Cherokee. John squinted at them and grinned. The one trailing behind was definitely Vinnie York. He was the exact image of his picture: darkly handsome, kind of Italian-looking, and wearing a long wool coat that had probably cost more than John's car. He moved with the kind of grace that made women take a good second look.

The second man was older. He wore dark trousers, stacked cowboy boots and a leather jacket, and he had a fisherman's cap pulled down low over his eyes. He walked with his head down, his hands bunched in the pockets of his jacket.

John jumped out of the car and crossed the road. 'Hey, Mr York!'

Both men turned and stared at him. John held out his hand. 'Vincent York, right? Hey, how you doing? I'm John Quigley.'

Vinnie York looked blankly at him. The second man kept his eyes firmly on the ground.

'You know, private investigator. Man, you're a hard guy to track down, aren't you?'

Vinnie pulled his wool coat tighter around his body. 'I'm sorry, this isn't a good—'

'Time?' John said cheerfully. 'No problem. If you can't talk now, tell me when you can, and we'll arrange it.'

'Open the car, Vincent. I'm freezing my balls off out here,' the other man said in a low voice.

There was something about his manner that interested John. He wore the flat tweed cap pulled down low across his eyes, and the collar of his jacket was turned up, shielding most of his face. Even when he spoke he kept his head down, mumbling his words from deep in his chest.

'Hey, how you doing?' John said. 'Yeah, the weather's really changing fast, isn't it?'

The man in the cap ignored him. Vinnie pressed a button on his key ring, and the central locking clicked loudly. The man in the cap slid into the passenger seat. He kept his face turned away from John, even though it meant holding an unnatural pose. John felt his antennae quiver.

Vinnie held out his hand and smiled with practised ease. '*Mon dieu*, Mr – Quigley, is it? My deepest apologies. I was going to call you later.'

John shook his hand. 'Where are you from? I thought you were from Dublin, like myself.'

'I am.'

'Yeah? That's some fancy accent you have. I bet the ladies love that.'

'Was there something you wanted?' Vinnie's smile remained glued in place, although it lost some of its brilliance.

'Maybe I'll try one. I could be Italian – *ciao, bella*… Nah, doesn't really work. Oh, and you can call me John – none of this "Mr Quigley" crap. You don't mind if I call you Vincent, do you?'

'You may call me whatever you like, *John*.' Vinnie said the name as if he'd bitten into a lemon. 'As I say, I got your message. I've been meaning to get back to you all day, but you know how it is. I'm up to my eyes at the moment.'

'Yeah.' John smiled and leaned an elbow on the bonnet of the jeep. 'It's a bitch when you're busy. You know why I was trying to reach you, right?'

'Yes, of course, my PR director informed me. It's about some missing girl. Dreadful business. I'm only sorry the club couldn't help more.' Vinnie pressed one hand against his chest and shook his head sadly. 'I believe the tape we provided was of little use, except to prove that she wasn't at Tempest.'

'Not downstairs, anyway.'

'Well, if that's all…'

'You know Ashley Naughton, don't you, Vincent?'

Vinnie eyed John warily. 'Know her? No, I can't say that I do. I'm sorry, I have to get on, I've a meeting at…' He pushed up his sleeve and took a long, exaggerated look at his watch. 'Oh, I'm already running late as it is.'

'But you know her friend, don't you?' John sounded confused. 'She's a member of your club.'

'To whom are you referring?'

'Ashley's a roommate of Claudia Delaney.'

'Oh, Claudia!' Vinnie forced a laugh. It was a harsh, barking sound. He was obviously more than a little rattled. John smiled back at him. 'Oh, I see. I didn't make the connection. Yes, I know Claudia – wonderful person.'

'And Ashley?'

'Let me see. You say she's a friend of this girl Claudia?'

John nodded. 'Blonde girl, very pretty.'

'Right, right. I seem to remember her…vaguely.' Vinnie furrowed his brow and attempted to look as if he was trying to remember her face. John glanced back at the man in the jeep: he was grinding his teeth and staring out the window as if he was trying to memorise every detail of the street.

Vinnie tapped John quickly on the shoulder and smiled apologetically. 'Look, John, I'm on my way to a meeting right now. As I say, I was going to call you this evening, but since you're here I can tell you everything I know – which, I'm afraid, is absolutely nothing.' Vinnie patted John's shoulder as if they were old friends. 'I mean, it's a terrible thing to say, but these young girls…they're so carefree and thoughtless. She's probably off having the time of her life with some boy somewhere.'

'You think that's what happened?' John said evenly. 'She's off playing love-nest with some boy she met?'

'Oh, I do,' Vinnie said sincerely. '*Cherchez la femme.*'

'What?'

'Please, give my deepest sympathies to her parents. They must be distraught.' Vinnie took a step back and jangled the car keys. 'I can only hope she returns safe and sound.'

'Yeah. They really are worried, the Naughtons – hey, maybe you know them?'

'No. Why would I?' Vinnie's eyes darted back to the jeep. 'Now, I really must—'

'You never heard of Edward Naughton? He's a builder.'

'No.' Vinnie clapped his hands together, acting like the cold was getting to him. 'Building really isn't my forte.'

'He used to be a friend of your father, back in the day. I'm surprised you don't know him.'

Vinnie's mouth dropped open, and it took him a moment to recover. 'Oh. Well, that's… interesting.'

'That's what I thought.'

Vinnie stared at his watch again.

'Oh, sorry, man – I'm holding you up.' John made no attempt to step away from the jeep. 'Hey, if I need to talk to you again, you have a mobile number or something?' He leaned in close and mock-whispered, 'Between you and me, I don't think your barman's the full shilling.'

Vinnie clutched the door handle so tightly his knuckles went white. 'I…I don't see why you would need to talk to me again. I've told you everything I know.'

'You never know.' John shrugged enigmatically and let the situation float. Inside the jeep, the older man must have been crippled with neck cramp.

Seconds ticked by. Finally Vinnie sighed. 'Fine. I assume you have a pen?'

John pulled out his mobile. 'I'll key it in here, that way I won't lose it.'

Vinnie recited the number in one short, angry burst. John tapped it into his phone and pressed Save.

'Is that it?'

'Yeah. Oh, no – wait, I've got one more question.' John pulled his notebook out of his back pocket and flipped through a few pages. 'Let me see now…what was it?'

Vinnie looked as though he'd like to wring John's neck. 'Mr Quigley, you know I have to be at my meeting—'

'Ah, yeah: here it is.' John held up his hand.

'Why do you think Claudia and Megan Lowry lied about going to your club?'

Vinnie released the door handle and took a step towards John. Nothing had changed in his face – at least, nothing John could put his finger on – but suddenly he didn't look so charming. He looked like the vicious, twisted little thug he was beneath the phony voice and the expensive clothing.

'You know, you're really starting to get on my nerves, *mon ami*.'

'I mean, it doesn't make sense, does it? Why would they lie about that?'

Vinnie smiled. Above his eye a muscle jumped and spasmed. A long, snaking vein stood out on his forehead. 'I think we're done talking here.'

'Don't you think it's odd – almost as if they were told to lie?'

'Perhaps they made a mistake. People make mistakes, don't they, Mr Quigley?'

'Do they?'

'Oh, yes.' Vinnie's eyes never left John's face as he stepped back. 'You're making a very big one now.'

'Are you threatening me, bud? Again? At least you didn't try to throw me across the street. Your right-hand man knocked the wind right out of me. Are you threatening me?'

'No, just offering a bit of friendly advice.' Vinnie yanked the door open, got into the jeep and slammed the door behind him.

The passenger was watching John with cold, flat eyes. John gave him a friendly wave and crossed the street to his own car. Behind him, the jeep roared into life and tore up the street so fast it left a trail of pale-blue smoke that hung in the frigid air like a veil.

John watched the jeep's tail lights disappear around the corner and smiled. He dialled Sarah's number. 'Honey-bunny?'

Sarah snorted. 'This must be good. What have you got?'

'York does a stand-up job of pretending he hardly knows Ashley Naughton.'

'You got to talk to him?'

'Sure did. He wasn't exactly thrilled about it, though.'

'Pick me up. I'm sitting on a bench across the street from his place.'

'What happened to the coffee shop?'

'Four euros for a half-cup of froth, that's what happened.'

'I'm on my way.' John hung up and climbed into his car.

Patrick was livid. He snapped the seat belt on and stared at his son's profile.

'You had Ed's kid in the club? She was there the night the gear went missing?'

'So what?'

'You had her there, and now that guy's looking into it, giving me the eyeball and—'

319

'He doesn't know a thing. He doesn't have any idea who—'

Despite the speed at which they were travelling, Patrick slapped Vinnie hard across the back of the head. Vinnie's head snapped back and cracked against the side window. The jeep swerved hard and sideswiped a row of parked cars. The side mirror snapped off, pinging into the air as if on elastic. Vinnie gasped and struggled to bring the jeep under control. He spun the wheel hard and jerked up the handbrake. Finally, after a heart-stopping skid, the engine cut out and the jeep stalled in the middle of the road

'What the fuck are you *doing*?' Vinnie stared at Patrick in disbelief. He lifted his hand to his head. A thin trickle of blood worked its way down from his upper ear where Patrick's ring had grazed him. He touched it and stared at his fingers in amazement.

'Get out.' Patrick unsnapped his seat belt.

'What?'

Patrick balled his fist and swung at him again. Vinnie jerked his door open and jumped clear of the jeep. Patrick scrambled over the handbrake after him. His skin was white as snow, and his pale eyes bulged with barely restrained fury.

Vinnie stood on the footpath and stared at the damage to his jeep. The front wheel arch had completely caved in and the paintwork was scraped and torn. His eyes travelled up to the jagged chunk of metal where the wing mirror used to be. Behind them, a tailback was building, and some people had emerged from their houses and were staring at their damaged cars.

'Fucking bollocks!' Vinnie said, momentarily forgetting all about the French accent.

'You have his fucking kid at your club?'

'You've destroyed my jeep.'

'Fuck the jeep!' Patrick punched the door, denting the metal and grazing his knuckles badly. If he felt the pain, it didn't show. 'Ever since I got here, you've been acting hinky. What the hell are you playing at? Why did you have her at the club? I don't want any fucking connection between me and Edward! I told you this a million times!'

'I don't even know her!' Vinnie snapped.

'Don't give me that fucking crap. I heard what you said to that private dick, but you're a lousy liar, Vincent. Even he didn't believe you. You think you can fool me? You knew who she was, you knew she was there, and maybe you know where she is now. What the fuck are you playing at?' Patrick ground his teeth together. 'You know something? That's it. You and me – that's it. When I sort this fucking mess out, you and me are through.'

'What are you saying?'

'I've had enough. You're out – got it? Out! No more deals, no more business with me. You're on your own.'

'You need me.' Muscles bunched in Vinnie's jaw. He took a step towards his father. 'I'm all you've got here.'

'I wouldn't trust you as far as I could throw

you.' Patrick stepped towards him, so that they were eye to eye. 'The sorriest thing I ever did was bring you in on this deal.'

'People are looking.'

'I don't give a fuck.'

Vinnie heard the white noise building behind his eyes. 'Get out of my face, Patrick.'

'I should never have got you involved with the business. Nothing is ever fucking low-key with you. I should have known you'd draw attention.'

'I'd say you're the one who's drawing attention.' Vinnie waved a hand towards a group of staring people.

'Over here living the high life, fucking gallivanting in the club' – Patrick jabbed Vinnie in the chest with his finger – 'instead of taking care of business.'

'Touch me again and I'll snap that finger clean off,' Vinnie said softly between clenched teeth.

Patrick snorted. He pulled his cap a little further down over his eyes and stepped back. 'If I find out you had anything to do with the kid's disappearance, I'll break your fucking neck.' He climbed into the jeep, slapped it into first gear and drove off.

Vinnie watched him go and pulled his mobile out of his pocket. He keyed in a number and waited, tapping his foot gently. While he waited, he calculated how much it would cost to repair the damaged cars and appease the owners who were making their way towards him with indignant expressions on their faces.

'Boss?'

'Davey, I need you to do two things for me.'

'Shoot.'

'First, *mon ami*, I'd like you to pick me up. I'll give you the address in a moment. After that, I'd like you to go see Claudia and that red-haired friend of hers.'

'Yeah?'

'Yes. I want you to make it clear to them that I am very unhappy, and that any future interest in my club stemming from their indiscretion will not be appreciated.'

Claudia Delaney raced along Dame Street, keeping her head down against the falling sleet. She bumped into people left and right, but she didn't slow down. Ever since Megan's frantic call, her heart had fluttered in her chest like a moth at a light bulb.

'Ow! Jesus!' She was spun almost one hundred and eighty degrees as she crashed shoulders with someone going the other way.

'Sorry – are you okay?' a man in a saturated denim jacket said, rubbing his shoulder.

'Why the fuck don't you watch where you're going?' Claudia steadied herself and took off at a jog. She clattered down the cobbles towards her building, opened the front door and took the stairs two at a time.

'Megan – Meg!' She burst into the apartment and raced down the hall. 'What happened? I couldn't get here any earlier—' She swung open the sitting room door.

'Some bleedin' friend you are.' Davey Clarke smiled at her from the sofa. He looked comfortable. His jacket was open and he sat with one leg resting on the glass coffee table. The other leg was stretched across Megan Lowry's lap, holding her firmly in place.

Claudia skidded to a halt. Meg was bunched as far away from Davey as possible. Her lip was split, and there was a thin line of dried blood smeared on her chin. She had clearly been crying.

Claudia put her hand to her mouth. 'Oh, Megan…'

'She's grand – aren't you, Redser? It's only a flesh wound.' Davey ruffled Megan's hair. She flinched at his touch. He laughed and lifted his leg off her.

'What are you doing here?'

'Bit of a tip, this. You'd think girls would be clean, but you're messy fuckers.'

'Get out of here before I call the Gardaí.'

'Go ahead, see how far that gets you.' Davey inclined his head towards the coffee table. 'Phone's right there.'

'Get out of here,' Claudia said, trying to keep her voice steady.

Davey lifted his other leg off the table and smiled. He understood why Vinnie liked this one so much. Even now, when she was scared shitless, she was trying to play it cool.

'You won't call anyone, 'cause if you do, them pictures we took of you and Redser at that party in Shankill are gonna get posted all around your college. Maybe I'll send a few down Wicklow way. Bet your folks would love that. Maybe they could blow them up, hang them over the fireplace and shit. Be great conversation over a dinner party.' Behind him, Megan began to cry softly.

'Get out,' Claudia repeated.

'Some arsehole was askin' questions about your little friend. Seems it's public knowledge she was at Tempest the night she upped and left. Vinnie reckons someone's been mouthin' off when they should have kept quiet.'

Megan groaned softly and closed her eyes.

'So what if *someone* did?' Claudia threw her bag down and rested her hands on her hips. 'Ash was there, but she *left*, remember? She said she was going home. What she did after she left the club was her own business – Vinnie said so himself. So it doesn't matter what *someone* said.'

'Well, Vinnie's upset that the club was mentioned at all. Any more hassle won't be appreciated.' Davey stood up slowly and tousled Megan's hair again. 'That right, Redser?'

Megan made a little strangled squeak.

'Leave her alone.'

'Or what?'

Claudia's face darkened. 'Did Vinnie send you here to tell us this?'

'What do you think?' Davey shrugged and

strolled towards her. Claudia moved away, but he matched her. Without warning, he grabbed the front of her coat and, with terrifying strength, lifted Claudia off her feet and bundled her out into the hall.

'Claudia!' Megan screeched, leaping off the sofa. Davey was too quick for her. He yanked the sitting room door closed and held it shut with his left hand. He transferred his right up to Claudia's throat and tightened it before she had a chance to make a sound. Her toes barely scraped the ground.

'You think this is all a game, you little cunt?' he said calmly. 'I'd watch myself if I was you. You might think screwin' Vinnie protects you, but let me tell you, girlie, it don't. Not from me.'

Claudia scrabbled at his fingers, trying to loosen his grip. She kicked at his shins, but with each kick his smile widened.

'And I'll tell you somethin' else while I'm here, will I?' Davey leaned in closer until his nose touched her cheek. 'Vinnie don't like big mouths discussin' his business, no matter how good they are at suckin' him off.'

Claudia's eyes widened. Davey saw uncertainty in them for the first time and felt something stir in the pit of his stomach. Oh, yes, he knew exactly what Vinnie saw in her: she was something special. He leaned in closer and brushed his lips against hers. Claudia tried to turn her head away.

'I like a girl with a bit of spunk in her,' he said

softly, nuzzling her neck. 'Maybe you and me can have some fun together when all this shit dies down.' He lowered his hand from her throat and gave her breast a rough squeeze. When Claudia whimpered, he laughed softly. 'Heard you're a right little goer, too. How about it? How about I come over here some night and show you how it's really done? Would you like that? You could be my secretary. I heard you're good at taking *dicktation*.'

The colour drained from Claudia's face. 'Please, let me go.'

'Not so tough now, are you?' Davey released her and the door handle at the same time and backed away towards the front door. Megan wrenched the living room door open and spilled into the hall.

'Get away from her.' She threw her arms around Claudia's shoulders. Claudia didn't move a muscle. She stood with her hand to her throat, panting, her eyes locked on Davey.

'Redser will fill you in on the details.' At the door, Davey winked and cocked his finger at Claudia. 'Be seein' you, babe,' he said softly, and with that he was gone.

'Oh Christ,' Megan cried, shaking Claudia's arm. 'He wouldn't leave! He told me he wanted to talk about Ash, and I...I let him up. But then he wouldn't leave. That's why I called – I couldn't make him leave... He hit me across the face, he wouldn't—'

'Shh, it's all right, Meg – it's all right. Calm down.'

Claudia patted her hand, double-locked the apartment door and leaned her forehead against it. Her stomach flipped slowly. She splayed her hand flat against the wood of the door, closed her eyes and fought the urge to be sick. Vinnie had sent him.

Behind her, Megan began to whimper. Claudia clenched her teeth together and turned. She took hold of Megan's chin and tilted her face up to the light. She could see Davey's hand-mark clearly against Megan's pale skin. 'That bastard. What did he say to you?' She put an arm around Megan's shoulders and walked her into the sitting room.

Megan sat on the sofa and sniffed. 'He said, if a-a-anyone else asks, we're to say nothing about the club, or about Vinnie. Oh God, Claudia, I think something terrible's happened to Ash.'

'Well, maybe she's just…maybe…' Claudia couldn't keep the tremor from her voice. She closed her eyes and tried to breathe slowly, but she couldn't shake the fear that Megan was right. Vinnie had always been interested in Ashley, always asking questions about her, about her family, her parents. Claudia had been so jealous, accusing Ash of playing up to him, leading him on. God…what if he'd only been using her to get to Ash?

'Claudia, are you all right?' Megan said. 'You look a little—'

Claudia pressed her hand against her mouth and raced for the bathroom. She barely made it before she puked violently. She retched until her throat hurt.

No, it couldn't be. Vinnie had said that he loved her, that she was special.

But he had told Davey Clarke about their private joke. How Vinnie liked her to take him in her mouth while he talked on the phone. How he called her his little secretary. They had probably had a good laugh over it.

She tried to remember when he had become interested in her. Certainly she had known him longer than Ash or Megan, but before he met Ash he'd hardly given her the time of day. Claudia gritted her teeth. He hadn't returned any of her calls this week. She needed to speak to him, not to his fucking machine.

She closed her eyes. He had told her he loved her. She would have done anything for him – had done anything for him. Claudia retched again, but nothing came up this time except a little saliva.

'What are we going to do?' Megan was behind her in the bathroom, blowing her nose hard into a crumpled tissue. 'Claudia, we've got to tell someone. We've got to call Margo.'

Claudia wiped her mouth with a wad of toilet tissue. 'Jesus Christ, no.'

Megan sat on the edge of the bath, her hands twisting frantically in her lap. 'But we have to talk to someone. What if they come after us?'

'They won't. That's just talk, Meg. Davey was trying to scare us.'

'But why?' Megan gazed tearfully at her. 'Why would he want to scare us? Oh God, what if something's happened to Ash? What if Vinnie…you know…'

Claudia clenched her jaw. 'Oh, don't be so bloody stupid! I told you, if we tell Margo she'll ring our parents, and then they're going to find out about everything – the E, the coke, the parties…everything! Think they'll be okay with that? My dad will kick us out of here. We could go to *jail*, Meg. Is that what you want?'

Megan fumbled for a cigarette. 'But why haven't we heard anything? Not even a call to say she's okay? I mean, even if Ash was angry or something…she would have called, right?'

He had told her he loved her. But he and Davey Clarke had laughed at her behind her back.

'How should I know?' Claudia flushed the toilet and brushed her fringe back from her forehead.

She remembered Ashley's face that night – the red mark where she had slapped her, the confusion in Ashley's eyes as she struggled to hold on to Claudia, screaming at her to come with her, to get the hell out of Tempest.

Oh God, Ashley, I'm so sorry, she thought. *I was wrong.*

*

Vinnie sat on the toilet in his bathroom and chopped out a line of coke. He was surprisingly calm. His ear throbbed where Patrick had struck him, and he'd had to have his jeep towed away for repairs. But really, he felt fine.

He listened as Patrick strode up and down the floor, pleading for more time. Vinnie heard him offer the Turks the deeds of Tempest as collateral, talking up how much it was worth, talking up how close he was to locating the delivery… Vinnie tittered softly. Nonsense. The bastard really thought that he would allow everything he'd ever loved to be destroyed.

His Nokia trilled. Vinnie slipped it out of his pocket and pressed Answer without even bothering to look at the screen. 'What?'

'Jaysus, that's some phone manner you have on you.'

'Dougie?'

'No names on mobiles, lad. Don't you know anythin'?'

'What have you got, *mon ami*?'

'You need to come down to the kennels tomorrow morning. Got that?'

Vinnie stopped chopping and sat bolt upright. 'Tomorrow?' he said. 'Have you heard—'

'No talkin' on phones,' Dougie said sharply. 'You come there, we talk there. Right?'

'Right, right.' Vinnie pursed his lips and glanced towards the locked bathroom door. 'I don't have to bring Pat—'

'Don't bring nothin' but yourself.'

'Right. I see, but—'

Dougie Burrows hung up on him.

Vinnie pocketed the phone, snorted the coke and let out a deep breath he hadn't even realised he'd been holding. Then, rubbing the remaining residue onto his gums, he slid off the toilet seat onto the mosaic tiles. He leaned forward and rested his head against the sink, closed his eyes and listened to the rising panic in Patrick's voice coming through the walls.

The cocaine gave him a nice little buzz, set his brain thinking and plotting. Soon everything would return to normal. He would be the lion. He would roar once more.

23

Margaret sat at her kitchen table, wrapped in a fuzzy pink dressing gown, a steaming cup of tea ignored on the table in front of her. It was six-thirty and still dark outside. She had barely slept a wink. She had tossed and turned all night before finally getting up at five thirty. Her thoughts were jumbled and fearful, exaggerated as thoughts always are in the dead of night. It had seemed easier to get up. She needed the solitude to think.

She had to catch her husband before he left for work. She needed to know what the hell was going on with her family. Edward was so ferocious lately. Every look, word or gesture from her seemed to spark off another fight. Normally this would have deterred her from pursuing him, but not this morning.

At seven-ten Edward Naughton ambled into the kitchen, fastening his tie. The bruising on his face had faded to a dirty yellow. His top button was open and his tie hung loose around his neck. He had cut himself shaving. Margaret's eyes were drawn to the tiny piece of tissue paper he had stuck on the nick.

Margaret cleared her throat and he spun around. He registered his wife with surprise.

'What are you doing up?'

'We need to talk.' She pushed a chair towards him with her foot.

'I don't have time to talk.' Edward refused the chair, leaned against the fridge freezer and fixed his tie. He adopted the pained expression he wore whenever he had to talk with his wife, and not for the first time Margaret wondered why he felt such contempt for her.

'Edward…'

'Well, what? I haven't got all fucking day.'

'I want you to tell me what's going on.'

Edward stopped knotting his tie. His sea-green eyes, the only attractive feature left to him, narrowed to slits. 'Tell you what? You got something to say, then spit it out.'

Margaret raised her head and stared at her husband of twenty years. What she saw disgusted her. He was fat and vulgar and he regarded her as less than worthless. She closed her eyes briefly, feeling a wave of nostalgia rush through her. He hadn't always been this way.

She remembered him as dark and hard-bodied, quick to laugh, flicking his hair over those piercing eyes. She remembered the mocking laugh and 'fuck 'em' attitude that had so thrilled her teenage, middle-class heart. She remembered his round, high arse in skin-tight stone-washed jeans. She remembered the smell of Brut and Brylcreem, the way his hair had glistened the first night he had taken her in his arms on the sand dunes of Dollymount Strand and made her a woman. She remembered her father warning her not to have anything to do with him, claiming – correctly, as it turned out – that he would break her heart someday. She had done exactly the opposite: she had fallen completely and utterly in love.

What had she known about love then, anyway? She'd thought Edward's coarse manner dashing and rebellious, free from the social constraints that had dogged her life. 'So what if he's been in trouble with the law?' she had yelled at her poor father one evening, as she left the house in a mini so short he'd thought she was wearing a belt. 'So what if he doesn't talk like us?' she'd screeched as she smeared more kohl around her eyes and backcombed her hair higher and higher. 'I love him! Remember love, Dad? You don't know what it's like!'

How stupid she had been back then. She had wanted laughs, excitement, romance, candlelight dinners for two. She'd wanted Sunday afternoon drives that didn't go anywhere and didn't need to, because they would be content in each other's company. She had wanted passion, adventure and commitment. And love; she had wanted love.

Why hadn't she been able to see what her father saw? Edward had wanted a wife who could give him the one thing money could not: class. She was his trophy, something brought out on special occasions to be shown off and admired. She was simply his way of saying, 'Look, I've pulled a posh piece. Look how far from the streets I've come.' She had married him for love. He had married her for appearances. Neither reason had been good enough.

'Why didn't you tell me Patrick was back?'

'What do you know about it?' Edward looked stunned. 'Who the fuck told you that?' He took a fast step towards his wife. 'Answer me, goddammit!'

Margaret flinched but held her ground. 'So it's true? He's here, in Ireland?'

'What about it?'

'Did you know Ashley was in that nightclub – his son's nightclub?' She stood up, pushing her chair back so fast it tipped over behind her.

'*What?*'

'The detectives. They found out Ashley was there. She was *there*, Edward. Did you know about it?'

'Christ, no! Of course not.'

'And now Patrick's back and you're acting so…so nervous and twitchy, and Ashley's gone, and I don't know what's happening—'

'Enough!' Edward banged his fist on the table. He was breathing hard and his skin looked patchy and flushed. He turned away from her and pressed his hand against his chest, desperately trying to ease the pressure there.

'Has that man done something to my

daughter?' Margo's voice rose higher and higher. 'Have you involved Ashley in some of your fucking *business*?'

'Margo, listen to me.' He spoke her name softly this time, in a wheedling voice she recognised as false. He lowered his hand and turned back to her. 'Please, Margo…I need to know. How did you hear about Patrick?'

'The detectives. They know about – about your past. They asked me what your connection to Vinnie York was.'

'Did you tell them I was connected to Vinnie?'

'Of course not! I didn't even know about him.'

'Thank fuck.'

'I told them you knew Patrick. '

Edward squeezed his eyes shut tight and pressed his hand to his forehead as though he'd just been hit by a migraine. 'Why'd you tell them I knew him?'

'Because Ashley was at that nightclub! Why wouldn't I mention it?'

'Oh Jesus…'

'Edward, I—'

'Shut the fuck up, will you! Let me think.' Edward turned away, breathing hard. God damn her! Now the detectives knew about him and Patrick, it wouldn't take them long to find out everything else. He swallowed, tasting acid from the ulcer he was sure he had developed in the last two weeks. What had Ashley been doing in Vinnie's club, anyway? He knew that lanky bastard had been behind her going missing – but what did he want? What was he up to?

'I couldn't believe it when I heard that name,' Margaret said bitterly from behind him. 'I thought you two were finished years ago.'

'It's business.'

'What business? What kind of *business* are you in with that lowlife?'

'Margo, I'm telling you to leave it.'

'My God, Edward, you're a successful businessman. Why do you keep in contact with the likes of Patrick York?'

'I said, leave it.'

'Is that why Ashley is missing? Is that why? Has something happened to her?'

'Look, don't worry, okay?' Edward grabbed Margaret by the shoulders and pulled her towards him, scaring her more than ever. 'But you've got to call those fucking detectives off. Do you understand me? For Ashley's sake, you need to get rid of them.'

Margaret stared into his eyes, her face stricken. 'What do you mean, for Ashley's sake?'

'If you don't…' He shook her harder than was necessary. 'You've got to call them off.'

Margaret jerked free. 'Why? Why? I don't understand what's happening! What are you saying?'

'Margo, if Vinnie York has her and he feels threatened…' Edward took a deep breath and forced himself to lower his voice. 'Margo, seriously, you've got to call them off. If they keep hassling Vinnie York, anything could happen – to me, to Ashley, to you.'

'Oh my God...' Margaret raised her hand to her mouth. 'Does he have her?'

'I don't know. Maybe...probably.'

'Then we've got to go to the Gardaí.' She grabbed his arm, her nails digging painfully into the folds of fat. 'Please, Edward, we've got to go to them. They'll listen now. We'll go right now, we'll explain—'

'Are you out of your fucking mind?' Edward pried her off and shoved her away from him. He grabbed his keys from the worktop. He couldn't bear her tears a moment longer, and he had no time and no answers to quell them. He wrenched the door open. 'I'm going to work now, Margo, but you listen and you listen good. You call them fucking detectives and get rid of them. I'm telling you, if you want to see Ashley again, then we go about this my way. No fucking cops, no more fucking outsiders. Got it?' He walked out and slammed the door so hard the glass above the handle shattered.

Margaret sank to the floor, her pink dressing-gown bunched around her small body as her legs failed her. She had never felt so alone and terrified in all her life.

Outside, Edward tried to start his car, but he kept fumbling his keys. When he dropped them for the second time, he gave up and left them where they had fallen. He loosened his tie and rolled down his window. He found it hard to breathe. A sharp stitch shot up his left arm.

His mobile shrilled into life, scaring him half to death. He groped it out of his briefcase and hit Answer. It was Pascal Mooney.

'Ed? Where are you?'

'I'm at my house. Actually, I'm just about to leave.'

'Any word on your girl?'

'Those detectives Margo hired – they've found out that Ashley was at York's club the night she disappeared.'

'So you were right, he has her.'

'I knew he was up to something. I just don't understand: if he has her, why doesn't he contact me? Why hasn't he offered to do a trade, Ashley for the drugs?'

'Ed, shut the fuck up. This is a mobile.'

Edward wiped a drip of sweat from his forehead. 'Why hasn't he said anything?'

'Even if he has her, you can't trade with him. You know that, right? Dougie Burrows expects his delivery. You and me, we have a deal – right?'

'I can't let him hurt my kid, Pascal.'

'You don't even know he has her!'

'I can't risk it.'

'Patrick will kill you if he finds out you've double-crossed him. He'll fucking kill you, Ed.'

Edward rubbed his eyes. This was a

nightmare. 'I need to talk to Dougie, let him know the situation – tell him I can't do the deal.'

'Look, here's what you're going to do. You lie low for a day or two, give me some time to sort this shit out.' Pascal lit a cigarette and took a deep drag. 'If Vinnie has your girl, I'll find out.'

'But where can I go? Lie low where? What about the…the delivery?'

'It's safe, isn't it?'

'Well, yes, it's safe. It's here… Maybe I ought to move it.'

'Nah. If it's safe, it's safe.'

'Don't worry, nobody'll ever find it. I have it in the pond.'

'You what?'

'The cases – they're waterproof. No one would ever look there.'

'It's not the gear I'm worried about, it's you. At least until Dougie gets rid of those fucking crazy Yorks.'

'I don't know…' Edward felt the pain in his arm subside slightly. 'What if I—'

'Ed, you don't make yourself scarce and you might not make it to tomorrow.'

Edward tried to swallow, but there was no moisture in his mouth. 'All right, tell me what to do.'

John arrived at the office ahead of Sarah for once. When she saw him sitting behind his desk, she threw her hand up to her forehead and mock-fainted against the door.

John glanced at her. 'Oh, ha-ha!'

'What are you doing here this early?'

John shrugged. 'Thought I'd take another look through those photocopies you got.' He waved his hand at the bundle of papers she'd brought in the day before.

Sarah put on the kettle and glanced at John. He was peering at one of the pages, and for once in his life he looked serious and thoughtful. She took the photocopied picture from his hand. It was a grimy shot taken as Patrick York walked down the steps of Kilmainham courthouse, a free man after an intimidation case against him collapsed. He was trying to shield his face from the cameras, but the photographer had caught him full on.

'What is it, John?'

'I think the reluctant passenger from yesterday was Patrick York.'

'I thought you couldn't really see his face.'

'When I said "Hey, Mr York", they both turned at exactly the same time.'

Sarah sat on his desk and looked at the photo. 'They probably turned for the "hey".'

'I don't think so. I'm pretty sure it's him.'

Sarah nodded slowly. 'Okay, it's Patrick York. What does that mean?'

'I called Steve last night, had him find out a little more about York, and guess what?'

'What?'

'He's regarded in Holland as a major cog in the cocaine trade. Been hauled in more times than they can count, but he's like Teflon: nothing sticks to the guy.'

'Steve rang the cops in Holland, for us?'

'Interpol. I don't think we can ask him for any more favours for a while.' John shrugged and stared at the photo again. 'So the question is, why would a guy who's wanted for questioning about a murder in this country risk coming back? Especially if he's got a good racket and a clean sheet abroad? And what's his connection to Naughton these days?'

'Who says there is one? Maybe it's all coincidence.'

'I don't believe that, and neither do you. They knew each other when they were growing up. Ashley Naughton went missing from York's son's nightclub. I'd say there's a connection, all right.'

'Did you tell Steve why you were asking about him?' Sarah said thoughtfully. 'Does Steve know he's back?'

John shook his head. 'I thought I'd keep that one between us for the moment.'

The phone on John's desk rang. Sarah reached across to grab it, but John got there first. 'QuicK Investigations, top of the morning to you.'

Sarah rolled her eyes, and John winked at her. She was forever warning him about how he answered the phone.

'Oh, hello… What's that?' John stopped

smiling. 'Oh? Where? … I see. Right. … Yeah, thanks for letting us know.' He hung up.

'Well?' Sarah said.

'That was Margaret Naughton.'

'What's going on?'

'We're being pulled off the case. She says Ashley has turned up.'

'What? Where?'

'At a cousin's house, in London.'

'Really?'

'So she says,' John said dryly.

'You don't believe her?'

'Not a word of it.'

'Think Davey Clarke visited her, like he did you?'

'Only one way to find out.'

'I'll get my coat.'

24

John and Sarah found Margaret Naughton hard at work in her garden. She was unloading compost from a green wheelbarrow and mulching it firmly over the flowerbeds to the left of the drive.

Margaret's eyes were swollen and puffy, but apart from that she looked as if she had stepped straight from the pages of a house and garden magazine. Her skin was free of make-up, her cheeks naturally pink from exertion and her hair was windblown. She wore gardening clothes – beige cords, a cream cable-knit jumper and soft, brown, fur-lined boots – and they made her look younger than the formal suits she had worn previously. At the sound of the car crunching across the gravel she looked up and waved, a faint frown on her face. John pulled up in front of the conservatory and he and Sarah hopped out.

'Cold day for gardening,' Sarah said.

Margaret brushed a lock of blond hair from her forehead. 'What are you doing here?'

'We thought we'd come down, see if you wanted to talk to us.' John wrinkled his nose at the smell of the compost. The country definitely wasn't his bag: too many creepy-crawlies, not enough concrete.

'About what?'

'About Ashley, for a start.'

'I…no.' Margaret rested the rake against the hedge and pulled off her gloves. 'Let's go in and have a coffee, shall we? I could do with a break.'

John and Sarah followed her into the kitchen and sat at a huge, pale-yellow Mexican pine table. They watched as Margaret filled a stainless steel kettle and put it on to boil. Sarah glanced around. It was a nice room, different from what she'd seen of the rest of the house. It was homely. The walls were painted rich ochre with orange ragging, the curtains were pale yellow with a scattering of cheery pineapples. A huge Welsh dresser occupied the wall opposite the back door, its pine shelves groaning with pretty yellow and blue crockery.

Margaret flicked at a piece of leaf on her jumper. 'I'm afraid you've had a wasted journey. There's nothing more to say, really.' She pulled three cups from a pine mug tree and spooned coffee into each one. 'You've been marvellous, and I truly appreciate everything you've done. Of course, I shall pay you until the end of this week.'

'So how was Ashley when you spoke to her?' Sarah said. 'Did she mention why she upped and left so suddenly? Why she scared you half to death?'

Margaret spilled some of the boiling water over the side of the first cup. She grabbed a dishcloth from the sink and began to wipe furiously at the granite counter. 'I think my husband is probably right. I'm sure this is some kind of…oh, I don't know – a prank.'

'A prank?' John said. 'You think Ashley disappearing was a prank?'

'Have you spoken with her?' Sarah asked.

'I… No. She hasn't called. I spoke to—'

'Then excuse me for saying this, Mrs Naughton, but I think it's a little peculiar that you want us to stop looking for her now. Has your husband insisted on this?' Sarah stared at Margaret's stiff back. Something was going on. Someone had made this woman change her mind about dealing with them.

John cleared his throat. 'Mrs Naughton, look, I don't know what's going on here. But, like Sarah said, we think there may be more to Ashley's disappearance than a prank. We're pretty sure Patrick York is back in Ireland, and we know he used to be a friend of your husband. We think Vinnie York told Ashley's flatmates to lie about her being in Tempest. Now, we've been doing a little checking into the York family, and let me tell you, they're not exactly the type of men—'

'Please! I've made my decision.' Margaret gripped the countertop hard and lowered her head. She took a deep breath, composed herself and turned slowly to face them, her expression carefully controlled. 'Listen to me. I am very grateful for all you've done, but I don't need your services any longer. Are we clear?' She carried their cups to the table, returned for her own and sat down heavily. 'This whole thing has been blown out of proportion.'

Sarah glanced at John and back at Margaret. 'Has someone put pressure on you to let us go?'

Margaret rested her hands flat on the table on either side of her cup. Her eyes filled with tears and her shoulders shook. 'Look—'

'I think your daughter is in real danger,' Sarah said sharply, 'and someone doesn't want us looking at Vinnie York.'

Margaret's head jerked up. What little colour she had in her cheeks from her work outdoors drained swiftly away. 'Don't say that.'

'And I don't know why you're backing out like this, but I hope you know what you're doing.' Sarah tried to touch Margaret's shoulder. The older woman jerked away as if Sarah's hand might burn her.

'I know what I'm doing,' Margaret replied softly, her voice breaking on the last word. She stood up and stared at Sarah. Her eyes were impossible to read. 'If you'll excuse me for a moment, I'll get my chequebook. And once you've finished your coffee, if you'll forgive me, I need to get back out there and finish up before it starts to rain again.'

'You know what I think?' Sarah said. 'I think someone has got to you, and I don't know how or why. Look, whatever's going on is obviously beyond anything John and I can help you with. You need to go back to the Gardaí, get them to listen to you, tell them about Vinnie York lying, go back to the flat—'

'Please stop lecturing me.' Margaret had stiffened at Sarah's tone.

'The detective you initially talked to about Ashley's disappearance, Michael Dwyer – I've met him, and he seems like a good guy. I'm sure if you went to him and told him everything, he'd help you. If you like I can call him and set up a—'

Margaret turned on her heel and marched out of the room.

John watched her go. 'Forget it,' he said. 'She doesn't want our help.'

'We hassled Vinnie York yesterday, and today we're pulled off the case.' Sarah flicked her dark hair angrily over her shoulder. 'Too coincidental for me.'

'Look, we'll get another job. Something will turn up.'

'It's not about the bloody money,' Sarah said, a bitterness John had never heard before creeping into her tone. 'It's got nothing to do with that. I wanted to find that girl.'

John threw his hands up into the air. 'You think I don't? But she's the one calling the shots, and if she says—'

Margaret came back into the room. She was carrying her chequebook and a delicate fountain pen. 'How much do I owe you?'

Sarah pulled a face and shook her head.

'How much do I owe you?' Margaret repeated, a hint of desperation creeping into her tone.

'If you can settle up for the two weeks, that would be great,' John said.

'Of course.' She leaned across the table, gripping the pen tightly, and opened her chequebook. She was stony-faced, her eyes over-bright, but they could hear the trembling hitch in her voice.

'Mrs Naughton,' Sarah began, 'I'm sure we can—'

'Here – take this. I've added a bonus.' They watched helplessly as she ripped the cheque out and threw it to John. 'Please, take it and leave.'

John picked the cheque up and read it. It was for four thousand euros.

'Mrs Naughton…'

Margaret waved her hand towards the door. She wouldn't look at either of them. The fleeting anger had left her body, and she seemed tiny and vulnerable. 'I want you to go.'

Sarah zipped up her coat and pushed her chair under the table. 'I really hope you know what you're doing.'

Margaret looked away. He mouth was pulled into a hard, thin line. 'Just leave, please.'

They drove back to Dublin in an uncomfortable silence. A couple of times John glanced over at Sarah, waiting for her to say something. She

350

pretended she didn't notice and kept her eyes on the road. Her expression was impossible to read. John lit a cigarette. Sarah said nothing about the plumes of grey smoke filling the car; she simply cranked open the window a little.

Finally John could bear the silence no longer. 'We'll be able to pay the insurance on the Fiesta for the year.'

Sarah shifted in her seat and stared out the window.

'Well, what do you think?'

'I think Vinnie York threatened Margaret Naughton,' Sarah said tightly. 'She gave us four grand, John. People don't do things like that. I say we hang in there for another day or so, see if we can get to the bottom of this.'

John tossed his cigarette out the window and sighed. He had long ago learned not to bother arguing with Sarah when she was in this mood. Anyway, though it bugged the shit out of him to admit it, he knew she was right: they couldn't abandon Margaret or Ashley now.

'What do you want to do?'

'Stay with the club.'

John sighed long and hard. 'Okay.'

25

Davey Clarke wound his window down and sucked the cold, damp air greedily into his lungs. Vinnie had on more aftershave than usual, and in the tight confines of Davey's Toyota it was making him feel sick. Between that and the fact that Vinnie kept humming 'I Believe I Can Fly' over and over again, his nerves were at breaking point. He rolled his neck and tried to flex the cramp out of his muscles.

Vinnie stopped humming and glanced at his watch. 'You know, I don't understand why he insists on keeping us waiting like this. He knows we're here. *Mon dieu*, it's like he's actually doing it on purpose.'

Davey jerked his head towards the window. 'There he is.'

Dougie Burrows stepped out of the cottage and walked languidly across the yard towards them. The rottweiler that had so petrified Vinnie trotted by Dougie's heels, her massive head stretched towards the car. Vinnie stared at her wall-eye; its weird, filmy blue made her look all the more sinister. If anything, he thought bleakly, she looked even bigger in broad daylight. He wished he were in his jeep. The extra height would have comforted him.

'There you are now,' Dougie said as he neared them. He wore filthy, ripped blue dungarees and green wellies with thick grey socks pulled up over the rims.

'Dougie.'

'Nah, don't bother to get out. Stay where you are,' Dougie said with a grin. It was clear Vinnie had no intention of exiting the car. 'Here.'

He tossed a piece of paper through the window, onto Vinnie's lap. Vinnie picked it up and read the name that was written on it, then he looked up at Dougie, his eyebrows drawing together. 'Who the hell is this?'

'A slieveen who contacted a friend of mine up North, late last week, about a big shipment of coke he was tryin' to offload. He wanted a fast sale, too. He was offerin' a cut-down price. I'll tell you something now' – Dougie leaned in at the window, and Vinnie almost gagged from the smell of dog – 'only that I've plenty of influence with the fella he contacted, we'd know nothing about this one. My friend wasn't too happy to be turnin' down such a good offer. Anyway…' Dougie tapped the paper. 'I located the fella in question, to ask where he might have come across a haul like that.'

'And where did he come across it?' Vinnie said, a little breathlessly.

'He tried to get cute with me at first. But

would you believe, after a bit of persuasion, he mentioned that fat fuck your old lad is so fond of?'

'Naughton?'

'Aye.'

'Are you sure?' Vinnie stared. 'Did he actually say it was Naughton?'

'Aye, he did indeed.'

Vinnie almost laughed out loud with sheer relief. 'I knew it! I *knew* the fat bastard was behind it!'

Dougie spat and scratched the rottweiler's head. He grinned at Vinnie. 'Tell you what: come on with me and ask him yourself, if you don't mind gettin' them fancy duds wet.'

'You have him here?'

'Down back. I needed a place we could talk – in private, like.' Dougie grinned, and his disgusting teeth beamed at Vinnie. 'Sometimes you get better results that way.'

'Indeed.' Vinnie climbed out of the car. He folded his coat around him and slid past the rottweiler with as much haste as she would allow. 'Davey? Are you—'

'Leave the quare fella here,' Dougie said. 'I don't want too many folk traipsing around. Upsets the dogs, like.'

Davey huffed softly.

'Yes, well, we can't have that, *bien sur*.' Vinnie closed the door, completely forgetting about Davey. He was thrilled, vindicated, on cloud nine. He was so close to the stuff, he could almost taste it.

'Come on.'

Vinnie followed Dougie through the cottage and out the back, past the kennels, the pups and breeding bitches, through a gap in a fence, over what could only be described as a bog and, finally, down a rutted track to a small concrete shed. The shed had a thick, padlocked steel door and no windows. A prickle of unease settled in the base of Vinnie's skull.

'You have him in here?'

'Sure, why else would we be here?' Dougie glanced at Vinnie as though he was a moron. He reached inside his dungarees, pulled out a small silver key, opened the padlock and stepped back. Cautiously, Vinnie moved into the shed. He slid his hand into his pocket and gripped his blade. Dougie followed him, shut the door and turned on the lights.

It took Vinnie's eyes a second to adjust to the startling brilliance of the light, but when they did he began to laugh softly.

'*Mon dieu,* Dougie, you are quite the craftsman.'

'Aye.'

The room was small, ten metres by fourteen, but it was a creative masterpiece. Every surface, including the ceiling, was tiled. The floor sloped slightly inwards, towards a drain set in the centre. There was no furniture, no porous substances to be stained, no skirting that might trap matter, no cloth or wood to become saturated. There was a jet hose fastened to one wall. Two halogen bulbs, recessed into the ceiling behind washable plastic covers, flooded the room with light. A set of blunt-nosed pliers and a vice-grip sat in a bucket of pink, sudsy water by the door.

The man hung by his wrists from a chain which ran from a stainless steel ring bolted into the roof. His head was slumped forward, his knees were bent and his feet trailed on the floor. They were swollen, shiny and purple from the settling blood; the man's heart had long ceased to pump it around his body.

Dougie walked over and lifted his head by the matted dark hair. 'Know him?'

Vinnie frowned slightly. 'I'm not sure. Should I?'

'Name's Dominic O'Driscoll,' Dougie said, smiling. 'Drove the quarry trucks for Naughton. He's from Donegal originally, has plenty of contacts there still. That's probably why Naughton thought he could slip through without me findin' out.' Dougie dropped the man's head. 'Tough old bastard, he was, too. Took a while to get him to talk.'

Vinnie stared at the battered and torn body. Even if he had known the man, he doubted he would have recognised him after the damage Dougie had inflicted. His body was pummelled black and blue; the face looked like fresh mincemeat.

'Is he…'

Dougie lifted the man's head again, peered at him and let it drop. 'Aye. Turns out he wasn't as tough as he thought.'

'Did he mention where Naughton's keeping it?'

'Said he didn't know. Tell you the truth, I'd be inclined to believe that.'

'*Merde.*'

'He did tell me one other thing.'

'Oh? What's that?'

'Naughton's goin' to ground.'

Vinnie scowled. 'Is he?'

'Yep.'

'Tell me, *mon ami*, where does the drain lead to?'

Dougie glanced down. 'Collected into a separate sewerage system.'

'Impressive.' Vinnie glanced around him. No matter what happened in this room, Dougie Burrows could have the whole lot washed down and clean in a matter of minutes.

'I'll look into where Naughton's gone, but this could get expensive.' Dougie scratched at his balls absently.

'I will, of course, see that you're well taken care of.' Vinnie leaned over and peered into the bucket. '*Sacré bleu*, what an interesting choice of tools you have there.'

'Seems to me, with Patrick headin' for the chop and Naughton on his way out, you might need a new partner.'

Vinnie straightened up and fidgeted with his cuffs. 'I don't think so.'

'Have a think about it.' Dougie fished a cob pipe out of his top pocket and stuffed it into his mouth.

Vinnie stroked his goatee. 'Find me Naughton's hidey-hole, *mon ami*, and we will talk again.'

Davey heard the dogs barking and switched on the radio to drown them out. He hit on 2FM just in time to catch the main news story.

> *'A man's body has been recovered from the water at South Pier in Arklow, County Wicklow. Gardai have refused to comment, although it is believed the body may have been in the water for some time. No formal identification can be made until the family of the man has been informed. The state pathologist is on her way to the scene. And now, in other news…'*

Stretched out on the pullout bed in Vinnie's spare bedroom, Patrick rolled over and switched off the radio. He stood up shakily and went into the guest bathroom to splash his face with cold water. The few days in Ireland had taken their toll on him: his skin was rough and pasty from lack of sleep, and he knew he had lost weight.

Patrick leaned his forehead against the mirror.

He hadn't needed to hear a name. He knew whose body had been recovered, and he knew the body would eventually be identified. Kelpie had been a soldier, he had been Patrick's man. How could he ever have doubted him? He had wasted so much time – and time was the one commodity he did not have.

He closed his eyes and listened to the traffic moving on the city streets below. He had asked to speak to Anouk, earlier, and Aziz had said she was sleeping. Patrick knew he was lying. Anouk was dead. Whenever he closed his eyes he saw her face, her trusting, innocent brown eyes. It made him gag to think what might have happened to her. He should never have got involved with her in the first place. What the hell had he been thinking? Men like him didn't take girlfriends like her. He might as well have killed her himself.

He splashed his face again. Aziz was suspicious and beginning to feel aggrieved. Even the offer of the club deeds hadn't appeased him. The last time Aziz had got suspicious of someone, that someone had been fished out of a filthy canal three weeks later, fingers and teeth missing, the rest of the bloated body too damaged for identification. Patrick knew it would be no different for him.

He watched the water swirl in the hand basin and drain away. It was as if his hope drained away with it.

Kelpie had not betrayed him, and that left only two men who could have: Naughton and Vincent,

his oldest friend and his only son. By the end of
the day he would know which of them had made
the mistake of crossing him.

26

John glanced at the address again. He hoped he had the right place this time. Obviously barmen made more than he'd thought. Churchview Apartments were a set of well-maintained red-brick buildings set back in their own grounds, off the Upper Rathmines Road. According to his information, Alan Roche lived in block B, number 16, and the nameplates outside the main door said his information was correct.

John pressed the intercom and waited. He'd finally tracked Alan down through his new job in Zanzibar, but only after the barman in the Westbury had fleeced him for twenty quid. He hoped he was early enough to catch Alan before he left for the evening shift.

Eventually a tired and cranky-sounding voice answered. 'What?'

'Alan Roche?'

'Who wants to know?'

'My name's John Quigley. I want to talk to you about Vincent York.'

'Alan's not here.'

John leaned against the wall. 'Hey, I can wait

here all day, Alan, so why not open up, eh?'

'Shit… Top floor.' The intercom buzzed. John hurried up the three flights and found apartment 16 at the bottom of the hall. The door was slightly ajar.

John tapped on it. 'Hey, Alan?'

'Come in!'

John pushed the door wider and stepped into a poorly lit hall that reeked of incense and Chinese food. Three pine doors led off the main hall. Two were closed, and the one at the end of the hall was open but had a set of multi-coloured glass beads strung across the frame. Through them, John saw a figure moving.

'Alan?'

'Yes, that's me. Come on in,' the figure said.

John closed the front door and took two steps towards the beads. Then someone behind him kicked him hard in the back. John felt the air rush out of his body as he fell forwards. He grabbed at a bright-red dado rail to keep his balance, missed and ended up in a heap on the floor.

'You stay there, motherfucker!' a high voice screamed. 'Alan, I've got him!'

'Wait!' John raised his arm to ward off another boot in the ribs. 'Wait, for fuck's sake!'

The beaded curtains parted, and John caught a glimpse of the man he guessed was Alan Roche. He was about John's age, but small and remarkably dainty. His head was shaved, and he had a platinum beard grown to about three inches

362

long and teased into a thin point. He wore a silver nose-ring and a mauve dressing gown. The thing that caught John's attention, however, was the large baseball bat Alan Roche carried in his delicate hands. It was obviously new. The price tag was still stuck to the shaft.

Alan Roche waved the bat threateningly. 'Who are you?'

John pushed himself back against the wall and splayed his hands in what he hoped was a non-threatening manner. 'My name is John Quigley. I'm a private investigator.'

'Oh, sure you are! And I'm fucking Madonna,' the second man yelled. 'Hit him, Al!'

John turned his head, slowly, and held his hands open. The man who'd kicked him in the back was almost as small as Alan. He was dark-haired, bare-chested and the whole of his left arm was covered in an elaborate Celtic tattoo. He wore candy-striped boxer shorts and flip-flops. For some reason he was posed in a Karate Kid stance, arms up in front of his face.

John put his hand into his jacket to get his wallet out. 'Don't do that!' Candy-stripe kicked him in the elbow.

'Stop!' John roared. 'I'm getting out my identification.'

The two tiny men exchanged nervous glances.

'Are you really a detective?' Alan Roche asked.

'Who sent you here?' Candy-stripe asked.

'Nobody *sent* me.' John handed his wallet to

Candy-stripe. 'I got your name from the club. I'm here about a missing person. Now will you let me up?'

Alan nodded to Candy-stripe. John stood up slowly and rolled his shoulders. 'Look inside the first pocket, you'll see my card.'

While Candy-stripe flipped through his wallet, John turned to the man holding the bat. 'Alan Roche, right?'

'So what if I am?' He jabbed John in the ribs with the head of the bat. 'If you try to hurt us, I swear to God, I'll…I'll bash your fucking brains in.'

'I believe you.' John rubbed his back and pulled a face. 'Hey, stop poking me with that thing.'

Alan lowered the bat, but only slightly. 'Who is it you're looking for?'

'Yeah, what the hell makes you think we know anything about it?' Candy-stripe said. He threw the wallet back to John.

John caught it and leaned back against the wall, making sure not to make any sudden moves. These two looked edgy enough to hit first and ask questions later. 'I'm working on a case involving a missing girl. Her name's Ashley Naughton.' He checked for reactions; there were none. Clearly these two hadn't the first clue who Ashley Naughton was.

'She was last seen at Tempest nightclub less than two weeks ago. Now the owner of the club,

Vinnie York, is saying he barely knows her. Only I happen to know otherwise. I think he's hiding something.'

'And what?' Candy-stripe snapped. 'What's that got to do with Alan? He doesn't even work there any more.'

'I was wondering if you might be able to help me.' John jerked his head towards Alan. 'You left the same weekend she went missing.'

'Ashley…' Alan put the bat down against the wall. 'Was she blonde?'

'Yes.'

'I think I remember her. She was a sweet thing, always really nice.'

Candy-stripe put his hands on his hips, his handsome dark face bunched up in anger. 'Alan, don't be stupid. Stay out of it.'

'Look,' John said, 'if you know something, you've got to tell me. Everyone else is dancing to York's piping.'

Alan looked at John sadly. 'Look, cupcake, I'm out of there. And I really don't want to get involved in Vinnie York's business.'

John frowned at being called 'cupcake'. 'A few questions, nothing more. He'll never know we've spoken.'

'Joey?' Alan tilted his head, his tiny features softening. 'She was a lovely girl.'

Candy-stripe tutted and threw his hands in the air. 'Oh, all right. Je-*sus*.'

'Thanks. I won't take up much of your time.'

John smiled wanly. 'Do you mind if I sit down first? I think I'm going to be sick. You kicked me straight in the kidneys.'

Joey yelped, jumped forward and grabbed John's arm. 'Oh Christ, I'm so *sorry*! I've been taking lessons, and we thought you were someone from the club – didn't we, Al? Shit, are you okay? Alan, get him some water or something.'

'Bring him inside and sit him on the sofa.' Alan disappeared behind the beads and began to rummage through presses. 'Shit, Joey... Where are all the clean glasses?'

'Over the sink – I *washed* them, remember?' Joey led John into a small, vermilion-red sitting room crammed full of oversized furniture. The windows were covered with golden, shimmering saris in place of curtains. There were photos of Alan and Joey everywhere, mostly in black and white. In every one, they looked as if they were having the time of their lives.

'I swear, I didn't think I could kick that hard,' Joey said, somewhat proudly. He shoved John in the direction of a yellow sofa covered in brightly coloured Indian cushions, and dropped into a pink plush love seat under the window. The smell of incense was overpowering in the tiny room.

John sat down and winced. The little shit had really clobbered him one. 'Jesus, who were you expecting?'

Joey pulled a face. In the light he was younger than John had thought first, about twenty-one or twenty-two. He crossed his legs under him, oblivious to the fact that he was almost naked. John made sure he kept his gaze at eye level. 'I thought you were that bastard, Davey.'

'Davey Clarke?'

'How do you know him?'

'Let's just say we've had a run-in.'

Joey pursed his lips. 'Well, let's just say he's been here before.'

The clattering in the kitchen stopped, and Alan appeared carrying a pint glass of water. 'Oh my God, you're as white as a sheet. Are you really hurt?'

'I'll live.' John accepted the glass gratefully and pressed it to his forehead. He was slightly embarrassed that Joey, who probably weighed nine stone wet, had floored him in the first place. That would never have happened to Philip Marlowe. 'Now, tell me why you two were planning to split Davey Clarke's head open with a baseball bat.'

'Show him your back, Al,' Joey said immediately. 'Go on, show him.'

Alan frowned at Joey, his face flushing. John knew he was embarrassed and caught off guard. 'I don't think he needs to—'

'Show him!'

Alan's pointy beard twitched with annoyance, but he opened his dressing gown and let it fall to the floor. Underneath he wore the smallest Y-fronts John had ever seen. Alan turned around, and John whistled softly under his breath.

'See? See?' Joey said, staring at him. 'See why now?'

'Davey Clarke did that?' John stared at the damage in amazement. Alan Roche's back was a mess of swollen, discoloured skin, covered with bruises ranging from palest yellow to deepest indigo. Tendrils of raw purple ran from his shoulder blades down to the top of the skimpy briefs. It looked to John like he must have had internal bleeding at some point. 'Jesus.'

'Yeah, Jesus. He likes to hit where the bruises won't show up, so he does,' Joey said angrily. He glanced at Alan, and his face contorted in blank rage. 'Likes to pick on people who can't fight back.'

'Jesus,' John repeated.

'For a scrap of measly fucking hash!' Joey said, his small features wracked with hurt. 'It was a favour for someone. It's not like he was dealing or anything. That right, Al?'

'Oh Joey, leave it,' Alan sighed, put his dressing gown back on and sat primly beside John on the sofa. 'I *was* dealing a little – nothing major, just a bit of grass, bit of hash. I didn't think anyone would give a damn, especially in that place.'

'I've been there. It's an anything-goes sort of place, isn't it?'

'Not so much downstairs, but upstairs anything goes, and I mean *anything*.'

John eased back on the sofa. The pain was beginning to subside. 'What can you tell me about Ashley Naughton?'

'Well, not much, really,' Alan said. 'I remember she was a little different from the girls she hung around with – shyer, more withdrawn. That other one, Claudia, she's Vinnie's main squeeze. Proper little bitch, but good fun, game for anything. Big coke fiend. She'd snort it out of a dirty carpet if you let her.'

'She's his *what*?'

'Girlfriend. Well, flavour of the month, more like.'

'I've met her,' John said incredulously. 'They were dating?'

Alan nodded. 'Only I wouldn't call it dating, I'd call it fucking.'

'And Megan Lowry?'

'Which one was that?'

'Redhead.'

'Oh, her.' Alan shrugged. 'Don't know much about her, really, except she was always wasted.' He tugged at the end of his beard. 'Vinnie was crazy about that girl Ashley. He used to use any excuse to get near her, but she wouldn't give him the time of day. She loathed him, you could see it.'

'What do you mean?'

'Well, she always made it her business not to talk to him alone, she wouldn't let him buy her drinks… That's why I remember her, really. I thought, *You go, girl. Don't get sucked in by that bastard.* The thing about Vinnie is that, once he beds them, he sheds them.'

'Did he bed Ashley Naughton?'

'I doubt it, but not for want of trying.'

'But I thought he was with Claudia?'

'That wouldn't bother him. He had some fixation on Ashley – I don't know what it was. Claudia's…well, she's part of that set, isn't she? Money, drugs, parties…they all think they can do what they like. And you know what? They can. Nobody looks up or down at them – not the parents, not the schools. But Ashley was in a different class, and even someone as fucking psychotic as Vinnie could see that.'

'Did Claudia notice his interest in Ashley?'

'Hard not to.'

John took a sip of his water and thought about the history between Patrick York and Edward Naughton. Had Ashley known of their connection? Maybe that was why she had kept her distance from Vinnie. And Vinnie wasn't used to being told no. Was it possible that he had lost it, hurt Ashley in some way? 'What do you mean, upstairs anything goes?'

Alan waved a tiny hand. 'Anything. Drugs, girls, deals. They're a rich crowd with no respect for anything or anyone. Their only objective is to have a good time.'

'York doesn't get any trouble from the cops?'

Joey snorted from the love seat. 'People like him get away with murder, don't you know that? That fucker greases the right hands and, hello, no fucking hassle.'

Alan nodded. 'Joey's right. Vinnie York is a

370

complete nut, but he's a clever nut. And he runs a tight ship. Everyone working for him is hand-picked, no squealers.'

'You left. You're talking to me,' John said.

'You're not the cops. If you were, I wouldn't even remember working in Tempest. Anyway, I liked that girl Ashley. She was sweet.'

John thought it through for a moment. 'Is Vinnie York involved in drugs?"

Joey and Alan tensed and exchanged furtive glances. Joey turned away pointedly. 'I wouldn't know, so don't be looking at me.'

John put down his glass and turned to Alan. 'Okay, give it to me.'

'Look, there's been talk…' Alan bit his bottom lip. 'Well, Vinnie likes his coke. He likes it so much he snorts it night and day. But then, he can afford to. It's common knowledge he sells it – well, common knowedge in the club. I think he makes more from selling cocaine on a Saturday night than the club earns in a month. It's always available up-stairs. I've heard him making deals with guys up there, too – big deals.'

'He talks like that in front of you?'

'When Vinnie's coked up, he'd talk to the devil himself. Anyway, people like me, we're just furniture to people like York.'

'Where does he get it from?'

'Well, he doesn't shit it out, does he?'

John pulled a face. 'Christ, I hope not.'

Alan smiled, but it was a grim smile. 'Look, I

don't know what any of this has to do with your girl being missing, but be careful when you're dealing with Vinnie.' He rubbed gently at his bruised shoulder. 'I hope you find that girl, but Vinnie doesn't put any value on people, Detective, and if she crossed him when he was up…'

He didn't finish, and John didn't push it. Suddenly the air in the apartment was cloying and he needed to get out. 'Listen, thanks for all your help. You've certainly cleared up a few things I was wondering about.'

Alan shrugged, a tiny, worn gesture. 'Okay, but remember: I won't be talking to anyone else. One hiding a year is my limit.'

As John let himself out of the building, the pain in his kidneys had subsided to a dull throb. Night was closing in fast and a chilly wind whipped about him, making his ears ache and chilling him to the bone. He pulled his mobile out and called Sarah at home. When she didn't answer, he tried her mobile. She answered on the first ring.

'Where are you?'

'I'm at the office. What's wrong with your phone?'

'Nothing. What's wrong with you?'

'You might try leaving your phone on once in a while. I've been trying to reach you.'

'Sorry, but hey – I've got news. Claudia Delaney was lying about York: she knows him – knows him on a slightly more intimate basis than she's been letting on. I think—'

'I know all that. I've got Megan Lowry here, and we've just had a long chat.'

'Oh.' That took the wind out of John's sails. He'd got himself bashed in the kidneys for nothing.

'I think you need to come over here.'

'She's there now?'

'Yeah.'

John unlocked the car door and slid in behind the steering wheel. 'I'm up in Rathmines. I'll be there in five.'

27

John had planned a better opening – something along the lines of 'There you are, you lying, coke-snorting hussy' – but the first words out of his mouth when he clapped eyes on the tearful Megan Lowry were, 'What happened to your face?'

'Davey Clarke did it,' Sarah said. She spoke softly, but John picked up on the tight set of her mouth and the undercurrent in her voice. Sarah was more than a little upset. 'He came around to their home and put the frighteners on them. Knocked them around a little.'

'Claudia too?'

'Yeah, both of them.'

'Why?'

'Vinnie York wants them to keep their mouths shut about Ashley.'

John gently tilted Megan's face up to the light. Her mouth was swollen and the bottom of her lip was scabbing over. 'You all right?'

Megan nodded and huddled deeper into an Eskimo-style jacket complete with massive, fur-trimmed hood.

'Why did he do this? What does he think you can tell us?'

'He doesn't…he doesn't want us talking about Ash to anyone else, full stop.'

'Did you contact the Gardaí? Your folks? Or are you two girls going to spin a yarn about this too?'

'John,' Sarah said, 'that's not helping.'

'Have you phoned the Gardaí?'

'No,' Megan said softly, her pale eyes brimming with tears. She glanced towards Sarah in desperation.

John sneered at her. 'Of course you haven't.'

'I can't! We—'

John released her face. He couldn't believe these girls, trying to protect scumbags like Davey Clarke and Vinnie York. 'Give me a fucking break.'

'John,' Sarah said, but he wasn't listening.

'Some guy comes into your home and knocks you around, and you're going to let him, just because your flatmate is balling some fucking coked-up French-spewing ponce?'

Megan flinched at the brutality of his words. 'I—'

'Yeah, did you think we wouldn't find out about that? What the hell's the matter with you? Your friend's missing, and it's likely that shit Vinnie York's done something to her! He sent that goon to rough you up. What the hell do you think he's done to your friend? I've had it with you two. You're going to come with me to the nearest station, and you are going to tell the Gardaí every stinking word you should have told us—'

'No! I can't!' Megan wailed, and drew back from him.

'*John*,' Sarah repeated.

But John was suddenly furious. He grabbed Megan by the arm. 'You want to lie to us, that's your business, but we don't have to sit here and take it. You want our help now? Well, that's too—'

'John!' Sarah yelled, rising from her chair. 'Let go of her and shut up for a second!'

'What?'

'They can't go shooting their mouths off because Davey has a videotape of Claudia and Megan *and Ashley* at some party. He's threatening to show it around the college and to their parents if they don't keep their mouths shut.'

'So?' John looked confused.

'It's not the kind of tape everyone needs to see. It could get them kicked out of college, for a start.'

'What are you talking about?'

'The girls are on there doing coke, drinking, having sex…' Sarah shrugged. 'Just your average night of debauchery, only these eejits let some guy film them with a hand-held camera.'

'It wasn't like that!' Megan bleated. 'We didn't think it was a big deal. It was a private party, and everybody was totally out of it, and this guy Richie …he was filming everyone. It was just a joke. We didn't think he'd give the tape to Davey. It was supposed to be a *joke*!'

'God, you lot are so stupid.' Sarah sat down and sighed. 'You're lucky it didn't end up on the Net. Never let anyone tape you doing anything. Ever hear of Paris Hilton?' She looked at John. 'Vinnie York organised the whole shebang. It's some invite-only thing for members of the club. He has one about once a month.'

John didn't reply. He glared at Meg, his jaw bunching. She tried to keep eye contact, but after a few seconds she gave a shuddering sob and buried her head in her hands. Sarah watched John carefully. His face was thunderous, and for a moment he looked like he was going to grab Megan and shake her until her teeth rattled.

But finally he blinked and let out a deep breath. He uncoiled his fists, walked around to his desk and sat down heavily. 'You kids kill me,' he said finally. 'You really kill me. What the hell were you thinking?'

'I don't think they *were* thinking,' Sarah said evenly. 'They're eighteen.'

John rubbed his hands over his stubble. 'Claudia Delaney was sleeping with Vinnie York up until a couple of weeks ago.'

'I know. Megan told me. But I think that particular romance is dead and buried.'

'Yeah, now that he got what he wanted.'

Sarah smiled bleakly. 'You really think he used her to get to Ashley?'

'I don't know. I don't know what to think any more.' John pulled out his cigarettes and lit one dispiritedly. 'I think he's got her.'

'We need proof.'

'Where are we supposed to get that?'

'John, think: why did Margo Naughton ask us to back off?'

'Clarke must have threatened her too.'

'Then what are we going to do?'

John nodded and blew smoke out through his nose. He had calmed down a little, and his mind had slipped into gear again. 'Megan, you sure Davey Clarke has this tape?'

Megan nodded but wouldn't look at him. She was crying again; big blobs of tears fell onto her jeans.

John looked at Sarah and raised his eyebrows. 'Well?'

'Well what?'

He glanced over at the softly sobbing Megan. He looked tired, and for the first time Sarah noticed a tight, determined set to his mouth. 'We have to get that tape back somehow.'

'What have you got in mind?' Sarah narrowed her eyes. 'I doubt he's just going to hand it over.'

'Megan, where does this guy live?'

Megan wiped her nose with her sleeve. 'I don't know.'

'Does Claudia?'

'I don't think so. See, the thing is, we...we never really liked Davey, none of us. He scares me, and Ash couldn't stand him either. I think even Claudia's scared of him, a little.'

'Do you know what kind of car he drives or anything?'

378

'No.'

'Okay, I'll find out another way.' John sucked on his cigarette, his eyes half closed, thinking. 'Megan, go on home – and for God's sake stay out of trouble for a day or two, will you?'

She looked at him with eyes that were full of anguish. 'Will you help us? Please, I don't know who else to ask.'

'Yeah, we'll help you – but from now on you don't lie to us about anything else. Got it? You lie to us, and you're on your own.'

Megan nodded wretchedly.

'Now get out of here. Sarah and I need to talk.'

After Megan left, Sarah ran her fingers through her hair and looked quizzically at John. 'What are you thinking?'

'I'm thinking I'm sick of being in the dark, and I'm sick of bullies like Davey Clarke and Vinnie York pushing people around.' John ground out his cigarette. 'I've got to go.'

'Where?'

John winked at her and snatched up his car keys. 'Need a lift home?'

'No, I'm okay. I'll lock up here and walk.' Sarah looked at him suspiciously. 'What about Margaret Naughton?'

'We'll go see her tomorrow.' John walked towards the door, his mind already planning his night's activities.

'What are you going to do?'

'I don't know.'

'John, promise me you're not going to do something stupid.'

'Me?' John gave her his best innocent look.

'Just promise me. It'll make me feel better.'

'Okay. I promise.'

Several hours later John sat behind the wheel of his car, eating a Mars bar and watching the club door. His plan was to tail Davey home after work and get his address. Davey had arrived at the club at twenty past ten and gone inside, and that was the last John had seen of him. He settled in to wait, not expecting much to happen before closing time, but at two twenty-five he got more than he bargained for.

Claudia Delaney appeared, staggering down the road in the direction of the club. She stumbled in her heels and almost fell, but somehow managed to keep upright. John could see she was plastered. Her normally sleek hair hung limp across her face, and her clothes were dishevelled. She stopped outside the massive steel door and had a brief but heated discussion with the ponytailed bouncer guarding the entrance.

John sat up straight and grinned. It looked to him as though Claudia was being denied entry. The bouncer spoke into his headset. A few seconds later he nodded, took Claudia by the elbow and tried to guide her off the step. Claudia grabbed the railings outside the door and dug her heels in.

The bouncer looked like he was getting annoyed. He tried ignoring her, but she made a clumsy attempt to push past him. Then he tried talking to her, but he clearly wasn't getting through. Eventually, after taking a quick look up and down the street to make sure no one was watching, he hoisted her off her feet and unceremoniously dumped her onto the street. With the windows rolled up, John couldn't hear what was said, but Claudia swung her fist and hit the bouncer in the jaw. The bouncer bunched his shoulders and looked like he might hit her back, but the moment passed and he backed away from her, a little more warily than before. Claudia burst into tears, turned on her heel and stumbled down the street.

John grinned. Jesus, Claudia Delaney was some girl for one girl.

Ten minutes after that, Davey Clarke came out and climbed into a dirty-looking beige Toyota Corolla. He turned the car in the middle of the street and drove off towards the south side. John wrote the number plate down and followed, keeping three cars between them in case Clarke was looking out.

In Rathmines, Davey stopped on double yellow lines and went into McDonalds. John parked in Leinster Square, where he could observe him without being noticed. Davey ordered enough food to feed a family of four and took a window seat to eat it. John lit a cigarette and tried to ignore the growling in his stomach. Three girls stumbled out of a house and swayed down the road, screeching at the top of their lungs. One of them banged her hip heavily against John's wing mirror. He scowled and watched six pale, flabby legs totter past on too-high heels. Some women weren't built to expose thigh on a cold night.

Eventually Davey finished eating. He strolled out of the diner and, after a quick glance around, hopped back into his car and pulled out. John waited for a few seconds and followed him. After the Swan Centre, Davey pulled an illegal left. John had no option but to follow, even though it meant drawing attention. He followed the Toyota down to Ranelagh, past the top of his own street, left again and on towards Donnybrook. The lights were a problem, but fortunately the Manta far outpaced the Toyota, and John caught up easily on the straight. When they hit the Stillorgan dual carriageway, John got a funny tingling in his spine. They were heading towards Wicklow.

It began to rain, a heavy, fast downpour that reduced visibility to nearly nothing. John craned his neck and almost pressed his nose to the windshield. The Toyota kept up a blistering pace. Clearly Davey didn't give a shit about speed cameras or penalty points. They were past Loughlinstown in minutes. John cursed the bad weather. It was making the road treacherous. At the new road works at the late lamented Glen of the Downs, a slew of water sent John skidding, missing bollards by inches. It took some fancy wheel-spinning and serious balls of steel not to lose control completely. Davey seemed to be having trouble too and he slowed the Toyota a fraction, allowing John to wipe the sweat out of his eyes and hang further back.

For the next forty miles John tailed him comfortably, letting a white bread van come between them to give him some cover. When they reached Jack White's pub and the Toyota swung left, John felt a quickening in his blood. He pulled in at the pub and waited for the Toyota's taillights to disappear. There was no reason to drive up its arse. He knew where Davey was headed.

John parked in the pub car park and lit a cigarette. He smoked it down to the filter, threw it out the window and started the car. The rain stopped. Slowly he travelled up the dark, winding road, swung left, knocked off the lights and cruised past the main gates of the Naughtons' house. They were open.

Half a mile further down the road, John parked in a field and jogged back towards the house. He moved silently up the drive, keeping close to the trees. He had no problem finding the Toyota: it was parked right out front of the house, as bold as brass. Davey had made no effort to conceal it.

John skirted around the noisy gravel and ran across the lawn, staying close to the hedge. The front of the house was in darkness. John eased himself backwards into the shrubbery and dropped to a crouch. He was sure he could see the glow of a light from the back of the house. Ignoring the drops of icy rainwater slipping from the branches and rolling down inside the collar of his jacket, he worked his way around to the back of the house.

He had been right: there were lights on back here. He took a deep breath, sprinted across the small yard and ducked behind a low wall running the length of the lawn. From his hiding place, he faced directly into the kitchen.

He saw Margaret Naughton, white-faced and tousle-haired, sitting at the huge table where he and Sarah had sat earlier that day. She was in a pale-pink dressing gown and had some sort of cream on her face. It shone waxily under the copper lights hanging down over the table. Beside her Emily Naughton sat wide-eyed, one claw-like hand clutching her blue quilted dressing gown closed at her throat. Clarke had obviously woken them up. Emily hadn't taken the time to put her teeth in, and her cheeks had collapsed like meringue when someone opens the oven door too soon. Her hair stuck out crazily from her head. She looked old and frail and terrified.

Davey sat in another chair, talking – unfortunately, his big bulldog head faced in John's direction. John crept along behind the wall on his hands and knees, edging closer to the house. He slid behind a half-barrel filled with begonias and peeped over the top.

Margaret said something. Her hands twisted furiously on the table in front of her. Clarke replied. Then he reached into the pocket of his bomber jacket, extracted a piece of paper and threw it across the table to her.

Margaret snatched up the paper, turned it over in her small, pale hands and looked at it. Whatever she saw, the effect was instantaneous. Her eyes flared wide and her body began to shake uncontrollably. She stood up and pointed her finger at a beige cordless phone hanging by the fridge. She staggered around the table and made a shuffling run towards it.

What happened next escalated so quickly that John would later have trouble remembering the exact sequence of events. Davey kicked a chair towards Margaret and gestured to her to sit. She flinched, sidestepped the chair and kept moving towards the phone. Davey didn't ask again. He lunged across the room, spun her by the shoulders and dragged her back towards the chair. Margaret struggled and tried to wrench herself free, so Davey slapped her across the face. Emily screamed. Davey roared at her, then dragged Margaret back to the table and shoved her roughly into the chair.

John curled his hands into fists and flexed his legs. He despised a man who would raise his hand to a woman. Incensed, and not exactly thinking clearly, John stood up from behind the barrel, raced across the small back yard, kicked open the kitchen door like a movie hero and charged.

Davey spun towards him, giving John just enough time to register the lack of surprise on the bouncer's face. Then, as the back door crashed against the wall, John roared like a bull and launched himself at the bouncer, throwing all his weight into the lunge.

Davey reacted as calmly as though John had written and asked permission. He turned his body to the side, squatted slightly on powerful thighs and balanced on the balls of his feet. He grabbed John's outstretched arm and dragged it across his chest. Using John's weight and momentum, he flipped him over one massive shoulder, sending him flying through the air and crashing into the Welsh dresser.

When John opened his eyes, he was on the floor, Davey was gone and Margaret stood over him, looking shocked and terrified.

John groaned.

'Are you all right?'

John tried a smile. Pain surfaced near his back and flared out across his body. 'Never better.'

She stared at him incredulously and her hands fluttered up to her face. 'What are you *doing* here?'

John tried to sit up. Chunks of smashed crockery slid off his chest and clattered into the wreckage around him. He lifted his head slowly. When that didn't kill him, he pulled himself up onto his elbows. He squinted at the devastation around him. Although he wasn't quite sure what had happened, it appeared Clarke had used him as a missile. The dresser was smashed to pieces. Drawers hung askew from split hinges, the backboard of the display section was split as cleanly as though with an axe and the contents were lying around him in a thousand pieces. He blinked a couple of times, hoping his eyes would stop fuzzing.

'I…I followed Clarke. I saw what happened.'

From her place at the kitchen table, Emily moaned as though she'd been kicked. John eased his legs out from the agonising knot they were in.

'You'll have to go.' Margaret nodded towards the door. Her face was deathly white, except for the red mark where Clarke had slapped her. 'Please, it would be better if you left.'

'I'm going nowhere until you tell me what the fuck is going on,' John said. When he spoke, the left-hand side of his mouth felt funny. He raised his hand to it and his fingers came away bloody; he realised his lip was ripped open. 'I mean it. What just happened here?' He tested his legs, found them in fairly decent working order and scrambled gingerly to his feet. 'Why was Davey Clarke threatening you?'

'Look, will you…can't you…' Margaret shook her head. She slumped into a kitchen chair and rubbed her eyes with the heel of her hand.

'What is it?' John pressed his hand to his lip again and tried not to puke from the pain.

She refused to look at him. Instead she reached

into her dressing gown pocket, pulled out a Polaroid and threw it across the table. John hobbled to the table and turned it over. *That bastard Clarke,* he thought. *No wonder she freaked.*

It was a photo of Ashley Naughton. She lay on a filthy mattress, her head turned towards the camera flash. She looked terrified. The room behind her was grim, full of rubble and old junk, and her bare legs were filthy and covered in bruises. John turned it over in his hands and put it back on the table.

'Those people have my daughter.'

'You've got to go to the Gardaí.'

'No!' Both women said it so quickly that they startled both him and each other.

'Jesus Christ, what is it with you lot? First Megan Lowry, now you?'

Emily recovered first. 'They'll kill her if we do that. They want Edward. They think we know where he is – and us out of our minds with worry for him.' She sounded weird without her teeth. 'That bastard said if we wanted to see the young one again, then we'd better make sure to get hold of Edward. But sure, how can we? We don't know where he is!'

'Your husband's missing too?' John glanced at Margaret in confusion. The pain in his back was like a thousand jackhammers pummelling his spine.

'Since yesterday afternoon,' Margaret said softly. 'He left here early that morning and no one's seen him since. His mobile's off, he won't return any of the messages I've left and nobody's seen him at the site.' She stood up shakily, went to the sink, soaked a dishcloth under water and handed it to John. 'Here – for your face.'

John took it gratefully and pressed it to his mouth. 'Do you know where he is?'

'Of course not!'

'Jesus, this just keeps getting worse and worse.' John shook his aching head. 'You need to call the Gardaí. Surely to God you can see the sort of people you're dealing with.'

'I know exactly the sort of people we're dealing with.'

The women traded looks. Something jumped between them, some signal John couldn't fathom.

'I think my husband has stolen drugs from the Yorks,' Margaret said softly. 'He's a greedy, stupid fool.'

Emily gripped the side of her chair so hard her gnarled knuckles turned white. 'Margo. Stop, now. You're talkin' nonsense.'

'Oh for Christ's sake!' Margaret banged her fist off the table.

'He told you not to involve anyone. He warned you what would happen. Maybe if you hadn't brought this shower in, she'd be back by now.'

Margaret snatched up the picture and threw it at her mother-in law.

John lowered himself into a chair. The pain in his back was almost unbearable. 'Here, come on, the two of you. There's no need—'

'No need?' Margaret turned on him, her eyes brimming with tears. 'Look at Ashley! Look what they've done to her!' The sob caught in her throat. She reached out and grabbed Emily by the arm. 'That bastard abandoned us, you and me, to that animal. I won't protect him any longer.'

The old woman tried to jerk her arm free. Margaret held on to her and stared over her head, her pale eyes fastened on John. 'Please, you've got to help us, Mr Quigley.'

'No, Margo. I'm warnin'—'

'Shut up!' Margaret screamed suddenly. She released her mother-in-law and pressed her hands against the sides of her head. 'I can't do it any more! I won't!'

Emily glanced nervously towards John. 'Don't mind her. She's upset, she's—'

Margaret shook her head as if trying to clear it. 'I knew something was up when you told me about York's son's nightclub. I knew Edward had…something must have happened. Now they want him… That man – he works for the Yorks, doesn't he?'

John nodded.

'He wanted me to tell him where Edward is. But I don't *know* where he is!'

'What's the connection between your husband and the Yorks?'

'It's drugs, I'm sure of it – drugs.' She pulled a disgusted face. 'My husband loves nothing more than a fast buck. And Patrick York is a vile, disgusting criminal who likes destroying lives.'

Emily lowered her head and began to cry softly. Margaret shot her a disgusted look. 'There's no time for that, Emily! Who are you crying for, anyway?'

'He's my son, Margo.' Emily pushed her chair back from the table and went to the kitchen door. 'So help me, he's my son.' She took one last forlorn look at John and closed the door behind her.

'Edward's been so jumpy lately… God, it's all starting to make sense.' Margaret turned to John, her eyes wide and glistening, her bottom lip quivering with unchecked emotion. 'Please, help us. Help us get Ashley back. I don't care about the other stuff. Whatever Edward's involved in…I don't *care* what it is. I only want my baby to come home.' Her face crumpled. 'That's all. I just want Ashley back.'

John could do nothing but put his arms around her. She sobbed against him for a few minutes. He patted her awkwardly on the back until finally she began to regain her composure.

'Look,' he said, 'start from the beginning. And this time, tell me everything you know. Don't leave anything out, no matter how daft you think it is… And you wouldn't happen to have a few painkillers handy, would you?'

Margaret stared at his swollen mouth. 'I'm so sorry. Of course I have. Wait here.'

She returned two minutes later with a box of painkillers and a bottle of Glenfiddich, three-quarters full. John raised his eyebrows. Margaret pulled two glasses out of a cupboard and set them down on the table.

'For the shock.'

'Okay.'

'I'm a total fool, do you know that?' she said softly. 'I should never have trusted that man, never. But I had myself convinced that he'd left all that world behind him.'

John filled their glasses. 'So let's hear it.'

She sat back down to tell him all she knew about Edward Naughton and Patrick York.

It was ten to six in the morning, dark and freezing, when John made it back to his car. He had finally convinced Margaret to get herself and her mother-in-law out of the house and into a hotel for a few days. With Edward missing, they were sitting ducks for Vinnie York and anyone else who might be looking for him. And, despite Margaret's protests, he had waited until they were packed and driving down the lane before he felt it was safe to leave them.

The frosted grass crunched under his feet and the cold air cut him to the bone. He scraped ice off his windshield with an empty cigarette box and climbed in. He didn't start the car. He wasn't even sure he could drive, in this state: his back was throbbing badly and his mouth ached, despite the six Solpadeine he had swallowed with a generous glass of Glenfiddich. He sat behind the wheel in the alien country quiet and tried to make sense of the night.

He took Ashley's photograph out from his pocket and stared at it. Where were they holding her? It looked like a shed or a derelict house. It could be anywhere. When had it been taken – last night? The night she'd disappeared? Was she even still alive? He put it back in his pocket and closed his eyes.

At least now he had some idea of what was going on. Edward Naughton and Patrick York had been in on some deal together, and something had gone south. Vinnie York had Ashley Naughton, Edward Naughton was missing too and nobody was willing to go to the Gardaí – and he still had no idea where Davey Clarke lived. Swell, just swell. John rested his forehead against the steering wheel. Suddenly he was exhausted. His earlier adrenalin rush had long faded. Now he was cold, confused and, he realised bitterly, no closer to finding Ashley Naughton. And he had made a promise to help, even though he had no idea what to do next.

28

Sarah turned her head and squinted at the electric clock by her bed. It read 7.10 a.m. If that was correct, then God help the lunatic ringing her doorbell. She threw her duvet back, padded sleepily into the hall and answered the intercom.

'What?'

'It's me. Did I wake you?'

'John, it's seven o'clock.' Sarah yawned and rubbed her eyes with the heel of her hand. 'What are you doing here?'

'Can I come up?'

'Now? Sure.'

Sarah buzzed him in, grabed a dressing gown from her bathroom and opened the apartment door. She gasped when she saw John's face. 'Oh my God! What happened to you?'

John leaned against the door jamb. He was so exhausted he could hardly stand. 'We're back on the case.'

'Who did this to you?'

'Davey Clarke.'

'How?' Sarah touched the side of his battered

face with her palm. John winced. 'He came to your house again?'

'No, this time I jumped him.'

'I don't understand.'

'I followed him last night, and guess where we ended up.'

Sarah stepped back. 'You did what?'

'I had to get an address for him. Look, Sarah, do you think you can make me a coffee or something? I'm about ready to collapse here.'

'Oh, right.' She ushered him inside and closed the door.

'And painkillers would be great. I suppose morphine is out of the question?'

Sarah only had Disprin. John swallowed three in a glass of water while Sarah made coffee. She listened, first in disbelief, then with growing anger, to his story. By the time he was finished, she was positively steaming.

'You complete *idiot*. He could have killed you! You promised me me you wouldn't do anything. I would never have left you if I'd known you were going to do something that stupid!'

John sat back on her sofa and closed his eyes. 'It's just as well I followed him. Who knows what would have happened if I hadn't been there?'

'You shouldn't have done a thing without talking to me first.' Sarah pushed her tangled hair back from her forehead. 'That's the problem with you, John. Despite everything you say, despite everything you promise, you just plough on regardless. Now Clarke knows you're on to him! What do you think is going to happen to Ashley Naughton now, John? You think about that?'

'You said yourself we needed to find proof they had Ashley!'

'Yes, but not by nearly getting yourself killed.'

'What was I supposed to do, let him knock Margaret Naughton around the place?'

'You should have phoned the Gardaí.'

'Margaret asked me not to.'

'She had no right to ask you anything of the sort.'

'It doesn't matter. She asked me not to, so we're not going to call them – not yet.'

'Well, I think that's just plain stupid. You've been assaulted twice by Davey Clarke, we know he and Vinnie are holding Ashley somewhere, it doesn't take a genius to work out that Edward Naughton is up to his fat neck in trouble...' Sarah threw up her hands. 'What are we waiting for? Are we waiting for a body? Is that it? Maybe after they kill Ashley and maim you for life, we can go to—'

'All right, Sarah!' John snapped. He was exhausted, in pain and in no mood for lectures.

Sarah took a deep breath and forced herself to calm down. She didn't want to shout at John. If anything, she wanted to throw her arms around him and squeeze him until it hurt.

'Are you okay?' she asked.

'No.'

'You look worn out. You need to get some rest.'

'I've got to get home.'

'John Quigley, you are going nowhere until you have some rest. Now stop being a stubborn arsehole and lie down. Just kick your shoes off and catch an hour or two, will you? Please, for me?'

'Sumo's at—'

'I'll go over and let him out. You need to lie down. Actually, you probably need to go to a hospital. That gash by your mouth looks like it needs stitches.'

'No hospitals.' John rubbed the stubble on the other side of his chin. His back was throbbing so much he felt a little sick. The thought of getting up and walking downstairs to his car was daunting. 'All right, if you check on Sumo for me, then maybe I'll lie down – just for an hour.'

'Right.'

'Sarah, I've had enough of being thrown around by that monkey.'

'I know you have.'

'We need to go see the organ-grinder. We go see Vinnie York, let that prick know we can't be bullied – let him know that we know he's involved, and if anything happens to that girl we'll go to the cops with everything.'

'John, take your shoes off and lie down, will you? I'm going to get a blanket.'

John did as he was told. He curled up on Sarah's two-seater, wincing slightly as he moved. 'We've got to let this crowd know we won't give up. We've got to let them know they can't push us around.'

'We will. We can do all that, but first get some sleep, okay?'

John closed his eyes. 'Okay.'

Sarah got a blanket from her hot press and carried it back to the sitting room. By the time she returned, John was already asleep. Sarah covered him gently with the blanket and sat down.

Davey Clarke could have killed John earlier, and she knew it. John was the stupidest, most reckless person she had ever known. He was also the bravest. To him, everything was a possibility, and he never knew when to quit. Sarah pressed her temples. The fact was, he *had* found the evidence they needed, and if he hadn't followed Clarke, Margaret Naughton might never have told them about the photo, and they could have sat on the club until the end of the week and found nothing. But he should have called her. Why did he have to be so reckless, so stupidly impetuous?

She stared at John, at his torn and battered face, and a sharp burst of anger surged through her – but not at him. John wasn't the one holding a girl hostage, John hadn't lied and threatened and bullied everyone around him. Vinnie York and Davey Clarke had.

Sarah snatched up the photo of Ashley Naughton and stared at it. Who the hell did these people think they were?

*

Patrick York woke up in a sweat. He had been dreaming about Anouk. In his dream she had been on a Ferris wheel and Aziz had been manning it, but he had been making it go faster and faster, and Anouk had been screaming, screaming to Patrick for help. He had tried to reach Aziz, to tell him to stop, but his legs had been too heavy and the distance too great. It didn't take Freud to work that one out.

Vinnie stood at the bedroom door, holding a mobile phone.

'What? What time is it?'

'Ten-thirty.'

'What are you doing up?'

'I'm going to my club.' Vinnie looked pale and washed out. His hair stuck up from his head and he stared at his father with gleaming, malevolent eyes. 'I'm going to my office. I'm going to sit there and enjoy it while I still have the fucking chance!'

'What are you going on about?'

'Edward Naughton has gone to ground. He's gone.'

'How do you know?'

'Yesterday I got a call from a guy I know who works at his site. So I sent Davey to investigate, and guess fucking what? It's true. Nobody has the faintest idea where he is.'

'How long?'

'Since sometime Tuesday.'

'You been keeping tabs on him, Vincent?'

'Somebody had to. I never bought his fucking

act.' Vinnie shrugged. 'It doesn't matter now, does it? He's gone, and we're fucked.'

'Get on the phone, check the airports and the ferries – find out if he left the country. If he hasn't, get a hold of his fucking wife. Beat the fucking information out of her if you need to.'

'It's a bit late in the day now, isn't it? I wanted to do that the day you got here.'

'This isn't the fucking time, Vincent. Get moving. It ain't over till I say it's fucking over.' Patrick rolled off the bed, brushed past Vinnie and went to the bathroom. He felt sick to his stomach and his heart was beating wildly, but he didn't want Vincent to see how panicked he was. His son was like a shark: if he smelled blood, he'd finish him off. It wasn't over, Patrick told himself; he shouldn't jmp to conclusions.

He stared at his reflection in the mirror. *Not bad for an old man,* he thought. The surgeon in Holland had done a cracking job. Even Patrick's own mother, God rest her soul, wouldn't have recognised him. His nose was perfectly reshaped, a huge improvement on the broken lump it used to be, and the new cheeks really altered his look, although the implants had hurt like fuck for weeks after. It had been costly but worth it. He could organise a new passport if he needed to. He could go anywhere in the world. Some of the old crew were down the Costa De Sol, a few others in Thailand. Sure, he'd be travelling light, with barely more than he had on him, but he could start again, he could build up a new life…

His shoulders slumped. Who was he kidding? Aziz would find him wherever he went. He was too old to live like that, constantly looking over his shoulder. He didn't want to start again. He didn't want to go anywhere but back to Holland, back to his flat, back to lying beside Anouk on a wet Saturday afternoon, talking, eating, reading the papers. That was his life. And it had been robbed from him.

The news that Edward had dropped off the radar had sucked all the wind out of Patrick's sails. Despite what Vinnie had been whispering in his ears, he had truly hoped his old friend was kosher. But Vinnie had been right all along. He had left it too long. He should have beaten the information he wanted out of Eddie. He had failed; he had let friendship cloud his judgement. And, in return, Edward Naughton had signed both their death warrants.

29

When John woke up, he was alone. It took him a few seconds to work out where he was and another few to remember how he'd got there. He sat up and groaned out loud. His body ached all over – every movement jarred him – and his face felt like a herd of wilderbeast had trampled over it.

He checked his mobile, but the battery had given up the ghost during the night. He sighed and slipped it into his pocket. Then he noticed a piece of paper on the table. It was a note from Sarah, asking him to hold off on speaking to Vinnie York and saying she'd contact him later. The photo of Ashley Naughton was gone.

He checked his watch and was surprised to see how late it was: ten past four. Shit, he'd been asleep for hours. He picked up Sarah's phone and called her mobile. She didn't answer.

John staggered into the bathroom and was stunned to see how much damage he had sustained. The skin around his jaw was ripped in several places, and the lower half of his face was bruised all over and covered in dried blood. He washed off the worst of it, amazed at how much pain even the softest touches of the facecloth caused him. He did the best he could and went home.

Sumo greeted him with more enthusiasm than John would have believed possible. 'Hey there, big fella.' John caressed the dog's wiry hair. For some reason he felt as though he had been gone forever. 'Hey there.'

He ate some Panadol, fed Sumo and noticed his answering maching was blinking. He hit Play, hoping Sarah had called.

The first message was from Cynthia. 'John Quigley, you are a complete shit. I can't *believe* you haven't called me! After the way you carried on last weekend, the very *least* you could do is be man enough to apologise! Sondra said I shouldn't call you first, but clearly *someone* has to make the first move. I'm in work, call me.'

John hit the button again.

'John! If this is some way of trying to punish me, then you better get over—'

He hit it again.

'Hey, asshole, if you think I don't have better things to—'

Jesus Christ, Cynthia again. There was one more message. John held his breath.

It was Sarah. 'John, it's me. I just called the apartment and you weren't there, so I figure you're either on your way home or passed out in bed. Either way, I've got an address for Davey Clarke. That Toyota he was driving last night is registered in his name, and I got Steve to pull the address for me. It's 27 Highroad Drive, Stoney-batter. I'll check in with you later. I'm on my way into town to meet up with Claudia Delaney, see if she knows whether York owns any places other than his apartment and the nightclub. Maybe we'll get lucky. I took the picture with me in case I need to rattle Claudia's cage – although, if what you tell me is true, she might be more helpful today. Talk later – hope you're feeling better. Bye.'

John listened to the message again and took down Davey's address. Then he went into his bed-room and dressed in a black tracksuit, black jacket, black boots and a black beanie cap. He packed a small rucksack with some essentials, locked Sumo outside again and grabbed his keys. He checked himself out in the hall mirror before he left and sighed. He was a mess, but it was the best he could do.

Pascal Mooney shivered and huddled deeper into his overcoat. He sat on the tombstone, picking at the moss and letting his feet swing – anything to keep the circulation going. Of all the fucked-up places to meet, this was surely the freakiest. Pascal didn't like graveyards at the best of times, but this badly neglected Protestant graveyard was giving him a serious dose of the heebie-jeebies. The grass was almost waist-high, full of briars and brambles, and the huge yew trees creaked and whispered in the wind. Pascal lit a cigarette and tried not to think about what lay a few feet under the soil. The sun was going down fast, its weak light barely clearing the old, ivy-covered wall. The shadows were long and impenetrable, adding to his growing unease. Why did Dougie Burrows want to meet him in the first place? He'd done everything he'd been asked, kept Edward out of harm's way, given everyone some breathing space.

After another ten minutes he heard the clear sound of the rusted gate being shouldered open. He tossed the cigarette away, climbed down off the tombstone and moved around to the overgrown path at the top of the bank. He watched as a lone figure walked briskly through the graveyard, a dark cap pulled down low over his face. Dougie was always worried that someone would recognise him.

Pascal clapped his hands together to keep warm. He didn't feel guilty about what he had done. He should have done it a long time ago. Edward was fucked. Even Patrick, the fucker, was nearing the end of his reign. By helping Dougie out, Pascal was looking out for his future. He had proved his worth. Dougie would see him right. It was survival of the fittest.

'I'm over here.'

The figure stopped in the shadow of the yew trees. Pascal waved to him. 'Quit fucking around, you bollocks. I don't think any of our present company would recognise you.' He laughed, shook his head and started to walk down the bank through the damp grass.

Dougie was still rooted to the spot. 'Hey, come on, will you?' Pascal called, irritated. 'I haven't got all fucking day. I've got to get back, I'm on shift.'

He climbed over the last patch of briar, stumbled and slid down the bank on his hip, coming to a stop inches from a patch of nettles. Pascal swore. The legs of his pants were saturated with dew. 'Jesus, you don't make anything easy, do you?' He pushed himself up off the ground and batted at his trousers angrily. 'I mean, for fuck's sake, why'd you want to meet in this fucking dump?'

He reached the yew trees and looked up. 'Hey, what the fuck are you doing here? What's going on? Where's Dougie?'

Davey Clarke stepped out from the shadows. 'The man's busy.'

'What the fuck's going on?' Pascal stepped back. 'How did you know I was going to be here?'

'How the fuck do you think?'

'Why would Dougie send you? I thought you were York's lackey.'

Davey stared at him with flat, cold eyes. 'I'm no one's anythin', bud, and don't you fuckin' forget it.'

Pascal raised an eyebrow and grinned slyly. 'Oh, I get it. You're playing all the sides. You're a crafty fucker, boyo, no doubt about it. Well, what am I here for?'

'Where's Naughton?'

'He's not missing if that's what you're sweating about.'

'Where is he?'

'You think I'm going to tell you? York would be there before I finished the fucking sentence.'

Davey sighed and backhanded Pascal across the face. Pascal's head rocked back and he stumbled but did not fall. He lunged at Davey and Davey hit him again. This time he went down.

'You fucking bastrard!' Pascal wiped at his mouth and stared up at the bouncer. 'You'll be sorry for this.'

'You old fucks are all the same, mouth mouth mouth.' Davey shrugged. 'Dougie want's to know where Naughton is.'

'Why doesn't he ask me himself?'

'I told you, he's busy.'

Pascal glared at Davey for a moment. He slowly got to his feet and wiped a drop of blood from his lip. 'All right, he's at my place.'

'Is Naughton gonna sell or what? Dougie's gettin' impatient, thinks Naughton might be tryin' to slide out of the deal.'

'Look, that's not going to happen.'

'Dougie's concerned.'

'He's nervous about his kid, that's all. He'll deal. Tell Dougie not to worry about it,' Pascal replied. 'That it?'

'If he backs out on us, do you know where he's got it stashed?'

'How the fuck should I know?'

'Naughton never told you?'

'Even if he did, you think I'd be telling you

shit?' Pascal lit a cigarette. 'Jaysus, what the fuck do you take me for?'

Davey smiled, reached into his pocket and pulled out a gun. 'Then what fuckin' use are you to me?' he said softly.

Pascal lifted his hands in front of his face and backed up. His cocksure sneer vanished. 'Hey, now, wait a minute – *wait*! What's—'

Davey lifted the gun and fired. The bullet punched through Pascal's hand and hit him square in the face with a dull squelching sound. It entered Pascal's soft palate and swung down for a few inches before exiting through his left cheek.

Pascal twisted and landed face down in the high, damp grass. Davey stepped forward, touched the gun to the back of his skull and shot him again. Pascal's body jerked up, twitched a couple of times and finally lay still.

Davey pushed his cap back and leaned down to study the cop. Satisfied that Pascal was well and truly beyond any kind of miraculous recovery, he turned away and headed back the way he had come.

While Davey Clarke was driving away from the graveyard, Sarah marched down Baggot Street like a woman with a purpose, her cheeks flushed with the cold, her long dark hair flying behind her. She had just come from Claudia and Megan's apartment, and her mood was at an all-time low.

The girls had been genuinely crushed when Sarah shoved the photo of their friend under their noses. Claudia in particular had wept openly. But they said they had no idea where the place could be, and in the end Sarah believed them. Actually, she had softened slightly towards them as they sat huddled together on the couch, looking less and less like the nightclub divas they thought they were and more like two frightened children in a situation they couldn't begin to understand. Her ire was now directed at at the person she was about to see.

She stopped outside the apartment building, checked the doorbells and rang the bell for the penthouse. A voice answered almost immediately.

'Yeah?'

'Open the door, Mr York. I want a word with you.'

'Mr York ain't here.'

'You want me to talk out here? Fine,' Sarah said coldly. She didn't bother leaning close to the intercom, and several people walking past glanced at her. 'I don't give a shit who hears what a deranged psycho you are. I don't know what Edward Naughton did to you and I don't give a shit, but I'm warning you: if you harm one hair on Ashley Naughton's head, I am going to go straight to the Gardaí and I am going to make sure you're the only person they look into.'

There was silence for a few seconds. Finally the voice said, 'Who the hell is this?'

'My name is Sarah Kenny. I'm an investigator with QuicK Investigations.'

'Well, Miss, you better come on up.'

The door clicked. Sarah hesitated for a split second, then entered the foyer of Vinnie York's apartment building.

On her way up in the lift, she tried to compose herself. This was madness, utterly ulike her, but whenever she thought of John's face and the girls crying, a flare of rage blazed through her like a white-hot light. John was right: it was time to see the organ-grinder.

She approached the penthouse with her heart knocking. As soon as she pressed the bell, the door opened and a man she'd never seen before grabbed the front of her jacket and yanked her inside.

'Stop!' Sarah struggled against him. The man ignored her, glanced out into the hall and slammed the door shut. He threw Sarah hard against the wall.

'Now, who the fuck do you think you are?'

Sarah was stunned from the impact, but she gathered her wits about her. 'I'm looking for Vincent York.'

'Yeah? Well, Vincent ain't here, cunt.' The man lifted his leg and kneed her in the stomach. 'I think I told you that already.'

Sarah reeled away from him. She dropped to her knees. 'You're Patrick York,' she gasped.

'How the fuck do you know who I am?' Patrick stopped pacing and stared at her.

Sarah took a deep breath and tried to keep her

voice from shaking. 'You can throw me around if you want, but you listen to me. I know you or your son has Ashley Naughton, and I swear, if anything happens to her—'

'You said all this shit already, too. Look, girlie, I don't know what the fuck you think you know, but let me make one thing clear to you: I don't know where the fuck the girl is. Got it?'

Sarah pulled the photo of Ashley out of her pocket and thrust it into Patrick's hands. 'Davey Clarke gave this photo to Margaret Naughton last night. So don't bother lying. We know you have her.'

Patrick stared at the photo for a long time. He stared at it for so long that Sarah began to babble nervously.

'Look, we were hired to find her, that's all… I don't care what you're doing over here, I don't care what deal you and Edward Naughton have going – that's none of my business. But that girl's mother is going out of her mind. She just wants her daughter back. She doesn't even want to involve the Gardaí. She just wants her girl back.'

'Shut the fuck up.' Patrick lifted his head and slammed his fist into the wall, inches from Sarah's head. Sarah gasped involuntarily and squeezed her eyes shut. 'Now, I'm telling you, I don't know jack about this.'

'I don't believe you.'

Patrick grabbed Sarah and jerked her close to him. She felt her legs begin to tremble. 'I don't

give a fuck what you believe. But I'll tell you this:
I'll look into it for you.'

'You'll look into it?'

'Yeah, I'll look into it. In the meantime, I don't
want to see your fucking face again.'

'I can't—'

'You tell Ed's old lady to back off. I'll find out
where her kid is. But if I see you again, I'm going
to rearrange that pretty face of yours. We clear?'

Sarah nodded.

30

Davey's house was a terraced ex-Council affair on a quiet residential street in Stoneybatter. John cased the place for a while to make sure the bouncer wasn't home. He didn't want any more run-ins with him, at least not until his face healed up.

It was dark, and the rain was picking up. John decided the time was right to make his move. He turned down a side street into a cul-de-sac, hefted himself over the wall of the house on the corner of Davey's road and dropped into the yard. He grunted on impact, but tightened the straps of his rucksack across his chest and ran swiftly across the yard. He had studied the houses carefully: there was nobody home in the first two, and only an elderly couple in the one next to Davey's. But he needed to work fast.

He scaled the wall on the far side of the first yard and peered over the top. There were only two more yards to go before he reached the back of Davey's house, and with any luck neither of them would hold a dog. Moving was incredibly painful and his back screamed in protest, but finally he dropped over the wall and made his way across the second yard.

'Shite!'

The wall had shards of broken glass embedded in cement running along the top – security Dublin style. Luckily, John had done his fair share of climbing. He dropped back down, slipped his rucksack from his shoulder and pulled out a thick blanket, which he unfolded and threw over the wall. He stuck his foot back in the crack, put the bulk of his weight on a half-grown fir tree and lowered his leg gingerly onto the blanket, praying he wouldn't end up singing soprano. With extreme caution he lifted his other leg over the wall and slid, as quietly as he could, down onto soft grass on the other side. He wiped the rain from his face, gritted his teeth and forced himself to keep moving.

He repeated the blanket trick on the far wall before finally dropping, wet but uninjured, into Davey Clarke's neatly paved back yard. He tugged the blanket down, refolded it and stuck it back into his bag.

The back of the house was in complete darkness. John crept along the back wall and checked the windows. None were open, and they were double glazed, but he couldn't see an alarm, and the 70s-style back door, complete with bubbled glass panels, looked invitingly easy.

John got the blanket and wrapped around his arm and smashed in the top pane of glass. He slipped his hand through the hole and drew back the sliding bolt on the inside of the door. It had taken him less than one minute to gain entry. He slipped inside, pulled the curtains and flipped on his torch.

Davey Clarke was not house proud, that much was obvious. The air in the small, dingy kitchen smelled stale and John's feet stuck to the faded lino. Dirty dishes were stacked high in and around the sink, and the kitchen table was covered with crumbs and well-thumbed weightlifting magazines. The sitting room was slightly better. It contained a nasty-looking three-piece suite, a sideboard, a wide-screen TV, a coffee table and a set of free weights. It was clear Davey didn't entertain much.

John tossed the room. In the middle drawer of the cheap coffee table he found a stack of ESB, cable and telephone bills. He scanned through them and was glad to see they were all paid by direct debit. Maybe Davey wouldn't mind if he borrowed an old phone bill. He looked through the sideboard quickly: nothing.

On the mantelpiece, John found a wooden box containing a Ziploc bag of grass and a pack of Rizla papers. He flicked the torch downwards – the fireplace was littered with twisted cigarette butts, tobacco and roach ends. John was surprised. He hadn't clocked Davey Clarke as the type who liked to kick back and smoke a little weed. He sniffed the grass and rolled his eyes in appreciation. It had been a long time since he'd smoked a joint. He wondered how long it would take to go through a bag this size. He put it back in the box.

John moved up the stairs and continued to search carefully and systematically. The bathroom was surprisingly neat. It was clean and the damp towels were hung neatly over a radiator to dry. The spare room doubled as a home gym, complete with bench weights and a rowing machine. A full-length mirror covered most of the wall opposite the bench.

In the master bedroom, an unmade king-size bed dominated the room. Davey had a portable television screwed onto a heavy wall bracket, with a brand new video recorder underneath. Some videos were stacked on top of the bedside locker. John flipped over the top one and grinned at the cover: Al Pacino holding a massive gun. *Scarface*; typical. He went through the rest of the tapes: nothing.

John opened the wardrobe and flicked through the clothes quickly. Like a lot of big men, Davey mostly wore tracksuits or jeans and T-shirts. The one decent suit John found was sealed in dry cleaner's plastic and didn't look like it saw the light of day too often. John rifled through a mound of dirty laundry piled up in the bottom of the wardrobe, grimacing at the smell of musty socks.

Next he turned his attention to the bedside locker. This contained many pairs of clean white sport socks, underwear and an open packet of Durex Extra Sensitive. John counted; there were none missing – surprise, surprise. He put the condoms back, bent down and shined the torch under the unmade bed, swinging it from left to right.

'Hello there.'

There was something under there, apart from an inch of dust and fluff. He reached in and pulled out an old leather suitcase with a brand-new, heavy-duty padlock snapped tight across the handles. John felt his interest rise.

He cradled the torch under his chin, hauled the suitcase into the middle of the floor and studied the lock. It was a heavy Triton model with a thick steel shunt, difficult to pick and almost impossible to break. Maybe Davey had been expecting visitors after all.

John ran downstairs and found a bread knife he'd noticed earlier in a kitchen drawer. He squatted beside the suitcase and, humming softly under his breath, sawed through the bases of the leather handles. The lock clattered harmlessly to the floor, still locked and as good as new.

John flipped the suitcase open and whistled softly under his breath. There were at least fifteen videos in there. He selected one, popped it into the video recorder and turned on the TV.

It was a homemade video of a party. People were dancing and talking, drinking, smoking. John grinned as he recognised one or two faces from national TV. Then he hit paydirt: a shaky shot of Claudia Delaney dancing on a table, a bottle of Jim Beam in one hand, a cigarette in the other, her eyes wide and unfocused. She was wearing nothing but a bra and a pair of red silk knickers. In the background, Vinnie York sat talking with another man on a sofa, his sardonic eyes watching Claudia with amusement. He grinned at the camera and waved it away.

The camera moved through the room, resting here and there on partygoers in various states of dress and drunkenness. John watched as whoever operated the camera put it down on a table and stepped in front of it. This must be the Richie Megan had mentioned. He was about nineteen, handsome, with floppy blond hair and a glazed, happy grin. When he spoke, his accent was educated and confident. He was pretending to be a commentator.

'Tonight, Mr Vincent York has provided us with entertainment on a grand scale,' Richie said to the camera. 'So tonight, for all your viewing pleasure, come with me to…ta-da! The pleasure zone.' He grinned again and disappeared from view. Seconds later he had hoisted the camera up and was moving off down the hall, opening doors and stepping into rooms.

In the first room, two giggling girls were chopping out lines of coke on a mirror, while a handsome boy of about seventeen, wearing a scarlet shirt open to the waist, looked on, casually smoking a cigarette. 'Get the fuck out, Richie!' one of the girls yelled, and tried to shield what they were doing. 'I swear, you're a fucking menace.'

'Hey, baby, be cool.' Richie laughed. 'Give us one for posterity.'

The girl flipped him the finger and continued chopping. The boy glanced at Richie and dropped the shoulder of his shirt. 'Richie, get a shot of me cherries.' He had a sing-song, effeminate voice.

Richie zoomed in on a fresh-looking tattoo. 'When you'd get that done?'

'Few days ago. What do you think?'

'Kind of small.'

'Now, now, Richie, *you* know it's not size that matters – don't you, hon?' The boy laughed and winked lewdly. The two girls started to laugh.

Richie coughed and shut the door. John stood up. He didn't have time to watch this all the way through. Davey might arrive back at any moment. He was about to eject the tape when, on screen, Richie opened the door of the second bedroom. John stopped, his finger in mid-air.

The camera grew shaky. Megan was flat on her back. A dark-haired, middle-aged man squeezed her small breasts and pushed into her again and again. Megan's arms were loose by her sides, her eyes open and rolling. Her legs were linked behind his back, but she didn't seem to realise what she was doing.

'Hey, man,' Richie said excitedly. 'Move around a bit. This is great.'

'Don't get my face,' the older man said. He turned his head away and slid down the bed, hauling Megan with him. Megan tried to grab at the covers, but Richie stepped forward and yanked them away. John could see Megan's face clearly now. She looked confused and out of it.

'Yeah, man, that's great – fucking great,' Richie said. 'Flip her over, get some doggy action.'

Megan blinked and tried to raise her head. She said, 'What?' in a confused voice.

'Hey, I told you, not my fucking face—'

John had seen enough. He ejected the tape and dropped it into his rucksack.

He wiped his hands on his tracksuit. He felt dirty, slimy. He stared at the other tapes for a few seconds. Were these more of the same – more girls caught up in a seedy world? He grabbed the whole lot and shoved them into his bag. Then he closed the lid of the suitcase, set the lock on top of it and pushed it back under the bed.

On his way out, he swung by the mantelpiece and pocketed the grass. He had already kicked the tiger's cage, there was no point in trying to be inconspicuous. Hell, it was good for pain – and Davey owed him.

Then he high-tailed it out of there as fast as his battered body could carry him.

When he got home, he wasn't the slightest bit surprised to find Sarah sitting on his doorstep, a Styrofoam cup of coffee steaming at her feet.

'You and me are going to have to talk about mobile phones, John,' she told him.

Edward Naughton pushed himself up from the sagging green sofa and paced around, as much as he could pace in the cramped mobile home. After three turns around the mangy brown carpet, he gave up and threw his body back on the sofa in frustration. He couldn't find anyone. There didn't appear to be anyone at his home, and Pascal wasn't answering his phone. What the hell was going on?

He was beginning to regret listening to Pascal Mooney. Pascal didn't know Patrick like he did. Patrick would take a seriously fucking dim view of him hiding out. It made him look as guilty as sin. Why had he allowed Pascal to bring him to this shit-hole – and why the hell had he told Pascal where the drugs were? Could he really trust a crooked bastard like Pascal Mooney about anything? Every word out of his mouth was always so carefully calculated and guarded. For all he knew, Pascal had collected the drugs and was on his way to either Patrick or Dougie. Goodbye middle man, hello riches.

Edward shook his head. The whole plan had been skew-whiff from the beginning. He had taken a huge gamble – and for what? For drugs he couldn't even move. Now he needed to take another gamble, if he wanted to have any chance of getting his daughter back alive.

Maybe the best thing he could do would be to throw himself on Patrick's mercy. Patrick would see to it that Ashley wasn't harmed; he'd rein Vinnie in. Maybe, Edward thought, that could be his way out of this mess: he could offer Patrick the

drugs back, as a trade. Sure, there would be reper-
cussions – but surely, once Patrick had the gear,
he'd find it in his heart to forgive him…

He thought of Patrick's face and swallowed
hard. Patrick would never forgive him; that was
ludicrous. The best he could hope for was that
Patrick would kill him quickly.

Maybe he could blame the whole thing on
Pascal? For a start, there was the whole question of
what had happened to Kelpie. Edward paced back
and forth. Pascal: now that was an actual idea.
Everyone hated cops, especially dirty ones. They'd
buy it. After all, Patrick and Edward went back so
far – and Edward couldn't be held responsible for
what Pascal did, now could he? Maybe he could
even make it look as though if it hadn't been for
him, they would have never found the cocaine. But
how would he explain where he'd been for the last
couple of days? Maybe he could say he'd had to lie
low to flush out the real person behind the drugs
heist…yeah, maybe that would be the way to go.

Of course, there was the other small problem
of what to do about Dougie. Dougie would want
his delivery. Edward frowned. One thing at a time.
For now, he just had to stay alive – and to do that
he'd have to make sure that Pascal was the fall guy,
but a silent one. He'd have to get rid of Pascal.

Edward chewed his knuckle. He wasn't a brave
man. He hated violence, and he wasn't particularly
good at it – not like Patrick. He preferred to let
others do his work for him. But this situation was

different. What choice did he have? It was either him or Pascal.

He glanced at his watch, feeling calmer than he had any right to be. It was pitch-black outside and his car was parked a good way behind the mobile home. He'd have to go and get it.

He was going home. He'd organise a meeting with Patrick immediately. They'd talk, come to some arrangement. He'd make sure Patrick understood that he'd had nothing to do with the theft. Patrick would have to accept his terms – he wasn't going to do a fucking thing until he got some assurance that he wouldn't be harmed and that his daughter would be returned in one very healthy piece.

He hurried down to the bedroom of the mobile to grab his coat. The bedroom was about the size of his bathroom at home, and the walls were damp and mottled with black mildew. The small double bed where he'd been sleeping looked crumpled and uninviting. Skirting around it, Edward yanked open the white Formica wardrobe and pulled his coat off a metal hanger. He was wedging the wardrobe shut again when he heard the front door open.

'About fucking time,' Naughton shouted. 'You're supposed to keep in contact, Pascal, not fuck off like that.' He scrambled around the bed. 'You know, I've been thinking. I'm not sure this is such a good idea, me staying here.'

He stepped into the hall and came face to face with Davey Clarke.

'How you doin'?'

'Fuck.'

For a fat man, Naughton reacted fast. He jumped back and tried to kick the bedroom door shut. But Davey was quicker. A heavily muscled arm shot out and hit Edward, a straight chop to the throat. Edward gagged and his legs buckled. The second blow hit him on the bridge of the nose. His head snapped back and he slipped into darkness. He slithered down the bed and came to an unnatural stop half in, half out of the bedroom door.

A second man stuck his head into the mobile and peered down at Edward Naughton's prone body. 'He out?'

Davey laughed. 'For the count.'

'What did you hit him for? We want to be able to talk to him.'

Davey shrugged. 'He'll come round.'

'You're a quare fella, Davey, no doubt about it. Go make sure there's no one else around this shitheap.'

Davey turned his head. 'There's no one.'

'Go make sure,' Dougie Burrows said, a note of steel creeping into his voice. 'I don't want no fuckin' cock-ups this close to the prize.'

Sarah stared at the tapes piled on the counter. 'You're stone mad. You know that, right? This guy kicks the shit out of you, and you break into his house?'

John handed her a fresh cup of coffee. 'You're

not much better. What were you thinking, going to York's gaff like that? Anything could have happened to you.'

'You don't see the irony in that, do you?'

'No. I don't.'

Sarah scratched behind Sumo's ears. 'I was so bloody angry – angry about you, Mrs Naughton, even about those stupid girls… I just wanted Vinnie York to know that he wasn't getting away with everything, that someone would stand up to him. I wasn't really expecting to have a confrontation with his father.'

'Guess you showed him.'

'The thing is, John, I think Patrick York was genuinely surprised by that photo. I know that sounds stupid, but I think he was.'

'Who knows? Maybe he's just a better actor than his son.'

'Maybe.'

'They know we're on to them,' John said thoughtfully, 'so they'll have to do something.'

'But who do we watch? Davey or the Yorks?'

'Both.'

'How?'

'Separate cars.'

Sarah sighed and ran her hand through her hair. 'I'll take Davey. He knows your face.'

'Or what's left of it,' John said, touching it gingerly.

'And this time we have to be in contact at all times.'

'Scout's honour.' John held up his fingers.

'Yeah, yeah, yeah,' Sarah said, and took a sip of coffee.

31

Edward woke up. He tasted blood in his mouth and felt someone's hands under his armpits. He was being dragged. He felt a hard surface scrape against his back. He groaned, feeling his pants slide further down his buttocks and his belt dig into the flesh of his hips. Finally he felt his back bump up against something, and he stopped moving.

'Ed, my boy, how's she cuttin'?' Dougie Burrows loomed into view.

'Dougie? What's going on?'

'Sorry about the entry. The big fella here gets carried away sometimes.'

Edward turned his head and blinked at a grim-faced Davey Clarke. The caravan suddenly seemed very tiny.

'What's he doing here?'

'He's what you might call a bit of a lever. Aren't you, Davey?'

Davey said nothing. He sat down on the saggy sofa and leaned his arms on his knees.

Edward eased himself up slightly. He felt queasy. A mild ribbon of pain circled his chest. His throat was burning and it was hard to swallow.

'What's going on?'

'Where's the coke, Ed?'

'What?'

'The coke. Where did you stash it?'

Edward rubbed his face. He could feel the ribbon tightening around his chest and a small tremor starting in his left hand. Maybe he had hit his head on the way down or something.

Davey slapped him across the face. Edward's head snapped back.

'The man asked you a question.'

'Dougie, why are you doing this?'

'Got a bad feelin' about yesterday, Ed – sort of a hunch that you'd try and weasel out on our deal.' Dougie pulled out his pipe and lit it, filling the caravan with sweet plumes of smoke. 'So, here's the deal: you tell me what the fuck you did with the coke, I'll pay you and everyone's happy.'

'Can't... Ashley.' Edward winced as pain shot up his arm. He tried to straighten up, but the vice-grip around his chest forced the air out of his lungs. Clouds of pain were rolling in across his body. Dougie's voice seemed very far away.

'Oh, don't worry about the young one. She'll be all right.'

Edward frowned. 'What?'

'Your little blondie one. Nice sort of a young one – has a bit of a mouth on her, mind, but sure they all do these days.' Dougie grinned at Edward. 'Need a firm hand, these young ones. Not so different from dogs: eat you one minute, all over you the next. You have to let them know who's the boss.'

Another spasm of pain, this one much worse, ripped down Edward's arm. His little finger jerked with it and he could feel his arm growing numb.

'So where's the coke?'

'Ashley…I…York has her.'

Dougie rolled his eyes. 'Faith, you and that fuckin' missus of yours must never talk. York doesn't have her, you gobshite.'

'What?'

'York doesn't have her.'

'Then where is she?'

'Where's the coke, Ed? Stop stallin' now, there's no point.'

'Answer him, you fuck!' Davey punched him again. Edward toppled sideways.

'Stop!' Dougie yelled, pushing Davey off. 'What the fuck are you hitting him for? He'll tell us – won't you, Ed? Ed?'

Edward stayed down, his cheek resting on the filthy carpet. There it was again, that bolt of pain – so sharp it was almost hot, like a poker jabbed straight into his heart. This time he didn't fight it.

Dougie dragged him into a sitting position again. Edward opened his eyes and stared into Dougie's face. His head flopped sideways and his peripheral vision was fading. He had trouble concentrating.

'Don't think about fuckin' playin' me, Ed. If you want the girl to see another day, you better tell me where the coke is.'

Edward felt another stab of agony. The ribbon tightened and did not release. The black clouds of pain rumbled on the horizon, and his vision blurred. He knew then it was all over for him. The only thing that mattered was Ashley. He saw her as she had been when she was small, not as the girl she was now. When she was small and he was Daddy, and he was the most important thing in her life.

'Baby,' he said, his mouth struggling with the word.

'There's something wrong with this prick.' Davey's voice came from far away; it sounded almost misty. Edward smiled at that.

'Ed! You tell me where the coke is, or I'll cut that girl's throat and feed her to the dogs, do you hear me?'

Edward closed his eyes. Funny, the pain wasn't so bad now – just hot, white-hot around his chest. He tried to speak, but he had difficulty getting the words from his head to his mouth. Maybe the connections were broken. Could that be it? He felt lighter, dizzy, filled with heat.

'Ed!' Dougie was shaking him and screaming. 'I'll kill her, I swear I will!'

Ah, but Ashley.

'The pond...I sunk it.' He hoped they'd heard that. He couldn't do it again. His head rolled forward until his chin rested on his chest.

'The pond? The fucking pond? Is that what you said? Did he say "pond", Davey?'

'Yeah, I think so.'

'Ed? You hear me, Ed? Did you say the pond?'

But Edward Naughton was gone.

'Fuck!' Dougie stood up and stared at him. 'Fuck.'

'Is he dead?'

'Of course he's fuckin' dead! What the hell did you keep hittin' him for?'

'You wanted him to talk, didn't you?'

Dougie stared at Davey. 'Well, for your sake, you better hope he was on the level with us – because if he wasn't, then we don't have any fuckin' idea what he did with the fuckin' coke.'

Davey grunted.

'Jesus, this is a fucking mess.' Dougie relit his pipe and thought for a second. 'Okay, get him into the boot of the car. We're going to go there and have a look around.'

'Now?'

'Yes, fuckin' now.'

Vinnie York was in his office, drinking a vodka and Red Bull, when his mobile rang. He reached for it glumly. 'What?'

'How's she cuttin', Vin?'

Vinnie sat up straight. 'Dougie?'

'Aye. I have somethin' for you.'

'What?'

'Somethin' you've been lookin' for.'

Vinnie's hands began to tremble. 'Are you telling me that you have the delivery?'

'Aye, I am.'

'Oh, sweet mother of fuck.'

'Thought you might be happy about that.'

'It is all there?'

'It is indeed.'

'But how? When? Where was it? Did—'

'No more questions for the moment. I wouldn't be doin' much talkin' over the mobile, if you know what I mean.'

'Oh, right – right. Oh, *mon ami,* you don't know what this means to me.'

'I have a fair idea. Now, are you gonna keep your end of the bargain?'

Vinnie smiled. 'If I have to wrap a bow around his neck.'

'Good. Bring him down my way later on. Give me a bell, let me know when you're leavin'.'

Vinnie hung up and whooped. He danced around the office, kicking his heels into the air. Suddenly the world was a wonderful place again, full of wonder and possibilities. He grabbed his mobile.

'Davey? It's me.'

'Boss?'

'Good news, *mon ami.* Our scruffy dog-fucker called. He has located the shipment.'

'He has?'

'Yes. You see? I told you going to him was a smart move.'

'I guess you were right.'

'Now I have to get Patrick down there

somehow. Shit, that's going to be tricky – he's so suspicious at the moment.'

'You could tell him I've located Naughton.'

Vinnie smiled. 'I could indeedy. That would get him moving.'

'I'll head down too, make sure there's no problems.'

'Excellent.' Vinnie shivered with anticipation. 'Oh, Davey, the lion will roar again.'

'Yeah.'

'I bid you *adieu*,' Vinnie sang, and rang off. He turned to the mirror, barely able to contain his glee. He had thought it was a long shot, but he had got it right. Was there any more proof needed that he was indeed the king?

'Time to celebrate,' he told his reflection. 'The king is dead, long live the king.'

He shot himself with two index fingers and toddled off to find his emergency stash of cocaine.

32

Sarah wiped at the condensation on the Fiesta's windscreen and shivered. The temperature had dropped dramatically in the last hour, and she was freezing.

She was also bored out of her skull. Stakeouts were never her forte at the best of times, and this one seemed plain stupid. Davey Clarke hadn't shown up, and she was beginning to feel foolish. Her earlier adrenalin had long since vanished and her doubts had returned. What the hell was she doing, sitting outside Davey Clarke's house in a car that had no insurance? They were way out of their depth. She would have laughed at the ludicrousness of her situation if it hadn't been so pathetic.

She wrapped her scarf tighter around her throat and blew on her hands. God, it was freezing. Where the hell was Clarke? She wasn't going to sit here all night watching an empty house, that was for sure. It didn't matter to John what she thought or said; once he got the bit between his teeth, he was off and running, no matter how harebrained the scheme. It wouldn't be the first time he'd got them into trouble doing things 'his way', either. It was as if he didn't understand her concerns – or if he did, he chose to ignore them.

She watched one of Davey's neighbours step out of his house, dragging a small, scruffy West Highland terrier behind him. The dog seemed reluctant to venture out in the cold, and Sarah didn't blame it. She grinned as it dropped its hindquarters and dragged its feet. The man gave a sharp tug on the lead and the dog relented and trooped off after him, its whole body curved in protest. Sarah sighed and went back to staring at the front of Davey's house. She had been there two hours now: nothing. And if he did come back, so what? It wasn't as if she really expected him to lead her to Ashley.

Whenever Sarah thought of Ashley, she thought of her as a hostage; she didn't want to think any other way. As a hostage, Ashley had value and was probably still alive – at least until the Yorks got whatever they wanted from Edward Naughton, Sarah thought sourly. What kind of man went to ground when his family was in danger? Or maybe he hadn't; maybe something had happened to him. *God*, Sarah thought miserably, *I wish we had just called the Gardaí and been done with it, let them worry about it all.*

Her mobile phone vibrated.

'Hey, it's me.'

'Hey, John.'

'Anything doing?'

'Nada. He's still not back.'

'I wonder where he is?'

'Dunno, not at the club, either,' Sarah said. 'How are you feeling?'

'Sore.'

'Well, if it's any consolation, I'm freezing to death here.'

John laughed. 'I know, it's not any better over here.'

'York still in the apartment?'

'Yeah – probably sitting by a nice hot fire, drinking brandy, as we speak.'

'This is bullshit. I've been here for hours. Who knows where he is? What if he doesn't come home at all?'

'Sarah, you said you'd watch him.'

'I said I'd watch *him*, not his house. Where are you parked? I'm coming over.'

'No, you're not. You'll stay where you are.'

'At least you know Vinnie York is in his house. This is a waste of time! I'm coming over.'

John sighed. There was no point arguing with her sometimes.

Patrick York sat in an alcove in Gig's Place, a small late-night café in Portobello. He was absent-mindedly picking candle grease off the table as he listened to the man seated opposite him recounting Davey's actions over the last couple of days. The excellent steak he'd ordered was pushed to one side, barely touched. The vodka, however, was going down a treat.

The man said his name was Sean. He was barely out of his teens. He was slim, lightly built, dark-haired, with flat black eyes. He was well dressed, but not showy; the suit was black, the shirt a metallic grey. His hair was neither too short nor too long, he wore no jewellery and he was clean-shaven. He was so average-looking he was remarkable, and Patrick guessed it would take serious hard work to give a good description of him, which made him invaluable in his line of work. He had no known loyalties, except to whoever was paying his tab. Alonso had recommended him highly, and Patrick could see why. He was impressed that someone so young could be so coolly professional. It seemed all the more impressive when he thought of the shambles that was his son, Vinnie.

When Sean finished speaking, Patrick nodded and threw back his vodka in one swift gulp. 'You sure the fat man was dead?'

'I can't be sure of anything, but they put him in the boot of an old-style beige Toyota, licence number 617 LNI. The car is now parked behind the cottage I told you about. The fat man was still there one hour ago. I doubt he's alive.'

'And they definitely took something out of the pond.'

'Yes. From my position I couldn't be sure what they retrived, but it was heavy.'

Patrick nodded again. He knew what they'd got their filthy hands on. He closed his eyes for a moment, thinking. Ed had betrayed him. And Vinnie was working with fucking Dougie Burrows. What a bunch of vipers they were, the lot of them.

'Give me the layout of the place again. I want to know all the ins and outs.'

Sean leaned forward and spent a few minutes describing every relevant detail of Dougie Burrows's house. Patrick asked only one question, and by the end he was extremely satisfied.

'You know,' Sean said, 'there was another man following Clarke the other night.' He described John and what had happened at the Naughtons' house.

Patrick waved his arm. 'It's this pansy-arsed detective agency Margo Naughton brought in. They still chasing him?'

'No.'

'Then fuck them – amateurs. You bring me the other thing I asked for?'

Sean slid a small grey duffle bag across the table. He did nothing to hide his actions, and nobody in the café paid the slightest bit of attention. 'Everything you asked for. American-bought .38 – clean, no previous use in this country, been cleaned and checked, extra rounds in case you need them.'

Patrick took the bag and put it under the table at his feet. 'Tell me, how's the boss?'

'Alonso sends his regards.'

'Business good?'

Sean inclined his head a fraction but didn't answer. Patrick understood: it was none of his business. He reached into the inside pocket of his jacket, extracted a brown envelope and slid it across the table. 'It's all there.'

'Of course it is.' Sean smiled without a trace of humour. 'Will you need any more of my services tonight?'

Patrick shook his head.

'It's been a pleasure.' He slid out of the booth and walked out of the café into the night.

Patrick felt his phone vibrate again in his shirt pocket. He didn't answer. He knew who it was; Vinnie had been calling him all night. But he needed some time – time to compose himself, time to come to terms with what had to be done. He ordered another vodka from the bored-looking waitress and settled back in his seat.

33

Vinnie was considering whether to chop out another line when he heard the front door slam. He leaped up from his cowhide chair and slipped the wrap back into his suit pocket. He opened his bedroom door and peered out. 'Patrick?'

'Yeah?' Patrick came down the hall, his hands in the pockets of his coat, his cap still on. He had ditched the bag in a bin outside Gig's.

'Oh, *mon dieu* – there you are. I've been trying to reach you for ages. Why haven't you returned any of my calls? Where have you been?'

'Here and there. Any word on Naughton?'

'That's why I've been trying to reach you. Davey's found where he's been hiding out.'

Patrick stared at Vinnie. 'You're shitting me.'

'No, he's watching him right now.'

'Is he sure it's Naughton?'

'Yes, Naughton. Jesus, what's wrong with you?'

'How did Davey find him?'

'I don't know. Someone probably called him, he went to check, and *voilà*.'

'*Voilà*?'

'Yes, *voilà*, it was Naughton.'

'And he's there now?'

'He is. Don't worry, he won't be going any-where. Davey will call if he moves.' Vinnie brushed imaginary lint off his shoulders. He couldn't be sure it wasn't just the cocaine making him paranoid, but there was something off about the way Patrick was looking at him, almost sizing him up. Maybe he shouldn't have had that last half.

'Ring him,' Patrick said.

'What?'

'Ring Davey. I want to be sure it's Naughton.'

'I assure you—'

'Ring the big fucker, will you, Vincent?'

'All right.' Vinnie pulled his mobile out of his shirt pocket and dialled Davey's number. 'Davey, it's me. Look, are you *absolutely* sure it's Naughton in the house? … Uh-huh… No, Patrick was—'

Patrick yanked the phone out of Vinnie's hand. 'Davey?'

'Yeah,' Davey said.

'You sure it's Naughton?'

'Sure as shit. He went in a couple of hours ago carryin' groceries and shit. Reckon he's plannin' to stay a while.'

Patrick nodded. 'Where is this place?'

'Already gave the address to Vinnie.'

'Sit tight;,we're on our way. Oh, and Davey? Good work. I'll make sure you're well rewarded for this.'

'Yeah. Thanks.'

Patrick passed the phone back to Vinnie. 'We better get a move on.'

Vinnie tried to hide his delight. He had thought it would be much more difficult than this. 'Yes, absolutely, we should.'

'You seem very jumpy, Vincent. You're not floating again, are you?'

'Of course not,' Vinnie said, as though the very notion appalled him.

'We don't know what might go down tonight. You need to have your fucking wits about you. We both do.'

'I'm fine.'

'You don't look fine. You're all sweaty and shit, and your eyes are like two piss-holes in the snow.'

'I'm fine.'

Suddenly Patrick threw his arm over Vinnie's shoulders, a gesture that almost spooked Vinnie into flight. ''Cause you know, it's you and me, lad. I know we've had a rough couple of days, but we're family, ain't we?'

Vinnie tried to ease out of Patrick's grip. 'We are family, yes.'

'And family sticks together. Right?'

'Indeed.'

'So what are we waiting for? Let's roll.'

Vinnie nodded, unable to trust his voice. He had a sudden urge to lash out at Patrick. His mind flashed back to himself at eleven, taking a beating from his foster father for using the last of the milk. And now Patrick was going on about *family*... It was a bit late in the day for that line. Family meant nothing to Vinnie. Even the word made him want to vomit.

'Tell you what,' Patrick said, 'I'm gonna ring the Turkish fucker first, let him know we've got a line on the gear.'

'Right, you do that. Make sure they know Naughton was behind it.'

'What?'

'Oh, nothing.' Vinnie took a step back into his room, then stepped out again.

Patrick frowned. 'You're making me nervous, the way you're hopping about.'

Vinnie forced himself to stop moving. Patrick's body language seemed to take on a new malice, and his eyes were full of weighted meaning. Vinnie tried to swallow. Shit, he really should have waited before doing the second wrap... 'Well, make sure you tell them we're going to Naughton's hide-out. Make sure they know Naughton was the one who had it.'

'Why do you keep saying that?'

'I just want them to know I had nothing to do with it vanishing.'

'See, now, I don't see how that's a problem.' Patrick rested his hands on Vinnie's shoulders and narrowed his eyes. 'Why would anyone think you were behind it? Vincent, you're my son. A son would never fuck over his father.'

Vinnie felt the hairs on the back of his neck rising. 'Well, of *course* not.'

'Then I'll make the call and we'll be on our way.'

'Right – good, good.'

'Man, they're going to be so fucking relieved we've found it, you've no idea.' Patrick hurried down the hall.

Vinnie waited until he heard his father moving about the guest room before he moved. He backed into his bedroom and dialled Davey's mobile frantically.

'Davey, it's me. We're on our way. Make sure you get down there first. Tell Dougie I'll be there in about an hour. Tell him to be ready.'

'Right.'

Vinnie paced the room. He was nervous and excited. Oh, to be finally free of Patrick, to have control of the supply route… He'd easily win the Turks back over, especially when they learned of Patrick's untimely death and Naughton's betrayal. Especially when he found their gear.

'I know he's your old man and all, but fuck, Yorkie, he brought this shit on himself,' Davey said suddenly, mistaking Vinnie's silence for doubt. 'He shouldn't have let this situation get so fucked up.'

'My sentiments exactly, *mon ami*,' Vinnie replied airily. He didn't want Davey thinking that he had no balls, that he couldn't see that for himself. 'Can you get me something to hold?'

'A piece? You?' Davey couldn't keep the incredulity out of his voice.

Vinnie scowled. 'Is that a problem?'

'Nah, man, but—'

'Then get me something. If you get there first, leave it under the driver's seat of your car. I'll find it.'

Vinnie snapped the phone shut and ran his hands over his clammy face. His stomach knotted and twisted. He tasted bile at the back of his throat and for a moment, despite his bravado, he thought he was going to throw up. He took some deep breaths and let them out slowly. Maybe he needed another line after all, to calm his nerves. He whipped out the wrap and, without bothering to chop out a line, snorted a third of it up his left nostril and another third up his right. He looked at the remainder; it was pointless to keep such a small amount. He swallowed it and rubbed the residue on his gums.

Patrick knocked. 'You ready or what?'

Vinnie flung the wrap in the bin and tried to smooth his hair. His gums were numb. He threw open the door and beamed at Patrick.

Patrick gave him a look of sheer impatience. He zipped up his leather jacket and fixed his cap more firmly on his head. 'You ready?'

Vinnie smiled. 'Oh, I'm ready. Ready as I'll ever be.'

'Vincent, do me a favour: at least brush the fucking nose candy out of your beard before you leave the house.'

Davey hung up and smiled. 'He's coming'

'Of course he is. That little fucker wouldn't miss an opportunity like this.'

'He wants a gun.'

Dougie started to laugh. 'Oh, does he? Well, sure, we may as well give him one, so.'

'Are we ready?'

'I've been ready for years.' Dougie pulled out a cloth bag from under his chair. He opened it and extracted another bundle of cloth, from which he produced a well-oiled Beretta. 'See this? This was my brother's. They don't even make these any more.'

'Nice-lookin' gun,' Davey agreed.

'It is, and I'm gonna see to it that this nice-lookin' gun takes the head clean off that fuckin' ratbag Patrick York. A kind of fittin' tribute, wouldn't you say?'

'Sure.'

'There's a Glock under the chair you're sittin' on. Take it out, and don't shoot yourself with it.'

Davey stood up and found the Glock. 'I don't need a gun.'

'You don't know what you need.'

'I can handle myself. Patrick's past it.'

'One thing I've learned over the years is you can never be too sure of anythin'. Take it, just to be on the safe side.'

Davey slipped the gun into the waistband of his trousers.

*

Sarah jabbed John in the ribs and inclined her head. 'See, I knew there'd be at least some action this side of town. There they are.'

John opened his eyes blearily. He had been dozing behind the steering wheel. 'They could be going anywhere. Maybe they're getting something to eat.'

'At one o'clock in the morning? Don't be stupid.'

They watched as Vinnie and Patrick climbed into a Mercedes. Vinnie gunned the engine and tore up the street, wheel screeching.

Sarah jabbed John in the ribs again. 'Let's go. We're going to lose them.'

'If you do that again, I'm going to dump you out on your arse,' John said. He started the engine and did a U-turn in the middle of the street. He was so sore he thought he was going to throw up, but he didn't want to mention it to Sarah. He didn't want to worry her.

34

The drive was pure torture for Vinnie. By the time they reached the motorway he was so high he could barely blink, let alone drive. He couldn't stop grinding his teeth and clicking his tongue off the roof of his mouth, either. His hands shook on the wheel of the rented Mercedes, and for some reason his legs kept cramping, making him accelerate in bursts. The silent, brooding Patrick wasn't making the journey any easier. Vinnie glanced at his father's tense profile and shuddered slightly. He was convinced that the silence was a trick, that Patrick could sense the excitement and anxiety flowing from him in waves, that any minute he would turn around and scream, 'I know what you're planning!'

Vinnie returned his eyes to the road just in time to avoid hitting the roundabout in Ashford. The car's tyres squealed on the wet road as he grappled with the wheel. By the time he shot out the other side of the roundabout, he had broken into a sweat.

'For fuck's sake, watch the road,' Patrick snapped. 'We don't want to end up minced before we get there.'

'This must be quite a thrill for you.' Vinnie slowed down from eighty mph to seventy-five. 'It's so different now, hmm, after all those years of roadworks? Well, *sacré bleu*, what a huge job that was! It must look very different from how you remember it.' Vinnie knew he was babbling, but he couldn't stop himself. 'All fields back then, eh?'

'I told you before to quit that French shit.' Patrick snapped on his seat belt and glowered at him. 'Just quit talking altogether. Get us there in one piece and shut the fuck up. Yak, yak yak…Jesus fucking Christ!'

Vinnie gripped the steering wheel hard and put his foot down. Let the old bastard sit there like a corpse, for all he cared. That was exactly what he would be in another hour, so let the prick practise. They drove on in silence.

Vinnie turned off the main road and drove slowly along a narrow country road. He passed through silent villages and dark, desolate open stretches, and with every mile his sense of paranoia grew stronger. The beech trees on either side of the road were eerie and skeletal in the sweep of his lights. He wasn't nervous about what he planned to do, he tried to convince himself, but about how difficult it might prove to do it. Patrick was no idiot at the best of times, and Vinnie sensed that he was well on his guard.

'I used to like the countryside when I was younger,' Patrick said suddenly, causing Vinnie's hands to jerk on the wheel.

449

'Did you?' Vinnie said weakly.

'Used to go down this way when we was kids – me, Ed and a fella called Albert Burrows.' Patrick glanced at him for a long moment before resuming his study of the passenger window. 'We had a laugh back then, before everyone split up – Albert disappeared and Ed got married. I never liked the stuck-up bitch. Don't know what the fuck Ed ever saw in her. Old Ice-Box, he used to call her, said it was like riding an iceberg.'

'I see.' Vinnie blanched. He'd forgotten all about Naughton, and didn't like to think of him having sex; his stomach wasn't able for it.

After another quarter of a mile Vinnie recognised the half-crushed six-bar gate lying against the ditch that signalled the beginning of Dougie's lane.

'This is it,' Vinnie squeaked. He braked hard and turned right. The lane was so narrow that the overgrown hedges scraped against the car. In his eagerness to be free from confinement, Vinnie accelerated too quickly, and he and Patrick were thrown about like ball bearings.

Patrick grabbed the handgrip over the door. 'Slow down! Are you trying to kill us?'

'Sorry.'

'Take it easy, Vincent. We don't know what's down here.'

'That's true.' Vinnie pressed his lips together and willed himself to calm down.

They bounced over another half-mile of

potholes, then the lane widened and the lights of the Mercedes picked out a vehicle parked across the gate of a field.

Patrick stuck a cigar into his mouth and lit it with the dashboard lighter. 'Stop here.'

Vinnie slowed the car and pulled up the handbrake.

'Who owns the van?' His father nodded towards the van. It was a dusty black Transit with blacked-out windows.

'I'm not sure,' Vinnie said truthfully. He cut the engine. 'Maybe it belongs to Naughton.'

Patrick glanced at the Transit and back at Vinnie. Vinnie attempted a smile. Was he being fanciful, or did Patrick look a little scared?

'Where's Clarke?'

'There he is.' Vinnie pointed: Davey Clarke, clad in his usual uniform of black jeans and bomber jacket, was climbing out of the passenger side of the van. 'It must be Davey's, then.'

'Go see what's happening. Find out where Naughton is.'

Vinnie got out of the car and rolled his neck from one side to the other, feeling it crack. He kept his face flatly neutral. He felt Patrick's gaze follow his every move. 'Davey.'

'Boss.'

'Where's Naughton?'

Davey jerked his head backwards. 'The cottage is right around the bend there.'

Vinnie felt his legs tremble. He pinched the

bridge of his nose and forced himself to breathe deeply until he had the composure to respond. 'You mean…'

'Yeah, everything's back on track.'

'What about my…er…'

'When Patrick comes with me, check out the van – left wheel arch. You'll find what you need there.'

'Okay, okay, okay.' Vinnie nodded vigorously. He pressed his hand against his chest, took a deep breath. 'I must think like the lion, Davey. The law of the jungle: be merciless, be brave, lead by example.'

Davey nodded, anxious to get moving. 'Yeah, do that.'

'After all, Davey, time and tide wait for no man, and this is my moment. Let's just say that after this *coup de grace*, everything will be *comme il faut*.' Vinnie racked his tired, addled brain for more expressions and came up blank.

Patrick got out of the Merc. 'What the fuck're you two whispering about? Where's Naughton?'

Vinnie reached out one shaking hand and squeezed Davey's shoulder. '*Bonne chance, mon ami.*'

'Yeah.' Muscles bunched in Davey's neck, and he looked away. Jesus Christ, there was no end to the crap Vinnie could spout. 'Better move, he's getting edgy.'

Vinnie turned and called to Patrick, 'Davey says Naughton is holed up in a cottage around the corner.'

Patrick stared at Davey. 'He alone?'

'Yeah.' Davey shrugged. His small eyes held no expression Patrick could read.

Patrick glanced towards the shadows and wondered where Dougie Burrows was hiding out. A hard rain began to fall, splattering off the gravel and the roof of the car.

'Are you coming?' Vinnie repeated impatiently.

Patrick looked between Vinnie and Davey and made a decision. 'Yeah.' He closed the car door and strode up the lane. Just before he stepped out of range of the headlights, he turned back. 'Vincent, toss me the keys of that car.'

'What?' Vinnie said. 'Why?'

'Gimme the fucking keys.'

'Give him the keys,' Davey muttered. 'You'll get them back.'

Scowling furiously, Vinnie tossed Patrick the keys of the Merc. Patrick caught them one-handed. 'And turn off those fucking lights. Davey, come on, let's get this show on the road.'

He rounded the corner and disappeared into the night.

Vinnie grabbed Davey's arm. 'You see? He's jumpy.'

'You think he suspects something?'

'No, but watch him anyway.'

Davey felt under his bomber jacket. He was glad he had heeded Dougie's advice and kept the Glock with him. 'Don't worry, he won't know what hit him.'

453

★

As soon as Patrick entered the darkness, he began to feel better. Back in the glare of the headlights, he had felt vulnerable, but here he was on a more level playing field. Unless Dougie used night-vision equipment, he was safe in the dark. Clearly the ambush was set up to happen at the house. Maybe Dougie meant to trap him inside, have Davey jump him before he got a chance to think; it would be less risky that way. Vinnie had been happy enough to stay behind, so his job had been simply to deliver Patrick, and he had done it. That narrowed the odds considerably.

Vinnie felt under the wheel arch. His fingers closed around the gun Davey had left for him. He pulled it out and stared at it. Vinnie didn't know the first thing about guns, but that didn't dampen his excitement. It was black, it was heavy, it stank of oil and it looked authentic. He held it out and turned it sideways, gangster style. Simply holding it gave him a thrill.

'Pow,' he said, twirling it around his index finger. 'Pow.'

Then he slipped it into his waistband, switched off the car lights and began to walk.

John stopped the car at the end of the lane. 'Well?'

Sarah glanced into the darkness. 'Well what? I saw the brake lights when we came over the crest of that hill. I don't see where else they could have turned off, do you?'

'No.' John stared out his window, trying to see through the inky darkness. The lane was little more than a rutted track with grass growing up the centre. The hedges on either side were thick, taller than him and completely overgrown. He didn't like the look of it at all. 'Do we drive down or walk?'

'I don't know.'

'It looks kind of narrow. If we did meet some-one coming the other way, we'd have to reverse all the way back to here.'

'They might hear us if we drive down.'

'On the other hand, we don't know how long it is.'

'It can't be that long. Anyway, if we drive down they'll see the lights.' Sarah chewed on her lip. 'I suppose we'd better park and walk down, then.'

John parked further down the road, pulling the Manta as far into the ditch as possible. Then he and Sarah got out and began to make their way down the lane. They hadn't gone ten feet when a heavy rain began to fall.

'Typical,' Sarah muttered, and hunched deeper into her coat. 'John, slow down. This ground is really mucky.'

'They have to be up to something,' John whispered. 'Come on, Sarah, maybe this is where they're keeping Ashley. Or maybe Edward Naughton's here.'

'Yeah, or maybe they just felt like a late-night

drive. Maybe this is just a wild goose chase,' Sarah said, but she sped up a little.

They walked in silence for a while. The going was getting harder; the surface of the lane was waterlogged and treacherous with mud. Although she tried to keep to the grass in the middle of the track, Sarah slipped and slid constantly, falling to her knees at one point and getting covered in freezing mud for her trouble.

She was beginning to regret her descision to leave Dublin when they rounded a bend and almost collided with the back of the Mercedes.

'Shit,' John said softly. He grabbed Sarah's arm and hauled her into the ditch. Icy drops of water fell from the brambles and branches as they pressed into the foliage. 'Shh.'

'There's no one in the car,' Sarah whispered after a few seconds. 'I can hear the engine ticking.'

John let out a deep breath. 'Where the hell are they, then?'

'Do you think they knew they were being followed?'

'I don't think so. I did my best not to get too close, but it's hard on these back roads.'

'I think there's another car over there.'

John wiped the rain from his face. His night vision was improving slightly. 'I see it, it's a van or something. You stay there for a second.'

'Why? Where are you going?'

'I'm just going to have a look, nothing else.' He stepped out into the lane.

'John, wait!' Sarah said, a note of fear in her voice.

'What?'

'Be careful.'

Davey and Patrick made their way up the lane. It was almost pitch-black, but Patrick's eyes were beginning to grow accustombed to the dark. They made no pretence of camaraderie. Both of them were fully aware that they despised each other.

They entered a small cobbled yard. The cottage, small and derelict-looking, stood in the centre, only a few feet away. A light shone in the window to the left of the door.

'He's in there,' Davey said. Patrick clenched his jaw. In the car on the way down, he had been sweating, filled with dread, but now that he was here, an icy calm had descended on him. His hands were rock-steady, his senses tuned to pick up any tiny signal. It seemed to him that he could almost read Davey Clarke's thoughts through his eyes.

'Okay. We go up to the door, I'll open it and you rush him,' he said.

Davey hesitated for a second. 'I should probably go round back, try and find another way in.'

'Nah, straight in – he'll never expect that.'

'I'll go round back in case he bolts.'

Patrick took his gun from the waistband of his trousers and touched it to the back of Davey's head. Davey froze.

'We're going to do it my way. We don't want any surprises, do we?'

'What are you doin'?'

'Shut the fuck up.'

Patrick shoved Davey ahead of him to the front of the house, keeping his ears trained for any sound. 'Open the fucking door, and do it slow.'

Davey didn't move. Patrick jammed the gun into the base of his spine. 'Don't think I won't use this.'

Davey dropped his shoulders and opened the front door. Patrick stepped in behind him, using him as a shield.

The first thing Patrick saw was Dougie Burrows, at the head of a massive, paper-strewn table, aiming a double-barrelled shotgun at the door. The second thing he saw was a huge black shape with teeth, soaring through the air at breakneck speed. Davey flinched, but Patrick brought up his gun and shot the rottweiler at point-blank range. The huge dog bucked silently and crashed to the floor, sliding to a halt inches froom Davey's feet, half her muzzle torn away.

'Fuckin' hell,' Davey said.

Patrick grabbed Davey by the back of his neck and manoeuvred him into the room. 'Put the gun down, Dougie.'

'Well, there's no foolin' you, you bollocks. Come on in and have a pew,' Dougie said sourly. He couldn't get off a decent shot, so he lowered the shotgun and rested it over his knee. He looked at the body of his dog and shook his head sadly. 'I told you, Davey, lad, this hoor's been around. He don't fall easy.'

'Doug.' Patrick nodded to him. 'I figured you'd be here. You want to put that piece of metal down altogether, before I blow you out of that chair.'

Dougie's eyes glittered. He leaned down and gently placed the shotgun on the tiled floor.

'Thanks. Now kick it over this way.'

Dougie kicked the gun across the floor and looked at Davey. Patrick noticed and understood the furtive signal. He patted Davey down expertly, removed the Glock handgun from his waistband and slipped it into his own jacket pocket. Then he smashed Davey behind the ear with a vicious downward swipe of his own gun. Davey grunted and toppled over onto the floor.

'That boy's gonna be fierce fuckin' sore when he wakes up,' Dougie observed. 'He's already taken a knock to the head this week.'

'Pity about him.' Patrick stepped over Davey, picked up the shotgun and put it on the sideboard behind him. 'Tell me something: where did you put my coke?'

'I don't know what the fuck you're talkin' about.'

Patrick smiled, raised the gun and pointed it at Dougie's legs. 'Take your pick. Left or right?'

'Patrick, I—'

Patrick shot him in the left leg, just above the knee. Dougie howled and flung himself out of the chair. He fell to the ground, clutching his leg and writhing in agony.

'Now, are you going to tell me what I want to know, or will I aim a little higher next time? Where's my—'

'Did you get him?' Vinnie kicked the door open and burst through it like a madman, a huge, ugly gun in his outstretched hand. He skidded to a halt, wild-eyed and staring, saw Patrick and gave a little startled squeak. Then he pointed the gun at Patrick and pulled the tigger.

The gun clicked as the hammer fell on an empty chamber.

Patrick raised his own gun and pointed it at Vinnie. Vinnie was sweating, and his eyes were black. The irises had been swallowed up by the pupils. In fact, he looked so coked up that Patrick was surprised he was still standing.

'What's wrong, son? Things ain't working out as you expected?'

'What?' Vinnie stared at Davey, who lay in a pool of dog blood, making strange, wet snoring noises. He blinked hard and wiped at his face, unable to grasp what he was seeing. Dougie was still rolling around the floor, cursing and holding his leg.

'Jesus Christ.' Vinnie backed up and massaged his temples. He had done another bump of cocaine out in the garden for courage, and he was three feet high and rising. His heartbeat was uncomfortably loud in his ears. He pointed the gun at Patrick and lowered it again. 'You…'

Patrick stared at his son. 'Vincent, you really are a dumb shit. You didn't think they'd arm you, did you?' he said, his voice mild and reasonable, as if the gun in his son's hand didn't exist.

'What? What?' Vinnie blinked at him. 'I don't understand.'

'Did you really think they were going to cut you in?'

Vinnie blinked again and looked down at Davey's unconscious body in confusion. 'Who? "They" who?'

'Davey was working with Dougie.'

'What?' Vinnie exhaled hard. He was finding it increasingly hard to think. 'What are you saying?'

'I know everything. I know you killed Eddie, Doug.' Patrick stepped on Dougie's shin. He jerked his head towards Davey. 'Well, either you or that fucker did it. But I'm curious, Doug: why am I here? Why didn't you just have me killed when you had the chance? Jesus, this one could have done it for you while I slept.'

Vinnie's hand wobbled crazily. 'He...I...'

Dougie snorted sharply. He wiped strings of saliva from his mouth and clutched at his bloody leg. 'He hasn't the balls to do it.'

'Shut up!' Vinnie screeched, and swung his gun toward Dougie, forgetting it was empty.

'I see.'

Vinnie waved a hand vaguely. 'I don't know what the fuck is going on here. Why are you saying Davey is working for Dougie? Davey works for *me*.'

Patrick grinned. 'Ask Dougie where the coke is.'

Vinnie wiped the sweat out of his eyes and glared at Dougie. He flung the empty gun down. No point in holding it now. 'Well, is it here?'

'Nice try, lad, but you won't back out that easy.' Dougie Burrows stared at Vinnie with loathing etched across his face. 'You know damn well it is. Isn't that why you brought your old man here? We were going to do a trade. Are you trying to back out of it now?'

Dougie stared at Vinnie balefully. Vinnie dragged his eyes away from Dougie and forced himself to concentrate on his father's calm face. He didn't like the way Patrick was handling the situation. Nothing was turning out like he had thought it would. 'I…I don't know what he's talking about. Trade? I don't know anything about a trade. He's mad.'

'Shut the fuck up, Vincent.'

'I…'

'Where's the girl?' Patrick asked Dougie.

'How should I know? The big fella handled that end.'

Patrick laughed softly. 'Vincent, take a look around this place.'

'Me? You're the one with the gun.'

'Right, so if you don't do what I say I'm going to fucking shoot you next.'

Vinnie goggled at Patrick. He had lost his momentum; he couldn't think any more. He felt queasy, light-headed. It seemed easiest to do what Patrick said.

Dougie watched him go. He took off his jacket and wrapped it around the wound in his leg. The bullet had gone straight through. 'You know what I'm telling you is the truth. He was going to trade: you for the drugs. Last week he sat in the fuckin' chair right behind you and offered you up, so he did.'

Patrick stared at Dougie. 'I'm not stupid. I know he has it in for me. It's only a matter of time before he lays me out. But it won't be with his own hand, you can be sure of that. It'll always be from a distance with Vinnie. Not like yourself, Doug. You always liked the personal touch.'

Vinnie came clattering back into the room, his face a mass of confusion. 'She's here! Naughton's fucking kid is here. All tied up in the fucking back room.' He gaped at Dougie. 'You had her? You were setting me up!' He charged across the room and aimed a kick at Dougie.

Dougie threw his hands up to protect his face. Patrick grabbed the back of Vinnie's coat and yanked him backwards. 'Stop acting the prick!' he roared.

Vinnie screeched, 'We had a fucking deal, Dougie – we had a fucking deal!'

'Shut up!' Patrick trained the gun on Vinnie, and Vinnie immediately shut his mouth. He was thinking at speed. It was bad luck that the girl was here. He had planned to clean the slate. Now he would have to decide what to do about her. Who knew what she had picked up over the last few days? She had probably heard his name mentioned, and that was a liability he couldn't afford.

'Now, Doug,' Patrick said coolly, 'I'll ask you again. Where the fuck is my coke?'

'I have it out back in the shed.'

'You have it in a fucking shed?'

'The shed I keep me dogs in. No cunt in his right mind would go in there.'

'Vinnie, go see if he's telling the truth.'

'*What?*'

'Go and see if he's telling the truth.'

'Have you seen the size of those dogs? I'm not going anywhere near the things.'

'They're penned, you fuckin' eejit,' Dougie said. 'You couldn't keep them loose, they'd kill each other.'

'There you go.' Patrick smiled evilly. 'So go check it out.'

'But it's raining and pitch-black out there, and I don't know—'

Patrick shot at him. The bullet missed Vinnie by about a foot and took out a fair chunk of Dougie's wall plaster.

Vinnie's jaw dropped, and the colour drained from his face. He turned and bolted out the door.

'I don't know where you got him from,' Dougie said.

'He's one of a kind, all right.'

464

'Aye, well. I tried to warn Davey to watch out for you, but sure he wouldn't be told. They thought you were past it, the two of them. Gobbin' on about how soft you'd gone.' He made a disgusted face and wiped his bloody hands on the sleeves of his shirt. 'Should have taken you out the moment you set foot in the yard out there. Could have blown you to kingdom come.'

'You should have.' Patrick nodded and regarded Dougie for a moment or two. 'What happened with Kelpie?'

With slow, deliberate movements, Dougie pulled his pipe from his top pocket and tamped down the tobacco. His hands shook when he lit it. 'Ed said Mooney took care of him. Knowin' Ed, he didn't have the stomach for it. Personally, I always thought that was a shame. Good fella, that Kelpie – loyal. Too fuckin' loyal.'

Patrick waited for him to get his pipe going. He kept his face neutral, but inside he burned with an icy fury. This jug-eared, tufty-haired fucker had been the cause of all his recent distress. Dougie Burrows wasn't fit to mention Kelpie's name. Because of him, Anouk was probably dead, Naughton was dead, his own son had betrayed him and his name was mud with the Turks. He wanted to rip Dougie's face off.

Dougie got his pipe going and puffed soft blue smoke towards the ceiling. He leaned against the chair, looking like an indulgent leprechaun, eyes half shut, head tilted slightly to one side. 'Mooney told

Naughton he only went to give him a tap of a shovel. Must've swung it a bit hard, like.' Dougie shrugged. 'Smashed the back of his skull like an egg.'

Patrick's gun hand twitched, but he kept his composure. There would be time to avenge Kelpie. Right now he needed to know a few things.

'Did Vincent know you had the cocaine from the word go?'

Dougie sucked his pipe contentedly. 'Pat, I wouldn't tell that useless fucker the time of day. I know he's your blood and all, but he's a junkie and a mouth. If he'd known, you'd have got wind eventually, and I didn't fancy my name getting back to your bosses. Anyway, I didn't have it. Naughton did. I *should* have had it, he was supposed to sell it on to me, but I didn't trust him not to back out. He was getting jittery. So I had Davey take the kid. That way, if Naughton tried to pull out, I'd use her to get my way. Next thing I know, we get wind you're on your way back. I needed to be sure that boy of yours would bring you to me. Davey there has a good head on his thick shoulders; he's played a blinder. Reeled Vinnie in like a bull trout.' Dougie sucked in more smoke and raised a ginger eyebrow. 'Always goin' on about how Vinnie should be runnin' the show and all that, when everyone knows the only thing he runs is his fuckin' mouth.'

'So why the big production? Why not give Ed his kid back and trade her for the coke? Be easier that way.'

466

'Because I wanted you to come lookin' for it. I wanted both you and the coke to disappear. Make it look like it was yourself that did a runner.'

'They'd still come looking for it. They wouldn't give up that easily.'

'They'd never find a trace of it.'

'Vinnie would squeal first time my Turkish friend put a blade to his throat.'

'You already know I wasn't plannin' to leave him around either.'

'Is Mooney in on this?'

'Mooney was a loose cannon. I don't deal with pigs, Pat. You of all people should know that.'

'Still, he'll be looking for his cut.'

'Not any more he won't.'

Patrick frowned. 'You killed him? Bad move, killing a cop, even a dirty fucker like Mooney. Messy, Doug. Not like you.'

'Like I say, he was a loose cannon.'

'Why was it that important that I come looking for it?'

Dougie narrowed his eyes. 'You killed Albert, you dirty fuck, you. I'd walk through the gates of hell to fuck with you.'

'That's your mistake.'

'Maybe so.' Dougie clamped his teeth down on his pipe and pressed his jacket tighter against his leg. 'Fuck, that hurts.'

Patrick went to the sink and filled a glass with water, keeping a sharp eye on Dougie in case he made a sudden move for the shotgun. He upended the glass over Davey's head. 'Wakey, wakey, fuck-face.'

Vinnie tramped through the cold and the muck, trembling. The bastard had shot at him – his own flesh and blood! He couldn't believe it. How had this happened? Why was Patrick holding a gun? Where had he got it from? Why was Davey out cold? How had Patrick managed to get the upper hand in this situation? Why was he meekly following Patrick's orders? Where were all the fucking dogs?

He stopped halfway across the yard and bent forwards to catch his breath. He had done far too much cocaine, and he knew it – he couldn't get his jaw to unclench or his hands to stop trembling – but it was the only thing keeping his mind and body together.

Was this a trick, a set-up? Maybe Patrick planned to grab the gear and get out. Surely he would kill Dougie – and what then? Would Vinnie be next? Could he back-pedal, convince Patrick that he wasn't trying to take over? Maybe he should get rid of Patrick after all…but how? He didn't even have a gun any longer – not that it had been any use, anyway. Fuckers! He did have his blade, but he'd have to get close to use it, and he wasn't sure he could make himself do it.

Vinnie rubbed frantically at his temples. All the questions were making him feel dizzy. He fumbled in his pocket for his wrap, turning his back against the rain. Maybe another little sniff would help him work it all out. After all, it wasn't like everything was ruined. He would summon the lion within himself. He could still turn this situation around...

Vinnie sniffed some more coke and wiped his nose with his sleeve. He felt instantly better, more in control of his faculties. What he needed to do was find the coke and get the fuck out of here. Which bloody shed was it supposed to be in again?

He clomped off towards the back of the cottage.

35

John sploshed back through the muck and slid into the ditch beside Sarah. 'There's no one in the van, either.'

Sarah was beyond cold. She could no longer feel her feet and she was shaking so badly her teeth hurt. 'Okay, so what now?'

'I say we keep walking. Find out who the Yorks are meeting.'

Sarah nodded miserably. 'I guess—'

There was a muffled bang.

'What the fuck was that?' John grabbed Sarah's shoulders and pushed her deeper into the ditch. Thorns scratched their cheeks and foreheads. They stood stock-still, although Sarah was convinced her heart could be heard over the crash of the rain.

'Was that gunfire?' she whispered against John's chest.

'I don't know. Sounded like it could have been, didn't it?'

'I don't know. I don't know what gunfire sounds like.' Sarah wiped the rain off her face and strained to listen. 'I don't hear anything else.'

'Did you think that sounded close by?'

'I can't tell with all this rain.'

'C'mon, let's move.'

They walked on, slower this time. When they rounded a bend and saw the cottage, they ducked into the brambles again.

'They must be in there,' John said.

'*Who*'s in there? We don't know even what they're doing here. Shit, John, I'm not even sure what we're doing here.'

'We need to get closer, have a look.'

Sarah slipped her hand into John's. 'I don't mind admitting this: I'm shit-scared.'

'Me too.' John squatted down and squinted through the rain. The light from the front window didn't exactly offer much illumination, but from what he could make out, the ditch ran the length of the yard and circled around the back of the cottage. A scraggy-looking yew tree grew to the side of the cottage. He could probably work his way along the ditch and get near enough to the window to take a look in. He took a step forwards.

'Sarah, I'm going to take a closer look. You wait here.'

'What?' Sarah yanked John back so hard he almost fell. 'I'm not staying anywhere.'

'Sarah, just for once, do what I ask you. I'm going to look inside. I need you to stay here and keep sketch. If you see anyone coming, whistle or something.'

'Whistle? Are you mad?'

'This place looks kind of run-down.'

'*So?*'

'In the photo, Ashley looks like she's been held in a run-down place, doesn't she?'

'Even if she's here, how are we supposed to get to her? What if the Yorks have guns? What if that *was* a gunshot?'

'What if they came here to kill her because you confronted them today?'

Sarah gasped. 'John, don't say that.'

'What if they came here to get rid of the evidence?'

'We don't even know that she's *here*!' Sarah hissed in exasperation.

'Exactly! All the more reason to look.'

'We should go to the Gardaí.'

'And tell them what?'

'Tell them...I don't know.'

'See ya.' John dropped her hand and made a dash for it. Sarah grabbed for the back of his jacket, but it was sodden and her fingers were too frozen to snag him. John was off and running.

There was another boom, louder this time. Sarah ducked low. 'Shit!' She watched John's departing back until the shadows swallowed him up. 'Shit.'

Seconds later, Vinnie York opened the front door of the cottage and ran out. Sarah could see him outlined against the light, as clear as day. She squashed herself further into the ditch and prayed to God that John had seen him too.

She needn't have worried: Vinnie never even looked in their direction. He stomped off across the yard, muttering and rubbing at his head. Then he too disappeared into the night, leaving Sarah alone, soaked and terrified.

When the water hit him, Davey groaned and tried to lift his head off the ground. The pain was unbelievable. He groaned again, louder this time. He opened his eyes and squinted at Patrick York, who was smiling nastily and holding a gun pointed at his head.

'You must have a head like a fucking cement block.'

Davey sat up slowly. He felt the huge, swollen lump at the back of his head. It was in almost the same place where Philo Redmond had clocked him with the toaster. 'Shit.'

'Davey, get up and take a seat over there, with your boss. There's a few things I'd like to clear up here.'

'Pat,' Dougie said, 'I don't know what you're playin' at—'

'Shut your yap.' Patrick waved the gun at him.

Davey hauled himself off the floor and staggered over to Dougie, who lay against his chair, smoking his pipe as if he hadn't a care in the world. Although his head was buzzing, Davey had picked up on the word 'boss', and he knew his days were numbered. He pulled out a chair and fell into it.

'Did you kill Eddie?'

'No.' Davey glowered at Patrick. 'I slapped him around a bit and the fat fuck had a heart attack.'

'Good.' Patrick smiled. 'Now, where's my cocaine?'

Davey rolled his neck again. 'Ask your son.'

'Try again. Doug here tells me Vincent's only the puppet in this show.'

'That puppet killed Philo Redmond.'

Patrick stopped smiling. 'You think I don't know that, you fucking lout?' His voice had a hard edge to it. 'Now, before I lose my patience completely, tell me where my cocaine is.'

'I'm not telling you shit.' Davey stared at him with naked hatred.

'Fine.' Patrick shot Davey square in the chest.

A dark trickle of blood ran down Davey's chest. He glanced down, surprised. He opened his mouth to say something, but couldn't form the words. A second later, he toppled off the chair onto the floor.

Dougie Burrows took the pipe out of his mouth. He didn't look quite so composed any more. 'Jaysus.'

Patrick crossed the room in two strides and stood over Davey, watching him desperately try to suck air into his shattered lungs. With every breath he took, a dark, foamy bubble pulsed through the hole in his chest. Patrick knew he wouldn't last long. 'You played it well, Davey, worming your way in with that halfwit son of mine. But it's over for you. Dougie already told me the gear's in the shed outside.'

Davey tried to say something, but a spasm of pain rocked him and his fingers curled involuntarily.

Patrick bent down and gripped his chin. 'I just wanted you to know that.'

'I…' Davey closed his eyes and drifted into unconsciousness.

Patrick stood up. Although the entry wound was small and had bled very little, a pool of deep-red blood was slowly spreading under Davey's back. 'All right, Doug. We're going to see if Vinnie finds my fucking gear where you say it is.' Patrick turned and looked into Dougie's eyes with the coldest, deadliest expression the Landlord had ever seen on a human face. 'And if you've been bullshitting me, God fucking help you.'

36

John lay as close to the ground as he could and waited until Vinnie walked into the dark before he moved again. Then he raced along, keeping flush to the ditch despite the thorns, nettles and three feet of water and muck. When the third shot rang out, John was in no doubt about what it was. He froze and listened, ready to run back the way he'd come if there were more, but there weren't, and after a minute John began to breathe easily again. He peered at the window through the rain, trying to make out the shadows that moved within. They were hardly shooting at him. The shot had seemed to come from inside the cottage. But if Vinnie was outside, who was doing the shooting – and what was he shooting at?

He picked himself up and crab-walked closer to the house. He made a dash for the yew tree, dropped behind it and sagged against its rough bark, panting with the exertion. His body was protesting against this further abuse, and he realised he was starting to feel slightly weak.

He took a few deep breaths and regained what he could of his strength and composure. He was only about twenty feet from the window, and even from here he could see someone moving behind the half-pulled curtains. If he could get close enough to see what was going on, he and Sarah would be in a position to decide what to do next.

Maybe Sarah was right: maybe they should go to the Gardaí. But what if they were wrong – or worse, what if Ashley Naughton was in there and something happened to her? John knew he would never forgive himself. He crouched down and crept towards the window. Under the sill he crossed his fingers and rose slowly, aiming for the gap between the curtains.

'What the hell is keeping that other arsehole?' Patrick said. 'I asked him to take a look around, not disappear altogether.' He walked towards the window, yanked the curtains back and looked out into the dark yard. He tilted his head this way and that, but he could see no sign of his son. There was only the rain, pelting against the windows.

'You sure there's no one else here?'

Dougie had managed to stop his leg from bleeding. He had been lucky; the bullet hadn't hit any major veins or arteries. He knew that if he got the chance, he could make an escape.

'I'm tellin' you, there was only meself and the big fella here.' He glanced at the bouncer. Davey was still breathing, but only just. It wouldn't be long before he was gone. Dougie winced and groaned slightly. His brother's gun, the one with which he'd planned to dispatch Patrick York, was under the cushion of his chair. He knew he had no chance of reaching it at this moment, not with Patrick watching him like a hawk. He'd be dead before he got his hands up. Unlike his fucking retard of a son, Patrick didn't mess around. No, he'd bide his time, think a little.

Sarah's heart almost leaped out of her chest. John had only barely ducked down when Patrick York's face filled the tiny cottage window. She had forced her fist into her mouth to keep from yelling his name. And now, as she watched John work his way back towards the ditch, she sank down onto the wet ground, her legs failing her with relief.

She waited, but when a minute had gone by, she realised that John wasn't coming back to her. That could only mean one of two things: John had had an accident, or he was going on further.

'Ah, crap.' Sarah shook her head with weary resignation. That was John bloody Quigley all over. Of course he'd gone on.

She pushed herself up, wiped the rain and mud from her face and, with a determined tightening of her shoulders, pressed on, following the line of the ditch to where she had last seen John.

John was making his way around to the back of the cottage. He had seen enough through the window to know that something seriously bad was going down.

He tripped over a long-abandoned lawn-mower jutting out of the ground and scraped his shin. Cursing, he hobbled his way into the back yard. He could just about make out the looming shapes of various sheds and outhouses. John pressed himself flat against the cottage wall. The rain battered him mercilessly. He felt his shin and found the sticky warmness there; he had ripped it to pieces. Great. He'd probably need a tetanus jab for that.

'Shit,' he muttered. He limped along, using the cottage wall for support. He came to another window, edged his way towards it and looked in. The interior was completely dark. A tattered net curtain covered the lower part of an ancient, half-rotted sash window.

John patted his pockets, searching for his Zippo. He found it, dropped it and, cursing furiously, retrieved it. He lit it, shielding the flickering flame against the rain. He held it to the glass and craned his neck to see into the room.

Ashley Naughton was lying on her side on a filthy mattress. Her eyes were closed, her hands and feet were bound and there was a gag in her mouth.

John gasped. He dropped his lighter. It flickered once and went out.

He was searching the soggy grass for it when someone said, 'You fuck, you!' Then he was grabbed and punched in the kidneys.

John grazed his head against the windowsill as

he went down. He fought for breath and swung his arm behind him, trying to catch his attacker in the throat. He missed by a mile, but his wild blow did manage to connect with Vinnie's cheek. But Vinnie was too coked up to feel it. He leaped on John, punching and kicking. Behind them the yard exploded into sound as the dogs in the sheds began barking and yelping at the top of their lungs.

John tried to get to his feet, but he was seriously winded. All he managed to do was roll up and protect his head a little. He knew he had to get up or he was a goner.

'Patrick!' Vinnie yelled. 'Patrick, quick!' He aimed another kick at John. 'You fuck! I'm going to kick the living shit out of—'

Sarah cracked Vinnie across the head with the only thing she could find in the dark, a rusty metal rake. She had swung it with every ounce of strength she had, and her aim couldn't have been better: she hit Vinnie across the eyes with a resounding clunk. Vinnnie crumpled as if he'd been shot.

'John?'

'Sarah?' The voice came out of the dark, winded but triumphant.

Sarah flung the rake away and groped around for John. 'Are you all right?'

'I've…found her. I've found Ashley.'

Sarah scrabbled forwards, practically on her hands and knees. 'We've got to get out of here.

They'll be out to see why the dogs are barking.'

'She's in there. I'm not leaving her.'

John uncurled and let Sarah help him up. He tried to stand, but his feet went out from under him again.

'Are you really hurt?'

'I'm okay…just winded. He hit me in my back.' John scrambled to his feet again. This time he stayed up, swaying slightly, but erect.

'Where's Ashley?'

'In this room – she's in there.' He reached for the window and tested the sash. It creaked and groaned, but wouldn't budge. He hadn't got the strength left to snap the lock.

'Help me with this.'

'We should go, get help,' Sarah said, but she stood beside him and grabbed the wooden ledge with her aching fingers. Together they pulled.

The wood was warped, and they managed to get some leverage. After a few seconds the lock in the centre of the window splintered away from the wood around it. Sarah gritted her teeth and pulled with all her might. There was another crack, louder than the first one, and finally, with a sucking sound, the window slid up about a foot and a half before jamming again. This time neither Sarah nor John could get it to budge another inch.

'I'm going in to get her.' John leaned in.

Sarah grabbed his arm. 'Not this time, you don't. I'll get her. You stay here. You're in no shape to do anything.'

481

John opened his mouth to argue, but closed it again. She was right: he was so battered he could barely keep himself upright, let alone help Ashley Naughton out.

'She's lying against the opposite wall. Her hands are tied, and I think her feet are too. Here, take my lighter – you can use it to burn those ropes off.'

'I hope to hell she can move,' Sarah said, her voice grim. She took the lighter and crawled through the window into the musty, pitch-black room.

37

Patrick York was rapidy losing what was left of his patience. With every second that passed his anxiety level rose, and when the dogs suddenly started barking he knew something was going on. Where was Vinnie? Maybe he had simply taken off, now that his scheme was busted, or maybe not. It was highly plausible that the idiot was still wandering around in the dark, lost or some shit. It was also highly plausible that Dougie had someone else outside, waiting to pick him off.

He paced across the room and peered out the window again. Nothing. This was fucking stupid. He couldn't sit around here waiting for Vinnie all night. Time to get his shit together and skip.

'What's up with those fucking dogs?'

'How should I know, the wind maybe.'

'Wind my arse.' Patrick frowned. 'Dougie, you and me are gonna take a little walk.'

Dougie looked up in amazement. 'Walk? Sure, how the fuck can I walk? You fuckin' shot me in the leg.'

Patrick gestured with his gun. 'You'll manage. Get up.'

'Patrick, I'm tellin' you, I don't think I can.'

'Get up or I'll shoot you, Doug. And you know I will.'

'You're goin' to shoot me anyway. May as well stay where I am.'

'Yeah, but you fuck with me and I won't shoot to kill. I swear I'll just shoot you in the gut. It'll be a long death, Dougie. Now stop fucking around and get up.'

Dougie ground what was left of his teeth and struggled painfully to his feet. 'You're a bastard, York. I'm sorry I didn't put a bullet in you when you walked through the door, Davey or no Davey.'

'Like I said earlier, that was your mistake. Now move it.'

Dougie hobbled to the door, and Patrick stayed close to him. Together they stepped out into the rising wind and the slanting, biting rain.

Sarah was struggling. She had found Ashley in the dark, burned through the ropes and slapped the girl into semi-consciousness – obviously they had her on some kind of drug. She was incoherent and frail, and getting her out the window was a nightmare. Her long, gangly body seemed to have no strength of its own at all.

'Ashley, come on, girl – slide your top half through, will you?' Sarah gasped. 'John, just grab her bloody arms, will you?'

'I'm trying.'

Between the two of them, they managed to

shove and pull Ashley through the tight gap. John tried to catch her, but they both fell in a tangle of arms and legs onto the wet grass.

Sarah climbed out and tried to work out which limbs were which. Somewhere off to her left, Vinnie York groaned, scaring her half to death.

'John, come on.' Sarah grabbed Ashley's arm – God, it was thin – and hauled the girl to her feet. They lurched away towards the ditch, half carrying, half dragging Ashley with them.

When they moved away froom the shelter of the cottage, the wind nearly blew them over and the rain stung their faces. It was getting worse with every second. John's breathing was laboured. The cut on his face had reopened when Vinnie York attacked him. It was bleeding profusely, his back was in agony and he was nearing complete exhaustion. Vinnie's swift attack had robbed his battered body of the last of its strength, and he was weakening with every stride.

They had barely made it to the ditch when Ashley said, 'I can't,' and collapsed onto her knees. Sarah felt her slip but couldn't stop her. John stumbled to a stop, panting harshly.

Sarah pushed her soaking hair back from her forehead and tried to think. 'John, this is ridiculous. I need you to do something.'

'What?'

'I need you to go ahead and get the car.'

'*What?*'

'We'll never get her all the way down the lane!

You know how mucky it is. You need to go ahead and get the car. I'll keep going with her. I'll meet you in the lane.'

'I'm not leaving you here.'

'You're not leaving me, you're helping me.'

'Sarah—'

'John, will you just do as I ask? Go and get it, drive it up that lane as far as it will go and I'll meet you there.'

John hung his head. Carrying Ashley was out of the question. He wiped the rain out of his eyes. He hated the thought of leaving Sarah behind, but he knew she was probably right.

'You've got to keep her moving, okay?'

'I will. She just needs a few seconds to get her strength back.'

John stood miserably for another second. He reached out and touched Sarah's face. 'Stay safe.'

Patrick stuck the gun into Dougie's side, and they struggled against the wind around the side of the cottage.

'Which shed?' Patrick bawled over the wind.

'That one.' Dougie pointed to a black shape on the other side of the yard.

'Where the dogs are?'

'They're penned, I told ya.'

Patrick looked around him uneasily. Where the hell was Vinnie? 'It's pitch-fucking-black out here. Don't you have any lights?'

'On the wall, there's a switch for the yard light.'

'Show me.'

Dougie limped across to the switch and flipped it up, and the floodlights overlooking the dog pens came on. And there, parked under a lean-to, was Davey's Toyota.

Patrick stared at the car, remembering what Sean had told him in Gig's place. 'Is Naughton still in the boot?'

Dougie looked startled. 'How the fuck did you know that?'

'Is he?'

'No, we took him out. Come on, I'll show you this shed.' He started to turn away.

Patrick tilted his head. Something in Dougie's tone interested him. 'You took him out?'

'Yeah.'

'Why?'

Dougie kept moving, dragging his leg, refusing to look around. 'I don't know. We thought it was best.'

'I'd like to have a look at that car.'

'For what? It's just a car.'

'Humour me.'

Dougie sighed. 'Look, Pat, I'm bleedin' to death here.'

'I want to see that car, Dougie. Do you have the keys?'

'Sure, why would I?'

Now Patrick was really curious. He grabbed Dougie by the back of the neck with his gun hand, patted him down and found the keys for the

Toyota in Dougie's trouser pocket.

'You're a shit fucking liar, Doug.'

'Pat, I —'

'Move, and no funny business.'

They made their way slowly across the yard to the car.

'Stand there,' Patrick said, several feet from the car. He backed away from Dougie and had a look. There was nothing special about the Toyota: late model, very common a few years back. He glanced at Dougie, noticing the stricken look on his face. Patrick smiled. He opened the boot.

'Hello there.' He beamed.

Two silver waterproof cases gleamed back at him. He looked over the boot at Dougie, grinning wildly. He opened the first one and said, 'Ahhh.'

There it was: his bounty, his road to long life and prosperity. He allowed himself the luxury of another fond look, then he closed the case and looked at Dougie.

'Guess that's that, then.'

'Pat, wait – we can do a deal. I can get you a price on that—'

Patrick shot him in the head. Dougie fell backwards and lay still. In the nearby sheds the dogs barked and howled like devils.

Patrick slipped the gun into his pocket. Now all he needed to do was get the car, transfer the load over and he was home free.

Patrick smiled. He was starting to enjoy his work again.

*

The sudden glare of the lights galvanised Sarah into action. Her heart thumped hard in her chest. She glanced along the side of the house and wondered if it was safe to move. A shiver ran through her. All she wanted to do was stay hidden, even if that meant lying in muck under a soaking hedge in the dark.

She turned her head and stared bleakly at Ashley's barely visible features. 'Are you okay?'

'I…' Ashley leaned to the side and vomited copiously. Some of it splattered Sarah's hand. The air was filled with a sharp, bitter odour. Sarah grimaced and tried to shift away.

'Okay, you probably needed to do that. Now listen to me: we're going to get up, and we're going to walk as fast as we can. Ready?'

Ashley groaned. 'I don't feel well.' Her voice was creaky and weak, but Sarah was overjoyed to hear her speak at all.

'Don't worry. I'll help you.'

'I can't…'

'Goddammit.' Sarah felt exhaustion wash over her. 'You can. Come on, get up. I'll help you.' Sweat ran freely down her back and under her arms. She dragged Ashley to her feet. The girl stumbled against her, almost knocking them both over. 'Come on, wake the fuck up.' She leaned Ashley against the hedge and slapped her face, hard enough to leave finger-marks. 'Come on! Please…you've got to help me.'

Ashley opened one glazed, bloodshot eye and stared at Sarah. 'Okay.' Her breath was stale, her voice barely audible.

'Okay, then.' Sarah felt a little more hopeful. Whatever they had Ashley on, at least she was starting to take her own weight. 'I'm going to get you out of here, but you've got to work with me a little. I can't keep half fucking carrying you.'

Ashley blinked again and gripped Sarah's arm with one slim hand. 'Okay,' she repeated, in a slightly firmer voice.

'Good. Let's go.' Sarah slipped her shoulder under Ashley's arm and staggered on. She would get them out of there, if it was the last thing she did.

38

Patrick was almost humming as he made his way to the front yard. Suddenly things were looking up. He didn't notice the rain any more, he didn't care about the last two weeks. He could get his life back. Okay, it might take a bit of time to convince Aziz that this kind of monumental fuck-up could never happen again – but, shit, time he could handle. And Anouk...maybe he'd been jumping the gun a little. Aziz had probably just been trying to scare him. There was a chance she was okay, scared but okay. She'd probably finish with him, of course, but... First things first: get the car and get the fuck out of here.

'What the fuck?'

There was enough light from the rear flood-lights for Patrick to make out two figures making their way along the ditch, towards the lane where the cars were parked.

'Hey!'

He saw the figures freeze. He was sure one of them looked around.

'Stop right fucking there!'

They broke into a shambling run. Patrick

491

cursed. He should have taken the shotgun from the house. He pulled his .38 from his pocket, raised it and fired.

Sarah was panting. 'Come on, Ashley, not far—'

Then something punched her forwards, knocking her off her feet. She pinwheeled and fell. Ashley screamed and staggered on towards the lane.

Patrick aimed again. This time the bullet went wide of the mark, and seconds later the other person was swallowed up by the shadows. Patrick lowered the gun and sprinted across the yard.

'Don't fucking move!' He slid across the mud to where Sarah lay, moaning, on her side.

He grabbed her hair and wrenched her head back. 'Who are you? How many are with you?'

Sarah screamed and clutched at her leg. Patrick looked down. He'd clipped her good: her anklebone had shattered like glass, shards of bone protruding through her sock. He hauled her face closer to his. 'Hey, I know you! You're that fucking detective.'

Sarah pressed one hand against his chest. 'Please…'

'Come on.' Patrick hauled her to her feet. Sarah wailed again, a thin, high-pitched sound that came from deep in her chest. 'Who are you here with?'

'Please don't kill me.' Sarah couldn't keep it in. The pain was unbearable.

'Shut the fuck up. No one can hear you out

here, anyway.' Patrick looked through the rain and cursed. The other one was as good as gone. Although he couldn't waste any more time hanging around, he needed to know if he was going to walk into some kind of set-up down the lane.

He hoisted Sarah over his shoulder as if she were a rag doll and carried her back across the yard to the house. He kicked open the door and threw her across the floor. Sarah screamed and tumbled to a stop. When she saw Davey, she began to sob uncontrollably.

Patrick picked up the shotgun. 'Who else is here with you?'

Sarah kept sobbing.

'I asked you a fucking question.'

'No one!'

'You're a liar. Who the fuck was running down the lane? I saw someone else; there were two of you.'

'A-Ashley Naughton.'

Patrick stared at her for a second. He left the room, but he was back before Sarah even realised he was gone.

'You telling me you came for the girl?'

Sarah nodded. She glanced at Davey, swallowed and looked away.

'You must have some set of fucking balls,' Patrick said admiringly. 'How'd you know where to find me?'

'I…I followed you.' Sarah clutched at her leg. If she moved even a fraction, the pain rocketed through her body. It was indescribable. She didn't know how long she could keep from passing out.

'This ain't turning out the way I'd hoped,' Patrick said tiredly. 'Now I've got to take care of you, and the girl's gone…' He set down the shotgun and shook the rain from his head. 'Who knows you're here?'

'N-n-no one.'

'Yeah?' He pulled out his .38 and pointed it at her head. 'That's too bad.'

'Please, please don't…don't do this.' Sarah held her hand in front of her face, cringing in terror. 'Please don't kill me.' She lifted her snow-white face to Patrick.

Patrick looked into her dark-brown eyes and something shifted in his chest. For a moment her eyes, the deep chocolate-brown of her irises, reminded him of Anouk.

The moment passed.

'I'm sorry, girlie, really I am. But I can't have you mouthing off about me.'

'I wouldn't – I won't tell anyone!'

'Sorry.'

Sarah sobbed out loud, closed her eyes and waited for the shot.

It never came. Instead there was a tremendous crash as John burst through the door and threw a wild punch straight at Patrick York's head.

Patrick caught the movement and darted to the side with lightning speed. The blow glanced off his ear, stunning him momentarily. But he still held the gun. John took the only chance he had: he launched himself at Patrick, throwing his full weight into the tackle. They toppled over the sideboard and crashed down in a tangle of arms and legs. The shotgun skittered across the floor, coming to rest in the treacly pool of Davey Clarke's blood.

John struggled to pin Patrick beneath him, but Patrick recovered fast: he brought his knee up between them, dug it into John's stomach and used it to roll him over while he struggled to free his gun arm. John bared his teeth and grappled desperately to hold on. Patrick twisted John's arm back and under him, using all his strength, and John felt his already weakened shoulder give slightly. Patrick must have felt it too: he snarled and yanked the damaged arm further. John grunted with effort, feeling his fingers lose their grip on Patrick's wrist.

Then he saw it – the look of triumph in Patrick York's eyes. In desperation, he did the only thing he could: he reared back and head-butted Patrick as hard as he could. Patrick grunted with shock. His new nose cracked and gave. Blood splattered over both of them.

Furious and half stunned, Patrick punched John in the side of the head. He released his hold on John's arm and tried to gouge him in the eye with his thumb. John twisted his head away, losing his grip on Patrick's gun arm. Patrick shouted triumphantly.

There was a huge explosion. Patrick's body stiffened, and he fell forward onto John. He twitched for several seconds, then lay still.

John scooted out from under him, dazed, his ears ringing. The top of Patrick's skull had been blown halfway across the room. It nestled comfortably on the dead dog's side.

John turned his head. Sarah put the shotgun down on the ground beside her.

'Sarah?'

Sarah smiled. Then her eyes rolled back in her head and she passed out.

39

'Sarah!' John crawled over to her and lifted her head in his hands. 'Sarah?'

To his relief, she opened her eyes. Her face was alabaster-white and expressionless. There was no surprise there, no shock or disbelief or anger. It was as if someone had pulled the plug on her emotions, taken the disk out for a while.

'There's so much blood.' Sarah gave him a terrible smile. 'He's dead, isn't he?'

'I reckon.' Patrick had split open John's eyebrow in the struggle, and he could feel the blood running down his face. He was dizzy and disoriented and could scarcely see. But, even half-blinded, he knew something was wrong with Sarah, something more than shock. There was so much blood on her...it had to be coming from somewhere. He ripped open her jacket and patted her body. She looked fine. So where was the blood coming from? It was all over her, her hands, her legs... Then he saw it: the gleaming white of her ankle bone, jutting out from under her jeans and through her sock.

'Oh, fuck.' John felt his stomach flip. 'Oh Christ.'

'Where's Ashley? Did you get the car?'

John ignored her and tried to roll up the leg of her trousers. Her ankle was completely shattered. He could see the tendons and muscle gleaming where her skin should have been. When he peeled back the sock slightly, a geyser of blood sprayed out. John stared at the damage in horror. He knew the dark blood had to be coming from a vein. Sarah was bleeding out.

'Shit.' He searched the cluttered room frantically for something to stanch the blood. He grabbed a tea towel, tore it into two strips and wrapped it as tightly as he could around the wound. 'Jesus Christ, Sarah, you're bleeding badly.'

'I really killed him.'

'Don't look at him, look at me, okay?' John said, fighting to keep the panic from his voice. The blood was already soaking through the tea towel.

'Where's Ashley?' Sarah said again. Her voice was becoming weaker.

'She's okay. She's safe. Don't worry about her. Sarah?'

Her eyes were closed. John pushed damp hair off her face. She was as white as a ghost.

'Sarah, come on! Can you hear me?'

She opened her eyes. They were black and her pupils were huge. John knew she was in shock.

'Hang in there.'

'He shot me,' she whispered, so softly John had to lean in to catch it.

'Can you sit up a little?'

498

'I don't…' She shook her head. Her lower lip trembled and she closed her eyes again. 'John…' Her forehead was criss-crossed with scratches from where she had pushed through the brambles. John wiped away some of the blood and dirt.

'Don't worry, don't worry – I'll get us out of here.'

He squatted on his hunkers and tried to think. His car was at the end of the lane. With his damaged arm, he could never carry her that far – even if he could pick her up at all.

'Sarah – Sarah, listen. I'm going to get a car, okay? I'll come back for you.'

Sarah murmured something, but she didn't open her eyes. John laid her head down as gently as he could and ran.

He sprinted across the yard and into the lane, running as hard as his exhausted legs would carry him. His mind was filled with Sarah's white, scratched face. Didn't people die from blood loss? Didn't people die from shock? Christ, the lane was almost flooded. By the time he'd made it down to the bottom and got the Manta, Sarah might be dead…

Then he saw the Mercedes. He skidded to a halt and ripped open its door: no keys in the ignition. Maybe he could hotwire it or something…no, that was stupid. He slammed the door and raced acrros to the van.

'Oh sweet Jesus, thank you.'

The keys swung from the ignition. John stared

at them like a man dying of thirst stares at a cool mountain stream. When he turned the key, the engine gunned to life immediately.

John parked as close as he could to the door and ran into the kitchen. It was a frightful scene. The room was spattered with blood and with matter that he didn't like to think about. John swallowed his nausea and crossed the floor, trying to avoid the puddles of congealing blood. He bent down and scooped Sarah into his arms. The pain in his shoulder was excruciating.

Sarah opened her eyes again and looked at him.

'You'll be okay.'

'John?' She closed her eyes again, and her head fell forward in a faint.

John turned and staggered outside, his damaged shoulder burning. Where would he put her? He opened the back of the van, balancing Sarah's weight on his leg, and laid her inside as carefully as he could. Then he climbed in and tore down the lane, the wheels spinning for purchase on the muck. Sarah whimpered once and was silent.

'Don't worry,' John shouted over his shoulder. He found a car phone and dialled the emergency services. 'You'll be fine. Just hold on, okay?'

The panic in his voice belied his words.

Vinnie sat up and pressed his fingers to his head. It felt like someone had it in a vice.

'Jesus.' He winced from the pain. He remembered now: he had caught someone – that fucking detective, what the hell was his name? There had been a fight. Then what? What the fuck had happened?

He climbed unsteadily to his feet and made his way across the floodlit yard. Where had the lights come from? Why was Dougie Burrows lying on the ground with a bullet hole in the middle of his forehead?

Slowly he made his way around to the front of the cottage. He stopped when he saw the half-open door. 'Patrick?'

No reply. He inched forwards and opened the door slowly.

'Jesus fucking Christ!' Vinne stared at the carnage before him. He stared at Patrick, then at Davey, then back at Patrick. Was he really dead?

'Patrick.' Nothing. Vinnie edged forwards and nudged him with his foot.

'Well, *mon dieu.*' Vinnie suddenly giggled. 'Hey, Patrick, your brain's showing.'

He bent down and gingerly looked through his father's pockets for the keys to the Merc. He found them, stood up and grinned. 'I guess you won't be needing these, hmm? Nope – not any time soon, anyway, *mon ami.*'

Then, laughing like a loon, Vinnie fled.

Ashley had gone half a mile before she found a house. She was barefoot and soaking wet. Her dress was torn from the brambles in the ditch, and she had fallen more than once and cut her knees open.

She stumbled into the garden and hammered on the front door of the bungalow with her fists. Seconds later, a light came on and the door was opened by a wild-haired, bewildered man in checked boxer shorts. Behind him stood a tiny woman with an angelic face, wearing a red fleece dressing gown. Ashley spilled into the hall and fell onto their floor.

'Please…help,' she cried, her breath coming in gasps.

'What?' The man blinked and took a step back.

The woman brushed past him impatiently. 'What's happened? Were you in an accident?'

Ashley clutched at her slippers. 'Oh, please, please… I think he shot her… Please, phone the Guards!' She laid her head on her arms and sobbed as though her heart would break.

Noleen was a no-nonsense woman who had raised a brood of children and she thought she had seen and heard it all, but she admitted to her sister the following day that she had never in all her days heard such piteous crying. She leaned down to pat the wretched girl's shoulder and ordered her husband to go phone the Gardaí at once. While he did that, she went into the sitting room and came back with a brandy bottle, a glass and a throw off the sofa. She wrapped the throw around the shivering, sobbing girl and cleaned some of the muck and debris off her face.

'There you are now, pet. Don't be crying. You'll be all right – you'll be all right. What's you name?"

'Ashley…my name's Ashley.'

'And who got shot, hon? A friend of yours?'

'No, I don't know her. She helped me get away from the men.'

'What men?'

'I don't know…I don't know. Davey – Davey took me. But there were more, they shot her…'

Noleen looked over Ashley at her husband, who was dialling the hall phone.

'Tell them to hurry.'

40

John had been in the waiting room of Loughlin-stown Hospital for two hours, wearing holes into the scuffed linoleum, when Detective Sergeant Owen Flannery finally caught up with him. Flannery was a tall, fit native of Wicklow, with almost twenty-five years on the force. He had snow-white hair, cut short, and a thick white handlebar moustache to match. It was a bitch to keep clean and it needed constant clipping, but his wife liked it, so he put up with the extra grooming.

'You took your sweet time.' John glared at the Garda as if he had crawled out of a sewer. He flicked his cigarette butt out the window and closed it with a snap.

'There's no smoking in this building.'

'So arrest me.'

Flannery held out his massive paw. 'I'm Detective Sergeant Owen Flannery.'

'Yeah, whatever.' John gripped the plastic seat in front of him so he wouldn't have to offer his hand. He had barely enough strength to stand, and his shoulder and face were killing him. Pleasantries weren't high on his list.

'You look like you've been in the wars.' Flannery lowered his hand, unaffected by John's rudeness, and nodded at John's split eyebrow. 'Anyone take a look at that for you?'

'I know how I look.' A doctor had earlier offered to look at his injuries, but he'd backed off when John warned him not to lay a finger on him.

Flannery nodded, pulled a battered notebook out of his coat and flicked through it. 'You must be John Quigley.'

John nodded.

'You say you're a detective of sorts?'

John bristled slightly. 'I don't *say* I'm a detective, I *am* a detective.'

'Got any ID?'

'It's in the glove compartment of my car, which is back at that house. I'm sure you found it, so why don't we stop pissing about?'

Flannery nodded agreeably. 'You left the scene of a crime, John. Bad move, lad.'

'I had to get my partner to a hospital.'

'How is she?'

'I don't know. They're operating on the ankle right now. It's a bad break and she's lost a lot of blood.'

Flannery nodded. 'You're all right, though.'

'Oh, yeah,' John snapped sarcastically. 'I'm right as rain.' He sat down heavily in a chair and rubbed his exhausted eyes with his filthy hands.

Flannery sat down opposite John. Rain dripped off his oilskin coat and puddled on the blue and white tiles. 'Tell me again what you said when you called the station.'

John rubbed his head wearily. 'I'll tell you the same thing I told that ignorant shit who answered the phone. I told him there'd been a shooting. I told him there had been a kidnapping, I told him there were people dead. He laughed at me, so I called him a dumb fucker. He wasn't as friendly after that.' He noticed the thick wedges of mud dried into Flannery's shoes and the splattered trouser legs. 'Looks like someone believed me, though.'

Flannery ignored that. 'You know a man called Dougie Burrows?'

'No.'

'You sure?'

John stared at him. 'Of course I'm sure.' He fumbled in his pockets for his cigarettes. The box was soggy and torn, but somehow two of his cigarettes had survived relatively unscathed.

'What about Vinnie York?'

'He was there at one point. He must have got away.'

'Tell me now, what's your connection to him?'

John lit up and blew a long stream of smoke towards the ceiling. 'I don't have a connection to him.'

'We have Vinnie York in custody, you know.'

'Good.'

'Would you like to know where we found him?'

'Go ahead.'

'Crashed into a wall outside of Killpedder. Blood all over him, gibbering like a lunatic.'

'Right.'

'You've had a few run-ins with him before, I believe?'

'Not with him – with his fucking guard dog, Davey Clarke. You may have noticed him. He was the dead man lying on the floor of that dump with a hole in his chest.'

Flannery ignored the sarcastic tone. 'Vinnie York says you tried to murder him.'

The cigarette dropped out of John's hand. 'What?'

'You heard.' Flannery's expression never changed, but his eyes were watchful and sharp.

'This is bullshit! I didn't do anything of the sort.' John picked the cigarette up and took a very long drag.

'The eight-inch gash in his head says otherwise. He says you clubbed him in the head with some kind of tyre iron and left him for dead.'

'I never touched him. He kicked the shit out of me.'

'So you admit fighting with him?'

'No, he jumped me.'

'Where?'

'At the back of the cottage.'

'Ah.' Flannery nodded and made a note in his notebook.

John blew out another stream of smoke. 'I was

trying to get the window open. Ashley Naughton was inside, bound and gagged.'

'Ah, yes, Ashley Naughton. This is the girl you claim you were hired to find.'

'I don't *claim* it. We were hired to find her by her mother, Margaret Naughton.'

'Vinnie York claims he was going to help her, then you came out of nowhere and attacked him.'

'Fucking nonsense.'

'That's what he says. He says he realised his father was planning on hurting her, and he was trying to save her.'

'So what?' John shook his head incredulously. 'He's a drug-using psycho. Who are you going to believe?'

'I don't know who to believe, but I want you to come with me and answer a few questions.'

'This is bullshit!' John jumped up and jabbed a finger at Flannery's face. 'I'm not going anywhere until I know how Sarah's doing.'

Flannery's voice was civil, calm, but firm. 'Come on, now. Don't let's go about this the hard way.'

John's head and shoulder ached and he was weak from exhaustion, hunger and pain. The last thing he felt like doing was going down to the station for questioning. 'You're acting like Vinnie York is the good guy.'

'We'll talk about it at the station.'

'What about York?'

Flannery rested a heavy hand on John's good shoulder. 'I told you, he's in custody.'

'At the station?'

'He's in Beaumont Hospital at the moment, under observation. He's got that head injury and a broken arm.'

'The slippery bastard!' John shrugged Flannery's hand off and stepped away from him. Flannery flexed his shoulders and narrowed his eyes. He took a dim view of John's attitude. He was seriously considering slapping cuffs on him, injury or no.

John clenched his jaw. 'Look, you saw Davey Clarke. He's dead, right?'

Flannery's expression betrayed nothing of what he was thinking. 'He is.'

'Davey Clarke works for Vinnie York. He shot him, or one of them did.'

'You saw him shoot Clarke, did you?'

'No, but he must have done it – or maybe Patrick York, I don't know.'

'I don't know who shot who,' Flannery said truthfully. He had never seen so much mayhem in his twenty-five years on the force – blood everywhere, bullets lodged in walls, guns turning up under chairs, a dead dog, bits of a man's brain drying on a wall... It would take the forensic officers weeks to work it all out.

'I didn't shoot anyone. I've never fired a gun in my life.'

Flannery took John's arm again. 'That doesn't alter the fact that I want to talk to you.'

'You've got to talk to Margaret Naughton,'

John said, his agitation growing by the second. 'She'll tell you Sarah and I were working for her.'

'We'll talk to her, don't you worry.'

Flannery steered him down the corridor to the main door – where, to John's surprise, an even bigger Garda stood, eyeing him warily. Flannery's smooth, reassuring voice rumbled again. 'You don't worry about anyone else. You worry about yourself and the hoor of a mess you're in.'

By the time John had repeated his story eight or nine times to the increasingly incredulous Flannery, written out and signed a painstaking statement, given his fingerprints and allowed swabs to be taken from his hands and cheek, it was almost twenty past five in the morning. They wouldn't have released him at all if Ashley Naughton, pale and exhausted, hadn't come in with Margaret and the family solicitor and backed up his story. Even then, Flannery had been reluctant to allow him to leave.

John felt like shit. He would cheerfully have lain down on the tiled floor of the Wicklow garda station and passed out, if they'd let him. But he remembered Sumo, locked up all day again, and forced himself to head for home. Unfortunately, his car had been impounded as evidence, and there were no buses or trains running at that hour. He stood on the steps of the station, zipped his filthy jacket against the biting cold and lit the weaker-than-shit Silk Cut he'd bummed off the desk sergeant. He pulled out his wallet, checked how much money he had and sighed heavily: not enough to even call a taxi. He finished his cigarette and went back into the station. It wasn't much, but at least it was warm and dry.

Finally, at six o'clock, one of the night duty officers tapped him on the shoulder and told him they'd organised a lift back to Dublin for him. A young officer who didn't look old enough to shave, let alone drive, was lumbered with the job. He wasn't impressed with John stinking up his squad car, and he wasn't much of a talker, for which John was deeply grateful. He leaned his head back against the headrest and dozed most of the way home.

When they reached Ranelagh and pulled up outside John's house, the young Garda said his only sentence. The suddenness of his voice frightened the wits out of John.

'Flannery says you need to give me your passport.'

John stumbled up his path and unlocked his door with great difficulty. Sumo sailed past him and peed all over the front yard. John found his passport and brought it back out to the waiting Garda, who opened it, looked at John and looked at the passport for a long time.

'Don't mind the picture. It's really me,' John said tiredly. He leaned on the gate, too exhausted to stand up straight.

'It doesn't look like you.'

511

Sumo, behind the gate, growled at the strange voice. The Garda eyed him, eyed John, and made a funny clicking sound. Finally he put the passport in the pocket of his immaculate uniform and left.

John went back inside, fed the dog and let him out into the back garden with a shoulder bone of beef. While the dog chewed contentedly, John phoned the hospital and learned that Sarah was out of surgery and asleep in one of the recovery wards. He thanked the sweet-sounding nurse, bolted the door, went into his bedroom and fell asleep without taking his boots off.

When the phone woke him ten hours later, he felt as if he'd just shut his eyes. He staggered out into the hall and groped for it blindly. 'Yeah.'

'John?'

He slid down along the wall in relief. 'Sarah?'

'How you holding up?' Her voice was weak and faraway-sounding, but it was her. John closed his eyes.

'I'm good. How are you? You must be better if you're making phone calls.'

'Okay, I guess. They repaired the ankle, put a steel plate in it. I can't put any weight on it for a few weeks.' She laughed, a forced sound that grated heavily on John's heart. 'They gave me morphine for the pain. It's great stuff. I can't feel anything.' She did the laugh again. 'I imagine when this wears off I won't be feeling quite so cheery.'

'What's wrong?'

'They came to swab my fingers for gunshot residue earlier.'

'God.'

'That's not the worst of it.'

'There's worse?'

Sarah sighed. 'Apparently Vinnie York's solicitor made some kind of statement this morning, naming you and God knows who else. He says Vinnie was set up, that you were probably working with Davey Clarke and that's why you tried to murder Vinnie.'

'Jesus.'

'It's total bullshit, it'll never stick, but he's using it to create confusion.'

'Jesus, how did you hear so fast?'

'John, *everyone*'s heard. This is big news. There was a reporter here asking the nurses questions and everything – I think they ran him out. Trust me, it's big. I'm surprised the reporters haven't been over to you yet.'

'I don't think I would have heard them anyway.' John picked at the dirt on the knee of his jeans. 'Do you need anything brought out to you?'

'Jackie and Helen are here.'

'Oh... I'll come out later.'

Sarah paused for too long. 'I wouldn't bother, John. They'll probably be here for a while, and...well, they're fairly...well. Helen's really pissed off.' Sarah sighed. 'It was all Jackie could do to convince her not to go around to your house this morning and give you hell.'

'I'd have set the dog on her.'

'John, they're my sisters. They're upset.'

'My fault, huh?'

Sumo scratched at the back door. John put the phone down, walked through the kitchen and opened the door. Sumo followed him back into the hall and lay down beside him.

'John?'

'I'm still here.' John scratched the top of Sumo's head, his fingers automatically kneading the wiry hair.

'John, I have to go, this isn't my mobile.'

'Okay. I'll see you—'

But she was already gone.

John slid down the wall onto the floor and pet his dog. The rain had finally stopped, and the last of the evening light filtered in through the hall window. The everyday sounds of horns blaring and car doors slamming were oddly comforting.

He forced himself up, left Sumo to amble about and took a long shower. Rivers of dirt rolled off him and drained away down the plughole. His body ached, and he let water pound it until his skin stung. When he got out and looked into the bathroom mirror, he was shocked at what he saw. He was black and blue from the back of his neck down to his third rib. The split in his eyebrow had reopened in the shower, and blood was slowly inching its way down his face. His lip was scabby and twice its normal size. In short, he was a mess.

Sarah was probably better off not seeing him today, anyway, he reasoned with his reflection. The sisters would probably be hovering around and cursing his name. This was a perfect excuse for them to put the boot in. And in his present state, the last thing he needed was a run-in with them. He might just wring their necks.

He was brushing his teeth, carefully avoiding his injured lip, when the phone rang again. John spat, rinsed and moved stiffly out into the hall to answer it.

'Mr Quigley, it's Owen Flannery. Sorry if I'm disturbing your beauty sleep.'

'I was up.'

'You'll have to come in. I've got a few more questions for you. I can send a car up, or you could—'

John leaned against the wall. 'I hear York's solicitor mentioned me to the newspapers.'

'We found Edward Naughton's body an hour ago.'

'Oh.'

'Dumped in behind the sheds at that cottage.'

'I see.'

'Not twenty feet from where you say you were.'

John said nothing to that. What was there to say?

'Did you know he was missing?'

'Yes. Margaret said, the night Davey Clarke attacked them.'

'So you knew he was missing and you still didn't think to come to the Gardaí?' Flannery sounded pissed off. 'What kind of eejit are you at all?'

John heard the contempt in Flannery's voice and bristled at it. 'Is my car ready?'

'I don't know, I'll have to check.'

'Don't bother sending a car, I'll make my own way down.' John hung up and instantly regretted not accepting the lift.

At half-seven he caught a bus to Wicklow and walked the kilometre to the station. As he walked, he was painfully aware of the looks people were giving his battered face. The evening was cool and the air crisp, and John should have enjoyed the walk, but he didn't.

The duty sergeant buzzed him in and directed him to Flannery's office. Flannery was in no mood for small talk either. As bad as John felt – and he felt pretty lousy – Flannery looked almost worse. Judging from his washed-out pallor and the rings under his eyes, he hadn't been to bed at all.

'You've got yourself into a right stinking shit-heap, lad,' he said, stroking the white caterpillar on his upper lip.

John shrugged. He folded his arms and held his tongue. Flannery's second-floor kingdom was a corner office with a small, pointless window. It was grey – grey furniture, grey carpets, dove-grey paint job on the walls. Someone had provided two acid-green mugs of cheap instant coffee.

'The whole thing stinks to high heaven. According to the girl's granny, Emily Naughton, her boy wasn't involved in any kind of trouble. She does confirm that you were brought in to find the girl, and that you said you thought Vinnie York had the girl somewhere. But Ashley Naughton says she never saw Vinnie in the whole time Davey Clarke had her, which matches Vinnie's story that he wasn't involved in any kidnapping. Then you go spinning me a yarn about drugs and all kinds of shite. There's bodies all over the place, and the only people we have as witnesses are Mr. York, two *private detectives* and a hysterical teenager.' Flannery shook his head. 'Suffering Jaysus. It's a mess.'

'I don't know what you want me to say.'

'Are you sure you're sticking to your story?'

John's eyebrows lowered. 'My *story*?'

'We did a search of York's place. The forensics crowd are over there now, but I'm telling you, lad, they won't find anything to back up your story that he had the girl.'

'Then maybe he didn't have her, maybe Clarke was working on his own. I don't know, do I?'

Flannery flicked through a folder on his desk. 'This fella Clarke – tell me again how you knew him.'

'I *don't* know him. Before this case, I'd never heard of him.'

'Tell me again what you and your partner were doing at that cottage.'

'We followed Vinnie York and his father there. You *know* all this.'

'And how did you know that the other man was Patrick York?'

'Are you saying he isn't?'

Flannery gave a noncommittal shrug. 'We've identified him, yes. Tell me this and tell me no more: would you be terribly shocked if I told you we recovered a substantial quantity of drugs from that farm?'

'No, I wouldn't.'

'You wouldn't?'

'We had our suspicions there might be some kind of drug thing connected with Ashley's disappearance. Patrick York and Ashley's father were friends. Margaret Naughton said she suspected her husband was involved in drugs.'

'Why would Vinnie York have left without the drugs?'

'I don't know! Why don't you ask him?'

'Did Sarah Kenny know who Patrick York was when she shot him?'

'He shot her first.' John glared at him. 'I don't know what you're getting at. Do you think this is all some big fucking conspiracy? We're all in something together?'

'Maybe ye are!' Flannery slapped the folder closed and stared at John. 'I don't know what to think! That's the problem. Ashley Naughton's kidnapping should have been a matter for the Gardaí in the first place.'

'Her mother went to you lot, and you laughed at her!'

'Did Margaret Naughton give you a cheque for a large sum of money a few days ago?'

'Yeah. So?'

'What was that for?'

'She wanted us to drop the case, so she paid us extra, hoping we'd leave it alone.'

'Why would she do that if she wanted you to find her daughter?' Flannery smiled craftily. 'Maybe she was paying you to leave her alone.'

'That's the stupidest thing I've ever heard. Look, we haven't even deposited it yet.'

Flannery tapped his fingers together. 'Davey Clarke…you knew him pretty well, didn't you?'

'You keep asking me that.' John's tolerance for Flannery's 'trick' questions was running on empty. 'And I keep telling you I didn't.'

'Vinnie York says you did.'

'He's a liar.'

Flannery glanced down at his notes for a long time. Eventually he let out a long sigh. 'Look, John,' he said, oozing faux country charm, 'look at it from my point of view. We've got people dead – Edward Naughton and Davey Clarke, Patrick York and Dougie Burrows. The only people to come out of all this virtually unscratched are yourself and Vinnie York. Now, your fingerprints were found on a .38—'

'I fought for that gun with Patrick York.'

'—which we've learned is the weapon that killed Davey Clarke. You left the scene of a crime. You struck Vinnie York what could have been a fatal blow to the head.'

'I didn't—'

'He says everyone was trying to kill him, including his own father, and he escaped – leaving behind one hundred and forty kilos of cocaine. He says he knew nothing at all about any drugs—'

'Of course he did!'

'—which, frankly, sounds like bullshit to me. But, then again, maybe he's telling the truth. It's a mess. And you were conveniently there to lend Margaret Naughton a shoulder to cry on the night she and her mother-in-law were roughed up by Davey Clarke. You have a cheque from Margaret Naughton for a large sum of money. And you claim Edward Naughton was smuggling drugs, with Patrick York – but, since both of them are dead, I can't prove a thing. Davey Clarke is dead. The only people to come out of this alive are you, your partner and Vinnie York.'

John stared at him. 'And Ashley Naughton.'

Flannery tipped his chair back and stared at John. 'How come, when Clarke assaulted Margaret Naughton, you were handily there to pick up where he left off? Very convenient, that. You seem to have a knack for being in the right places at the wrong times, eh? Jaysus, I wish I had that talent, I'd be the best Garda in Leinster.'

John had taken enough. He leaned forwards and slammed his hands onto the desk. 'I was there because I followed Clarke that night! I was doing my *job*!'

'Your job.' Flannery smiled suddenly, untroubled by John's outburst. 'You know, I did a bit of checking into you and *your job*. You're the same smart-arse who ruined the careers of two good Guards in Dublin. Aren't you?'

'That's me. So what?'

'You're a piece of work, all right. Maybe you are telling the truth – or maybe you're just one lucky little bollocks who should have been put away years ago.'

John sank back. It was all he could do to keep from reaching across the desk and slapping the sceptical look off Flannery's face. Bad enough he was injured, bad enough his partner was lying on her back in Loughlinstown Hospital, bad enough he had screwed up and people had died. How this hick fucker didn't believe a word he was saying, and Vinnie York was putting the knife in and twisting it. He clenched his hands in frustration.

'We through?'

Flannery rubbed his hand across his eyes and dropped back into his chair. He closed his eyes and said nothing. Every so often he blew air out through pursed lips and his moustache jiggled. John waited. Around the building phones rang and doors slammed, voices dipped and rose, but the only sound in the room was the tick of Flannery's wall clock.

After two minutes of silence, Flannery opened his eyes. 'You can go now. Go home and stay there. I want you where I can contact you.' He was obviously struggling to keep his cool.

John knew this wasn't the time for smart-alec answers. He stood up. 'Where's the car?'

Flannery jerked his head towards the window. 'It's locked up out back. Get the desk sergeant or someone to release it. You'll have to sign for it at the front desk.' He fussed with the papers on his desk. He could hardly bring himself to look at John.

John walked to the door.

'Mr Quigley,' Flannery called after him, in a tight voice devoid of his practised charm.

'What?'

'Your tax disk is out of date.'

John walked out and left the door open.

41

It was after eleven when John made it back to the hospital. It was after lights out, everyone else had left and Sarah was asleep. He had to plead with the night nurse to be let in. He was prepared to cry if need be, but for whatever reason – and John doubted it was because he looked cute – she took pity on him and let him have a few minutes.

Sarah was in a semi-private ward with another woman. John pulled the curtains around her bed for privacy and sat down on a hard plastic chair. He gazed at Sarah as if seeing her for the first time. She looked deathly. Her skin was pale even against the white pillow, and there were deep blue shadows under her eyes. Her dark hair fell in a thick fold over her right shoulder, tangled and held in a loose ponytail. Her foot, in a heavy cast, was hitched to a traction brace at the end of the bed.

John had brought a bag of Maltesers and a bottle of Sprite. He put them on the floor by the bedside locker. A vase of white chrysanthemums took up most of the locker itself. John plucked out the card that was stuck amongst the stems and read it. The flowers were from David Fenshaw, the 'gentleman' with whom Helen had set Sarah up on a date. Typical.

'Hey, you came.' Sarah was watching him through her eyelashes.

John put the card back. 'Nice flowers.'

'They found Edward Naughton's body.'

'I know. I heard.'

'How you feeling? You look pretty rough.'

John nodded and ran his fingers through his hair. 'Tired, I suppose. Been on the go since early this morning. Flannery's had me tied up – although not as literally as he'd like.'

Sarah stretched out her hand to him. An IV drip was taped across the back of her hand, and her veins looked very blue against her pale skin. John took her hand and gently rubbed the tape with his thumb.

Something caught in his throat. He wanted to tell her he was sorry – sorry for letting her get hurt, sorry for dragging her into a situation they weren't prepared for, sorry for not listening to her and going for the Gardaí, sorry for leaving her in a water-filled ditch on a freezing cold night. He wanted to say it, but he couldn't form the words. For once in his life, he couldn't think of a single thing to say.

Sarah sighed and shifted under her covers. 'I know, I got it all day too – only I got a Ban Garda with a lisp. "Do you theriouthly ecthpect me to believe that, Tharah?" You would have loved her, she was something else. And then my sisters arrived and started giving out to me, *together*. I almost jumped out of the window, foot or no foot. Helen's voice…it can even pierce through morphine.'

John's gaze never moved from her hand. 'Kept you busy, eh?'

She smiled. 'You should have heard them. They really went to town on you. Your ears must have been burning all day.' She stopped, wondering why John wasn't smiling. 'John? What's wrong?'

'Maybe they're right.'

Sarah stared at the top of his head. 'What?'

'Maybe they're right about me. Shit, Sarah, you got *shot*, and it's my fucking fault. You wanted to go to the Gardaí, but no – I had to play the hero.'

'John, it's all right.'

'Patrick York could have killed you. He very nearly did.'

Sarah pulled her hand out of his. 'John, look at me.'

He raised his head slowly and gazed at her cheek. He couldn't look her in the eye. He was afraid he might start howling like a baby if he did. 'What if Patrick York had hit you a little higher?'

'I'm all right,' Sarah said firmly. She didn't want to think about that possibility any more than he did. Helen had already done enough of that for the two of them. 'None of this is your fault.'

'You could have been killed. I should have listened to you when you wanted to go back and ring the Gardaí.'

'We got Ashley Naughton out. If we'd left her… I saw Patrick York, John, I saw his eyes. He wasn't going to leave anyone to point the finger at him. If we'd left Ashley, she'd have been dead.'

'I dragged you into this.'

Sarah took a deep breath. 'Nobody drags me anywhere I don't want to go, John Quigley. You know that.'

'Yeah, I know.'

'Look at me.'

He raised his head a little.

'John…' She looked at him so earnestly he almost felt his heart break. 'John, listen, we're on a learning curve in this business. We can't expect to get everything right first time. Hindsight is twenty-twenty and all that crap, remember? Next time, we'll be brilliant. Next time we'll ring the Gardaí first.'

John lowered his head again. He felt responsible, no matter what she said.

'What else did Flannery say?' Sarah asked, changing the subject quickly. She was horrified to see John so upset, so cowed. She wouldn't have thought he had it in him.

John sighed. 'He still thinks I'm making half of it up. I think he thinks I was in cahoots with Davey Clarke somehow, or with Vinnie York. He can't decide how to pin it all on me.'

'I take it he knows about your poor history with the cops.'

'It's just as well our stories matched. I think Flannery would jump at any chance to lock me up and throw away the key. Vinnie York's playing dumb, saying he was an innocent victim and I'm the villain, and I think Flannery likes that version of events.'

'Let him say what he wants, the evidence will back us up.' Sarah waved a hand feebly. 'We didn't do anything wrong. God, I wonder if Vinnie York's actually telling the truth? Maybe he didn't know anything.'

John smiled. 'Who knows?'

The chubby nurse who had let John in popped her head around the curtain. 'You've got another visitor, lovey. I can tell her it's too late if you like.'

'Who is it?'

'She didn't give a name. Young girl, blonde.'

John and Sarah exchanged glances.

'No, she can come in,' Sarah said.

The nurse checked her watch and glanced pointedly at John. 'All right, but only for a few minutes. You need to get some rest.'

Sarah nodded.

A minute later they heard the nurse's soft voice again. '…very tired, and it's nearly time for rounds.' Then the curtain was pulled back, and Ashley Naughton's gaunt face seemed to float above the end of the bed.

'Sarah Kenny?' Her voice was low and very deep, almost mannish, wrong for her girlish appearance. Her hair was freshly washed and gleamed in the low lights. She was dressed in a black polo-neck and dark-blue jeans. She wore no make-up, and her skin was as smooth and pale as porcelain, but her eyes were exhausted and haunted. She stared at Sarah, an expression of mild puzzlement on her delicate features.

Sarah pushed herself up slightly. The movement made her wince a little. 'Yes.'

'I'm sorry, I can't really remember your face.' Ashley nodded to John and stood awkwardly at the foot at the bed. Now that she was here, she didn't seem to know what to say. Her hands plucked at the bedsheets, and the skin under her eyes had the bruised blush of someone who hadn't slept for a long time. The silence grew.

'I'm sorry about your loss,' Sarah said gently.

'Thank you.' Ashley's hands stopped moving. Her fingers were long and thin, the nails were chipped and broken.

'And I'm glad you're all right.'

Ashley took a deep breath and raised her head to look at Sarah. 'Is it true, what you've been telling the Gardaí – that my father…that he was involved with those men, and that's why they kidnapped me? Why would you say something like that?'

Sarah looked into her eyes. 'Because I believe it. Your mother believes it.'

Ashley dropped her head again. 'I wanted to see you. I thought maybe you could… I can't understand what happened. Is it true…' Her voice wobbled for a second. 'Was my father…you know, mixed up with drugs?'

John gave Sarah's hand a light squeeze. She glanced at him, and he shook his head once. *Don't lie.*

'Yes,' Sarah said, looking back at Ashley. 'We think he was working with the Yorks.' There was no point in softening the blow. It would come out in the end, one way or another. 'We thought Vinnie York found out who you were when you started to appear at his club, and decided he would try a little shift of power.'

'He always gave me the creeps. People have the wrong idea about him. They think he's so smooth, so charismatic. He's no such thing.' A tear slipped down Ashley's cheek and landed soundlessly on Sarah's cast. 'But this…this seems like too much even for him. Davey Clarke…he…he… he's the real monster.' Her voice broke and for a moment it looked like she might crack, but she checked herself, and her eyes, so like her mother's, held firm.

'I'm sorry,' Sarah said again.

'I couldn't last night, but I wanted to thank you for getting me out of there. One of the Gardaí told me you carried me… I just wanted to thank you.'

'There's no need.'

'Yes, there is.' Ashley stiffened.

'We were doing our jobs,' John said. 'I'm glad you're okay, though.'

'Yes, I'm okay,' Ashley said, a flash of bitterness creeping into her voice. Her hands tightened around the bed rail until her knuckles went white. 'My mother's had some kind of…episode. The last few weeks have been very hard on her – and now, with Daddy… I have to take care of things now. There's nobody else. Poor Granny's hopeless.'

John held his tongue. He stared at Ashley with raw admiration. This slip of a girl had had her whole world shattered. She was holding herself together with sheer willpower.

'If you need anything…' he began, and stopped. What could he offer her? What did you offer a person when her life had been torn asunder?

'No. I only came to say thank you.' Ashley cleared her throat and slid her hands into the pockets of her jeans.

'Ashley, wait a minute,' Sarah said. 'Look, I don't understand everything yet, but I'm sure your father wouldn't have let anything happen to you.'

'My father was a weak, stupid man…but I loved him.' Her face began to crumple.

'Ashley, I'm sure you did. I'm sure he loved you too.'

Ashley trembled and again pulled herself back from the brink, barely. She raised her head and jerked it towards Sarah. 'Thank you both again.'

Then she turned and walked away. The click of her heels echoed across the tiled floors. Sarah lay back on her pillow and closed her eyes.

'That poor girl.'

John nodded. 'We should have known from the start Naughton was bad. Dammit, we *did* know.' It was yet another mistake in a whole line of them.

'John, I'm glad you came, but I'm really tired. I'm still suffering from the bloody anaesthetic.' Sarah smiled thinly at him. Ashley's raw pain had upset her terribly. She needed some time alone.

John patted her hand and rose to go. 'I'll see you tomorrow.' He turned to leave.

'John,' she called, so softly he almost missed it.

He came back to the bedside. 'Yeah?'

Sarah reached out and took his hand in hers. 'Don't be so hard on yourself. We're a team, and we did our best.'

In that moment, John made himself a solemn promise. He was going to change. No more skiving, no more cutting corners, no more stupid stunts. He would pull out all the stops, take every job that came in, even if it meant wandering around Fairview Park in the dead of night looking for lost cats. He would make Sarah glad she had taken him up on the flippant offer he'd made her that fateful day when she'd walked back into his life.

He leaned over her and kissed her cool forehead. Sarah closed her eyes again and was asleep in seconds.

42

Somebody once said there is no such thing as bad publicity, and John discovered that this was true. Even though QuicK Investigations had cocked up the whole Naughton case from the word go, it still ended up working out in their favour.

Once the press picked up on the dramatic events of that night, the QuicK office phone spent three solid weeks hopping like it was possessed – journalists pleading for interviews, parents of missing and wayward children convinced that John was some sort of divining rod for problem kids. John took on as much work as he could possibly manage. Once he was rushed off his feet, he couldn't think about Sarah's absence all the time.

Flannery had pulled out all the stops. Although Vinnie York still professed his innocence – very convincingly, it had to be said – the evidence against him was mounting steadily. There was the small matter of the gun with Vinnie's fingerprints on it that had been found at the scene. It had been empty, but it had been there, and Vinnie hadn't been able to explain it away. There was also the small matter of the cocaine found in Vinnie's blood sample and in his pockets at the hospital. That cast a slight shadow over his innocent-bystander act.

Gardaí found eight Kalashnikov rifles and four nine-millimetre Berettas under the floor-boards in Dougie's kitchen. A more thorough search of the property unearthed a bunker, situated under the wire cages of three particularly vicious-looking, battle-scarred pit bulls, which contained a virtual arsenal of weapons. The shed Dougie had constructed intrigued the search team, and when they followed the pipelines they were able to detect at least four different samples of human tissue embedded in the drains.

John laughed until he gave himself a stitch when he read in the papers how Vinnie had come to crash in Kilpedder. Apparently the dope had tried to self-medicate his cut with cocaine and had got some in his eyes. Blinded and numb, he had driven across two lanes and ploughed into the only wall for miles around. When Gardaí arrived on the scene, they found him sitting on the grass verge holding a broken arm and gibbering. John wondered if Vinnie had known the coke had been in Davey's car, and if the fact that he had missed such a valuable haul kept him awake at night.

Things were starting to fall into place. The decomposing body of Pascal Mooney had been found by a couple of kids playing hooky from school. A search of his home turned up several references to dealings with Edward Naughton and Patrick York, although this was played down in the papers. Jason Healy was arrested driving out of the car park of Annabel's nightclub one Saturday night and charged with drunk driving. A subsequent search of his person yielded class A drugs, to which the smiling Gardaí added a charge of attempting to drive a car under the influence of the aforementioned drug without licence or insurance. In return for a considerably lighter sentence, Healy sang like a canary, spilling everything he knew about Vinnie York, Patrick York and the drug-smuggling racket. Surprisingly – since everyone who knew Jason thought he was as thick as pig shit – this was quite a great deal. He turned out to have an almost photographic memory for names and dates. Up and down the countryside, dealers and bag-men began to sweat. The boys from the Criminal Assets Bureau rubbed their hands together with glee, took down every name Jason mentioned and began eagerly totting up exactly how much Vinnie York's empire was worth, starting with the club, the jeep and the penthouse apartment.

The real nail in Vinnie's legal coffin came in the large, looming shape of one Josie Molloy, Kelpie's sister. Dressed in her finest, she hauled her considerable bulk to the Gardaí and proceeded to give a long – and, on occasion, fictional – account of the day Vinnie York and Davey Clarke had come calling to her house. By Josie's account, Vinnie not only knew about the cocaine but was a major drug player, and her own brother had frequently spoken of his nefarious deeds. She showed the sergeant the mark where Vinnie had slapped her, and she cried over her televison. It was a magnificent performance, and it sealed the deal on Vinnie York.

Detective Sergeant Owen Flannery finally, with ill grace, conceded that John was not a black-mailing, drug-smuggling master criminal, and grudgingly mentioned QuicK Investigations in one or two interviews without spitting. John's fin-gerprints had been found in Davey Clarke's home, and for a day or so Flannery had thought he had him.

But when Megan Lowery, looking very sweet and demure, called to Wicklow station and ex-plained just how heroic John had been in retriev-ing some personal effects from Clarke's house, Flannery had grudgingly relented and John escap-ed a charge of conspiracy and whatever the hell else Flannery had been cooking up. Flannery later called John personally and warned him that he was now on his radar and wasn't to go round bending the law willy-nilly – and that included breaking and entering, even if the place being broken and entered was the home of a crook. John promised he wouldn't do it again. He uncrossed his fingers after he hung up.

The papers delighted in Vinnie York's fall from grace, guffawed over his many appearances in the back of *Tatler* and lampooned him mercilessly. Photos of Ashley looking cool, blonde and refined only heightened the national sense of outrage. The papers named her an angel, him the devil incarnate. When they learned of Vinnie's coke-parties-cum-orgies, the whole story went into the stratosphere. Claudia Delaney did a kiss-and-tell story in *It* magazine and was a bit of a celebrity for about a week. It was tabloid heaven.

John kept his head down. He couldn't bask in the publicity, not with Sarah still injured. He hired a painter and a decorator and had the whole office cleaned up and a new carpet installed. He had screaming matches with Helen on the phone at least once a week, most of them resulting in either him or her hanging up. He bought a flat-screen iMac to replace the crappy computer Sarah had been using. When he wasn't working, he spent a lot of time with Sumo, taking him for daily walks in Phoenix Park. Sumo was delighted with all the attention and only tried to kill three deer. John turned down Cynthia's offer of a fresh start, in person – something he'd never done in his life. Cynthia called him a selfish shit and chucked a drink over him, but they both knew that was a bit staged.

And he waited. He waited for Sarah to be released from hospital. He waited for her to decide whether she would return to work. He felt restless, on hold. It hit him hard that he missed her so much. They hadn't spoken much over the past few weeks. John sensed that Sarah needed time, and he was giving it to her.

At nine o'clock on a grey, overcast Monday morning, John drove along the Grand Canal, parked the car behind Portobello College and walked down Camden Street towards the office. He bought a bunch of bananas from his favourite street stall on the way. It was bitterly cold and threatening rain. Heavy grey clouds rolled over Dublin, so close they seemed to skim the rooftops.

On Camden Street, the vendors had rows of sparkling tinsel tied to their stalls. Poinsettias in terracotta pots, their blood-red flowers in full velvet bloom, fought a losing battle against the artificial sprays of holly and rolls of bright, cheap wrapping paper. John admired them while he waited for his fruit. One or two of the older women on the stalls seemed to think he was a bit of a hero these days. Their catcalls made him laugh as he passed by.

John broke a banana from the bunch and munched it as he walked past festive windows and listened to the hawkers calling, 'Five for fifty the wrapping paper,' up and down the street. Although he pretended to hate Christmas, like a good adult, John had to admit he enjoyed the build-up, the air of expectation and seasonal bonhomie. By the time he reached the office building he was in sparkling form.

'Going up?' Rodney appeared at his shoulder, wearing a Santa Claus hat with flashing stars, reeking of scotch and the aftershave he used to cover it.

'Yeah.' John headed up the stairs. 'How've you been, Rod?'

'Great! How's Sarah? Any word on when's she coming back?'

John's good humour faded a little. 'Don't know exactly. She needs physical therapy on the ankle. It could be a while before she's fully mobile.'

Rodney nodded, stumbled outside his door and righted himself. 'Tell her I was asking for her, will you? I miss our chats.' His eyes clouded over for a second.

'I'm sure she misses you too.'

'Do you really think so?'

'Sure.'

Rodney slapped John heartily on the back and fumbled for his keys. The back of his suit jacket was rumpled and grubby, as if he'd slept in it. John climbed the last flight, thinking that Rodney wouldn't make it to the new year at the rate he was drinking.

He put his key into the new mortise lock and turned it. The lock clicked open on the first half-turn. John stopped in his tracks. He knew he hadn't left the office unlocked. He put down the bananas and carefully flattened himself against the wall. Then he pulled a thick leather sap out of his pocket and kicked the door open. After that night in Wicklow, he realised just how dangerous people could be. He'd been carrying various weapons ever since.

'Jesus! Come in, will you, and close the door. You're letting the heat out.'

John released his breath, picked up his bananas and stepped back into the doorway. Sarah sat at her desk, clutching a cup of coffee. Her foot was still encased in thick plaster, and her crutches rested against the wall behind her desk. She wore a short, faded denim skirt and red woolly tights with dancing reindeer racing up her long legs. She had cut the foot out of one leg of the tights and rolled it up to her knee.

'Nice reindeer, baby. They go all the way up to the North Pole?'

Sarah blushed and put her cup down with a bang. 'Please, John, spare me your feeble attempts at humour. I can't get this bloody thing into most of my trousers.'

'How's the pain?'

'No ballroom dancing for a while.'

'No, seriously.'

'Pretty much under control. Cold weather affects it a bit.'

John closed the door and shrugged off his jacket. 'I was wondering if you were going to get up off your arse any time soon. Ever since our Starsky and Hutch routine, we've got more work than you can shake a stick at.'

Sarah looked away, and John felt his stomach lurch. He knew then that she had only come to break the bad news. He looked at her, waiting for it, waiting for her to ruin his day, his week, his life.

'I like what you've done with the place,' she said. 'Very sharp.'

'Nothing to do with me. I showed the guy in and told him to clean it up.'

Sarah whistled softly. 'Jesus, he had some job.'

John leaned against the wall and crossed his arms. Was she deliberately stalling? 'I don't think he'd ever seen wallpaper like ours before. He reckoned it was museum-worthy.'

Sarah grinned and looked around at the freshly painted magnolia walls. 'I don't think much of the colour, but the iMac is great.'

John smiled at her. 'Glad you like it.' He went to his desk and sat down. His legs suddenly felt a little weak. 'So, how are you?'

Sarah brushed a thick lock of hair away from her face and regarded him coolly. 'Why didn't you come see me the last few weeks?'

'I got the impression I wasn't wanted.'

'By who?'

'By everyone.'

'You mean Jackie and Helen.'

'They said you'd recover better if I didn't keep putting you under pressure about work and stuff.'

'Since when have you ever taken any notice of them?'

John picked up a pencil from his desk and doodled on his brand-new blotter. 'It seemed like a good idea not to keep getting their backs up.'

Sarah shrugged. 'Let them get their backs up all they like. I won't be bullied into anything, especially not by them.'

John glanced up. She was still too pale and she

looked thinner than ever, but there was a sparkle in her eye and a note of determination in her voice. 'You came for me, John, even when you knew it was dangerous. You came for me.'

'Of course I did.'

'So I told Helen to back off.'

'Good.'

It was all he could think of to say. He knew she had decided to stay. There was no reason to make a drama of it.

Sarah took a sip of her coffee. 'By the way, I've taken about three dozen calls since I came in this morning. You'd think with all the money we've made recently you'd buy a bloody answering machine. Christ, do I have to think of everything? Come on, John, you can't keep relying on…'

John sat back in his chair and glanced out the window. A couple of twirling snowflakes drifted past the freshly cleaned glass. Down on the street below, cars honked as traffic slowed to a crawl.

John popped a cigarette into his mouth and lit it while Sarah, his partner and his friend, lectured him on what she thought he was doing wrong. All was right with the world – or, if it wasn't, it was close enough.